The
Eagle
and the
Snake

The Eagle and the Snake

Douglas Boyd

WARNER BOOKS

A *Warner* Book

First published in Great Britain in 1992
by Sinclair-Stevenson

This edition published by Warner in 1993

A CIP catalogue for this book
is available from the British Library

ISBN 0 7515 0012 7

Photoset by Rowland Phototypesetting Ltd
Bury St Edmunds, Suffolk
Printed in England by Clays Ltd, St Ives plc

Warner Books
A division of
Little, Brown and Company (UK) Limited
165 Great Dover Street
London SE1 4YA

ACKNOWLEDGEMENT

Many people contributed to this book.

I talked with legionnaires and ex-legionnaires from seventeen countries about their experiences wearing the white kepi from the time of Dien Bien Phu to the Gulf War. If they remain anonymous, it is because men of the Foreign Legion like it that way. The insight they gave me into this legendary army and its unique code of honour was invaluable; any inaccuracies are mine.

The women who helped I can name and thank in person.

First was Caroline Upcher who saw a possibility and stayed with it all the way. Then Mandy Little who knew a good idea when she saw one and Atarah Ben-Tovim who re-paid a debt.

When we met, Atarah and I made an agreement to give each other ten years' full-time help and support so that we could both achieve all our unrealised ambitions. First I gave up my career as a BBC Television producer and director in order to work for her. The ten years became twelve but we made it. Then it was my turn to collect and Atarah stepped down from a pinnacle of showbusiness success to work for me researching, making contacts, fixing travel schedules and doing all the myriad unglamorous things that authors' wives do.

Mine was the greater gamble, waiting for the second bite of the apple. This book is the first instalment of my pay-off.

This is a work of fiction. Any resemblance between the characters and any person living or dead is purely coincidental. And yet, where the Foreign Legion is concerned, fact and fiction mix. It is hard to say which is more fantastic.

For example, in December 1940 Legion engineers were dragging the Lang Son river in northern Vietnam to recover a number of 105mm. guns which had been dumped there months before to prevent their capture by the Japanese. From the bed of the river the divers brought up – in addition to the guns – a number of iron-bound chests containing mint-condition Mexican silver coins. This considerable treasure, recovered entirely by chance, proved to be the *caisse noire*, or pay-chest of a French general, ambushed in that same spot by Chinese mercenaries in 1885.

As to the gold of Dien Bien Phu, officially nobody knows what has become of it . . .

My name is Raoul Duvalier. To look at me now, you wouldn't think I was once an officer in the most extra-ordinary elite army the world has ever known. Yet at twenty-eight, when all this began, I was a captain in the Foreign Legion – fit, tough and confident. I had money, good looks and a beautiful wife. On leave I drove racing cars for Ferrari and rode for France in the Olympics. I played polo, ski'd and excelled at every sport I touched. It was a wonderful life in every sense; I had the world in front of me.

In the tradition of my family – we Duvaliers have served France as generals since Napoleon's time – I was marked out to become a general myself one day but things turned out very differently . . .

Fate has tricks in store that take us all unawares, however golden the future appears. Now I am just a man in a wheelchair – and not even a wheelchair hero. On the contrary, I am a cripple who was dismissed from the service in disgrace. Even the hundred per cent disability pension for wounds incurred in my country's active service, was revoked.

My country? There's so much to explain. The Legion is composed of men from a hundred different nations, speaking God knows how many tongues, but our motto is Legio Patria Nostra. That means: The Legion is Our Country.

Although we fight and die for France, every few years the government tries to abolish the Legion because they are afraid of

1

us. *Are we so terrible? Are we devils not men, as an enemy once called us? There are days and nights when every recruit thinks he has landed in hell, that's for sure. Our discipline is harsher than in other armies and the training is mercilessly tough. It has to be that way. How else can you weld men from so many cultures and classes and countries – men from mud huts and Manhattan skyscrapers – into a perfect military machine? Yet the Legion has never been short of volunteers wanting to serve in a white kepi despite knowing that they will get the shittiest, most dangerous jobs to do and no thanks at the end.*

We don't need thanks or medals. We have something better: pride and a code of honour.

Pride because every legionnaire who stays the full course knows he has proven himself for life. Three out of four men are rejected in training. Those who survive never forget that they are the best: better soldiers and better men than the ones who couldn't take it, the rejects and deserters.

And our code of honour is unique. It binds every legionnaire as a brother to every other man who ever wore the white kepi. On the battlefield or in a bar-room brawl, if one of us in trouble shouts: 'A moi, La Légion!' *the rest will come running.*

Which is why . . . I've been avoiding this because it hurts.

Which is why I chose a small group of legionnaires to help me when I wanted to set right the great wrong I had suffered. I knew I could rely on them all the way, cost what it may, simply because they were legionnaires. But now I have to face the fact that one or more of these men has betrayed me. It's like finding out that God has bad breath.

The raid had been well planned and was carried out like clockwork.

The first guard dog died without a sound. The short steel bolt transfixed its head from eye to ear, terminating the Alsatian's life before its brain had registered the dull *thwack!* of the bowstring.

Through the starlight scope fixed to the matt black crossbow, the marksman watched the animal crumple into an inert heap. He panned the weapon slowly upwards, studying the side of the ancient tower which had stood on its spur of rock overlooking the Dordogne for seven centuries. The Swarovski image-intensifier magnified starlight 80,000 times to give a ghostly green image. There were no gaps between the finely dressed stones which an enemy might use to scale the wall. The thick, iron-bound oak door would have taken a battering ram and a party of strong men to force it open. The windows of the lower floors were narrow and protected by stout iron bars. On two sides, limestone cliffs dropped sheer to the river below.

A grid of infra-red proximity detectors was wired to switch on floodlights concealed under the medieval gargoyles that jutted from the masonry at each corner. Video cameras pointed at the ground in front of the lights. The tower was better guarded than many banks' strong rooms in that summer of 1974.

The crossbowman lowered his weapon and moved forward, a black figure in the moonless night. Counting paces, he stopped just outside the invisible field swept by the infra-red beams. On the full-scale mock-up of the tower where he had trained, there had been a chalk line on the ground exactly where he stood.

A professional, relaxed and alert, he waited for the signal telling him that the other dog had been dealt with. He retensioned the crossbow and dropped into the slot a quarrel to which was attached a fine terylene cord that led to a reel clipped onto his belt. When he heard the call of a hunting owl, he knelt on one knee and held his breath for a moment. Then came the muted *thwack!* and the bolt arched upward through the blackness, towing the cord above the invisible beams and high over the top of the tower.

A second owl call confirmed that everything was going as planned on the other side of the tower. The crossbowman slung the weapon across his shoulder and pulled hand over hand on the thin cord until he came to the thicker nylon scaling rope, which he lashed to the branch of a tree, using a quick-release knot.

The third owl call was the signal that the other end was

secured. The man in black echoed the call, clamped a pair of carabiniers over the rope and began hauling himself upwards, safely above the infra-red beams.

Minutes later, there were four raiders on the roof of the tower. A light was flashed once in the direction of the river. From the far side of the Dordogne came the answering flash of a car's headlights. The four black-clad figures split into two teams: one pair attending to the security systems and clearing up all traces of their entry while the others slipped noiselessly into the bedroom of the tower's single occupant. It was dimly lit by a small night-light and sparsely furnished without any of the touches that might indicate a woman's presence.

The sleeper awoke to find a powerful torch shining into his eyes, blinding him. Before he could speak, a gag was thrust into his mouth and tied firmly in place. Beyond a brief thrash of panic, he made no resistance as the blankets were pulled from the bed, revealing his crippled legs that made identification beyond any doubt.

The two raiders lifted their prisoner from his bed and placed him in the wheelchair that stood beside it. Swathes of sticking plaster secured his wrists, knees, elbows and ankles to the wheelchair. A swathe of tape around the temples immobilised his head against the back-rest and two final turns of tape went over his eyes, making an effective blindfold. The only parts of his body that the prisoner could still voluntarily move were his eyeballs and his tongue.

Only then did his captors remove their hoods. They wheeled him without speaking into the lift and pressed the button for down.

They know what they are doing, these faceless, silent men who locked me up in the dungeon. They know all about me and I know nothing about them. There's no escape from here, even if I were not bound hand and foot, and gagged into the bargain. The Knights Templar who raised the tower in which I made my home built this place as a fortress overlooking the ford where pilgrims crossed the Dordogne on their way to Santiago de Compostela. I wonder whom they incarcerated down here. Who panicked in the darkness then, as I am panicking now?

Sensory deprivation! Oh, they know what they're doing all right by locking me up in darkness. They must know how I so nearly went out of my mind during the months of agony when I was kept in a black, lightless box unable to stand or lie down. These people want to break my spirit fast.

To fight them I have only one weapon: my will. I must conquer the fear of the dark that has me whimpering like a child with the night terrors. For twenty years I have been unable to sleep without a light on, so great is my fear of the dark, but I must take charge of myself or go out of my mind.

That's better! I hear the animal whimpers quieten and cease. Now my ears are full of the raucous breathing and racing heartbeat of panic. Gradually my breathing quietens and my pulse slows.

I've done this before, you see. Many times!

The trick is to hoard sensations like a miser counting his louis d'or.

Each precious feeling, however small, is a piece of reality. As long as I hang on to reality, my captors cannot win.

So what sensations can I find?

Hearing? I can hear two sounds: my breathing and my heartbeat. What can I smell? The musty cloth of the gag and the damp stone of the dungeon walls, that's all. Sight? There is nothing to see down here, even if I were not blindfolded. . . . Touch? My fingers are taped together very thoroughly. But yet . . . I can feel beneath my forearms the arm-rests of the wheelchair. I may hate it, but nothing reminds me who I am so much as this chair!

I have a thousand simple tricks like that to regain control of my body – all learned when I was a prisoner in a black box on the other side of the world.

To regain control of my mind, the best and simplest trick of all is to recite like a prayer my name and what I am:

My name is Raoul Duvalier. To look at me now, you wouldn't think I was once an officer in the most extraordinary elite army the world has known. Yet at twenty-eight, when all this began . . .

*

The prisoner moaned. It was the worst kind of pain to think that he had been betrayed by a fellow legionnaire, a man bound by the same code of honour as himself. He wanted not to think about it. And yet, he must find out who had given him away, or end by suspecting them all. That meant starting at the beginning of a long chain of events and going over everything he knew about each man. Some small detail from the past might indicate the Judas.

He heard the noise of the trap-door opening and the click of a light switch. He could see nothing through the blindfold, but heard feet coming down the stone steps and across the flags towards him. A hand pulled up his pyjama sleeve. A strap was tightened around his biceps and a needle sought a vein. The strap was released. A sensation of heat travelled up his arm and into his brain . . . and a vortex sucked him down and down.

PART 1

SEPTEMBER 1953–JANUARY 1958

1

The morning of 20 September 1953 was just another Sunday at the Cercle Sportif, the exclusive club patronised by the elite of Hanoi's French colonial society.

Beneath the slowly turning ceiling fans of the long bar, a pianist was playing a clever medley of Gershwin tunes, mainly for his own pleasure: there were few club members sitting in the comfortable chairs at eleven o'clock in the morning. Outside, on one of the impeccably maintained grass courts that would not have shamed Wimbledon, four unbelievers played a leisurely game of mixed doubles under a cloudless blue sky. The lightest of breezes teased ripples along the surface of the Olympic-size swimming pool in which no one swam. Most of the top people in Hanoi, from the Governor down, were at mass in the cathedral.

It was after midday when the members flooded into the club for their ritual aperitifs. White-coated Vietnamese servants moved silently with trays of drinks between the low tables, waiting on their European masters with a deference that was servile. There was a smattering of elegant dress uniforms in the bar but most of the men wore white cotton tropical suits. They were planters and mine owners who made their money from tin and rubber, the two main exports of the colony. The board of the Michelin company had more

9

influence on the *colons* of Vietnam than did the government in Paris; to them, commodity prices on the world market were more important than politics.

The pianist was crooning songs from the shows into a microphone. It was difficult to hear his words above the animated conversation in which the principal topic was the new French Commander-in-Chief, General Lépine who had just been sent out from Paris with his new plan to crush the Viet Minh guerrillas. Like the British in Malaya, the French in Vietnam wanted the Communist menace to be eradicated from their colony so that business could get back to pre-war levels.

On a high stool at the bar, drinking alone, sat a lean, hard-faced man of about thirty, wearing the uniform of a captain in the First Infantry Regiment of the Foreign Legion. A well-worn black beret lay on the bar top beside his glass of beer, the cap badge showing the emblem of an intertwined eagle and snake. His combat boots, though clean, were unpolished. His body language said plainly that he was no regular fixture of the Hanoi social scene but would have been more at home in the field with his men. His smallest gesture seemed fuelled by a controlled anger. After one baleful glare at the settlers and garrison officers by whom he was surrounded, he contented himself with a detailed study of the bottles behind the bar.

His face creased into a grin of pleasure as he saw, in the mirror glass behind the bottles, the arrival of the friend he had been waiting for.

'*A moi, la Légion!*' he roared over the buzz of after-mass conversation. The call by which any legionnaire in a brawl summoned to his help all other legionnaires within earshot, cut short the small talk. Well-groomed heads turned in surprise at such uncouth behaviour.

The only person who looked pleased was the newcomer, dressed in the ceremonial uniform of a Foreign Legion captain.

Raoul Duvalier's Sunday morning duty had been to escort a general's wife to mass in the cathedral. From his kepi – the flat-topped forage cap of the Legion – to his spit-shined shoes, he gleamed with smartness as he hurried across the room and clapped his old comrade on the shoulders, embracing him warmly.

'Koenig, you old bastard!' He grinned. 'It was good to get your call. I didn't even know you were in Vietnam.'

The two men stood looking at each other with unselfconscious pleasure for a long moment.

'How are you keeping?' asked Raoul.

Without bothering to lower his voice, Koenig replied, 'Feeling sick.'

'Sick?' Raoul's voice was incredulous. 'You've never been sick in your life.'

'These people make me feel sick.' Koenig waved a hand vaguely at the crowd in the bar. 'Listen to them yapping like lap-dogs. All they've got to talk about is how 3,000 socialites tried to gate-crash senator Kennedy's wedding last week or how the price of rubber and oil is too low. Don't they know we're fighting a war? Jesus, I'd rather be sharing a bowl of rice with a platoon of Viet Minh than sitting among people like these, waiting for you to show up!'

'Well, it's their club,' said Raoul, easing himself on to a stool next to Koenig. 'So calm down and keep your voice low or you'll get us both thrown out.'

Koenig took a long look at his former classmate at the officers' academy of St Cyr. They had lost touch as their postings led them on separate careers. He did not seem to like what he saw. 'Two weeks in-country at headquarters and you already look as though you belong on the Hanoi scene,' he commented ironically. 'A real general's bum-boy.'

'Knock it off,' said Raoul, with a hard punch in the other man's guts. 'Do you think I enjoy being dressed up like a fugitive from some comic opera? Or that I asked for the job of keeping the general's arse clean all morning, going to cocktail parties every afternoon and dancing half the night with bored garrison wives who keep trying to drag me into bed?'

'You poor bastard!'

'Someone has to do the job,' shrugged Raoul.

'And how is your beautiful wife?'

'Huguette is as beautiful as ever.'

'I saw her picture in *Paris Match* recently.' Koenig's dislike of his friend's wife was plain to Raoul's ears.

Raoul swallowed half the beer Koenig had thrust at him. 'So tell me how it is out in the field, *mon vieux*.'

Koenig barked a command for two more drinks, his voice cutting like a whiplash through the clamour of other voices. 'It's tough,' he answered. 'The Viet Minh spent five years fighting the Japs. The ones who survived are bloody good soldiers.'

'And this General Giap of theirs?'

'Brilliant. You better believe it. He runs rings around our top brass.'

'My general is planning to change all that,' said Raoul.

'His fucking Plan!' Koenig laughed derisively.

'At least he's got one.'

'Every general has a plan,' sneered Koenig. 'It's idiots like me out in the boonies who have to try and make them work, or die trying.'

'This plan is different. I'll show you.' Raoul led his friend away from the bar to a less exposed position at a vacant table. He took a starched napkin from round the neck of an empty champagne bottle and used his fountain pen to draw on it a rough map of the country.

'Up to now,' he explained, 'we have been fighting the Viet Minh piecemeal wherever they choose to attack us.' The pen blobbed ink like a blue rash to illustrate his words.

'You don't have to tell me,' Koenig observed. 'Each one of those ink blobs is where I buried one of my men.'

'Shut up and listen,' said Raoul. 'General Lépine is going to change all that. His plan is to set up an impregnable military base here.' The fountain pen stabbed a large cross in the top left corner of the map. 'We're going to move some 20,000 troops backed by 155mm artillery into the valley of Dien Bien Phu. There will be an airfield so that even if the

Viet Minh manage to cut the road, the base can be resupplied indefinitely by air . . .' Details of logistics and timing rolled easily off Raoul's tongue while Koenig listened without interruption, absorbing it all.

'At Dien Bien Phu,' Raoul ended, tapping the map, 'we shall annihilate the Viet Minh once and for all – or at least crush General Giap's balls so badly that it will take years before the bastard can walk properly again.'

Koenig snorted: 'That's not a plan; it's a pipe dream, a game on a sand-table.' He leaned forward in his chair and stabbed a finger at Raoul. 'Just tell me one thing, *mon vieux*. If your general's new base is so bloody impregnable, why the fuck should Giap play into our hands by attacking it? The guy's not a fool. He's a military genius! So answer me that.'

'He hasn't any choice.' Raoul echoed the words he had heard General Lépine use so many times in Paris and in Hanoi. 'Dien blocks the path of the Viets' advance into Laos, anyone can see that. It's only ten miles from the border. Giap can't bypass it. So for strategic reasons, he must take Dien Bien Phu or die trying.'

'Maybe.' Koenig was unconvinced.

'We have artillery, aircraft, supplies,' argued Raoul. 'And what has Giap got? Just the *bo-doi* – his barefoot soldiers.'

'He has a limitless supply of them,' warned Koenig.

'You are wrong, Duvalier.' The dry-voiced correction came from an artillery colonel with one hand who was standing behind Raoul's chair. 'Giap does have some artillery up on the Chinese border.' He picked up Raoul's pen and drew a symbolic gun at the top of the map.

'However, there's no way the Viets could move anything heavier than mortars across the mountains that surround the valley of Dien Bien Phu.' He cross-hatched a series of mountain ranges between the gun on the Chinese border and the cross that was Dien Bien Phu.

'Are you sure of that, sir?' asked Koenig.

'I'd stake my life on it.' With a polite nod, the colonel left them and went to join some friends at another table.

Who's that guy?' Koenig was impressed. 'He seems pretty sure of himself.'

'That,' answered Raoul, 'is Valentin. He commands the artillery at Dien Bien Phu.'

Koenig laughed. 'Then he ought to know what he's talking about.' He grabbed his beret off the table. 'Let's go somewhere we can get drunk in private.'

'I can't,' said Raoul apologetically. 'I'm meeting some people for lunch. Why don't you join us?' Anticipating a refusal, he put a hand on his friend's arm. 'The lady is a cousin of mine, married to a planter out here.'

'A planter and his wife.' Koenig smiled wryly. 'Just the sort of people I don't want to meet.'

'You're an uncouth peasant,' decided Raoul.

'Better than being a chocolate-box soldier like you.'

'Well, you're too late now.' Raoul's strong grip forced Koenig back into his chair. 'Here they come. The brunette . . .'

'. . . is beautiful. And my type.'

'I didn't know you had one, you old monk.'

'I didn't until now. But she takes my breath away, Raoul. I'm glad I stayed.'

Raoul relaxed. There was never any guarantee how his impulsive friend would behave. He wanted Koenig to like the woman who was approaching their table. 'That's my cousin Marie. We grew up together. You know, long summer holidays at the family home in Brittany. Teenage crushes on each other, reading poetry by moonlight on the beach . . . that sort of thing.'

Koenig guffawed. Without taking his eyes off the woman in question, he sneered, 'Nice life if you can get it. As a teenager, I spent the long summer holidays hanging around the street corner in Belleville, trying to get a free jump from the tarts in the local bar.'

'Stop flaunting your working-class background,' grinned Raoul.

'It's quite obvious enough without you working at it. And . . .' He put a restraining hand on Koenig's knee.

14

'Before you say anything wrong, the man with Marie is her very possessive husband, Gustave. His family have been out here in tin and rubber for three generations.'

'Oh great! One of the fat cats I'm fighting for.'

'Belt up, Koenig,' warned Raoul. 'Gustave's not stupid.'

The couple who greeted Raoul and his friend warmly were, on the surface, typical members of the Cercle Sportif. Gustave Laval had the clear eyes and healthy tan of a planter who spent most of his life in the open air. His wife, dressed in a light Thai silk dress, held his arm and watched her husband's face a great deal while he was talking. She had the same brown Duvalier eyes as Raoul. Her high cheekbones, pale skin and fashionably cut dark hair seemed to hold Koenig spellbound. Her husband exchanged an amused glance with Raoul.

A waiter placed drinks on the table.

'Did you sell?' asked Raoul when the man had gone.

It was Gustave's turn to tell Raoul to keep his voice down. He nodded at a group of planters' and officers' wives seated on rattan loungers at the edge of the pool. 'The gossip machine. If they so much as get a sniff that I've sold two of my plantations in the last month . . .'

'Why?' interrupted Koenig.

Gustave's intelligent eyes rested on his questioner. 'Hedging my bets,' he said calmly. 'Prices are not marvellous, but . . .'

'They'll be a lot worse in six months' time –' Koenig roused himself from his contemplation of Marie – 'the way the war is going.'

'Exactly.'

'You're both being defeatist,' said Raoul. 'Lépine's Plan . . .'

'. . . is a mousetrap in which he's trying to catch a larger beast,' finished Gustave. 'OK, if General Giap is stupid, it'll snap shut and maybe crush the yellow rat. But if Giap is cleverer than us, the trap will snap on our elegant European fingers instead.'

'Meaning what?' asked Marie.

'Have you seen Valentin's hand?' asked her husband rhetorically.

Koenig leaned across the table and shook Gustave's hand more warmly than he had when they were introduced. 'Monsieur Laval,' he smiled, 'you may be a civilian, but you have a better grasp of military strategy than all the fucking generals sitting in headquarters down the road. Excuse my language, madame.'

We like to pretend our mistakes were inevitable, that anyone pointing them out afterwards is using hindsight. Yet Gustave knew even then that Giap and his nameless thousands of bo-doi were going to win and push us out of their country. Gustave knew the Vietnamese people. He had felt a change in their pulse that warned him it was time to go.

Koenig knew too. He had learned the hard way to appreciate Giap's military brilliance, by watching his men die one after another not from disease and bullets and mines, but from something far more lethal: the better generalship of the enemy. No, I am underestimating my friend. I think Koenig knew before they died. Unlike me, he understood history, whereas I had only studied it, learned it for exams and comprehended nothing.

What greater anguish for such a man than to do his duty as an officer, knowing that he was spending men's lives fighting the inevitable?

And why was I so blind?

I was not alone, but that's no excuse.

The fundamental difference between Koenig and me when we first met as cadets at St Cyr was that we were perfect examples of the two kinds of soldier. I was a man of action and he was a philosopher, a poet, a scholar of war.

I, born in the lap of privilege, the son of a general and the grandson of a general, took for granted the trappings of authority and did not enquire why I should carry out orders or give them to others. So on the larger scale I did not enquire as to their historical validity, whereas Koenig, reared in a slum, had fought every step of the way to his captain's bars. In order to have no inner weakness, he had trained himself to question everything in terms of morality, logistics, physical and political feasibility. Oh, only in his own mind . . . outwardly he was the model of unquestioning obedience. Individual thinking was not appreciated in those days at St Cyr.

Even as a cadet-in-training – and God knows our life was tough – I lived by the motto Carpe Diem. Each day I rose like a young giant, revelling in the mental and physical challenges of our training. I took for granted excelling at the game of life. We Duvaliers always did.

Everything came so easily to me; I was perpetually high on being first. But Koenig agonised over the meaning of what we were doing. Whilst outwardly obedient, inwardly he had to have a reason for everything and lay awake at night in his cubicle wrestling with doubts, like a novice in his cell.

Unlike me – born French and never gave a thought to it – Koenig even had a reason for his nationality. His father chose to leave the Saar when Hitler's troops marched in, not because he was Jewish – he was an ardent Christian – but because he believed Nazism was an evil creed. He left his home and business and brought his wife and son penniless to France, which he regarded as the haven of all refugees of conscience. To the son, growing up in the shabby streets of Belleville, being French was almost a religion.

I became a soldier without thinking. In my family it was the natural thing to do. Koenig, however, defied the pacifism of the father he loved in order to dedicate himself to the service of France as though in payment of a family debt. He kept his sense of mission private as other men hid their religious beliefs and taught himself to act the part of a tough, fearless, conscienceless man-at-arms. Perhaps the greatest struggle he fought was between his duty as a soldier and his vision of history which was in direct conflict with what was expected of us. But, as I say, he kept all this to himself; few people saw through the outward façade.

Later circumstances inverted Koenig's role and mine, but our real natures were true opposites, which perhaps explains a friendship that survived great upheavals: we were so different that each could wholeheartedly admire the other.

*

The group of French wives whom Gustave had labelled the gossip machine were also discussing the Lépine Plan. The subject made a change from cavilling about the dishonesty and ingratitude of native servants.

'If we must talk about soldiers,' asked one woman, grown bored with the subject of troops and logistics, 'who is that gorgeous hunk in uniform talking with Gustave and Marie Laval? Not the killer in khaki. I mean the other one with lanyard and epaulettes and those deep brown eyes you could melt in.'

'Bad luck,' her friend replied. 'He's married. Name of Raoul Duvalier.'

'Duvalier the rider?'

'That's right. Bronze medal in the '48 Olympics.'

'Wouldn't mind being ridden by him.'

There were a couple of sighs and a giggle from the other women.

'At your age! Anyway, he's married to one of Mr Dior's models.'

'Of course.' The first woman put two and two together. 'Huguette Duvalier . . .' She deliberately left the sentence unfinished.

'And what does that mean, pray?'

'I heard – 'A sip of lime juice to aid the timing – 'she sleeps around a lot.'

If it was pleasantly cool sitting beside the Cercle Sportif's pool in the middle of Hanoi's winter, the heat inside the pump and filter shed behind the swimming pool was stifling. Fumes leaked from the exhaust pipe of the diesel generator and made the atmosphere almost unbreathable.

One of the barefoot sweepers, dressed only in vest and shorts, was brushing dust and leaves from the concrete pathway. After a careful look round, he laid down his broom, opened the door of the shed and vanished inside.

'What news, comrade?' he asked the waiter who was squatting on his heels beside the pump in order not to be visible through the grimy window.

'Everyone is talking about Lépine's new Plan.' The waiter answered with his mouth close to the sweeper's ear.

'What do they say?'

'That the French are going to make Dien Bien Phu into . . .' The waiter had difficulty in translating the metaphor he had overheard, of a hammer and anvil. He used his hands to clarify the meaning. 'A trap where Lépine will crush our forces as one crushes rice between two stones.'

The sweeper was thoughtful. 'Did you hear any numbers?'

'Twenty thousand men,' the waiter recalled.

'Which regiments?'

'Mainly colonial troops.'

'Good.' The sweeper was pleased. Africans and Arabs of the colonial regiments had no reason that he could see to fight and die for the commercial interests of French rubber companies. And as for the local Vietnamese and Thai troops. . . . He spat derisively. 'They will run away when the fighting starts. They always do.'

'Plus 4,000 men of the Foreign Legion,' said the waiter.

'That is bad news,' the sweeper sighed. In 1954, eighty per cent of Legion NCOs in Vietnam were German veterans. They would not run away; in their own country jail sentences or worse awaited them. Nor would they ever surrender.

'I must go now,' said the waiter.

'*Hu Chu Tich, muon nam!*'

'Long live President Ho!'

The sweeper lit a cigarette and squatted on his haunches, untroubled by the heat and fumes. The deafening noise from the broken exhaust made for privacy, which was the overriding consideration in his clandestine life. He stubbed out the cigarette when a second waiter slipped into the pump house.

'Well, comrade?' asked the sweeper.

This waiter was younger and more nervous. He spoke rapidly: 'They are talking about artillery. A whole battery of 155mm guns are to be trucked into Dien Bien Phu.'

'Who said so?'

'Today I work in the long bar. I overheard a group of army officers talking to the one who has a wooden hand.'

'Ah, Valentin,' breathed the sweeper.

'Is it useful?'

'All intelligence is useful, comrade. You have done well. *Hu Chu Tich, muon nam!*'

'Long live President Ho!' the waiter echoed. 'Long live He Who Enlightens!'

2

Six months later, the scene at the reception in the Governor's Palace in Hanoi gave no hint there was a war going on a few miles away. Virtually everybody in the ballroom, apart from the waiters, was European. Planters in smart suits mingled with officers from the Army, the Legion and colonial regiments. Their womenfolk were dressed in the height of fashion, copied by Chinese tailors from the pages of *Vogue* magazine. Champagne was the drink of the evening.

On the small bandstand at one end of the room a trio of off-duty Foreign Legion bandsmen were playing current hits. 'Rags To Riches' and 'Diamonds Are a Girl's Best Friend' were followed by the pianist crooning softly into the microphone the words of Maurice Chevalier's big hit of the year, the boulevardier song, 'I Love Paris'. A spotlight played over the dancers and lingered on Gustave Laval and Marie. Raoul, watching from the balcony, felt a twinge of jealousy and put it down to loneliness; his own wife was 12,000 miles away.

As Gustave led Marie off the dance floor, she squeezed his wrist to draw attention to her best friend, who had just entered the ballroom alone, looking pale and thin. 'Have the next dance with Mireille,' she whispered. 'Please.'

He kissed the back of her hand. 'I'd rather dance with you,' he murmured.

'I know.' Marie felt warm and secure; many planters' wives worried when their husbands went into town alone but she trusted Gustave totally. 'I know. But Mireille has been through hell, out there in Dien Bien Phu. Take her out of herself, Gustave. Tonight, she needs to forget.'

'De Bonneville should never have taken her to Dien,' said Gustave gruffly. 'What's a general thinking of, to take his secretary with him into a siege?'

He excused himself, pushing a way for them through the throng of dancers leaving the floor. 'If you ask me, Marie, it's that sort of thing which demonstrates more clearly than anything else how little our generals appreciate what they're up against in this war.'

'Shh, she'll hear,' Marie cautioned him as they drew near. 'Make her dance, even if she says she doesn't want to. And don't talk about You-know-where.'

'You don't have to tell me.'

When the two women embraced, Marie felt her friend trembling. 'You're looking better, darling,' she lied.

Mireille Picard's face was thin to haggardness and there were deep lines of strain around the eyes.

'. . . and you're so slim.' Marie said the wrong thing out of concern and could have kicked herself.

'On the same rations the men eat in Dien Bien Phu, I've lost seven kilos.' Mireille clung to her friend. 'And, as to being slim – see me in a bathing costume. I'm not slim, I'm skinny as a rake.'

Gustave took her hand and led her on to the dance floor. He was a good dancer, making Mireille relax in his arms as he found a path through the press of bodies. He could feel some of the tension drain out of her as they danced, chatting about trivia.

At the end of the music, she disengaged herself with a wan smile. 'I'm sorry, Gustave,' she said. 'I can't.'

'Can't what?'

'Can't dance and talk of nothing.' She looked him in the eye. 'You and Marie are very sweet, and I appreciate what you're doing, but how the devil do you expect me to foxtrot and make small talk as though –' she looked angrily around the crowded ballroom – 'as though men are not dying out there at Dien Bien Phu at this very moment just so we can drink champagne and try out the steps of some new-fangled tango.'

'It's OK.' Gustave tried to quieten her. He pulled a handkerchief from his pocket for her tears. 'Take it easy.'

'It's not OK.' Indignantly she ignored both the handkerchief and the embarrassed looks being directed at her. 'And I don't want to take it easy, Gustave. If I'm distraught, it's not from being under constant shellfire until twenty-four hours ago. It's because I spent the last weeks watching men die because nobody in Hanoi understands what's going on. Nobody!'

'What is going on?' Gustave guided her discreetly away from the dance floor. Behind Mireille's back, he was signalling to Marie to join them. She broke off her conversation with Raoul and followed as Gustave led the way through the open french windows on to a terrace overlooking the river, where they found chairs and a table under the stars. A waiter appeared and placed three glasses of champagne in front of them.

Mireille picked hers off the table and threw it into the gardens.

In the darkness, Gustave squeezed his wife's wrist and murmured, 'Better to let her talk and get things out of her system.'

To the tense woman on his other side, he said, 'Tell us about it, Mireille. We only have rumours to go on. You've been there. You know what it's like.'

'What do you want to know?' she asked perversely. 'That our soldiers are fighting and dying on half-rations since the Viets cut the road? That sort of thing amuses you, does it?'

'But the Lépine Plan . . .' Gustave wanted to understand. 'Surely it allowed for the road being cut? Our revered C.-in-C. had this lovely new term for Dien. It was to be *une base aéroterrestre* – a base designed to be supplied by air.'

'In war,' said Mireille bitterly, 'new ideas rarely work. The

Viets under general Giap now have 105mm artillery ranged on the airstrip. No supply planes can take off or land. So, you've got it in one, Gustave, you clever bastard. Dien is a base designed to be supplied by air . . . that can't be supplied by air.'

'Giap has artillery? You mean mortars?' Gustave corrected her gently.

'Don't patronise me,' she snapped. 'I'm secretary to a general and I know the difference between mortars and artillery better than you do.' A brittle laugh showed the strain she had been living under. 'Giap has the camp ringed by at least 200 heavy guns, transported in pieces by coolies across the mountains all the way from China.'

'That's a logistical impossibility,' Gustave exclaimed. 'I heard Colonel Valentin himself say so.'

Mireille took a sip from the glass Marie pushed towards her. 'When he heard the ranging shots of the Viet heavy guns, Valentin killed himself – unable to face the fact that Giap had achieved the impossible.' Her voice was shaking despite all efforts at self-control. 'He did it with a hand grenade, Gustave. When you think about it, that is a difficult way for a man with one hand to commit suicide. He had to pull out the pin with his teeth.'

For a moment, neither of her listeners spoke. Then Marie asked quietly, 'How did you get out of the camp and back to Hanoi?'

Her friend was calmer now. She took a long drink. 'The general ordered me to leave on a tiny artillery spotter plane that had been repaired in a bunker. We got off during a lull in the shelling. There was only one other passenger on board: a wounded Vietnamese para. No one else will escape from Dien, I can tell you that for free.'

Gustave turned to Raoul, who had just joined them. 'These Viet guns around Dien Bien Phu, Raoul. We'll bomb the hell out of them, won't we?'

'Do you want the official reply, or my private thoughts?' Six months in Lépine's HQ had given Raoul a cynical outlook on the war. On the first day of each month he requested a combat posting to Dien Bien Phu itself, but each time his master refused permission.

'I'd like both,' said Gustave soberly. He thought from Raoul's voice that the other man had been drinking.

'Officially,' Raoul announced loudly, 'we have total air superiority, my friends. So, it's unnecessary to worry about this temporary setback. You didn't read our press handout of this afternoon? Quote: "The Air Force is carrying out aerial reconnaissance to locate the Viet batteries. We shall then drop *n*. tons of H.E. to blow the bastards to pieces. Meantime the camp will be resupplied by airdrop." End of quote.' He spat.

'Unofficially?' asked Marie. She felt a chill of fear and wished she had brought her young daughter to Hanoi and not left her on the plantation a hundred miles away.

'Unofficially,' Mireille answered for Raoul, 'General Giap has been one step ahead of us from the start. In addition to his 105mm guns blasting hell out of our positions, he also has a ring of anti-aircraft guns around the camp that effectively interdict air support. A Dakota flying in a straight line on a supply drop has to fly through a wall of flak. Airborne reinforcements are out of the question.'

'Jesus!' from Gustave. Even a civilian could appreciate what that meant.

'I don't think He's going to help us, either,' said Mireille desperately. She stood up and said, her voice breaking, 'There are men I love out there, Gustave, and they're all going to die. All of them. And nobody here cares.' She ran from the terrace into the darkened gardens.

'Let her go!' Gustave held Raoul back. Together they watched his wife hurry after her friend.

A waiter appeared from the shadows to place two more glasses of champagne on the table and withdraw as silently as he had come.

'I heard a rumour this afternoon,' said Gustave soberly, 'that one of the outposts held by the Legion has been overrun.'

Raoul swallowed his drink in one gulp. 'Not just *an*

outpost,' he said. 'It was the vital one, on the hill which overlooks the airstrip. In a sixty-minute bombardment, 600 shells from the Viet heavy guns wiped the position right off the map.'

'I don't know anything about military operations,' Gustave interrupted, 'but this is incredible. Why weren't our men – what's the phrase? Why weren't they well dug in? We've had four months to get ready for this siege.'

'We were dug in against mortars,' Raoul said sourly. 'Nobody dreamed that the Viets had heavy guns until the first rounds fell this afternoon. We thought we were fighting savages. At the end of the bombardment, the men who were still alive on that hill waited for the sound of horns and gongs and the usual screaming as human waves of *bo-doi* hurled themselves forward to be cut down on the barbed wire.

'Instead, Giap used modern tactics, sending in well-trained sappers with plastic explosives and Bangalore torpedoes to cut the wire. His troops had bazookas to destroy our machine-gun emplacements. In five hours it was all over. A whole battalion of the Legion was wiped out to the last man.'

As Gustave sat silent, trying to absorb the news, Raoul clapped his hands to summon a waiter. He pulled a wad of piastre notes from his pocket and thrust them at the man. 'Whisky,' he ordered. 'Get me a bottle.'

'Tonight,' he said to Gustave, 'I'm going to get drunk.'

'Monday, 19 April 1954: Situation report at 0700 hours . . .'

Raoul suspected that General Lépine was not listening. He continued the morning briefing none the less, tapping loudly on the wall map in the general's office. 'Outposts Béatrice, Anne-Marie and Gabrielle are now in the hands of the Viet Minh, *mon général*. Latest intelligence indicates that Giap has over 50,000 combat troops ringing Dien Bien Phu, supported by more than 75,000 coolies transporting food and ammunition supplies.'

'Our casualty figures?' Lépine did not turn round but remained at the window, staring out at the sandbagged courtyard. To the open dismay of the civil authorities, he had given orders that all public buildings in Hanoi were to be protected by walls of sandbags. The Opera House and the cathedral were sandbagged and shut. The Paul Doumer suspension bridge across the river was choked by tanks and lorries. Both ends of the massive structure were protected by heavy machine-gun emplacements. The city's shady, tree-lined avenues were being desecrated by untidy sprawls of barbed wire. Army checkpoints were stopping and searching all Vietnamese traffic.

'It makes the place look like a military camp,' the mayor had complained. 'And it's very bad for business.'

'Hanoi is a military camp,' Lépine had retorted.

Even the sandbagging had been done against the orders of his political masters in Paris. Spread no alarm, they ordained with habitual Olympian detachment.

The monsoon was due in two days' time. Even without the Viet guns, the weather would halt flying for days on end. The leaden overcast through which the sun had not penetrated for the last two weeks seemed to squat above the town like a bad omen. The build-up of heat and humidity did nothing to help Lépine's temper.

'I wanted yesterday's casualty figures checked,' he snapped.

Raoul covered a yawn with the sheaf of papers in his hand. He had spent the night drinking with Gustave, had a shower and shave and then reported for duty.

'A casualty level of 150 per cent –' Lépine turned to meet the eyes of his ADC – 'is excessive. How did De Bonneville explain that?'

'He instanced the First Legion para battalion, *mon général*. On paper, it's one of his strongest elements. In fact, it has ceased to exist. Of the original 700 *effectif*, less than one hundred are still alive. Almost all of them are wounded. The confusion in the figures is because many men have been wounded two or three times but are still fighting.'

Lépine stopped listening. *Never reinforce failure* was one of the first maxims an officer cadet learned. But he had no choice: his orders from Paris were that the struggle at Dien Bien Phu must continue at whatever cost until the politicians haggling with the Viet Minh representatives in Geneva could find a way out of the mess. Yet any soldier could see there was no way the French could win this battle without American help and . . .

'I had an EYES ONLY cable from the Ministry this morning . . .' The general interrupted Raoul's recitation by pulling out of his trouser pocket a much-folded piece of paper. 'Decoded, it informs me that: IN WORDS OF PRESIDENT EISENHOWER COMMA THERE WILL BE NO UNITED STATES INVOLVEMENT IN VIETNAM WAR STOP.'

Stunned, Raoul put down the clipboard. It was the decision they had been waiting for: the fate of Dien Bien Phu had already been decided in Washington.

Lépine continued reading, as though voicing the words that were going to cost so many lives made them more credible:

'UNITED STATES PACIFIC FLEET INCLUDING CARRIERS WITH SIX TACTICAL ATOMIC BOMBS ON BOARD DESTINED BY PENTAGON FOR AIRDROP ON VIET ENCIRCLEMENT DIEN BIEN PHU NOW STEAMING EASTWARDS REPEAT EASTWARDS AWAY FROM VIETNAM COAST MESSAGE ENDS.'

'Then it's all over.' Raoul let out his anger by hitting the map on the wall with the back of his hand.

Lépine's shoulders slumped. He sat down in one of the visitor's chairs as if denying that his arse belonged in the seat of responsibility behind the elegant Louis XV desk. 'Someone has to tell De Bonneville,' he said bleakly.

'I'll go up to the radio room straight away.'

The general shook his head. 'The Viets monitor every transmission,' he said wearily, 'and Intelligence suspect they have broken our codes. So this message has to go by word of mouth, Duvalier.'

'My mouth?' suggested Raoul quickly.

'You've asked me before,' said Lépine, irritated. 'Each

time, I have told you that as the son of a general, who will one day be a general himself, your place is here.'

Raoul drew himself up at attention. 'With respect, *mon général*, I didn't ask to be seconded to you from the Legion in the first place. Frankly, I suspect my father's hand in this appointment as your ADC, but I've carried out my duty conscientiously, detesting every hour of every day I have worked in this office. I wasn't made to push paper. And now . . . after the news you have just given me, it doesn't matter a monkey's fuck who is your ADC, whether it's me or Donald Duck.'

The unexpected outburst of pent-up emotion made Lépine reflect for a second. Then he nodded, cold and unemotional to the last. 'Your assessment is correct, Duvalier. You can go. I shall be sorry to lose you.'

Raoul's spirits soared for the first time since he had been posted to Hanoi. He threw the wad of paper he was holding into a waste bin. It was all meaningless.

'With respect, *mon général*,' he said, 'I rather hope never to see a clipboard again.'

With a brisk salute, he spun on his heel and left the office before his master could change his mind.

Poor Lépine! History is cruel to generals who lose a campaign. Yet he did the job he was trained to do:

> *Whatever happens, we have got*
> *the Maxim gun, and they have not.*

It wasn't Lépine's fault that Giap had a better Maxim gun than ours. Of course, the Americans had an even better one which they had been dangling in front of us, but at the last moment they snatched it away. . . .

It all sounds mock heroic now, but I left that office walking on air. It's a good metaphor to describe my emotions, looking forward to jumping out of an aeroplane for the first time in my life – under battle conditions! I knew it was a one-way ticket, even if I survived the landing. Yet I was as eager for the experience as I would have been to ride a good horse I didn't know or go skiing alone hors piste *in an avalanche area. You could say I needed to feel adrenalin coursing through my veins after all those months serving as Lépine's lackey, but it was more than that.*

As the position of the beleaguered garrison grew daily worse and the world seemed less and less interested in its fate, a clamour had arisen in the Legion regiments spread over the length and breadth of Vietnam. Thousands of men volunteered to parachute in and fight to the end alongside their comrades. If I had bothered Lépine time and again to let me go, I was only one of many. There was no question in our minds of a rescue operation; you didn't need to work in HQ to know that the garrison's position was hopeless.

It was as if one man going down beneath impossible odds in some bar-room brawl had cried: 'A moi, la Légion!' *Our code of honour made it impossible not to hear the call of our brothers-in-arms who were dying out there – and doubly impossible not to answer the call.*

3

Raoul watched carefully as the burly para sergeant with tattooed forearms clipped the release line of his parachute to the static line which ran the length of the stripped-out Dakota.

He followed suit and checked for the tenth time that the fire selector of his MAT 49 machine pistol was on safety with the magazine rammed firmly home before shuffling towards the rear hatch of the Dakota. The dorsal parachute packs banging against the back of their knees made the men waddle like bandy-legged frogs. As the plane lurched in a wind pocket all the frogs swayed first one way, then another.

The legionnaires preparing to jump into what remained of Dien Bien Phu were of two kinds. Half of them were tough pros from the elite Deuxième Bataillon Etranger de Parachutistes; jumping out of a plane was what they were trained for. Seven hundred others that day were, like Raoul, untrained volunteers about to jump for the first time in their lives.

There was a crash that sounded loud even to ears deafened by the roar of the engines. One engine coughed and belched black oily smoke. The Dakota lurched and slipped sideways, losing height as men clung to each other for support while the pilot fought for control. The plane levelled out for the drop run to the irregular accompaniment of further anti-aircraft bursts.

Grinning with excitement, the tattooed para sergeant hauled Raoul up from the floor. He pointed to a small light blinking above the open jump hatch.

'Green light, captain. Here we go,' he shouted over the noise of engines, the shell bursts and the wind rushing in through the open hatch.

Once out of the plane, Raoul swung in comparative silence beneath his canopy as the aircraft disappeared towards the horizon, bursts of ack-ack following them as they went. Two of the Dakotas were trailing black smoke and losing height visibly.

Raoul checked the chute billowing above his head. So far as he could tell, it was normal. He looked down. The ground seemed very close. It was impossible to reconcile the scene below with his memory of the neatly drawn maps of the valley in front of which he had given his daily briefings at Lépine's HQ in Hanoi. Apart from some shell-shattered and burnt-out planes on what had been the landing strip, there were no landmarks or features of any kind left in the area of the camp. Trees, the road, even the village and the airstrip had all vanished in a wasteland reminiscent of a First World War battlefield.

With no sense of personal danger he watched a gently curving line of Viet tracers which climbed lazily up towards him. Two figures hanging from parachutes nearby twitched as they dropped through the stream of bullets, then hung limply from the shrouds.

The shock of landing took him by surprise. The para sergeant in the plane had told him it was like jumping from the second storey of a house. Raoul recalled being thrown during an outing with the Cheverny hunt and rolled on by his horse. This was worse: all the breath was driven from his lungs, his ribs felt as though they had been squeezed in a gigantic fist. The concerted noise of artillery and small-arms fire both near and far blended into a sustained roar.

Dragged along the stony ground by the chute, unable to

get back his wind and release himself from the harness, Raoul watched helplessly as a group of paras who had just landed spun in awkward attitudes like ungainly puppets and fell to the ground.

He felt a sharp and violent pain in his right knee. A short burst of automatic fire from close at hand threw across his body the corpse of the Viet commando who had attempted to slash his belly open and missed as Raoul was dragged along the ground by the parachute. A knife spun through the air and landed in the churned-up gravel. A few metres away a para in the act of unclipping his harness was suddenly sprung upon from behind by another Viet in black pyjamas whose knife slit the Frenchman's throat from ear to ear. A stutter of shots from a MAT 49 and both bodies fell to the ground locked together.

Above the billowing of the wind in the silk of his parachute and the cacophony of explosions, Raoul could hear the demented screams of a man whose belly had been ripped apart by a burst of machine-gun bullets. The high falsetto was like an obscene piccolo playing solo above an infernal orchestra. The wind was pulling Raoul's chute towards a tangle of barbed wire in which several men struggled, impaled and unable to free themselves. Machine-gun fire washed over the wire, hosing down the bodies, which jerked and slumped inert.

In a final effort of desperation, Raoul found the quick-release button of his harness and slammed the heel of his hand hard against it. The dragging momentum stopped. He rolled over to get clear of the shrouds and found himself staring up at the silhouette of a black-clad Viet in the act of bayoneting a legionnaire who was entangled in the lines of his chute. Safety catch flicked off, Raoul loosed two short bursts into the Viet's face and saw it disintegrate in a pink spray.

He scrambled to his feet. One look at the legionnaire's face told him he had been too late. Two more Viets rose out of a shallow ditch only metres away. One, unarmed, scrambled across the gravel in a desperate attempt to salvage a weapon while the other drew back his arm to hurl a grenade. Raoul loosed another short burst from his MAT 49, smashing the grenade thrower back into the fold of ground where he had been lying. Then he turned his machine pistol on the second Viet, who was in the act of picking up the fallen legionnaire's rifle. The boy – he could not have been more than fifteen years old – looking surprised, stared at his crimson belly and crumpled to the ground beside the legionnaire. As Raoul crouched instinctively to change magazines, the grenade exploded, raining gravel and pieces of flesh over him.

The morality of it never entered my mind. Perhaps I lack a conscience and that is why a code of honour is so important to men like me.

Those Viets would have killed me, so I killed them first, but I felt no more emotion about the act than if it had been a game. The legionnaire's code we all learn to chant in unison says it well: In combat, legionnaire, you act without passion and without hatred.

I felt neither emotion for those men. They and I had played a game in which the stakes were their lives against mine. I had won – as I usually did at games – and they had lost. That was all. If I had lost, I should not have borne them any ill will in my dying thoughts or felt that I had been cheated of my destiny.

I felt no fear, crouching there and ramming the fresh magazine home; I was a soldier doing what I was supposed to do. I can understand men being afraid who are in action for the first time, or whose nerves are frayed by shellfire, or too long exposure to combat. . . . I can understand them being afraid, but I had been under fire before, I was healthy, fit, well fed and fresh to the battle. I was neither afraid nor was I brave, for bravery – in my book – is what you have to summon from within to overcome the paralysis of fear.

To be honest I felt good and, in the midst of all that hell, more peaceful than the man who had spent six months chafing at the bit in Lépine's elegant office. I can't explain it – I draw no moral – but there it is.

*

A hoarse voice yelled in French: 'Over here. Keep low!' Raoul obeyed without thinking and found himself in what had been a trench and was now just a shallow declivity littered with torn sandbags and twisted pieces of corrugated iron. Facing him were two haggard, wounded men with dirty bandages on legs, heads, arms. Red-rimmed eyes glared over the top of an FM 24/29 machine-gun at the carnage outside their frail shelter.

'Welcome to Dien Bien Phu, *mon capitaine*,' one of them gasped hoarsely. 'Do you have any water?'

Raoul unbuckled the two canteens strapped to his belt and handed them over. The men drank with groans of pleasure, ignoring the stream of bullets passing only inches above their heads. Dragging his injured leg behind him, Raoul snaked his way along a shallow trench to the field hospital.

His first sight of the underground casualty dressing station defied belief. The single surgeon in Dien Bien Phu had volunteered to be parachuted into the camp when it became obvious that continued evacuation of the wounded was out of the question. Since arrival, he had been operating night and day with one or two hours' sleep in twenty-four. He had just one trained helper: a French army nurse who had scrambled off the last ambulance plane to land only seconds before a Viet shell had destroyed the aircraft. Assisting her were a dozen Arab women. They were whores from the Bordel Militaire Controlé – the Legion's mobile brothel. When custom dwindled they had volunteered, as the only women among 18–20,000 men, to help care for the flood of wounded and dying.

On paper in General Lépine's office, the hospital was described as 'fit to grace the Maginot Line with forty beds, operating theatres, X-ray room, dental surgery and all the paraphernalia of modern medicine'. The reality was that, overwhelmed by the thousands of casualties, and lacking blood, plasma, oxygen, drugs or even clean bandages, the hospital of Dien Bien Phu had been reduced to a stinking charnel house.

After one look at the long lines of mud-covered

wounded – some waiting patiently for attention, others screaming in uncontrollable agony – Raoul took a scarf from the neck of a dead para sergeant and tied it tightly around his injured knee. The wound was an ugly gash, but he could not bring himself to ask for proper treatment, surrounded by men who had lost arms and legs, men whose intestines spilled blue and red from slashed bellies, men whose blood was pumping out past tourniquets until they collapsed into coma.

Raoul recognised the French nurse in bloodstained khaki fatigues as a girl with whom he had often danced at the Cercle Sportif. As she came towards him between the rows of stretchers, he opened his mouth to speak to her, then shut it again when he saw her glazed eyes and zombie-like walk. She was asleep on her feet.

The injured man on whom the surgeon had been working, sat up on the filthy operating table. A re-used bandage held in place a large and blood-soaked dressing where his left eye had been. His right hand was also swathed in bandages through which fresh blood already showed.

Instead of complaining of his injuries, the patient joked: 'Excellent modifications, *toubib*! Now I shan't have to shut my left eye when taking aim.' He held up the bandaged hand. 'And as to my two missing fingers, they always did get in the way on Saturday nights.'

The dirty, unshaven face – what there was visible – was that of a man of fifty, but the voice was the same. . . . 'Koenig?' Raoul called.

'Duvalier, by God!' The injured man looked in Raoul's direction. He tried to smile but only one side of his face moved. 'What are you doing here?'

Raoul embraced his friend.

Koenig did not bother to duck as a near hit brought a shower of dirt from the ceiling. 'Are you the reinforcements we've been waiting for?' he asked sarcastically.

Raoul shook his head. 'There aren't going to be any.'

The single eye in the pain-racked face studied Raoul. 'You surprise me,' he snarled. 'They've really fucked up this time, in Hanoi and Paris – your generals with their arse-brained plans.'

'This whole place is a shit-storm,' Raoul agreed.

Koenig closed his good eye. 'I can't see anything wrong,' he said.

Raoul grinned at the Nelson joke. It was typical of Koenig to deny by humour the pain he was in. They sat on a pile of spilled sandbags, waiting for a lull in the shelling. Raoul lit two cigarettes and passed one to his friend.

Koenig inhaled deeply. 'The quack gave me the last of his brandy,' he muttered. The last reserves of energy he had summoned up for the operation without anaesthetic were used up. 'It was Bisquit. Very nice of him.' The twitching eye closed and his head slumped on to his chest, the cigarette still in his mouth.

Raoul grabbed the other man's shoulders and shook him. Koenig awoke with a start.

Raoul started to apologise. 'I thought . . .'

The single bloodshot eye blinked. 'No such luck. Give me back my fag, you thieving bastard.'

Raoul retrieved it from the ground. It was blood-stained and grimy but Koenig did not mind.

During a lull in the shelling, they left the hospital dug-out. Koenig headed back to his few remaining men on the perimeter while Raoul limped in the direction of De Bonneville's command post to report his arrival. Under the leaden skies burdened with the monsoon rains, no birds sang. A solitary machine-gun was firing steadily on the other side of the camp, like a demented woodpecker. There were no trees, only churned earth and rubble and refuse. A stench of explosives mingled with the odours of decay hung in the humid air.

In the command bunker General De Bonneville looked as though he had not slept in months. He and his staff moved like automata. For several moments the defeated commander of Dien Bien Phu stared at Raoul's face, unable to focus his eyes sufficiently to recognise the man in front of him.

'I'm glad you're here, Duvalier,' he said at last.

When Raoul gave the news of Eisenhower's decision, which had travelled from Washington via Paris, De Bonneville laughed bitterly. 'It was never going to happen,' he said. 'I knew the Yanks wouldn't do a thing to help us, when it came to the crunch. Lépine didn't need to send you here to tell me that.'

'He didn't send me,' said Raoul. 'I volunteered, sir. I never wanted to be his ADC in the first place. I'm a legionnaire. I want a combat command, sir.'

Leroux, the senior Legion officer present, laughed. He swept an arm in a 180-degree arc. 'Take your pick . . .'

'No.' A glint came into the tired eyes of the man behind the table. 'Le Mans,' he said in a voice hoarse with tiredness, too many cigarettes and too little to drink. 'Didn't I read in *L'Equipe* some time, Duvalier, that you've driven that circuit in a Maserati?'

'It was a Ferrari.' Raoul was impatient; he had not dropped into the middle of a battle in order to exchange small talk.

'So it was.' A thin smile crept over De Bonneville's wolfish features. 'I need a driver,' he said.

Raoul fingered the trigger guard of the sub-machine-gun slung across his chest. 'And I want a combat command, sir.'

'And I,' said the general, 'want a man who can handle a jeep on a battlefield as though it were a Ferrari at Le Mans. It's a strange assignment I'm giving you, Duvalier, but it's an important one, so listen hard.'

4

The monsoon broke next day exactly on time at eleven o'clock in the morning.

As the downpour cut visibility to a matter of feet, the drumming of rain on corrugated iron shelters almost drowned the noises of battle. Within minutes the arid wasteland of Dien Bien Phu became an obscene swamp of mud, blood, refuse, faeces and decaying flesh through which wounded and bone-weary men hauled themselves back to their posts. There was no longer any pretence at probing the enemy or even of repulsing the encroaching Viet trenches that were now within grenade-throwing range of the shrinking perimeter at many points. Life for the remaining legionnaires and other French troops had become a matter of staying alive another hour, another day if they were lucky. Some men huddled in a burrow they had dug and pulled a few sandbags over the entrance, determined to stay there until the fighting ended, come what may.

The jeep in which Raoul sat, shivering with cold, all rank insignia torn from his uniform, was the only French vehicle in the valley still in running order. On either side of the jeep was mounted an FM 24/29 machine-gun. Both weapons were being constantly oiled and polished by two lean-faced, stubble-chinned German legionnaires. They called themselves Hans and Franz, like a music hall double act. They were, in De Bonneville's words, to be Raoul's guardian angels.

The vehicle was parked under a roof of logs covered by several feet of earth in a bunker which could resist anything short of a direct hit by a 105mm shell. The constant noise that pervaded the rest of the camp was reduced in the shelter to a distant hum, punctuated by an occasional explosion nearer than the rest.

Rainwater dripped continually through the roof. The driver's seat was the only dry place. Behind Raoul's back a stack of ammunition boxes filled the rear of the vehicle. Most were discarded empties now packed solid with over a million dollars' worth of gold coins which made up De Bonneville's *caisse noire*. The black box, as it was traditionally called by the French in Indo-China, was the pay-chest for the 15,000 colonial troops who had been under De Bonneville's orders at the start of the siege. Since – unlike European soldiers – the Thai and Vietnamese levies could simply put down their weapons, exchange their uniforms for local garb and melt into the countryside, they had to be paid daily in gold to keep them fighting. When the situation worsened and even this could not keep them at their posts, they faded away by hundreds every night.

The pay-chest was one of the few things in Dien Bien Phu that was worth saving. Raoul's orders were to get it away from the Viets at all costs. Three miles to the south of the main camp lay strongpoint Isabelle, the only position outside the main perimeter which was still holding out against the masses of Viets. At Isabelle, a Foreign Legion colonel by name of Lafont had decided not to surrender, but to lead his surviving men in a fighting break-out. Raoul was to drive the gold to Isabelle and join the break-out party.

Even talking about it in De Bonneville's bunker, the mission had sounded like a more arduous alternative to suicide: to reach Isabelle meant driving right through the centre of the encircling Viet Minh forces.

Hans and Franz had looked at each other as though Raoul were crazy when he briefed them: 'We are to wait until dark before driving the jeep through the encircling Viet positions until reaching Route 41. We then follow the road south to reach Isabelle.'

For the sake of their morale, he affected confidence, repeating De Bonneville's own words: 'The last thing the Viets will be expecting at this stage of the battle is a jeep driving straight through their lines. With surprise on our side, we may just make it.'

It was the biggest gamble of my life – with odds of several thousand to one against.

As Franz said, even if we did get through, it was quite likely that the trigger-happy defenders at Isabelle would disbelieve their own eyes at the improbable sight of a French jeep belting through the night towards them – and simply blast the jeep and us to pieces!

That was the least of our worries. To begin with, nobody knew whether the road was still passable by jeep or had been cut into a thousand pieces by trenches and shell holes.

Ours not to reason why, as the poet said. The Legion's code of honour puts it more prosaically: Your mission is sacred. You carry it out at any cost, come what may.

To stop the men thinking too much, I set them to work. First I had them practise changing the wheels of the jeep in seconds. If we hit a small mine or a lucky shot pierced a tyre, they would need to be quicker at the job than any pit team at Le Mans. When I was satisfied, I dispatched my two guardian angels to comb the battlefield for two extra jeep wheels with serviceable tyres which we could carry as spares.

In obedience to De Bonneville's order not to expose myself to any unnecessary risk, I stayed at the wheel of the jeep and did what soldiers do at times like that. Out of my wallet I took the latest batch of pictures Huguette had sent me. She regularly sent copies of her latest proofs. I can see those particular images still; the memory of them had to last me a long time. . . .

In one pose she gazed haughtily at the world in a Dior dress, a hand lightly resting on a Grecian pillar. In another, she relaxed in a swimsuit on the beach at St Tropez. At some smart stud farm, in jodhpurs and tailored riding jacket she posed beside a racehorse. The pictures, false and posed as they were, summed up my life with her. It consisted of night clubs and smart restaurants and the beautiful, preferably rich, people who inhabited her world.

When Hans and Franz came back with the tyres and some biscuits they had scrounged, they exchanged whistles of appreciation at Huguette's icy beauty. In return they showed me their dog-eared, out-of-focus snapshots of wives and kids back home, wherever that was.

And I felt a great emptiness within me. I had never been given to introspection; my life was the way it was and I enjoyed it. But – perhaps with a premonition of what was to come – I looked at those men's family photographs and felt lonely. I realised for the first time that I did not know Huguette's private face. Even in the bedroom, she had never been off guard. The pictures she sent had all been taken for newspapers and magazines; any with a suggestion of intimacy or warmth had been blue-pencilled on a contact sheet by strangers. It seemed that our whole marriage had been a public event.

My reverie was interrupted as a nearby Tannoy speaker crackled into life and I recognised the voice of Colonel Leroux, reciting a story that every legionnaire knew by heart. We learnt it in training and heard it every 30 April, the Legion's birthday. That day was the anniversary of the battle of Camerone in Mexico some eighty years before. Leroux's ritual account of great valour against overwhelming odds held for us all the comfort of a favourite bedtime story. We listened like Catholics following the familiar litany of the mass.

'On 30 April 1863, Captain Jean Danjou, a thirty-five-year-old veteran of the Crimea, Italy and North Africa volunteered to lead a small company of legionnaires in an endeavour to keep open the highway between Vera Cruz and Mexico City, along which a convoy was bringing three million francs in gold to French headquarters.'

Neither of Raoul's Germans had taken any special interest in the jeep's cargo. Like Danjou's men of ninety years before, they were simply doing a job. To them, the important crates in the jeep were the ones marked with a white cross, which contained ammunition.

Raoul wondered whether future generations of legionnaires would listen to the story of the gold of Dien Bien Phu, as he was listening to the story of Danjou and his heroic men.

Leroux's voice continued: 'After marching non-stop from one o'clock in the morning until 0700 hours, it was decided to make a stop and brew some coffee. The Mexican commander chose this moment to attack. Captain Danjou organised a fighting withdrawal of his men to the farmhouse at Camerone. The legionnaires were now surrounded by at least two thousand Mexicans. Of Danjou's original sixty-four men, sixteen were already dead, wounded or missing.

'Mortally wounded, Captain Danjou made each legionnaire swear to fight to the death. By six o'clock, after a day of continuous fighting, the original company of three officers and sixty-two men had been reduced to one officer and eleven legionnaires. They had had nothing to eat or drink for twenty-four hours.'

There was a crackle of interference on the Tannoy. Colonel Leroux's voice continued: 'Surrounded by the bodies of 300 Mexican dead, the single surviving officer ordered the last four unwounded legionnaires to fix bayonets and follow him in a charge against the enemy.'

The Tannoy went silent as a shell cut the cable for the thousandth time. Franz crossed himself, his lips moving in prayer.

Another loudspeaker took over; the Viet psy-war team was in action again. They had stopped using Vietnamese, Thai and Arabic since virtually all the colonial troops had ceased fighting or run away. Clearly borne on the wind from somewhere very close, came the repeated call in French and German: 'French soldiers, legionnaires! Why continue this useless fight? Why die for the profiteering bankers who exploit the French colonies in Indo-China? Why die for Michelin? Why do what the legionnaires did at Camerone and get yourselves massacred?'

Then, faintly at first, to cover the noise of the Viet loud-speakers, men of the Legion began singing the most famous of the Legion's slow nostalgic marching songs, 'Le Boudin'.

'Le Boudin' is a nonsense rhyme about black pudding! In the Legion messes, we sing it at each meal-time. That day, there were no meals but we sang it all the same, to block out the invitation to surrender. The three of us in that jeep joined in at the top of our voices. After listening to the story of Camerone, we were as one man with legionnaires 12,000 miles away in Sidi-bel-Abbès. I don't know how the magic worked, but it did. Not a single man singing in the mud of that death-starred valley gave a bugger for Giap and his men with victory on their side.

The Viet loudspeakers fell silent; either we had won the battle of words or they didn't care any more. Hans and Franz shared their handful of mouldy biscuits with me. We dozed and waited. Whoever said that war is long periods of boredom interspersed by short periods of terror was certainly right about the waiting.

Before midnight we pushed the overloaded jeep through knee-deep mud as far as the French front line; I didn't want to give any warning to the other side by starting the engine too early. Surprise was our main weapon. My orders to Hans and Franz were not to start firing until the jeep was fired on – and then to spread a hail of lead ahead and to both sides of the speeding vehicle.

According to the sappers who silently cut us a way through the wire on what had once been a track leading to Route 41, the Viets had lifted most of the mines – theirs and ours – in readiness for the final assault on our positions. Most of them! they said. I joked that one would be enough. . . .

Raoul reached behind and shook each man's hand. He felt the involuntary tensing of sphincter muscles and the same surge of adrenalin as on the starting grid. One of the Germans was muttering a childhood prayer. Neither of them had commented when the sappers wired a demolition charge under the floor of the jeep. The detonator was under Raoul's seat; if the jeep became immobilised, he would blow it up, whether or not they were still in it.

Raoul took a deep breath, reached by habit to pull down the goggles he was not wearing and pressed the starter. It felt good to be back at the wheel. The jeep was no Ferrari, but, given the terrain they had to cover, it was the best wheeled vehicle in the world. He gunned the motor, listening to the revs, then thrust the gearstick into first and slammed the accelerator to the floor. The jeep skidded in the thick mud and leapt forward, heading southwards into the night.

From this reconnaissance before dusk Raoul knew that the track was dead straight for half a kilometre, until it joined the highway. He had decided to drive semi-blind until that point, flashing the headlights on and off to make a more difficult target.

Spotting obstacles, he changed gear fast, up and down, wrestling with the steering wheel as ruts and potholes twisted the wheels first one way then the other. He was driving with lights off when there came a thump and a scream as they ploughed through the sleeping bodies of a squad of Viets who had been bivouacking on the road itself. As the vehicle bounced over terrified men trying to roll out of the way, Raoul hit the headlight switch and kept going, trying to chicane his way through a nightmare of legs and arms and faces that flashed past in the darkness.

The jeep crashed into and out of shallow depressions – shell holes that the Viets had filled in. Then came a louder crash as they hit the road itself. By sheer luck, no tyre burst and the steering linkage did not snap. Raoul wrenched the wheel hard round and headed south. The road became a series of bends for two kilometres. He had decided not to worry about mines. If they hit an anti-personnel one, with luck they might just blow a tyre; if they set off anything bigger, they'd be blown to hell before they knew about it.

They skidded sideways between the burnt-out carcasses of two French tanks which almost blocked the road. Raoul was aware of the two Germans hanging on for dear life behind him, feeling the same exhilaration as he felt. All three men ducked their heads instinctively as they smashed through a flimsy barrier of oil drums.

'Thank Christ they were empties!' Raoul shouted.

A trench cut right across the road appeared in the head-lights' beam.

'Hold on,' Raoul shouted, accelerating up the low ramp of earth. The jeep took off and landed on the far side of the gap with a bone-shaking crunch. Raoul could hear himself laughing with pure joy: 'We made it!'

At that moment, two Viet soldiers appeared in the beam of light with sub-machine-guns trained on the jeep. Before they could squeeze the trigger, both men were blasted off the road by a roar of fire from Hans' side of the jeep.

A crowd of coolies carrying loads suspended from bamboo poles across their shoulders stood gaping in stunned aston-ishment as the jeep rounded a bend and bore down on them. Raoul held the jeep straight until the last moment, when he decided that the sheer mass of scores of bodies would slow and stop the vehicle like a sandbag stops a bullet. He jerked the wheel savagely to the right and bounced off the road, scraping over rocks and through stunted, shell-torn bushes, hoping he was driving in a curve that would intersect the road again.

They drove through the centre of a cooking fire, scattering embers on to the men sleeping alongside it and bumped back on to the road. A grenade – or it could have been a small mine – exploded just behind the jeep, spraying them with mud. Hans and Franz were firing in short, disciplined bursts, each spraying a quadrant of fire ahead of the jeep. From a captured concrete blockhouse straight ahead, a stream of tracers spat back at them. In the nick of time, Raoul swerved off the road-way just as an anti-tank grenade fired from the blockhouse exploded where they would have been.

And then there was silence, broken only by the noise of the jeep's exhaust. They drove through the night as in a dream landscape. Wet tree trunks, glistening mud banks on either side of the road, faces and figures of men and draught animals flashed by as Raoul skidded, braked, accelerated and drove onto and off the carriageway a thousand times to avoid shell holes and trenches. All the Viets, it seemed, were either asleep or too busy with preparations for the next day's final assault to believe their eyes as the jeep hurtled through the night.

High on adrenalin, I felt invulnerable and godlike. I knew no bullets could touch me.

The ancient Greeks might have said that the gods were letting me be divine for a few minutes in compensation for the incredible ordeal that lay ahead. But I had no thought for the future or the past, except to offer mental thanks to Enrico Ferrari and his drivers who had taught me so many tricks at the wheel on the circuit of Le Mans.

At that moment, nothing mattered – not the gold, or victory or defeat – except getting to the end of that impossible drive. As we crashed through the last barrier before Isabelle, I was in an almost religious ecstasy with a sense of destiny fulfilled. I had been obsessed with fast cars since the age of sixteen. At that moment, I knew why. All had been preparation for one drive. It was the greatest sporting performance of my life and no one would ever know.

We came through the encirclement around Isabelle without a single round being fired at us. Perhaps everyone was looking the wrong way. The jeep crashed through the wire barriers on the French side of the line and careered to a stop with a broken front axle inside a candlelit dug-out where gaunt-faced, hollow-eyed men reached for their weapons until Hans, reverting to his mother tongue in the nick of time, leaped out to stand in the headlights' beam with both hands up in the air, yelling: 'Nicht schiessen, Ihr Frontschweine. Wir sind Freunde.'

It was a good choice of language; there wasn't a Frenchman within earshot! The entire complement of the dug-out was German.

I kept shouting: 'We did it! We did it!' Adrenalin pounding in my veins, I turned to embrace my other guardian angel. Franz gave me a crooked, lopsided grin and fell forward on the smoking breech of his machine-gun. His left ear and half the back of his head were missing.

5

At 1700 hours on Friday, 7 May 1954, General de Bonneville shook hands with his surviving officers. Like a sleepwalker, he led his staff out of the command bunker into the warm drizzle. Past two legionnaire sergeants who were dousing half-burned code books in petrol, they squelched through foul-smelling mud to meet their captors. From hollows and slight indentations in the swamp around them, mud-covered men arose, wounded, hollow-eyed with fatigue, but able to stand up straight for the first time in weeks.

De Bonneville was not to know that of the 12,000 men being taken prisoner with him at that moment, almost 9,000 would never go home, but be written off at the negotiating table in Geneva and vanish into some nameless limbo in the swamps and jungles of Vietnam. Nobody could have guessed that the last returnees would only see France again after sixteen years of captivity.

A group of disembodied white pith helmets were bobbing through the clinging ground mist as the Viet Minh officers entered the camp to accept the surrender. The silence, after 169 days of siege and 56 days of continuous shelling, was unnerving. As men's hearing threshold adjusted, they picked up the faint noise of battle continuing eight kilometres to the south.

De Bonneville's last words as a free man were: 'Isabelle is still holding out. With luck, Lafont will break out tonight under cover of darkness.' He stumbled with tiredness and nearly fell. 'Lafont has his orders. He'll make sure Duvalier gets away tonight, if no one else does.'

Like most prophets about Vietnam, the general was wrong. By 0800 hours next morning, the sound of battle ceased at outpost Isabelle as Lafont too surrendered. Half an hour later, the sound of gunfire broke out again as the victorious Viet Minh turned their machine-guns and assault rifles on their captives and killed every one of the 800 men.

Of all that I knew nothing until much later. Just after dawn, I recall hearing the sound of a heavy mortar walking closer and closer to the bunker where I had taken shelter. The last round I didn't hear. I recovered consciousness to find myself lying in silent blackness and thought I was dead.

Death was very painful; waves of agony pulsed from my legs through my body into my brain. Unable to breathe, I panicked but could not move. Some formless weight was pressing me down in the airless dark: I was buried alive beneath an immovable heap of sandbags.

I suppose it was the pain that stopped me going out of my mind. I tried to lift an arm or even move a finger. Impossible. Nose crushed flat into my face, unable to open my lips I thought I was going to suffocate. Then I realised that there was a narrow gap between the sandbags covering my face, through which enough air filtered to keep me alive. A few shallow breaths later, I fainted from pain.

It was like a dream when I was dug up and recovered conscious-ness for the second time to find my belly being prodded with the sharp end of a bayonet. I was still deaf from the blast. It was a long time before my hearing returned to normal, and my sense of smell took even longer.

In the corner of my field of vision, strangely bent, lay the damaged legs from which pain pulsed through my entire body. No more than four or five metres away, Hans and a couple of other men sat in the attitudes they had held before the explosion, frozen in mid-gesture but dead, their internal organs ruptured by the blast effect of the shell that had buried me. My brain was slow in absorbing the obvious; below the knees, my legs were dead, but Hans and the others were dead all over.

I recognised the rifle pointing at me as a French MAS 49 which the Viets had captured. The skinny little peasant holding it was alternately clenching his teeth with rage and screaming abuse at me, his face contorted with hatred. Although unable to hear a word, I understood very well that he was winding himself up to deliver the killing blow. Behind him, three soldiers had slung their rifles and were wrestling a large flag with the Viet Minh star into position on the pile of rubble that had been Lafont's command bunker.

I watched the MAS 49 lifted high above me, silhouetted against the grey sky, and waited for the thrust that would drive the bayonet through my guts. I waited for this teenage peasant to end my life without any emotion. Then I became aware that a can bô – one of the Viet Minh political commissars – had caught the rifle in mid-thrust and was wrestling for control of it. He was screaming abuse at the bo-doi, to distract him from sticking the bayonet through my belly.

My thoughts were strangely remote, dwelling on the irony of my situation: suppose the sandbags that had saved my life by soaking up the shell blast had also suffocated me! What even greater irony if the man who dug me out of my living tomb chose to end my French life with one thrust of a French bayonet on the end of a French rifle! Such are the thoughts that precede death.

I fainted from pain again before the screaming match was over. When I came to this time, there were no drugs to fight the waves of agony that broke over me. As each receded, I felt myself growing weaker, dragged down by the undertow.

At intervals I was lucid, at other times adrift. Chronology went haywire. Events imprinted themselves on my mind randomly like a badly cut art film full of flashbacks, so that I have never been able to sort out in what order things happened that day. Did I see or imagine the final shell bursts of the Viet Minh assault? Either way, I recall our tracers and theirs spitting through the relentless drizzle . . . men dropping and writhing in agony . . . a dance of *death in which bodies and pieces of bodies flew magically through the air as the Viet Minh cleared the last minefield by the simple expedient of walking a punishment battalion through it.*

It was mid-morning when Raoul opened his eyes to find himself lying in the rain, on the muddy ground beneath a leaden sky. Through the ringing in his ears he heard for the first time a voice which he would never be able to forget: 'My name is Captain Minh.'

Squatting beside the stretcher was the unarmed *can-bô* who had saved him from being bayoneted. 'You smoke, Captain Duvalier?'

'No,' Raoul grunted.

'But you do. I know. Here.' The commissar rummaged in the green canvas satchel on the ground beside him and took out a bloodstained packet of French cigarettes. He lit two and put one to Raoul's lips. 'How are you feeling?' His French was perfect with just a trace of singsong.

'I need medical attention.' Raoul spoke through gritted teeth. His voice sounded alien and distant in his own ears.

Captain Minh nodded. The nicotine was clearing Raoul's head. He looked around to find himself on a moonscape of debris-strewn gravel, alone apart from Minh and three bodies lying a couple of metres away.

'Where am I?' he asked. 'Why am I not with the other wounded?'

Squinting through the smoke, Minh savoured his reply. 'There are no other wounded at Isabelle.'

'You're lying.' Raoul tried to raise, and fell back as waves of pain engulfed him. 'There were several hundred men alive here this morning.'

'All dead,' smiled Minh. 'All dead.' With a mounting sense of excitement, he surveyed the man lying on the stretcher in front of him. The medics had informed him that this casualty would probably die without treatment, but not immediately.

'You killed everyone?' A total massacre was hard to believe.

Minh threw away his cigarette end. 'Colonel Lafont should have surrendered at 1700 hours yesterday. That was the agreed time. He chose to fight on, hoping to break through our lines under cover of darkness. In failing, he forfeited the right of his men to surrender.'

'You killed them all?'

'Except for you.'

'Why me?'

Minh chuckled. 'Because I found you in time, Captain Duvalier. That is why you are alive. If I had reached you a few minutes later, you would be as dead as your comrades. As it is, you are now alive and my hostage.'

'Hostage?' The word did not belong in Raoul's military vocabulary.

A nod. 'During your so-called age of chivalry in Europe, a knight whose life was spared in battle became the property of his captor until ransomed by friends or his own wealth. Am I not right?'

The effect of the cigarette had worn off. The pain came back in black relentless waves, worse than before. Despite all his determination, Raoul could not fight it. 'I need medical attention,' he moaned.

Minh stood and picked up the canvas satchel that was the *can-bô*'s badge of office; there were no insignia of rank on the olive-green uniform he wore. He looked down at the man lying on the stretcher, trying to gauge his strengths and weaknesses. 'Yes,' he agreed. 'You need medical attention urgently, Captain Duvalier. But in the People's Republic of Vietnam, we have no privileges; everything must be earned. So you must now earn the right to medical attention by giving me some information.' He brushed dirt from the underside of the satchel.

'Under the Geneva Convention,' claimed Raoul, 'I have the right to give you only my name, rank and number.'

Minh was walking away. 'The People's Republic of Vietnam is not a signatory to the Geneva Convention. I have said what you must do.'

*

I tried to guess the time by estimating the position of the sun through the grey overcast, but it was impossible. My watch had been stolen while I was unconscious. I would have given a lot for a drink or another cigarette. I must have been hallucinating from the heat, the thirst and the pain, for at one stage I thought Franz sat up and talked to me. I could not understand more than a few words; he was talking German. And did Minh return to squat beside the stretcher and eat his midday bowl of rice, watching me, biding his time? Or was that a hallucination too?

The only thing that was real was the pain from my legs. To distract myself I felt for my wallet, but someone had rifled my pockets. I wondered what skinny Asian peasant was looking at those photographs of my elegant wife modelling the latest Dior fashions.

The Duvalier family had two homes: the old villa by the sea in Brittany where they came together en masse in the long summer holidays and a large nineteenth-century mansion south of Paris, full of portraits of generals in gilt frames. Built by a prosperous merchant in the 1880s when the railway turned the peaceful village of Bourg-la-Reine into a suburb, the house stood in a garden of well-tended lawn and mature trees – a setting for an Impressionist painting. A delicate Chinese pavilion peeped through the shrubbery to complete the illusion.

Raoul's mother welcomed her daughter-in-law on the sunlit terrace. She placed the gift-wrapped box of handmade chocolates from the rue de Rivoli beside the bottle of white wine in its crystal glass cooler on the marble drinks table, and dismissed the maid with a wave of her hand.

For her weekly visit to Bourg-la-Reine, Raoul's wife was dressed in a trim little polka-dot cotton suit, tight at the waist, with a matching pillbox hat. Her three-inch stiletto heels gave her the navel-before-nose stance of her pictures in the pages of *Vogue*. Slight shortsightedness created the air of distant aloofness which Mr Dior required of his models. Cool, pale and distinguished, with a classical profile and violet-coloured, slightly oval eyes, Huguette looked on the world and found it ugly by comparison with herself.

Raoul's mother poured wine into two glasses and gave a toast that had more meaning that day than usual: '*A la santé de Raoul!*'

Huguette took the minutest sip of wine and replaced her glass, crossing her legs and wondering how soon she could cut short the duty visit and leave.

'Have you heard the news from Indo-China?' Her mother-in-law came straight to the point.

'People are talking of nothing else,' Huguette complained. 'It's really boring. All day long in the show room yesterday I heard nothing but Dien Bien Phu, Dien Bien Phu, Dien Bien Phu.'

Raoul's mother wondered how her daughter-in-law would react. 'It's the biggest defeat we've had since 1940, Huguette. In addition, I'm afraid I have some bad news for you. The general rang me from the Defence Ministry half an hour ago. One of his old chums told him that Raoul parachuted into Dien Bien Phu just before the surrender.'

Huguette smiled vaguely. To cover an incipient yawn she thought of checking her make-up but knew that the older woman regarded doing that in public as bad manners. Trying to show an interest, she asked, 'Does that mean Raoul is a prisoner?'

'I hope so.'

Huguette stood and turned round, pretending to admire the flowers in order to steal a surreptitious look at her watch. Behind the professional smile, she was thinking: How damn, bloody boring. And how typical of Raoul! It's bad enough to get himself posted to China or wherever, without this. . . .

She was a woman who needed admiration. Her husband's own stunning good looks had attracted her for the narcis-sistic reason that he looked good with her – as a gorgeous piece of jewellery or a wonderful new dress might set off her natural beauty. His reputation as a playboy sportsman amused her; it made him into a sort of trophy she had won. His military life meant no more to her than a series of glamorous uniforms in which he looked dashing and manly beside her.

In public she liked seeing other women look at him, knowing that he was her property. And when they were alone together, she enjoyed the repeated lovemaking that told her just how much she turned him on. But she was an addict who needed regular fixes of admiration, so when Raoul was away – playing soldiers, as she called it bitterly – she had to get her daily dose elsewhere.

Next to jewellery and clothes, mirrors were Huguette's favourite objects. The sight of herself reflected in the long windows of the house reminded her that in less than half an hour she would be standing in front of the bedroom mirror with her lover behind her. She would watch his hands caress her, slowly undoing buttons. He would slip her clothes off one by one, exposing the body on which she lavished so much care. Throughout she would watch his eyes feasting on her body while his hands explored her. . . .

Huguette shuddered and squeezed her thighs together in anticipation.

'We shall have to be very brave,' Raoul's mother was saying. 'Now sit down and let's have a talk about what we're going to do – and say. To the press, for instance.'

'*Merde!*' breathed Huguette to her reflection. 'I'm going to be late.'

6

The flies were the worst nuisance. Attracted by the stench of decomposing flesh, millions of them made a continuous noise like distant buzz saws. Raoul used the little energy he had left to keep the insects from his eyes, blocking out the thought of what they were doing to his damaged legs.

He turned his head away from the sun. Through half-closed lids, a photograph swam into focus. It lay, half trapped beneath a tattooed forearm, together with a couple of letters written in German. A bare foot had crushed the three value-less items into the muddy gravel as the *bo-doi* stripped Hans naked. In the photograph a woman and a small boy of about eight were standing in front of what looked like a hair-dresser's shop. Raoul made out the words MULLER – DAMENFRISEUR on the shopfront behind them.

A footstep crunching in a patch of gravel caused him to turn his head and see the *can-bô* holding out a lighted ciga-rette. He took it and dragged smoke into his lungs greedily. The small cupful of muddy water he had been given an hour before had done little to quench his raging thirst.

He had to ask for each favour – a drink, a cigarette – and was aware that in accepting them he was participating in Minh's conditioning: the carrots would be forthcoming as long as it suited his captor and the stick would be kept never entirely out of sight behind the trainer's back. It was the way wild animals were broken. He had heard that, during the Korean war, the Chinese in Korea had systemised the psychological conditioning of prisoners in the same way, and called it brainwashing.

The *can-bô*'s next visit came after nightfall.

The rain had ceased and moonlight flooded the battlefield from a clear sky. I became aware that my captor was squatting on his heels a few paces away, smoking a cigarette and watching me silently. As a deep inhalation lit up his face, I wondered what kind of man Minh was. Of one thing I was sure: my end would have been easier if he had arrived a few seconds later on the scene. The bo-doi's *bayonet would have pierced my belly once, perhaps twice. A few moments of agony, some blows and oblivion.*

Minh's way, I already knew, would be both longer and far more painful. It was time to start trying to form a relationship, to sound him out. 'You speak excellent French, Captain Minh,' I said tentatively. 'Have you studied in France?'

He ignored my question and asked the one I had been fearing. 'The pay-chest,' he said. 'Where is the gold, Duvalier?'

It was the longest night in my life. A thousand times, Minh put the same question to me.

With dawn there was a noise of vehicles not far away and voices nearer. The smoke of cooking fires rose in straight columns through the heavy, moist air. High above the scene of defeat, a solitary French photographic reconnaissance plane flew figures-of-eight, tempting the Viet anti-aircraft batteries into a spasmodic barrage.

'Here,' said Minh. He loomed above the stretcher and held out a wooden bowl. Watching me shovel the few handfuls of soggy rice into my mouth, he said thoughtfully, 'I may not be the right person for this job, you know. It may be necessary to replace me with some other can-bô *who is psychologically tougher.'*

I said nothing.

'Unfortunately,' Minh explained, 'I acquired many bourgeois Western ideas in my youth and have not truly re-educated myself since returning to Vietnam.'

'*Bourgeois ideas?*' I was wary of saying the wrong thing. '*Like what, for instance?*'

'*For instance, I take no pleasure in watching you suffer, Captain Duvalier. I want you to know that.*'

'*Then why don't you get me some medical attention, Captain Minh?*'

The scream of rage seemed to come from another man. He leaped up and delivered a kick to my injured legs that had me sobbing uncontrollably. I dropped the rice bowl, which rolled out of reach.

In an equally abrupt return to his usual mild voice, Minh explained what he wanted. '*We know that the majority of De Bonneville's troops were local levies that had to be paid in gold daily to stop them deserting,*' said Minh. '*That's no secret. The only secret is what happened to the pay-chest, Captain Duvalier.*'

'*How should I know?*'

Minh pursed his lips as though reproving a difficult child. '*We know that you brought it here to Isabelle. Some time between 0400 hours when we drove Lafont's men back inside the perimeter and 0800 hours when our victorious soldiers finished mopping up, you buried or hid the gold. Didn't you?*'

Still I said nothing.

'*It is no use to you now,*' said Minh patiently. '*The imperialists have lost not just the battle of Dien Bien Phu but also the whole war in Vietnam. That gold is the property of the people of Vietnam. If you want to live, you must tell me where it is.*'

I hoped I was going to die.

Later that day Raoul was carried to a flat-bed truck and driven over bumpy ground to a prison compound. There he was thrown into a corrugated iron box. It was completely dark inside, with not even a chink of light showing through. The box was too low for him to straighten his neck. He had to sit, head over to one side, with his injured legs bent. The torture of a thousand cramped muscles was now added to the agony of his wounds. And at night dozens, maybe hundreds, of mosquitoes managed to find their way into the box. He swatted them in handfuls but always there were more.

His eyes puffed up from the bites and would hardly open. His face swelled.

In the box, time stood still. When it was black and hot, it was daytime outside. If Raoul relaxed and let his skin touch the metal of the box, it burned. At night he shivered with cold and fever. By counting feeding times, he kept track of time for the first couple of days, but then gave up. He became unsure whether he had been in the box for a week or a month. It could have been longer, much longer.

The pain in his legs grew less severe. He wondered if that was a good sign or a bad one. In the darkness he could not see what had happened to the wounds and his probing fingers gave little information. He wished his sense of smell had come back; at least he would then know if the wounds were infected – although, lying day after day in his own filth, it was perhaps better not to have a sense of smell.

There were several other boxes in the compound; he had seen them when he was thrown into this one. Minh had made a joke: 'These are my black boxes, Captain Duvalier. You will live in one until you tell me where yours is.'

Raoul wondered who were the occupants of the others and what they had done to merit this treatment. Were they all Minh's creatures, or was there a team of *can-bôs* at work?

A small bowl of rancid rice and some tepid water constituted the daily meal. From the start Raoul disciplined himself not to gobble the rice like a starving animal as soon as it arrived but to make his own decision when to eat.

In the black box there were only two decisions he could make: when to eat and not to speak to Minh. The persistent *can-bô* came several times a day – sometimes at night – to ask the same questions through the tiny feeding hatch. With always the same offer of trade: '. . . in return, you get medical attention, Captain Duvalier. Talk now, before it is too late to save your legs.'

It is indescribable torment to be locked in a cage where you cannot stand or lie down properly. I tried to die by the only weapon left to me: not eating. Yet when I awoke and anxiously checked the feeding bowl, I found that, asleep or half-asleep, the body had betrayed me and taken nourishment.

Some nights I dreamed of hearing screams and the sound of men being beaten. Yet sometimes when it was day and I was not asleep I heard those sounds too.

The guard took me out of my box once. They were having a beast show: baiting with long sticks what had been a white man, wearing an iron collar attached to a heavy chain. He was bearded, naked, filthy and covered in sores. The poor creature's mind must have gone, for they had trained him to bark like a dog and to beg for food. They kept pointing to him and asking me a question to which I replied: 'Khuong biet.' I repeated the answer, changing languages in the hope that one or the other would awaken some echo in the brain of the dog-man. 'Je ne sais pas. Ich weiss nicht. I don't know. Yo no sé. Io non so.'

All he could do was bark.

Drawn by the laughter of the guards and the noise the dog-man was making, Minh appeared on the scene. He was furious with the guards for letting me out. He must have ordered some punishment for them. At any rate, they took revenge by throwing me back inside the cage, overturning my water bowl in the process. Thirst tormented me.

I began to fear that I should end like that poor chained creature.

The feeding flap banged open, showing a square patch of sunlit earth with a pair of feet.

'I have some news for you,' said Minh.

From Minh's feet, Raoul judged that the *can-bô* was squatting in his usual position. 'News?' he repeated dully.

'Yes.' There was a trace of excitement in Minh's voice. 'Your government has asked our representatives at the peace talks in Geneva for a truce. This is the direct result of your defeat here at Dien Bien Phu.'

'And will there be a truce?' Despite himself, Raoul could not help hoping.

'Oh no,' laughed Minh. 'Instead, our representatives have demanded freedom from the imperialist yoke for the peoples of Vietnam, Cambodia and Laos.'

'I'm a soldier,' said Raoul, 'not a politician.'

'Many of your comrades,' said Minh, 'are signing a petition supporting the legitimate demands of the peoples of
Indo-China to be liberated from French colonial
oppression.'

'That's up to them,' said Raoul. 'I don't blame them, but
I won't sign.'

'If you sign the petition,' said Minh, 'it will count in your
favour.'

'I swore an oath of loyalty to France.'

'So did the others.' Minh's voice was smooth. 'But their
political education while in our hands has opened their eyes.
They have experienced a political awakening.'

'How did you educate them?' Raoul asked sarcastically.
'By locking them up in boxes not fit for an animal, like this
one?'

'You think,' said Minh calmly, 'that this accommodation
is the worst we have. There, as in so many things, you are
wrong, Duvalier. Down at the river we have some cages
almost entirely under water, where the prisoners must hold
on to the bars, night and day. When they let go, they drown.'

He slammed the feeding hatch closed.

*That information, intended to demoralise me, did the reverse. I
was comforted to know that some French or Legion prisoners were
in even worse conditions than mine. It showed that some had the
courage to fight back and that I was not alone in spirit.*

*I determined not to show less valour than those men. The first
thing was to regain control of my mind. I began compiling lists,
beginning with my class at St Cyr.*

*First names: Adrien, Antoine, Bernard, Dominique, Edgar,
Fabien, Georges . . . . Was there no one after Patrice and myself?
Surnames similarly, from A to Z. I wonder what happened to
Koenig. Was he a prisoner too or did he get away? If he was in
the hands of the Viets, it was ten to one he was among the men
hanging on to the bars of the cages in the river.*

*At first there were gaps in my lists, names I could not recall.
Yet when I woke up next day some unconscious process had plucked*

them out of oblivion and the list was complete. And I felt somehow better and stronger, as though sleep does the body more good when the subconscious has a job to do.

To recall the faces was harder; I may have cheated with some. When I had assembled them all in my mind's eye, I photographed the entire class on our passing-out parade and stuck the right name under each face. It was strange to be looking at my own face and writing underneath: DUVALIER, *Raoul.*

I reconstituted my class in the first year at cadet school: further back in time, so more difficult to recapture. To begin with, there were several gaps. I had never been a reflective person, but since the only entertainment I had was my own memories, I determined to explore them all. It was exhilarating: like primitive man discovering a secret cave into which he could crawl and where God could not see him.

The simile is telling; Minh had become like a god. He was all-powerful, as far as I was concerned.

Inside the box, the prisoner's teeth were chattering audibly with fever, his skin covered in sweat.

'What does it matter to you about some gold coins?' Minh's soft voice asked rhetorically. 'They are not your property, Captain Duvalier. The gold was raised in taxes stolen by your imperialist masters from the people of Vietnam. If you now help the people to recover what is theirs by right, they will be your friend.'

Interspersed with the invitations to betray were threats, odd items of news and menacing little asides: '. . . if you wish to sit in your mother's garden in Bourg-la-Reine again . . .' or '. . . forget what your father the general would think. He will never know.'

Dawn was breaking when the *can-bô* murmured between puffs on his cigarette: 'I think you have gangrene, Duvalier. The wounds on your legs stink. You should decide soon, before it is too late.'

And, most insidiously of all, 'You can tell me where the gold is hidden, Captain Duvalier. No one else will ever know. Only you and me.'

7

On the day after the fall of Dien Bien Phu the Viets herded their thousands of wounded and half-starved prisoners into long straggling columns and marched them into the jungle. They headed north, then east then south and north and east again on a route that took them through jungle and over mountains which would have been a severe endurance test for healthy men. Unless the purpose was to kill off all except the toughest, the march was a senseless exercise in cruelty. During the four months it lasted, three-quarters of the prisoners died of wounds, illness and malnutrition.

It seemed to the survivors that they had never known any other life. One day like all the others they stood in hot mid-September sunshine, suffering yet another re-education session. Some of the wounded had fainted and been left on the ground where they fell. The others remained in their ranks, sullenly trying to block their minds to the stereotyped arguments of Asian Marxism that bombarded them from the clusters of loudspeakers hoisted on bamboo poles.

The *can-bôs* had chosen this site well, for their captives were lined up on the parade ground of the former Legion barracks at Tuyen Quang, scene of an act of French heroism in 1885. For legionnaires it was a hallowed spot, the most symbolic place in Vietnam on which to be humiliated by the victors of Dien Bien Phu.

Captain Minh finished his speech and stepped down from the podium, to be replaced by a similarly anonymous colleague who continued the verbal relay race aimed at deadening the minds of the French prisoners before they were marched on their way. The repeated theme of the harangue was the moral bankruptcy of the former colonial powers.

'The next colonial war will be in North Africa,' the speaker chanted again and again. 'The next colonial war will be in North Africa! The next . . .'

Many of the men in front of him concentrated their thoughts on food, clean water and shade. A few, hopeful of favours, chanted the words of the chorus, avoiding their comrades' eyes.

Captain Minh was buttonholed after his speech by the senior commissar present. He was dressed in the same drab uniform devoid of insignia as the other *can-bôs*, but held the rank of colonel. Standing beside him was a Chinese adviser, a Red Army psychologist who had made his name by developing the brainwashing procedures used on American prisoners in Korea.

'Comrade Chang,' said the colonel, 'is very interested in your progress reports on the prisoner Duvalier.'

Chang smiled. In badly accented Vietnamese, he said, 'Good reports. Bad progress, comrade Minh. You are too soft with this man, I fear.'

Minh bowed his head. 'Duvalier is a man of honour, a professional soldier, comrade colonel. I have done everything you suggested to isolate him, to break his spirit. He has not seen a human face, or been out of his cage in four months. Although physically very weak, his resolve is strengthened by his code of behaviour.'

'An Olympic-class sportsman like him,' said Chang thoughtfully, 'must have a very strong will. That sort of man gave us many problems in Korea.'

'In Duvalier's case,' interrupted the colonel, 'we are not

interested in re-educating him. We want only the information which he is withholding. And we want it before he manages to die on us. That –' a bony finger stabbed Minh's chest – 'is your responsibility, comrade.'

'I may have found a way through his defences,' said Minh deferentially. He held up a Russian-made Zenith 35mm camera.

'Tell me,' said Chang.

When Minh explained his plan, the Chinese smiled. 'Very original, comrade. Let's hope it works.'

'For your sake, Minh, let's all hope it does,' said the colonel.

Minh smiled, bowed his head and continued photographing the prisoners. Every picture he took had a purpose: the purpose of breaking the will of a man crouched in the fetid heat of a lightless cage one hundred miles away.

Minh thought I was in the cage, but in fact I had escaped!

Oh, not in reality. . . . Even if they had opened the door and let me go, I could not have dragged myself more than a few feet along the ground, much less run away.

But in my mind, I had discovered a secret door into another world: the world of fantasy where there were no mosquitoes or heat or hunger or thirst – and, best of all, no Minh!

Since reality was an insane world where men were turned into dogs, I had invented an alternative reality to live in. It was the only way not to let Minh and the guards win.

That phrase is the clue: I didn't want to let them win. It wasn't a coldly worked out decision, just a reflex deep in my psyche. The first time it happened, I was thirteen and in my first term at cadet school. We had boxing lessons 'to make men of us'. My best friend was matched against me. Instead of just tapping me for appearances' sake as I was doing to him, he began to hurt. I could not see the point of that, but when he knocked me down and I saw stars, I picked myself up off the mat and – still dazed – cut his face over both eyes and knocked him out before they could stop the fight. Minh's mistake was to push me so far down in the miasma of pain and degradation that in the end I fought back by instinct. What saved my sanity in his black box was my sportsman's reflex not to let the opponent get the upper hand.

It didn't always work of course. There were still days when the pain, the guards, the heat and the hunger did their work on me. But, for whatever reason, Minh never came on those days. Could a guardian angel have been watching over me even in that hell? I don't know, but on the days when my morale was lowest and I would have cracked, Minh didn't come. Sometimes – I admit it – I asked for him by name, wanting to tell him everything.

Was I seeking some reward? Not even that. I wanted to please my keeper. That's how low I had sunk.

But on the days when I was able to find that secret door, he could not touch me. I wasn't even in the black box. I was skiing in the Alps, or riding or driving at Le Mans. Second by second I lived every inch of a descent I knew. I rode one horse and then another round a course I knew by heart. I drove the circuit in one car and then did it again in another with different handling characteristics.

But life in the secret world was not all fun; that would not have been real. I re-wrote drill manuals, took a squad of recruits on the battle-training course and slogged alongside them all night on forced marches. I gave Lépine daily briefings and attended cocktail parties and receptions. I filled every hour and left no time for idleness.

I also began to plan for the future. Realising that I would not be eligible for military quarters – that officialese circumlocution avoided acknowledging to myself that I should be pensioned off as a cripple – I started to plan my future home. It had never interested me what happens when you press a light switch or flush a toilet, but now I began to plan a home in which I could one day lead an independent life. For a man unable to walk up a flight of steps, it had to be a very special home. In fact, I planned a series of homes, for as fast as each was completed, I grew bored with it and – as it were – moved to a new address where building had to start all over again. Until I 'moved into' my dream house: the Templars' tower above the little village of St Martin beside the wide Dordogne.

I had never been to this part of France in my life, yet two years later, I found that my dream was real. There really was a tower above a village exactly like the vision that came to me then. Some mystics say that fasting frees the mind from the physical constraints of the body. Well, certainly I had been fasting for a long while! Perhaps my mind travelled back to France and saw this place? Or did I look across a loop in time and see myself here in the future? Impossible to explain, but it's true.

There were bad days in my fantasy life as well. One morning I was in Lépine's office and rang Huguette a hundred times. There was something urgent I had to tell her. In front of me was the picture of her standing by the Grecian pillar. Each time I dialled, a man's voice answered and would not let me speak to my wife. After trying a hundred times, I tore the picture up in anger.

But that evening wasn't so bad. Koenig and I were in Paris on leave, so we went on the town together and had a wonderful meal just off the Champs Elysées with a group of old classmates. Several of them were dead but had been given a twenty-four-hour pass to celebrate with us. We ended up at a rather risqué night club just off Pigalle, drunk as lords.

With my friends around me that night I felt secure, not knowing what Minh had up his drab olive sleeve.

In ten years of war the French had never set foot in the squalid fishing village of Hai Thon. No Westerner had even heard of the place until it was designated at the cease-fire conference in faraway Geneva as a place for the hand-over of prisoners.

With the Zenith around his neck, Captain Minh mingled with photographers from several Communist newspapers who were taking pictures of the injured prisoners.

Despite their previous experience, the French army doctors and nurses had been horrified to see the condition of the men waiting to be exchanged. They were lying on stretchers under a thatched roof with open sides. Many were in a desperate state after the death march of several hundred miles. Those from Dien Bien Phu were not the worst; some of the others had been in captivity for as long as four years.

Few could walk unaided. All were suffering from dysentery and malaria.

There were long speeches in Vietnamese, laboriously translated, before the French party was allowed formally to accept responsibility for the prisoners. Names were checked off the official list as men hobbled or were carried up the ramp into the landing craft which would take them back to the world. All the while, Minh kept clicking away, as assiduous as any pressman.

A lieutenant and a captain from the Legion's *deuxième bureau*, dressed in white coats with Red Cross armbands, were working their way through the prisoners. They met at the end farthest from the landing craft and deliberately turned their backs as Minh swivelled his camera in their direction.

'No luck,' said one laconically.

'No sign of Duvalier,' agreed the other. 'No one has heard of him since the surrender. He's vanished from the face of the earth. It looks like he's dead.'

Several days later, at dusk, Raoul was hauled out of the box and lifted bodily by two guards who carried him to a primitive shower where they hosed him down until he was more or less clean. They had to help him dress in a fresh set of the ubiquitous black pyjamas; even his fingers would not function properly.

Then they carried him into an interrogation room where Minh sat behind a desk, smoking. Raoul was allowed to collapse on the chair like a sack of potatoes. After five months in almost continual darkness, the light from the naked 40-watt bulb above the bamboo table hurt his eyes excruciatingly.

'No trousers!' Minh screamed at the guards. 'Take off the prisoner's trousers.'

'No,' Raoul screamed back when he understood what they were doing. He had kept his eyes averted during the shower, not wanting to see his legs. It was one thing to know they were useless, but he did not want to see them. He fought the guards with feeble, atrophied muscles, ignoring their blows. But it was to no avail. Two minutes later he sat on the chair, clad only in the pyjama jacket.

'Look at your legs,' ordered Minh.

Despite the burning pain in his brain, Raoul kept his eyes fixed on the bulb, trying to make himself blind so that he would not see. On another command from Minh, one guard forced his head down and down, while the other held the lids of both eyes open until Raoul had no choice but to see the twisted, broken legs that hung obscenely from his body like those of an overgrown child with rickets.

'And to think you were once an athlete and a sportsman,' Minh sneered. 'Look at you now, Duvalier. You are nothing. Less than a dog.'

As Raoul's resistance weakened, the guards let go of him and stood back.

His world of make-believe was no defence against the first proper sight of his broken legs. Defences gone, he sat on the chair weeping. He felt the tears rolling down his bearded cheeks and could not stop the sobs shaking his whole body. He had been proud of the health he enjoyed, of his fitness and physical prowess as a rider, a driver, an athlete. To see the twisted, atrophied, useless legs was to know that he would never again ride a horse, or ski, run, walk or even stand unaided.

Minh motioned the guards to leave; he was in no danger of being attacked by the cripple in front of him. He dropped the cigarette, half smoked, into a bottle of beer, deliberately wasting both in front of the prisoner who had neither, then said, 'I have news for you.'

Raoul said nothing. After a time he stopped weeping and stared dry-eyed and hopeless at the bamboo wall of the hut.

'I have news for you.'

Raoul turned his half-closed eyes to Minh. Curiosity, after all the months without any news, prompted him to listen.

'On 8 October,' said Minh, 'the last French troops withdrew from the Republic of North Vietnam.'

Raoul closed his eyes against the light. The words meant nothing to him.

'On 9 October, our victorious troops occupied Hanoi after eight years' guerrilla warfare. Our victory is complete.'

Still Raoul stayed silent.

'And . . .' Minh clapped his hands to attract Raoul's drifting attention. 'Listen to me, Captain Duvalier. I have another item of news that is directly relevant to you.'

Through one half-closed eye, Raoul regarded his captor.

'All the other French prisoners have been repatriated,' said Minh. He repeated the sentence slowly, as to a handicapped child. 'A cease-fire agreement was made three months ago in Geneva. Under its terms, all prisoners have gone home.'

'I don't . . . believe you,' Raoul growled hoarsely.

Instead of getting angry, Minh smiled. 'I don't expect you to believe my word,' he said reasonably. 'But perhaps you will accept the evidence of the camera.' Like a conjuror with a trick, he spread fan-wise on the bamboo table a dozen of the photographs he had taken at Hai Thon.

Raoul screwed up his eyes and peered at the pictures.

The first was of a beach where men lay on stretchers, some in shade and some in sun. The faces were European but the bodies were thin as Asian peasants'. In another photograph, a number of women in the uniform of French army nurses were bending over some of the stretchers. In another, several French officers stood with a group of Viet Minh on a beach. A landing craft was in the background. Stretchers were being carried into it. The last shot was of the landing craft putting out to sea with its French flag fluttering in the stiff breeze. Someone on the stern was waving at the camera.

'Well?' Minh was watching Raoul's face. 'What do you make of my amateur reportage? Technically it's not up to the standard of *Paris Match*, but I think it tells the story quite clearly. Don't you?'

It was so long since Raoul had spoken that his voice was

hoarse and croaking. 'What am I supposed to make of it?'

'Your comrades have all gone home.' Minh spoke slowly, allowing each word to sink in.

He lifted the photographs and let them fall to the table. 'The pictures tell you that much. There has been a cease-fire agreement in Geneva, Captain Duvalier. All the French prisoners in Vietnam have been repatriated. Only you are left. Your government has abandoned you.'

It was difficult to concentrate his mind after the months in the black box, but Raoul knew there was something wrong with Minh's logic. He fumbled for the photographs, peering closely. 'There's maybe a hundred, hundred and fifty men in these pictures. You're not going to tell me that's all the prisoners you had?'

Minh smiled. 'Of course not. The hand-over was conduc-ted at many different places and I could not be everywhere. The pictures are – what do you say? – a fair sample. Believe me, Captain Duvalier, you are all alone. There is no longer any reason to be stubborn in the belief that you are helping your country by your continued refusal to talk.'

Minh had been prepared to argue, to threaten, to promise. He was not prepared for the tears that were running anew down Raoul's thin and bearded face. His pulse racing, the *can-bô* leaned forward. 'Now you'll tell me where you hid the gold?'

Like a dog who is anxious to please, Raoul cringed. 'Yes,' he whimpered. 'I'll tell you.'

Minh's immense relief spread through his whole body. It invaded his bowels and made him clench his buttocks as though against dysentery. The Chinese psychologist had been wrong and he, Minh, had been right. Months of humiliation and pain had not broken this man, but the simple idea of showing him photographic evidence that he had been abandoned by his country had done the trick. The snivelling wreck of a man opposite him was a creature with whom he could now do what he chose.

With an effort, Minh kept the triumph from his voice and softly reassured his prisoner. 'You did all that honour demanded, Captain Duvalier. I have great respect for you. Truly.'

He stood and put on his soft cotton cap with the red star above the peak. 'I salute you, comrade.' He raised his hand to the peak of his cap and hurried from the room, heading for the latrines and hoping that he would get there before he soiled himself from sheer excitement.

8

The battle had effected a gigantic landscaping of the whole valley in which Dien Bien Phu lay. Little distinguished the hill that had been outpost Isabelle from the rest of the terrain. Gaping craters of naked soil showed where the bunkers had been sited but there were also gentle slopes covered in brilliant green vegetation, where formerly had been desolation and filth.

Raoul was carried in a primitive sedan chair by two scowling *bo-doi*. His face – sensitive to even weak sunlight after so long in the dark – was shaded from the burning midday sun by an enormous conical hat of woven palm-fibre, as worn by the peasants in the rice paddies.

'It may be difficult to get your bearings.' Minh blinked repeatedly with a nervous tic. He had been chain-smoking since they left the prison camp. 'Take your time.'

They were on a knoll surmounted by a new hoarding on which was written in Vietnamese and French:

This is the scene of the heroic struggle in which several thousand members of the people's army of the Republic of Vietnam sacrificed their lives to destroy the soldiers of the so-called Foreign Legion, mercenary lackeys of the imperialist government of France.

The words meant nothing to Raoul, whose fantasy life did not include the battle of the previous May. More important was the pain in his eyes. Even in the shade of the peasant's hat, the sun hurt. It was like a red-hot rod stabbing directly into his brain. Pain came in so many different rhythms, intensities, wavelengths. To identify the one he was now experiencing meant thumbing through a catalogue of misery. Snow blindness . . . that was it. He had once suffered from snow blindness after losing his goggles while climbing high in the Alps.

The memory made him frightened of losing his sight totally this time. After five months in the darkness, it was quite possible. So he kept his eyes screwed tightly shut and squinted through the slits between the lids.

He focused on the hills first, recalling a dream in which a man with one hand promised that the Viets would never bring a single gun across that skyline. Dream or reality, it made no difference now. Below the hills, Dien Bien Phu dozed in the heat like any other peaceful valley in the fertile tropics. Peasants went about the daily business of living. Animals grazed, supervised by small children. Smoke rose from the rebuilt huts in the villages. Some of the blasted trees had already sprouted new branches. There was no sign of all the dead thousands whose lives had ended here. It was as though all the gallantry and daring, the self-sacrifice and suffering had never been.

Only two recognisable features survived: the Nam Youm river flowing sluggishly from north to south and the road running roughly parallel, which the French had known as Route 41. But Raoul had taken all that into account when choosing the place to hide the gold.

It was along the road at which he was now looking, that he had driven with Hans and Franz a lifetime before, in the crazy adrenalin-fuelled dash that was more like a dream than all the fantasies he had conjured up since.

Suddenly his memory became sharp, as though an optician had put the correct lens in the frame.

'Take your time, Captain Duvalier,' Minh interrupted his

thoughts. The *can-bô* lit another cigarette from a half-smoked stub and, to disguise his tension, strolled away in the direction of the fatigue party of *bo-doi* equipped with picks and shovels, waiting for orders.

Raoul had chosen the place to bury the gold in the middle of the night because it was easy to find without relying on landmarks. Yet a prisoner's cunning stopped him from directing his bearers straight to the site of the cache. He had them carry him along the bank of the Nam Youm for several hundred yards to the north as though having difficulty orienting himself. He shook his head and ordered his bearers south. Then east. After months of confinement, he became inebriated by movement and the power to give orders.

Minh watched his every move like a cat with a mouse, until Raoul grew tired of the game, like a child whose attention has snapped.

'By the bridge,' he said sullenly. 'That's the spot.'

The *bo-doi* shouted for Minh, who came running, his team of diggers trailing behind.

The span of the bridge had been destroyed when the Viets stormed the position five months previously. The metal structure had been replaced by a swaying temporary bridge of bamboo and rope, strung across the Nam Youm between the foundations of dressed stone which still stood on either side.

'Beside the footings of the bridge. . . .' Raoul pointed an emaciated and claw-like hand.

There was an excited chatter among the *bo-doi* when they found the disturbed earth of the original hole. As they went deeper, sweat poured off them and the chatter grew less, until the only noise in the valley was the incessant buzz of insects and the rhythmic noises of pick and shovel biting into the red earth.

The explosion was like a divine bad joke, refilling the hole with most of the earth that had been removed and lifting three diggers high in the air before scattering surplus soil and pieces of bodies across the sunlit ground. A forearm with the hand attached landed soggily beside Raoul, who stared at it for several seconds before realising what it was.

As eardrums recovered from the blast wave, the moaning of the survivors made a dull backing to Minh's repeated screams: 'That was a booby trap. A trap.' He stood over Raoul threatening him with a cocked 9mm Makarov pistol.

Raoul's eyes hurt from the sunlight and his ears from the explosion. 'No trap,' he protested repeatedly. 'Your men must have driven a pick into an unexploded shell.'

'It – was – a – trap!' screamed Minh, punctuating the words by pistol-whipping Raoul's face.

Excited by the *can-bô's* violence, the two bearers tipped the sedan chair over. Once Raoul was on the ground they began kicking him in the chest and kidneys. He curled his body into a ball, trying to protect his head by wrapping his arms around it but not resisting the blows landing elsewhere.

Suddenly all was quiet. Raoul lay, hardly able to breathe from the pain of broken ribs. He was aware of the sun burning his back where the thin cotton of the black pyjamas had been torn, but his body seemed to weigh a ton and he had no strength to move it. He watched inertly as the remains of the three dead men were laid to one side under a French groundsheet. The wounded were carried out of sight towards the nearest village and a new team of *bo-doi* was commandeered by Minh to carry on digging.

They propped Raoul on a heap of wet earth dug for a second time from the hole, his legs dangling uselessly over the edge. Each breath cost a stabbing pain where his back touched the stone foundations of the bridge. One eye was swollen and closed. Through the other, he watched the men's feet puddling the mud with the water that seeped into the diggings now that they were below the water table of the nearby river. He recalled Hans and the other diggers up to their thighs in liquid mud, cursing in German as they toiled.

The new group of diggers worked slowly and carefully, fearful of another stray shell.

'At least,' said Minh viciously, 'my men will have the satisfaction of knowing that you die with them if there is another booby trap.' To show his solidarity with the workers, the *can-bô* stationed himself beside his prisoner at the edge of the hole, chain-smoking.

Raoul lay as still as possible to reduce the pain from his ribs, making no move even when they found the first ammunition box and Minh leaped down into the hole, tore it open and spilled a thousand *louis d'or* in a glittering golden stream into the mud.

During the weeks that followed, the *can-bô* paid regular visits to the prison hospital, bringing cigarettes and once a bottle of warm beer.

Medical care amounted to little more than some bandages for Raoul's broken ribs; no adhesive plaster was available. A few herbal infusions replaced the Western drugs which the Viet Minh lacked. The prison doctor was an ex-trainee radiologist who had flunked his exams after a year's study at the Jesuit hospital in Hanoi. He took one look at Raoul's twisted legs and the wasted muscles, then simply shook his head.

But there were luxuries like water to wash in and clean clothing, after months of filthy rags. The food was simple but clean: fresh rice with a dash of *nuoc-mam*, the foul-smelling condiment of Indo-China. Twice a week, slivers of dried fish were added to the rice.

The worst thing for Raoul was to meet other French prisoners and realise that Minh had tricked him with the photographs. A large number of French and Legion prisoners had still not been handed over; some were kept back for punishment, for re-education or simply as bargaining counters of one kind or another.

Raoul knew nothing of the debate over his future that raged between Minh and the Chinese psychologist, Dr Chang. It was Minh who won the day by insisting: 'I know Duvalier inside out, comrades. Duty and honour run in his veins, not blood. There is no greater punishment for a man with that code of honour than to be sent back to his own country, knowing that he has betrayed it.'

The smiling little commissar chose to accompany Raoul's stretcher to the miserable fishing village of Hai Thon – to be with him right up to the last moment when he was formally handed over to a representative of the French Red Cross.

I could not untangle my emotions as I said goodbye to Minh in the poverty-stricken village that stank of fish drying in the sun. Like lovers who have to part, we had nothing to say, but shared a bottle of warm beer as we waited. The hand-over was late; the landing craft had to anchor in the estuary until high tide enabled it to pass over the mud flats. When it grated on the shore and the ramp came down, I felt closer to Minh than to the French medics who were coming to collect us.

At the debriefing later, I gave the answers that my questioners wanted to hear: that I hated Minh, that I would kill him if we ever met again. But the reality was far more complex.

Could you hit God in the teeth for something he had done to you? Well, Minh had been God for a while. I felt no hatred, despite all I had suffered. If I say that I loved him, that sounds perverted to anyone who has not lived through what I endured. Yet pain makes love, as any mother knows. Let's settle for describing my feelings when we said farewell as a sort of yearning. I looked back from the ramp of the landing craft and saw Minh on the fish-strewn beach, waving goodbye He was dwarfed by the Frenchmen standing near and looked frail and delicate by comparison with their Western bulk.

Was I just imagining it, or did he too feel some emotion at seeing me go? He called out almost shyly: 'Au revoir, Captain Duvalier.' And I felt ... I felt like a dog must feel when its master gives it away to strangers: worried, yearning, straining to catch one last glimpse of him as the ramp came up and the engines started throbbing.

Could I have explained that to the men in uniform who plied me with questions when I got 'home'? Of course not. Which was perhaps just as well, for it cautioned me not to disclose other things to them. And that may have saved my life.

*

'Please remember always that I have great respect for you – not for the system you serve, but for you personally I have ... great respect.'

Raoul remembered Minh's final words three weeks later as he was being carried down the gangplank at Marseilles. The February weather was grey and raining, with a cold onshore wind. On the bleak, windswept quayside, curtains of drizzle alternately veiled and revealed the principal band of the Foreign Legion, which was playing a selection of the most nostalgic slow marches in its repertoire. It made a fitting accompaniment to the occasion, emphasising as only music can the unspeakable tragedy of war.

The returnees who could walk hobbled down the gangway under their own power, holding on to the chains at the side or lurching on crutches with a nurse to steady them. Raising his head off the stretcher as he was carried down, Raoul could distinguish among the reception party the tall figure of his father in general's dress uniform, with his wife and Huguette flanking him on either side.

As Raoul's stretcher came level, the general's white-gloved hand held a rigid salute, his eyes staring straight ahead. Raoul's mother and wife looked in vain at the sad procession. As his stretcher was carried past, they saw only a pair of dark brown eyes staring back at them from an unrecognisably pale and emaciated face.

'Poor man!' said the general's wife in a low voice, as her eyes rested for a moment on the hump of blankets where the wounded man's legs should have been. Anxiously, her eyes travelled along the file of stretchers, seeking a face, a shape she could claim as her son.

Respect! I lay there thinking: That's how my father would have saluted my coffin – ramrod stiff and clear-eyed. Perhaps he would have preferred that less complicated alternative? The short drama of a firing party, the ceremonial last volley over the open grave and the earth covering me. . . . A nice, clean stone with the name engraved and gilded. . . . And, once a year, an expensive wreath to show how much the family respected my sacrifice. From their point of view that would have been a better end than to have me brought back a cripple.

I should not sneer at them. Perhaps for me, too, it would have been better.

A few minutes had been allowed for the families to greet their sons and husbands and fathers. In the huge echoing customs shed a fleet of army ambulances was waiting discreetly under cover. The relatives had been told that there would be no press reporters or photographers present, out of respect. The truth was that wounded ex-prisoners were no longer newsworthy in France. Even a general's son and former Olympic sportsman who would never walk again was not worth a paragraph. That morning, for the second time in a year, France's colonial problems had brought down her government. Premier Pierre Mendès-France, who had put so much energy into getting the prisoners back from Vietnam, had been sacked after a vote of no confidence in his policy in France's newly troubled colonies across the Mediterranean in North Africa.

The Duvalier trio picked its way among the stretchers to where Raoul had been deposited. A large, handwritten card pinned to the red blanket gave Raoul's name. Seeing it, his mother turned to one of the orderlies and said: 'There's been a mistake. This . . .' She looked from the man in the white coat to what remained of a man on the stretcher at their feet. 'This can't be . . .'

The orderly pulled Raoul's arm from beneath the blanket. Written on the inside of his wrist, like an epitaph in indelible pencil was: DUVALIER, *Raoul, Capitaine, Légion Etrangère.*

The arm was thrust back under the blanket. The general's wife covered her mouth with her hand and forced herself to say, 'Raoul?' She bent and kissed the pale forehead, still convinced there was a mistake.

Raindrops dripped off the points of Huguette's flowered umbrella and fell on to my face. I looked up and wondered how I could ever have made love to such flawlessness. *Standing beside the stretcher, she looked so feminine, so delicate and so clean!* Since the hand-over I had been washed and daubed in antiseptic a thousand times, but I felt in my imagination the filth and scabs still clinging to my body, as though I should never again be clean – as though my rightful place were in Minh's dark cage rather than between her scented satin sheets.

After one brief glance at me, Huguette blinked. When the long mascaraed lashes parted again, out came a powder compact. She checked her make-up, examining her own image intently, then snapped the compact shut and gazed into the distance as though the men on stretchers were nothing to do with her. I recognised the gesture. It was Huguette's way of mentally effacing anything unpleasant that intruded into her self-centred world.

My father seemed even more remote, like the ancestors whose portraits glared down from the walls of the old family home and whose names I had learned as a child without being clear whether they were three or six generations distant. Every inch a general, he looked me squarely in the eye and uttered platitudes about a soldier's duty. The words 'sacrifice' and 'noble' were repeated several times. The peroration sounded like a formal speech of which copies would be handed out afterwards. During it, I watched my mother's controlled face and Huguette's unfocused smile, trying to remember whether those two women in my life had always looked like that.

'We shall visit you in the hospital,' my father said. His white-gloved hand gripped my shoulder firmly. The general saluted again as the attendants lifted my stretcher and carried it into one of the ambulances.

I had not spoken one word.

9

The remote Val de Torrens lay high in the Pyrenees, close to the Spanish border. It had been chosen as the site for a tuberculosis sanatorium in the 1930s when mountain air was still considered the best treatment for consumptives. Made obsolete by drugs, it had lain empty for years until taken over by the Army to accommodate the flood of seriously wounded men returning from Indo-China. The buildings, in a mock-Corbusier style of concrete and glass, squatted like an insult in the natural beauty of the valley which swept up to the raw peaks where Africa was colliding with Europe.

On the second day after Raoul's arrival, a psychiatrist in captain's uniform pulled up a chair beside Raoul's bed. 'I'd like to have a chat with you, Duvalier,' he said amiably. He waited a few minutes before adding, 'The nurses tell me you haven't said a word since your arrival.'

Raoul looked at him with the brown eyes that seemed to grow ever larger in his wasted face. He could think of nothing to say to the man, so he turned his own face to the wall and pulled the sheet over his head. He had lost the habit of talking during all the months of solitary confinement and was in any case grappling with something too important to interrupt with a trivial conversation.

Since leaving Minh's cage, he had been unable to find

the way back into the fantasy world where he had spent so much time. The real world of the hospital ship, the brief meeting with his family and the hospital routine, with its treatment and operations, was a reality he did not want to accept. So he tried to escape, but could not. He dozed and daydreamed but could not recreate the intense fantasies that had replaced reality for so long. It was as though he had left in Minh's black box the key to the secret door. It was a great loss.

The chief surgeon at Torrens was a rather aloof colonel with grey hair, grey skin and grey eyes. He was a tall thin man with a stoop that came from thirty years of leaning over operating tables. He took his time with each new arrival. There was no need for haste; if a patient was going to die, it would have happened long before he reached Torrens.

Raoul weighed less than seven stone. He was poked and prodded, weighed and measured. He was examined by the colonel and a team of students. The analyses of his urine, faeces and blood were discussed in detail. The colonel spent a long time examining the X-rays of Raoul's legs and feeling the wasted muscles.

'First we'll have to get you fit enough to stand the anaesthetic,' he murmured in an almost inaudible voice. 'I've got to put you on a diet which will fatten you up, Duvalier. . .'. He used the verb *gaver* which means to force-feed geese for the production of *foie gras*. 'Then we'll see how the first one or two operations go, before making up our minds about your eventual prognosis.'

He was about to leave the bedside, his train of students and nurses following, when Raoul spoke for the first time. 'Tell me the worst and the best, colonel.'

The colonel patted Raoul's foot under the bedclothes. 'It's a little early for . . .'

'Fuck you!' snarled Raoul. 'Give me an answer.'

'I remind you,' said the colonel in the same remote tones, 'you are under military discipline, captain. Kindly address me by my rank.'

Raoul hauled himself half out of bed. Controlling himself

and stressing the man's rank, he said, 'Give me an answer, colonel. I want to know.'

'The worst,' said the surgeon, talking to the X-rays rather than the patient, 'is that we can't really do very much to straighten things out after all the months you've been without treatment.'

'And the best?'

The colonel put down the X-rays. 'That we can straighten your legs enough for them to hang decently in a wheelchair.'

'That would be the best you can do?'

The cold grey eyes met Raoul's. 'That would be the best we can expect, captain.'

Raoul stayed sitting upright as the party moved on. Despite the efforts of the nurses to make him more comfortable in the bed, he remained in that position for several hours.

The stooped grey figure appeared regularly at Raoul's bed to poke and prod the useless legs, stick pins in them and tap them with little hammers. There was usually a retinue of students in tow and at least one visiting colleague who had come to Torrens just to examine Raoul's legs. In professional jargon that excluded the patient, amazement was expressed that anyone should survive such injuries in the fetid heat of Vietnam and without medicines.

'Captain Duvalier was an extremely fit sportsman,' the colonel explained to his students. 'But even so, in that climate, most combat wounds of any importance lead to gangrene if not immediately treated. We therefore surmise that the fractures were caused by a barrier of sandbags being blasted at his legs, cushioning the skin so that the bones were broken without laceration of the skin.' Students and visitors alike were fascinated.

Raoul did not listen to the surgeon's lectures. He was bored with having his body poked and measured and weighed and tested by captains and colonels, bored with being washed by nurses, bored with being X-rayed by the radiologists, bored with being fed and washed and exercised like a broken toy.

Lacking the key to his former world of fantasy, he had only one escape. Whatever the weather, he spent hours every day in his wheelchair on the balcony, staring at the mountains through binoculars. Through the glasses, he became familiar with the villagers' small herds of cows with bells on their collars, munching their musical way through the lower reaches of the valley. High above, on the crags, he could see the natural fauna: marmots, foxes, eagles and the occasional izard, the delicate Pyrenean chamois.

The binoculars were a tunnel through which Raoul looked at the real world, while the physical reality of wheelchair and crutches was a dream from which he would one day wake up. When low clouds or fog made observation of his valley impossible, he pored for hours over a large-scale map of the area. The hospital was represented as a group of small blobs, insignificant against the immensity of mountains in which wild swirls of black contour lines twisted and turned, intersected only by the thin blue lines that denoted streams and rivers. Roads had no place up there.

Surgical operations succeeded each other in monotonous series. 'We want to try such-and-such,' the colonel would say. It was unclear to Raoul whether he was patient or guinea pig and a matter of indifference to him. He signed the consent forms without reading them, irritated to be dragged away for a day or two from the real world high above the man-made enclave of concrete and glass.

On the day of his wife's first visit to Torrens, Raoul could not eat. All morning his emotions were so confused that he vacillated between wishing not to see her at all and wanting to ask her to take him away from the hospital with her that very day.

There was a mix-up in reception. The young trainee nurse on duty was overawed by such a haughty visitor, dressed by Dior and perfumed by Chanel. She allowed Huguette Duvalier to sweep past and make her way to Raoul's room before anyone had briefed her on what to expect.

The four men in the room stared at this apparition: an

elegant woman followed by a uniformed driver carrying champagne and flowers. Huguette stood, one gloved hand on the door handle, making her entrance in a fur coat over a black cocktail dress and a hat more suitable for the racecourse at Longchamps than a hospital visit.

'*Bonjour, messieurs*,' she greeted them.

Nobody replied. Her shortsighted eyes examined them one by one before settling on Raoul. She had put out of her mind the memory of his emaciated physique and the thin, feverish face with eyes that burned like coals in their sockets – and recognised him only by discarding the others one after another.

It was a mistake to come, she thought, hiding her panic behind a professional smile. His mother should have come, not me. . . .

Her reflection in the large window reassured her. It was not how anyone else would have dressed to visit Torrens, but that was her style. She took a deep breath and steeled herself to plant one unfocused kiss on Raoul's cheek.

'My God, it's warm in here.' She slipped off the fur coat to reveal jewellery and an inappropriate cocktail dress. As she unpinned her hat, Raoul's room-mates stared at her hungrily. The driver placed the champagne and flowers on Raoul's locker and left.

Huguette shook hands with the other men, talking briefly with each one like royalty on a visit, Raoul thought. Then she opened the window – it was difficult to breathe in the room where four men chain-smoked all day out of sheer boredom – and leaned out into clean air. The snow-clad mountains seemed to hang over the hospital buildings, so steep was their rise from the valley sides.

'My God!' Huguette shuddered, a city-dweller appalled at Nature. 'This is the end of the world. What a boring place, Raoul. Whatever do you men do to pass the time here?'

For half an hour she gave a performance, chattering brightly about friends who now meant nothing to Raoul. They were just names; he could not be bothered to search dim and distant memories for faces to fit them. Huguette seated herself side-saddle on the edge of the bed where he could see the swell of her breasts through the vee of her *décolletage*. Raoul's sense of smell had still not returned. He wondered what perfume she was using, or whether there was a faint hint of her body's natural odours. Then he remembered that his wife had never smelt of anything that did not come out of an expensive little bottle.

The other men's eyes devoured her. Raoul felt his erection grow under the thin blanket and wondered if the others had the same problem.

Huguette was repulsed by Raoul and the three men who shared his every waking moment. And yet at the same time she was excited by the undercurrent of sexuality she was provoking in their ravaged bodies. The fact that they, crippled in the prime years of their lives, could not do anything except admire her from afar satisfied a need in her. Their hollow eyes stared at her hungrily out of pain-sculpted faces. None of them said anything apart from an occasional grunted yes or no. The sexual tension in the air was palpable.

When she first walked through that door, I was angry that Huguette should humiliate me and my friends by walking in dressed like that. And then I saw her clearly for the first time in our lives – as a deeply insecure woman who needed clothes, make-up, jewellery, cars and all the reassurance her glamorous way of life could provide, so that she could face the world with confidence.

She, I thought, is the real cripple in this room. Her crutches cost a fortune!

And paradoxically I felt for her more affection in that split second than I ever had before. I understood that I had never loved her. I had wanted her sexually and married her because I felt proud to own such a beautiful animal, but I had never loved her before that moment, when it was too late.

At a loss for something to say, Huguette asked, 'How long until you can walk properly again, *chéri?*'

She might as well have asked him to take her to dinner

at Maxim's that same evening and on to a trendy night club for dancing.

Raoul was stunned. 'A few more weeks, I suppose,' he stammered, then hid behind: 'You'll have to ask the *toubib*. He doesn't tell us things like that.'

One of the male nurses entered with a polite invitation for Huguette to take coffee with the colonel. On her return to the ward after this briefing, she was frigidly polite, unable to cope with the news she had received. Raoul wanted to comfort her but could think of nothing to say. She clutched her hat and fur coat, excusing herself with 'It took me two hours to get here from Lourdes in a taxi with no shock-absorbers, over terrible roads. If I miss the train back to Paris, it'll mean spending the night.'

It was typical of her lies: from the window they could all see the chauffeur sitting in her car, parked in front of the Admin. block.

Leaving, Huguette planted a single kiss on Raoul's temple. Something about her manner reminded him of a maiden aunt kissing his grandma's forehead in her coffin when he was six years old. As the swing door closed behind her, the major in the next bed who had lost both arms said, 'Your wife is very beautiful, Duvalier.'

Raoul was observing some distant sheep through the binoculars. He did not reply. There was a thumping sound from the next bed. It was the major banging his head on the pillow. Between thumps he sobbed through gritted teeth: 'I – can't – even – wank – myself.'

The visits from Raoul's parents were no more successful. In fairness to them, thought Raoul, there were few parents who did adjust to the different physical, mental and emotional relationship with a son who had become a *grand mutilé de guerre*.

He was in a wheelchair on the balcony the first time they came. Raoul's father was in civilian clothes to make the point that he was just a relative and required no special treatment because of his rank. In contrast to Huguette's sartorial excess both parents were dressed in sombre colours as though in mourning. The general shook Raoul's hand, complimented him on the binoculars, examined the maps with which his son spent so much time, and then took himself off to the chief surgeon's office where he spent more time talking with the colonel than he had with Raoul.

On his mother's subsequent visits, she brought apologies: 'The general was called to the Ministry at the last moment.' Or: 'The general is at a conference in Algiers.'

Among the books his mother brought was one about the painter Toulouse-Lautrec. Raoul thought it a strange choice: he had never been interested in art. Leafing through it, paying more attention to the sketches of horses than to the more famous, later works, he read how the artist's father, a fanatical horseman, had disowned him after an attack of polio when it became clear that his son would never be able to ride a horse. The book fell open naturally at that page, as though his mother had bent the spine repeatedly at that point. It was the way messages were passed in the Duvalier family.

It came as a relief to Raoul when his mother wrote to tell him that they were going to live in Washington, where the general had been posted for three years. He wrote a polite letter back, congratulating his father on the posting. From that day on, he never opened his mother's letters.

It was not so easy to come to terms with my feelings for Huguette when she came a second time to Torrens. It was a sunny June afternoon, and she arrived without notice. She told me that she no longer worked for Dior as it had become too boring. Poor Huguette! Did she really think a man in hospital would not have seen the gossip in the newspapers? The truth was that she had been sacked for having an affair with the husband of a client. At first humiliated, then angry, I had ended by feeling sorry for her. In a different way, her life was as devoid of privacy as mine.

She looked that day as remotely beautiful as ever. Her story was that she had come from a location in the mountains where she was filming a cinema commercial and had not known until the very last moment that she would be able to come. I wondered if all her little excuses had been clever ways of avoiding big ones. The car in which she arrived was certainly no hire car.

She was dressed that day in a blue tubular shantung dress, with matching shoes, gloves and hat and a contrasting light cream coat. In regulation striped pyjamas under a dressing gown, I felt underdressed!

She was playing the part of nurse, wife and bitch in turn. Huguette is a woman who can change roles so fast that it is sometimes hard for a man to keep track.

When they were alone on the balcony, Huguette was over-solicitous, finding Raoul drinks, lighting his cigarettes.

'You don't expect me to stay with you, darling?' she asked apropos of nothing, blowing smoke into the cool summer air.

'I don't expect anything.'

She bent to kiss him on the lips, playing some role, or maybe a part in her commercial. 'You were such a wonderful lover. I want you to know that.'

'I still want you.' Raoul had not understood what she was telling him.

'Darling,' she said softly. 'How could I? Be realistic.' She glanced over her shoulder at the three pairs of eyes watching them through the open window.

Slipping on the coat, she said, 'I want a divorce, darling. My lawyers will write to you. Don't make any problems, please. People would say I was such a bitch to get rid of a wounded veteran. But I'm not cut out to be a nursemaid, you know that.'

'You've found a new lover,' he said, knowing the moment the words were out of his mouth that it was a stupid remark.

Huguette smiled at herself in the mirror of her powder compact. Behind her, she saw the three crippled men hungrily watching her every move. 'Lots,' she said. 'But this is more important. I'm marrying a count, darling. I shall be a countess. What do you think of that?'

'Tell me how many you've had.'

Huguette picked up her bag and gloves. 'Oh God, I don't count them.' She threw Raoul a rare glance that focused on him, and looked away as he tried to hold her gaze. 'The first one was ten days after we got married, if that helps you to get rid of me.'

Ten days? The thought hurt, but was it true? 'Anyone I know?'

'That friend of yours with the German name.'

'Koenig?' He laughed at her.

'That's right. He wasn't any good.'

'You're lying.'

'Am I? Look, darling, some women . . .' She was examining her nails critically, flexing the long tapering fingers. Her future husband, the count, adored kissing them in public. '. . . need to love a man, to devote themselves to him. I'm the other kind, Raoul. I need to be loved, to be adored, to be submerged in attention . . .' She stopped in mid-sentence, surprised at her own honesty.

'I fucked you a lot,' he said savagely.

She agreed straight away. 'I said you were a good lover, darling. But I needed more than that. I needed to be taken to smart restaurants, to go dancing, be given clothes, to stay in the best hotels.'

'When I was on leave . . .'

She laughed. 'It was fun. But most of the time you were stationed in some boring place I'd never heard of, where you spent the whole time shouting at men in boots with short haircuts.'

'You never loved me,' he accused her.

'Didn't I?' Huguette sighed. A final touch of lipstick and the compact snapped shut. 'Now don't let's have an argument and say cruel things. The fact is, there's no point in us being married any longer, is there?'

Raoul's pride wanted to say: 'Don't come here again. I don't want to see you.' But it would not have been true. Looking at her untouchable beauty was like looking into a strange mirror which reflected through time instead of space and where he could still see, behind her in the glass, a faint image of the man he had been when he was whole in mind and limb.

10

After Huguette had gone, the tangle of emotions generated by her visit was tearing Raoul to pieces. He propelled himself angrily along the corridors in his wheelchair, deliberately crashing open the fire doors in the hope of hurting someone on the other side. He ended in the only place where anger could safely be expended – the physio wing.

The senior therapist of the hospital was a French Canadian from Quebec. Although entitled to be addressed by rank, Louise Lacrosse insisted that the patients use her first name. She was a plain woman in her late twenties who wore no make-up, kept her hair pinned up tightly in a bun and had never been seen in a skirt. Because she had no special relationships with any of the surgeons, there were whispers among the gay male nurses that she was butch.

She watched Raoul punishing himself on the wall bars and with weights but left him alone. When the anger was all gone, he felt a fire of resolve burning within him.

Huguette had floored me. I had to come up fighting or not at all. Occasionally men killed themselves at Torrens; lacking hands and arms, they invented some ingenious methods of suicide. But that wasn't my way. Looking back, I owe a lot to Huguette being her narcissistic self that day. By kicking the crutches out from under me, so to speak, she triggered my reflex to save myself by rejecting my dependency on others.

I waited in the gym until the rest of the men had left before taking a pair of crutches that were leaning against the wall. Heaving myself upright on them, I managed to put some weight on my legs just long enough to move the crutches a few inches. I dragged my feet forward and repeated the manoeuvre until I had crossed ten lines painted on the floor at one-metre intervals. The exhilaration of crossing the finish line was greater than at the end of the mad dash in the jeep through the Viet lines. I nearly fainted from the excitement of walking – if you can call it that – for the first time in a year.

'Fantastic!' Louise had come up behind while all my attention was concentrated on staying upright. She caught me just as I was falling. 'The colonel's going to love you, when I tell him . . .'

'I didn't do it for him,' I shouted. I wanted the world to know. 'I did it for me.'

She must have seen the tears in my eyes but knew how to keep the conversation neutral. 'It's his surgery. The colonel did a brilliant job straightening your legs.'

'It's my willpower,' I snapped.

She grinned. 'You deserve a reward.'

'Like what?'

'How about a nice massage? Lie down on the bench.'

'You've had some bad news?' Louise's skilled fingers kneaded the tight and twitching muscles in his back.

Head down, Raoul grunted, 'My wife's divorcing me.'

Oh Christ, she thought. Everyone knew that was coming, except him. Make a joke, Louise. . . . 'I never go out with married men, but this makes a difference.'

'Where shall we go?' he asked, playing along with her game.

She gestured at the wild mountainside above them. 'I grew up on the shores of Hudson Bay. It was a tough place to live but I learned a lot about animals from my father and brothers. Working indoors all day long, I miss it. So every now and again, I go up on the tops and get close to the wildlife for a while.'

'And how do I travel?' asked Raoul. He rolled over and sat up, a towel over his loins.

'One of the water company engineers who works on the dam is a pal of mine. He's lending me the four-wheel-drive jeep tomorrow afternoon. Wanna come?'

Her no-nonsense manner made the invitation seem less frightening.

'It'll make a change from my usual afternoon stroll.'

'I'm not joking,' she said.

'Why me?' he asked. 'Or do you reward every cripple who staggers a few paces?'

Careful . . . she turned her back to wash the liniment off her hands. 'I've seen the interest you take in what goes on up there, Raoul. Binoculars are OK, but I reckon you deserve the chance of a closer look. And . . .'

'And what?'

'Tomorrow's your birthday . . .' she said, as though joking.

To Louise the men she worked on were not just broken bodies. However horrifying their injuries, they were still individuals with personalities. Raoul had arrived at Torrens little more than a corpse clinging stubbornly to life. She had helped him rebuild the wasted muscles; his reconstructed identity was his own creation.

She had witnessed so many times what a rejection, usually by a woman, could do to destroy a wounded vet.'s precious morale. After all that Raoul had achieved in the past few months, she did not want that to happen to him. Silently she finished the sentence: '. . . and I have a present for you'.

The track curled upwards out of sight of the hospital buildings and the village of Torrens below, doubling back on itself time and time again to take advantage of the contours. The jeep bumped over rocks and through streams up to the axles. To Raoul, finding out what was hidden behind each outcrop of rock and spur of mountain was experiencing the three-dimensional reality of all the close-packed lines on the map over which he had pored so long.

On the way up, the weather changed. During the half-hour drive in second gear up to the dam, clouds raced in from the peaks of the range and rain was now making the track slippery. As Louise hauled the jeep round a bend above a precipice, wheels skidding on wet rock, Raoul hung out of the open side of the vehicle and gazed down to where a waterfall leaped in showers of spray from rock to rock on its eventual way to the sea.

'It would solve everything,' she panted, fighting the wheel straight, 'if I took a wrong turning.'

Raoul wondered how she knew what he had been thinking. He tore his eyes away from the abyss and saw the woman beside him flushed with the exhilaration of the drive, her eyes sparkling. She was a different person from the calm, unemotional therapist who ordered patients always to do ten more press-ups or another five lifts. She looked, he thought, quite sexy.

The track evened out as they came into a narrow hidden valley, invisible from below. 'I'm sorry about the weather,' she apologised. 'It's unpredictable at this altitude.'

'I know,' Raoul said tersely. 'I used to climb in the Alps.'

A squall of colder air blew the dark clouds apart. Bright sunshine filled the valley, the waters of the dam flashing it back on the bald scree slopes so that for a moment, until their eyes adjusted, the view was like a burnt-out picture on overexposed film. A tiny stone-walled cabin with a sheep pen beside it nestled in the lee of a huge rock that had detached itself from the main mass and rolled into the middle of the valley floor. There was smoke coming from the chimney.

'Someone lives up here?' Raoul asked.

'No.' Louise laughed at the idea. 'It's a mountain refuge – for the use of benighted walkers and climbers. The shepherds use it in winter when the weather catches them.'

'Who lit the fire?'

'The guys from the water company were up here this

morning,' she said. 'I asked them to leave the fire going. It's already chill at this height.'

Black storm clouds sat above the valley, bringing a sudden dusk. Louise parked the jeep near to the door of the refuge and vanished inside. Raoul dragged himself on his crutches the few paces that separated the jeep from the cabin, thinking bitterly of the times when he would have arrived at the 3,000-metre contour line on his own feet, sweating but not out of breath. He placed his crutches against the wall as once he had stacked his skis and sticks at the end of a day, and stood in the doorway holding on to the woodwork with both hands to support himself.

Inside, Louise was on her knees blowing on the embers in the crude hearth. A tiny flame caught the tinder she had stuffed under some twigs and dead branches from the back of the jeep. The dry wood ignited with a crackle and a roar.

'Shut the door,' she said. 'You're making too much draught. I've got no more wood once this has burned.'

With difficulty, Raoul perched on a stone jutting out from the dry-stone wall and heaved the heavy door to. He leaned against the rough stones, sweating.

The gaps between the stones had been plugged with mud and moss. With the door closed, the noise of the wind died away. It was strangely quiet in the refuge. He took out a cigarette and lit it. As his eyes grew accustomed to the gloom broken only by the flames in the fireplace, Raoul saw that there was no furniture, only a sleeping platform and a few pots and pans for cooking, placed on a stone ledge above the fireplace.

Louise stood and stretched. Her arms locked behind her head, silhouetted against the flames, she asked unambiguously, 'Well, are you going to take advantage of the situation?'

'I won't be any good to you,' Raoul warned her. The words reminded him of what Huguette had said about his friend Koenig. All lies, he thought angrily.

Louise rolled her anorak into a pillow for the bed, then undressed swiftly, keeping her back to him without artifice as though she were alone in her bedroom. As she bent over to add each garment to the sleeping bags she had brought in from the jeep to make a bed for them, Raoul watched the flickering firelight caress her thighs and buttocks, all the female curves that were normally concealed beneath her hospital uniform and the unfeminine clothes she wore off duty.

He licked his dry lips. 'I won't be any good,' he warned again.

She turned and let him see her nakedness for the first time. The sight of her nipples and pubic hair was like a pain that made him want to close his eyes.

'I'm a physio,' she said softly. 'I know what's wrong with you. You're not a paraplegic, Raoul. It's just your legs that don't work. The rest of you is OK, if your mind will let it be.'

Her eyes on his, she unpinned her long hair and let it fall down below her shoulders. He blinked at the change it made to her appearance. Framed by rich auburn hair, in the soft light from the log fire her face was ten years younger.

'Why are you doing this?' he asked, clinging to the rough wall for support, unable to take his eyes off her.

'Because I want you,' she said. Her eyes said it was true. 'Come to me.'

Louise held out her arms in a timeless gesture of invitation, then slowly subsided on to the sleeping platform. She did not move or say anything as Raoul laboriously hauled himself past the fire and collapsed beside her.

There he sat shivering until she grasped his hand and placed it on her breast, then gently guided the other between her thighs. He jerked his fingers away from her skin as though it stung. 'No. No,' he said through clenched teeth. 'I can't.'

Her reaction stopped him. 'You don't find me attractive?'
'It's not that . . .'
'It's OK, Raoul,' she said in the brisk tone of voice she used in the gym. The Canadian accent seemed stronger than usual. 'I should have known better. I guess with a wife

as beautiful as yours, I was too ambitious. I'm pretty fit and my figure's OK but my face is nothing special, is it? Still, I did fancy you, you know.'

'I'm sorry.'

'Don't be.' She laughed to herself. 'I brought some champagne. If you don't mind drinking it from paper cups . . .'

'I'd like that.'

She put on her blouse and padded bare-legged across the earthen floor to the duffel bag she had dropped just inside the door. The bottle of champagne she handed to Raoul to open.

They drank watching the flames.

'When this squall is past, I'll drive you down again,' she offered.

Maybe the champagne helped. Or the fact that they were cut off from the world by the storm raging outside and by the desolation of peaks and valleys that isolated them from the rest of the human race.

They sat side by side not touching, watching the flames, and talked in low voices about the wildlife they had seen in different countries.

'Do you miss hunting?' she asked.

'If you gave me new legs,' he said, 'I don't think I'd shoot any living creature ever again.' He finished his second cup of champagne. 'Louise . . .' he began and hesitated.

She caught the change in his voice and looked at him, her eyes wide and searching his to be sure of the meaning. This time, as his hand lifted the blouse and touched her breasts, it was she who flinched. She shut her eyes as he undid the buttons and bent to kiss her breasts.

Gently, Raoul laid her back on the bed. A paper cup tumbled from Louise's hand. The champagne was soaked up by the dry earth of the floor. She felt his lips on her skin and wrapped her arms around him, wanting him desperately. And then they were laughing, she helping as he eased himself out of his clothes, touching him, kissing his body until he sat naked from the waist up.

'Don't stop,' she pleaded. 'Don't stop now.'

'I can't take my trousers off.' Raoul wanted to keep his legs hidden.

'It's not your legs I want to feel,' she said playfully. And then, a moment later, she whispered, 'I knew it would be all right.'

He grunted as she wriggled on top, tantalising him with her moist lips, touching and moving away before he could catch her.

'*Doucement*,' she breathed. 'There's no hurry.' But she could feel the urgency in him that threatened to spoil the magic of the moment, so bent and kissed his flesh, caressing him with lips and tongue. 'You're beautiful,' she said between mouthfuls.

He groaned with shame as the hot semen burned its way out of his body. 'Oh God, why did you make me do that?'

Louise raised her head. 'Because I wanted to,' she said gently. She wriggled up the bed, pulling the covers with her, and kissed his lips long and tenderly.

Those eyes of his, she thought. I wish I could write a poem . . .

'I'm ashamed.'

She kissed his ear and murmured, 'Don't be. It was something you had to get out of the way, after all this time without a woman. In a few minutes, we'll start again. This time, you can make love properly to me, Raoul. For me, not you.'

11

Arguments between the patients at Torrens had a way of boiling over into physical violence. Raoul had one day found himself finishing an argument by attacking his friend, the major without arms. Beside himself with fury, he was raining blows on the defenceless torso in the next bed when forcibly dragged away by two of the male nurses. The beds were moved apart. Raoul and the major glared at each other from opposite ends of the room for a whole day, unable to remember what they had been fighting about.

A young Foreign Legion lieutenant who had lost a leg fighting in the new war in Algeria, picked a fight with Raoul for no reason: 'I don't blame the *fellagha* for trying to kill me, Duvalier. I was doing the same to them. That's what war's all about. But I do blame –' His voice rose to a shout – 'the French government for not equipping us with the tools of modern war, like helicopters to evacuate the wounded. I didn't need to lose this leg.' His fist pounded the arm-rest of the wheelchair. 'Do you know why they had to cut it off? Because it took my men three hours to carry me on a litter from the *djebel* where I was shot down to a road where a jeep could drive me to hospital. That's why.'

A nurse, passing with a covered bedpan, tried to smooth things over with a joke. 'If we were Americans, *mon lieuten-*

ant, we'd have helicopters to bring supplies of iced Coke to the front line, never mind evacuate the wounded.'

'That's it!' The lieutenant thumped the arm-rest. 'You'll see, Duvalier. The key to modern warfare is equipment. It was American equipment that won the Second World War.'

'It didn't do the Yanks much good in Korea,' objected Raoul. It was a sport: baiting the newcomers. 'In any case, you're wrong, lieutenant. In this new kind of war – Korea, Vietnam, Algeria – we've come full circle, back to one man pitting his strength against another's.' He was thinking of his own dark combat with Minh.

'Korea?' sneered the lieutenant. 'If MacArthur had been given a free hand by his government to bomb red China . . .'

'If, if, if,' Raoul interrupted. 'Just suppose the rumours are true and the Yanks are about to go into Vietnam with all their know-how and equipment. Do you expect they'll do any better than we did, under-supplied and under-manned? Or any better than your men are doing in Algeria right now?'

'You're out of date, Duvalier.' The lieutenant was ten years younger than Raoul. 'Did you know, for example, that the Yanks have weapon sighting systems that can see in the dark? Give my platoon a dozen of those and I guarantee we'd wipe out the whole FLN within one year.' He punched Raoul's arm to punctuate his remark.

'You're wrong,' said Raoul. 'The whole philosophy of war has changed.'

'Bullshit! The point of any armed confrontation is to win.'

'Wrong again,' said Raoul. 'In the new war in Algeria, the FLN don't have to win.'

'What kind of crap are you talking?' The lieutenant wanted to hit his adversary, but confined his anger to gripping the arm-rests so hard that it hurt.

'The FLN doesn't have to win,' Raoul repeated. 'They just have to avoid losing. Day by day, month by month, one bullet at a time, they're bleeding away our military strength. If they can do that for long enough, in the end every village in France will have lost one of its sons. At that moment, political pressure will force the government out of office.

The FLN know that. It's the whole philosophy of colonial war.'

He felt an obscure perverse pleasure in quoting Captain Minh's teaching to his fellow alumnus from St Cyr.

'You're both talking a load of bullshit!' said a voice behind him.

Raoul turned his chair to see standing in the doorway a man in sports jacket and grey flannels.

For a moment, I did not recognise my visitor.

We lived in a closed world. Visitors – even regular ones – were embarrassing intrusions from 'down there' at the foot of the mountains where people all had two legs and two arms. Visitors reminded us that we were freaks. We looked forward to their coming anxiously but, more often than not, felt confused, disappointed and angry afterwards.

In any case, I did not remember ever seeing Koenig in civilian clothes before. Of course I had seen him in mufti sometimes, but he was one of those men who, once they put on a uniform for the first time, seem to belong in it so that ever afterwards they look wrong in ordinary clothes. He was dressed that day in a nondescript sports jacket and trousers. His mutilated right hand was in his pocket. In the left he carried a briefcase. He looked more like an unsuccessful commercial traveller than one of France's best soldiers.

He told me later that it was a shock to stand in the doorway of that sordid room and see me for the first time since we had parted at Dien Bien Phu. I seemed to have shrunk – not just my legs but my whole body and even my head. The eyes alone, he said, were the same.

For my part, I saw this stranger staring at me and thought he was someone else's visitor, come to the wrong room. Then I recognised him and my first thought was the allegation that Huguette had made. Had Koenig made love to my wife within two weeks of my marriage? Would he have done such a thing? I could not believe it of him. Huguette told so many lies. If anything, her saying that about my best friend meant that he had probably rejected some kind of overture from her. . . . But that was rationalisation. The worm of suspicion was eating away at me.

*His face was leaner and browner than I recalled – although
perhaps that was because I had grown used to the pallor of inval-
ids. There was a black eye-patch where his left eye had been. It
didn't stop the grin of pleasure from covering his whole face. The
bad moment past, I felt a flush of warmth radiate from my bowels
throughout my whole body, just to see him. I didn't care what, if
anything, had transpired between him and Huguette. 'You old
bastard,' I shouted. 'I thought you were dead.'*

*'I should be,' Koenig admitted. His grin was different, twisted
by the scarring around the eye. He put down the briefcase on my
bed and embraced me. That hug meant more than Louise giving
herself to me.*

'Who the hell do you think you are, busting in here?' The
Legion lieutenant had been spoiling for a fight and was
angry at the interruption.

Koenig grasped the handles of his wheelchair and propelled him along the corridor. 'Fuck off,' he said laconically,
'before I break your other leg.'

'He's OK,' said Raoul, as the door slammed. 'We get
wound up in here.'

'I'm not surprised,' said Koenig. 'They wanted to keep
me in a hospital when I got back to France. I told them what
to do with that idea. How long have you been in this dump,
Raoul?'

'Nine months, nearly ten.'

'Time you got out. How are your legs?'

'I can hobble a few paces.'

'And that's it?'

'I kid myself, but that's as good as it's going to get.' Raoul
grimaced. 'So what are you doing?' he wanted to know.

'What I always was: soldiering.'

'You lucky bastard. Where?'

'Algeria. We have a new war out there, as your argumenta-
tive young friend knows.'

'You didn't come here to talk about that.'

Koenig winked mysteriously, took half a dozen bottles
of Johnnie Walker Black Label out of the briefcase and

presented one to each of the other three men in the room. They chatted like old friends while Raoul wheeled himself along the corridor trying to borrow a couple of drinking glasses.

On the balcony – the only place they could have a private conversation – Koenig raised a tooth mug full of whisky and gave the only toast possible: 'To absent legs and eyes, wherever they may be!'

The sight of his old classmate had shattered Koenig more than he had anticipated. He forced himself to compare the handsome outgoing sportsman Raoul had been with the tense, withdrawn cripple in the wheelchair. A parallel thought compared the code of honour they shared with what some men were planning to do to his friend. As though, he thought, Raoul hasn't suffered enough already. . . .

'Aah, that's good.' Raoul closed his eyes and felt the alcohol burn its way through his stomach, working through arteries and veins to his skin. 'There's an embargo on hard liquor here. We get wine with our meals, but this . . .'

'You'll need a good stiff drink for what I'm going to tell you.'

Koenig's hint meant nothing to Raoul. He poured another mugful of whisky.

When he had finished it and reached for the bottle again, Koenig clamped his disfigured right hand over Raoul's wrist. 'That's enough,' he said. 'You can get pissed later when I've gone.'

'You can't stay?' It was the question that always slipped out.

'My disguise –' Koenig flicked the civilian clothes he was wearing with disdain – 'is because I'm AWOL, on the wrong side of the Mediterranean. I don't want to stick around here too long. Somebody might recognise me and then we'd both be in the shit.'

Raoul laughed and then sobered up, seeing the look in his old comrade's eye. 'You on the run, Koenig? What did you do? Kill someone?' It was an old St Cyr joke.

'The reverse,' said Koenig harshly. 'I'm trying to save somebody's life. Now shut up and listen . . .'

*

The investigators came the day after Koenig's visit. After introducing the two *deuxième bureau* officers with obvious distaste, the colonel left them alone with Raoul in his office, instructing his patient to ring for a nurse if the questioning tired him.

The investigators wore casual civilian clothes. One talked while the other listened and made shorthand notes in a reporter's notebook. The talker was the quiet-voiced officer with fair hair who had been looking for Raoul during the first hand-over of prisoners at Hai Thon, over a year before.

He sat on the corner of the colonel's desk, smoking a pipe, hands in the pockets of his jacket. 'We don't seem to be getting very far,' he said after an hour.

'No,' agreed Raoul.

'We have to establish, captain, exactly what happened to the pay-chest that was in your charge at Dien Bien Phu. We need to know how much had been paid out to the local levies and how much remained. We also need to know exactly when and how it fell into the hands of the Viets. This is not a criminal investigation. It's a question of tidying up an outstanding file. But it's a file worth rather a lot of money.'

'Difficult,' grunted Raoul. Koenig's news had knocked him down again. He wondered how many times he would get up off the mat. It was easier this time with someone in his corner. 'There was a battle going on, you know. I didn't write out a neatly itemised receipt when the pay-chest was handed over to me.'

'That was irregular.'

Raoul despised them. It was tempting to confront them with what he knew, but that would involve Koenig too. He contented himself with sarcasm. 'Blame the officer who had previously been in charge of the *trésor* for not insisting.'

'And why did he not ask for a receipt?'

'Because he was dead.'

'Yet afterwards,' the investigator persisted, 'you say that you broke the gold up into loads more easily carried in old ammunition boxes. Didn't you count it then – from interest, Captain Duvalier?'

'There was a battle going on,' said Raoul. 'Do you people know what that is? There's a lot of noise, it's dirty and people try to kill you. You try to kill them. Oddly enough, that seems more urgent than counting some bloody coins.'

'I have to ask all these questions,' the investigator excused himself. 'But we're still not getting anywhere, are we?' A pause. 'I'd like you to tell me again what little you do remember about the last hours of Isabelle. Any small clue could help me to reconstruct what occurred.'

'I recall hardly anything.' Raoul gestured to his legs under the blanket. 'I was blown up some time before dawn and lay unconscious for hours. Certainly it was daylight when I came to, late morning probably. I was concussed. I don't remember anything clearly.'

'But the gold was with you at the time of the breakout?'

'I assume so. The whole idea of me driving it to Isabelle was to deny it to the Viets.'

The investigator puffed at his pipe. If the bastard turns the chair round and sits astride it, I'm going to call him Maigret, Raoul promised himself.

'So –' a stab of the pipe stem in Raoul's direction – 'at a guess, you buried it when the breakout failed and it became obvious that the position was going to be overrun by the enemy?'

'I suppose so.' Raoul had been watching the mountains when called to the colonel's office. The binoculars still hung around his neck. On the slopes high above them, sheep stopped grazing and stood all looking in the same direction. He scanned the hillside through the binoculars to see what had alarmed them, but could find nothing. It felt like a warning to be on his guard.

He put down the glasses and turned the wheelchair to face the investigators. 'I suppose we did bury the ammo boxes with the gold inside, but I don't know where. I don't recall anything about that night. Amnesia. Shell-shock. Call it what you want.'

'One of my problems,' said the man from the *deuxième bureau*, 'is that you are the sole survivor of Isabelle. Every

107

single officer and man in the position was massacred by the Viets in the morning of 8 May 1954. Between 600 and 800 survivors were killed in cold blood and you alone were spared.'

'So I'm told,' said Raoul. 'Being unconscious at the time, I was hardly in a position to know what was going on.'

The investigator seemed fascinated by the patterns in the wood of his pipe. 'It's curious that you alone should survive, Captain Duvalier.'

'If you call this surviving.' Raoul lifted the rug over his knees and pulled up both trouser legs to show them the damage.

An intake of breath and the investigators looked away. 'Your survival suggests that the Viets knew about the gold, captain. It suggests they kept you alive deliberately, in order to get their hands on it.'

Anger boiled over in Raoul. 'I was bloody near to death. The reason I was not killed was that I was lying unconscious under a pile of sandbags whilst the Viets executed my comrades.'

'You remember that much, then?' A glint of satisfaction in the man's eyes warned Raoul to keep a grip on himself.

'I have a hazy recollection of being dug up,' he admitted. 'Then, I think, I was kept all day in the sun on a stretcher with no attention or water to drink. There was a dead German legionnaire from the first infantry regiment lying a few metres away.'

'How do you know he was German?'

'He was one of the two machine-gunners on the jeep I drove through the lines to Isabelle.'

'Name? Rank?'

'Jesus! I don't know.'

'And yet you know the man's regiment?'

Raoul kept his temper. 'They'd stripped the poor bastard naked. He had the regimental emblem tattooed on his arm: an eagle and a snake intertwined.'

'Everything you can tell us is helpful.'

The second investigator was scribbling in his notebook.

Raoul forced himself to calm down. 'He was a sergeant. Called himself Hans.'

'Surname?'

'I don't remember!' Raoul shouted. 'We weren't properly introduced. It wasn't a ballroom. We met on a battlefield where crawling maggots like you two don't exist!'

An eagle circled in a thermal. A symbol of nobility, he thought, flying free among the pureness of the high peaks. And not maggots but snakes, the lowest of the low, wrapping themselves around the eagle, trying to pull it down into the mire – that's you two.

A page turned in the notebook. 'We're still making no progress,' remarked the one who was doing the talking.

'No.'

'If you are the sole survivor of the massacre at Isabelle and you can't remember anything material – which of course is understandable in the circumstances – then, speaking hypothetically, we can go no further with this investigation.'

'So it would seem.' Raoul felt relieved that he was over the hump.

'On the other hand –' the second investigator spoke for the first time – 'perhaps we ought to come clean and tell you, whilst you are the only man to have survived the Viets' overrunning the position, some of the men who were in Lalande's breakout are still alive.'

'I was told everyone else was killed.'

'Everyone in the position on the morning of 8 May was killed.' A pause for that to sink in. 'However, when Lalande and the main force were driven back into the perimeter during the night, a small group managed to hide in an abandoned Viet trench about a kilometre outside the lines. It took them several weeks of living off the country and most of them died on the way, but some eventually made it home via Laos.'

Like Koenig, thought Raoul. My one-eyed friend spent six weeks hacking his way through hostile jungle, watching his comrades die one after another from wounds, infection and starvation, while you snakes were eating regular meals and making plans to trap eagles. . . .

The sheep were running now, bounding down the mountainside in great leaps to get away from the unseen threat. An eagle? A fox? 'I'm tired,' said Raoul ringing the bell.

'We mustn't tire you,' said the pipe-smoking investigator politely. '*Au revoir*, Captain Duvalier. We'll be back.'

12

The hospital chapel had been cleared for the court martial. With Christmas only two days away, the chaplain had protested but been overruled; someone in Paris was in a hurry.

Three judges in uniform sat at a long trestle table placed where the altar normally stood. The fair-haired investigator from the *deuxième bureau* sat beside the major who was presenting the prosecution's case. On the opposite side of the court, Raoul sat beside his defending officer. Everyone was in No. 1 uniform.

From some stores, smelling of mothballs, Raoul's best uniform had been forwarded. The last time he had worn it had been to take General Lépine's wife to mass in Hanoi cathedral.

Like an insult from the past, it hung on him several sizes too large until a local tailor had taken the jacket in. Even after the alterations it still fitted badly but looked sufficiently smart from the front which was all that counted. The altered trousers hung slackly around Raoul's spindly legs. In place of his felt bedroom slippers a pair of polished shoes had been borrowed and put on his feet by the nurse who had helped him to dress. A Legion officer's kepi was on his lap.

*

The deuxième bureau *men got the confession out of me on their third visit, as Koenig had advised. Having renounced my right to address the court, I sat now waiting for the verdict, next to my defending officer who was making notes on a pile of papers, interrupting to make a point, bobbing up and down, going through all the motions. But in my mind, I was free! Sitting there at my own court martial, I had rediscovered the door into the secret world where I had taken refuge from Minh.*

By turning my head to look through the plain glass side windows of the chapel, I could see the mountain tops that I had studied for so long. In a shaft of sunlight, I thought I could see the chimney of the cabin where Louise and I went to make love. And then I was transported on a sunbeam into that high, hidden valley. I was above the cabin, running and leaping downhill, feeling the scratches of the stunted, windswept bushes on my strong, bare legs. Hearing my shout echoing round the valley, Louise appeared at the door of the cabin, her face radiant. . . .

Beside the other 'me' in the wheelchair, the defending officer's voice droned on: 'The son of a general, a hero of France . . . the top cadet of his year at St Cyr . . . outstanding marksman, pilot, skier and horseman . . . medals . . . rapid promotion.' His eulogy was nothing to do with the real me.

Above and behind the judges the altar window of stained glass glowed as a weak sun shafted through breaks in the cloud cover. The window depicted a saint in the uniform of a Roman soldier, cutting his cloak in half with his sword in order to share it with a beggar. I searched my memory of Wednesday catechism lessons, trying to recall which saint had done that. I relived those lessons while the others in the chapel went about the banal business of my court martial.

St Martin. . . . The name that had been eluding me surfaced from the subconscious like a piece dropping into a jigsaw. The saint in the window was a tribune's son who had left the Roman army to become a hermit and then a bishop.

My thoughts drifted to the fox I had been watching the previous day fretting behind a wall not 200 metres from the hospital, hungry for the gardener's chicks in their wire run. And I was the fox, slinking slowly closer to its prey. The sensation was so real

that saliva dripped from my lips. I had to dry them with a
handkerchief that the nurse had thoughtfully placed in my pocket.

The pipe-smoking investigator from the deuxième was speak-
ing now. '. . . according to Captain Duvalier's own confession, he
revealed to the enemy the location of the pay-chest which had been
entrusted to his keeping. In the absence of exact accounts, it is
estimated that the value of the contents was approximately two-
and-a-half to three billion francs at then current values.'

I made a rush, grabbed a chicken, broke its neck with one jerk
and raced for the den where the hungry cubs were waiting.

The defending officer was entering his plea. 'Whilst Captain
Duvalier had not been tortured as such, there are extenuat-
ing circumstances. He was weakened by starvation, wounds
and months of deliberate sensory deprivation. If you will
look at the medical evidence, it is clear that the accused
officer was also suffering from fever and dysentery. He was
not responsible for his actions.'

Above the peaks, the sky darkened as snow clouds lurched
into view. Raoul watched them build and darken the sky
while the voices droned on around him. The knowledge
that he could once again escape at any time was almost
inebriating.

The blizzard fell on the buildings savagely like a freak
wave intent on swamping a vessel at sea. It hammered at the
chapel windows, snow building up rapidly on the bottoms
and edges of the frames. In the resultant twilight, someone
switched on the chapel lighting and Raoul realised that the
judges had adjourned to the vestry.

His accusers avoided looking at him. They sat in silence
until the judges filed back. The sentence was as Raoul had
foreseen. What could the snakes do to drag him down, worse
than stripping him of his rank and dismissing him with
ignominy from the life he had loved? That was the limit
of the degradation they could impose. Thanks to Koenig's
warning, he had cheated them but there was little satisfaction
in it. Raoul felt soiled and angry.

*

A clatter of helicopter rotors from the car park of the snow-bound hospital announced the departure of the officers who had come to Torrens specially for the court martial. The lieutenant with one leg hurled a crutch impotently at the huge machine as it lifted off. He sat in the falling snow on one of the balconies, clad only in pyjamas and heedless of the temperature, screaming insults.

In the staff quarters, Raoul and Louise lay in her bed. It was against the regulations, but there was no other place they could be alone whilst the hospital was cut off by the drifts. Raoul had been savage and unloving. He had needed to hurt someone and Louise was the only person he could reach.

For Louise, it had been like making love with a stranger. She felt the anger burning within him at the verdict and wondered at the irony of the timing. The television was full of coverage for the coming Winter Olympics at Cortina d'Ampezzo, where several of his former friends were competing in the French team. That must really hurt a man who can't even stand properly, she thought.

She kept such reflections to herself. There were many things they tacitly agreed not to talk about. Although the affair had been going on for nearly three months, Louise knew there were whole areas of Raoul which he kept hidden from her. And lately, he seemed to have withdrawn not just from her but from everyone. She tried again to make some contact.

'You didn't have to confess, Raoul. You made everything easy for them.'

'What does it matter?' he said sourly. There was no way he was going to tell her what he had learned from Koenig.

'It matters that you have to leave the hospital.' And me, she wanted to add. 'I saw your movement order being made out when I was in Admin. this afternoon. You're being transferred to a civilian hospital near Paris.'

'I'm not going,' he said.

'You don't have any choice,' she said gently. 'This is a military hospital. Now you've been kicked out of the Army, you can't be treated at Torrens any longer.'

'What I meant was, I'm not going to another hospital. It's time I picked myself up off the mat.'

'What does that mean?'

He laughed. There was no point explaining.

'How will you manage to look after yourself?'

'Other men have done it.'

'When did you decide this?'

He lit a cigarette against her wishes – Louise disliked the smell of smoke in her room – and exhaled. 'When I was listening to the defending officer telling the court about my sporting achievements, that's when. Who is this paragon of masculine virtues they are talking about? I asked myself. Me? If I could do all that with a pair of legs, I can certainly learn to look after myself without them. Above the thighs, my body is only thirty-one years old, Louise. I could easily live for another thirty years, despite my injuries. So I'd better get started.'

'But what'll you do for money? They've taken away your pension.'

'And my father won't give me a penny after this disgrace. . .' He paused at the thought. 'I'll learn to live frugally. I've always had all the money I wanted – to buy a car, a boat, a horse. So being hard up will be a challenge, a *raison d'être*.'

He laughed. 'The Army taught me to be an accountant, among other things. Everyone in business has to have an accountant and you don't need legs to keep people's books. Maybe that's what I'll do.'

'Where will you live?'

On the spur of the moment, he said, 'In a village called St Martin.'

'Where is that?'

'I don't know yet. There must be many St Martins in France.'

'I don't understand.'

'St Martin,' he said, 'was a soldier. He'll look after me.'

'Why are you talking like this, Raoul? You're not religious.'

'No.'

'And even with a saint on your side, you'll need help.'

'Are you offering?'

Louise played with the hairs on his chest. 'They've grown thicker,' she said, 'since we've been making love regularly.' Touching his skin, she knew it was all over and bent her head so that he should not read anything in her face.

'I asked you a question.'

When she did not reply, he lifted her head so that he could see her eyes. She tried to pull away but he would not let her.

'You're hurting me, Raoul.'

'Answer me.'

'The woman in me would like to say yes.'

'Then say yes.' He willed her to agree.

She freed herself and sat up in the bed, a million miles away from him. 'It wouldn't work, Raoul.'

'We could try.'

Louise shook her head. 'In my job as a physiotherapist I've learned too much about the way handicapped men's minds work. And don't tell me you'll be different from all the others, because you won't.'

'At least tell me why it wouldn't work.'

She wanted to scream at him: Because you don't love me, that's why. Instead she said calmly, 'Because, however well we started out you'd eventually come to regard me as a poor substitute for your legs ... as a servant whose function is to fetch and carry and do your impatient bidding night and day. You'd get frustrated with yourself but let out your anger against me ... like just now, when we were making love. I couldn't take that, day after day, however much I love you.'

There was a long pause before he said, 'Well, that's set-back number one.'

'There is another reason ...' Louise spoke hesitantly. 'I don't know whether I should say this.'

He waited.

'You're still in love with your wife.'

'Huguette's divorcing me.'

'But are you divorcing her? Or will you – like many div-orced women – continue masochistically loving the person who's rejected you?'

'I don't love her.' Raoul had difficulty finding the right words. 'But when I look at her, I know that I wasn't always like this.' He stubbed out the cigarette in a glass by the bed and threw the duvet off his legs.

'Maybe.' She stroked the legs into which she had put so much work. 'Trouble is, I can't compete with someone as beautiful as Huguette.'

'You have a soul,' he said. 'Hers comes out of a bottle each morning.'

Louise searched the depth of his eyes. They're the only part of him that hasn't changed, she thought. They're the real man. He must have been so handsome . . . too hand-some to look at me. 'I'll tell you this, Raoul, and it has nothing to do with being jealous. You must get rid of Huguette. Push her right out of your life. Be the man you are. Don't try and remember what you used to be. It doesn't matter any more.'

'It matters to me,' he said harshly. 'This –' he hammered his useless legs with a clenched fist – 'This isn't good enough for me, don't you understand?'

'Then I'm not good enough for you, either.' And that's the truth, she thought.

'At least say you'll come and visit me, Louise, when I've found a home.'

'In your mythical St Martin?'

'Will you?'

'I don't know.' Louise pulled a dressing gown over her shoulders and got out of bed. 'If you still want me, write. Then I'll decide.'

Huguette was never one to let the grass grow under her feet when she wanted something.

The first vehicle to make it through the drifts behind the snow plough was a taxi from Lourdes bringing a lawyer's clerk and two envelopes. The one in Huguette's flowery handwriting was

117

addressed to Monsieur Raoul Duvalier. There was no mention of my rank of captain. And the lawyer's writ was also addressed to 'Monsieur DUVALIER, Raoul'.

Huguette's single sheet was a polite request for my signature on the papers setting out the terms of an uncontested divorce. I suppose she saw the letter as a crafty appeal to my sense of chivalry: '. . . anticipating that you would not expect me to renounce any hope of a normal marital life, I have instructed Maître So-and-So . . .'

She needn't have bothered to plead. I would have signed anyway. I raised the paper to my nostrils and smelled a faint trace of Ma Griffe, the perfume that Huguette used to wear. My sense of smell began returning that day.

The pale-faced clerk who had travelled from Paris offered me his fountain pen with which to sign. I scrawled my signature on the forms and handed them back. One of the nurses acted as witness. The taxi departed.

I sat in the hospital minibus waiting for the driver. It was cold with no heating on. There was frost on the inside of the windows. Despite all my resolve, I felt just as bleak inside myself. I had never known what it was to be a civilian. The previous day's stripping of insignia from my uniform, the withdrawal of my rank and the termination of my status as war hero had held all the symbolic violence of rebirth. I was a newborn babe out in the cold with no warm breast to suckle me.

Through a hole my breath had melted in the ice, I saw Louise walking between two of the buildings, a cape wrapped round her. Her face was turned away and she did not look back. As the minibus bumped slowly down the road, over the ridges of refrozen snow, taking me away from Torrens and back into the world 'down there', my chief emotion was of relief that it was all over.

13

'Drive on. Don't stop.' Huguette turned her head as the car passed the turn-off to the old tower. 'It's a ruin, Chauvin. Nobody lives there.'

'Very good, madame.' The driver glanced in his rear-view mirror and pulled back on to the road.

'You did check the address, down in the village?'

'Yes, madame.'

She was twisted right round in the seat now. 'There's a chimney behind the tower, with smoke rising from it.'

'Then somebody must live there, madame.'

'Stop the car.'

'Very good, madame.'

It was drizzling. The car windows began to steam up. Huguette sat in the back seat, clutching the New Year card. Raoul's signature was the same bold flourish it had always been. And the address: The Templar's Tower, St Martin-sur-Dordogne. There was no mistake.

'Would you like me to knock on the door and check this is the right house, madame?'

'Yes,' she said. 'Do that, Chauvin. I'm looking for a Monsieur Raoul Duvalier.'

'Very good, madame.' The driver was a middle-aged man used to her caprices. He reversed back to the turn-off, opened his door, put on his cap and started to get out.

'No.' She changed her mind again. If Chauvin knocked first, she would never know how Raoul reacted to her walking back into his life after two years' absence. It was that first split second of unguarded reaction she had come to see. 'Drive right up to the tower, Chauvin.'

'Yes, madame.'

The smoke was from a stovepipe which emerged from the side of a large, dilapidated barn at the base of the tower proper. There was a light at the window. When the car's engine was switched off, loud classical music was audible from inside the barn.

Huguette felt an excitement that was almost sexual. She slipped out of the car as soon as the door was opened and before the driver could raise an umbrella over her head.

'Get the presents,' she called, hurrying across the cinder-strewn yard past an ancient and obviously hard-driven Citroën V6 to shelter under the porch of the barn. On the way across the yard, she noticed that the car had been adapted for a driver unable to use the foot-pedals.

She knocked on the door. No reaction from within. She knocked again, harder. The music stopped. She knocked a third time and heard a man's voice: 'Wait, can't you? I'm coming.'

Of course, she thought. Poor Raoul. He can't hurry.

He opened the door to find her standing there against the background of the grey January sky like some gorgeous butterfly that had got its timing wrong.

Huguette was wearing a sable coat swathed around her. Behind her stood the uniformed chauffeur holding some gift-wrapped boxes, and behind him was the gleaming body-work of a burgundy DS, the same de luxe model that the President used.

Thrown into confusion, Raoul felt a welter of memories rise and choke his power of speech, leaving him wordless as Huguette swept in.

He was used to the way people avoided looking at his legs. This was different. Huguette managed somehow to avoid seeing any part of him except the face, at which she

120

smiled conspiratorially. Apparently satisfied with what she saw there, she moved past him and surveyed the interior of the converted barn as impersonally as an estate agent showing round a client in the absence of the owner.

The tower and its outbuildings had been purchased cheap by Raoul as a derelict ruin that nobody wanted. He had converted the barn into one large studio where he worked, ate and slept. All unnecessary walls had been taken out and the floor concreted, with ramps instead of steps. The bed was in an alcove, like a wall cupboard without doors. Beside it, a saucepan caught drips from a leak in the roof. A toilet and shower cubicle in what had been the milking stalls gave the only privacy. The walls were limewashed stone. The single luxury was a large hi-fi and a huge collection of opera LPs that overflowed the shelves and were stacked neatly on the floor.

Huguette blinked at him and smiled. 'What an adorable little place,' she said. 'And so practical, like an artist's studio.'

He found his tongue at last. 'It suits me.'

To the waiting chauffeur, she said, 'Put the boxes here on the table, Chauvin. Then wait for me in the car.'

She indicated a space in Raoul's papers which sprawled over the massive table made from two old doors placed over simple trestles. The driver put the boxes down carefully, made a half-bow in Raoul's direction and left the house, closing the door behind him.

'Cigarette?' Raoul asked. His pulse was normal now. If Huguette was a ghost from the past, it was he who had conjured her up by sending a card. So he determined to enjoy the entertainment of her visit.

'I'll have one of mine.' She perched on the edge of the table, took a black-paper cigarette from a tortoiseshell case and fitted it into a long holder. She let him wheel himself across to her with a light.

He answered her questions truthfully. No, he wasn't making much money, but it was enough. Yes, the car was specially adapted. He drove himself on business. 'And the business is interesting. You'd be amazed how much an accountant knows about his clients' lives, never mind their business activities.'

'Oh really?' She wasn't listening. She never had, he recalled.

Huguette launched herself into a story about being nearby to film a television commercial on location. He wondered whether she had forgotten that she had used an almost identical excuse for her last visit to Torrens. Why had she really come?

It was hot in the studio. Unable to keep warm by exercise, Raoul had to keep the temperature high. Huguette shrugged off her fur coat and turned completely round to show him the tight black wool dress she was wearing, as though she were on a catwalk and he a client. It was one of the last dresses designed by Christian Dior before his death, she explained.

'Oh really?' Raoul in turn was polite. The world of dresses and mannequins was long behind him. To his surprise, it did not hurt to have his ex-wife so near. She was an alien creature from another planet and he a zoologist, observing but not involved.

Politely, he asked, 'How is your new husband?'

'The count –' she was looking behind the toilet partition for a mirror but there were none in Raoul's home – 'is well.'

'And you have the stepchildren, or so I seem to recall reading in the papers?'

She brushed the idea of children away with an elegant puff of smoke. 'One child. He is away at boarding school. I insisted on that. You can't see me playing nursemaid to a grubby little boy of eight who wants to shoot guns the whole time, can you?'

'Poor kid.' Raoul was on the boy's side. 'I know what that's like, to be sent away to school at eight.'

'I met your parents recently,' drawled Huguette. 'At the Elysée reception for the English queen on her state visit. They looked well.'

For name-dropping – ten points, he thought. 'I don't keep in touch with my parents any longer.'

'Tell me, darling –' Raoul knew from her inflection, a sort of gasp with the speech fighting an inhalation, that this was what she had come for – 'did you really give away a fortune in gold to those awful Vietnamese?'

For a moment, he was stunned. He had thought he was in control of the meeting but Huguette had somehow managed to get behind his defences. It was always the same. She did it by flitting from one subject to another faster than his logical masculine brain could keep up.

The court martial had been kept secret, he knew. 'Where did you hear that?'

'The Minister of Defence is a friend.'

'Well, he ought to know.' The bitterness showed in his voice.

'I don't believe it.'

'Oh, it's true.'

'Is it?' She leaned forward so that his face came within her focus. 'I can't believe that of you, Raoul. You were always so damned honourable. You'd die rather than give away a centime in your charge.'

This was not the conversation he wanted. Angrily, he snapped, 'Oh, go and read the report of the court martial your political friend arranged so very efficiently. All the details are there in black and white.'

'I think you stole the money,' she said, probing him with a joke.

Raoul waved a hand at the home he had made. 'Look around you, Huguette. Do you see what my friend the tax-man calls evidence of wealth?'

She moved swiftly with the grace of a former mannequin and kneeled beside the wheelchair. 'Would you tell me if you had stolen a fortune, darling?'

Raoul looked into her great violet eyes – as wide open and innocent as a child's. Didn't she understand anything? he wondered. He was going to ask: What did you think I had been doing, when you saw me carried off the ship at

Marseilles, more dead than alive? But there wasn't any point. . . .

Her lips parted in subconscious invitation. He seized her and pulled the perfect face close to his, smelt her, saw the alarm in her eyes and kissed her savagely on the mouth. She whimpered at the strength in his arms. He was surprised how pleasurable it was to hurt her. When he let go, the only sound in the room was his own harsh breathing and the regular *plip*, *plip*, *plip* of the drips in the saucepan.

And then she was gone, leaving behind a whiff of perfume and Turkish cigarette smoke and a tangle of memories.

He undid the prettily wrapped boxes, to find that one was full of magazines containing photographs of the beautiful Countess of Mesnay-Sèvres. Only a completely uninhibited narcissist like Huguette, he thought, could give anyone such a present. He dumped the lot into the wood-burning stove and put some Mozart on the hi-fi. The genius in the music put the afternoon's tawdry entertainment into perspective.

He could not concentrate on business and finally put aside the balance sheet on which he had been working when Huguette arrived.

Her visit had cleared something in his mind. It was time to write to the only other woman in his life. He pulled the wheelchair up to the typewriter, inserted a sheet of paper and made several false starts before he was satisfied.

> Templars' Tower
> St Martin-sur-Dordogne
> 6 January 1958

Louise,

I address you without any endearments because I hope that since I last held you in my arms and felt your touch and heard your voice you will have found someone else. Not for my sake, but for yours, I wish this.

It takes more courage than I had thought to write, but if you are still free and feel the same about me, may I invite you to visit me here in my simple home overlooking the Dordogne river? Come for an hour, for a day, for a weekend.

Life was hard at first after I left the hospital at Torrens; I had grown dependent on other people for so many things. However, everything is possible if one puts one's mind to it. I learned to drive a car adapted to my needs, to find food, to cook and do housework. All the menial things for which I was brought up to use others, I now do for myself. I tell you this so that, if you decide to visit me, you know I invite you as a companion – literally a sharer of my daily bread – and not as 'a substitute pair of legs'.

I told you I should live in a village called St Martin, remember? There are 246 communes in France which bear the name. Why this particular one? I'll explain.

I don't know whether my experiences as a prisoner in the hands of the Viets have made me a little mad. It's quite probable. Certainly I was never a mystic or a believer in any way before. Yet, after leaving Torrens I had what I suppose the religious would call visions.

I began my search for a new home by marking on a map of France all the places named St Martin. I worked my way from St-Martin-d'Arrossa in the high Pyrenees to St-Martin-des-Champs in stormy Brittany and from St-Martin-du-Bas-Rhin, almost in Germany, to St-Martin-de-Crau in Provence. In my long odyssey I visited more than half of the towns and villages that bear the saint's name.

And in every St Martin where I passed the night, I had a dream. Maybe the first night, maybe not for a couple of weeks. But the dream was always the same: of a man on horseback riding away from me, whom I had to follow. There was a clinging ground mist in the dream, so that the legs of his mount disappeared into greyness. The rider was muffled in a cape against the cold. He never turned his face towards me or spoke, but he had what I can only call the charisma of a commander used to being obeyed. As a soldier, I knew that I owed a duty to follow him.

To begin with, I resisted the dream. (I never believed in the supernatural.) When I refused to follow, the dream returned the following night and the next, more urgently, until I learned to follow obediently. Gradually the rider and horse became clearer. The mist thinned. The hoofprints on the ground were strange until I realised they were made not by modern horseshoes but by Roman hipposandalae, which were differently shaped. And the clothes of the rider which I had at first taken for medieval became definitely of the late Roman period. I realised then that my nocturnal guide was St Martin.

Other things became clearer too: I could see that the mist came from a river nearby. It was the main feature of the dreamscape which included a small village, a bridge, a church and what looked like a ruined castle on a cliff overlooking the river.

I began asking in each St Martin whether anyone knew of a namesake village which was near a river, with a very old church and a small castle. Eventually I found my way here, to the exact landscape of my dream. I have dreamed no dreams nor seen any visions since the first night I slept here. Nor have I any other signs of insanity!

I hope you will come to visit me. If not, I wish you peace and happiness.
Raoul

I sealed the envelope of the letter to Louise before I could change my mind. I had deliberately omitted any mention of the crystal-clear visions of the tower during the months in Minh's cage. Someone as matter-of-fact as Louise would have thought me mad if I had said that I already knew every detail of the view from the top of my tower because of all the hours I had spent there when I was a prisoner in Vietnam! Yet before I restored the tower, there was only a narrow spiral stone staircase leading halfway up which I could never have negotiated, so I had never been up there in the flesh.

I left many things out of the letter. If Louise came, I wanted it to be her decision and not a response to my need.

That night the music on the hi-fi was Mozart's Magic Flute. *I had started listening to opera as a way of weaning myself off the dangerously seductive fantasies in which I could spend hours at a time, whole days even. Opera, with its exotic stories and magnificent music, was a safe substitute for a dangerous drug. It had the advantage that it ended with the last note of the score, and not after I had wasted a day in fanciful imaginings.*

I consumed my new, non-habit forming drug in large doses, very loud, especially late at night when I couldn't sleep. Sometimes my legs gave me hell. Then I preferred to doze off in the wheelchair while listening to the music. It was better than taking pills.

That night sleep eluded me for a long time. The end of the opera left me neither asleep nor awake. I was dreaming that the part of Papageno – Mozart's birdcatcher – was being sung by Koenig. He was dressed in Papageno's fantastic costume of feathers, with a bird-mask concealing his face. More an eagle than a bird-man, he swooped down and snatched me from the two snakes who had come to trap me at Torrens. They entwined themselves around me, pulling me down and down. Koenig strained and strained but could not lift me out of their reach. Just as we seemed to be rising, I knew it was a trick; that I should not trust him too far. I let go. He soared upwards into the blue while I fell on to the centre of a vast empty opera stage. Two Papageno-eagles appeared from the wings and circled me at a distance. There was a snake entwined around each one.

To the background of the birdcatcher's perky little tune, one of the Papageno-eagles danced up to me. The bird-mask was slid upwards to reveal Minh's face, mouthing a question I did not want to answer. I turned to the other Papageno.

'Help me, Koenig!' I cried.

The second mask slid up to reveal, not Koenig's face but Huguette's, her big eyes holding me hypnotised as she moved closer and closer until all I could see were the eyes. And the question she breathed was the same as Minh's: 'What did you do with the gold, Duvalier? What did you do with the gold?'

PART 2

1958–1964

1

The small town of Enfida was only two hours by train from Oran, the second city of Algeria. It boasted a school and a score of backstreet garages. There was a single main street with a few shops and a small hotel. The *hôtel de ville*, the gendarmerie and the railway station were so French as to look out of place on this side of the Mediterranean.

The mail arrived at Enfida's station each morning promptly at 10 a.m. Before the two-carriage train had steamed away down the single track there was always a small group of settlers waiting at the local post office; mail was important to people who lived on lonely farms in the hinterland.

Marie Laval took the batch of letters handed to her by the smiling postal clerk.

'*Bonjour*, Madame Laval.'

'*Bonjour*, Ali.' She glanced past him at the Laval pigeonhole.

'Isn't that parcel for us as well?'

'Ah yes. So sorry.' He seemed flustered.

Marie took the parcel from him. It was nothing very exciting. She could see from the label that it only contained a dress for her eight-year-old daughter, Marie-France, and a couple of bush shirts for Gustave, ordered from a catalogue company in France.

She flicked through the letters. They were mainly type-written business correspondence addressed to Gustave, but one stood out. The bold handwriting could only be Raoul's. She moved away from the counter, turned her back for privacy and tore the envelope open there and then. His news was not of himself. Like most of Raoul's letters, this one was full of anecdotes about the illicit doings of his clients in – she glanced at the postmark on the envelope – the little village of St Martin where he had settled. From his vivid descriptions she felt she knew the landscape, the people, their friendships and feuds, the atmosphere of market days, the tricks they played on one another and especially on out-siders like the taxman.

It was so many years since Marie had lived in France that Raoul's regular letters had taken on the mystique of once-upon-a-time and the compulsion of a favourite soap opera. It was rare for her to wait until getting home before she opened and read a letter from him. At the beginning of the correspondence she had not known how to reply to the undertones of bitterness she sensed: bitterness at his injuries and bitterness at the way he had been treated by life. It had been so unlike the optimistic, devil-may-care man she remembered that she had wondered how anyone could change so much. Then, as Raoul settled into life in his new home, the letters had changed: humour had crept back into them and a kind of compassion for other people that the old Raoul had never had. Marie knew that her cousin had been divorced and wondered sometimes if he had found a new woman. Was she the reason for the change, for his content-ment and new sense of purpose? If so, he never mentioned her.

She read the letter twice before stuffing it back into the envelope. The contrast between Raoul's word-pictures of life in provincial France and her life in Algeria hit her as she stepped out of the door of the post office: the dry, dusty heat was a far cry from the gentle climate of the lush and fertile Dordogne where he lived. She wondered what he made of her letters in which she tried to describe in detail the life that Gustave and she had built up from nothing in the three years since they had arrived in Algeria after the French exodus from Indo-China.

It was not yet midsummer but the sun beat down from a sky of cloudless blue. Marie kept to the shady side of the street. Most of the Europeans wore hats and light clothing. Almost all the Arabs – men and women – wore thick traditional robes which protected them from the sun.

She had parked her car in the shade of the tamarisk tree, unlocked and with the windows wide open. She tossed the letters and parcel on to the rear seat and chatted with some friends who had also been to collect their mail. In the school yard, European and Arab children played together, all wearing identical blue overalls.

Marie waved at some of the children who recognised her. Her own daughter was not at school that day due to an attack of asthma. Mentally she checked off the chores. She had collected the mail, bought some groceries and picked up the medicine prescribed for Marie-France by the local doctor, an Arab who had been trained in France. There was nothing else that needed doing; it was time to get back to the farm.

She was just getting into the car when a young Arab wearing paint-covered blue dungarees and carrying a pot of paint, touched his forehead to her in a symbolic greeting of respect. Marie recognised him as a brother of Ali the post clerk and also because he had worked on the Laval farm as a casual labourer the previous autumn during the grape harvest.

'Madame Laval,' he said with a wide smile. 'I do apologise. I have spilled some paint on your car. I was so careless. Please, allow me to wash it for you.' He spoke rather fast in perfect French, but with a thick accent. Unlike many Arab men, he did not stare at Marie's body in her thin white cotton dress, but kept his eyes politely on her face.

The paint was the ubiquitous white limewash with which all the Arab houses were coated every year. Marie knew that it would wash off with water and not leave a mark, providing the job was done quickly. The incident was mildly annoying, but the youth was so polite and respectful. . . .

'Where can you wash it?' she asked.

He gestured to a nearby side street. 'My cousin has a garage, madame. I shall wash it there for you.' With repeated apologies, he took the keys and drove the car carefully into the garage as she watched.

'If you've nothing better to do,' a familiar voice hailed Marie from the terrace of Enfida's small French-owned hotel, '. . . come and join us for a coffee.'

Marie crossed the street and greeted Henri and Josette Rodriguez warmly. Theirs was the nearest farm to the Laval property. Of Spanish extraction, Henri's family had been living in Algeria for four generations. He was tall, with dark hair and face tanned to the colour of leather. When he smiled, which was often, he showed a mouthful of perfectly white teeth. His wife, Josette, was a petite Parisienne, always smartly dressed and with a sparkling sense of humour.

The couple had been a great help when Marie and Gustave first came to Algeria. Far from resenting the newcomers, Henri had loaned equipment, given advice on treating diseases, and advised which vineyards to keep and which to replant. He had helped Gustave to hire reliable labourers and avoid taking on idlers. Josette had been equally friendly to Marie. They were the best kind of neighbours in a country where neighbours were important.

Their conversation that morning – indeed the sole topic among the Europeans sitting on the terrace of the Enfida Hotel, under the medlar and albizzia trees – was about the demonstration in Algiers the previous day. Forty thousand French Algerians had taken to the streets, demanding that the great wartime hero General de Gaulle assume the premiership of France in order to save the North African colonies.

'Do you suppose De Gaulle will accept?' Marie asked, handing back Henri's copy of *L'Oranais*, the local daily paper, whose front page featured a report and photographs of the demonstration.

'If he does, our troubles are over.' Henri Rodriguez tapped the newspaper headline. 'Tuesday, 13 May 1958, will be a day to remember – the day when the people of Algeria called and De Gaulle answered their need. The general will sort everything out, you'll see.'

Josette nudged Marie and rolled her eyes. 'Politics!' she said. Neither of the women was interested in the subject; they left that to the men. In any case, all the FLN violence which had provoked the demonstration in Algiers had been hundreds of miles away in the interior; there had never been any trouble in the Enfida valley where the local Arabs depended on the European farms for their livelihood.

Henri was right. The date was one Marie would remember all her life, but not because the old man of Colombey-les-deux-Eglises had returned to power.

To Marie's annoyance, the splash of paint was still there. The car had not been washed at all. She called several times but there seemed to be nobody about. On closer inspection the garage looked as though it had been derelict for years. She found a piece of rag on a workbench and wiped off the worst of the paint, although some had already dried hard and would need scrubbing. She found a tap, but no water came, which left her swearing mildly at the Arab who had caused the problem. Typical, she thought. Why don't they ever do what they say they will?

She backed the car angrily out of the garage and drove out of town. Apart from a convoy of army trucks, there was no other traffic on the road back to the farm. Marie accelerated, raising a cloud of dust as she turned off the highway on to the dirt road which led into the low hills where the vineyards lay.

Gustave's last words to her had been, 'You're not at Le Mans. Drive carefully!' He was always nagging about her driving.

Remembering the warning, Marie slowed and changed down to take a bend between two low hills. As she crested the rise, she braked at the sight of an ancient pick-up van parked askew across the road. An Arab was standing beside it, dressed in traditional robes and headgear. As she drew near, he held up both hands and gestured to his vehicle, then started walking towards her as though to ask for help.

He came to the open window with a wide smile. His face was half hidden by the hood of his dark brown jellaba. Only when he was close, did Marie see that it was Ali's brother – the youth who had spilled paint on her car.

'What are you doing here?' she asked. 'And why didn't you wash the paint off my car, as you said you would?'

She could see that he was sweating in the thick jellaba. Why was the hood up, covering his face? Had he thought she wouldn't recognise him?

'*Je suis en panne*, madame.' One brown hand gripped the driver's window, which was half wound down.

'I can see you're broken down.' Sweat trickled down Marie's neck as soon as the cooling effect of the breeze was lost. 'Can't you push your car off the road so that I can get by?'

He seemed nervous, his eyes darting from her face to the van and back.

'What is it?' she asked. 'What's the matter? Are you ill?'

From the corner of her eye she saw another man emerging from under the tarpaulin in the back of the pick-up. He was wrestling with something black and metallic that looked like a gun. It was caught in the folds of the tarpaulin. Ali's brother shouted something to his companion and tried to grab Marie's arm through the half-open window. She wrenched it free. The Peugeot was still in third gear. She slipped the clutch part-way in and stamped on the accelerator, praying the engine would not stall as she pulled away from him.

He screamed as a rear wheel ran over his feet. The car ran down the slight embankment on to the stony earth of a ploughed field. With the extra momentum, Marie risked letting the clutch right in. The Peugeot fish-tailed in the loose earth, then straightened up. It hit a rock with a crash that sounded to Marie as though she had torn the sump off the engine. Then a ragged burst of shots rang out and she saw the rear window splinter. With the sun behind her, the view in the mirror was a brilliant pattern of shattered safety glass with two distinct bullet holes in the centre, like a pair of demonic eyes glaring at her.

A dust screen blanked out the Arabs' vision as Marie hauled the heavy estate car in a long arc through the loose earth and stones back to the road, aiming for a point a couple of hundred metres past the two Arabs and their van. They were both firing now, but wildly into the dust cloud. Marie heard a couple of shots hit metal. The rear side windows, which were not safety glass, disintegrated in a thousand splinters. Please God, don't let them hit a tyre, she prayed.

She bounced the car up on to the tarmac of the roadway with a crash that tore the exhaust off. For a terrifying moment she thought she had smashed the steering too. As the dust cleared, the last couple of random shots rang out, which she did not hear above the noise of the broken exhaust.

The steering wheel had a will of its own; it was hard to hold steady and the broken shock absorbers made the car swing wildly on the bends. Marie took one hand off the wheel for a moment to wipe away what she thought was a river of sweat running down the left side of her face. Her hand came away dripping blood: a sliver of glass had gashed her scalp.

She fought the gear-stick, trying to push it into top gear and gain some speed, but the car was jammed in third. The rear mirror useless, she stuck her head out of the window and risked a quick glance behind. The pick-up truck was moving now, one Arab at the wheel and the other kneeling on the back. He was leaning over the roof of the cab, taking aim at the Peugeot. A chance shot crazed Marie's windscreen, leaving her blind in front as well as behind.

She remembered Gustave once telling her that the only thing to do with a broken windscreen was to punch a hole right through it. She balled her right fist and punched several times to make a hole large enough, cutting herself in the process. Now both hands were covered in bright red blood, which dripped on to her clean white dress. It had arrived, ordered from a catalogue, only the week before. Irrationally, she thought: Damn, this is only the second time I've worn it.

Marie could see enough roadway through the hole in the screen to try and hold the car straight. She hit the steering wheel with a clenched fist, willing the car to go faster. On the dashboard, the needle of the temperature gauge was going up and up and the car seemed to be slowing down despite the accelerator pressed flat to the floor. The boundary marker of white stone, which Gustave and Henri had set up, came into sight. She fixed her eyes on it like a high-wire artist fixes his gaze on the pole at the far end of the wire and willed the car towards it. Please God, let me get back to my husband and child. . . .

At the fork where the tracks to the Laval and Rodriguez farms split off from the road she took another look behind. The pick-up was turning the other way. Faint with relief, she drove the last couple of kilometres to the house and Gustave. The Peugeot's exhaust was by now coughing black smoke and it was losing speed visibly. If the Arabs had not given up the chase, they would have caught up with her just before she came in sight of the house.

Alerted by the sound of gunfire, Gustave came running out of the farm office as she drove up, with a loaded hunting rifle in his hand. When he saw the stalled, wrecked car and his wife in her blood-spattered dress sitting trembling in the driving seat, her hands locked round the wheel, unable to get out or even to speak to him, his face was a mixture of incredulity and horror.

Marie's only coherent thought was: Thank God I didn't put the handbrake on when I stopped as Gustave is always telling me to. If I had, I'd be dead by now.

2

'It's a write-off. I smashed the sump, the suspension and the steering. The exhaust's completely torn off. The bodywork is riddled with bullet-holes. It's a miracle the car got me home before the engine seized.'

Despite a sedative injection and Josette Rodriguez' calming influence, Marie had been unable to stop talking since the ambush. Words poured out of her.

'And supposing Marie-France had been with me. . .'. Her voice trailed away as she looked at the parcel on the back seat. It was slashed to pieces by shards of glass from the shattered windows. '. . . she'd have been cut into little pieces.'

'I want you to call in the Army,' Gustave interrupted angrily. He was talking to Legendre, the gendarmerie inspector from Enfida. 'Get them to throw a cordon right round the valley and pick up every Arab male in five miles' radius. Marie has identified the one who spilled paint on the car. I've given you his name. Obviously, he's the ringleader who planned the whole thing. So get out there and catch him.'

'He'll be far away by now.' The inspector lit a Gauloise from the stub in his mouth. He looked as though he had been up all night. His creased jacket had sweat stains under the armpits and down the small of his back and he was unshaven.

139

'So what are you going to do about it, Legendre?' Henri Rodriguez backed up his friend.

'Calm down,' said the inspector. 'Marie was lucky.'

'Lucky?' Gustave shouted.

'The kids who attacked your wife were amateurs.'

'Kids? Jesus! And you call that the work of amateurs?' Gustave grabbed the inspector's shoulders and forced him to face the ruined car. 'The men who attacked my wife had at least one automatic rifle, probably two.'

The inspector shrugged himself free. 'If they'd been hard-core FLN, Marie wouldn't have been able to drive out of the ambush.'

'But what are you going to do?'

'Keep this to yourselves . . .'. The inspector eyed the bunch of Arab labourers who were huddled nervously at the other end of the yard. The mayor of Enfida, Hassan Abou-Bakr, who was present in his capacity as doctor, stood uneasily with the Europeans.

'There's a censorship clamp-down,' said Legendre quietly. 'But I'll tell you people, and Abou-Bakr already knows. This hold-up – or attack, call it what you will – is not a solitary incident. There have been four other attacks on Europeans, on my patch alone, during the last twenty-four hours.'

'Oh God,' moaned Marie. 'It's going to be like Vietnam all over again. Soon we'll only be able to use the roads in the daytime. We'll spend the nights behind barbed wire, in houses with sandbagged doors and windows. I can't stand it.'

She turned to her husband and grabbed his lapels with both hands, shaking him. 'I can't face that again, Gustave. D'you hear me? I can't face it . . .'. There were tears pouring down her blood-streaked face.

Henri and Josette separated her gently from Gustave. Still talking frantically, Marie let herself be helped into the house by Josette.

'Now the women have gone,' said Legendre quietly, 'I'll tell you men how the doctor and I managed to arrive so quickly. We were already halfway here at your neighbours', the Zecchinis'.'

'Are they having trouble too?' asked Henri.

'Not any longer.' The inspector looked grim. 'When their maid arrived for work this morning, she found the old couple in bed with their throats slit and their bodies hacked to pieces. They were still warm.'

'Bastards,' swore Gustave.

'Zecchini had farmed that land for sixty years,' said Henri softly, 'since he was a boy.'

Gustave turned to the doctor. 'We've had no trouble in this region before, Abou-Bakr. So why now?' His voice rose. 'You're the mayor. Go on, tell me. Why all this violence now?'

The doctor's sad brown eyes looked from Gustave to the group of labourers muttering among themselves. He felt as never before that he belonged in neither camp. By race and religion, his place was at the other end of the yard; by education and way of life – for better or for worse – he was tied to the Europeans.

It was Legendre who answered for him. 'The FLN has a plan of campaign, Gustave. For whatever reason, they've deliberately left the Enfida valley alone up to now. Maybe they had a big arms cache here and didn't want to draw attention to it. I'd be the last to know. But there was a country-wide outbreak of violence last night. There was nothing on the radio or in the papers because of the censorship, but it was pretty bad. What we've got here is just the tip of the iceberg. I'd say it was the FLN's reply to the demo in Algiers. It seems someone on the other side has at last put a cross against Enfida on their map. From now on, we're in the front line.'

'You've got to protect us,' said Henri angrily.

'Be reasonable,' said the inspector. 'What the devil can I do, with one Frenchman and half a dozen Arabs under me? And probably two of the Arab gendarmes are undercover FLN. How can I protect a hundred Europeans living in ones and twos on properties that are miles apart? I can't even offer any effective protection to people who live in Enfida itself. I don't know for certain that my own wife is safe in town at this very moment.'

'Nor do I,' said the doctor.

'You're an Arab,' said Gustave rudely. 'You're safe enough. It's us Europeans they want to kill.'

'You are wrong,' the doctor spoke gently, as though to a feverish patient. 'They hate people like me far more than they hate you, Gustave. First, because I am a doctor. They hate my European education. Second, because I am mayor ... because I work with the French administration. For that, they call me a traitor, a collaborator with the enemy. I assure you that I share your danger.'

Legendre backed him up. 'I've seen the threats Abou-Bakr has received. There's nothing I can do to protect him against his own people. What we can do, without delay, is get all the European women and children off these isolated farms.'

Gustave looked around at the new buildings he had put up, the farmhouse he had extended and restored, the neatly tended vineyards stretching away in all directions, the washing on the clothes line, the swing and the doll's pram in the pretty, flower-lined garden Marie had made.

He had spent every penny of the capital salvaged from Vietnam on buying and building up this farm. He had worked seven days a week and fifty-two weeks of the year to get the fields and vineyards looking the way they did that afternoon. He could not grasp the disaster in which they were all involved and spoke slowly, like a man just woken up from a deep sleep. 'Are you saying we've got to abandon our home?'

'Do what I say –' Legendre's voice was harsh – 'or you risk coming back from the fields one day in the not-too-distant future and finding your wife and kid with their throats cut.'

'No!' Henri's eyes were flashing with anger. 'I'm not running away, Legendre. This land was desert when my grandfather came here. He cleared it with a couple of mules and dug the first wells with his own hands. My family made this valley fertile. So we're staying. We pay taxes. You get the bloody Army in. It's their job to protect us.'

'Like they did in Vietnam,' said Gustave bitterly.

He turned on his heel and walked across the sunlit yard towards the crowd of chattering labourers. They fell silent at his approach.

They know who attacked Marie, he thought. They know who killed the Zecchinis. He looked at their faces one by one. They were like strangers. Ali, Mahommed, Abdul ... Selim the foreman. ... Men he had employed, shared jokes with and worked beside in the fields day after day for more than three years now looked away, refusing to meet his gaze.

You're the enemy, thought Gustave, walking up close and staring at each face. Marie is right. We're back in the nightmare of Vietnam. Which of you will come in the night with a knife and an axe to hack my wife and child to death, like you killed the Zecchinis this morning?

'Go home!' His voice was harsh, alarming the two vultures who perched on the ridge of the house. They flapped noisily away into the afternoon heat. Gustave shook his balled fists at the Arabs, wanting to hit them. 'Go home, all of you!'

Like children who had been naughty, they scattered and hurried away in ones and twos across the sun-baked brown landscape in the direction of their village.

Five single shots rang out as Marie was closing the shutters of Marie-France's bedroom that evening. Three bullets went wide, two hit the house. One broke a tile on the roof, ricocheted and went whining away into the dusk while the other lodged with a thud in the shutter only six inches from Marie's face.

For the sake of the child, she was trying to control herself when Gustave ran into the room, alerted by the shots. He was holding a heavy Colt revolver in his hand. On the bed Marie-France, frightened by the shots and her mother's obvious fear, was sobbing between the strained rhythm of

143

asthmatic breathing, clutching her favourite doll for comfort.

Gustave tried to embrace both his wife and eight-year-old daughter simultaneously. 'It's all right,' he kept saying meaninglessly. 'It's all right.'

Marie fought for some control over her emotions. The shots had come from a dried-up wadi 500 metres away. The shutters are still open, she thought. Those madmen outside could walk right in. Why doesn't Gustave . . . ?

'Go round the house,' she said to him, keeping her voice calm for the child's benefit. 'Quickly. Lock and bar all the shutters, Gustave. And barricade the outside doors with heavy furniture. Do it now while I look after Marie-France.'

He looked relieved at being told what to do.

When she joined him in the dining room after her daughter had quietened and was sleeping, Gustave was holding the telephone in his hand. He put it down almost guiltily.

'I was trying to ring Henri and Josette, to make sure they're all right, but the line's been cut,' he said. 'So we can't call for help.'

'We're cut off?' The news was frightening.

He tried to reassure her with bravado. 'Whoever is out there knows I've got a rifle and the Colt. I don't think they'll attack us. Those shots were more to frighten than anything else.'

At that instant the lights went out. The house was silent as the murmur of the generator stopped. It was in the tractor shed only fifty metres from the house. So they were that close, Marie thought. She felt her way to the kitchen to find a candle.

When she returned with it, Gustave had not moved. She sat beside him, expecting him to make some move, to tell her what to do.

Instead, all he could manage was to pour a stiff whisky for them both. He kept repeating, 'I don't understand it, Marie. I don't understand it.'

Angry at him, she snapped, 'What don't you understand?'

He sighed. 'I know some of the *colons* treat their workers badly but I've been fair to our labourers and paid them good wages. Henri is always telling me I'm too soft. So why pick on us?'

'Does it matter why?'

'I thought they liked us. And now this . . .'

'Perhaps,' she suggested, controlling herself, 'perhaps it's because we've always got on so well with the locals.' The alcohol burned her empty stomach; she realised she had not eaten or drunk anything except water since the coffee in Enfida that morning. 'And perhaps it's deliberate – to show they're not just settling old feuds, but that they want to drive away or kill all the French in North Africa.'

'I was listening to the radio after everyone left this afternoon,' he said. 'The censors let some news out. Last night and this morning 500 Europeans were killed in Algeria and another 200 injured. Some of them were shot. Most were knifed or hacked to pieces with axes, like the Zecchinis. It's as bad as Vietnam.'

'Worse,' she said.

There was a sound of men's voices speaking Arabic outside. Some laughter. 'Sleep well, Laval,' someone called.

'The maid's left,' whispered Marie. 'She just walked out, without saying anything.'

Gustave was listening. 'The cook's gone too,' he muttered. 'We're alone.'

'I'm not a courageous person,' said Marie. 'I wish I was. But I can't live here under siege like this, Gustave.'

'It's our home,' he said. 'It's all we've got.'

Marie heard a great sigh as though all the air had left Gustave's lungs. He slumped on the table beside her, head held in both hands. 'We got up this morning living in paradise. It's not even bedtime yet and paradise has turned to hell.'

His impotence angered her. Since their marriage, Gustave had always made the decisions. When he consulted her, which was rarely, she did what he wanted. In return, he had taken all the responsibility for the family. She waited in the candlelight for him to tell her what they would do now. Instead, he was rocking himself backwards and forwards silently, head between his hands, like a child comforting itself.

'Josette,' she said, 'is moving tomorrow with her daughters to stay with Henri's aunt in Oran. She's a widow who runs a bar near the Foreign Legion depot.'

'Oh?'

'She has offered me and Marie-France a room there, if we want it.'

'Until this blows over?'

'It's not going to blow over, is it, Gustave?'

He avoided answering by asking, 'Well, do you want to go?'

It was the first time in their marriage he had asked her to make a major decision.

'Yes,' said Marie firmly. 'If we're still alive in the morning, we'll leave straight away for Oran.'

If we're still alive, she thought. It's come to that . . .

Her mind went to the car still standing in front of the house where it had seized up – and to the letters on the back seat under the broken glass. She had forgotten about them until now. How would Raoul behave if he were there at that moment? She looked at Gustave rocking himself backward and forward. Raoul might be a cripple in a wheel-chair, but he'd . . . he'd be fighting back, not pouring himself another drink. She was sure of that.

She knocked the bottle over with a gesture of anger.

Gustave stared at her as though she were mad when she said, 'I want you to teach me how to shoot that revolver of yours.'

He recoiled. 'You couldn't shoot a man, could you?'

Marie felt that the shots aimed at her daughter's bedroom had taken her across a moral watershed. When she was attacked that morning, her reaction had been hysterical and feminine. She had been aware of it but could not control herself. Now that her child was being threatened, she felt different: coldly resourceful and determined.

'Could you shoot a man trying to break in here tonight?' she asked.

'I don't know,' said Gustave wretchedly. 'Henri could and would, but I'm not like him. I never expected this to happen to us twice in a lifetime.'

'Could you shoot a man?' she insisted.

'I just don't know,' he cried. 'Leave me alone.'

'Well, I know,' she said with quiet determination. 'I could and I will. So give the gun to me and show me how it works.'

3

I knew the trouble was building up in Algeria long before it happened, not because I had Koenig's grasp of history, but for a much simpler reason: Minh and the other commissars had made no secret of the plan to drive the French out of North Africa as soon as they had torn down the last tricolour in Indo-China. They had even given us prisoners the precise timetable! But no one in Paris believed the news we brought back from those jungle camps.

The first FLN assassinations were carried out exactly on schedule in November 1954 while I was still a prisoner. At the same time the FLN numbered about seventy men. There was no Liberation Movement. But those seventy men were determined to stop at nothing. They set out to destroy the infrastructure of Algerian society, drive the French out and take over the country for themselves. They had received their political training in Moscow and Peking but most of their military training had been by French officers, in our Army!

Aping Lépine, I plotted the first outbreaks of violence on the maps of Algeria that decorated the walls of my home. The place looked like a general's HQ, but I was only a spectator – even more impotent than Lépine had been to alter the course of events. At first, the violence was not directed against the French; it was the Arab population who suffered and bled. The purpose was both to terrorise them into obedience and show that the whites could do *nothing to help. When both aims had been achieved, the FLN declared open war. The timing was brilliant. Once again, we were out-generalled. It took a general on our side to recognise the fact.*

A hundred times I thought of sending some word of caution to Marie and Gustave living on that lonely farm. Why didn't I? Well, in her letters to me, so full of details of family life and the excitement of starting again with her husband and child in a new country, I glimpsed the idyll they were living. I wanted to believe in it. I needed to. At Torrens and after, I had been oppressed by a growing sense of hopelessness, a feeling that my generation of officers had been crushed between relentless forces; the past and the future colliding, with us between and tearing us to shreds. Most of my friends were dead and most of the survivors wounded, some worse than myself. So I wanted to believe that Fortune was smiling on our generation again, that some things would turn out happily ever after, making all the sacrifices worth while.

Was that why I said nothing to alert Marie and Gustave? Or was it simply that it seemed too cruel to tell them that a lunatic hand from the future had pressed the button on a political alarm clock which would go off one day soon – to shatter their dreams and much else besides? For whatever reason, I said nothing. I betrayed them by my silence and felt both at the time and afterwards that I bore some of the blame for what happened to them.

Chez Mimi was a large, high-ceilinged, airy bar whose clientele included many off-duty Foreign legionnaires. Their uniforms with colourful epaulettes, badges, lanyards and the white *kepis* which were their trademark, added colour to the scene. Across the wide tree-lined boulevard from the bar was the depot where recruits were processed straight off the boat from Marseilles, but they were confined to barracks for the few days they spent in Oran. For them, the idea of a cool drink on the shady terrace was as remote as a mirage in the desert.

Mimi herself was a short, chubby woman with dark hair, unmistakably Spanish in looks and accent. Her ready smile showed half a mouthful of gold teeth, of which she was very proud. She was as cheerful dealing with a drunken legionnaire at 2 a.m. as when she reopened the bar five hours later to sell a cognac to a labourer on his way to start work in the docks. She prided herself on never having called out the military police in thirty years of running the place. The legionnaires loved her and called her *'la mère* Mimi'. She acted as their banker, advancing money when they were broke and keeping their pay safe when they went on a binge and were liable to waste every penny on girls and booze. She listened to their troubles and helped them write letters home.

Mimi's warm smile and open arms embraced Marie and Josette equally as members of her own family.

'You and your beautiful daughter can stay with me as long as you wish,' she told Marie on their arrival. 'I always pray for big family of girls, but God, he plan different. *Pobre de mí!* All of these years, running a bar, I been surrounded by men. So now I'm a-going have fun with a house full of women and girls, you see.'

If she was worried about her nephew living alone in an isolated farmhouse, virtually under siege, she never spoke about it. 'Don't a-worry!' was Mimi's favourite saying.

Oran was a sprawl of white buildings in every style, from modern concrete office blocks in the centre of town to traditional Arab houses in the *medina* and new European bungalows on the slopes of the hills overlooking the blue sweep of the harbour and the open Mediterranean beyond. Trees, shrubs and flowers were planted along the centre of the boulevards. Twice a day the streets were swept. During the heat of summer, water trucks sprayed all the streets and squares several times a day to keep the dust down.

All the races of the Mediterranean basin mixed freely in public places like Mimi's bar where the varied clientele was a constant source of entertainment for a lively eight-year-old like Marie-France, especially after the lonely life she had led on the remote farm at Enfida. Josette's twin daughters were too young to be friends, so Marie-France sat in the bar or on the terrace for long hours after school, watching the customers and listening to their conversations in French, German, Italian, Spanish, Hebrew, Arabic and Greek.

The legionnaires, with their rough ways and loud talk, fascinated her. The younger ones were often both homesick and shy of the heavily made-up and flashily dressed girls of their own age who were in the bar for business. So they adopted Marie-France as a sort of younger sister. They taught her phrases in their own languages and spoiled her with lemonade and ice creams.

She had vaguely understood from Mimi's conversations with the other women that these young men were soldiers, like the ones who were supposed to track down and kill the bad men at Enfida, but . . . 'They're so kind to me,' she told her mother.

The same doubts worried Marie. 'Mimi,' she said one day when they had been living several weeks above the bar, 'those boys from the Legion don't look like the tough veterans we had out in Vietnam. They worry me.'

'Don't a-worry,' answered Mimi. 'Those boys . . . they relaxing when they in my bar. I don't want them shootin' guns and smashin' things here. But when they fightin', they tough. Best soldiers in the world, they are.'

A couple of trucks in matt olive paint, returning from the docks, drove through the gate of the depot opposite. The morning's intake of tired recruits clambered out.

A couple of NCOs were shouting at the recruits to move faster. Two dozen bewildered young men aged between eighteen and twenty-four ran hither and thither in confusion. Their ill-fitting old fatigue overalls and shaven heads made them look like convicts.

'Why do they shout at them so?' Marie-France asked.

'That the way of the Legion,' smiled Mimi, taking a tray of clean glasses from Yasmine, the cook.

Across the road, the recruits were doubling round and round the square in bright sunlight to the whistled commands and shouts of the NCOs.

'Is the training that makes them tough,' said Mimi. 'When they unhappy, they tell me all about it. You would no' believe

151

the things those NCO make them do. And the punishment they hand out . . . *Díos mío!* But it work. Those boys, they raw kids when they arrive. You see, six months later, they are killers, every one!'

'Mummy! Look, it's Daddy come to see us!' Marie-France was dancing with excitement as her father's car pulled up outside the bar.

She ran to greet him and stood back hurt as he walked past without touching or even looking at her. Henri was with him. The two grim-faced men explained something to the waiting women. The child's eyes travelled from one grown-up's face to another as smiles of welcome faded from the women's faces. For once, Mimi did not say, 'Don't a-worry.' She too looked unhappy.

When her mother and father went upstairs, Marie-France slipped after them before Mimi could distract her. She could hear Henri's angry voice shouting at Josette downstairs in the kitchen. She peered round the edge of the doorway to see her father kneeling on the bedroom floor with his head in Marie's lap. She was trying to comfort him. Gustave was crying. Marie-France had never thought that a grown man could weep like a hurt child. It was very frightening.

She stood silent in the doorway, watching her parents. Gustave's anguished shaking and sobbing reminded her not so much of any person she had ever seen as of the pet puppy which she had found poisoned the morning they left the farm to drive to Oran. It had lain on the ground shaking in spasms, with blood-flecked foam around the mouth, until her father had carried it away and shot it behind a shed.

Gustave's tortured voice rang out again and again with the same words: 'I heard a noise like a wasps' nest all night long. They must have had half a dozen chain-saws going, working by moonlight. They have chopped every single vine down to the ground, Marie. Every single vine. They have chopped . . .'

The convoy left Oran at dawn, in order to drive to the Enfida valley, load up what furniture could be saved from the Laval and Rodriguez farms and get safely back to Oran before nightfall.

In the first car, Henri and Josette travelled with two loaded rifles. Then came two hired removal vans driven by tough-looking men recommended by Mimi from among her clients. Bringing up the rear were Gustave and Marie, both armed. They had asked for army protection and been told that there was not a soldier to spare in the whole of Algeria. The entire country was in a state of emergency.

The journey to Enfida was eerie. Once they had left the outskirts of the city, there was no civilian traffic on the roads. The only vehicles they saw were a few army and Legion patrols, travelling at speed on the crown of the road with headlights on and horns blaring, all in a hurry to get somewhere. Gustave concentrated on the road, saying nothing to Marie. He had not spoken a word since his breakdown the previous day. Marie knew he had not slept a wink that night.

Nearing Enfida, Henri led the small convoy across country, skirting the town itself to take a short cut that led to the two properties. As they came over the brow of the hill where Marie had been ambushed, Gustave braked and pulled up behind the vans. Henri was standing in the road-way, signalling them to stop.

The plain below was like a scene from a war film. In the middle distance the Laval farm buildings were ablaze from end to end, a thick column of black smoke soiling the cloud-less blue sky as it spiralled vertically upwards in the still air from the tractor shed where fuel had been stored. There was no sign of movement around the buildings, although dotted here and there in the fields were inert lumps which proved through binoculars to be the livestock, slaughtered to the last beast and left to rot in the sun. The vineyards had been bright green when Marie last saw them. She gasped as she saw the arid rows of sawn-off vines lying on the brown sun-baked earth, good for nothing except firewood.

As far as the eye could reach, the same scene repeated itself. All the European farms in the valley had been torched, a column of smoke rising from each property. Gustave shifted the binoculars from one to the next. He and Marie were newcomers but Zecchini, Rodriguez and the others were names of landowners that had been important in the Enfida valley since the area was settled and made fertile in the 1830s. The columns of smoke marked the funeral pyres of the Spanish, Italian and French families who had taken this semi-desert area under the terms of the *pax gallica* and made it a green and fertile land.

As he scanned the further distance, Gustave saw that the modernised Arab properties had been similarly dealt with. Only a few fields farmed by villagers with oxen and irrigated by hand had been spared. They stood out, green and promising in the wasted landscape. That night, while he and Marie had been lying sleepless in the little room above Mimi's bar, the FLN had put agriculture in the valley back into the Middle Ages.

Not a soul moved in the deserted landscape.

Henri put down his binoculars after studying the ruins of his home. 'There's nothing to save,' he said harshly. His face was white beneath its tan and his eyes screwed up as though to avoid a blow. 'Turn the vehicles round. Let's go.'

'No, wait.' Gustave restrained him. 'There's a vehicle heading this way. See that cloud of dust coming from the town?'

Henri reached beneath the dashboard and took out a heavy Mannlicher rifle. He slid the bolt to load a cartridge into the chamber. 'If the driver's an Arab,' he said grimly, 'I'm going to shoot the bastard.'

'But you don't know . . .' Josette began.

'Shut up,' he said. 'Get back in the car and stay there.'

She caught his arm. 'Henri, you can't just kill . . .'

His back-handed blow knocked her reeling against the wing of the first van. The driver caught her and raised an arm to fend off a second blow. 'Take it easy, Rodriguez,' he gasped.

'Get her out of the way,' snarled Henri. 'Someone has to pay for all this.' He jerked his head at the scene below. 'So

I'm going to kill the first Arab I come across – *pour encourager les autres*. Don't anyone try to stop me.'

Gustave grabbed his own rifle, uncertain what to do. The car drew nearer until they could make out the word GENDAR-MERIE in large white letters beneath the coating of dust. Legendre braked to a halt and got out, one of his Arab sergeants with him.

Henri raised his rifle, aiming at the sergeant's chest. 'Get out of my way,' he roared at Legendre.

The gendarmerie inspector walked steadily towards him, blocking the line of fire. For once there was no cigarette in his mouth. When the muzzle was pressing against his chest, he stopped. Nobody moved in the frozen tableau.

'Put the gun down, Henri,' said the inspector. 'It doesn't solve anything.'

'Look at my farm!' Henri's voice was more a cry of distress than a shout.

'I've seen it – and the others.'

'I swore I'd kill the first Arab I saw.'

'Don't bother, old friend.' Legendre's red-rimmed eyes met Henri's glare without flinching. The voice from his parched throat sounded like gravel. 'They've done that job for you. The first telephone call I got this morning was from Madame Abou-Bakr, the doctor's wife. They came for her husband in the night and tied his hands and feet to four tractors. Then they started the engines and made her and his five-year-old son watch as they tore him apart.'

Legendre stepped aside. 'Now, if you still want to kill a brave man in cold blood, go ahead and shoot my sergeant.'

4

'Feeling thirsty are you, soldier?'

Frank Hansen stiffened at the Glasgow accent close behind him. Like the other recruits, he had assumed that the NCOs screaming orders and abuse at them in the Legion depot were all French. After a choppy sea crossing from Marseilles, the new intake had been put to work immediately on arrival. They had spent the whole morning and afternoon in burning sunshine on hands and knees, cleaning the concrete parking lot of the depot with hand-brushes. The backs of their fatigue overalls were no longer black with sweat but rimed with a succession of white salt rings where their perspiration had dried.

Warily, he agreed with the stocky little corporal standing over him: 'Sure, I could do with a drink.'

'Stand to attention when I talk to you, lad!' the corporal roared. He stood, thumbs tucked into his belt, boots polished, uniform immaculate, kepi at regulation angle, rocking on his heels.

Frank stood up painfully; his knees were stiff and bleeding in several places from the sharp ridges in the burning concrete.

'Yes, sir!'

'Say "corporal" when you talk to me, you lump o' shit!'

'Yes, corporal!' Frank shouted.

'That's better.' The informal tone crept back into the corporal's voice. 'Where are you from, Yank?'

'Idaho, corporal.'

'They don't know how to stand up straight in Idaho, then?'

Frank pushed his head and shoulders back, only to feel the corporal's hard fist crash into his belly, winding him. 'Tuck your stomach in, Yank. That's better.'

I must be mad, thought Frank as he gasped for breath. His first day in the depot was a long way from his fantasies of the Foreign Legion, in which he had pictured himself holding a rifle, crouching behind a wall of sandbags and peering desperately across the moonlit desert from which a shot had just come – or fighting back to back with his last surviving buddy as some nameless enemy closed in for the kill.

Each time the little corporal inspected the result of the recruits' cleaning efforts, he found something wrong. Like a fiendish conjuror pulling rabbits from an empty hat, he pounced on a cigarette end deliberately thrown down by one of the drivers or a fresh oil stain on the concrete which had not been there minutes before. The sweating recruits groaned inwardly as their tormentor pronounced the whole area filthy and made them start all over again in the blazing sun.

The corporal was the first person Frank had heard talking English. Cautiously, he tried to make some contact. 'It's pretty hot today, isn't it, corporal?'

The idea made the little Glaswegian laugh.

'You'd fancy a nice cool beer, then?' He pointed across the boulevard to the terrace outside Chez Mimi. A crowd of customers were taking their evening aperitifs beneath the shade of large Cinzano umbrellas. Although Frank did not yet know it, Chez Mimi was one of the few bars in Oran not to be wired in or protected by sandbags; the proximity of the Legion barracks had so far discouraged extremists of both the Arab FLN and the settlers' counter-organisation known as OAS.

To Frank, with his dust-dry throat and mouth, the bar was impossibly remote. He watched a little girl in a white dress come to the edge of the terrace and stand with her back to the patrons. She stared with large serious eyes at the soldiers on the other side of the road. Frank thought she looked worried.

The corporal waved to her: '*Bonjour*, Marie-France.'

'*Bonjour, caporal*,' she called in reply.

'My girlfriend,' grinned the corporal. 'What do you think of her, Yank?'

'She's pretty.' Cautiously Frank took advantage of the moment's informality and put his weight on one leg to rest the other knee.

'If only she was ten years older, eh?' the corporal nudged him knowingly.

A dust devil corkscrewed its way across the sun-heated surface of the road, dragging a train of sand and pieces of paper through the gates of the depot and strewing it across the concrete. The corporal's mood changed abruptly. 'You!' he shouted at Frank. 'This place is like a fucking pigsty. Get down on your knees and clean that shit up. *A genoux!*'

'We've got to fight,' said Henri. He was sitting in the small kitchen behind the bar, where he and Gustave had been drinking steadily since returning to Oran from Enfida.

'No,' said Gustave. 'What's that motto they're writing on the walls? *La valise ou le cercueil.* That's it. For us Europeans in Algeria the choice is between packing our bags or picking a coffin.'

'No!' Henri's clenched fist hit the table. 'I'll not accept that. I'm going to fight. It's too late to save our farms and homes, but by God, I'm going to make those FLN bastards pay in blood for what they've done to me.'

'You're too old to join the Army.'

A laugh as Henri downed another glass of the unlabelled home-distilled eau-de-vie. 'Fuck the Army, my friend. They're fighting in the dark, doing what Paris orders. And

158

what the hell do they know in Paris? I'm joining the OAS. They're men like me who were born here. They know what to do.'

'You're crazy,' said Gustave. 'The OAS are criminals with a price on their heads.'

'Don't you believe it!' Henri reached over the table and pulled his friend close. He waited as Yasmine, the Arab cook, carried a tray of dirty glasses through the room to get to the kitchen sink. Henri lowered his voice. 'Out there, drinking in the bar, are five OAS men that I went to school with. And there are probably others I don't know.'

'There are?' With the alcohol and the day's events befuddling his mind, Gustave could not think clearly.

'Have you got the balls to join us?' asked Henri.

'I don't know.' Gustave felt as hopeless as he sounded. 'I have to talk to Marie.'

'Well, fuck you then!' Henri lurched to his feet and grabbed the bottle, heading into the bar.

School was closed next day and so was Chez Mimi. The OAS had called a strike of all European-owned businesses and institutions in retaliation for a FLN strike the previous week.

Marie-France was watching from the first-floor balcony as Yasmine returned from the daily shopping expedition to the market where she bought fresh vegetables. Seeing the familiar chubby form turn the corner from the street where the market was held, Marie-France ran downstairs to see what treat Yasmine had brought her. There was usually a sticky Arab sweetmeat or some other small present in the cook's ample basket.

On the ground floor the shutters were still up; it was dark in the restaurant. Marie-France heard Yasmine put down her shopping on one of the outside tables and insert the key in the lock of the restaurant door.

'*Bonjour, chérie*,' called the Arab woman, outside in the bright sunlight.

She turned to pick up her purchases from the table behind

her. At that moment the gunman in the rear seat of a dusty black Panhard cruising past Chez Mimi at walking speed opened up with a hail of 7.65mm bullets from his stolen MAT 49 sub-machine pistol. At a range of less than ten metres, the impact of the shots shredded the Arab woman's back and buttocks to a bloody pulp.

The car accelerated and turned the corner on screaming tyres before the Legion sentries opposite had time to cock their rifles or decipher the mud-bespattered number plate.

Marie-France stood in the doorway and watched Yasmine's habitual smile turn to a look of astonishment. The mouth that had just said *bonjour chérie* hung slack as the plump body spun sideways to the ground, spilling vegetables in all directions. An aubergine from the torn shopping bag rolled through the pool of blood and spun a sticky red train from the supine body across the tiles to Marie-France's feet.

Despite the shutters, there was glass everywhere – except by some miracle on the small patch of floor where Marie-France was standing.

The first person to arrive on the scene was one of the recruits from the depot whose quick reflexes had him sprinting across the road before the astonished sentries had got their wits about them. He knelt beside the woman lying on the ground in a pool of blood, her legs spread wide. One look told him there was nothing he could do for her. A whimper caused him to look up and see Marie-France standing in the doorway, staring wide-eyed, one hand stuck in her mouth.

'It's OK, little girl,' said Frank Hansen, stepping between Marie-France and the remains of what had been Yasmine's body to block her view of the blood and the indignity of death. 'It's OK. Take it easy.'

He searched in his memory for the right words to say in French. All he could think of was '*Ça va. Ça va.*'

Thinking that the soldier coming towards her was the person who had killed Yasmine, the girl screamed, '*Ne me touchez pas! Ne me touchez pas!*'

She backed away from him, still screaming, a long high-pitched note of terror that went on long after Marie Laval had wrapped her trembling daughter in her arms and carried her upstairs away from the carnage on the terrace.

5

'It happens all the time. The French call it *une sale guerre*, a dirty war.' The tough little Glaswegian corporal was talking Frank out of his shock in the recruits' dormitory of the depot.

'But why kill an Arab cleaning woman who had just been to the market?' Frank's face was pale. 'She wasn't doing anyone any harm.'

'Och, I don't know. Perhaps she was carrying arms.'

'She was carrying vegetables! I picked them up, all covered in her blood.' Frank shook his head. 'Who could do a thing like that?'

'Who did it?' The corporal took another drag on his Gitane and flicked ash on the floor. 'That's another question altogether, laddie. It could ha' been the FLN, using terror to show the Arabs you canna' get away with working for the French any longer. It's a tactic that works.'

He picked a piece of loose tobacco off his lower lip. 'Or it could ha' been the OAS, the settlers' underground army. They just kill Arabs for the fun of it, as far as I can see – although they call it retaliation. Last Thursday they shot fifteen Arab postmen in one morning.'

'Fifteen postmen!' exclaimed Frank.

'Aye. And a while ago they killed a whole lot of Arab cleaning women on the same day, so it might ha' been them.'

'It's insane,' said Frank.

'It is that,' agreed the corporal. 'But you're in trouble, laddie.'

'I am?' Frank tore his thoughts away from the little girl screaming and the body lying in a pool of blood. It was the first corpse he had seen.

'You're in deep shit,' said the corporal, relishing every word. 'All recruits are confined to the depot, Hansen. I told ye that when you arrived. That was an order. And you left the depot without permission. You disobeyed an order. No sooner you'll get to Bel-Abbès than you'll be on jankers for a week, laddie. And that's a tough way to start your five years in the Legion, I can tell you.'

The heel of his boot ground the cigarette butt into the polished floor. 'Now get this place cleaned up, Hansen,' he spat. 'It's a fuckin' pigsty in here.'

Oran, Algeria
Wednesday, 3 August 1958

Dear Mom,

I've joined the Foreign Legion. This is the regulation postcard we have to send our families. Then no more mail for six weeks. I'll send you an address when I can. We don't have uniforms yet, but the food's OK and I'm learning French. Don't worry, I'm having a great time.

Your loving son Frank

Two thickset brutes with corporals' stripes and MP armbands met Frank straight off the truck bringing the new recruits to the main Legion barracks at Sidi-bel-Abbès and double-marched him to the *gnouf* – the lock-up.

Stockade, glasshouse ... by whatever name, it was the same the world over. Frank was stood to attention for two hours in the broiling sun of the exercise yard, watching a squad of men under punishment climbing senselessly up and down a wall with heavy packs on their backs. Another MP with a rope's end and a whistle was driving them faster and faster until one of the men collapsed from heat and exhaustion. He was left lying where he fell.

What am I doing here? thought Frank miserably. Me, a boy from Cook County, Idaho who's voluntarily signed a piece of paper writing off five years of his life, to live like this. . . .

He jumped when one of the MPs shouted the name to which he would answer for the next week: 'You, shitface, come over here.'

Understanding the meaning, if not the French slang, Frank ran to stand in front of the MP.

'*Tu piges pas?*'

'No, corporal. I don't speak French.'

'Well, Hansen, you're lucky.' The MP's accent was German. He lit a cigarette and blew smoke into Frank's face. 'You've got seven days to do in here for disobeying an order. Think you can take it?'

Frank swallowed. He felt frightened of what lay ahead. 'I hope so, corporal.'

The MP leaned forward and lowered his voice. 'Well, don't shit your pants yet, Yank. We heard why you ran out of the depot, so nobody's going to lean on you, unless you ask for it. Keep your nose clean. Do everything you're told and you'll be out of here in seven days.'

'Right, corporal.'

The door slammed behind Frank leaving him alone in a bleak, cold cell. A patch of blue sky was visible through the tiny barred window high in one wall. As his eyes adjusted, he saw a plank bed with one folded blanket, a pot and a bare wooden table. He sat on the bed. Within minutes, the door was thrown open and an MP he had not seen before was shouting at him to stand up and not sit down until ordered.

Throughout the long afternoon Frank heard other cell doors open and close, boots march along the corridor, always at the double. Commands were shouted. He could hear the whistle and the crack of the rope's end outside in the yard. At dusk, the door was opened and a metal mess tin of unappetising food thrust inside. Frank sat at the table to eat it and was immediately shouted at for sitting down without being told to. It dawned on Frank that he was being punished for having disobeyed an order, but that someone had decided to give him privileged treatment. If he could learn the rules of this mad world he had thrust himself into, he would be left alone with his thoughts for a few days and could then begin to be a legionnaire.

Only two months ago, he thought, my biggest worry in the world was what to write in the school yearbook! And who to take to the graduation prom, which was how all this started. . . .

The problem was Joanne Foster. From the day she took up residence in the executive suite at Hansen's Foods as the President's secretary, her boss's son had a wild crush on her.

Whenever Frank had to meet his father at the canning factory, he prepared in his imagination entire conversations to hold with Joanne. Yet each time he got there his heart was beating so fast that he had to hurry through what seemed like a cloud of perfume in her office, eyes averted, unable to do more than mumble, 'Hi, Miss Foster!'

'Why, hallo Frank!' Joanne's sexy drawl, the modish skirts that revealed her fully fashioned stockings and the swish of nylon as she crossed her legs, all haunted his dreams. She had come from the state capital, lured by the high salary Sven offered her; in Jacksonville, women did not wear perfume or dresses like hers, at least not to work.

When the other boys in the Jacksonville High football team started dating girls, Frank did the same. He kissed and fumbled, sometimes alone and sometimes in groups, but none of the girls his own age took his breath away like Joanne did.

Frank was aware that his mother did not like the new

secretary. When clients who did business with the Hansen fruit-packing company came to dinner, his father told jokes about businessmen and their secretaries. The men roared with laughter but Frank noticed that the wives did not laugh.

Came the graduation prom and Frank left it too late to ask the girl of his choice, only to find that she had already promised Big John Summers, the captain of the football team. He couldn't go to the dance without a girl, but there was no one else he fancied. So he did what he always did when in doubt: he went to ask his father's advice.

The Hansen family's hunting lodge was ten miles' drive out of town, on the edge of a lake. Frank drove there in the Ford convertible which had been his seventeenth birthday present. He saw his father's Cadillac parked at the end of the track that stopped 100 metres short of the cabin, with a woman's jacket draped over the seat. Frank parked beside the new-model Cadillac and walked the rest of the way. There was no sign of Sven on the landing stage. Nor was he out fishing in the dinghy on the lake. Sven's favourite toy, a power-boat with twin Evinrude outboards, bobbed gently at its moorings.

It wasn't the hunting season, so Sven wasn't in the woods either. He had to be in the cabin, thought Frank. Yet that didn't figure. . . . His father loved noise. Where Sven was, there was always either the sound of a motor, the roar of the machines in the factory, the revving outboards on the boat, or at least a radio turned up high somewhere nearby. And here all was quiet except for the birds and the lapping of wavelets against the piles of the landing stage.

Frank mounted the wooden steps to the porch, which he and his father had built the previous summer. One of the cabin windows was open. Through it he heard someone breathing heavily. There was a gasp and a cry of 'Oh God!'

Frank pulled aside the flyscreen of the open window to find himself looking into Joanne's eyes, upside down. She was stark naked, lying on a sofa, her lipsticked mouth open in ecstasy only inches from his staring eyes, her arms and legs widespread. Sven's close-cropped blond head was buried between her thighs. In the instant Joanne's eyes registered his face, Frank could see that his father was as naked as the woman he was making love to.

Crash! Frank slammed the screen shut and leaned against the wall of the cabin, feeling that he was going to be sick. How could his father do *that*? There was a commotion inside the cabin. A door slammed. Frank started running, at first towards the landing stage then in a curving path through the bushes to get back to his car and away before his father could catch him. He was starting the engine when Sven, still naked except for a towel around his waist, ran up. 'Hey, Junior! Wait, there's no need to get excited!'

As the car bounced over the ruts in the track, Frank repeated tearfully to himself again and again, 'How could you, Dad? How could you?'

At supper, his mother fretted over Frank, worried at his lack of appetite and inhabitual silence. Sven did not show up for the meal, but that was nothing unusual; he often worked late or rang from another town, saying he was still in a meeting and would be staying the night. Until that day, Frank had believed his mother when she said how lucky they were to have a father who worked all hours and provided for them so well. Now, he wondered how often Sven had been working and how often he had been cheating on them – doing *that* with Joanne Foster.

His mother, trying to distract Frank from whatever was on his mind, asked, 'How about the prom, Junior? Have you decided who you're going to ask?'

'No,' he shouted at her. 'No, I haven't. I don't want to ask anyone. I'm just not going to the prom, so there!'

He stomped upstairs, slammed the door of his bedroom and locked it. He lay on the bed fully dressed, with the light off, going over and over the same unanswerable questions. How could Joanne do *that*, she who was so ladylike with her perfume and smart clothes and immaculate make-up? How could Dad come home and sleep in the same bed as Mom after doing *that*? Did Mom know? Is that why she didn't laugh at the boss-and-secretary jokes?

Frank had heard all the locker-room boasts of sexual conquest. He knew all the names for *that*. Giving head. Eating pussy. Tastes like white of egg, someone had joked. Oh yeah? I take it with salt . . . and a leer to go with the laugh.

It was past midnight when Sven's heavy car rolled into the driveway of the Hansen ranch, crunching gravel. The radio-controlled garage door beneath Frank's bedroom went up and down. He heard his father moving about downstairs, taking a beer from the icebox. A radio was switched on and a burst of 'I'm All Shook Up' filled the house before being cut off in mid-word. It was Sven's usual routine on coming home late, deferring the moment of going to bed.

Footsteps came upstairs. Then there was a tap on the bedroom door.

'Frank?'

He lay silent on the bed.

'I want to talk to you man to man, Frank.'

'Well, I don't want to talk to you.' He heard the quiver in his own voice, tried to convince himself that it came from anger, not pain.

Sven's quick temper was audible in his voice through the locked door. 'Open this door, Frank. Or I'll smash it down.'

'No.' If he kept the sentences short he wouldn't give himself away . . .

The handle turned. Sven rattled the door angrily but kept his voice down. 'You don't have to take it like this, Frank. You're nearly eighteen. You know what girls like Joanne are good for. A roll in the hay and a fuck every day – isn't that what they say in school?'

Frank heard his mother's voice calling from the other end of the landing.

'OK, honey,' replied Sven in a different tone. 'I'm just coming.' And through the door he hissed, 'I'll talk to you in the morning, Junior.'

How could you? Frank thought miserably as the footsteps receded along the landing. He put on the light. The pine-clad walls, the crossed paddles and pennants from summer camps, the athletics trophies he had won, all meant nothing.

He pulled out of the custom-built wardrobe the tray holding his collection of medals. From it he took the ones Sven had won in the Second World War and Korea. He opened the window wide and threw the medals out into the night. There was a splash as one landed in the swimming pool and a tinkle as another hit the concrete pool surround.

Frank tipped the other medals out on to the bed. He had swapped them and bargained for them, always imagining that one day he would have medals pinned on his chest, like his father had – by General Patton, he of the pearl-handled revolvers. Growing up while his father was away at the war in Europe, Frank had had only one ambition: to be a soldier. It was partly his mother's fault for making Sven into a hero for the small boy who had hardly ever seen him. But after Korea finished, the idea of peacetime soldiering had seemed pointless to Frank. The whole idea was to fight, to risk one's life and be a war hero like his Dad. So Frank had let the idea drift.

Staring at the medals, he wondered about the men who had won them. There was an Iron Cross he had bought by mail order which set him thinking. It didn't have to be an American war. . . .

Frank recalled watching television a few nights before while his father had been sorting out some fishing tackle in the den, a can of beer beside him and a portable black-and-white television tuned to the network news.

The picture cut from the newscaster in the studio to film footage of the scenes in Algeria where, after four years of guerrilla insurgency, the settlers were confronting the Paris government in open revolt.

'Whilst the new President, General de Gaulle, negotiates with leaders of the revolt in Algiers,' the reporter was saying to camera, 'the Muslim quarter of the city of Oran is quiet today after a night of rioting in which thirty-two Europeans lost their lives. Order was restored by detachments of the French Foreign Legion, who are now policing the city to prevent further trouble.'

The camera panned to a wide-angle of the street in which

the reporter was standing. A burnt-out bus and two over-turned cars were mute testimony to the violence that had taken place. Shots broke out anew and the cameraman did a whip-pan with the camera still running to focus on a jeep with four legionnaires skidding to a halt as they came under fire from a rooftop.

The soldiers threw themselves from the vehicle and sprinted into cover behind the bus, where they began returning fire. The picture shook as the cameraman ran across the street after them for a closer shot, keeping the camera running. A close-up of the legionnaire sergeant showed his eyes staring upward through the empty windows in the blackened coachwork. Blood was running down his face from a graze. He was breathing hoarsely through his open mouth. Bullets could be heard ricocheting off the metal above him.

He waited for the gunman in the house to exhaust his magazine, then turned to the camera and shouted, '*Suivez-moi!*' The camera zoomed wide to show him and two of the other legionnaires hurling themselves across the street into the shelter of a doorway. They kicked in the door of an Arab house after blasting off the lock with a burst from a machine pistol, then vanished inside, leaving the fourth legionnaire lying on the road outside. The camera zoomed in to a close-up of the inert body.

'What did that guy say?' asked Frank.

'The sergeant?' grunted his father. 'Nothing much. *Suivez-moi* means: follow me.'

Frank was certain from the intensity of the sergeant's expression that the message had been more important than that. 'Is that all he said? Just, come with me? And those other guys ran across the road through the bullets, just like that. Wow!'

'Listen, Frank . . .' The commercial break was starting. Sven punched the button that turned off the television. 'When you're in combat and your sergeant gives an order, you don't think. You just up and do it.'

So, thought Frank, staring at the medals on the tray, there

were still heroes like the man who had won this Iron Cross. Those men in the French Foreign Legion had run through a hail of bullets when ordered to. . . .

He shoved the collection back into the wardrobe. In the tray below was what he called his travel kit. It included the money saved up for a trip to Florida that winter and the passport Sven had got him for a trip to Mexico City last fall. Picking it up, Frank's mouth twisted as he realised sourly that his father had probably only invited him along as an alibi. Joanne had travelled with them. . . . Now everything fell into place.

Frank switched off the light and sat in the semi-dark room, thinking. It was past 1 a.m. when he had worked out what he was going to do. He stepped out of the window on to the flat moonlit expanse of the garage roof and hurled his prized bunch of car keys into the middle of the pool.

There was a cleaner, more manly way of leaving home than at the wheel of a car which had been a present from his father. By taking the Greyhound bus that left town in the early morning, Frank reasoned that he wouldn't owe anything to anybody.

6

The shouts and whistle blasts ended. Boots thudded along the corridors of the *gnouf* and cell doors slammed for the night.

'Hey, Yank!' The whisper seemed to come from the water pipe.

Frank rolled off the uncomfortable bed and knelt on the cold concrete floor.

'Hey, Yank! Can you hear me?'

There was a gap in the wall where the plaster had been laboriously scraped away with a spoon handle. Frank put his face close to the pipe. 'Yeah,' he said. 'Who are you?'

'My name's Buddy.'

'Are you American?'

'Nah. Belgian.'

'So how come you speak American?'

'I worked in a bar on a US base.'

'How did you know I was an American?'

There was a snigger. 'I got ways of finding things out.'

Even in here? Frank looked up at the light, which was on. There was no switch in the cell. 'Hadn't we better be careful? If the MP catches us talking . . .'

The man in the next cell laughed quietly. 'Don't worry. It's Franceschi on duty tonight. He drinks. He won't be back for a while.'

Lying on the cell floor passing messages to another prisoner he had never met was the first romantic thing that had happened to Frank since he had knocked on the door of the Legion recruiting office in Marseilles; the brief violence of the assassination seemed more like a dream than a real happening.

Frank answered question after question from the other side of the wall. His unknown friend seemed to have an insatiable appetite for information about America and all the trivia of Frank's daily life in Jacksonville. He also had a sixth sense about the guard. After half an hour's conversation he interrupted Frank's reminiscences with a sudden hiss. 'Here comes Franceschi. Get back on your bed, quick.'

Frank lay on the bed and narrowed his eyes to slits. A minute of silence later, the peep-hole opened and an eye stared into the cell. Frank had heard nothing. He did not hear the MP go away either. Several minutes passed before he heard, 'Frank the Yank? It's OK to talk now.'

Frank nestled down in the corner next to the pipe. 'How did you know the MP was coming? Did you hear him?'

A snigger. 'I been in here before, man. Franceschi walks around in his socks at night, hoping to catch guys jerking off. I just know how long it takes the Eyetie to drink a bottle of beer, that's all.'

'Oh.' Frank added the MP's voyeurism to the catalogue of new experiences that day. 'You didn't tell me your name.'

'It's Buddy. Buddy De Burgh.'

'That your real name?'

'Sure.' The voice sounded defensive. 'Why not?'

'Why d'you join the Legion, Buddy?'

'Oh that? I had some trouble with the police.'

'Wow!' Frank had never knowingly met a criminal. 'In Belgium?'

'No. On the base. American MPs.'

'What happened?'

'They caught me stealing.'

'Money?'

Another snigger. 'Everything. You've no idea what I walked out of that base with before they caught me.'

'So why didn't you go back to Belgium?'

'Why do you think, man?'

'I don't know.'

'I already been in trouble there.' There was a pause, then an eagerness crept into De Burgh's voice. 'Say, Yank, do you know Buddy Holly?'

'I don't know him. I like his records. Why d'you ask?'

'He's the greatest musician ever born. I'm going to work with him when I get out of here.'

Frank was out of his depth in this stream of fantasies – or were they fact? 'When you get out of this prison?'

'No, sucker. Out of the Legion. I'm going to join Buddy Holly's group when my time's up. I play guitar.'

Frank laughed.

'What's so funny?' De Burgh sounded hurt.

On the morning of his release, Frank was hustled out of the cell, eager to meet De Burgh at last. He knew that his cell neighbour was also due for release that day. An MP double-marched him *hup-hup-hup* along the corridor to the orderly office where Frank was left standing to attention in front of the first officer he had seen in the twelve days since he had been sworn in.

Men came and went. No one took any notice of Frank. He could have been a piece of furniture. There was another prisoner awaiting release standing in front of the officer's desk when he arrived. Frank sneaked a look at him and was immediately shouted at to face front. The other man, he saw, was a hard-faced legionnaire of twenty-five or more with a livid scar on his cheek. He gave Frank a surreptitious wink.

So that's what De Burgh looks like, thought Frank. A real hard man. And he promised to look after me until I know my way around . . .

They had been waiting twenty minutes when one of the MPs double-marched into the orderly office a third man to be released that day. He was a shaven-headed recruit like Frank, but a stunted, rat-faced little fellow with a sallow skin who looked little more than a boy. Frank's heart sank when the lieutenant behind the desk addressed rat-face as legionnaire De Burgh.

Quartier Viénot, Sidi-bel-Abbès
16 September 1958

Dear Mom,

I've survived the first six weeks' training! In case that doesn't sound a big deal – several guys flunked out. It's physically very tough and the NCOs have weeded out the ones who weren't ever going to make it. I'm glad I was pretty fit from all that football training.

Everything in the Legion is rules! Rule One is: recruits are not allowed to walk anywhere! Outside the dormitory we have to run all the time. And the corporals shout at us the whole time. We have about eight hours' drill every day. They've been teaching us to march the Legion's way. Apparently no other army in the world marches at eighty-eight paces to the minute. That's very slow. And all the time we march, we have to sing! The most famous song is about *le boudin*, which is a kind of sausage! I don't understand all the words, but I have to sing them just the same. My French is getting OK because non-French-speakers have language instruction each day.

After a whole day on the parade ground, we are often out on exercises half the night. When we get back to barracks, the corporal will call a kit inspection and deliberately dirty everyone's kit. We have to stand at attention by our beds and watch him. Then we spend two or three hours of precious sleep time getting everything clean again before morning inspection at 0530!

Luckily for me there are a couple of Germans in my dormitory who speak English, as well as a Belgian guy I've teamed up with, named Buddy. At least, that's what he says his name is, but I think he made it up. He says he's on the run in three countries and that's why he joined the Legion. His dream is to come and live in the States and be a musician with Buddy Holly. I heard him show off, playing on another guy's guitar in the canteen last night. He may think he's good, but actually he's terrible!

De Burgh has not slept in his bed once! Can you imagine that? He's not the only one. Several of the guys in the dormitory sleep on the floor so they don't have to re-make their beds in the regulation way each morning!

The first weeks – I have to say it, Mom – I cried a lot. Not in the daytime, but at night. Mainly because I was tired, so tired you wouldn't believe it. I think I might have done something stupid just to get away, if it hadn't been for Buddy. Nothing ever seemed to get him down. He helped me clean my kit and showed me a million tricks to make life easier. I owe him a lot. I guess that's the best thing about this life: it doesn't matter what a guy did in civilian life. Nothing counts before we joined up.

We're allowed to have mail now the first six weeks are over, so write me, please.

Frank

De Burgh finished his beer. His shifty eyes glanced round the neighbouring tables but there were no unfinished glasses left unattended. 'Lend me the dough for another round, Frank.'

Frank shook his head. 'What do you mean, lend? When you going to pay me back?'

'Aw, come on. Look . . .' De Burgh took Frank's much larger hand in his, 'I got no more money till pay-day, Frank. Buy me another beer and I'll tell your fortune.'

Frank chuckled. 'That's a new one.'

'I'm not kidding. I can, you know.'

'Where d'you learn to tell fortunes?'

'My mother was a gypsy.'

Frank laughed outright. Several times he had caught De Burgh out, tripping over his own lies. 'You told me you were an orphan, Buddy.'

The brown eyes in the thin rat-face were wide and innocent. 'I told you I was brought up by nuns, Frank. Even an orphan's got a mother and father someplace, stupid.'

'What happened to your mother, then?'

'They took her away. She was pure Romany. They rounded them all up and put them in camps. But she could see the future. That's why she gave me to the nuns to look after, before the Germans came. I guess she knew they wouldn't think to look in a convent for a gypsy kid.'

Frank fought his way to the bar through the crowd of recruits. The air of the canteen was thick with cigarette smoke. He placed the beer in front of his friend and stuck out his hand. 'OK, Buddy. Tell me what you see.'

'Gotta cigarette, Frank?'

'First you tell my fortune. Go on, man. You promised.'

'OK.' De Burgh traced the lines on Frank's large paw with a dirty, broken nail. 'Aw shit, I don't want to do this.' He pushed the hand away.

'You can't stop now,' Frank insisted. 'I paid you a beer. What did you see? A short lifeline, five wives or what?'

'Nah. It's nothing for you. You'll be OK.' The little Belgian gypsy avoided looking at Frank.

'That's good then?'

The shifty eyes flickered back to Frank for a moment. 'Anybody you know ever die, Frank?'

'I don't think so. Why?'

'You got the smell of death on you, man. That's why. It's on your hand.'

'You're having me on.'

'No, I'm not.'

'Well, that's a good thing, isn't it? We're soldiers. We're supposed to kill people.'

'Maybe.'

'What about reading your own hand?'

'Look. I'm going to ask you to do something. Just do it. Don't ask me why. See that slob Grunwald drinking on his own at the bar? Say: Grunwald's my best friend.'

Frank laughed. 'OK, Grunwald's my best friend. What's that mean?'

'You'll see,' said De Burgh mysteriously. He finished the beer, looking a little happier. 'Come on, we got some blanco-ing to do.'

1 January 1959

Dear Mom,

Thanks for the Xmas food parcel. I shared it around. How's this for a Foreign Legion tradition? When you get a food parcel, the post corporal gives you, say, 2,000 press-ups to do as punishment! No kidding. No press-ups and you don't get the parcel. The idea is that you have to share the press-ups among your buddies. Then they have a right to share the parcel, in return. A lot of the guys here come from pretty poor homes and never get parcels, so it's a good idea, all round. Actually, the food for Christmas day in the canteen was pretty good – real French cuisine.

Another tradition is that all the guys make little nativity cribs as Xmas decorations, complete with the stable and the animals and of course the baby Jesus, Mary and Joseph. I don't just mean the other recruits like me. I'm talking of the hard men. We dropped into one of the para units the other day whilst we were on an exercise. There were all these real tough guys with tattooed arms and scars on their faces, busted noses and all, sitting there making nativity cribs! Weird!

On Christmas day, the officers served us at dinner and we called them '*tu*', which is kind of a friendly way of saying you. The rest of the time, discipline is tight and we'd get a week's field punishment for calling an officer '*tu*'.

You asked me about my friend De Burgh. He's four years older than me and pretty streetwise. He knows a million tricks to keep his nose clean – and mine. But I'm physically a lot stronger than him, so we take turns helping each other out.

The corporal says we're over the worst of the training now. Another month to go until we pass out and get presented with our white kepis. At that moment, we are real legionnaires! I hope you understand that means a whole lot more to me than graduating from Jacksonville High.

Love, Frank

7

The truck ground its way for hour after hour through the monotonous landscape of south-eastern Algeria. The combined noise of the engine and the whine of the transmission were brain numbing. Frank and De Burgh with six other new legionnaires alternately stood in the lurching open-top vehicle and sat on the spine-crunching wooden benches. Neither position was comfortable for more than a few minutes. All the men had loaded rifles in their hands, which they were forbidden to lay down. Dust thrown up by the jeep in front got in noses and mouths despite the *chèche*, the sand-coloured scarf that each man wore tightly wound round his face below the eyes.

The desert through which they drove had not been designed in Hollywood; there were no beautiful sand dunes, gracefully waving palm trees or green oases. The view from horizon to horizon was of gravel and rocks, with a few stunted bushes clinging to cracks where moisture was to be found.

In the jeep two alert legionnaires sat by the machine-gun mounted behind the driver. One of them turned at last and shouted something to the driver of the truck. The new men rose wearily to their feet to get a first sight of their new home.

Fort Lesieur could have come out of a film. It looked –

and was – hundreds of years old. It had been built and destroyed several times by different armies. The battlements, parapet, firing step and all the buildings inside were of the same limewashed adobe. Officers and men slept on metal beds above beaten earth floors where bugs and scorpions ran free.

As the truck drove through the gate of the fort, the new arrivals were confronted with their commanding officer. He seemed to match the bleak landscape and the comfortless fort: a tall thin man with a black patch over one eye and no insignia on his uniform. With a loaded MAT 49 slung over one shoulder, Captain Koenig strode across the small parade ground and mounted the jeep to watch the new intake clamber stiffly down from the truck which had brought them from Sidi-bel-Abbès. The close-cropped head turned from side to side, assessing each man with its single eye.

A sergeant with a thick Greek accent brought them to attention, kitbags lying on the ground between them. Without preamble, Koenig announced: 'I am your commanding officer. My name is Koenig. In German, that means king. I am the king of Fort Lesieur, to which you have been posted.'

There were a few tired laughs, which he ignored.

'You men belong to the First Infantry Regiment of the Legion, body and soul. I mean that. The First is the best regiment in the best army in the world.'

He swung round dramatically and pointed to the east where the Tunisian frontier lay. 'Here you are up against the best enemy in the world. He is worthy of you and he's waiting for you. Less than five kilometres away, on the other side of the frontier the FLN have one of their training camps.'

He stepped down from the jeep and walked along the line of men, stopping one pace in front of each one, as though to brand his face into their souls. At the end of the line, he turned and faced them. His hard voice echoed off the sun-baked brick walls all round. 'You men are here for one reason: to kill every *fellagha* from that camp who dares to cross the border in my sector. I am personally going to teach you how.'

The sergeant ordered them to check their magazines and put one up the spout. Within minutes of arriving at the fort, Frank, De Burgh and the others were being marched in extended line out into the shimmering heat haze behind the lean figure of Koenig. Each man carried his pack and rifle. The kitbags were left lying on the parade ground.

The captain was setting a hard pace. 'Jesus,' muttered Frank, trying to disguise the excitement Koenig's personality aroused in him. 'I have a feeling we've got some real soldiering ahead of us at last.'

De Burgh was looking unhappy. He seemed to have shrunk inside his olive drab uniform. 'That one-eyed captain looks a real hard bastard, Frank. He's got the smell of death all over, he has.'

'You and your gypsy superstitions.'

'You can laugh. I tell you, I don't like this place, Frank.'

As the sergeant overtook them, striding easily over the scorching stony ground alongside the column, Frank asked, 'What's the captain like, sarge?'

The sergeant gave an evil grin. In the accent of his native Salonika, he grunted, 'Koenig? The Arabs call him the bastard who never sleeps.'

'Great,' muttered De Burgh. 'I guess that means we don't either.'

The sergeant laughed and passed on.

'You got any spare water?' Frank asked when he had gone.

De Burgh looked sly. 'I've got brandy. You want some?'

Frank took a swig. 'That's good. It's going to be a thirsty day. They could have given us time to refill our canteens at the fort before we moved off.'

'I've a feeling,' said De Burgh prophetically, 'that's going to be the story of our lives in this dump.'

Frank scratched his arm, which was sore from the tattoo De Burgh had talked him into having done before they left Sidi-bel-Abbès, so that he could get his own tattoo at a cheaper price. Now the motto *Legio Patria Nostra* decorated

Frank's skin below the eagle-and-snake emblem of the regiment. He wondered what his mother would say when she saw it.

As each pace succeeded the one before and he grew thirstier and thirstier, his thoughts started drifting. A burst of firing very close brought him back to reality with a start. A bullet buzzed close to his head and he found himself lying in the dirt flicking the safety off by reflex and looking for the enemy.

The enemy was Koenig. The one-eyed captain was standing on a low rock, his smoking MAT 49 pointing skywards over the heads of the men.

'You were all asleep,' he shouted, his harsh voice echoing off the bare hillsides all around. 'If I had been a *fellagha*, you'd be dead now.'

Surveying the line of men prostrate below, he added, 'To help you remember you're not still in training and that there are men in the *djebel* whose job is to kill you, you are now going to march an extra five kilometres. But first, empty your canteens. Sergeant, make sure they do.'

An hour later, throats parched and sand itching their eyes, Koenig's men marched into an Arab village, which the Greek sergeant called a *bled*. There were no young men in sight. The old men, women and children watched the legionnaires sullenly. Frank apologised to the woman inside the hut he was ordered to search for weapons. In reply, she spat in his face. He wiped the gobbet from his cheek and raised the rifle. She backed away in the gloom, cursing him in Arabic. The hovel was filthy: chickens were nesting in the single bed where mother and six children all slept. Frank could not bring himself to search the pile of old rags. There seemed to be very little food in the place and the smell in the poorly ventilated and smoke-filled hut made him gag.

Most of the children in the *bled* seemed to have eye trouble. After the search, which drew a blank, Koenig set up a defence perimeter while the medic ran a clinic for the children.

A few mangy donkeys and some goats clung to the shade

of the buildings. Frank envied them. He stood with his back to the *bled*, squinting against the setting sun as he kept watch.

They returned to the fort well after dark. Captain Koenig and the sergeant looked as fresh as when they had begun the march. Most of the newcomers looked and felt dead on their feet; they were too tired to eat and crashed out on the thin mattresses and creaking metal beds. Frank had carried De Burgh's rifle the last couple of miles in addition to his own. He pulled De Burgh off the bed and forced him to walk to the canteen and consume a full helping of the unappetising food they would get to know as the staple diet of Fort Lesieur, washed down with *pinard*, a cheap, rough wine.

De Burgh fell asleep in seconds. On the next bed, Frank lay exhausted but strangely elated that he had passed the first test set by the lean, tough captain with one eye. Also, he had the feeling that he had at last completely swapped roles with De Burgh. Here in the desert, it was the under-sized Belgian who needed looking after; all the smart tricks in the world didn't make a pack and a rifle any lighter.

By the light of a candle, Frank finished a letter to his mother:

... are you kidding I enjoy your news? The clipping you sent, about Buddy Holly's plane crashing in a snowstorm last month, upset De Burgh. He can never get enough of that music. On our last night in bel-Abbès, he was driving everyone mad by playing over and over again the only Buddy Holly number on the jukebox 'That'll be the Day – The Day When I Die'.

Write me soon.

Love, Frank

P.S. De Burgh hasn't had a letter since the day he joined up. I think his family are all dead. He doesn't talk much about it. Do you think you could find some nice girl in Jacksonville who would be willing to write him now and again?

*

There were voices talking low outside the barrack block. Frank blew out the candle. Cautiously he climbed up on the end of the bed and peered out of the unglazed ventilator. Silhouetted against the moonlit parade ground he saw two figures at the row of cold-water basins that were the fort's only toilet facility. As his eyes adjusted to the moonlight, he made out the unmistakable figures of Captain Koenig and the Greek sergeant, Grivas. They were dressed in Arab robes and busy blacking their faces and hands with night camouflage. Frank could see that they were armed only with knives.

The two men slipped silently through a gap in the main gate, which was immediately closed after them. They headed east, towards the frontier and the enemy training camp. Frank lay down on the bed. The bastard who never sleeps . . . the nickname seemed to sum up Captain Koenig pretty well.

The *fellagha* knew every inch of the land in the sector of Fort Lesieur and had a million escape routes and bolt-holes to hide in after each ambush. Like all guerrillas they also had the great advantage of being able to secrete their weapons and merge back into the local population – or simply walk across the frontier into Tunisia where the Legion was officially not allowed to pursue them.

As the summer of 1959 wore on, the heat, the arduous patrolling, the constant risk of ambush and mines combined with shortage of sleep to hone Koenig's men down to tough, efficient fighting machines. Even De Burgh stopped complaining, because nobody listened. Marching all day in temperatures of 110 degrees Fahrenheit and higher, no one carried an ounce of fat. The discipline of a hundred firefights welded them into a fast-moving, competent team. There were moments on operations when even Koenig's harsh face showed pride in his men.

Unable to stand the relentless discipline and harsh regime, one of the less popular men in Frank's intake deserted. Given the choice of taking his gun with him and being hunted down like an animal by his own comrades, legionnaire Grunwald chose to go unarmed, hoping not to be pursued. His plan was to walk to the nearest town across the border, travelling by night and hiding up during daylight hours. His naked, mutilated body, with penis stuffed into the mouth, was found next day at dawn less than a hundred metres outside the fort. It was buried in the small graveyard that same morning.

Captain Koenig stayed at the graveside after the firing party had been marched away. There were ten man-length piles of stones on the dry ground to mark the ten men who had died since he had taken command of the lonely outpost. Each had a plain cross bearing the name of the legionnaire beneath.

Koenig stood for a moment in front of each grave, remembering the man's face and the voice. An Australian, two Germans, three Frenchmen, a Canadian, a Dane, a South African . . . and another German, Grunwald.

And all of them were – mentally, Koenig completed the phrase – *morts pour la France*. But was that true? Did France any longer care? Or was the sacrifice in vain? Were he and his men fighting a war that had already been decided at a conference table behind closed doors? He looked around at his kingdom of bare and stony earth that was no good to anyone and wondered how many more men he would bury at Fort Lesieur, allegedly in its defence. He came to attention and saluted the men who had died. As his hand came down, he executed a smart right turn. Facing east, he wondered whether, just a few miles away, some FLN officer was burying one of his men.

That evening, Frank got into an argument with De Burgh, who had been acting morose all day. 'Snap out of it, Buddy. Grunwald was a loser, that's all. Doesn't mean anything. Or were you hoping to run away as well? This spoilt your plans, has it?'

'It's not that.'

'What is it then?'

'You remember the spell I cast in the canteen at bel-

Abbès, Frank?' De Burgh asked gloomily. 'You see how it worked?'

'You're crazy. You're talking gypsy hocus-pocus. Grunwald ran away because he had no friends.'

'I'm not talking about why he ran away.' De Burgh emphasised the *why*. 'I'm talking about death. That man was going to die, whether he ran away or not.'

The little Belgian gypsy seemed to shrink each day, as though he could make a smaller target for the enemy that way. The wise-guy self-confidence that had taken him through training was ebbing away.

As his friend grew increasingly morose and silent, Frank felt better and better. Fit and strong, he recuperated easily, even after the long marches by which Koenig toughened them up, day after day. The indifferent food did not bother him, or the lack of sleep. He felt a growing confidence in himself and felt proud to be a legionnaire serving under Captain Koenig. It was the life of which Frank had dreamed as a kid while playing with his collection of other men's medals.

8

The only thing Frank questioned about life at Fort Lesieur was the routine torture of suspects. It sickened him when a dozen frightened and sullen Arabs were rounded up while working in their poor stony fields and strapped to a metal workbench behind the MT section in the fort. Electrodes were clipped on to mouths and genitals and the current was turned on.

'What *willaya* do you belong to? Who is your commanding officer? Where are the weapons hidden?' Like a monotonous chant, the *harki* – an Arab soldier acting as interpreter – repeated the same questions again and again until one of the victims could no longer stand the increasingly severe electric shocks.

The first time Frank saw this, he turned his face away and wanted to be sick. He kept in the shadows of an overhanging roof, hoping to be invisible. It was Captain Koenig's restless eye that spotted him.

'You!' he shouted at Frank. 'You in the shadows! Hansen! Turn around and watch.'

Reluctantly, Frank did as he was told. Each time the switch was thrown, the contortions of the suspects' entire bodies would have hurled them right off the metal bench if the straps had not been so strong.

The stench of vomit and faeces in the still, hot air was

appalling. From time to time, a legionnaire played a water hose over the squirming bodies on the bench – not for hygiene but to improve the electrical conductivity of the victims' flesh.

Captain Koenig walked round the workbench and planted himself in front of Frank. 'You don't like this, do you, Hansen?'

'*Non, mon capitaine.*' Frank stood to attention.

'Neither do I,' said Koenig evenly. 'That is why I am present at every torture session in Fort Lesieur.'

Frank's confusion showed in his eyes.

'*Faut qu'ils parlent,*' said Koenig tersely, jerking his head at the men on the bench. 'We have to make them talk, Hansen. In this war, ninety-nine per cent of our intelligence is obtained by the method you are witnessing.'

'There must be other ways,' said Frank desperately.

'We didn't invent the rules of the game.' Koenig shook his head. 'We're up against men who decided from the outset to use terror as their main weapon. We have to use the same methods, Hansen, whether we like it or not.'

A chorus of sobs and screams rose from the men strapped to the workbench as the voltage was raised.

'War shouldn't be like this. Is that what you're thinking?' Koenig's voice softened. He remembered his own horror, the first time he had seen a man tortured.

'*Oui, mon capitaine.*'

'Wrong,' said Koenig. 'Two and a half thousand years ago, the greatest military philosopher, Sun Tsu wrote: Kill one, frighten a thousand. That's the basic philosophy of all our modern terrorists. Nothing is new.'

'With respect, *mon capitaine*, it doesn't justify this . . .' Frank's eyes indicated the men twitching and moaning on the metal bench only two metres away from where they were standing.

Koenig thrust his face within centimetres of Frank's. 'Listen, Hansen,' he hissed. The single eye searched Frank's eyes, willing him to understand how a soldier had to override his own conscience. 'I lost two of my men yesterday in an ambush. And this *ordure* . . .'

Koenig jerked a thumb at the men being tortured. 'This vermin was within two kilometres of the spot when it happened. Some of them probably did it. Certainly one of them knows something about it.'

Frank stayed rigidly at attention. To his surprise, Koenig slapped him on the shoulder. 'At ease, Hansen. These bastards are lucky. At least the French army has drawn up *The Code of Humane Torture.* The other side has no such code when they catch one of my men.'

'We have a written code of torture?' Frank could not believe what he was hearing.

'That's right,' Koenig explained. 'For example, there must always be an officer present. And children must not be tortured.' He shrugged. 'That is something the other side does all the time.'

'I know that, sir.'

'Most importantly, Hansen, under the French code torture must stop the moment the suspect is prepared to talk.'

Perhaps understanding what Koenig had said, one of the men on the bench moaned something that caught the attention of the *harki* who, in turn, shouted out in French.

'Cut the current,' Koenig snapped.

Frank watched blankly as the man who was ready to talk was unstrapped from the bench and half-carried into the intelligence office.

January of 1961 was cold. There was snow in the Aurès mountains. At the end of each day's gruelling patrol, Koenig's men slept close to the camp-fire, too tired to talk much.

'Hey, you guys! Come and listen to this.' Martinez, the Mexican radio man called to Frank and De Burgh, the only other English-speakers in the group.

They rolled out of their blankets and scrambled across to where he lay. In the flickering light of the fire, he held out to them the headphones plugged into the illicit multi-band radio which he carried everywhere. Frank and De Burgh each put one earphone to an ear and found themselves listening to a Voice of America station relaying live the inauguration ceremony of President John F. Kennedy.

Reception kept fading and surging. At the end of the ceremony, Frank stayed hunched by the radio man's blankets for a while. When he walked back to his bed-roll, De Burgh said sympathetically, 'Made you homesick, huh?'

'It wasn't that,' said Frank.

'Whatsamatter then?'

'You remember what Kennedy said when he was talking to people of our age? The President said: Ask not what your country can do for you – ask what you can do for your country.'

'So?'

'It sounds corny, but that's why I'm here. I want to serve. And the Legion, like it says in our tattoos, is my country.'

'You're crazy,' muttered De Burgh.

'You must feel the same,' Frank insisted. 'Else, why did you have this tattooed on you?' He tapped the regimental emblem on De Burgh's arm.

'Shit,' sneered his friend. 'That's to pull the chicks, man. What did you think it was for?'

It was noon when Sergeant Grivas halted the patrol in the shade of some cedar trees growing beside the Wadi Warène, a seasonal river they had been following for several days in pursuit of a small party of FLN believed to be transporting arms. There was water running in the middle of the stream-bed. The bitter liquid was no good for drinking, but they could cool their faces in it and soak their feet at the end of the day.

The men had been marching since dawn. They eased their Bergen rucksacks off aching shoulders and sagged against the tree trunks for a smoke break in the shade. Then came a crackle on the radio beside Ramirez. He jammed the headphones on his ears and held them tight. Reception was bad due to the topography.

'I have Bluebird,' he muttered. Bluebird was Koenig's code name. 'Oh, shit! Old One-Eye has seen something.'

'What is it?' Frank rolled over and looked in Ramirez' direction.

'Don't ask,' grunted De Burgh, his soft bush hat tipped over his face to keep the flies off. 'We'll hear soon enough.'

Frank had never mastered the art of smoking while keeping his face covered. He slapped a token mosquito from the crowd having lunch on his neck, removed a cigarette from the pack in De Burgh's breast pocket, lit it and exhaled.

The Alsatian war dog whose lead De Burgh was holding licked the back of Frank's arm, hungry for salt.

Frank fondled the furry ears. Since Koenig had talent-spotted the little gypsy's natural ability for tracking and made him a dog-handler, De Burgh's morale had gone up; it was the first time in his life that he had earned respect from men like Captain Koenig and Sergeant Grivas. Frank saw a new side to his friend. De Burgh seemed to have been born for the job. Walking point, his busy little eyes, which people thought shifty because they were forever on the move and never looking straight at anyone, picked up the smallest traces where a man had trodden or a leaf had been crushed by someone pushing through the bushes. He could see where a foot had scuffed bare rock or a stone had been recently displaced. His peripheral vision caught the smallest movement; he saved Frank's life on one occasion when they walked into an ambush, spoiled only by De Burgh's warning shout half a second before the first shot rang out.

Time after time when the quarry they were pursuing took to scrambling over bare rock and left no visible traces, De Burgh led the patrol apparently by telepathy until he picked up the trail again. He swore to Frank that he could talk to the Alsatian and that his furry friend talked back, '. . . inside my head, Frank. Honest.'

While not believing what he called 'all this gypsy hocus-pocus', Frank was as impressed as the other men when De Burgh and the dog were in action. They seemed to work as a single creature with six legs and at least six senses.

A light flashed on the hilltop just above where the patrol was resting. Instinctively Frank grabbed his loaded machine pistol and slipped the safety off, then relaxed as the light became the reflection of sunlight on the perspex canopy of Koenig's Alouette. The tiny reconnaissance helicopter danced in the air currents as it skimmed over the ridge and filled the wadi with noise. Ramirez cursed as the suddenly increased volume of Koenig's voice hurt his ears.

'Understood,' said Ramirez. 'Over and out, Bluebird.'

Within seconds, leaving two men to guard the pile of rucksacks, the squad was mobile again, rifles and sub-machine-guns slung on their backs as they scrambled on all fours up the nearly vertical slope above which Koenig flew in a loose circle. As always, when they crested the ridge, panting and sweating, there was nothing to be seen. To the north a blue smudge could have been the sea, fifty kilometres distant. In every direction closer at hand extended a succession of ridges and valleys, all seemingly identical. In the sunlit valley below was a timeless scene: a cedar-strewn slope and a few piles of rocks. Nothing moved. They stood, getting their breath back while De Burgh and the dog cast around for scent or inspiration.

Ramirez, relaying Koenig's voice from the Alouette, was pointing towards the rocks below the trees.

'Spread out,' yelled Grivas. 'Keep your distance. Bluebird definitely reports three men carrying something heavy when he popped up above this ridge just now. They went to earth as soon as they saw the helicopter, somewhere down there by those rocks.' He pointed.

The men moved down the slope. The cedars gave little cover. They were looking for a cave mouth, a fallen tree, a pile of stones – for anything in, under or behind which a man could hide.

The helicopter dipped behind the skyline. In the sudden quiet Frank was aware of his own breathing, the crunch of boots on shale and rock and De Burgh's voice echoing off the hillside. He was talking to the Alsatian, encouraging it. 'Come on, boy. Come on. Let's find them. Let's flush out those big, bad *fells*. Where they gone, eh? Come on . . .'

Near the valley bottom, the dog caught the scent it had been taught to recognise. It bared its teeth in a low snarl and started tugging on the long leash. Fifty feet away across the scree-strewn slope, Frank heard the noise and turned to see De Burgh running and jumping over rocks, letting the dog pull him.

Frank alerted the sergeant with a shout. As he turned back, he saw the dog leap through the air in front of a dark shadow which was a cave mouth. A shot rang out. The dog dropped to the ground. Another shot and De Burgh dropped too.

Frank's long strides brought him to the cave, his MAT 49 at the ready. Inside cowered three Arabs, their eyes wide with fear. Two were boys of fourteen or fifteen in peasant clothing. They were unarmed. The other was older and wore a militia jacket above civilian trousers. His faded khaki cotton cap had a simple red star above the peak. Two worn leather bandoliers of cartridges criss-crossed his chest. He was holding an M-1 carbine with a 30-round magazine. With a grimace, he lowered the weapon and threw it outside where it skidded on the gravel until stopped by Frank's boot.

'*Nous nous rendons*,' he said clearly: we surrender.

All three raised their hands as far as the low roof of the dug-out permitted. Frank looked from De Burgh's open eyes to the dog lying with half its head torn away. Then along the leash, the end of which was still wrapped round his friend's hand. Then back to the Arabs in the hole.

Frank shook his head; something was blurring his vision, like a mist behind the eyes. He shook his head again, but the mist did not go away. There was an equation of pain that he could not solve. De Burgh had been his buddy. It had been Frank's duty to look after the little Belgian runt, but he had let him down.

He felt no anger as he fired a short burst from the MAT 49 into each of the men in the hole. Like a silent prayer, he mouthed the words of the legionnaire's Code of Honour: '. . . *in battle, you act without passion and without hatred* . . .'

It was true, there was no hatred in his heart, just a terrible emptiness. From where he stood, his face in the bright sunlight of midday, it was impossible to see any wounds on the bodies in the dug-out. Only the stillness and their unnatural attitudes told him they were dead. One of the bodies toppled sideways, revealing at the back of the hole the outline of the German Maschinengewehr 42 the men had been carrying. Frank squeezed the trigger again. On sustained fire, the spray of bullets drifted high and to the right. The magazine held 22 rounds; any more strained the spring. He let them all go, then training took over. Without thinking about it, he switched the empty magazine for the full one that was taped to it end-to-end.

A gale of wind-blown dust and gravel swirled around Frank as Koenig's helicopter landed. The captain was running towards him through the dust, followed by Ramirez and the sergeant.

Koenig took one look in the hole and turned to Frank.

'The one in uniform,' he snarled. 'I wanted him alive, Hansen. I wanted him to talk.'

'They killed De Burgh,' said Frank dully.

The blow from the captain's fist caught Frank on the cheekbone and made his ears ring. Like a sleepwalker, he brought the MAT 49 up, aimed straight at the captain's belly. His finger tightened on the trigger.

'Put that weapon down, Hansen.' Grivas' thick voice came from close behind Frank and the muzzle of a rifle was jammed into the small of his back painfully hard. There was the sound of rocks rolling down the slopes as the other men converged on the hole De Burgh had found.

Frank let his own weapon fall to the ground, then slumped beside it. Squatting beside the body, he closed De Burgh's eyes. The third eye, the neat hole in the centre of the narrow forehead, would not close. He pinched the edges of the wound together several times but it made no difference. Gently he undid De Burgh's *chèche*, pulled it free and placed it over his friend's face.

'What happened?' the sergeant asked.

'I lost a man,' said Koenig savagely. 'That's what happened.'

Frank stooped and lifted De Burgh's body. It seemed to weigh nothing, stripped of all life's cares. As he straightened up he smelt a faint sweet whiff of perfume or blossom on the air and wondered if that was the smell of death that the little gypsy had talked about. When he took the next breath, it was gone.

Grivas was talking to him. 'What did you say?' Frank asked.

'I said to put him in the captain's helicopter, Hansen.'

Frank shook his head.

Captain Koenig stood in front of him. 'It's OK, Hansen,' he said gently. 'I'll take care of him.'

'No.' Frank pulled away. His eyes were unfocused. 'I want to carry him back.'

He lurched up the steep hillside carrying his friend's body over one shoulder, his feet slipping and sliding in the loose shale. For every two steps up, he slid one backwards.

The other men watched him go without talking. To Koenig standing below, Frank looked like a medieval penitent bearing a cross through the biblical landscape. He blinked the image away; reality was enough.

As Grivas started after Frank, Koenig caught the sergeant's arm and said quietly, 'Let him go, sergeant.'

. . . there are worse ways to die, I know that, Mom. One minute De Burgh was alive, the next minute, he was dead. I miss him.

Can you do something for me – for him? He didn't talk much about Alice, or flash her photograph around like some of the guys do, but I know he enjoyed getting her letters a lot. He was always asking me questions about what Jacksonville was like. He wanted to know if I could help him get a work permit for the States after we get demobbed, and whether Dad could find him a job in the factory. So maybe D.B. and Alice were planning something together, I don't know. Perhaps you can break the news to Alice? I tried several times to write her, but I can't do it.

Love, Frank.

9

*I*t was many years later that Frank talked to me about his feelings after De Burgh's death. Even then he had still not come to terms with what he called 'my guilt'.

I tried to explain to him that what he felt was not guilt.

Nor was it a question of debt, although Frank insisted, 'De Burgh had saved my life. I owed him – and I let him down.'

Frank was seeking reasons for something you can't explain.

An uncle of Marie's fought all through the First World War without a scratch. One after another he watched his friends die. When he came back to his fiancée in 1918 it was not to marry her but to say goodbye. He returned to trench-scarred, treeless Flanders where he joined that small group of quiet men who cycle from one crowded war cemetery to the next, keeping the gardens between the simple crosses in order. They are old now, those Frenchmen, Belgians, Canadians, New Zealanders, Americans and Scotsmen who tend the fields of crosses. They still spend their years weeding and cutting the grass above their comrades who fell more than half a century ago. They do it not to repay a debt, but to be near them.

There are women who mourn their beloved for half a century and husbands who mourn their dead wives just as long. Yet when a man feels the same way for a fallen comrade, all too often he fails to recognise his feelings for what they are: a selfless love – what the Greeks called agape. And the mourning can last a lifetime *because, of course, the dead do nothing to adulterate the love we feel for them.*

I remember Koenig saying, when we were both innocent young lieutenants only a few months out of St Cyr, that our regimental emblem symbolised the two aspects of warfare. The eagle stood for the exaltation that men feel in battle when they rise above the selfish human condition, when they are prepared to sacrifice them-selves – to throw away their lives if need be – for a wounded comrade or even to recover the body of one already dead. Greater love hath no man . . .

The snake, said young Koenig as though looking into the future, was the dark underside of war: the destruction, the pain and degradation that we inflict on each other beyond reason.

Well, Algeria was a snake war. There was little exaltation. It was a campaign fought by ambush, lies and terror on both sides.

I heard nothing from Koenig during those years in Algeria. My letters to him evoked no answer. Much later, a man on the run hiding in my house, he told me something of the war he fought with his own conscience as one by one all his ideals had to be sacrificed in the execution of his sworn duty as an officer in the Legion. He confessed to having committed every crime in the course of duty. In the end, he clung fanatically to his code of honour because it was all he had left. It was then he took up arms against France, the country that he loved so much.

There's no ambiguity about what he did. He became a traitor and was sentenced to death in absentia. And where does treachery stop? Could not a man who has betrayed his country also betray a friend? I would never have suspected him of betraying me, yet I should not have thought him capable of torturing men. And I know he did that. He told me so himself. So it could be that he is the one who has betrayed me now. Koenig certainly knew all my secrets, all the security precautions I had taken. It could have been him. . . .

In 1961 when Koenig took the fatal step, nothing was simple, nothing clear cut. During the French President's visit to the Algerian capital, Arab crowds danced in the streets crying: 'Vive De Gaulle!' while gendarmes and soldiers turned fire hoses on the same European demonstrators who had clamoured to bring De Gaulle back to power only a few years before. No wonder men's loyalties got tangled.

'*A vos ordres!*' Frank saluted his commanding officer, took one pace to the rear and executed a right-turn smart enough for the parade ground at Sidi-bel-Abbès.

Like the rest of the men in Koenig's company, Frank would have charged a machine-gun position on a word of command from the one-eyed captain. Yet he would willingly have given up his new corporal's stripes to avoid carrying out Koenig's last order. Soldiers of the Legion's infantry regiment were to arrest their own comrades of the legendary First Parachute Regiment for taking part in armed revolt against the government in Paris.

'*C'est dingue,*' Frank muttered under his breath. It was crazy: one regiment of legionnaires was going to round up another and send it off to the *gnouf.* A dozen generals and hundreds of officers were to face courts martial. The politics of the situation was beyond Frank. All he knew was that he and his men had been ordered to arrest other legionnaires. The order went clear against the code that they had all sworn to uphold: *Every legionnaire is your brother-in-arms, whatever his race, his nationality or his religion. At all times you bear him that unswerving solidarity that unites members of the same family.*

The spring which had gone slack within Frank when De Burgh died, had finally snapped.

'That's an order, Hansen!' Koenig shouted. 'Get on with it!'

Frank handed his MAS 49 rifle to the legionnaire beside him and walked unarmed across the street in downtown Algiers.

He had to pick his way carefully between the pot-holes where cobbles had been torn up to make the barricades behind which students and renegade army and Legion troops had been holding out for several days. There was a smell of burnt rubber in the air from a bus that had fallen victim to a Molotov cocktail, its burnt-out skeleton used as part of the barrier.

The para sergeant in leopard-spot camouflage suit on the other side of the barricade stood firm as a rock, his pistol aimed at Frank's belly. 'One pace nearer and I'll shoot.' The voice with a heavy Italian accent was quite matter of fact.

Frank looked sideways. Twenty paces away, Koenig was having the same conversation with a group of para officers.

'*Sois pas dingue*,' he said: don't be crazy. 'The rebellion is over, sarge. You've got to lay down your arms.'

'And then what?'

Frank jerked an arm at the open lorries waiting at the end of the street. 'Tell your men to embus on those trucks.'

'I'm not ordering my men to go to prison.' The sergeant lowered his pistol. 'We've been betrayed.'

'By whom? Your officers?' asked Frank.

'No. By you bastards who've sided with De Gaulle.'

'I didn't side with anyone,' said Frank, disgusted. 'I'm just following orders, sergeant.'

The para on the other side of the barricade tapped his arm, which bore a tattoo of a flaming grenade and the words: *Legio patria nostra*. 'This doesn't mean anything any more?'

Frank pulled up his sleeve to show the same words tattooed on his own arm.

The two men glared at each other. Then the sergeant leaped over the obstacle and spat in the gutter at Frank's feet. He walked, staring straight ahead, towards the waiting trucks. It was up to his men whether they followed him or not. Halfway down the street, he turned and shouted bitterly at Frank, 'This is the end of the Legion. *La Légion est morte!*'

He slipped the safety catch on and threw his pistol deliberately into the crowd of civilians watching silently on the far side of the barricade. A hand reached up and caught the weapon adroitly. One by one, his men followed him over the barrier. In sullen silence they marched towards the waiting trucks, looking neither right nor left.

Frank avoided looking them in the eye. Nor could he meet the eyes of his own men. He knew they felt as sick as he did at the thought of sending comrades to a military prison.

When the trucks were full, an order was given. Engines started up and the convoy jerked its way in low gear over the broken road surface. The legionnaires on board started singing. At first it was 'Le Boudin', the Legion's favourite song. Then someone with a voice stronger than the rest led the singing men into Edith Piaf's famous refrain 'No Regrets'.

From the houses on both sides of the street, women started running towards the lorries, blowing kisses to the men who had risked the penalties of mutiny for them. Some threw flowers into the trucks; the legionnaires responded on the chorus by hurling their berets and kepis into the air.

As the trucks vanished from sight at the end of the street, hundreds of men's voices were singing in unison the words of Piaf's brave, sad philosophy of the streets. They did not regret what they had done; their code of honour had left them no alternative.

The ground was littered with berets and kepis. Frank recrossed the street to the line of armed men facing the barricade. He took back his rifle from the legionnaire who had been holding it and shouted to his men to open ranks, allowing the civilians to leave the area and return to their homes. Some of them spat at the Legion uniforms; most just looked tired and dispirited.

Ordering his men to police the area behind the barricades and collect any abandoned weapons or ammunition, Frank felt empty.

Something had gone terribly wrong for the Legion to be split in two like this. Some of the officers, he saw, had tears in their eyes. By contrast, Koenig's face was set in a stern mask, devoid of feeling: a face of stone. Frank had seen his commanding officer like that only once before, when a patrol in the Aurès had found hanging in an olive grove the bodies of five children who had been executed by the FLN for the counter-revolutionary crime of being inoculated by a French doctor.

*

Frank's hero, the one-eyed veteran of Dien Bien Phu, deserted the day after the arrest of the paras. His code of honour left him no choice.

Three months were to pass before Frank saw Koenig again. Frank was coming out of the gate of the Legion depot in Oran with a couple of other corporals, to take a drink at the café opposite. Since De Burgh's death, he had been drinking heavily. The sun was low in the evening sky. Frank shaded his eyes and looked again. It was hard to be certain but the tall, lean figure in a dark civilian suit and dark glasses, standing on the terrace of Chez Mimi and staring at him across the road, was either Captain Koenig or his double.

An army convoy drove past, blocking Frank's view. After the last truck had passed, he ran across the boulevard but the man had gone. And Koenig was on the run, a deserter with a price on his head. So logic said that it was unlikely he would show himself so near to the Legion depot where he might be recognised and arrested.

Frank waited for the other corporals to arrive and took a table on the terrace. They ordered three pastis and were halfway through their drinks when the unshaven, sad-faced man who was serving behind the bar approached their table and whispered in Frank's ear, 'There is a telephone message for you, monsieur.'

Frank did not bother to rise. 'You're mistaken,' he laughed. 'I haven't had a telephone call in three years.'

'No mistake,' insisted Gustave Laval. 'A Monsieur Koenig is asking for Corporal Hansen.'

Frank shot a look at his drinking companions, who had not overheard. He followed Gustave through the restaurant, noticing a pretty dark-haired girl of eleven talking to Mimi behind the bar. He recognised her as the child he had picked up in his arms the day of the cook's assassination, three years before. Marie-France, used to soldiers coming and going, did not spare him a second glance.

A telephone was off the hook, lying on the counter. As Frank went to pick it up, Gustave replaced the instrument and said from the corner of his mouth: 'In the back room, corporal.'

The door was guarded by Henri Rodriguez, whose loose jacket did not hide the shoulder holster he wore. 'Put your hands on the wall, corporal. Legs apart,' he grunted.

After a moment's hesitation, Frank allowed himself to be frisked.

Satisfied that he was clean, Henri threw open the door. In the room, wreathed in the thick smoke of Gauloises cigarettes, sat six men.

'Corporal Hansen!' Captain Koenig's voice had lost none of its parade-ground bark.

Frank sprang to attention. '*A vos ordres, mon capitaine!*'

'*Repos!* I'm not your captain. You can stand at ease.' Koenig stood up to face Frank. He took off the dark glasses, revealing the puckered scar where his eye had been. 'I won't mess you about, Hansen. First, I don't have to tell you what organisation we all belong to.'

'No.'

'Second: you joined the Legion for the same reason I did: to fight. You're not the type to surrender.'

'Who's surrendering, captain?'

'The government in Paris. But I'm offering you a choice, Hansen. We want you to join us and continue the fight.'

Frank was aware of the five other pairs of eyes watching his reactions. 'I'm only a corporal,' he shrugged uneasily.

'Rank doesn't matter,' said Koenig. 'There's a job you can do. We need someone with your knowledge of explosives but he has to be an American who can pass as a tourist in Paris.'

'You want me to desert, captain?'

'Desert?' Koenig made a gesture of irritation. 'We are living in extraordinary times, Hansen. Words like honour and duty no longer mean what they did. France is being governed by a traitor . . .'

'A madman,' Henri interrupted.

'Traitor or madman,' said Koenig, 'our duty is to save the country from him. There is a tradition of Americans and

Frenchmen helping each other in times of emergency. So we are asking you to join us.'

Frank moistened his lips. How would the other OAS men present react to a refusal to join their plot to assassinate President de Gaulle? Some if not all were armed . . .

'No,' he said, his pulse racing. 'I understand how you feel, *mon capitaine*, but France is not my country. I'm a legionnaire first and an American second.'

'I'm sorry,' said Koenig. His single eye pleaded silently with Frank, which made the man in uniform uneasy.

There was a long pause, broken by Frank. 'May I go, captain?'

'Hold it, Koenig!' One of the other men spoke for the first time. He was a fleshy, pale-faced man with bags under his eyes and spoke with the distinctive *pied noir* twang of the Oranais region. Frank guessed him to be one of the merchants who had made a fortune importing subsidised goods from France.

'I'm not having that man walk out of here, knowing that we are in this room. If he's not with us, he's against us, that's the rule.'

'I trust Hansen,' said Koenig coldly. 'He won't give us away. In any case, he knows only my name. The rest of you are safe enough.'

'So you say,' said the flabby merchant. He heaved his bulk out of the seat and came between Frank and Koenig. 'Listen, Yank. You will go back to the table on the terrace where you were drinking just now. You will stay there thirty minutes. If you leave before then, your back will be full of lead before you're halfway across the road to the depot.' He looked at Henri. 'Understood?'

Henri nodded.

'And, Hansen,' said Henri. 'Don't make any telephone calls in the next half-hour. Savvy? The same goes for either of your pals, so make sure they stay in their seats, too. Don't even get up to go and have a piss.'

10

Raoul opened the door of the barn and sat framed in the light. The magnificent voice of Maria Callas singing the Habanera from *Carmen* drove the silence away. He looked out into the night to see who had knocked. A rim of crescent moon was reflected in the ripples on the dark water below the cliff where the Dordogne swirled around the piers of St Martin's bridge.

'Hallo?' he called. 'Anyone there?'

A man's voice asked softly from the darkness, 'Are you alone?'

Raoul hesitated. 'Yes,' he said, 'I'm alone.'

From the shadows came the figure of a man dressed in the blue overalls of a peasant, with an old hat pulled down low over the face. Raoul recognised his friend only by the black eye-patch. Koenig slipped through the doorway, pulled the wheelchair inside and slammed the door.

The two old comrades embraced. Koenig grabbed a loaf of bread from the kitchen table and tore lumps off it, wolfing them down with slices of salami, hacked with a pocket knife off the long home-cured sausages dangling from the beams.

There was no need for Raoul to ask where Koenig had come from or why he was dressed in nondescript working clothes. This was not the first time he had sought refuge for the night in St Martin. It was 10 September 1961 – two days since the attempt on General de Gaulle's life at Pont-sur-Seine, for which the OAS was claiming responsibility.

Raoul poured a glass of the local red wine for Koenig and watched his friend eat. 'Thirteen years ago . . .' he voiced his thoughts, '. . . you and I were rivals to gain the Sword of Honour as best cadet of the year at St Cyr. We had everything ahead of us.'

'And look at us now,' said Koenig bitterly.

'Me a cripple and you a criminal on the run.'

Koenig swallowed the wine at a gulp and belched. 'Excuse my eating habits. I haven't had a bite for forty-eight hours.'

'What happened?' asked Raoul.

'We were betrayed,' his friend said bitterly. 'De Gaulle's security people were on us like a ton of bricks the moment the first shot rang out. I was lucky to get away.'

'You're not getting anywhere with all this violence.'

'It worked for the FLN,' said Koenig obstinately. 'They used violence to drive us out of North Africa.'

'It won't work in France,' Raoul disagreed. 'Terrorist tactics depend on terror. You were always quoting Sun Tsu, remember? All that stuff about "Kill one, frighten a thousand." It sounded so simple in theory. Yet it took the FLN thousands of assassinations of their own people in order to panic the entire Muslim population against the government of Algeria. Are you and your comrades prepared to start doing that to French men and women and children? Could you mount a random campaign of terror to drive the nation against De Gaulle?'

'No,' admitted Koenig. 'We wouldn't go that far.'

'Then you can't win. There's no middle course with terrorism.'

'We can't win, but we can't stop.'

'Give up this futile blood-feud, Koenig. It's not De Gaulle you're up against. It's History. You of all people ought to know that.'

'Give up?' Koenig was bitter. 'I can't settle down in France unless I want to spend my life under cover, waiting for the midnight knock on the door. I can't go back to being a regular soldier and I don't know how to do anything else. One way and another, this fight has become my identity.'

He was prowling around Raoul's spartan home, taking in the neat stacks of clients' accounts on the single large table and the collection of opera LPs. As a soldier he was more interested in the wall maps of South-East Asia, and the filing systems and racks of cardboard boxes full of press cuttings and research on the continuing Vietnam war, to which President Kennedy had contributed several thousand Green Berets. 'What's this all about?' he asked. 'You playing generals or something?'

Raoul was struck by an idea. To him, Koenig had the look of a man who would do something stupid soon, just to end the struggle inside himself. So he said, 'I might have something else to offer you.'

'Like what?' The bitterness in Koenig's voice embraced losing an eye and a hand or both legs.

'If you're on the run, how do you slip into and out of France?'

'There are always ways.'

'Your photograph has been in all the newspapers. With a missing eye and a damaged hand, you're pretty recognisable. They must keep a strict watch for you at the borders?'

Koenig laughed. 'We come and go by courtesy of the Union Corse.'

'The Corsican mafia?'

A nod. 'Someone did a deal with them. Or maybe they just want to damage the government. I don't know. Anyway, they bring us into and out of France through Marseilles with the little packets of dope that originate here –' he tapped the Golden Triangle on the map of Burma, Thailand and Laos – 'and end up on the streets of New York.'

'That's more or less what I guessed.' Raoul concealed his mounting excitement. 'And supposing you wanted to bring some luggage with you, from just that part of the world – all the way back here to France. Could they handle that too?'

'At a price, anything's possible.' Koenig stretched tiredly.

'What's on your mind? You want me to smuggle you in a machine-gun so you can hold up the local bank?'

Raoul's eyes were bright with excitement. He took a bottle of bootleg *marc* from a shelf under the sink, poured two glasses and held one out to Koenig. 'We've had a raw deal,' he said. 'I'm not crying about it, neither are you, but I think life owes you and me a favour.'

In a moment of intuition, Koenig looked from the large map of Vietnam to his old comrade. He leaned forward and placed a hand on Raoul's arm. 'Would this have anything to do with Dien Bien Phu and that bloody court martial?'

Raoul smiled. 'How would you like to become a partner in an operation to recover my gold?'

Koenig slapped him on the shoulder. 'So you didn't give it away to the Viets, you old bastard?'

'I'll tell you . . .'

Koenig listened without question to Raoul's story of the day he had taken Minh to where the gold had been hidden, the unexploded shell suddenly erupting earth and bodies from the pit, the beating, the resumed digging by the fresh fatigue party of *bo-doi*. Knowing the country and the conditions, he could see Raoul lying on the edge of the pit with Minh in his commissar's uniform standing over him chain-smoking. He saw the *can-bô*'s leap of triumph into the pit when the first ammunition box containing the treasure was unearthed and torn open to spill gold coins into the mud.

'So you told them where the pay-chest was hidden. After four months in a black box, I'd have done the same.'

'Correction!' Raoul rapped. He manoeuvred the wheelchair so that he could watch Koenig's face closely. 'I told Minh where half of the gold was hidden.'

'Jesus H. Christ!' As the words sank in, a huge, crooked grin of admiration spread slowly over Koenig's face. 'You had split the gold into two lots? And hid them in two separate caches?'

Raoul nodded.

'And you gave one away. Which means that the other half of the gold is still there?'

'So I believe.'

Koenig knew what the chaos of the battlefield was like. 'There must have been all hell breaking loose on the last night when you attempted to fight your way out from Isabelle with Lafont's men. So why go to the trouble of burying the gold in two caches?'

'It was fortuitous,' Raoul shrugged. 'I wasn't trying to be clever. Gold is heavy. There was no way we could have carried all of it on our backs, fighting our way through the Viet lines. So I buried half before the breakout and distributed the rest among a squad of men who were unwounded. When we were driven back into the perimeter and it was clear that the fight was all over, I ordered a second hole to be dug, to hide the second half of the gold. It was that cache which I betrayed to Minh.'

His eyes, focused somewhere on the other side of Koenig, were seeing again the incredulity on the exhausted faces of the German legionnaires when he had ordered them to start digging the second hole. They had obeyed, cursing the Legion and the Viets, but Raoul most of all. . . .

Koenig's thoughts too were far away. He pictured the scene as it must have been: exhausted men spending their last reserves of ammunition and energy in the attempt to fight their way through the encirclement, their despair when they were driven back, their last chance gone and death staring them in the face.

His admiration for the man in the wheelchair was boundless. As no civilian ever could, Koenig appreciated what reserves of inner strength it must have taken for Raoul to survive his wounds and resist Minh's psychological pressures. That he had still had the cunning or the courage to cheat his captors of half the treasure after the long months of pain and torture, was almost beyond belief.

'And now you want me,' Koenig was thinking aloud, 'to go back to Dien Bien Phu and get the other half of the gold, whose whereabouts you did not give away?'

'It's not as simple as that,' said Raoul hoarsely. His palms were clammy with perspiration. 'First I have to know: are you in or out?'

'In,' said Koenig without hesitation. 'Count me in.'

Neither man slept. It was dawn before Koenig had asked all the questions to which he wanted answers. Some Raoul had given him neatly and concisely in words. Others had been in the form of maps swiftly retrieved from Raoul's filing system or passages marked in books on which he put his finger in seconds. Raoul's barn, as Koenig realised, was exactly what it had seemed to him at first sight: a command centre for a military operation. He had discarded the idea only because it seemed unlikely that a man in a wheelchair could be masterminding a military operation.

'Is it possible?' asked Raoul anxiously, when he was finished.

Koenig laughed. 'I walked out of Dien Bien Phu. Most of my companions died, but it is possible. I'm the living proof. We need three or four men. They'll have to be fit and in the peak of training.'

'*Le deuxième REP?*' Raoul named the Legion's crack para regiment. The first REP had been disbanded as punishment for its part in the Algiers rebellion.

'Probably,' said Koenig. 'They must be a team, used to working together without wasting time asking questions. To get the gold, they've got to be quickly in and quickly out of Vietnam. There'll be no time to make mistakes.'

'You'll go in with them?'

'No.' Koenig had already decided this. 'I trust my Corsican friends, but not too far. So I'll stay on the Laos side of the border, to hold both ends of the operation together and make sure there are no nasty surprises when the recovery party gets back with the goods. The crucial member of the team – the hardest to find – will be a man who speaks Vietnamese and Meo. He'll have to recruit bearers from the Meo hill people on the way in. We'll call him Mr A. The others are B,C and D.'

'They all have to be men we can trust,' said Raoul.

'Trust?' Koenig drew a loaded Mauser automatic from an inside pocket.

Raoul shook his head. 'I meant afterwards. If any one of them talks, the trail will lead to me.'

'Now that is a problem,' agreed Koenig. 'We both know what most legionnaires are like. They get drunk, spend too much and talk big, boasting to girls or bartenders of their exploits.'

'So we need three or four men who are among the best professional soldiers in the world and who won't spill the beans afterwards, but will be happy to settle quietly down here where I can keep an eye on them.'

'That's all?' The irony was plain.

'No,' said Raoul. 'At the moment there's a war going on in Laos. NVA troops and Pathet Lao are all over the place. No way we could get even a small party safely in and out. So we have to wait for the right moment. Sooner or later, there'll be a truce. We have to be ready for it and grab the moment.'

'*Carpe diem?*' grinned Koenig. 'Your old motto . . .'

There was the sound of a car driving up to the house and stopping. Koenig was instantly on his feet.

'Relax,' said Raoul. 'That'll be Louise, coming to stay for the weekend.'

'Who's she?' Koenig slipped the safety catch off the Mauser and stood behind the door. 'A regular woman?'

'That describes her quite well.'

The look on Raoul's face told Louise as soon as she came through the doorway that something had happened. He looked younger, transformed; all the bitter lines that had made him look so much older than his years were gone – wiped away by a new sense of purpose. She embraced him and only then saw the tall, lean man standing behind the door with a gun in his hand.

'I know you,' she said calmly. 'You're Raoul's friend who came to warn him in the hospital.'

Koenig held the revolver awkwardly as Louise stood on

212

tiptoe to plant a kiss on his stubbly cheek below the missing eye. She took no notice of the weapon.

'You must be hungry,' she said, knowing what he was doing there. 'There's never much food in Raoul's house, but I've got coffee and fresh rolls in the car. I'll make you breakfast.'

Koenig, the gun hanging at his side, turned to Raoul when she was gone. 'Can I trust her not to blab?'

'You can trust Louise with your life.'

'It comes to the same thing, my friend.'

11

*T*he offer I made Koenig was genuine enough. Without him, I knew that my chances of recovering the fortune I had buried in Dien Bien Phu were slight. But I also knew from the way the American war was building up in Vietnam that our partnership was premature. It was going to be years before anyone could go into north-east Vietnam, let alone come safely out again.

My motive in making the offer was to keep my friend alive. I hoped that knowing how much I needed him might stop Koenig throwing away his life in some desperate and pointless act of violence. It depressed me more than I admitted even to Louise, to see reduced to the level of a hired killer the man I had always pictured as a gallant knight fighting beneath the fleur-de-lys banner.

Of course it was easy for me in my enforced capacity of spectator to see that the clandestine violence of the OAS would lead nowhere – as it was impossible for someone at the very heart of the turmoil like Koenig to gain any perspective on the events in which he was enmeshed.

But events moved fast. Nine months later, the last French troops were leaving Algeria. There were many in the Legion who wanted to blow up the Quartier Viénot at Sidi-bel-Abbès rather than let it fall into the hands of the enemy – an enemy which, so we believed, had been beaten militarily and yet been accorded victory *for political reasons. For longer than a century the barracks had been a kind of martial cathedral, a holy place where men were dedicated to the traditions and glory of the Legion. To leave this shrine and allow it to be defiled by les bicots was an order that stuck in the gullet. Yet discipline prevailed and the Legion contented itself with a ceremonial burning of the precious trophies and relics that were subject to oath 'never to be taken back to French soil'.*

On one issue, the Legion stood firm. To avoid its certain desecration by the FLN after the French withdrawal, the Monument des Morts in bel-Abbès was taken apart by the pioneers. Designed, sculpted and cast in bronze by legionnaires to commemorate the names of all those men who had died since 1830 fighting for France, it was shipped across the Mediterranean and rebuilt on the parade ground of the Legion's new headquarters at Aubagne in Provence.

The convoy bearing Frank Hansen to the docks for shipment to France stopped outside the depot in Oran. With an unspecified delay ahead of them, Frank and several others strolled across the boulevard for a last drink in Chez Mimi.

Behind the bar, Gustave Laval was stacking clean glasses carefully under the counter. Marie was watching him. There were days when her husband seemed to have shrunk mentally to being just a barman. He had no thoughts that went beyond the confines of their lives in Mimi's bar – as though anything bigger was too painful to think about. More and more she was running the family, what few decisions there were left to make.

Marie called Mimi from the kitchen and helped her and Gustave serve the legionnaires their drinks. Even Mimi had lost her good nature. She no longer told anyone not to worry about things. Her nephew on the run with a price on his head, her business worth nothing, she had taken to praying and spent hours each day in a scruffy little church run by a Spanish priest down by the docks.

Most of the men took their drinks inside. There were no other clients in the once busy bar. The OAS had dynamited

Oran's oil terminal the day before and the air on the terrace was thick with falling smuts. The conflagration was a symbolic funeral pyre: the town was dying at the end of a state of undeclared civil war which had reigned for two months. The civilian population had been in armed insurrection against French regular army troops under the ruthless General Katz, while Oran's own General Jouhaud languished in a condemned cell on the other side of the Mediterranean, convicted of high treason. The civil administration had stopped working: dustbins were not emptied, traffic lights did not work. The town was falling to pieces. Marie-France had not been to school for weeks and hung about the bar, chatting to the soldiers. Marie hated to see her twelve-year-old daughter mixing exclusively with prostitutes and soldiers, but could think of no alternative.

'And now the Legion is leaving,' she said to Gustave. 'Once they're gone, it won't be safe here.'

'Nothing we can do about it,' Gustave said glumly. It had become a refrain whenever she asked him what he thought about anything.

Marie had set to with pen and paper several weeks before, trying to find an avenue out of the hopelessness into which Gustave and so many others were plunged. Some of the friends in France to whom she wrote did not reply; they did not want anything to do with Algeria or *pieds noirs*. But her cousin Raoul had replied by return with a list of questions. She had answered them at once and received a firm offer of help.

Their bags were packed. That had been easy, despite the baggage restriction of two suitcases per person; the Laval family's few remaining possessions had filled only three cases, which now stood ready at the end of the bar. The taxi was due any moment.

Marie took Raoul's letter from her pocket and read it again:

Don't worry about money! There are some advantages in having a cousin who's a respected accountant. I've been through the whole project, costed it and put together a package which adds up to 100 per cent financing. Don't ask me how! The short answer is: perjury.

The big thing is that, for someone with Gustave's drive and energy, it's a chance to start again.

She put the letter away. Gustave's drive and energy.... She had not dared to tell Raoul that her husband's only interest was in anaesthetising himself each morning and staying that way till nightfall.

Gustave saw her tuck the letter away. She had not read it to him and so far he had not asked what was in it. 'What's Raoul doing these days?' he asked.

'He's an accountant.'

Marie hated the mirthless laugh with which he greeted the news.

'That sums up the world we live in, Marie,' he said bitterly. 'Raoul Duvalier, the once-glamorous playboy-sportsman-hero is now a cripple, reduced to earning his living as an accountant.'

The legionnaires waited through the long, hot afternoon, leaning against their yellow desert-camouflaged trucks still painted with the names of bases in towns to which they would never return. A column of civilians shuffled themselves and their baggage a few inches at a time along the quay. Among them Frank recognised the girl from Chez Mimi. It seemed a strange quirk of fate that one of the last faces he should see as he left Algeria was the same girl he had met under such traumatic circumstances on his second day in-country.

At twenty-two, after nearly four years of war, he felt old. He thought about De Burgh lying in his stony grave. The legionnaire's code of honour commanded: *In combat, you never abandon your arms, your wounded or your dead.* Yet by leaving De Burgh and the others behind, Frank felt they were doing just that. In a sense they were all casualties.

Beside De Burgh's grave lay the ghost of an innocent boy from Jacksonville who had wanted to serve – to give and not to count the cost, as the old Jesuit prayer put it.

There was still one year to go before the end of his five-year engagement but from now on, Frank determined, he was going to look after Number One.

He wondered where Koenig was and what he was doing.

At last the overcrowded ship pulled out of the harbour. The legionnaires at the stern rail looked back across the blue water at the town. Many of the civilians were weeping openly. Others stared out to sea, not wanting to see where their homes had been. There were fires burning unattended in the town and the dockside was littered with abandoned, looted cars.

'Can this be the right place?' Marie wondered aloud as Gustave stopped the car outside Raoul's tumbledown barn above the little village of St Martin. The rusting old *deux chevaux* purchased in Marseilles represented the sum of their capital.

Raoul's address – Templars' Tower – sounded picturesque. The reality was a ruined heap of masonry that towered several storeys high and a lean-to barn with a roof in bad repair and cracks in the walls against which several ugly concrete buttresses were fighting a losing battle.

Recalling the elegant house at Bourg-la-Reine where Raoul had grown up and the grandiose family home in Normandy where they had spent the long summer holidays together, Marie shuddered.

A note on the front door said: Use Side Entrance. They followed the high wall that surrounded the cottage garden and found the *porte cochère* held open by a woman of about Marie's own age in a light summer dress and flat-heeled sandals. She had obviously heard the car drive up and greeted them all with a warm smile, kissing Marie on both cheeks.

'Come in,' she said with a strong Canadian accent. 'I've been longing to meet you all. Raoul has told me so much about you. I'm Louise.'

She embraced Marie-France laughingly. 'Raoul said you were a little girl and you're a young woman, almost as tall as your mother.'

With an adolescent's uncertainty, Marie-France blushed at the compliment.

They were standing in a courtyard garden, cut off from the world by high walls. Raised flower beds, which a gardener in a wheelchair could look after, held sage and thyme, basil, tarragon and other herbs she did not recognise. There were no flowers; it was a masculine enclosure in which straight paths made it easy to negotiate a wheelchair. There was a table at the far end of the garden with a bottle in an ice bucket and some glasses.

'Oh, I love champagne,' said Marie-France.

'I've got a confession.' Louise took her hand and led the way towards the house. 'I'm afraid we haven't the money for real champagne. It's only a *blanc de blancs* but it tastes just as good if you like the people you're drinking it with.'

There was the sound of a man's voice, talking on the telephone near an open window.

'Raoul won't be long,' she said, inviting them to sit. 'He's on the phone to Monsieur Marassin.'

'Who's that?' asked Marie.

'The man who owns the farm you're buying. Apparently Marassin has changed his mind about selling and Raoul is now changing it back again.'

'We haven't even seen the property yet,' said Marie hesitantly.

'Oh, it's very beautiful,' said Louise. 'You'll love the house; it's a dilapidated eighteenth-century château in a glorious situation, with a big lawn stretching right down to the Dordogne. But it'll be hard work; the whole place has been neglected since before the war. . . .'

'Did you have a war here too?' Marie-France was curious. 'In France? There seem to have been wars everywhere.'

'It was before you were born,' said her mother.

An avid student of body language, Louise was watching

Gustave. He had hardly met her eyes since he arrived and sat listlessly in his chair, not really listening to the conversation. His dull eyes seemed more interested in the bottle of wine than the future. Not the man to take on an old dilapidated château and a farm gone virtually wild, she decided. Whatever was Raoul thinking of?

'How is Raoul?' asked Marie.

'Oh, he's fi . . .' Louise stopped herself. That wasn't what Raoul's cousin was asking. Cautiously, bearing in mind how some people felt about the handicapped, she said, 'You know that he lost the use of his legs?'

'He told us that in his letters.'

She thought it only fair to give them a warning. 'What Raoul went through has changed him in many ways. I never knew him before, but I imagine you may find it hard to recognise your cousin.'

'Are you Uncle Raoul's wife?' asked Marie-France.

'Not really,' Louise laughed. 'I'm more like a friend. I visit him most weekends. The rest of the time he lives alone here, except that he's always buzzing about in his car, seeing clients and arguing with the tax people.'

'Huh!' Gustave spoke for the first time since his arrival. 'Raoul . . . an accountant!'

'He's a very good one,' said Louise defensively. 'He's managed to get you a loan to buy Château St Martin – if you want to buy it, that is.'

'Of course they'll want to buy it.' The strong, confident voice came from the doorway where Raoul sat in his wheelchair. 'It's too good an opportunity to pass up.'

Oh God! thought Marie, covering her mouth with one hand. Can that be Raoul? Is that thin man hunched in a wheelchair, with the sallow, lined face and a shock of grey hair . . . is that all that is left of the tall, handsome athlete I remember?

She turned away before he could read her thoughts and stared down the garden. Raoul a cripple with a broken body. Gustave crippled inside, a man broken in spirit. Herself? She tried not to look in mirrors. . . . Of their generation in that strange garden, only the Canadian woman seemed intact.

Then the energy of Raoul's enthusiasm for the project of putting Château St Martin back on its feet infected her. He had done all the financial work for them: cash flow, interest repayments, subsidies, tax advantages – everything was worked out on paper. The body might be damaged, she thought, but Raoul's will was as strong as ever. Poring over the sheets of paper he had prepared, she began to believe it might be possible – if Gustave could get a grip on himself.

Raoul ignored their first reaction to his crippled legs – he was used to that – and talked persuasively over a glass of *blanc de blancs* about the opportunities that lay ahead.

'You're young,' he said, 'and healthy. If you put your energy into this, in ten years' time you can recuperate all your lost fortunes.'

'Oh yes,' sneered Gustave. He had not bothered to look at the file of paper. 'Like we did with our farm in Enfida.'

'That's behind you.' Raoul dismissed the past. He slapped his legs derisively. 'If I've learned one thing, *mon vieux*, it is. . . . What was that song Piaf sings, Louise?'

' "No Regrets".'

'No regrets.' He raised the glass in a toast. 'Ever.'

His eyes dared them all to disbelieve his philosophy. Marie raised her glass and chinked it against his. In that moment he looked so young and boyish that she saw him not as a crippled version of the man he had been, but as what he was. Forget the legs, she thought, and he's still a stunning man. His movements have energy. He radiates will-power and those mocking brown eyes of his make me feel like I'm sixteen again.

She felt a blush spread over her face and neck. Louise was looking at her oddly. Marie coughed to cover her confusion and Raoul laughed at her. She wanted to hug him for being alive, for still having drive and enthusiasm. His eyes, she thought, they haven't changed. And in his soul he's still Olympic class.

Raoul checked his wristwatch. 'Marassin's expecting you

in fifteen minutes. Don't listen to him about the problems – how the place is run down, the ground's no good, etc., etc. He's just trying to put you off. And don't talk money with him. He's a cunning old devil. On the one hand, he'll frighten you off the place and in the next breath, he'll put the price up. He wins by confusing people. Just tell him I'm your financial adviser and leave it to me to make the deal.'

Marie embraced him. It was confusing; he was so like Gustave had been and yet so different.

His arms hugged her with surprising strength. 'I'm happy you came,' he said.

She felt warm tears run down her cheeks and let them fall on his face. They were tears of happiness, after all the anguish. 'It's going to be all right,' she said. 'I don't know why I'm crying now.'

Her daughter was not able to kiss him. Raoul helped by stretching an arm to shake Marie-France's hand so she did not have to move close to the wheelchair. 'Come and see me again,' he said. 'If all goes well and your parents like Château St Martin, we'll have some real champagne next time *pour arroser la maison*.'

She blushed again. 'I didn't know you'd heard me.'

He winked.

Gustave was halfway to the gate when he turned and asked, 'This other project you mentioned in the letter to Marie. You didn't tell us about that.'

'Ah . . .' There was a trace of disappointment in Raoul's voice, swiftly concealed. 'That fell through. In fact, it wasn't a good idea anyway, Gustave.'

As Louise walked back up the garden after closing the gate behind their visitors, she said, 'I liked your cousin Marie. She must have been very beautiful when she was young.'

Raoul was listening to the sound of the car starting. He stared at Louise, examining her from head to foot as though he had not seen her for a long time. 'She was,' he said absently. 'Very beautiful.'

*

Louise! Now there's someone who should bear me a grudge. And she certainly knew all my secrets. For a long time she was the only person in whom I confided all my plans. As to motives for betrayal, I gave her so many over the years.

I took her love, which was mine for the asking at Torrens. I spurned it and took it again. And she took nothing from me ever, except for one thing that she desperately needed.

I think she knew from the beginning that I could never love her. The irony is that but for her I should never have learned to love anyone ever again. For years I needed all my emotional energy for myself in order to rebuild a personality in the empty husk that had come back from Minh's black box. By the time that was accomplished I had lost the habit of loving anyone except myself. Or perhaps I had never had it; it is hard to be certain of anything in my life before Dien Bien Phu, so intertwined are memory and my fantasies of that time.

Louise gave me everything and in return I gave nothing. I could have lied and pretended, to make her happy. I could have learned to love her as she deserved. But I didn't. Instead I humiliated her many times, which was cruel and unnecessary. I chose to hurt her because she was the only person I could reach and I needed to hurt someone.

And I lied to her and cheated, by pretending to need her when I was whole again and should have let her go. Clinging to a crutch we no longer need is a trick the handicapped learn fast, but it's a nasty one.

So a detective would have her high on his list of suspects. That woman must bear a grudge against a man who treated her so badly, he would say. But then, I don't think detectives very often meet angels.

'I beg your pardon,' Raoul apologised. 'I wasn't listening.'

'I said, that husband of hers is not up to much, is he?'

Raoul stretched out a hand to grasp Louise's. 'Gustave is what's meant by the phrase "a broken man".' He sighed. 'Another one of our generation crushed by forces none of us could control.'

'Not what you were looking for, for this mysterious other job?'

He shook his head.

Sensing the disappointment, she sat on the ledge of the flower bed next to the wheelchair. 'So how will he sort out the château? That's not a job for a man with a broken spirit.'

'The answer is Marie,' mused Raoul. 'When I knew her, she was the soft and clinging type, content to let Gustave make all the decisions. Now, after what they've been through in Vietnam and Algeria, she's twice the person she was.'

'But can she take on a job like this?'

He laughed softly and squeezed her hand. 'If she decides to, she'll do it. Remember she's a Duvalier by birth. Back us into a corner and we come out fighting.'

Koenig rang when it was 6 a.m. in his part of the world but only midnight in France. 'Well?' he asked.

'No good,' said Raoul.

'*Merde!* He's not the man we're looking for? Not Mr A?'

'Definitely not.'

12

Invited twice to desert by men who had had enough of the endless spit and polish of garrison life in metropolitan France, Frank refused. He did, however, stick to the private deal he had made with himself on the boat crossing the Med. He became an old soldier, serving his remaining time without looking for trouble. He sought out the cushy jobs, especially those that took him away from base on detachment, like courier duty, escorting prisoners, delivering equipment – anything to get away from the daily round of the barracks in Aubagne.

Much of his free time was spent in a bar near the Vieux Port of Marseilles which was run by a former sergeant in the Legion's paras, a heavily built Swede by the name of Larsen who had been invalided out with wounds received in Vietnam and still walked with a noticeable limp.

'Another brawl last night,' Larsen greeted Frank, who was helping himself to a beer behind the bar.

'I heard you called in the MPs.' Frank's only concern was that the bar might be placed off limits.

'You think I'm crazy? It was the neighbours who called them in, not me. The locals lose no chance to drop a legion-naire in the shit.'

'Why do they hate us so much?' asked Frank.

'Beats me,' said the big Swede. 'I've been running this

bar for eight years and some of my neighbours still don't talk to me. They seem to think that all legionnaires are rapists and drunks.'

Frank summed up the French attitude to the Legion. 'They're proud to have us die for them, but we can't marry their daughters.'

The Swede swept a meaty paw round in a semicircle. There were a couple of dozen off-duty legionnaires drinking, chatting up the girls and playing billiards. He guffawed. 'Would you want a legionnaire to marry your daughter, if you had one?'

Frank had to laugh. 'I don't think I would, Larsen.'

At the next table a couple of middle-aged American tourists from Kansas were running through a catalogue of complaints which ranged from the lack of a bath in their hotel room to the prices they had to pay for meals and the general lack of hygiene in Europe. They didn't like the food either, on account of the garlic. And why didn't the natives speak English. . . ?

Behind their backs, Frank exchanged a grin with the barman who understood every word the tourists were saying.

The couple from Kansas left the bar and headed, cameras dangling, downhill towards the port. Frank crossed to their table and picked up the newspaper they had left behind. It was the European edition of the previous day's *Herald Tribune*. The front-page headline was of President Kennedy's decision to set up MACV – the Military Assistance Command, Vietnam. The first American combat troops, Frank read, had already disembarked on Vietnamese soil, where the 57th Helicopter Company had been in action against North Vietnamese troops a long way south of the seventeenth parallel agreed as the demarcation line during the Geneva conferences.

Frank spun the paper on the bar.

The Swede stopped polishing glasses and read the piece. 'Kennedy's a Yankee bastard,' he said, unimpressed.

'What do you have against him?'

'This guy –' a finger thick as Frank's thumb stabbed the

president's photograph in the newspaper – 'was telling us a year ago to get out of Algeria because the country belonged to the Arabs. Now he thinks South-East Asia is his own backyard. In fact, he's left it eight years too late to do any good in Vietnam.'

Frank looked blank.

'It's their fault,' said the barman, nodding at the couple from Kansas, 'that we lost Dien Bien Phu. Because of that defeat, the Yanks are now having to go back in and take on the Viets. I wish them luck.' His face contradicted the words.

'Still,' he added more calmly, 'for you it's a piece of good luck, Hansen. Your time in the Legion's nearly up. You can go home and enlist for Uncle Sam. Take my advice and get shipped to Vietnam. With five years in the Legion behind you, you'll make sergeant in no time.'

'Not me,' laughed Frank. 'I've had enough soldiering for a lifetime. You won't catch me in uniform again.'

'You're right.' Larsen had every bartender's agility at changing sides. 'When your time's up, get out of uniform and stay out.'

Someone put a coin in the jukebox. Frank's face fell as Buddy Holly's voice started belting out 'That'll be the Day'. The song brought a wave of guilt that he was alive and drinking beer, listening to music and picking up a girl now and then while De Burgh and thousands of other men who had died to no purpose lay rotting in alien soil on the other side of the Med.

The Greyhound bus was already leaving Jacksonville when Frank tapped the driver on the shoulder. 'Pull over, will you? I want to get out.'

It was 5.30 a.m. and most of the other travellers were asleep. The driver glanced at the tough-looking passenger with the short haircut and the new denim suit who wanted to alight. With a squeal of brakes, the coach stopped in a parking lot on the edge of town. 'You nearly missed your destination,' the man yawned. 'It happens on the overnight buses. Folks sleep their way from one state to the next.'

'I wasn't asleep,' said Frank. 'It's just that Jacksonville isn't as big as I remember. Everything looks kinda different.'

'Been away long?'

'Five years, six weeks, three days.'

'You've been counting?'

'Sort of.'

The driver looked away and hit the button that released the door with a hiss of escaping air.

Frank stood on the bottom step and stuck his head out of the open doorway. 'I don't recall this parking lot.'

'It was the school,' said the driver, wanting to be rid of a man who had spent five years counting the days. 'Some local big-shot bought it up and made it into a supermarket.'

'Jacksonville High?' Frank looked again. Where the school buildings had stood five years before was just a flat cinder-strewn parking lot.

'Have a good day,' said the driver. For good luck he made the Indian hand sign for peace, to which Frank replied with a loose legionnaire's salute.

With another hiss of air, the pneumatic door closed and the coach ground its way up the road, heading south to the state boundary. The keenness of pre-dawn reminded Frank of early morning patrols in the desert. He sniffed the air, which smelt clean after the all-night fug inside the bus. On the far side of the car park stretched a blank brick wall, the rear of the new supermarket. A delivery truck labelled *Hansen's Foods – Fruit Division* was unloading crates of apples at a loading bay. Nobody else in Jacksonville seemed to be awake.

Frank hefted his holdall over one shoulder and walked round to the front of the supermarket. The building was dwarfed by a huge illuminated sign which towered above it: *Hansen's Foods.* A simplified portrait of his father wearing a stetson beamed goodwill at the empty parking spaces. Frank saluted the sign ironically, 'Hi, Dad!' Some local big-shot, the driver had said. That had to be Sven.

He took his time walking through the town. After the medieval French towns he was used to with their narrow

228

streets of old stone houses, Jacksonville's wide modern main street and timber-frame buildings seemed insubstantial and temporary – more like a deserted film set than a real town. He headed up the main street, looking for memories.

The drugstore was unchanged. Still the same tall chrome stools on which he and the other boys in the football team had ogled the girls. Every other store seemed different.

A fine drizzle started to fall but he kept walking. He heard the swish of tyres behind him. 'Where are you going, fella?'

It was a police car with the sign unlit. Frank bent to see inside. He did not recognise the driver. 'Home,' he said.

'And where's that, wise guy?'

''Bout two miles out of town.'

'What's your name, fella?' The voice was hard and unfriendly.

'Hansen.'

'By golly, it's Frank.' The second patrolman, seated on the far side of the car, explained to the driver, 'Sven's boy.' He got out and pumped Frank's hand. 'You've been away a long time.'

'Too long,' Frank smiled. It was the right thing to say.

'Can we give you a lift?' the driver asked, to make amends.

'Nope. I'll walk.'

'You're gonna get wet.'

'That's OK by me.'

'Have a good day.' The car sped off into the drizzle.

Frank lifted his face and let the rain wet it all over.

Through the glass kitchen door Frank could see his father sitting alone in the kitchen, drinking coffee and listening to the radio news.

He was about to turn the handle, then stopped. Five years before, he had rehearsed a hundred savage things to say to his father on his return. Why was I so angry? he wondered now. I was such a kid. . . . Why shouldn't the old man have some fun?

The dog came into the kitchen, scratching itself with a

hind leg. It stopped, sensing someone outside. When it barked, Sven looked up to see a rain-drenched man with his collar turned up and a holdall on his shoulder. 'Who the hell are you?' he shouted.

Frank grinned. His father hadn't changed. When in doubt, shout! was one of Sven's sayings. He stuck his face into the light.

'Jesus! Frank!' The door was torn open and Frank found himself wrapped in Sven's powerful embrace. 'It's good to see you back, boy.' A fist was thumping Frank's shoulder blades, another pummelling his kidneys. 'It's so good to see you back. You don't know how good it is.'

'It's good to be back, Dad.' Frank dropped his bag on the floor and extricated himself from his father's welcome to pat the dog and ruffle its ears.

Sven stood back and looked at his son proudly. 'By God they made a man of you in that Foreign Legion, Frank. You're as tall as me.'

Frank grinned lopsidedly. 'I didn't win any medals though,' he apologised.

'You threw mine in the pool,' Sven recalled.

'I wanted to teach you a lesson.'

It was Sven's turn to grin. 'Lotta people tried to do that, Frank.' There was a brief silence between them.

'I don't believe in apologies,' said Sven, 'but I'm sorry you were upset by that incident out at the cabin.' He stopped. 'I was going to call you Junior. That doesn't seem right any more.'

Frank shrugged.

'Am I hell sorry?' Sven corrected himself. 'Did you the world of good, leaving home like that. Look at you, built like a football forward. What do you weigh? Over two hundred pounds, huh?' He punched Frank's biceps none too gently. 'Solid muscle.'

'Ninety-five kilos,' said Frank. 'I don't know what that is in pounds.'

'Coffee?'

'Thanks.'

They sat at the long table drinking the strong black brew.

'How's Joanne?' asked Frank, man-to-man.

Sven closed the door conspiratorially. 'I got rid of her just after you left. They're all the same. After a while, they take liberties and you have to kick 'em out.'

'Oh?'

'But . . .' Sven's eyes lit up. 'I have a beautiful creature works for me now, name of Marlene. Makes Marilyn Monroe look like a nun. Wait till you see her.'

'Does, er . . .' There was one question Frank had to ask. 'Does Mom know about your girlfriends?'

Sven dropped his eyes. 'Well she does and she doesn't, if you get my meaning.'

There was something in his father's voice that made Frank ask, 'How is Mom? Recently some of her letters have been weird, disconnected.'

'She drinks.'

'What?'

'I shouldn't say this about my own wife, but she does drink too much.'

'You mean she has a problem?' Frank whistled. He looked at the closed door.

'Let's talk about you,' said Sven. 'What are your plans?'

'Jesus, Dad! I just got home.'

Outside, a motor horn sounded one discreet blip. Sven looked at the clock on the wall. 'That's my driver. Time to go. Look, I'll put my cards on the table, Frank. I'm starting a new line in food products: Sven Hansen's Swedish Range. Not just for our own stores, but nation-wide. The investment in publicity alone will be colossal, so I don't want any problems with this one. I need a line manager I can trust to look after things when I'm away – which is a lot of the time. D'you want the job?'

'I'm a soldier, Dad. I don't know how to manage a food factory.'

'I'll teach you on the job.' Sven grabbed a rechargeable electric razor from its bracket on the wall and started shaving. 'Don't forget I was a soldier too.' He negotiated the point of his chin carefully. 'What did they pay you over there in Europe, Frank? Peanuts, I guess.'

'Not a lot.'

'So it's time to start earning. You had a good time. Now you settle down and make some money. That's what life's about. I'm offering you –' Sven felt his chin and put the razor away – 'twenty thousand dollars a year, Frank. Plus benefits and a new car each year. If you don't want the job –' he snapped his fingers – 'I'll find someone else who does, easy as that.'

'You don't change, Dad.'

'Why should I?' Sven flashed the big, wicked grin that made people smile at him even when they knew he was railroading them, using them, conning them. 'I like the way I am. What d'you say about the job?'

'I'll think about it.'

'I'll give you till tomorrow.'

'That's not long.'

Sven was shrugging into a light cotton jacket. 'If I was advertising the job, I'd say: The successful applicant will make quick decisions – and be right every time. So, if twenty-four hours isn't long enough, you're the wrong man for the job.'

The door slammed and Sven was gone.

Frank felt the excitement that his father had always generated. It was like living at twice the speed of ordinary people. He prowled about the silent house, the dog following. Not much had changed, except that one of the guest bedrooms seemed to have been converted for his father's use. Frank's own bedroom had been redecorated and the adjoining bedroom converted into an en suite bathroom. He took a shower and lay on the bed, wide awake and wondering if he had come home.

13

On 22 November 1963 all America stayed glued to its television sets from mid-afternoon onwards. A CBS reporter outside the book depository in Dallas was grappling for words on-screen as Frank calmed his mother, whose hysterical phone call had brought him home from the factory long before his usual finishing time.

'It's a terrible thing.' She sat staring at the television. 'Who would want to kill the President?'

'I don't know, Mom.'

She was wearing a hostess gown and high-heeled shoes. Half her hair was in curlers, the other half partly brushed out. It was unclear to Frank whether she had been getting ready to go out, or just returned from a luncheon engagement. Her bedroom looked like a cross between a hairdresser's salon and a bar room.

Frank took the glass from her hand. 'This stuff doesn't help, you know.'

She contradicted him. 'Sometimes it does, honey.'

He turned the sound up and sat on her bed to listen to the reports coming in.

His mother was pouring herself another glass of brandy when the telephone rang.

'That'll be Dad.' Frank picked up the extension phone beside the bed.

'We mustn't disturb Sven,' she said vaguely. 'The new line's very busy.'

It was often hard to follow her train of thought. Frank thought she meant telephone line. 'Which new line?'

She laughed in a completely normal manner. 'Not telephones, Frank. Products. The new Swedish range. They're very good.'

He smiled at her. 'I know. I make them.'

'Answer the phone,' she said.

It was a woman's voice Frank did not recognise. 'Mr Hansen? Mr Frank Hansen?'

'Speaking.' He kept his eye on the screen. The police were hunting a lone assassin.

He heard a sigh of relief at the other end of the line. 'I thought it might have been your father.'

'He's out of town. What can I do for you?'

'I need to talk to you, Mr Hansen.'

'Right now,' he said, 'I'm a bit tied up. If you ring me in the office tomorrow . . .'

'No, I mean face to face. And it's private.'

'Who is this?'

'My name's Alice.'

His mother turned the sound up still louder. A policeman in Dallas had been shot and killed while trying to make an arrest. Frank clamped a hand over his free ear. 'Alice who?'

'. . . about Willem.'

'I think you're making a mistake. I don't know anyone called William.'

'Willem De Burgh.'

'Oh Christ!'

The trailer camp was a mile the other side of town. Frank pulled his car into the space marked '199 – Koszinsky'. It was a tidy emplacement with some evergreen shrubs in plastic tubs outside the door of the trailer, which was open.

Alice was quite composed but Frank could see she had been crying. The fresh make-up didn't cover the damage completely and her lipstick was crooked. He recognised her immediately from the photos De Burgh always carried and wondered how he could have spent three months in the same small town as her without meeting by chance.

Awkwardly, they shook hands.

'Come in,' she said. 'I made some coffee. I made it strong, you being over there in Europe. Willem said the French drink it pretty strong.'

He gasped at the taste and put the cup down. 'Not that strong.'

'D'you want some milk?'

'Thank you.'

There was a small black-and-white television standing on the plastic laminated sideboard by a bowl of roses. The vision was on, with the sound turned down. The furniture was just about comfortable. Alice's home was clean and tidy but poor. She matched it. Dressed for work in an office, he thought. A tight skirt and plain blouse, no jewellery. Her hair was done in a cheap perm.

On the table in the dining area there was a pile of letters in airmail envelopes.

'I didn't mean to bother you,' Alice said. 'When I heard you'd come back to Jacksonville in August, I wanted to talk to you about Willem. I was going to call you a hundred times, but then I thought, what's the good of opening up old wounds.'

She tried to smile. 'Memories, I told myself, are better. And then,' Alice echoed the words of Frank's mother, 'this terrible thing happened. I was watching the television this afternoon. I work nights because the money's better, so I watch a lot of daytime television. I saw it all. One minute the President was driving along with Mrs Kennedy beside him and the next he was lying there in her arms, dying. And I thought: Oh God, that's how it was with Willem. But I wasn't there at the end.'

Her face crumpled. 'It wasn't my arms he died in. So I had to call you, to find out. I rang your office and they said you'd gone home. So I rang you there.'

He shied away from her emotion and took refuge in anger.

'How d'you get my number? It's not listed.' Immediately he felt guilty and thought: I'm getting to sound like my father. The girl's unhappy. At least I could listen to her. . . .

'I work for the telephone company.'

He nodded. 'That figures.'

'We're not supposed to call unlisted numbers.'

'I won't tell anyone.'

'Is the coffee OK?'

'It's very good.' He thought she was going to cry again.

'I'm sorry.' She sniffed and blew her nose. 'May I call you Frank?'

'Go ahead.' He sat down on one of the bench seats and touched the pile of letters. Had De Burgh written all these?

'You were there when he died.'

'I haven't thought about it for a long time.'

'But you were there, Frank.'

'What the hell can I tell you?' He was angry at her and at himself for being so stupid as to come. 'Dead is dead.'

'I loved him,' she said quietly. 'We were going to be married. Did Willem tell you that?'

'I loved him too!' he shouted.

'We all loved him,' a voice called from outside. In the doorway of the next trailer, three women were talking about Dallas.

'We'll have to keep our voices down,' Alice pleaded. 'Mobile homes have thin walls.'

'I didn't mean to shout at you.'

'I know.' She touched his arm momentarily. 'If you can tell me how it was, I won't ever bother you again, I promise.'

He stood up, feeling trapped in the confined space. 'You never even met De Burgh,' he snapped at her. 'How can you say you were going to get married?'

'I'm religious.' Saying it seemed to calm Alice down. 'That's how I met your mother, through the church. And she gave me Willem's address to write to. And . . . I don't know whether you believe in these things. The first time I got a letter from Willem, I held it in my hand . . . I was sitting right there where you are now, Frank.' Her eyes willed him to believe. 'And I thought: This letter is from my husband. I just knew. Can you believe that?'

Frank avoided her eyes. She's as crazy as D.B., he thought. They'd have got on well, reading palms and having premonitions together.

He made himself sit down. 'What do you want me to tell you, Alice?'

With a sigh she turned suddenly businesslike. 'I'd like to know what the place was like where he died. What time it was. And how it happened. Did he suffer? And where he's buried.'

A fucking shopping list, he thought. He sat down again and took a deep breath. 'Buddy was a funny kind of guy. He'd lived in towns all his life but he loved animals and the countryside . . .' He paused.

'Go on.' Alice's eyes were closed; she wanted to remember each word.

It was a fairy story. Frank forced himself to continue. 'Especially he loved dogs. He never volunteered for anything but he did volunteer to become a dog-handler. If it hadn't been for the dog that day, he'd have had both hands free . . .'

When he had finished, she kept her eyes closed. Her lips were moving in prayer.

Why not? he thought, making a path through the Red Sea of letters with the back of his hand.

'Willem's captain,' she said suddenly, startling him. 'He must be a very nice man.'

'Koenig? Nice? Why d'you say that?'

'He wrote me a most beautiful letter and enclosed a poem,' said Alice. 'It helped me a lot.'

The thought of Koenig sending anyone a poem was unreal. 'Have you got a drink?'

'My church doesn't allow alcohol . . .'

And you met my mother there? he wondered.

'. . . but I've got a friend two doors along. She'll have a bottle of bourbon, if that's any good.' Alice was out of the door and back fast.

Frank turned off the television. He poured himself a glass of the bourbon and swallowed it in one go.

'The truth is,' he began, 'De Burgh was a scruffy little gypsy runt with bad teeth. He came from the back streets of some Belgian town that doesn't have any front streets He wasn't much taller than you. He dreamed all his life of making it to live in America. I often wondered if that's why he made friends with me. It's probably why he wanted a pen-pal to write to. I guess he thought if he could con some American girl into a promise of marriage, he was home and dry. To my certain knowledge, he was a liar, a thief, a cheat and the best friend I'll ever have. I miss him still.'

Alice's eyes were bright, but not with tears.

Frank stood up to go. She hugged him, her face turned away. His muscles tensed. Then he relaxed and put one arm around her shoulders.

When Alice let go and opened the door, she said simply, 'God bless you for coming.'

The conversation with Alice brought back all the unresolved trauma of De Burgh's death nearly three years before.

It surfaced mainly at night. Frank staggered half-awake up an endless hill of guilt, slipping and sliding in the loose shale. In the daytime he could suppress the memories by working hard, but every night he lay awake and climbed that hill again with his friend's body slung over one shoulder. He felt no guilt for the act of killing the three unarmed men in the cave, but agonised about why he had not been there beside De Burgh to shoot first or maybe take that single fatal bullet in his own body.

A thousand what-ifs went through his thoughts until his brain was spinning. If Sergeant Grivas had not spaced the patrol out so far apart, he might have been near enough to save De Burgh. What if De Burgh had unleashed the dog to attack, then he would have had both hands free and. . . . Why couldn't Buddy have been wounded and not killed outright?'

Each sleepless night, Frank relived every detail of the

seconds that elapsed from the two single shots up to the landing of the helicopter and the blow from Koenig's fist. Every tiny detail of the scene was complete except for one thing: he could not remember what De Burgh's face looked like. In the dreams and visions of the small hours, the face was blown away, like the dog's had been, although Frank was aware consciously that his friend's face had in reality been untouched apart from the third eye that would not close.

Each time he knelt in imagination to close the open eyes, the face was not De Burgh's, but one of the Arabs'. And the eye to which Frank's hand was reaching became an empty socket of red flesh and white bone, crawling with maggots.

He would have liked to talk to his father about it but could not find an opening until two weeks after the meeting with Alice. They were shooting skeet at the butts behind the house one Sunday lunchtime when Sven observed, 'You're looking tired, Frank.'

The skeet sailed through the air. Frank followed it and waited to the last moment before firing. A hit.

'Am I working you too hard?'

'No, sir,' said Frank. 'I'm fine.'

'I hope so.' There was a pause as Sven squinted along the barrel, waiting for the next release.

Bang! A shower of fragments littered the ground.

'You need a woman, Frank.'

'You're probably right.'

Another skeet sailed through the air. This time, Frank took it exactly at the zenith.

'Nice shot,' Sven approved. He broke the gun and reloaded, watching his son. 'I'm getting rid of Marlene. How d'you like to take her on?'

'I've already got a secretary.'

A chuckle. 'That old bag? Get rid of her. You'll have a lot more fun, in and out of the office, with Marlene. I tell you, Frank, that girl is one hell of a lay.'

'Is that all these women mean to you?' Frank felt angry at

his father's selfishness. 'You'd pass Marlene on to me like a piece of office furniture you no longer want? What about Mom back there in the house? What the hell kind of life is she leading, drinking herself to death whilst you're fucking everything in skirts?'

The barrel of Sven's gun was laid across Frank's chest. 'Don't you lecture me, boy. I live my life my way, understand? And if people can't live at my pace, there's nothing I can do about that.'

Bang! Bang! Two more skeet met death in mid-flight.

Sven lowered his smoking gun. 'Don't blame your mother's condition on me. I look after my people, so long as they're lookable-after. It makes me sad, but I don't think she is salvageable. So let's talk about you. Lately I'd say you've been acting like a man with a problem. Tell me what's on your mind, son.' The clear blue eyes bored into Frank's.

Frank heaved a sigh. This was the opening he'd been looking for. 'It's something I did in the war, Dad . . . while I was in Algeria.'

The black gardener who had been operating the skeet thrower was collecting the spent shells off the ground around where they were standing. Sven Hansen took Frank's gun, broke it, removed the unspent shell and handed it with his own gun to the gardener before leading Frank out of earshot. 'Tell me about it.'

'I don't know whether I can.' Despite the mild weather, Frank was shivering. He recognised the reaction as fear – like the physical fear he had felt in combat. 'This thing has been bottled up inside me for quite a while.'

Sven took a dark thin cheroot from the pocket of his shooting jacket and lit it. As he waved out the match, he said tersely, 'I wasn't asking you, Frank. I gave you an order.'

'Yes, sir.'

'So, do it.'

After Frank had recounted the end of the search in the Aurès mountains and the death of De Burgh, Sven was silent for several minutes. He chewed the end of the cheroot and threw it away. Trying to be helpful, but misunderstanding the problem, he said: 'So these three guys you shot were unarmed?'

'That's correct.'

Sven Hansen studied his son. He liked what he saw. 'I've been lucky, Frank. I was a supply officer. I got my decorations for moving supplies from one place to another more efficiently than other people, so I never directly caused the death of anyone. I don't know how I'd feel if I'd killed a man, let alone three unarmed men. But I think in the circumstances, I would have done the same as you did, that day in Algeria. Does it help you to know that?'

Frank's mouth twisted in a grimace. His father had completely missed the point. He wondered if Alice would understand and decided there and then to pay a visit to the trailer camp that afternoon.

'Right,' said Sven briskly. 'Now you've got that off your chest, you can relax. Take my advice and find a woman. Forget what I said about Marlene. Find a nice girl. Get married, if you want. But for Christ's sake, get out and have some fun.'

'I'll try.'

'Just one more thing,' said Sven. 'This buddy of yours, De Burgh, was he a faggot?'

'De Burgh?' Frank shouted. 'No, he was not.'

'You're sure?'

Frank was near striking his father. Breathing heavily, he spat the words out. 'As sure as you're standing here.'

'OK,' said Sven. 'Calm down. I believe you.'

It was a tradition at Hansen's Foods that Sven's birthday in mid-December was celebrated each year by shutting the production lines and giving all the employees a paid day off. In the evening, the staff and their families were invited to Sven's party. The food and the drink were good and generous, the climax of the evening being the ceremonial carving by the host, dressed in cowboy costume, of a whole steer which had been roasting over an open fire in the garden for twenty-four hours.

On the floodlit dance floor which had been specially set up in the barn behind the Hansen house, a square-dance trio was playing in jeans and check shirts, the caller going hoarse trying to make himself heard above the shrieks of the girls and the whoops of the men dancing. Frank did his duty at the bar and danced with several of the older women, then excused himself and drove into town and out the other side.

It was Alice's night off. Frank knocked at the door of her trailer. He could see the light of the television screen through her curtains.

She looked surprised but pleased to see him. 'You're supposed to be helping at your father's party.'

Frank stood on the step and held out a hand. 'I want you to come,' he said.

Alice shook her head and stepped back. 'I don't belong there, Frank. I'm not right for you.'

His hand was still held out. 'I want you to come.'

'No, please.' She touched her hair and looked at herself in a mirror. 'I can't. I'm not dressed to go out and my hair's a mess.'

'It looks pretty to me. I'll wait while you get ready.'

'Please don't make me do this.'

'Alice Koszinsky,' he said patiently, 'I have to tell you I'm fed up with sneaking over here to be with you on your nights off – meeting you in lay-bys and cafeterias and sitting in my car or yours talking, so your neighbours won't gossip about you. What have we got to be afraid of? We're both adults.'

'But I don't belong in your world, Frank.'

He stepped inside the trailer and put both hands on her shoulders. 'I want to look after you,' he said. 'You belong wherever I take you. Get that straight.' He kissed her on the lips. 'Either you come to the party with me or I spend the night here – and I swear I'll make such a noise when I leave in the morning that everybody in the trailer park will know.'

She dropped her eyes with a tiny sigh. 'I'll do what you want.'

*

'Who's the girl talking to your mother?' Sven asked. It was the only time in the year that he allowed himself to drink too much and his speech was slurred. The party was in full swing both inside the house and all over the garden.

'You don't know her,' said Frank. 'Her name's Alice Koszinsky.'

'Does she work for me?'

'No, she's my guest.'

'She is?' Sven sounded surprised. 'You could have picked yourself a more . . .'

'. . . a more sexy piece of tail, is that what you were going to say?'

Sven laughed and slapped Frank on the shoulders. 'That's exactly what I was going to say. Still, I have observed –' he pulled his son conspiratorially close – 'that some girls who look like butter wouldn't melt in their mouths give you a real good time in bed.'

'I wouldn't know,' said Frank. 'I've only known Alice three weeks.'

'I'm saying all the wrong things.' Sven burped. 'Forget it. Have fun.'

14

Marie straightened up and rubbed her aching back muscles. Her right hand was cramped from a long day's labour with secateurs and she had bleeding blisters on both hands where the metal handles had rubbed the skin raw. Her mud-covered boots were heavy. Her face was red from wind and rain and streaked with mud where she had brushed away strands of hair that escaped the hood of her ancient anorak.

The regular *snip, snip, snip* of Gustave's secateurs was far ahead of her, almost at the end of his row. He worked like an untiring automaton. Simple repetitive labouring seemed to heal his soul a little. From being an alert, educated, shrewd man of business, he had become a bent and prematurely aged peasant who laboured without any apparent emotions day after day in the fields. He ate his meals in silence and had no interests apart from work, eating, drinking and sleep.

As Raoul had foreseen, the estate of Château St Martin was run by Marie. With his help, she made all the financial decisions. She decided what should be planted where and when. Gustave seemed happy to accept her decisions. Luckily the principal crop was grapes for wine-making. Once they had been picked, they were delivered to the local *cave cooperative*, where the wine was made.

To put the property back on its feet after decades of neglect and bad management was going to take several more years' hard work, Marie knew. There had been many times since coming to St Martin when she would have given up. She kept going, thanks to Raoul's will-power and his unswerving belief in her. He also had a comforting conviction that the price of wine would rise astronomically within a few years. This Marie thought a pipe dream, although she never said so.

'One day,' he would say, pointing to the decrepit buildings of the main house, 'you'll be having balls in the ballroom, elegant dinners in the dining-room, croquet parties on the lawns and wine buyers from all over the world in Rolls-Royces and Mercedes will be queuing up to buy your wine.'

Such was his enthusiasm that for a moment she would see it all with his eyes. Once he had gone she would walk back through the largely derelict house with its empty, echoing salons and corridors and broken windows to the few rooms in which she lived with Gustave and Marie-France. Alone in the bedroom she planned wallpapers and colour schemes as an escape from the drudgery of working seven days a week to do no more than pay the interest on the bank loan. At times depression would set in and Raoul's vision would seem an impossible dream. Yet overall, he had a way of making her believe that the work ahead would be far easier than the beginning.

If she had one regret that Raoul could not lift, it was that her teenage daughter seemed to be drifting further and further away. It was normal in France for a growing teenager to be a weekly boarder at the *lycée* in Bergerac who came home only for weekends and holidays. Her mother accepted that it was better for her Marie-France to become a fully integrated French girl rather than a returned expatriate like her parents, but she missed the companionship of another woman in the household. Marie's only close friend was Louise, who also spent most of her time away from St Martin.

The row of vines as yet unpruned stretched endlessly

away into the clammy December mists. Marie's back hurt. Her hands hurt. She was wet and cold. She wiped a strand of hair from her eyes and peered towards the house. Through the mist she could make out the distinctive outline of a large white Mercedes parked in the carriage drive. It seemed so improbable that she thought she must be imagining things. She blinked rain from her eyes. It was still there when she looked again.

She clomped back to the house in her heavy gumboots, to find Raoul getting out of his old Peugeot which was parked beside the Mercedes. In the rear seat of the Mercedes sat Huguette, looking as always like a fashion plate. Marie identified her more from magazine photographs than from the single time they had met in the flesh, years before. A chauffeur was holding open the door.

'Marie darling, I wanted to see where you lived,' drawled Raoul's ex-wife. 'Raoul was telling me what great things you are doing up here. I just had to see for myself.'

'Oh my God!' Marie was acutely aware of her muddy boots, old trousers and torn anorak. Her hair was in a mess. She turned to Raoul angrily. 'You should have warned me you were coming.'

'It's been years,' said Huguette before Raoul could speak. 'I think we last met when Raoul and I got married.'

She took no notice of the other woman's embarrassment, mimed a kiss on both of Marie's cheeks without actually touching and walked self-confidently up the crumbling steps into the main entrance of the château.

Marie followed, feeling like a stranger in her own house. She kicked off her boots and walked flat-footed in socks, mumbling answers to Huguette's stream of questions, none of which seemed to be listened to. Like most of Huguette's spur-of-the-moment ideas, the visit was simply a way of passing time and simultaneously exhibiting herself to an admiring public.

Raoul joined them in the empty ballroom with its parquet floor warped and cracked by the damp. He had propelled himself into the house via the kitchen where there were no steps to hinder him. Expecting some moral reinforcement, Marie was puzzled by his behaviour. He did not greet her, indeed seemed unaware of anything else except Huguette's physical presence.

He sat immobile in the wheelchair, following her every movement with his eyes as though mesmerised. Huguette basked in this blatant adoration. She walked up and down the length of the room, posed by the long windows and preened herself like some gorgeous feline creature on two faultless legs, keeping up a stream of egocentric chatter the whole time.

Marie felt hatred welling up inside her, mostly for what Huguette was doing to Raoul. His behaviour was totally out of character with the man she knew. Where in this silent sycophant was the veteran who had carved out a new life for himself against all the odds, the sportsman who had overcome a shattering disability, the man whose support gave Marie the strength to go on when her own was flagging? She wondered what power made it possible for such a selfish, shallow narcissist as Huguette to make a weak and wordless admirer out of such an extraordinary man.

It was a great relief when Huguette cut short her tour of the house by announcing that she was late for an appointment in Bordeaux where her new husband, now Minister for Culture after some cabinet reshuffle, was opening a new theatre.

Feeling betrayed, unable to summon the energy to escort her visitor to the door, Marie sat emptily on one of the cracked window-seats that smelt of dry rot. She let Raoul show his ex-wife out. There was a mumble of voices and the thud of a heavy car door. When she heard the wheelchair returning, squeaking on the wooden floor, Marie got up quickly, opened the french windows and walked back to her work in the vines without staying to talk to Raoul.

The following day, Louise drove up to Château St Martin while Marie was eating lunch alone. She accepted a plate of salad and listened to the story of the surprise visit without comment.

'I felt so humiliated,' Marie finished. 'How could Raoul do that to me, here in my own house?'

'I know what it feels like,' said Louise. She seemed to have something on her mind. 'I've had the doubtful pleasure of meeting Huguette Whatever-her-name-is-now . . . oh, too many times. She makes me feel so ugly.'

'But how does she do that to Raoul?' Marie shook her head at the memory. 'He didn't say a word, just sat gazing at her like a dog. He must still be in love with her. Doesn't that make you sad?'

Louise laughed. 'Raoul only thinks he loves that beautiful bitch goddess. But it's not love, what he feels for her.'

'Then what is the attraction?'

This was not what Louise had come to talk about. 'I think,' she said, 'although it took me a long time to work out, that Huguette comes to see Raoul because he adores her. You've seen the way he looks at her. That sort of woman will travel a long way to be adored.'

'. . . Which doesn't explain what he sees in her.'

'Memories,' said Louise. 'Don't begrudge him those.'

They had finished eating when Gustave arrived late for the meal. He often missed meals altogether. Marie placed his plate on the kitchen table in front of him. He grunted, started to eat and took no notice when the two women left the room.

'I have to talk to you,' said Louise when they were alone. They were sitting on the bed in the cluttered bedroom that Marie shared with Gustave. It was the only comfortable place.

Marie noticed a strange look on her friend's face. 'What's up?' she asked. 'Is something the matter with you and Raoul? Forgive me, I've been so full of my own feelings.'

Louise came straight to the point. 'I'm leaving.'

'Leaving Raoul?'

'Leaving France. Leaving Europe. It's time I got on with

my own life. I'm not needed here any longer, now the war in Algeria is over.'

'How do you mean?'

'I'm one of the best physiotherapists in the world for major traumatic amputations, Marie.' It was not a boast, just a statement of fact. 'I've been offered a job by the US Veterans' Administration, working with men who've been injured in Vietnam. It's a wonderful opportunity, so I'm taking it.'

'What does Raoul say?'

'I haven't discussed it with him. This is my decision.'

'But . . .' Marie was at a loss for words. 'How can you just walk out of his life? He needs you. He loves you.'

Louise smiled a little wistfully. 'Right and wrong. Needs me a bit . . .'

'And loves you.'

'No.' Louise stood up and looked out of the window. 'Anyway, I've made up my mind.'

'When do you go?'

'The end of the week.'

'That soon!' Marie joined her friend by the window. 'What will Raoul say?'

'I'm not telling him.'

'But you must!'

Louise shook her head. 'I don't want our last memories of each other spoiled by lies.'

'Where are you going?' Marie asked.

'I'm not telling anyone.'

'Not even me?'

'Especially not you, in case Raoul tries to trace me. I've said goodbye to him in my way.' Louise tried to sound braver than she felt. 'Today I shake the dust of St Martin off my feet and never come back.'

There was a silence as Marie unravelled her thoughts.

'I'm telling you this for a reason,' continued Louise. 'So try and understand.'

She turned to Marie and embraced her. 'I don't know why it's so difficult to say this. But it is hard, so I'll just blurt it out. Raoul is in love with you and I think you're in love with him.'

Marie's face blanched under the tan she had gained from working outdoors in all weathers.

Louise smiled. 'I see I was right. He's been in love with you since you were both teenagers.'

'We had a crush on each other,' Marie stammered. 'That's all.'

'Is it?' Louise studied her friend's face. 'Remember that I watch people's bodies professionally, Marie. It comes with the job. I saw your face the first day you came to St Martin. Your eyes when I met you at the garden gate that day were like a lamp with the bulb gone out. You were shattered when you first saw Raoul and then he did something to you, you flushed and your eyes came to life. I see him do that to you every time you meet.'

'I thought I hid it.'

Louise turned away. She did not want Marie to see her face; it would give away too much. 'And I watched Raoul too that day, because you were, after all, another woman in his life. I saw you do something to him that I had never been able to do.'

She willed herself not to cry; there was no point. 'You made him light up with joy. I wondered why. The answer was so simple.'

Marie digested the conversation. 'Is this your way of telling me to have an affair with my cousin?' she asked.

The first smile of the day crossed Louise's features. 'Contrary to what you may think, he's a very good lover.'

Marie looked at the corner where Gustave's clothes were hanging. 'I'm a married woman.'

'Are you?'

Neither spoke for a moment, then Louise said, 'Gustave's sick, Marie. Look, I'm not trying to play doctors, but how long is it since you and he made love?'

Marie searched her friend's eyes to see where the conversation would end. 'Years,' she said.

'It looks like it.' Louise paused. 'And how long is it since

250

he showed any awareness of you as a person? Or had a normal conversation? Or expressed an abstract thought?'

'A long time.'

'What do you think is wrong with him?'

Marie sat down on the bed. By talking about Gustave she was aware of taking an irreversible step. 'It's though some worm inside Gustave has eaten away all his personality. The skin's intact but there's nothing inside.'

Betrayal comes in so many guises; Koenig's treason was only one. But Marie knew in her heart where that conversation with Louise was leading. The fact that she and her husband had not been intimate for years did not, by her standard of values, excuse loving another man.

So, if I can suspect Koenig, then Marie should figure on my list of suspects. She betrayed Gustave mentally that day, long before there was anything a lawyer could call infidelity. Sitting on her conjugal bed with Louise's soft, persuasive Canadian voice making it sound so easy, so logical, so good, Marie decided on a course of action that is betrayal of a kind.

'Gustave will get worse, not better,' Louise explained. 'Maybe fast, maybe slowly. The brutal fact is, he's ill and there's nothing you can do about it.'

'It's easy for you to talk like that. He's not your husband.'

There was a pause, the two women looking at each other in the mirror.

'It will make no difference to Gustave,' said Louise. 'He doesn't want your loving but Raoul does. To begin with, he needed me more than anyone else I've ever worked on. That's why I gave him more. And for a while I thought he'd really fallen in love with me. But I have to face it, I'm not a woman who inspires great love. The moment he was cured of being a cripple in his own mind, he didn't need me any more.'

'And I just happen to be here, ready to take him over?'

Louise grabbed Marie's wrist and squeezed. Her voice was tense. 'Listen, you saw what Huguette did to him yesterday. She does that every time she comes . . . reduces him to a nothing. And he's not nothing. He's a wonderful man. There are some women who consume a man. Huguette is one. Raoul deserves better than that. You and he would be good for each other. And he will be able to break off his mad, pathetic relationship with that greedy, shallow ex-wife of his.'

'You think I can compete with Huguette?' Marie looked at herself in the small mirror on the dressing table. She saw only age staring back.

Louise shook her. 'OK, so you've got no make-up on and your hair needs doing. Even more to the point, at the moment you're obviously a woman who's unloved and it shows, even in a mirror. But if you admit what you feel about Raoul and let him love you, you'll be a beautiful woman again, you'll see.'

Marie stayed in the bedroom long after she had heard Louise's car drive away. Gustave's heavy footsteps clomped through the yard on the way back to work. Her reverie continued until she heard Marie-France calling out, 'I'm home for the weekend. *Maman*, where are you?'

Marie felt a cold ache deep inside her which had nothing to do with the weather. She had made up her mind what she was going to do. She could wait until Gustave died, but even with the amount he was drinking now, that could be five or ten years away. By then it would be too late.

'I'm in the bedroom,' she called.

There was a piece of Shakespeare she had learnt at school. Something about a 'tide in the affairs of men which taken at the flood . . .' How did it go on? 'Omitted, all the . . .' No, that wasn't right. 'Omitted, the voyage of their life is bound in shallows and in miseries.'

Marie looked at herself in the mirror. The grey winter light coming in the window was enough for her to see that, for a woman, it was even more imperative to catch the tide. And this was probably the last time it would come in for her.

15

'I'm coming in.'

'Please, Frank, no.'

'Yes.'

Alice had made Frank park his car outside the trailer camp, so as not to awaken the neighbours. It was 5 a.m. and snowflakes were drifting down in the light of the street lamps to land on the neat miniature lawns between the mobile homes. Frost-crispened grass crunched softly beneath their feet.

'I need to talk to you,' he said.

Alice turned her key in the door. 'Is it about Willem again?'

'If I said yes, you'd let me in. But no, it's about me. About us.'

'We've talked a lot, Frank.'

'There's something I want to say to you, which I haven't said before.'

She shut the door quietly behind him.

'I love you.'

Alice shut her eyes. She was remembering the coffee grounds, the first time he had come to her home. 'It's too early,' she said.

'Too early for what?' he asked forcefully.

'To know. First, I need a sign.'

A sign? Frank let that go. 'You said you knew when you held Buddy's first letter in your hand,' he argued. 'And I know now, Alice. I knew the first day I came here. When I was driving away afterwards, I felt like you'd dipped your fingers into my soul. That's why I've told you things I've never told anyone else.'

'I feel very humble that you trust me...'

He shook her roughly. 'I don't want you to feel humble. I want you to feel happy and proud that I love you. I want you to marry me.'

'Keep your voice down, please.' Alice subsided on to one of the bench seats and sighed. 'Oh, Frank. I wish you wouldn't hustle me. Give me time.'

He sat beside her, full of tense urgency. 'I need you, Alice. I want to care for you, to give you a home, to have kids with you – all those things that a man's supposed to feel about the woman he loves. But the fact is, I need you too. I can't sleep nights. I told you why. But when I'm near you, I feel more peaceful than I've ever felt in my life. You make me feel good and I think I deserve you.'

Alice turned in the seat and looked him full in the eyes. 'You're a good man,' she said solemnly. 'And I respect you. I feel very...' She was going to say happy, but changed it to '... secure when you're near me. At first I felt close to you because you loved Willem. Now, it's a lot more than that. But I'm a very serious person, Frank. I know it would be wonderful marrying you and living with you, but I have to be certain first – before I say yes.'

'What do I have to do?' He was desperate.

'Don't you know?' Alice brought her face close to his and smiled. 'Make love to me.'

With four words she seized the initiative. It was the last thing he had been expecting her to say.

Alice took both his hands in hers. 'I believe that making love is like a sacrament, Frank. When we do, I'll know.'

'What about the neighbours?' he said weakly.

'Kiss me.'

It was the first time Frank had felt Alice's whole body

embrace him, soft and yielding as she sank back on the seat beneath him. Through the dress she had put on for the party, he felt her nipples harden. Her legs parted to the pressure of his. He kissed her ears and neck and eyelids. Trained by the girls to whom he had made love in Algeria and France, he waited for her passion. But where they had wanted to suck and bite and grab and scratch, Alice seemed to be floating on the current of his lust. She was not passive, but accepting rather than passionate.

They left a trail of clothing from the living area to her bedroom, which Frank had not been in before. He inhaled the air that smelt of her and wanted to make love to the whole room. In the bed, Alice touched him gently, caressed his face, his arms, his chest, his belly. Her eyes flicked from one detail of Frank's strong and healthy body to another like a camera freezing close-ups from which a composite whole will afterwards be built up. It was unlike any other love-making Frank had known. There was a strong lack of urgency, as though the important thing was that they lay naked in each other's arms, not as a prelude to orgasm but as a statement in itself.

When Frank lifted himself off her to feast his eyes on her breasts, belly, pubic hair, she watched him with eyes wide and lips parted for the next kiss, taking pleasure from his pleasure in her. Neither spoke until at last he entered her.

'Oh Frank,' she breathed, feeling him fill her with a joy that was pain as well.

He had a flash image of Sven saying, 'Girls who look like butter wouldn't melt in their mouths . . .'

Frank came too soon, after the months of abstinence.

'You were perfect,' she said when they were lying side by side afterwards.

'It wasn't so good for you.'

'It was right.' There was a smile on Alice's face he had not seen before. She looked quite beautiful. 'I told you, I wanted it to be like a sacrament, Frank. I didn't want to be carried away by passion. Not the first time. I wanted to remember everything clearly. And the answer's yes.'

'The answer?'

'If you still want me to.'

The positions were reversed now. It was Frank who felt very solemn as he sat up in the bed. 'Will you marry me, Alice?'

She was smiling, her eyes wide open. 'Oh yes. Till death do us part.'

'Why'd you say that?'

A cloud passed. 'I don't know. Perhaps because I don't believe in divorce.'

'It's a funny thing to say.'

She pulled the bedclothes off herself and her voice went husky. 'Make love to me again, Frank.'

This time her passion matched Frank's. Her kisses devoured him. Her hands explored and caressed his body. Her belly returned his thrusts. By some subtle physical magic, she taught him to transport her to a plane of bliss on a tide of tenderness and then suck her back in an undertow of aggression and savagery that alternately sated the two women she was: the gentle one the world knew as Alice Koszinsky and the passionate animal she had kept hidden even from herself until that night.

At dawn, she woke him with a kiss. 'You have to go to work.'

'My God!' Frank looked at his watch. 'I'm late.'

Alice held him back in the bed. 'The morning after Sven's party, I should think half the factory is late.'

'They will be.' He kissed her briefly and tried to go. 'I'm the boss. I have to be there first.'

'No,' she said firmly. 'This is a very special morning. As far as I'm concerned, we're married now. So I'm going to make you breakfast, like a good wife. You'll get orange juice, coffee and toast and anything else you want.' She rolled out of the bed naked and watched him watching her slip into a towelling bathrobe.

'Anything?'

'Anything you want,' she said. She bent and kissed him on the lips. His hands opened the bathrobe and touched her

256

breasts gently. He loosened the cord around her waist and then they were both in the bed again, making love slowly with a thousand caresses.

Afterwards, Alice said drowsily, 'Breakfast.'

The mobile home was centrally heated. Frank put on a Japanese kimono from Alice's wardrobe and padded barefoot into the living area. He bit into a piece of toast.

'Sit down,' she ordered. 'You work hard all day, you'll take the time to sit down and have a proper breakfast first.'

She seated herself opposite him and curled her feet snugly underneath her, hands clasped around a mug of coffee. There was something different about her eyes and the set of her face, he thought.

'You're beautiful,' he said.

'For you.' She smiled and it almost broke his heart. He reached across the table to touch her. 'Oh God, Alice, I want you so much.'

'Tell me,' she said, 'who you are.'

He was puzzled. 'You know who I am.'

She stared at her cup. 'You never talk about yourself, Frank. Did you know that?'

He laughed. 'There's not much to talk about. I'm just a regular joe who's lucky enough to be American and reasonably rich. What more could I want?'

'Just Sven Hansen's son? Is that all you are?'

He scratched his head and stretched both arms. 'Well, I don't have any hang-ups, like wanting to stick a knife in the old man and take over his empire, if that's what you mean. I wish he was kinder to my mother, that's all. But I still like Sven for what he is. I think he's a great man.'

'Yet you ran away and joined the Legion because of something he did.'

'I was a kid then.' He laughed at the boy he had been. 'No, I shouldn't say that. I still find it hard to handle any deep emotion, Alice. I mean, running away to join the Legion was pretty excessive, wasn't it? Other guys would have had a violent shouting match with their father maybe, but I had to throw away five years of my life to make a point.'

'Was it a waste, your time in the Foreign Legion?'

He thought a moment. 'No. I learned about myself. I liked the life. In fact, I'd still be in uniform, if the French government hadn't fucked up and just about crucified the Legion during my term of service.'

'It's not the same any more?'

'Oh, the Legion will recover. It's just that the men in it during those crisis years got their loyalties somewhat chewed up.'

'I should be glad it all went wrong.' She sounded thoughtful. 'Otherwise you wouldn't have come back and we might never have met.'

'And you'd have been Mrs de Burgh?'

'We have Willem to thank for bringing us together,' she agreed. A sip of coffee and then, 'What are your vices?'

'You ask weird questions,' he laughed. 'I'm so boring, I don't think I have any. Except . . .'

'Except what?'

Encouraged by her stillness and the way she gazed at him, feasting her eyes, he continued, 'Well, I'm just as happy foot-slogging through the desert with nothing but a canteen of water as I am driving a new-model Chevvy, staying in the best hotels and wearing a Brooks Brothers suit. Most of the time, I get on with just about everybody. I don't especially hate or love anyone.'

'Those aren't vices. They're virtues.'

'Oh hell . . . I'm putting this so badly because I don't think about these things, Alice. But I would say my main character defect is that I rarely feel deeply about anything. So when some strong emotion hits me, I act irrationally.' He was embarrassed. 'Look, I'm not explaining this well.'

'You're doing fine.'

'What I'm trying to say is that I have in me a terrible violence, Alice. When I'm hurt, I go over the top.'

'I'll never hurt you, Frank . . .' She was gazing past him as she spoke, looking into the future. '. . . As long as I live.'

*

Sven's idea of a suitable wedding present was a brand-new house on a survey less than a mile from the Hansen ranch. It had been the show house of a speculative development in which he had a financial interest. He called at Alice's trailer one sunny January afternoon a week before the wedding and insisted on taking her to see it.

The house was completely furnished and had a swimming pool. Alice walked from room to room. It was larger than any house she had been in, except for the Hansen ranch. Its size did not bother her. She felt remote and peaceful with her secret and the sense of inevitability that was growing within her.

She made suitably impressed remarks as Sven demonstrated how the gadgets worked, from the radio-controlled garage doors to the waste disposal under the sink. His pleasure at seeing her reactions reminded her of a child demanding that someone open a present there and then.

Alice had grown to like Frank's volatile father and found him fascinating but not frightening. The only embarrassment for her was the outsize name-board reading Wonderland which Sven had had specially hand-carved for the driveway.

'What else could your home be called, Alice?' he asked, with his usual excessiveness.

Standing in the living room by the huge picture window looking on to the snow-covered lawn and the pool under its winter wraps, Sven took both of her hands and Alice understood why other women went to bed with him so easily. He was like a big, happy, uncomplicated boy.

'I want you to be the happiest young woman in Jacksonville,' he said seriously, the light-blue eyes locked on hers. 'And in case you wonder why I'm so generous, this house isn't just for you, Alice. It's to make a home for my grandchildren.'

He grinned at her startled look. 'I can always tell. Does Frank know?'

She blushed. 'I haven't told him yet. I wasn't sure.'

'Twins,' he said. 'They run in your family.'

'Have you been checking up on me?' She was half angry and half amused.

'Of course.' The blue eyes were twinkling. He pulled her down on to the jumbo-sized settee. 'I'm a very rich man. One day Frank will inherit all I own. So I had to be sure you weren't just a gold-digger after the Hansen fortune.'

'You had private detectives making enquiries?'

'The best. Don't worry. They're very discreet. I've used them before. No waves.'

'And supposing I'd failed the test?'

'I'd have got rid of you,' he said simply.

'You're a ruthless man, Sven.'

'I don't deny it.' He grinned, pleased with himself. 'I tell you one thing, honey. When I first set eyes on you at that birthday party, I thought Frank had made a mistake. But now – I don't know what that boy of mine has done to you – you're truly a very beautiful young woman.'

No, he thought. That's a load of horse-shit. The fact is, I owe this girl a lot more than the price of a new house. If she hadn't happened, Frank would have left Jacksonville for good by now. I don't know exactly what happened to him when he was away at his war but I do know it was something he couldn't live with – until this strange, quiet girl with her honest eyes came into his life. I don't want Frank running away again. And thanks to her, he won't.

PART 3

SUMMER 1967–FEBRUARY 1968

1

The ancient black London taxi, pensioned off to end its days in Belfast, joined the stream of traffic heading for the docks in time to catch the night ferry to Liverpool. In the rear sat a small, wiry priest in a stained cassock and much-mended shoes. Seated beside him was a young man dressed as a seminarist.

As they passed the Springfield Road police station, a poster was being pasted on the noticeboard outside the main entrance: *Wanted: Sean Carey.*

The priest made the sign of the cross. 'God help me,' said Father Callaghan, 'I've become more of a thief than a shepherd.'

As though to excuse himself, he added, 'It's in keeping with the times. There were 5,000 people at a rally in London today to legalise smoking pot, I ask you! And there's the Parliament in Westminster passing a law that makes abortion legal. I don't know what the world's coming to.'

He handed to the taciturn young man beside him the passport taken with some clothing from the cell of a newly arrived novice at the Redemptorist monastery in Clonard, a slum area of west Belfast.

Sean Carey glanced at the photograph. 'It's like enough,' he grunted, fingering the clean upper lip and the cheekbone where he had shaved off his sideboards. His distinctive tangle of red hair had been cut short and dyed black, the single gold earring removed.

'The feller's eighteen, same age as you,' said Father Callaghan. 'Memorise his name. Now you don't have to show a passport on the boat to Liverpool, but you'll need it at Dover and when you land in France. When you get to Paris, get rid of it.'

'I don't go much for these clothes you got me.'

'You're supposed to be a seminarist,' said the priest. 'So you've got to look like one. Shaving off a moustache and having your hair cut is no great price to pay for getting away from an army snatch squad that comes knocking on your mother's door at two o'clock in the morning.'

'If I ever find out who informed on me,' Sean threatened, 'I'll be back here and deal with him.'

'It's sometimes a jealous girlfriend,' said the priest vaguely.

'I don't have one.'

The taxi slowed and stopped near the armed police checkpoint at the dock gate. In the summer of 1967, security in Belfast was still in the hands of the police. The death of the first British soldier was still nearly four years in the future.

'I'll have to drop you here,' said the driver. He waved the priest's money aside and spoke to Sean. 'Good luck across the water.'

The young man's cold grey eyes fixed the priest's as the taxi drove away. 'That driver, does he know who I am?'

'No,' said Father Callaghan. 'He's a good Catholic who knows you're in trouble, that's all.' To deflect Sean's thoughts, he ordered, 'It looks odd to have no baggage, so carry this holdall I've got for ye. And keep this bible in your other hand at all times. Read it when you're sitting in the saloon on the boat and on the train to London.'

With a rueful smile, he added, 'You'll find it stops people talking to ye. Unless they're religious, of course. And then, God help you. I don't suppose ye remember much of what's inside the book.'

The priest was chatting loudly about the bishop's monthly

newsletter as they walked through the police checkpoint where there was only a cursory examination of Sean's ticket. The crowded, dreary waiting room at the foot of the gangway smelt of beer and urine. Father Callaghan passed an envelope of money to Sean.

'You've got enough cash in there,' he said. 'After you arrive in Paris, get in a taxi and show the fellow what I've written on the back page of the bible.'

Ever suspicious, Sean looked at the writing. 'What's it mean?'

'You don't even trust me, do ye?' said the priest. 'It simply says in French: Take me to the Old Fort at Vincennes.'

'The taxi driver will know where that is?'

'He'll know.'

A barrier was moved aside and people started moving up the gangway towards the overnight boat.

'I wish you luck, Sean,' said Father Callaghan softly. 'And I pray that the Foreign Legion can use the terrible talents God has given you without making you a criminal.'

Sean had learned the importance of details during his months on the run. He bent his head for the priest's blessing then merged with the passengers shuffling up the gangway, leaving Ireland without a second of regret.

Two boat journeys and three trains later, he was washing the dye out of his hair in the men's room at the Gare du Nord in Paris. After waiting a few minutes in the queue for a taxi, he grew tense with a feeling that he was being watched by a policeman on duty nearby. He left the queue when the *flic* was looking the other way and tracked a cab down outside the station by the simple expedient of waving a banknote in the air.

After a look at the back page of the bible the driver said in English, 'You want to join Foreign Legion, Johnny?'

'Take me there.'

'I show you sights first? Eiffel Tower? Champs Elysées?'

'Just take me there, pal.'

'I know a bar with very nice girls, Johnny.'

'Take me to Van-Sen or I'm getting out right here.'

With no sense of the geography of Paris but knowing by instinct that he was being cheated, Sean ignored the driver's attempts to make conversation during the circuitous journey. At the Foreign Legion recruiting office in the Old Fort of Vincennes he considered breaking the driver's nose as a mild gesture for consumers' rights, then thought better of it, not wanting to attract attention from the French police. He contented himself with tearing in half the strange-looking notes Father Callaghan had given him and showering the pieces on the pavement for the driver to pick up.

Pursued by a stream of abuse, Sean was admitted to the Old Fort. The night's catch of a dozen other young men were playing cards or trying to sleep in a comfortless dormitory with the lights on. No one spoke English. For the first time Sean wondered how he was going to cope linguistically. He ate a cold help-yourself supper in the bleak refectory. Back in the dormitory with no one to talk to, he rolled himself in a blanket on one of the uncomfortable metal beds and shut his eyes. He was used to sleeping in strange places at all hours of the day and night, and was not disturbed by the comings and goings, the arguments, the all-night card game or the sound of drunken vomiting.

Five miles away on the Champs Elysées, the crowds of late theatre-goers had thinned, leaving the pavements to a few insomniacs, tramps and prostitutes. Seated at a table in one of the glassed-in pavement cafés was a young man the same age as Sean. To judge by the pile of screwed-up paper in the ashtray beside him, he had been trying for a long time to write a letter.

Dear Vanessa,
    As you see, I pushed off to Paris. I am writing this note while drinking champagne in a charming little pavement café on the Champs Elysées, prior to joining the Foreign Legion . . .

Roger Milton tore up the sheet of paper and placed the pieces neatly in the ashtray with his previous attempts. It would be nice to write in verse, but he couldn't find any decent rhymes. He tried again:

Dear Vanessa,
Just a line to say goodbye.
From the postmark you'll see where and why
I spent my eighteenth birthday
Wish me luck and wave goodbye . . .

That was no good either. He tore it up. On the last sheet of paper he wrote:

Dear Vanessa,
Sorry I said all the wrong things the other night. To give you a decent interval in which to reconsider my proposal, I have joined the Foreign Legion.
I shall put the question again in just over five years' time, providing I survive.
My regards to your father, and to Mr Hackett, my respected house-master.

A cough. The waiter was hovering by his table with the bill. The café, Roger saw, was empty. All the other chairs were already stacked on the tables.

'Good God,' he gasped at the bill, 'did I drink all that?' The amount was exorbitant.

'You did, monsieur. If you would like to pay now, we can both go home.'

Roger counted out the bills from his wallet. He had just enough left for the taxi fare to Vincennes.

'There's a fifteen per cent service charge,' said the waiter. He looked bored and tired. 'It's normal, monsieur.'

'It is?' Roger shovelled the rest of his cash on to the man's tray. As an afterthought, he grabbed back just enough for a Métro ticket.

The waiter had already locked the door when Roger

remembered his gold-nibbed Parker pen. He could see it still lying on the table beside the pile of torn-up letters. He hammered on the glass wall.

'Go 'ome,' the waiter called. 'It is late.'

'Open up,' Roger begged. 'There's a good chap. I left my pen . . .'

The lights went out. The waiter disappeared into the rear of the bar, leaving Roger alone on the deserted Champs Elysées. For some reason he had imagined that French cafés stayed open all night. It was 3 a.m. and it was drizzling. Roger looked at the letter in his hand. The ink was already blurring with raindrops. He shoved it into the envelope and dropped it into a post-box by the nearest Métro. The bad news was that there were two hours to kill before the first train.

The woman had been watching him from a doorway. She was well made-up and smartly dressed. In the light of the street lamps she looked attractive. Holding a white umbrella over her head she walked up to the lanky, fair-haired English boy.

'Are you looking for company?' Her voice was warm and friendly.

He knew what she was, although he had never been this close to one before. 'Well, actually . . .'

'Are you alone?' she asked. 'Perhaps you like to come 'ome with me? I like Englishmen.'

'Frightfully nice of you.' Did he look as English as that? She hadn't even spoken to him in French. He felt rather unsteady on his feet. 'But as it happens, I don't have any money.'

'No?' She took in the well-cut suit and expensive shoes. The fact that he was good-looking in his rather shy English way was unimportant. 'How will you manage to get 'ome wiz no money?'

She had hold of Roger's arm now – he was not quite sure how it had happened – and was leading him into a side street. A green neon sign at the far end winked on and off: *Hôtel. Hôtel. Hôtel.*

He pulled away with an apologetic laugh. 'No really, I'm

not kidding. I'm broke. Completely broke.' He pulled both trouser pockets inside out to make the point and the coins he had kept for the Métro tinkled on the pavement. He stooped to pick them up and nearly lost his balance. She was still there when he straightened up, waiting under the next street lamp with her back to the light. They were alone in the street.

'I'm going to join the Foreign Legion in the morning,' he explained, 'but I haven't got a penny to give you.'

'Is a joke?'

He shook his head.

She smiled. 'You really join Foreign Legion?'

He nodded.

'Oh dear.' She sounded genuinely sad. 'Your girlfrien', did she jelt you?'

He laughed, more at himself than her accent. 'How did you know? Is it that obvious?'

She was lifting his cuff. 'That's a good watch,' she said.

'It's an Omega. Solid gold. A present from my pa.' Should I be telling her this? he wondered.

'They will steal it,' she said. 'They steal everything from you when you join the Legion. Better you make it present to me.'

She moved her whole body close to his and planted a kiss on his lips. He could smell her scent on the chill night air.

'I pay for the room,' she said. 'You don't worry about a thing, darling. Come on.'

She turned and walked ahead of him along the glistening pavement, her three-inch heels clacking in the silence. Roger followed her silhouette: the shoes, the legs, the short skirt, the tight jacket and a halo of frizzy back-lit hair beneath the umbrella turning green with the light from the neon sign. Inside the dingy hotel foyer and up two sets of stairs close behind her, watching her shiny shoes, the gold bracelet on one ankle, her legs disappearing into the tight-stretched skirt that showed the outline of her panties as she negotiated the steep steps on the corners.

Roger saw nothing in the tiny, dimly lit room except her.

He stood watching, his back against the door as she removed her jacket, unzipped her skirt and wriggled out of it.

She sat on the edge of the bed wearing just her bra and panties. 'You like?'

'Oh yes,' he said. 'Rather.'

She waited a moment. When he made no move, the woman spoke in a husky whisper. 'Ees it the first time you been wiz a girl?'

He was going to lie. 'Actually,' he said. 'It is.'

'Oh.' She pretended to be excited. 'Then I will show you everything. Everything. Come 'ere, darling.'

It was nearly dawn when Hans-Peter Muller stood in front of the main gate of the Old Fort at Vincennes. He wondered whether his father had walked through this same grim portal when he enlisted. If he did, thought Hans-Peter, he must have felt a bit more confident than I do. . . .

He was a slim young man with long blond hair beautifully cut that hung down the back of his well cut leather jacket. He looked younger than his twenty-two years and had an innocent wide-eyed expression that attracted a certain kind of older man.

He screwed up his courage and knocked. The sentry, who relieved the boredom of his job by making instant assessments of the volunteers, summed this one up at first sight: German, gay and too soft to stay the course.

'You sure you come to the right place?' he asked in a heavy Spanish accent.

'*Absolument certain.*' Hans-Peter's French was perfect and almost accentless.

The sentry shrugged and stood aside. With three men out of four currently being rejected there was no chance this one would get through.

The oak door slammed shut behind Hans-Peter's back. His heart racing, he followed the sentry across a courtyard and up several flights of stairs, following literally in his father's footsteps.

An all-night card game was going in one corner of the

dormitory. The players stopped and stared at the newcomer. One of them blew a kiss. Hans-Peter grimaced to himself. That was what he was trying to get away from.

He put his small holdall on a bed and took out a new toilet bag. Someone whistled. Several men laughed as he walked to the toilets. After cleaning his teeth, Hans-Peter braved the same reaction on the way back. He peeled back the blanket to find dried urine stains all over the mattress. The next bed was the same. And the next. In the end he chose the one adjacent to Sean, who was still an inert heap under his blanket.

Hans-Peter lay down, fully clothed. Sleep would not come. He fidgeted on the thin mattress, wondering what his mother had made of the farewell note: Dear Mutti, I have to sort out my life. . . .

He had deliberately not said where he was going, for fear she might be able to stop him somehow. Poor Mutti, he thought. She'll be worried stiff. I ought to have telephoned her.

Two men, more sharply dressed than the others, rose from the card game. With a vaguely menacing air, they sauntered to the foot of Hans-Peter's bed for a closer look. '*C'est une gonzesse*,' said the one with a Corsican accent: it's a tart.

'It's very pretty,' agreed the other. 'Those shoes must have cost a packet, *eh pédé*?' He tweaked Hans-Peter's toes.

There was a movement in the next bed as Sean woke up, sensing the proximity of trouble. He opened one eye and said quietly, 'Fuck off! You're disturbing me.'

The threat in the words was plain, despite the language barrier; for what remained of the night they were left in peace.

'*Toi!*' The duty corporal pointed a finger at Hans-Peter. '*Viens ici!*'

He shook his head at the long hair and well-manicured nails. Still, it wasn't his job to weed them out and this was the only English-speaker in the net, so . . . '*Tu parles anglais et français?*'

'*Oui, caporal!*' Hans-Peter tried to stand at what he imagined was the position of attention.

'OK. In the Legion, we operate the buddy system. Know what I mean?'

'*Non, caporal.*'

'The Irishman over there doesn't understand any French. So you're his buddy. You translate for him. Make sure he knows what's going on. That's your responsibility.'

'*Oui, caporal!*'

'Dismiss!'

Hans-Peter was the last person in the room Sean Carey would have chosen as a buddy. He had mentally labelled the German boy a fucking kraut poofter. But the corporal was right: he needed someone to translate for him.

'What's your name, Irish?' asked Hans-Peter.

'Patrick O'Reilly,' said Sean coldly. 'That's me name.'

'Where you from?'

'Dublin,' came the answer. 'Where else? I'm Paddy O'Reilly from Dublin.'

Conversation, thought Hans-Peter, was not the Irishman's strong point. It was uphill work to get anything out of the buddy he'd been ordered to look after. He was relieved when, halfway through the morning, the corporal shoved Roger Milton through the door. There was a stare of curiosity from the card game at the tall public schoolboy in the old-fashioned three-piece suit.

'Hey, kraut,' called the corporal. 'Here's another one for you to wet-nurse. It doesn't speak anything but English.'

At midday the recruits were given a hot lunch and told they were getting the train to Marseilles the next morning. The news was anticlimactic; they had expected something to happen sooner than that. To kill time they sat or lay on the beds in the dormitory chatting or playing cards.

Hans-Peter translated the news for his two charges. Apart from exchanging names they had hardly spoken to each other. Roger seemed to be in a reverie and the Irishman answered Hans-Peter's questions with a glare from the cold grey eyes that made the German boy shiver.

Their civilian clothes had been taken away; they wore clean but ill-fitting old fatigues. Most of the men in the dormitory were smoking. Those who had money were drinking beer purchased in the canteen. One man had vomited twice in the wash-basins. To make some contact, Hans-Peter bought three bottles of beer to share with his two charges. The Irishman refused his without thanks. Roger thanked him politely, drank all three, one after another, and sank back into his reverie.

Two sleepless nights travelling caught up with Hans-Peter. He gave up trying to talk and turned his face to the wall to get some sleep. In the next bed Sean lay on one elbow, watching everything that went on.

Roger lay on his back staring at the ceiling, recalling all that had happened in the sordid little room near the Champs Elysées. Five times he had come. He felt drained and had a pain in his groin. He wondered what the woman's name was.

He scratched his crotch. Ought to have a shower. . . . He had probably had more fun with the nameless girl than in a lifetime with Vanessa. He wished now that he had not posted the letter.

He wondered what the other chaps in the Upper Sixth would say at the beginning of term when they learned that he was not coming back to do the third year for the Cambridge entrance examination. Mentally he composed an Epistle to the Upper Sixth Common Room:

Dear Chaps,
While I should have enjoyed the privileges of being a Senior Prefect, I have decided instead to take up with a monosyllabic bog-walloper, a gay Teuton and various whores, drinkers and card-sharps in the Foreign Legion. . . .

He giggled at the idea of the effect the letter would have. Pity the beer was all gone. Very generous of the kraut. . . .

273

Sean's eyes flicked to him. 'What's so funny, English?'

Roger glanced at his questioner, seeing him for the first time. Scruffy bloke, he thought. Looks like a criminal.

'Women,' he said grandly. 'It'll be good to get away from them for a while.' He rubbed his wrist, which felt naked where the strap had been. Never had a watch been so well spent, he decided.

2

Even in Provence, it can rain in July. The heavy downpour made the scene look forlorn as the canvas-topped truck bringing the recruits from the main railway station in Marseilles drove past the guardhouse of the barracks at Aubagne and the heavy metal gates clanged shut behind them.

Their nervous eyes took in the first sight of their new world. Identical blocks of buildings stood in rigid lines, as though on parade. Even the shrubs, the grass and the perfect flower beds looked under military discipline. In every direction, men in immaculate uniforms walked, marched and ran smartly about their business.

Before the vehicle had stopped, the newcomers were being shouted at by two corporals working on the principle by which all armies have functioned since Caesar's time and before. It's called Hurry Up And Wait.

Like two dogs harrying cattle to their fate in a slaughter-house, the corporals split the recruits into two squads for processing. The morning became a painful race between the two squads, as though the corporals had a bet on who would finish first. Each herded his squad from one anonymous block to the next without a word of explanation. Outside each building the men waited in sodden clothes for reasons unknown. The bouts of waiting in ranks forbidden to speak were interspersed, once inside the buildings, with frantic orders and hectic activity as items of kit were thrown at them, or their bodies dispassionately examined by wordless orderlies in a variety of uniforms. Needles were repeatedly stuck into various parts of them to inoculate or take samples.

Before the last man had been processed, the corporal would announce that they were behind schedule and double-march them through the rain to another identical building. Sometimes they passed the other squad, looking as dejected as themselves. Kitbags bumping on shoulders, the corporal running backwards alongside and shouting at them to keep in step, they progressed wetly through the morning and the afternoon and the next day and the next. The men came to feel dehumanised, disorientated, as though their bodies were anonymous cogs of flesh enmeshed in a machine that would mince them to nothing if they ever stopped turning in synch with all the other cogs.

The first taste of the Legion's many rituals came in the canteen at lunchtime on the first day. Forbidden to talk, the recruits followed the example of their seniors and waited outside the mess in orderly lines until a whistle blew and everyone filed into the canteen in silence.

As each man entered, he removed his kepi and stood to attention in front of a metal stool. A *caporal-chef* entered and shouted something meaningless to the recruits. A single voice was raised in one of the Legion's many marching songs. It stopped abruptly and the singer shouted, '*Trois!*'

In silence the old hands counted off four paces, then shouted in unison, '*Quatre!*' At the top of their strong, male voices they belted out a song which the newcomers would later know as 'La Légion Marche'.

The recruits were awed by the sheer power of 300 men singing in an enclosed space and by the esprit de corps from which they were excluded by their inexperience. The song ended abruptly; the silence was palpable. The corporal who had started the whole ritual shouted, '*Asseyez-vous. Bon appétit!*'

Three hundred voices shouted as one, '*Merci, caporal!*'
There was a scraping of boots and stools as each man sat.
To Sean, who had lived most of his life on a diet of sand-
wiches and fish and chips, the meal on the serving dishes
was enormous; his problem was to work out an order in
which to tackle the hors-d'oeuvres, entrée, meat and cheese.
Pouring himself what looked like fruit juice from a jug, only
to find that it was wine, he passed it across the table to
Roger, who pronounced it 'Nearly drinkable. Nice colour.
Good nose. Well, cheers! Have some yourself, old chap.'

'I don't touch alcohol,' said Sean.

Roger, who was a slow eater, saw all of the main courses
disappear before he had finished eating the hors-d'oeuvres.

'If you don't eat fast, you'll starve,' advised a Canadian
legionnaire who had heard them speaking English.

The noise of conversation grew until no one could hear
his neighbour's voice. A scream from the corporal for silence
was obeyed instantly. Gradually the noise level grew again
until cut short by another shout. Even this seemed to be a
ritual, thought Hans-Peter. He wondered whether it had
been the same in his father's day.

He was straining his ears to hear something Roger was
saying when the corporal in charge appeared behind Sean
and delivered a rabbit punch hard on the back of his neck.

Sean gagged on a mouthful of food. His eyes glazed and
he shook his head violently to recover his vision. Before he
could make any protest, the corporal walked on down the
lines of feeding men as though nothing had happened. The
Canadian put a hand across the table to restrain Sean, who
was in the act of getting up to retaliate.

'What was that for?' gasped Hans-Peter, appalled at the
casual violence. 'He wasn't doing anything.'

The Canadian explained with a grin, 'You new guys have
to learn these things.'

'What fucking things?' Sean was angry. There was a click
in the vertebrae as he moved his neck.

'You had your feet on the bar of the stool,' the Canadian
explained. 'That's not allowed at mealtimes. You gotta keep

them on the floor the whole time. Or . . .' He made a chopping gesture with the side of his hand on the table.

Sean rubbed the back of his neck ruefully. 'I'll get that bastard before I'm out of here!' he vowed when the corporal was safely out of earshot.

La boule à zéro was the name given to the Legion's traditional billiard-ball haircut.

The bare walls, concrete floor, harsh strip-lighting and lack of equipment made the camp barbershop more like a sheep-shearing shed than a hairdressing salon. There were no scissors and no mirrors, just a huge electric trimmer for each barber.

The new recruits watched in fascination as the trimmers ploughed through the hair of those ahead of them in the queue. It was like seeing lawn mowers cut a swathe through overgrown gardens. The first stroke carved a path from the nape of the neck to the brow. A dozen others removed every hair on the head.

When it was Hans-Peter's turn to squat astride one of the plain wooden stools, he was rigid with fear; his hair was a part of his identity. He glanced by habit at where the mirror should have been. In front of him was a blank wall; here the client had no say. He shivered as the barber grabbed a handful of the long blond hair and switched on the trimmer. The hair fell in heavy hanks on to Hans-Peter's shoulders and slipped to the floor, where it joined straight European hair, crinkly African hair and black Asian hair in a carpet that completely hid the concrete.

In memory Hans-Peter smelt again the perfume and the chemicals, the smell of nail varnish from the manicurist's cubicle – all the feminine smells that had been the background to his childhood. He heard the buzz of women's chatter and the whirr of the driers and his mother at the door wishing a departing client goodbye. For him, nothing could have symbolised the abnegation of civilian identity more keenly than that first regulation haircut.

A tap on the shoulder. 'Next!'

He stood and looked at Sean rising from the neighbouring stool, more ugly than before with his now completely hairless skull, the ears protruding like in a child's drawing. It did not seem to bother the Irishman. At the far end of the barbershop, Roger was staring at a piece of broken mirror, making faces at himself.

He laughed when Hans-Peter could not bear to see his reflection: 'You a hairdresser,' he jeered. 'If you could see yourself now . . .'

With their shaven skulls and identical shapeless overalls, the squad now looked like a group of half-starved convicts.

Hans-Peter stuck his head out of an open window, feeling sick. There was not a woman in sight. There were men of all complexions: tall, blond Germans and Scandinavians, swarthy Spaniards, Greeks and Italians, pale Anglo-Saxons and one or two Africans, a few Arabs and some Vietnamese. Men in uniform were everywhere. They all looked healthy, confident, strong, masculine.

There could have been no greater contrast with the exclusively feminine world of the ladies' hairdressing salon where Hans-Peter had grown up. He told himself that this men-only life was what he needed in order to sort himself out, what he had travelled from Berlin to find. Yet what he felt was not a thrill of anticipation so much as a chill of fear – the fear of the unknown, both within himself and all around.

The only time that recruits to the Legion regain their separate identities is when the Intelligence Branch – the deuxième bureau *– vets each man to weed out undesirables. Contrary to legend, we don't want thieves or anti-social elements in the Legion. No man guilty of a blood crime is knowingly accepted and even a history of petty crime will result in a would-be recruit being put on the next train home. If his crimes were committed in France, he is simply handed over to the civil police.*

The weeding-out takes place after a few days of hectic processing, by which time men who have something to hide are generally off their guard.

The system is simple: the new intake is marched into a classroom where each man sits at a desk. There are two sheets of lined paper in front of him, which he is required to fill with the story of his life. What he writes may be the truth or a tissue of lies; that's up to him. Frenchmen have to invent a story. Since citizens of the Republic are not allowed to enlist in the ranks of the Legion, they must make up a non-French identity that accounts for them speaking the language fluently. Most claim to be Belgian or Swiss and are known thereafter as the Gauls – les Gaulois.

The catch is that every recruit is afterwards grilled by two or three NCOs in his own language. They take him several times through the details of his story, shouting questions all at the same time, trying to trick him, throw him off balance and confuse him. If he passes the test to their satisfaction, the Legion accepts him as the man he claims to be.

Muller, Milton and the Irishman were not at all the kind of material I had in mind when Koenig and I went seeking three men for a lightning clandestine mission inside Vietnam. I was frankly angry that an old classmate like their colonel should try to foist them on to me.

It was Koenig who drew my attention to the first document in Muller's personal file, which I had not bothered to read.

He handed me two sheets of paper covered with rather effeminate handwriting. When I read them I saw a face, a tattooed arm and a photograph lying in the mud.

'I was guessing,' said Koenig, watching my reaction.

'You guessed right,' I replied. 'Let's see this young man. It seems I owe him a debt.'

Frank Hansen, I remember, had an instinctive dislike for Muller from the start, but I overrode his objections. If I had been less cavalier, I might have avoided the bad blood between them, but as to taking Muller on. . . . Well, once I had read his brief life-story, my code of honour left me no alternative.

3

Hans-Peter sat at the desk in the *deuxième bureau* classroom. The two sheets of blank paper mocked him. What are you going to write? they asked. How are you going to get out of this?

He had rehearsed a hundred times the story he would use, assuming that the questioning would be perfunctory and oral. Wasn't the Legion supposed to be full of criminals, drunks, rapists and brawlers? Hadn't it been a haven for hundreds, maybe thousands, of war criminals on the run like his father? How had they got in?

Perhaps they hadn't had a written test in those times? He willed his pulse to slow down and pulled the first sheet of paper to him. He had always enjoyed calligraphy and even using an issue ball-pen his handwriting was flowing and artistic.

There was no need for him to tell any big lies, he decided. He would simply omit the real reason for running away to join the Legion.

My name is Hans-Peter Muller. I was born in 1945 in west Berlin where my mother runs a ladies' hairdressing salon in Wedding, which is a district within the French sector of the divided city. My father, Hans Muller, was a sergeant in the German army. Unable to get work after the war, he left Germany and joined the Foreign Legion in 1947. My mother received some letters and photographs from him, posted in Algeria. Later he wrote from Vietnam. She has the letters still. In 1954 they stopped coming. Much later we heard from an uncle who had also enlisted in the Legion, that my father had died at a place called Dien Bien Phu.

Hans-Peter studied what he had written. It was close to the truth, except that his father had not been in the Wehrmacht, but the Waffen SS. And unemployment was not the reason why Hans Muller had left home in 1947.

He had come home after the war in civilian clothes with somebody else's identity card. A phone call from an old comrade working as interpreter with the Four-Power military police gave Hans five minutes' warning to grab the cash from the till and disappear minutes before a jeep-load of military police skidded to a halt outside. The Russian and the American sat in the jeep while the French and English MPs stomped around the house, looking for evidence of a man in residence. They searched Ingrid Muller's bedroom and threw all her underclothes on the floor. They even searched under the bed of her two-year-old son, who was crying at the intrusion.

They told her that they were rounding up former SS men suspected of participating in the atrocity at Oradour-sur-Glâne during the Allied invasion of France in 1944, when men of the SS Das Reich division had murdered the entire population of a small town in central France for no known reason.

Years later when Hans-Peter asked his mother, 'Would my father have done a thing like that?' she didn't want to answer.

Eventually she said, 'I never knew your father, Hansel. He left for the Russian front only a week after we were married. He came home once on leave for two days and we made you. Then he lived with us off and on for three months when you were a baby and he was on the run. I never saw him again after the day the MPs came for him. How can I say what kind of man he was?'

School ... thought Hans-Peter. I must write something about school. They'll expect that. But I must be careful not to drop any hints.

At school I was good at languages, art and sport. My mother had many French and British customers – wives of troops in the garrison – so I learned very young to speak French and English by talking to them in the salon whilst they were under the dryer.

I was always able to draw well. When there was a new hairstyle and my mother could not afford photographic enlargements, I used to draw charcoal sketches of it to decorate the salon.

And that's what got me involved in my first relationship. To begin with, Herr Stoss was just an art teacher taking an interest in a talented pupil. Mutti was glad when he asked her permission so politely to take me with him to *vernissages* at art galleries on the Kurfürstendamm and to museums. She had always said I hung about the salon too much. 'It's wrong for a boy to spend all his time with women, Hansel. You need a man to take an interest in you like a father would.'

Like a father would! Berlin was short of men after the war. And Stoss with his limp from an old leg wound and pale blue eyes and curly hair, was a man – if not the kind that Mutti had been hoping for. Looking back, I can see how careful he was, not to alarm her or me. He certainly took his time before making the first approach.

I must have known him for three years by then. Yes, I was fourteen. It was in a cinema off the Ku-damm after we had been to the opening of an exhibition of modern art. He'd made sure I'd had a drink or two there. I don't remember the film we were watching. He took my hand. When I realised that his flies were open and he wanted me to touch him, I didn't mind. I did it to please him. I wanted to please him because he'd been good to me . . . and because it excited him.

'Write!' A clenched fist thumped down on the crown of Hans-Peter's head. He looked up, blinking at the corporal who stood over him, glaring. '*Schreib! Napishi! Escriba! Ecris!*'

Feeling sick from the blow, Hans-Peter bent his head and continued writing:

I won many prizes for sport. I also have a gift for mending machines. When I was twelve I repaired a motor bike for a neighbour, which was otherwise to be written off. By the time I was fourteen, I worked evenings and weekends in Steiner's Garage, at the end of our street. I wasn't even an apprentice, properly speaking, but I could often mend things when the boss gave up and wanted to fit a new part. There was a shortage of spare parts in Berlin, so I was very useful to Steiner.

And I had trouble with him too. He used to take me into that grubby little office of his at the back of the garage and show me photographs of men and women doing things to each other.

'Which ones excite you more, *Junge?*' he would ask, licking his thick rubbery lips and watching my face.

Then he would lock the door and tell me what I had to do, to get out. Sometimes he would just grope me. I was frightened of saying no. But I was more frightened because I liked it. I wanted to go there, but I hated myself for going. Sometimes I would stay away from the garage for a week or two. Then Mutti would say how I ought to keep in with Herr Steiner because he could get me a job when I left school. So I'd go back there and it would start all over again. I stopped going near the garage when I was sixteen and told Mutti that I had . . .

. . . decided to become a hairdresser because there were not many jobs in Berlin for a boy of my age with no *Abitur*. I could have gone to art school . . .

but I knew that would lead me back to Stoss, or someone else like him. Mutti was disappointed, but

. . . she needed an extra pair of hands in the salon – and I had a flair for cutting. The money was fine, but I decided to look for a job where I could do more sport and if possible work with machines. There is no conscription in west Berlin, so I thought of joining the Foreign Legion as my father had done.

Hans-Peter put down his pen. Several of the others, he saw, had completed the stories of their lives. Some had written only one paragraph, despite the supervising corporal's unimaginative endeavours to increase the flow of inspiration. Not wanting to attract attention again, Hans-Peter kept his head down.

Keep your head down! He remembered Chantal Borne's advice when she saw him off at the railway station, less than a week before. 'You'll be all right in the Legion so long as you keep your head down and don't attract attention.'

Like Stoss and Steiner, she had set out to seduce him, from her first appointment at the Muller salon. Each week, Hans-Peter had been aware of her eyes watching him in the mirror whenever he looked up from working on her hair.

As a Parisienne and the wife of a French officer in the Berlin garrison, Chantal Borne was better dressed than the German customers. Hans-Peter liked her clothes as much as her conversation, which was fast and witty and kept him mentally on his toes. She in turn appreciated his perfect command of her language. She laughed at his puns. She lent him books of French poetry and novels to read. Eventually she suggested that he call at her apartment on his afternoon off to collect a copy of the latest Françoise Sagan novel.

She lived at the top of an old house which had survived the war intact, apart from bullet-holes on the ground-floor walls. From her windows there was a view over the rooftops.

In the distance loomed the Brandenburger Tor and the bomb-damaged remains of Hitler's ministries. Inside the apartment, there were no sounds from the neighbours on the other side of the thick walls. The furnishings were tasteful, with silk cushions everywhere, the walls lined with books and records. There were paintings on the walls too, some original.

Hans-Peter soaked up the atmosphere: books, records, paintings.

She watched him savouring each pleasure. 'Do you like my home, Hans-Peter?'

He nodded, unable to speak. He was feeling the same conflict as when he went into the darkened cinema with Stoss or entered Herr Steiner's office and heard the lock click. He wanted what was going to happen, and wanted not to want it.

Chantal had given a lot of thought to how she should be dressed; she wanted to excite but not frighten. He was only a boy, she thought, and probably a virgin, while she was almost old enough to be his mother. The choice had been earrings, a silk blouse and a flowing bias-cut skirt that swirled as she moved. Hans-Peter had done her hair the previous day, in the same style as Hildegard Kneff.

She took Hans-Peter's coat, exuding a free sensuality as she brushed against him and murmured, 'Let me get you a drink.'

She put a record on the turntable and curled her legs under her on the opposite end of the sofa from her visitor. The music was Kneff's latest recording, 'Ich hab' noch einen Koffer in Berlin'. The low, throaty tones were like Chantal's own voice.

She lit a cigarette and studied Hans-Peter, stroking her neck thoughtfully.

'You're a very beautiful boy,' she told him.

His pulse was racing. All his senses were heightened but he could not move. He watched helplessly as his hostess stubbed out her cigarette and slipped towards him along the sofa. Her high-heeled shoes fell on to the carpet with a soft thud. Two buttons of her blouse fell open as she removed her earrings.

Her mouth was only inches from his when she said, in the husky Kneff-like voice, 'Do you want to kiss me?'

He closed his eyes and felt her bear him gently backwards into the cushions, her hair on his face. Her lips were cautious, seeking a response which did not come. Her tongue entered his mouth. She began undoing his buttons, caressing his chest and kissing him. There was no haste. Seduction, as she had learned young, was an art that should never be hurried. It took half an hour for her to get to the point where they were both naked on the carpeted floor – and even longer before she realised that Hans-Peter could not make love to her.

She touched, stroked and kissed his body. She rubbed herself against him like a cat pushing for attention. She buried his face in her breasts, while he lay soft as a girl, waiting for something that could not happen.

Hans-Peter visited her several times on his weekly afternoon off. They sat and talked on the sofa, discussed literature and poetry. She tried one more time to arouse him sexually and after that concentrated on helping him in other ways.

Even the briefly sketched two-page outline was enough for me to be certain that young Muller was the son of one of my guardian angels at Dien Bien Phu.

I recalled that interminable day of agony when Minh had kept me thirsty and pain-racked on a stretcher in the sun. I saw again the naked body of the man I had known simply as Hans. I saw one arm tattooed with the eagle and snake emblem reaching out across the mud and gravel of the battlefield in my direction. And just out of reach of the dead fingers, I saw again the handful of letters thrown away by the bo-doi who had looted his pockets.

I could see so clearly everything that happened that day. Each image was burnt into my memory by pain.

The photograph lying with the letters in the mud came sharply into focus. I saw the woman and a boy of about eight standing in

front of a hairdressing salon in Berlin, with MULLER DAMENFRIS-
EUR across the top of the shopfront.

There could have been half a dozen men named Hans Muller
at Dien Bien Phu. After all, eighty per cent of our NCOs there
were German. But how many would have had a wife who was a
hairdresser in Berlin and a boy of that age who would grow up
with no father?

It seemed that fate, by sending his son to me was saying: Take
care of this young man.

But perhaps I was deluding myself. For now it seems to me
that, given the circumstances, young Muller is the most likely
traitor of all.

4

'You've got to fill both sheets of paper.' Hans-Peter had translated the instructions for Roger and Sean. Head down over the desk, Sean panicked. He had never written that much in his life. He looked at the men on either side. Hans-Peter stopped writing for a moment and stared into space. On the other side of Sean, Roger was writing steadily, a slight smile on his face. The glint in his eye made Sean wonder whether Roger was writing the truth. What had he got to hide?

Sean had hated every moment spent in a classroom. The humiliation of those who are always bottom of the class was something he knew all about. It gave him a savage pleasure to be writing in his ill-formed handwriting what was a pack of misspelled lies from start to finish. Only the date of birth was correct:

Me name is Patrick O'Reilly. I burn in Dublin and live ther all my live till now. My fater werk in the Guinnes brury. Me moter clean ofis fer mony . . .'

The writing was large, very large.
As Koenig remarked, 'Was that due to semi-literacy? Or was

289

it a cunning way of filling up the paper? There's no evidence the man's stupid, quite the reverse.'

His opinion was the same as mine. The story of Patrick O'Reilly rang false. However, whatever his true name, the Irishman had stuck to his fiction throughout a tough grilling, and O'Reilly was the name he went under for five years in the Legion. In any case, as far as Koenig and I were concerned, his file had other, far more interesting items in it.

Sean's earliest memory of his childhood on the Clonard estate, a poverty-stricken Catholic ghetto in west Belfast, was of his mother saying, 'Yer gonna die, son. Yer got noomoniya.'

She lit a candle, borrowed from the neighbours, and placed it on the shelf behind the door where she hung his clothes at night so the mice did not get into them. The electricity had been cut off for non-payment, but the candle was not for light. Its flame was supposed to show his soul which way to go.

Other memories of early childhood were too shameful to remember. His second conscious recollection was of the summer after he had nearly died of pneumonia. He was four years old.

'Lemme in, will ye? There's a good boy.' Michael Carey's glazed smile swam through the raindrops running down the window pane. He was standing beneath a hole in the rotten gutter but did not notice. Three days' stubble covered the weak chin; the mouth was slackly open, showing broken and discoloured teeth.

Sean said nothing. After a moment, his father stepped back from the window and patted the bulging raincoat pocket where the boy could see. 'I've got something nice for ye. It's a present.'

The boy let the curtain fall back into place and stepped sideways, standing with his back to the wall as though his father could see through cloth but not masonry. His mother was out scrubbing. There was no food in the house until she returned. He scuffed a shoe along the cracked skirting board that had come away from the wall, toying with the idea of opening the door.

It was tempting for the four-year-old to believe that his father did have 'something nice' for him. More likely, thought Sean, what's in the pocket is a bottle and if I let the old man in I'll get a beating, or worse. . . .

He heard the singing outside grow fainter as his father lurched away down the street. He hoped his father was heading back to the pub on the corner.

Sean waited, hoping his mother would not be long. If she was there, the worst would not happen. . . .

Then he heard the noise of breaking glass by the back door. His father must have come down the narrow passage between the houses and be climbing over the pile of bottles in the backyard to force his way in. There was no lock on the back door, which did not even fit properly since the jamb had been splintered by a drunken kick the previous winter.

The noise in the yard stopped. Silence, broken only by the gush of rain from the broken gutter and the sound of the radio in the house next door.

Cautiously, Sean crept to the kitchen door and peered through the crack where the wood was broken. His father lay head down on the bottle pile where he had fallen after climbing over the low wall. The eyes were staring open and blood oozed from nose and ears, diluted by the rain on the blotchy skin. One hand was stretched out reaching for the full bottle he had been trying to save when he fell.

Fascinated, the boy watched the grimy fingers clench on empty air and then relax. He wanted badly to go to the toilet, but that would have meant opening the door and walking past the dying man to reach the outside lavatory, so he sat down on the floor with his back against the door and accepted the bowel cramps as he accepted the cold, the damp and the hunger that were normal parts of his life.

. . . I got no skil so thers no werk for me in Dublin an I don wanter join te Irish ermy . . .

Sean was nine when Father Callaghan – the new priest, as he was called in Clonard – came into his life.

The wiry and cheerful little man of God from Connemara spent a morning in the dreary corridors of the education offices arguing with the overworked psychologist who specialised in truancy.

'It's the shame of it,' sobbed Sheila Carey when the priest brought her son home. 'The neighbours knowing and all.'

She tugged at the curtain in the front window as though it were a cloak of invisibility that could hide her disgrace. The shabby furnishings of the tiny parlour were Sheila Carey's only pretence at respectability in a rented house that did not conform to any building regulations. Her few possessions were all on display: unused wedding presents on the second-hand sideboard with chipped veneer and a few family photographs on the mantelpiece. Beside the fire that was never lit was an uncomfortable armchair, never sat in.

'Enough!' the priest said sharply. 'It's the sin of pride that makes ye think like that, woman. Never mind the neighbours. You'd do better to think about your son.' He let go of Sean's arm. Immediately the boy moved out of reach, near the door.

When Sean was eleven, his champion defended him in the juvenile court, argued with probation officer and judge and brought him home again.

'What will we do about this son of yours?' Father Callaghan asked Sheila Carey. 'I had a hard job convincing that probation officer who's looking after him. She wants to put Sean in a special school for boys who've been in trouble and run away from home.'

'I won't stay there,' said Sean.

Sheila Carey looked desperate. 'My boy's never run away from home, father.'

'He has,' the priest reminded her gently.

'Only once,' she said. 'When he was six. His uncle Patrick

had beaten him, so he said. That's why he ran away. He wasn't –' she ran out of words – 'he wasn't running away from me, like.'

'The psychologist says the root of Sean's problem is that he needs a man's influence.'

'I'm too soft on the boy,' she said. 'I know that.'

'What about this uncle of his?'

'Fockin' bastard, he is!' the boy swore.

'Be quiet!' ordered the priest.

'Patrick's me dead husband's brother,' she explained. 'Sean doesn't like him.'

'Why not, Sean?' asked Father Callaghan.

'He won't say,' she put in.

'The boy needs a father's hand,' said the priest. 'Had you ever thought of marrying again, Sheila?'

She looked him straight in the eye. 'Who would want me, father?'

He avoided the question. 'Well, there it is. We've got to do something with the boy. I saved him from being sent away this time, but I won't be able to do it again if he goes on like this.'

'They're all against my boy.' It looked as though she would sob again.

'He makes it easy for them,' said the priest. 'Playing truant all the time and stealing, what do you expect?'

Sheila Carey was getting ready to cry. 'They're trying to take my son away, father.'

'No, they're not.' The priest grew impatient and shook her shoulders roughly. 'I told you, the judge listened to me, woman, which is more than you do. For six months, they'll leave things as they are, providing I take a personal interest in Sean's moral welfare. But we can't have the boy setting fire to a supermarket again just because the manager has warned him off the premises, can we?'

'The manager made a mistake,' she said. 'I know it wasn't my Sean that did it.'

'Unfortunately for your son,' snorted the priest, 'he's got the reddest hair in west Belfast. Nobody could mistake him.

I talked to the manager. Most of the kids round here steal from shops, of course, but he says Sean is one of the ring-leaders. That's why he made an example of him.'

'I can't believe it . . .' She twisted her handkerchief between her fingers.

'Well I'm afraid I can,' he said shortly. 'So let's stop talking rubbish and get down to the facts. What we are dealing with here, is not a boy of ten who's got himself into trouble.'

'Sean's eleven,' she interrupted.

'Will you be quiet?' he shouted. 'I'm not talking about his age. We're talking about something much older than that. We're talking about something as old as the human race. Older, even.'

'Are we?'

The priest leaned forward and paused to give his words the emphasis he wanted; there were times when a sermon for an audience of two merited all he could put into it. Enunciating each word, he said, 'We are talking about the devil, Mrs Carey.'

Quick as a flash, he grabbed Sean's thin shoulders before the boy could move and thrust him in front of his mother. 'I can see the devil in your son.'

5

It was for boys like Sean that Father Callaghan had planned St Mary's Youth Band, hoping they would join it to compete with the Protestant marching bands that drew the crowds each year when they processed along the Shankill Road in high summer. But the boys of the Clonard estate were lone wolves; each had his own excuse not to join even a Catholic band.

'I haven't got the proper clothes,' said Sean sullenly. 'So I can't go.'

'If you mean the beret and the jumper,' said Father Callaghan, 'I think I can fix that.'

He waited for some reaction, but none came. 'If I can scrounge ye a jumper and a beret, Sean, will ye go along to the rehearsal tonight?'

The boy scuffed the toe of his boot on his mother's clean doorstep and drew a black line on the scrubbed white stone. 'I'll think about it,' he said, his eyes avoiding Father Callaghan's gaze.

'Well, that's arranged, then,' said the priest hastily. 'I'll drop by your house this afternoon with the clothes and I want to see ye at that rehearsal tonight without fail.'

He released the boy and watched him run along the pavement and dart into an alleyway, not wishing to be seen with the priest in his black cassock.

'Keep your fingers crossed, God.' Father Callaghan spoke

to the sky. Then, changing religion, 'And where the devil am I going to find a beret and a jumper before teatime?'

The priest made a point of not speaking to Sean at the rehearsal that evening, nor the following week. He let a month go by before dropping in 'for a cup of tea' one afternoon. Sean's enthusiasm took him by surprise.

'It's great,' said the boy. 'It's really fantastic, being in the band.'

'Good,' said Father Callaghan cautiously. 'I'm glad you like it. Can you play anything yet on your fife?'

They were sitting in the Careys' kitchen. Sean had just returned from school. He was eating a slice of bread and marge, which his mother called tea.

'He hides the instrument when he goes to school,' she said. 'He thinks somebody might break in and steal it. And he sleeps with it under his pillow too.'

'But can he play it?' asked the priest, teasing gently. When Sean did not reply, he sat back in the only unbroken chair. 'No, I expect it's too early yet. He's only been going to the band for a few weeks. It takes longer than that to learn an instrument.'

'I'll show you,' said the boy defiantly, licking the grease off his fingers.

'Go on, then.' The priest spoke quietly, hoping nothing would break the spell of the moment. 'Get that fife and show me what you can do.'

Sean moved silently through the house, not wanting to betray the hiding place even to the priest. When he came back, he was dressed in the beret and the jumper of the marching band.

'What do you want me to play?' he asked.

'Can you play a couple of notes?' the priest asked, humouring him.

'Of course I can.' Sean was scornful. 'Anyone can play notes. I'll do better than that. I'll play yez a tune.'

'And what tune did they teach you already?' the priest wanted to know.

'I taught meself,' boasted Sean. 'It's easy. I'll play yez a tune by that Acker Bilk. I heard it on the wireless.'

He raised the fife to his lips, took a breath and started to play. His eyes narrowed with concentration and then closed completely. His whole body swayed with the music.

The indulgent smile left Father Callaghan's face. He had been expecting a poor, fumbling imitation of one of the band's Irish marches. Instead the haunting melody of 'Stranger on the Shore' filled the room. The composers would have recognised it from the first few notes, but they would also have known that the boy had taken the music and made it his own. The priest had only his untutored instinct to go on; a shiver ran up his spine, for it seemed impossible that a scruffy, semi-literate, undersized, ignorant child could make real music as Sean was doing.

When the last note had died away, Father Callaghan clapped his hands.

'What'd you do that for?' the boy asked suspiciously. He wiped his lips on a sleeve and held the instrument behind his back, as though frightened it might be taken from him.

'Because you're good,' the priest answered.

The boy's freckled face flushed with pleasure.

'You're just saying that, father,' said Sheila Carey.

'Oh no I'm not.' Father Callaghan turned to her. 'I don't know much about music, Mrs Carey, but I tell you that son of yours has a gift. He's maybe even what they call a prodigy.'

In Sheila Carey's life, the unknown had usually proven to be dangerous; even an unknown word could contain menace.

'It won't get Sean into trouble, will it, father?' she asked anxiously.

Rosemary Keogh was the doyenne of Belfast's woodwind teachers. Her home was an elegant Victorian family house near Queen's University. The walls of the teaching studio were decorated with photographs of a host of young men and women in dinner jackets and evening dress, her pupils who had become professional musicians in orchestras and chamber music groups all over the world.

A mixture of elegance and toughness that had driven many of her pupils to professional level, she sat at the piano of her teaching studio with the natural authority of a tycoon at his desk or a bishop on his throne. For once the indomitable Father Callaghan knew he had met his match; this quiet woman in the tweed skirt and grey cardigan would not be persuaded to do anything she did not want to do.

'You're going to think me uncharitable,' she said, fingering the keys of the piano as she thought over Father Callaghan's proposition. 'But, remember that I've had many slum children from west Belfast brought to me over the years by well-meaning people – priests like yourself, teachers and social workers. What you don't understand is that free lessons never work.'

'But this boy's different.' Father Callaghan sat tensely on the edge of his chair. 'If you'll just listen to him . . .'

'No.' Her mind was firm. 'There wouldn't be any point. You see, most of the work of learning an instrument is done between the lessons, father. At the weekly lesson, I just move the pupil on to the next step, so to speak.'

She held up a hand to stop his interruption. 'Now some children practise each day because they want to, but most do it because a parent makes them. If the parents aren't involved, it's a waste of my time.'

To soften the decision she went on, 'Oh, I don't blame the children themselves, father. It's the environment they live in and the negative values all around them. But what can we do?' She stood up to indicate the end of the conversation.

Father Callaghan remained obstinately seated. 'This boy's different,' he repeated.

A shake of the head. 'I'm sorry.'

The priest took a deep breath. He disliked telling lies, even for good ends.

'I can find the money from a charity,' he said. 'If I pay you a term's fees in advance, Mrs Keogh, you can take the boy on just like any other pupil. Then, if he's no good at the end of the term, you can kick him out with my blessing. How's that?'

'You're a persistent man.'

She seated herself and looked out at her garden. The first lilacs were in bloom, splashing bold mauve and green against the weathered red bricks. A faint hum of traffic from the Lisburn road penetrated the double glazing. There was the distant sound of an ambulance heading for Belfast City Hospital. They could have been a hundred miles, not two, from Sheila Carey's house in Bombay Terrace with its broken windows and unpainted doors.

'I already have a full quota of pupils,' she said, her mind made up. 'I really don't think I could fit one more in.'

The doorbell rang as if to prove her point. There were voices of a woman and a child in the hallway.

'Will you listen to the boy?' pleaded Father Callaghan, playing his last card.

Mrs Keogh pursed her lips; priests like this were always a nuisance. Why had she agreed to let him come?

'Very well, father,' she said. 'I'll give the boy two minutes of my time at the end of my next lesson. Two minutes and no more.'

Sean waited in the corridor. He refused to sit, but stood close to the door of the studio, listening to the sounds within. His feet were braced defiantly apart, showing how ill at ease he was in this house with its elegant wallpaper, antique carpets and polished boards. It was like no home he had ever been in before. He intended asking Father Callaghan when they left if this was how all Protestants lived. In which case, the devil was certainly taking care of his own.

At the end of the lesson, the door opened and a girl of about Sean's age came out. She was carrying a flute case and a music case. Her mother hurried her past Sean and out of the front door.

'You can come in,' called Mrs Keogh.

To Sean's ears her well-modulated voice had an English accent like the newsreaders on the BBC. He walked into the room nervously, eyes large and darting from one picture to another on the wall.

'You brought your instrument, I see.' She held out a hand to inspect the fife.

'Give it to the lady, Sean,' ordered Father Callaghan.

Reluctantly, Sean handed over the fife.

Mrs Keogh looked at it. As she had thought, some of the pads were split and one spring was broken. It was hardly playable.

Irritated, she handed back the instrument. 'How many lessons have you had?' she asked.

'He's not had any proper lessons,' Father Callaghan answered for Sean. 'Just a bit of help from some of the lads in the band, you know.'

'Well, I'll give you an easy piece.' She leafed through a pile of beginners' music and selected one at random, smoothing it out on a music stand which she lowered to Sean's eye height.

'I can't read them dots,' he said sullenly.

'Then how are you going to play to me?'

'I make up me own music,' mumbled Sean. 'What I've heard on the radio and that.'

'Why don't you play the tune for Mrs Keogh?' suggested the priest hurriedly. 'The one I liked so much.' He was sweating from tension.

'Do you like Acker Bilk?' asked Sean.

'Who?' she queried.

'It's pop music,' explained the priest.

With an animal's instinct, the boy sensed he had said something wrong but did not know what. 'You've not heard of him, have ye? He's very good.'

'Oh, play me whatever you like,' she said, patience gone. 'As long as it's short.'

When he had finished, she said nothing for a moment.

'I'll be going,' said Sean, thrusting the fife inside his dirty jacket. 'Ye're in a hurry, aren't ye?'

'Never mind that.' She sat at the piano and pressed a key. 'Sing me that note.'

'I don't sing,' the boy said. 'I don't like to.'

'You'll sing it for me,' she said. 'Or you'll not come here again.'

He sang the note, ashamed of his voice. The sound was hardly audible.

'Louder,' she ordered.

'Now this note . . .

'And this . . .

'Now I'll play three notes, one after another and you sing them in the same order.'

Father Callaghan was silent, his eyes travelling between them, fascinated.

'Now I'll play a chord,' she said.

Sean blinked. 'Whassat?'

'Three notes at the same time. You have to identify them and sing them back to me one after another.'

'That was easy,' said Sean. ''Ave I passed the test, missus?'

'Do you know what an opera is?' she asked.

He shook his head.

'Well I'm going to play a tune on the piano. It's from Rossini's opera *William Tell* and I want you to play it back to me.'

Sean listened to the first four notes. 'That's the *Lone Ranger* music,' he said.

'Maybe,' she said. 'Play it on your fife.'

When he had finished, she smiled. 'Ten out of ten, Sean. Can you play it faster?'

'I played it the same speed you did,' he said accusingly.

'You did,' she agreed. 'Exactly the same tempo. But now I'm asking you to play it faster.'

And at the end, he said, 'Playing fast's easy, missus. It's playing slow I find 'ard. The notes sorta wobble, if you know worra mean.'

'They do indeed.' Mrs Keogh was excited. 'That's why you must come to me for lessons, Sean.'

6

The Ulster Hall, Belfast
Saturday, 15 December 1962
The BBC Symphony Orchestra
Soloist: James Galway . . .

S ean kept his eyes glued to the wording of the poster.
That way he didn't have to look at the stream of
smartly dressed people crowding into the foyer of the
concert hall. From time to time he glanced wildly about,
hoping to catch a glimpse of Mrs Keogh's tight grey perm.
To the boy's ears, tuned to the diphthongs and soft conson-
ants of west Belfast, the middle-class voices in the foyer
sounded unfriendly, clipped and English.

Inside the foyer was a boy of about sixteen in a smart
worsted suit and a white shirt with collar and tie. He was
talking animatedly to two teenage girls in boarding-school
uniform and grey walking-out cloaks, both of them holding
flute cases. Several times the three turned to look at Sean
on the other side of the doors.

To the outsider looking in, his reflection stood in the glass
between them. He felt ashamed of his threadbare flannel
trousers and handed-down jacket with sleeves that were too
long. His short crew cut made his ears stick out: Jug 'andles
was his nickname in Clonard, but only ever used by boys
big enough to get away with it.

'Why there you are, Sean! Don't skulk outside, boy. Come on in and meet my other pupils.'

Mrs Keogh appeared at the critical moment, just as he was about to retreat into the anonymous darkness. Dressed for the occasion, she swept him into the hall, to be introduced to her three pupils waiting inside. 'This is Sean. He started lessons with me this summer. And this is Robert, my star pupil. And these two convent girls with the giggles are Ginette and Dorothy.'

'Hallo,' said Robert.

The girls contained their giggles and nodded at Sean, who kept his head lowered and mumbled to no one in particular. He tagged on to the end of the line as Mrs Keogh propelled her protégés upstairs to the balcony and seated them in the front row.

'You'll hear better up here,' she said, leaving them with the tickets.

'Where are you goin'?' Sean asked uncertainly.

'Backstage,' she said, 'to talk to the orchestra.'

Trapped by Mrs Keogh's seating arrangements between the girls and the smartly suited Robert, Sean sat in a spastic contortion, hoping to hide both the frayed cuffs of the jacket and an oil stain on his trousers by clamping his arms firmly to his legs and not moving.

'Can't you talk?' asked Robert after several unanswered questions.

Sean shook his head.

'A mute,' Robert said to the two girls on the other side of Sean.

'Perhaps he's a mutant?' suggested one of the girls, teasing.

'A mute mutant,' agreed Robert. 'Definitely an extra-terrestrial being from the dark side of Belfast.'

The girls giggled. Sean blushed to the roots of his cropped red hair. If he had not been trapped in his seat he would have got up and left the hall before the concert even began.

*

'What do you think of Galway?' Mrs Keogh asked at the start of Sean's next lesson. 'He started in a marching band, just like you.'

'Who did?' queried Sean.

'The young man who played the solo flute at the concert.'

'Him!' Sean stopped putting his flute together. His face lit up with remembered pleasure. 'He was great. Did ye hear him at the end when he picked up that fife just like the one I have in the band? And then he played them little Irish jigs as an encore and got everyone clappin'.'

'Which music did you like best, Sean?' She was testing him. 'The jigs or the Mozart flute concerto?'

'The jigs was excitin'.' Sean's rare enthusiasm boiled over. 'Bejasus he can play fast when he wants to, that fellow!'

'You preferred the jigs to the Mozart, then?'

'I dunno.' The boy's thin freckled face was screwed up in concentration, recapturing the sounds he had heard. 'The jigs was . . . well, they wasn't nothing, really. It was the way 'e played 'em what got you, like. But the music by that Mozart. . . . It made you think, dinnit?'

'Yes.' Mrs Keogh was looking at the roses in the rain-damp garden. 'Music like that makes you think, Sean.'

'Do you suppose . . .' He hesitated. He would not have asked anyone else such a question.

'Do I suppose what?'

'Do you suppose I could be as good as that Galway fellow, one day?'

He could, she thought, if only he has enough ambition.

'Well . . .' She felt her way cautiously. 'Jimmy Galway is twenty-three. You're thirteen. If you work as hard for the next ten years as you have this term with me, you could be another Galway by the time you're his age.'

'Playing on that platform in them fancy clothes, with an orchestra and all?'

'All that,' she agreed.

Sean was grinning at the prospect. 'Bejasus, I'd like that, Missus Keogh. I really would.'

*

304

A year later, Mrs Keogh held up the certificate that had come in that day's post. 'You've passed your Grade 5 examination, Sean. With distinction.'

He took the piece of paper and read it slowly, mouthing the words to himself.

The fact that he's hardly literate, she thought, makes his achievement all the more significant. . . .

'You can stop congratulating yourself, Sean,' she smiled. 'In music, you can never let up. Today we start work for the next exam. I want you to learn this.'

She passed him a copy of the Badinerie from Bach's Suite in B Minor. As his eyes alighted on the musical notation, they flicked at lightning speed along each line, sight-reading the music.

'Hey, this is great stuff,' he said.

'It is,' Mrs Keogh agreed. 'Let me hear you play it.'

She spun the piano stool and sat with her back to Sean, listening to him play. The garden was bleak, a few dead rhododendron heads on the bushes. The music Sean was making was like a breath of spring, lighting up next year's blossoms in her mind's eye. Not for the first time, she wondered where such gifts as his came from.

It was almost three years after his first lesson with Mrs Keogh that Sean auditioned at the Mozart School, a specialist school for musically gifted children in Birmingham.

The trip to Birmingham with Father Callaghan was the first time Sean had been far away from Belfast. The night crossing of the stormy Irish Sea to Liverpool had been an adventure; the two-hour train journey from Merseyside to Birmingham he had spent wide-eyed and wary, watching and listening to the English around him. Even the side trip with Father Callaghan to see the new cathedral of Christ the King being built in Liverpool had been an event for a youth who had only been outside Belfast once before in his life.

The auditions at the Mozart School, Sean had taken in his stride – as he did everything to do with music. Afterwards he and the priest had stayed the night in a modest religious boarding house which had seemed like the Ritz to Sean.

He arrived at his next weekly lesson bubbling over with confidence; there was hardly any need for his teacher to ask how he had played.

'Did you listen to any of the other flute candidates, like I told you?' Mrs Keogh asked.

'I did.' Sean looked serious. 'There was one flute girl who was better than me on the piano. But my flute playin' was better than hers by a long way. I was the best one there.'

'Then we'll keep our fingers crossed,' she smiled. 'It'll be a week or so until we know the results.'

'You said they 'ad three places for flute players,' he accused her.

'I did.'

'Well, I'm definitely in the best three, so they gotta take me.'

'Don't count your chickens, Sean,' she said seriously. 'I'm sure you're good enough to merit a place at the Mozart School, otherwise I wouldn't have entered you for the auditions. But that doesn't necessarily mean they've accepted you.'

His face fell. 'Why not? 'Cos I'm a Catholic?'

She grew impatient at the way he thought the entire world was polarised by religion. 'It's nothing to do with that,' she snapped. 'They make the selection on several grounds, not just according to the way you play. You must understand that, Sean, and not take it to heart if you're not accepted this time.'

He glared at her.

She noticed he was putting on some weight at last and was not quite so skinny and undersized for his age as when she had begun teaching him three years before. Unfortunately the effect was, if anything, to make Sean look more aggressive. The tousled red hair, a suggestion of a straggling moustache across his unshaven upper lip and the gold earring he wore in his left ear would not have won the approval of the selection board at the Mozart School.

Accompanying his first piece on the piano, Mrs Keogh

wondered whether they had looked at Sean and seen a young thug or closed their eyes and heard an angel play.

She was shortly to find out the answers to both questions.

From the Principal

The Mozart School
Aston
Birmingham
14 May 1965

Mrs Rosemary Keogh, LRAM, ARCM, ALCM
Holly Bank
Eglantine Avenue
Belfast

Dear Mrs Keogh,

AUDITIONS FOR ACADEMIC YEAR 1965/6: CANDIDATE'S NAME: SEAN CAREY

I am writing personally to you about Sean, rather than simply sending an audition form because it was not easy for us to reach a decision about him. Technically, I would say that he undoubtedly has the technique and musicianship that could lead to a performing career.

However, since the Mozart School is residential, other considerations do affect which pupils we accept and which we regretfully have to turn down. In Sean's case, it was felt after a great deal of discussion here that he would not adjust to the discipline and standards of behaviour required by the school. It is therefore with regret that I have to tell you he has not been accepted.

As we all know, young people can change a great deal in the course of a year. If you should feel that Sean's personal development and improved social skills warrant this, please do enter him as a candidate in next year's auditions.

Yours very sincerely,

Andrew Small, DMus, MA (Cantab), FRCO

Holly Bank
Eglantine Avenue
Belfast
1 June 1965

Dear Dr Small,

I don't believe in special pleading, nor do I think that you lightly rejected Sean Carey. Having taught him for three years, I am all too well aware to what extent he lacks the social graces. But in all honesty, another year of living in west Belfast is unlikely to improve anyone. For a boy of Sean's age, the reverse is likely.

So I am putting my pride behind me and breaking a lifetime's rule by asking you to reconsider your decision. Sean has set his heart on becoming a professional musician. I fear that the sense of rejection he is experiencing may cause him to fall by the wayside. It would be a pity for the world of music to lose his talent. Playing like his is rare, as you know.

If you can see your way to accepting Sean, I know he would work hard to make himself an acceptable pupil at the Mozart School.

Yours sincerely,
Rosemary Keogh.

From the Principal

The Mozart School
Aston
Birmingham
8 June 1965

Mrs Rosemary Keogh, LRAM, ARCM, ALCM
Holly Bank
Eglantine Avenue
Belfast

Dear Mrs Keogh,

Thank you for your letter regarding Sean Carey. I have thought about it a great deal. However, the standard of playing in our woodwind auditions was extraordinarily high this year and all the places for the academic year 1965/6 are now filled.

Yours very sincerely,

Andrew Small, DMus, MA (Cantab), FRCO

7

The graffiti on the wall of the demolition site were in letters six feet high. The first read: *Workless of the world, unite!* Someone else had written equally large: *IRA = I Ran Away*, a reference to the previous Saturday when a Protestant mob had stormed through the Catholic area and set fire to a tobacconist's shop with no sign of life from the dormant Republican organisation.

'You've got some smart clothes, Sean,' said Father Callaghan, eyeing the new leather jacket and Levi jeans.

Sean continued smoking. He had been avoiding the priest for weeks.

'Have you got a job, then?' Father Callaghan asked.

Some boys of eight and nine were setting fire to a pile of old tyres. The wind changed and smoke billowed chokingly across the site.

'I make a bit of money now and then.' Sean coughed. It was the neighbourhood euphemism for stealing.

'What about a regular job?' asked the priest.

Sean laughed. 'Oh sure. I'm gonna change me name to Billy Wilson and get a job in the roofing business.'

The reference to the Protestant domination of many job areas in Belfast saddened the priest. At seventeen, he thought, to be so cynical. . . .

'I could maybe help,' he offered.

'I don't want no help,' said Sean. 'Not from you. I got me friends, if I want help.'

He turned and walked off, deliberately heading into the smoke.

The priest hurried after him. 'Don't be so bitter, Sean,' he called. 'You took that audition too much to heart. It wasn't a rejection, they said . . .' A coughing fit stopped him in his tracks.

The youth walked on. ' I learnt me lesson,' he threw over his shoulder. 'I shouldn't 'ave got involved with all that music stuff you tricked me into. It was a waste of time.'

'It's never a waste of time,' said the priest, getting his breath back, 'to reach for something better in life.'

'Says you!'

'We don't always get what we want, but we have to go on trying.'

'Maybe you do. I don't.'

Father Callaghan was hurrying to keep up, the skirt of his cassock lifted high. 'Mrs Keogh tells me you've not been to a single lesson this term. And the bandmaster says you don't turn up to rehearsals any more.'

Sean turned. From the set of the leather-clad shoulders, the priest thought a blow was coming. Then he saw that the look in Sean's eyes was not anger, but pain.

'Listen, father,' said Sean. 'I never 'ad a girlfriend. At school I was always bottom of the class. All I ever did right was play the flute, but they don't want that, see? So why should I want what they got? Huh? You tell me that.'

The fire went out of the priest for a moment. 'I can't give you a reason, Sean,' he said wearily.

''Cos there isn't one!' In bitter triumph, Sean poked the priest in the chest with a gesture that was halfway to a blow. 'Now leave me alone, will you?'

Father Callaghan watched him cross the street and enter a Republican drinking club. There was the sound of an out-of-tune piano. Somebody was trying to play 'A Walk in the Black Forest', but kept getting lost in the undergrowth after the first few steps. The sound cut off as the door slammed shut behind Sean's back.

For a half-pint of lemonade, Sean would play two requests. Most of them he knew by heart; the others he improvised. Nobody in his audience appreciated what they were hearing. Sean despised them musically and as people. As the evening wore on and the beer flowed, the talk got wilder and the boasts more empty.

To hear them talk, he thought scornfully, you'd think they had personally put the IRA bomb under Nelson's column in Dublin. And even if they had, it was four months ago and they're still talking about it . . .

He crashed both hands down on the piano in the flourishing chords that began Rachmaninof's piano concerto. Nobody heard. His uncle Patrick's alcohol-reddened face reminded Sean of the night he had watched his father dying on the pile of bottles in the backyard. The two men had been alike as twins in looks as well as behaviour. If asked which one he hated more, he would have found it difficult to answer.

'Play us another tune on the piano, boy,' Patrick Carey ordered tipsily. 'That song I like about the Easter Rising. Whassit called?'

'I already played that once this evening,' snapped Sean.

'Did ye? Well, play it again, I say.'

'Play it yourself, you drunken old fool.' Sean slammed the piano lid closed and slipped beneath Patrick's lunging right fist. He left the club in a hurry and stood in the cool air outside to clear his head of the alcohol and tobacco fumes.

There was a light in the vestry of St Mary's church at the end of the road and the door was open. On Wednesday evenings after confession, Father Callaghan would listen to anyone with a problem. A few men came, asking for money or booze, which the priest never gave; mostly, it was women wanting someone to talk to.

From the shadows, Sean watched his mother emerge from the church and head for Bombay Terrace. Above her the great stained-glass window of the church was lit up from within, the blue-veiled madonna dandling the naked infant on her lap with a bland and vacant smile, framed by angels.

'Fuck you, Jesus!' shouted Sean. He turned away, angry with the priest who counselled, angry with his mother for believing, angry with the men in the club for their futile, vain boastings and angriest of all with himself for being like them.

'It's all talk,' he shouted accusingly at the deaf façade of the club. 'All talk! Nobody round here ever does anything!' The words echoed between the walls of the church and the club.

To vent his energy Sean grabbed a small lump of concrete from the rubble-strewn pavement and spun round to hurl it savagely at the stained-glass window. It flew straight as a bullet in the direction of Jesus' right eye but bounced harmlessly off the wire netting.

8

In the summer of 1966, maintaining law and order in Belfast was still police work. Apart from having to put down occasional disturbances which were afterwards officially whitewashed as football hooliganism, the uniformed force known as the B Specials ran few risks worse than insults by day. At night, stones were thrown and sometimes softer, less pleasant things as well.

Searching for a stolen car on the edge of the Catholic ghetto, the young policeman knew he was in hostile territory. He was eighteen and, like most of his colleagues, came from a Protestant area of Belfast, on the other side of the Shankill Road.

He looked down the dark street with the broken street lamps and waved to the sergeant on the next intersection, then waited for the older man to turn and look in the other direction before taking a half-smoked cigarette from the pocket of his uniform pocket.

Fifty metres away, Sean lay full length on the corrugated iron roof of someone's wash-house. Under the cloudless, starlit sky the air was icy. His feet and hands were cold from lack of movement but he did not mind that.

He watched the police for twenty minutes, picking the one who was least alert. His choice made, he eased the old Lee Enfield rifle into a firing position and squinted along its barrel. It felt good. The fingers of his right hand caressed the round metal head of the well-oiled bolt. He eased it back and heard the click as the spring of the magazine fed the first round into the chamber. He had been able to find only three bullets, but hoped that one would be enough.

His uncle Patrick had been boasting for years that he would use the rifle 'to kill a Protestant or an English soldier one day when the order comes from the South'.

Well, thought Sean, I'll show the old bastard I don't have to wait till I'm bent and grey.

His thoughts came back to here and now as the B Special cupped his hands to light the cigarette.

An eye shot, thought Sean. Like a tune of Mozart's: simple but perfect. An eye shot. Right in Jesus' eye . . . .

Time slowed down and stretched until each elastic second became an infinity of delectable sensations in Sean's mind. The gun in his hands felt light as a flute. Following the target's movements over the sights was like the sway of his body when playing the slow movement of Mozart's flute and harp concerto.

The difference lay in the power that was his. With a gun in his hand, he did not have to ask anyone to like him.

As the policeman looked up, before shaking out the used match, the momentary pinpoint of reflection on his eyeball gave Sean the aiming point he sought.

He squeezed the trigger and the .303 bullet sped straight to Jesus' right eye. It blossomed red for a split second before the match dropped from lifeless fingers.

Only then did Sean hear the sound, echoing off the blank walls of the houses. As the echoes died there was a scratching noise like rats behind a skirting board. It was the spent cartridge case rolling down the iron roof to fall on the cobbles below.

There was panic all around: shouting and running feet and torches shining into every dark corner. But Sean did not run. He took his time, moving quietly from cover to cover back to Bombay Terrace.

The first thing he saw on entering the kitchen by the back

door was the bruising on his mother's swollen face; her left eye was nearly closed. Clutching her belly in pain, she crouched on the floor beside the old iron cooking range.

Patrick Carey stopped his boot in mid-kick. He was nearly sober now, and frightened.

'You stupid little bastard,' he roared, coming at Sean like a human wall. 'What do you mean by going to my house and taking that old rifle from behind the wardrobe?'

Without giving Sean a chance to reply, he rained blows and kicks in a technique of battery that worked as well drunk as sober.

Sean landed one blow on his uncle's nose. It was something he had wanted to do for years.

Before he could get in another blow, he was borne backwards by the older man's body weight and beaten to the floor. He had been thrashed by Patrick many times in the past and lay curled tightly, arms over his head, letting the blows land but trying to take them on legs and arms rather than anywhere vital.

When the storm of kicks abated he looked out from between his elbows to see his uncle sitting on the only unbroken chair, breathing heavily and dabbing at the blood from his broken nose.

Keeping his eyes wearily on Patrick, Sean clambered to his feet. Behind him, a voice in the doorway said coldly, 'That's enough of the violence, Patrick Carey.'

Sean turned to see the Man standing in the kitchen doorway. He was shorter by a good couple of inches than Sean's 5 foot 8, and as pale-faced as a newly released prisoner. The Man was never referred to by name. He sat each evening in the Republican club alone but never drank more than half a pint of Guinness. Nobody, drunk or sober, ever argued with him. His word, when he settled disputes or gave orders, was law. There was a man like him in every neighbourhood of Catholic Belfast.

'I'm told there's been some foolery with that gun you're looking after for us, Patrick,' said the Man. He spoke without raising his voice, a man of natural authority.

'The boy here . . .' His uncle's bloodshot eyes jerked at Sean. 'He went to my house and took it while I was out having a drink. I was trying to find out what he's done with it, like.'

'You should have tried asking him with your tongue before using your boots,' said the Man unemotionally.

Patrick made as if to speak then shut his mouth out of respect mingled with fear.

'Get out,' said the Man. 'Leave us alone.' As an afterthought, he added, 'You'd better take the woman with you, Patrick. Get some of the neighbours to look after her. I'd say you've broken a rib or two. But no doctors, mind.'

'Now,' he said to Sean, when they were alone. 'It was you shot the B Special tonight, wasn't it?'

Sean stopped feeling his teeth that were loose.

'Aye,' he said. 'I was fed up with all the talk. I thought it was time to do something.'

The Man nodded. 'Ye did something all right. Ye stirred up a hornet's nest. And you've lost us a rifle.'

'I didn't lose it,' said Sean. 'I hid it between a shed and a brick wall.'

'Did ye now?' As calm as a judge in court, the Man weighed up the alternatives. 'Well, I'll let you make amends.'

'What's that mean?'

'It means you'll have to go and get back our rifle that you took.'

'They'll be looking for me,' said Sean.

A ghost of a smile crossed the Man's pallid face. 'So you'll have to go careful, won't you?'

As Sean slipped out of the back door, he caught the Man's orders, delivered in the same flat monotone. 'Two things, Sean Carey. If you're caught. . . . One, you never saw me tonight. Two, you found the rifle on a demolition site where someone had thrown it away.'

Sean sneaked through the night. It took all his knowledge of the alleys, roofs and yards of west Belfast to penetrate the cordon of armed police and soldiers around the intersection where the B Special had been shot. The return trip, carrying

317

the rifle, left him bathed in perspiration and high on his own adrenalin.

The Man took the heavy Lee Enfield, removed the magazine and said, 'You only fired the one bullet, then?'

'Yeah. An eye shot. I got him in the eye.'

'You were lucky.'

'No,' said Sean. 'I waited till he lit up a ciggy. The stupid bastard made it easy for me.'

'Could you do it again?'

'Easy,' Sean boasted. 'I could have shot a British soldier on the way back just now. They were all over the place, looking for me. One of them was only twenty feet away, with his back to me where I was in the shadows. It would have been easy.'

'Leave it, boy,' the Man ordered coldly. 'From now on, you shoot the people we tell you to. When we tell you.'

It took Sheila Carey many sleepless nights to work up the courage to broach her son's problems at one of Father Callaghan's Wednesday evening sessions in the vestry of St Mary's.

She was still the same wizened little creature she had been when the priest had first come to the parish; the decades of misery seemed not to change her one way or the other. The priest, though, had lost the sparkle in his eyes. Imbued with a sense of hopelessness, he had twice asked the Bishop to relieve him of his pastoral duties and twice been told firmly that his place was with his flock in Clonard.

'From what you tell me, Sheila,' he said heavily, 'your son has got himself involved with the IRA.'

The word *involved*, in local usage, meant using weapons for one side or the other. It meant killing, or at least being prepared to kill.

'He goes out at night with guns, father,' she said. 'It was bad enough when he was stealing, but this is worse. He'll end up shot dead one night. I know he will.'

Father Callaghan agreed. 'If Sean shoots at people, they'll shoot back. One day, they'll get him. It's a matter of time till I'll be saying a requiem mass for him right here in St Mary's.'

She looked at him in despair. 'Isn't there anything you can do, father?'

The priest walked with her into the empty church. 'I could pray,' he said. He could have added: But I don't think there's anyone listening. . . .

Aloud, he said, 'Sean is on what the IRA call active service. Your son has signed a pact with the devil.'

He raised his eyes to the window of the Virgin and Child. Blessed Mary, he thought, this boy's not the only one here who's come to terms with evil. What kind of priest am I, sitting in my vestry wishing this poor woman would take her burden somewhere else? The Lord said: Come unto me, all ye that travail and are heavy laden. . . .

'There is one thing you could maybe do, Sheila.' He was thinking aloud and trying to be positive. 'If you want to save Sean's life, you could inform on him. He'd go to prison, but he'd be alive.'

'Inform? On my own son? I couldn't do that.'

It was not the first time he had given the advice. 'There's a special telephone number written on a board outside the Springfield Road police station. You ring it. When they answer, you don't have to identify yourself. Just tell them and ring off.'

'I couldn't do it,' she said.

'No,' said the priest, 'I didn't think you could.'

He followed the Virgin's eyeline to the window above the altar where God sat enthroned on a cloud, dispensing a frozen blessing.

The message seemed clear. Father Callaghan heaved a sigh. So it has to be me, God. . . .

9

At the Quartier Lapasset in Castelnaudary near Toulouse, God was 5 feet 8 and immaculate from the top of his perfectly white kepi to the gleaming spit-shined toe-caps of his boots. Corporal Grohmann was notorious in the training regiment as the drill instructor whose squad had won the drill competition more often than any other. As he explained in the first sentence addressed to the new intake which included recruits Muller, Milton and O'Reilly, he intended to win it again.

God's First Commandment was: 'March!' The Second was: 'Sing at the top of your lungs!'

As the recruits marched and counter-marched across the parade ground, the traditional marching songs of the Legion helped to maintain the slow cadence that Napoleon would have approved, eighty-eight steps to the minute. Each time Grohmann's squad passed another group of marching men, the manic corporal screamed at them to drown the competition. The other squad's NCO yelled the same order. As the two songs merged, a cacophonous crescendo bounced off the walls of the barrack blocks lining the square, fading again as the squads separated and the two songs became distinct once more.

When God commanded 'Halt!' every boot in the squad had to hit the ground at precisely the same instant, to give a sound like a single gunshot. Grohmann had an ear like an orchestral conductor and could pick out the one man who was a millisecond late. The miscreant was made to identify himself by shouting his name out loud, so that the whole squad knew whose fault it was they had to march and halt again. And again. And again.

'Is Roger Milton your real name?' the orderly sergeant translated.

Surprised by the ripe Cockney accent, Roger glanced sideways and was deafened by the command: 'Face the front.'

'Yes.' Roger licked his lips. 'That's my name, sir.'

Behind the desk sat a lean, hard-faced officer Roger had not seen before. In front of him were Roger's passport, the two-page life story written at Aubagne and a letter from the British Embassy in Paris.

The officer picked up the handwritten pages. 'In your life history, Milton, you said: "My old man's a dustman. He wears a dustman's hat." Is that true?'

The Cockney sergeant coughed. Roger began to feel uneasy. 'Yes, sir.'

'Then he's been promoted.' Nobody laughed. 'It appears he is now a Member of the British Parliament who has received a letter from your headmaster, telling him where you are. He is also a chum of the British ambassador, who wishes to know whether you are happy in the Legion or whether you wish to be released.'

That bloody letter to Vanessa, thought Roger. She told her father and he wrote to the old man and . . .

'Well, Milton?' the Cockney accent asked. 'Don't keep the officer waiting.'

'I'm quite happy here, sir.'

'You're sure?'

'Yes, sir.'

'Then sign this piece of paper. We'll send it to the ambassador, so he can sleep at night.'

Roger signed below the words: *I Roger Milton confirm that*

I have enlisted in the Foreign Legion of my own free will.

'Take care of this man, sergeant.' The officer seemed bored. 'Dismiss!'

Roger about-turned smartly and was marched at the *pas gymnastique* out of the orderly office. It could have been worse, he thought.

Instead of turning right, back to the parade ground, the Cockney voice ordered him to turn left. At the end of the corridor he found himself at the back of the building where Grohmann was waiting. The little corporal had taken off his jacket. Hans-Peter was holding it for him, looking worried.

Grohmann thrust his face close to Roger's. Despite a difference of nearly six inches in their height, he managed to make Roger recoil.

'Stand fast!' Grohmann hissed. 'You've dropped me in the shit, Milton. I don't like the commandant being bothered by letters about my men. It reflects on me.'

The orderly sergeant was watching from the doorway. There was no one else in sight.

Without any warning Grohmann's right fist crashed into Roger's guts, doubling him over. Roger tried to defend himself.

'Attention!' Grohmann shouted. 'Stand to attention, you filth!'

The rain of blows stopped as suddenly as it had begun.

The orderly sergeant picked his nose. 'Don't annoy Corporal Grohmann again,' he said calmly, 'or he'll take you apart.'

'No, sergeant.' Roger's lips were swollen and he could taste blood.

'Now we've got that out of the way –' the Sergeant sounded friendly, or maybe it was just the London accent – 'perhaps you can clear up one other thing, Milton?'

'Yes, sergeant!'

'In your life story you said that you attended a secondary modern school in Brixton and never learned no languages.'

Roger said nothing.

'And yet the ambassador's letter says you was a Senior Prefect at Blenheim School.'

'That's right, sergeant.'

'Strange . . .' The sergeant was smiling. 'Now I never 'ad the benefit of what you might call a good education, Milton, but surely they teach you French at one of Britain's best public schools, don't they?'

'Yes, sergeant.'

Grohmann's fist thudded into Roger's bruised ribs. '*Méchant*,' he said. 'Very naughty.'

Hans-Peter winced and looked away. He would have done better not to move.

'Hand my jacket to the sergeant,' Grohmann ordered him.

Hans-Peter was unprepared for the same savage assault that Roger had just undergone. When Grohmann had finished with him, he gasped, 'What did I do?'

'Say "corporal", shit-brain.'

'What did I do, corporal?'

'You were laughing at me, shit-brain. Weren't you?' Grohmann's face was inches from Hans-Peter's. He spoke through clenched teeth. 'Fucking double act – you and your clever English pal, pretending he couldn't speak French.'

'But he can't, corporal.'

Roger felt responsible for what Grohmann was doing to Hans-Peter. 'It's not Muller's fault,' he stammered, speaking French for the first time. 'I never let him know, corporal. I played the same trick on him. Honestly.'

'Now we're getting somewhere.' Grohmann wiped his fists on Roger's overall, leaving a smear of blood. He stood close and looked up at the tall recruit's bloody face. '*Tu piges très bien, après tout?*'

'*Oui, caporal.*'

'Then, what the fuck was all this crap about not speaking French?'

'It was just a game, corporal.'

'Just a fucking game?' Grohmann's voice rose to a scream. 'Where do you think you are! In a bleeding kindergarten? You stupid sod!'

At the second blow to his jaw, Roger felt a tooth crunch. The sharp stab of pain cancelled all the bruises from the first attack.

When he opened his eyes, the sergeant was holding out Grohmann's jacket for him to put on. 'I'll give you a word of advice, Milton,' he said. 'You're in the Legion and you've just signed away your last chance of getting out. So don't tell lies to anyone. In the Legion we may do many things, but we don't lie to each other.'

'You look filthy,' snapped Grohmann. He buttoned his jacket and brushed down his lapels. 'Double back to your billet and change into clean fatigues, both of you. I want you both back on the parade ground inside two minutes.'

I read the brief report of this incident in Milton's personal file. There was a further letter from the ambassador to which the Legion did not bother to reply. If a man is between eighteen and forty and in good health, once he's signed on, he's in for five years unless the Legion rejects him.

The report interested me because Milton is a type you don't often find in the Legion: an intellectual liar who habitually tells untruths as a game because he knows himself cleverer than other people and enjoys pulling the wool over their eyes. Too clever for his own good, Milton.

When Koenig and I interviewed him, I asked him why he had written that letter to the girl.

'I was in love,' he said.

'You're a liar,' I told him. 'You wrote to your headmaster's daughter knowing that your father would find out where you were and throw you a life-line.'

'Did I?' he asked.

I was curious. 'So why didn't you grab the life-line?' It would have been in keeping with my reading of his character.

'I suppose I'd got to like Muller and Irish,' he said. 'Didn't want to cop out on them.'

I think that was the truth. The trouble with Milton is that he is a fundamentally untrustworthy person, so one never knows.

*

One by one the other squads finished the morning's drill and doubled off to the canteen. At last only Grohmann's men were left on the parade ground. On the order to halt, their feet crashed as one pair. The sound echoed and died away to complete silence. For once even Grohmann appeared relatively pleased with the result.

'You three,' he said pointing at the rear rank where Sean, Hans-Peter and Roger Milton were standing. 'You stand fast. The rest – dismiss!'

The men broke ranks and doubled away to the mess, already late for the midday meal. They were always last to arrive in the canteen. Several times they had arrived too late to be served.

On the parade ground Grohmann rocked on his heels and surveyed his three victims. There was an unseasonably cold wind driving across the open square, cutting through the men's thin cotton fatigues.

'*Mes trois inséparables*,' Grohmann sneered. 'You'll get no lunch today. You've got Milton to thank for that. He's a liar and I don't like liars. So I'm going to make all three of you suffer. That's how the buddy system works.'

He walked round the three recruits, inspecting their noses and behind their ears like cattle in a market, while they stared rigidly to the front.

'I want you back on the parade ground in seven minutes, shaved, washed and dressed in *tenue de campagne* – full battle order.'

'Yes, corporal!' they shouted in unison.

Civilians always wonder what is the point of such harsh discipline. Is it necessary to treat men this way? they ask.

The answer is yes. The job of the little tyrants like Grohmann is to weld men together and turn them from a collection of individuals into a disciplined body of men. They do it as their counterparts in every army for the last 3,000 years have done it: by humiliating the trainees until they bond together against their common foe. Esprit de corps thus born may later be cemented by shared achievement, but the humiliation must come first.

And training in any elite corps must drive each man to the limit of his physical and emotional resources. It is vital to know how he will behave one day on a battlefield when hungry, thirsty, fatigued beyond words, shocked and frightened. If he is going to crack up, far better he does so in training than in a moment of crisis with a loaded weapon in his hand.

One of Grohmann's time-proven techniques was to select one or two men in each group and make examples of them. It's a way of warning the others: stay in line or this will happen to you. In that particular intake he picked on Muller, Milton and the Irishman. Milton he did not forgive for tricking him; the smart-ass always gets it in the neck from men like Grohmann. Muller he disliked because he was gay. And he wanted to break the Irishman just because he was tough, because he would not knuckle under, because the cold grey eyes met Grohmann's and said: Fuck you, I can take it.

By meting out his special treatment to these three men, he bonded them into a team that could stick together for a lifetime.

Who else but a Grohmann could make Roger Milton decide to stay in the Legion with his pals when he was given his chance to escape? Who else could weld together such an unlikely trio: a mischievous intellectual, an illiterate killer and a man who was running away from what he was?

At midnight the kit inspection had been going on for two and a half hours. From time to time Grohmann broke off the inspection and shouted without warning, 'No. 1 dress uniforms. Three minutes!' Or 'Full battle order!' Or 'Walking out dress!'

In wild confusion, the recruits scrambled out of one uniform into another. At the same time the discarded clothes had to be folded neatly and laid out on the beds in the regulation box display.

Two hours later Grohmann was still at it. He found a hundred faults with each man's kit and tore items of clothing off the wearers on the pretext that they were dirty or wrongly worn. To make an example of Roger, he threw his best uniform out of the dormitory window, where it fluttered down five floors to the wet ground below.

I must have been mad, thought Roger, standing rigidly to attention. I could have been on a train back to Paris right now. I didn't have to sign that piece of paper, so why did I?

It was Sean who retrieved the uniform, running up the five flights of stairs with it over his arm.

Next Grohmann picked on Hans-Peter's kit and threw it in all directions around the dormitory while his victim had to stand ramrod stiff until even his bed was demolished and lay, broken into its separate components, on the floor beside him. Only Roger's and Sean's help made it possible for Hans-Peter to be ready for the next inspection.

It was well past 1 a.m. when Grohmann suddenly tired of his game and slammed the dormitory door. The light was switched off from outside and the recruits subsided on to their beds in the darkness with a chorus of moans. Morning parade was at 6 a.m. Most of them had at least an hour's cleaning to do before then and the morning was going to be hell: they were due on the *parcours de combattants*.

It was on the combat training course that the first men cracked up.

To make it to the end of the course meant going through, under or over a succession of obstacles that would have exhausted an Olympic athlete. Doing it against the clock and under simulated battle conditions, harassed the whole time by the screaming NCOs, demanded every ounce of fitness and determination.

The recruits were made to run through thigh-deep mud, jump across mud-filled ditches, climb rope ladders, scale walls, swing on frayed ropes across swamps, belly-crawl under barbed wire and through concrete drains that had been blocked with tangles of razor wire. At intervals, without warning, live ammunition was fired on fixed lines just above their heads or close behind their backs.

At the end two recruits lay inert in the mud, unable even

to summon up the necessary adrenalin to be frightened of the bullets flicking above them. When the firing stopped, they lay still despite the NCO's kicks. One just groaned aloud; the other eventually sat up and wept from nervous and physical exhaustion. Both were driven from the course under a storm of abuse and a hail of blows. They were last seen in a military police jeep, handcuffed to the rear rail like criminals.

As the weeks went by, more men cracked up and disappeared. Grohmann took a fiendish delight in humiliating them to the last moment. Occasionally the squad was addressed by other NCOs and officers but it was Grohmann who decided when or whether they could sleep when they were out on their feet. It was Grohmann who awarded punishments and saw that they were carried out. It was Grohmann who kept them at it when the other squads had already finished for the day.

The immaculate little corporal was hated by every man in the squad. He revelled in the knowledge and would have regarded popularity as a sign that he was failing in his task – to make fighting men out of the handful of raw boys. On morning parade or at the midnight *appel* in the dormitory, his cold eyes took in every detail but betrayed no emotion. To the recruits he appeared inhuman: a cloven-hoofed god with horn and tail, into whose power their very souls had been consigned.

At first the men openly envied those who cracked under the harsh training and were allowed to return to civilian life. Then a perverse pride began to grow in them as they came to know in every fibre of their bodies that they had proven something by simply staying the course, that they were tougher, stronger, more resolute than the rejects. They were, quite simply, better men. They felt proud to be in the little corporal's squad, called themselves 'Grohmann's mob' and boasted to other men in the canteen of his excesses instead of complaining about them.

Their bodies continued toughening up day by day. The ones who had been flabby, grew lean. All of them built muscles where none had been before. But the changes were not just physical. Sean lost the sly underdog look he had worn all his life; he stood straight and looked taller. Hans-Peter lost the languid manners of the hairdressing salon, although even with shaven head and dressed in muddy fatigues at the end of a tough day, he still had more the look of a dancer than a soldier. And Roger lost the gangling, lanky look of the dilettante public schoolboy. Despite the arduous physical regime, he fleshed out and his shoulders grew broader. If he still created fantasies in his own mind, he kept them to himself, having no wish to lose another tooth.

At first, it had been Roger who most often helped the other two out of trouble. After ten years in English boarding schools, he grasped the tricks of military life quicker than they did. Hans-Peter was slow to adapt and rarely able to return any favours. Strangely it was Sean, the born loner, who made the biggest and most costly gesture of comradeship.

10

If Grohmann was lord of the parade ground, the king of slime was Corporal Cecchi. A swarthy little Corsican with rat-like eyes, he was the meanest man in the Quartier Lapasset, delighting in all the deadly, dirty tricks of unarmed combat. His chosen empire was a slippery slope above a mud pit formed by a bend in the river which carried run-off from the Black Mountain above Castelnaudary.

Cecchi's idea of a learning incentive was to trip or throw each recruit who made a mistake into the mud pit. In summer his victims emerged stinking and wet. In winter they were cut by underwater rocks and quickly froze in the vicious wind that blew off the mountain.

At 7 a.m. on a September morning Grohmann's mob was handed over to Cecchi. A few miles to the east, at resorts on the Mediterranean coast, early-rising holidaymakers were looking forward to a day's idleness on sun-drenched beaches. The recruits were already wet through with sweat after a five-mile run from the camp and stood shivering in the mountain air, trying to concentrate on what the unarmed combat instructor was saying.

'Try again,' he jeered as his current victim climbed out of the mud and staggered back up the bank for another go.

The men collected bruises and cuts and became wetter and more demoralised under Cecchi's taunts. Cracked ribs, dislocated shoulders and the occasional broken leg were routine results of his kind of instruction.

'It's your turn, kraut.' Cecchi picked his favourite victim. 'Take this rifle off me.'

At the first sessions with Cecchi, some of the trainees had laughed when the instructor baited Hans-Peter. Now they preserved a noncommittal silence, trying to memorise the little Corsican's encyclopaedia of dirty tricks and learn from Hans-Peter's suffering.

Each time Hans-Peter came for him the instructor side-stepped like a matador fooling a novice bull and tripped, threw or pushed his victim off the bank into the mud pit. Six times Hans-Peter climbed back for more punishment. He was bruised and cut in several places.

Sean watched with mounting anger. He resented the way Cecchi was making a spectacle out of Hans-Peter. In all his years in Belfast he had never had a friend but watching Cecchi's baiting, an irrational anger rose in his throat. He clenched his fists, digging the nails into the palms.

Finally even Cecchi grew tired of his sport. He pinioned his victim to the ground in a crude embrace and kissed him on the lips in the Mediterranean gesture of insult to a man who was not masculine.

'Next customer!' Cecchi rolled upright in one smooth movement, bounced to his feet and booted Hans-Peter in the arse, sending him sprawling in the mud below.

He spun round, scanned the faces of the men watching and picked on Sean. 'You, Irish. Let's see if you can do better than the *pédalo*, your nancy boyfriend.'

Sean ended up in the mud less often than the others because the street-fighting tricks he had learned in Belfast were more use against Cecchi than the Marquess of Queensberry rules. But this time he slipped on the wet grass, allowing Cecchi to get an arm-lock on him before he could regain his balance. He was forced to the ground and then knocked over the edge of the bank by a blow from the rifle butt.

Sean landed awkwardly in the river, not in the mud pit

but further out. He sat almost submerged among rocks for thirty seconds or more before bringing up one hand and rubbing his ribs as though the fall had broken something.

'Try again,' shouted Cecchi at him above the noise of the water. He waved the rifle tauntingly. 'Come and take this off me, you slob.'

Sean took his time wading to the bank, hunched over as though in pain from a broken rib. He negotiated the slippery incline with only one hand, the other still clutching his side. Arriving at the top where Cecchi stood in a crouch, waiting for him, Sean appeared to stumble, putting out both hands to save himself. He fell against the instructor's leg. There was a loud crack and a scream as Cecchi's body arched through the air. Sean stood with the rifle in his left hand, looking down at the Corsican instructor, who lay clutching a broken leg in the mud.

The other recruits stood open-mouthed, stunned by the speed of Sean's attack. It was Roger who reacted first. Before any of the other NCOs ran up, he kicked out of sight the sharp-edged lump of rock that Sean had carried up from the river bed to use as his weapon.

Hans-Peter, Sean and Roger stood on the parade ground, the wind gusting around them. Their fatigue overalls were still wet from the mud pit and the sweat of running back to camp. The rest of the squad were sitting in clean dry clothes in the canteen, enjoying the hot midday meal and regulation quarter-litre of wine.

A trickle of blood ran slowly around the rim of Hans-Peter's left ear where a cut inflicted by the butt of Cecchi's rifle had broken open. He was itching to raise a hand and wipe the blood away, but waited until Grohmann's back was turned before twitching his head almost imperceptibly to shake the drop off.

Grohmann's eagle eyes caught the movement. 'Well, pretty boy,' he sneered. 'This business is all your fault. You don't like fighting another man face to face, do you?'

'I was doing my best, corporal.'

'I know your type,' continued Grohmann. 'You don't want to grip another man's body and throw him to the ground. You'd rather grip his prick and suck it, wouldn't you?'

'No, corporal.'

'Don't lie to me, pretty boy.'

Hans-Peter felt a blush on his cheeks. Grohmann's face broke into a contorted smile. He swung abruptly away to face Sean.

'You, Irish,' he hissed. 'You think you're a mean little bastard, don't you?'

Sean stayed silent, meeting Grohmann's eyes levelly. Neither man blinked.

'It's called unarmed combat,' said the corporal, stressing the adjective. 'Picking up a rock and using it to bust Corporal Cecchi's leg was not a good idea.'

'He asked for it,' said Sean. 'He told me to take the rifle off him. And I did.'

The corporal's bellow of wrath only inches from his ear caused even Sean to jerk his head sideways. 'You say "corporal" when you talk to me, you lump of Irish shit!'

Sean lowered his gaze. His mouth was still sullen. 'Yes, corporal,' he muttered.

'Louder!'

'Yes, corporal!' The shout echoed off the blank barrack blocks around the parade ground.

'That's better.' With deep satisfaction, Grohmann announced:

'You've got two weeks in prison to look forward to now. That's broken harder men than you, Irish.'

'Yes, corporal!'

'And as for your pals,' he turned on Roger and Hans-Peter, 'we'll see if you're still smiling after two hours of *la pelote*.'

After twenty minutes of the Legion's traditional field punishment, Hans-Peter felt his lungs would burst at each breath. No matter how deeply he filled them, there was never enough oxygen for his pounding heart to force into the punished muscles.

His back-pack contained twenty-five kilos of bricks. Instead of straps, it had wire loops that cut into the skin and tore the flesh even at a walking pace. He heard Roger's grunts of pain beside him. Running was agony; steel helmets without liners banged on their shaven skulls at every step, rubbing the scalp into bleeding sores.

Grohmann stood in the centre of the punishment compound with a whistle in his mouth and a rope in his hand. As Hans-Peter and Roger doubled round in circles, the corporal blew random blasts on the whistle. One blast meant they had to execute a neat forward roll in which the hard, lumpy back-pack threatened to dislocate the spine. Two blasts meant crawling on their stomachs with no daylight showing between their bodies and the ground. Three blasts had them marching at knees' bend, an agonising position in which the back-packs threatened to overbalance them at every step.

Whenever they slowed up or misinterpreted the whistled commands, the corporal lashed out with the rope's end using all his strength. Each time they rose to their feet swaying like drunks, the back-packs felt heavier and the wires cut deeper into their flesh.

The whistle blasts grew more frequent. Run. Crawl. Run. Crouch and march. Run. Forward roll. Run. Crawl. Run. Crouch and march. Run. Forward roll. '*Magnez-vous le cul!* Move your asses!' Grohmann screamed. 'Faster! Faster!'

'Cecchi is a mate of mine,' Grohmann had explained at the start of the punishment.

The words rang in Hans-Peter's brain, changing with the rhythm of his pounding feet to the message: 'Sean is a mate of mine. It's my fault he's in prison. Sean is a mate of mine. It's my fault he's in prison.'

Through tears of pain and hopeless rage he saw Roger beside him, his face a mask of fatigue and pain.

My God, thought Hans-Peter. Do I look like that?

Another whistle blast.

Please God, help me, he prayed. I can't go on. A forward roll. No, I was wrong: it should have been knees' bend marching. . . .

The rope sliced across Hans-Peter's chest, stinging through the sweat-sodden fatigue blouse.

I must concentrate. Another whistle blast. Belly crawl. Another blast.

Hans-Peter lurched to his feet and doubled round the compound, the helmet banging his brains with every step.

'I can't take any more. I've been in hell for three whole months.'

It was 2 a.m. Stars burned bright in a moonless sky. In a small pool of light behind the cook-house, Hans-Peter scrubbed a grease-impregnated wooden table with a nail-brush and cold water. The only result of an hour's work had been to cover the brush and his hands with grease; the table was as dirty as when he had started.

'Don't let Grohmann get you down.' Roger was scrubbing another table just as greasy.

'I can't help it.' Hans-Peter sounded close to tears. His head hung down. His eyes kept closing from sheer fatigue.

'At least, don't let him see that he's getting you down. If he ever does, he'll hound you to hell.'

'I'm there already, Roger. I've got boils all down my back that hurt so much I can't sleep. The medic lances them and they just swell up again. And that bastard Grohmann has given us jankers every night this week. I never slept so little in my life.'

The infection in Hans-Peter's ear that had begun with a blow from Cecchi's rifle butt was painful and made him dizzy. There were cuts on his hands that would not heal, mainly due to the hours of scrubbing fatigues that he had to put in each night. His mother would not have recognised the haggard convict face.

'Where's Irish gone to?' Roger paused for a rest and indicated the third greasy table.

Hans-Peter was not listening. 'I'm beginning to think that African guy had the right idea.'

'Stop talking like that!' The image of the stiff black body swinging in the showers made Roger shudder. 'He was a loner. He had no friends. That's why he couldn't take it.'

Sean rejoined them, moving silently on bare feet despite the freezing wind blowing off the mountains. He took out of his fatigue blouse a twist of newspaper full of white powder.

'Grease solvent from the MT garage,' he said, spilling a third on to each table. 'As long as we wash it all away, nobody'll know.'

'You took a risk,' said Roger. 'If the night picket had caught you wandering around the camp, you'd be back in prison.'

Sean laughed at the thought of the booted night patrols catching him in bare feet. 'They'll never send me back there,' he said confidently. 'It was worth two weeks inside for the pleasure of breaking Cecchi's leg, but I'm not goin' back for a second dose, I'll tell ye that.' He touched his cheek where two teeth had been removed by a corporal's boot as the price of insolence when Sean had answered back on his first day in the prison.

'Now scrub your guts out and we can be back in bed inside ten minutes, if we're lucky.'

'Don't do it!' a voice hissed in the darkness of the toilets.

Sean's arm reached over Hans-Peter's shoulder and took the length of webbing from his hand before he could tie it to the overhead pipes.

Hans-Peter grabbed for the strap. 'Give that back to me,' he sobbed. 'It's mine. It's mine.'

A rough blow in the chest landed him on one of the toilets in the row of doorless cubicles.

'Keep your voice down or you'll wake Grohmann. Then we'll both be in the shit.' Sean moved into a patch of moonlight and deliberately coiled the webbing strap in his hand. He was clad only in a pair of shorts.

'I can't go on, Irish.' Hans-Peter was rocking himself on

the toilet, arms wrapped round his body. 'I can't take any more.'

'What's so special about you, kraut?' asked Sean. 'Why should you be let out when we have to stay here?'

'The rest of you are tougher than me,' Hans-Peter moaned. 'I've had enough.'

'We've all had enough, you stupid bastard. Why's it any worse for you than it is for the rest of us?'

'Leave me alone.'

'No.' Sean sat on the floor in the pool of moonlight, his back to the wall, facing the toilets. 'I'm not goin', you know.'

After a while, tired of watching Hans-Peter rocking himself in wordless anguish, he said, 'You ought to be ashamed, kraut. Did you know that?'

'Ashamed I can't take it?'

Sean laughed quietly. 'There's no shame in that. Ashamed of letting us down, is what I meant.'

Hans-Peter sniffed and wiped away the tears on his cheek. 'Who am I letting down?'

Sean crossed the cold concrete floor and knelt in front of his friend. He gripped the other man's shoulders fiercely.

'Me, for one,' he said. 'I went to prison for you, you selfish bastard. And if you think life with Grohmann is hard, I can tell you that in the *gnouf* they could make Grohmann himself weep ten times a day.'

'I'm sorry,' Hans-Peter sniffed again. 'You're right. I am letting you down.'

'Not just me,' said Sean urgently. He stood and shook Hans-Peter vigorously. 'There's Roger, too. He must have done jankers a dozen times because he'd lent you a piece of equipment when yours wasn't ready for inspection.'

'I know.'

'Did you ever think of desertin'?' Sean asked, to change the subject.

'Desertion?'

'That's what I said. Meself, speaking French like I do, I wouldn't get very far, but with you talking the language like a native, we'd make a go of it.'

337

'Where would we head for?' Hans-Peter asked. 'Back to Ireland?'

Sean laughed sourly. 'Not there. No way.'

'Then where?'

'Spain maybe. The frontier's not far,' said Sean vaguely.

Hans-Peter felt drained but calm; his crisis was over. He raised a hand to touch his friend's naked chest. From there it seemed natural to slip both arms around Sean's hips and pull him close. He buried his face in Sean's belly.

'Please let me,' he murmured, all the old excitement rising within him. His voice was husky with desire. 'It'll be good, I promise.'

His fingers sought Sean's erect penis and raised it to his lips.

Sean slipped out of reach. 'That's enough,' he said. He grabbed Hans-Peter's wrist and pulled him roughly to his feet.

Hans-Peter gazed into his friend's eyes, so close in the moonlight. He could feel Sean's penis pressing against his own leg. 'You want it too,' he said. 'Don't you?'

They stood close without moving for a long time, Hans-Peter acutely aware of the sound of his heartbeat pulsing in his ears. Slowly he slid down to a kneeling position and took his friend's penis into his mouth, licking, caressing, wanting to swallow it all.

Sean closed his eyes, breathing heavily. He came quickly, his fingers digging into the muscles of Hans-Peter's shoulders and leaving a pattern of nail-marks like a brand on the skin.

'Let's get back to our beds,' he said harshly. 'I need the shut-eye, even if you don't.'

11

Koenig's lean face was red with anger.

'It's not my government,' he shouted. 'It may be yours, that pack of baying shit-hounds in Paris that made the amnesty last year. The law of 18 June 1966, they call it. And under this so-called law traitors are welcomed back to the country they betrayed.'

He threw in front of Raoul a newspaper folded to show an article on the reinstatement at a French university of a left-wing sociologist who had taken a leading part in the brainwashing of French prisoners of war in Viet Minh death camps.

'It's democracy,' said Raoul. 'Do you think I don't get angry too? The man was a deserter apart from being a traitor. Now he's an honoured member of the middle classes he affects to despise, while we who did our duty are stuck in wheelchairs for life or on the run, sneaking in and out of France like common criminals.'

Koenig slipped the black patch off and massaged his weeping eye socket. 'There's no point in bitterness,' he said. 'But how can we stretch our code of behaviour to encompass things like that?'

Raoul sighed. There was no answer to his friend's question. Koenig had arrived unannounced and, as always, in darkness. Though years separated his clandestine visits, their conversation picked up each time from where it had left off as though they had seen each other only days before. The two old comrades had eaten well on plain soldiers' fare and split two bottles of local red wine between them, discussing the American war in Vietnam.

'It's bad,' said Koenig. 'The Yanks aren't getting any-where. They're doing everything wrong, the same as we did. Foot by foot, kilometre by kilometre, the Viets are taking over the South. Back in Washington President Johnson announces a new list of bombing targets in the North, while college kids drugged to the eyeballs throw dog-shit at their own soldiers outside the Pentagon. Democracy, you call it?'

'But Laos?' asked Raoul. 'That's the shortest route. That's the way we have to go in.'

'No chance with the Pathet Lao on the warpath. At the moment, *mon vieux*, the only way into and out of Dien lies through two war zones.'

Raoul gazed at the maps on the walls of his home, updated each morning. 'I hoped things might seem easier to someone who lives out there. I thought, from close at hand, Koenig, you might see a way through. Or is my plan just a pipe dream after all?'

He put out a hand to restrain Koenig, who was about to rise on hearing the front door open. 'That'll be Marie.'

'Another woman in your life?' Koenig's tone was ironic. He slipped the eye-patch back on. 'Last time I was here, I met a lady called Louise.'

Marie had shed ten years since the start of her affair with Raoul. She had the lively look of someone who spends much of their life in the open air, but happily and not as drudgery. Her eyes were bright and her dark hair danced round her face; her dress was a floral print. It was the way Raoul liked her to be, simple but feminine.

The two-inch heels of her open sandals clattered on the uncarpeted concrete floor. She kissed Raoul and looked Koenig in the face. 'I remember the last time we met. You stared at me. I had the feeling you didn't much like me. It was in the Cercle Sportif in Hanoi and you were talking rather loudly about useless civilians.'

'Koenig hasn't changed,' said Raoul happily. 'Still talks too loud.'

'. . . except I use the Cercle Sportif in Saigon these days.' Koenig kissed her hand and took his time letting go.

'You still live out there?' Marie was surprised.

Koenig made a grimace. 'At least there I don't have to hide my face. I live openly under my own name and nobody's going to arrest me for it.'

'What do you do?'

'For a living?'

She nodded.

'I run a rubber estate in the Central Highlands. Most of my neighbours are French – ex-OAS like me who can't come openly back to France because there's a price on our heads. We make a bit of money and watch the war.'

She was looking from him to Raoul and back again, comparing them.

Koenig searched his memory. 'I just remembered. You had a husband who was a planter.'

Marie turned her face away. 'That's right.'

'Do you have any trouble on your plantation?' Raoul asked hurriedly.

Koenig shrugged. 'Sometimes the Yanks drop a few tons of bombs and kill some of my trees,' he shrugged. 'They probably add them to someone's body count. Unlike bodies, the trees grow again.'

'Are you married?' Marie asked.

'Not as far as Europeans are concerned.'

With a colonial's understanding, she said, 'But you're married all the same?'

'We think we are,' said Koenig. It was his turn to blush. 'We had a Buddhist ceremony.'

'Have you children?' she wanted to know. It was hard for her to picture this tough, masculine friend of Raoul's enjoying a family life.

'A boy of three and a girl of four.'

341

'That must be nice,' she said, 'after all your bachelor years as a soldier.'

'It is.' Koenig took a photograph from his wallet. His voice softened. 'Here they are.'

Marie looked at the picture of the smiling Vietnamese girl in her white *ao-dai*, standing in front of an estate bungalow not unlike the one where she and Gustave had lived. Koenig's wife looked very young. A child held each of her hands.

'She's very beautiful,' she said. 'They're all beautiful.'

'They're the best thing that ever happened to me,' said Koenig.

Raoul had pulled one of the maps off the wall. 'Show me where you live.'

Koenig put away the photograph and stabbed a finger near Pleiku.

'That's a VC-controlled area,' observed Raoul, 'according to my information.'

'Right.'

'They don't bother you?'

'Only for taxes.'

'Taxes?' queried Marie.

'They come up to the house at night and tell me how much. I haggle and pay up, then they go away. Sometimes they take a few local men and girls as conscripts at the point of a gun. There's nothing I can do about it. It's the way the country runs itself.'

Raoul granted.

'Can I get you another drink?' Marie asked.

Koenig shook his head. 'Thank you but I must be on my way.'

He shook hands with Raoul and was about to do the same with Marie when she stood on tiptoe and kissed him on the lips.

'I've wanted for a long time to meet you,' she said. 'Raoul talks of you often. Go safely home to your wife and children.'

'I will.' Koenig studied her face close to. 'You're a lucky bastard,' he said to Raoul.

Marie stood in the doorway and watched his tall, thin silhouette outlined against the starlit river as he walked away from the village to where he had parked his hired car in a copse half a mile away.

But in the bleak studio Raoul was staring at the maps over which he and Koenig had pored for hours.

'Did I drive your friend away?' Marie asked.

'Koenig never stays long.'

'Is he really on the run, after all these years?'

'He's under sentence of death if caught on French soil,' said Raoul.

'Why does he come to France, if it's so dangerous?'

'Because it is dangerous. No, that sounds too flippant. He comes here because he feels he has a right to. It's difficult to explain, but that's Koenig. As a kid he wanted to be a lawyer but his family had no money, so he went into the Army. He comes here to prove to himself and me and a few others that *they* haven't won completely.'

'They? How long have you known him?'

'Since I was at St Cyr. Must be more than twenty years ago.' He folded the maps and placed each carefully in its drawer.

'And you didn't know he was married?'

'Men don't talk about things like that.'

'You didn't tell Koenig about me?'

'Not a word.'

'Because you're ashamed?'

Raoul smiled. 'I'm not ashamed, Marie. I told you, in twenty years Koenig and I have never discussed anything emotional.'

'What are you doing now?'

'Staring at you. You pleasure me. That's the dress I bought you last week in Bordeaux.'

'I thought you hadn't noticed.'

'I always notice what you're wearing.'

'Yes.'

'You're very beautiful.'

With Raoul's eyes fixed on her, Marie did not see the

crippled legs or the wheelchair. She felt the power of his desire. It was hard to breathe, as though his arms were already around her, constricting her lungs. She sucked air in. I ought to feel guilty, she thought, betraying my husband with my lover twice every week. But I don't. I feel happy, happier than I can remember being for years.

Raoul wheeled himself around the room, switching out the lights one by one until there was only a single lamp left on.

Marie turned and the new dress flared out around her stockinged legs. Raoul was sitting on the bed. 'Come here,' he said. 'I want you.'

It was almost a ritual. He could not stand and embrace her, undress her and lead her to the bed as a normal lover would have done. Instead he ordered her to walk across the room to him. The first time, if he had asked her to go to bed, she would have said no although she wanted to say yes. But he had done the same then and ordered her to join him on the bed. So she had walked the five fateful steps, magnetised by his eyes.

And so it was now. Marie felt she had no choice and so there was no guilt. She sat, embraced her lover, closed her eyes and felt his lips, his tongue, his fingers explore her. The new dress slipped to the floor and was followed by her slip, her bra, her suspender belt and stockings. It was a game they played. Raoul would ring her and say, 'Don't wear any stockings today.' Or 'No bra this morning.' At first she had thought him kinky but then she came to enjoy the secret thrill of spending the day dressed ready for her lover.

'You're wonderful,' he breathed in her ear. 'I love your body.'

'I'm glad.' Marie's voice was husky with desire. She felt his fingers open her, probing, caressing. Some nights when his legs hurt, he lay still and ordered her to make love to him. This night, he wanted to be active. She lay and let him touch her, arouse her, enter her. Once he was in her body, he felt so powerful that he forgot he was ever otherwise.

They made love three times. Marie could not remember

Gustave doing that ever, not even on their honeymoon. Afterwards, lying in his arms, she wondered whether Raoul thought often about Huguette. There was a subtle feminine battle every time Raoul's ex-wife paid a visit to St Martin, but at least he no longer sat wordless in Huguette's presence, following her with his eyes like a dog watching his mistress. . . .

Perhaps, thought Marie, it was the right moment to ask a question that had been waiting for years.

Raoul felt the change in her. 'What is it?' he asked drowsily.

'Was it odd,' she asked softly, 'to see the picture of Koenig's wife and children?'

He laughed. 'No.'

'Don't you regret not having a child to call you Daddy?'

'I don't have regrets,' he said shortly.

'Louise said once that you were frightened of being a father.'

'It wouldn't be fair,' he said, meaning his legs. 'Not fair to the kid.'

Marie thought of her daughter, just starting her first term at university in Paris, and how she had adjusted to living with a father who was now little more than a vegetable.

'There are worse things,' she said, 'than a father in a wheelchair. Look what Marie-France had to put up with, these last few years.'

'You couldn't foresee that. With me, it's different.'

'She told me I could tell you when I thought you were ready.'

'Marie-France?'

'Louise.'

'Tell me what?' he asked irritably. It always made him sharp when her mind butterflied from one subject to another.

'The way she put it to me was: "I've taken the only present I want from Raoul." Do you understand?'

'You're wrong. Louise didn't take a thing from me.'

'She was pregnant when she went away.'

Raoul lifted himself on to one elbow and searched Marie's face. 'Louise has my child?'

Marie nodded.

'She never wrote.'

'She writes to me each Christmas. She calls the boy Raoul. He's three years old this month.'

Marie watched the tears run down Raoul's face. The eyes that could turn dark with anger, that could lure her to his embrace or make her laugh, now were full of pain. She pulled him down and buried his face in her breasts.

'I wish it was me,' she said. 'I wish I'd had your child, my love.'

12

The sound of firing echoed off the slopes of the Black Mountain above the ancient town of Castelnaudary. The sustained bursts of the FM 7.5 light machine-gun drowned the spasmodic coughs of the FAMAS 5.6 assault rifles – the French answer to the Armalite M 16. In the occasional lull, a trained ear could pick out the solitary bark of a single shot loosed off by a carefully aimed F 1, the chosen weapon of the Legion's snipers.

Far below the firing range, motor traffic followed the old trade route along which British tin had travelled to the Mediterranean in exchange for oil and wine long before the Romans came. Not far to the south, the tops of the Pyrenees danced in the haze. Beyond lay Spain, the goal of Hans-Peter's plan, which was based on a newspaper article about Jewish refugees who had escaped over the Pyrenees to Spain during the Second World War.

Sean had learned that the local gendarmerie were only alerted to watch for deserters in a radius of thirty kilometres from the Legion's base. The problem was that the recruits were escorted by armed NCOs whenever they went outside the barracks. Roger said that their best chance was to scale the barracks wall immediately after evening *appel*. They could put at least thirty kilometres between themselves and Castelnaudary before dawn. It would be tough going, but without packs they could do it. Then they would live off the land, making their way through the mountains by travelling only at night and sleeping in the daytime. Once in Spain, they would pose as tourists who had lost their passports.

Hans-Peter clung to his dream of desertion. It was the last thing of which he thought at night; it surged up from the subconscious whenever there was a free moment during the day.

His daydream was interrupted by a shout from Grohmann. 'You two, Muller and Milton. Get that weapon firing! You hear me?'

'Get a move on,' Roger hissed.

Hans-Peter threw himself flat and fed the belt of ammunition into the light machine-gun Roger had been carrying. It looked to his naked eye, screwed up against the dust that was blowing into their faces, as though his friend was doing too well. He fed another belt of fifty rounds into the weapon and looked behind to make sure neither Grohmann nor the armourer corporal was near.

'Ease off, Roger,' he advised in a whisper. 'If you score too high, you'll be made section machine-gunner.'

'Doesn't bother me.'

'You want to end up lugging ten kilos of machine-gun everywhere? Plus ammo? You're crazy.'

Roger grinned at the thought. The FM 7.5 was a powerful weapon. To compare it with the FAMAS was like confusing a moped and a 1,000 cc motorbike. And Hans-Peter was the best server: he could strip the weapon faster than anyone else and feed the fifty-round belts seemingly without interruption. They made a good team on the machine-gun.

He squinted over the sights. 'We'll show Grohmann what we can do,' he decided.

At the other end of the range, the cardboard target disintegrated in a cloud of fragments. Roger eased the weapon on to the next target, shattered it, moved to the next and destroyed that.

In the lull, as their ears adjusted, they heard Grohmann talking with the armourer.

'Hey, Milton.' The little corporal was standing over them. 'You're the section machine-gunner from now on. That's your weapon. Look after it and love it.'

'Yes, corporal.'

'That was good shooting,' said Grohmann.

Roger rolled over on to his back and grinned. He felt pleased with himself. Grohmann's praise was rare indeed.

'He'll need a server,' said the armourer.

'I volunteer.' Hans-Peter spoke without looking up.

'You?' Grohmann eyed him disparagingly.

'Him,' said the armourer. 'When a gun jams, Muller's the fastest recruit I've ever seen at getting it working again.'

'A small miracle,' sneered Grohmann. 'Muller is good for something at last.'

Apart from the attack on Cecchi, Sean had kept a low profile, concealing his prowess with weapons. He stayed resolutely in the average scoring bracket each time they were on the firing range. Assault rifles and machine-guns held, in any case, no appeal for him.

It was when he saw an F 1 sniper rifle equipped with telescopic sight for the first time that he could not resist raising a hand to volunteer. Grohmann threw the weapon at him. He caught it in mid-air and felt the balance. It had a feeling of class that no mass-produced assault rifle could ever have.

Sean concealed the thrill it gave him to handle a precision weapon again. He lay on the stony ground, pretending to listen to the instructions of the armourer squatting beside him and enjoying the feel of the smooth stock against his cheek. With the first shot, he knew he had found his weapon. With each recoil, he felt again the sensation of playing the flute. Three sighting shots. Then he took five bulls neatly out of the targets, as cleanly as if they had been punched by machine.

Grohmann squatted down on the other side of Sean. 'Where did you learn to shoot like that, Irish?'

'I never did before today,' Sean protested.

349

'You've handled a rifle before,' the little corporal snorted.

'No,' said Sean, getting slowly to his feet. 'It's a gift.'

Grohmann held Sean's five targets in his hand. He measured him with a new respect. 'It doesn't matter,' he said. 'But don't lie to me, Irish.'

The two men stared at each other without saying a word, Sean determined he would not blink first. It was Grohmann who turned away and, after a brief consultation with the armourer, led Sean to the far end of the range. 'We'll see what you're like at 500 metres,' he said.

Sean settled the sniper rifle on its bipod. He shrugged away the binoculars offered by Grohmann with 'I can see all right.'

There was an almost religious silence between them as Sean nestled the stock of the rifle against his cheek. The trigger was like silk to his index finger. He ran his left hand along the telescopic sight, which was smooth as the polished wood of a flute.

When he was comfortable, he fired three sighting shots, adjusting the lunette minutely after each. A light wind blew at an angle across the range. Sean took in the way the clumps of grass and small bushes were moving while the branches of trees were still; he aimed off without even thinking. Grohmann, prepared to give instructions, saw that none was needed. He watched the performance through binoculars without speaking.

Sean's pulse was racing and his lips were dry as he tried to resolve the inner conflict. Instinct tempted him to back down and not attract attention, but his narcissism had been touched. He wanted Grohmann – the sneering, insatiable bastard – to know he was good at something.

Five bulls.

'Now, 1,000 metres,' said Grohmann.

Three bulls and two inner circles.

'How do you like the F 1?' Grohmann asked.

'It's a beautiful weapon and no mistake,' said Sean. His fingers caressed the stock lovingly.

'I was a *tireur d'élite* before my eyesight changed.'

350

Sean looked questioningly at the corporal lying beside him. Grohmann removed his kepi. The recruits had joked many times that it was welded to his skull. A livid scar ran from above the right temple to a hairless patch of mauve skin above the right ear.

'Algeria,' explained Grohmann.

Sean waited.

'A *fellouze* got lucky. My right eye never saw straight again.'

Sean said nothing as the corporal replaced his cap. He was thinking of the unknown Arab sighting on Grohmann's immaculate kepi, squeezing the trigger and seeing the corporal fall.

Reading the thought, Grohmann laughed. 'You'd like to be looking at my face through that sight, wouldn't you?'

Sean did not reply.

Grohmann shrugged. 'You're not the first and you won't be the last, Irish.'

He sat up and tossed a cigarette to Sean, who let it fall to the ground.

'I don't smoke, corporal,' he said.

Grohmann lit up and squinted through the smoke. 'You don't smoke. You don't drink. And you shoot like an angel. Can you walk on water?'

Sean did not reply.

The performance of each squad was scored continuously and competition among the drill instructors was fierce, which made a natural marksman like Sean an asset to Grohmann's squad.

The corporal threw away his cigarette. There was a subtle change in the tone of his voice.

'Listen, Irish,' he said. 'I want you practising with that rifle every time we come on the range. Don't waste your time with the FAMAS. I want you winning the inter-squad 1,000-metre marksman competition. And I want your two pals to win the LMG prize on the FM 7.5. for me as well.'

From that moment, he stopped victimising them.

13

O n the other side of the Atlantic, the summer of 1967 passed without great upheavals. The racial troubles of the previous year were quiescent, Shirley Temple announced she would stand for Congress and boxer Muhammed Ali got married. North of the border, President de Gaulle stirred up separatist hopes in Quebec, while President Johnson escalated the war in Vietnam step by futile step.

Life in Jacksonville was good for Frank. That year the Swedish Range of products made more money than the supermarket division of Hansen's Foods and Frank was promoted to vice-president. It was a life lacking in adventure but full of challenges. Each day brought problems which he solved with good humour and tact. He was popular with his staff, not least because he seemed able to anticipate his father's thinking, which avoided on the Swedish Range production line those volcanic outbursts of Sven's temper that were legendary in Jacksonville. At twenty-eight, Frank was a rich young man in his own right who would be a millionaire by the time he was thirty.

His children saw little of their father during the week, for Frank was at work by 7 a.m. and rarely returned before they were asleep. Alice never complained, knowing that the weekends were hers and the twins'. At the ritual Sunday lunches where all the family ate together, Sven insisted on calling her the Queen of Wonderland, but she was still outwardly quiet and unassuming. Few people saw the inner strength that enabled her to hold her own in the Hansen family.

Frank's fears that she would be overwhelmed by Sven's crude energy and confused by his mother's semi-alcoholic evasiveness were unfounded. Indeed, becoming a grandmother and having a daughter-in-law with whom to go to church seemed to have lessened his mother's drink problem.

So when tragedy struck, it was all the more shattering.

The day began like many summer Sundays. Alice left the twins for Frank to look after while she and her mother-in-law were driven to church by some neighbours. Frank slopped around the house and garden in a dressing gown, enjoying the company of his two excited three-year-olds who changed visibly from week to week. They were fascinated by Sven's latest toy. His present for their birthday the previous week was a mongrel puppy he had impulsively saved from the local dog pound and called the Mutt. For Frank, one of the pleasures of Sunday was the two solid hours in the morning when the telephone did not ring once and nobody said: 'Frank, we seem to have a problem . . .'

It was tacitly understood that no questions were asked about where Sven spent his sabbath mornings. On this particular Sunday, Frank drove the twins to church in his station-wagon and collected Alice and his mother after the service. From there, they headed for the cabin by Jackson's Lake where Sven was waiting beside the barbecue with a pile of steaks ready for cooking.

Sven tolerated religion; women could go to church if they wished, but piety in the home was banned. When Alice quietly said grace for herself and the twins, Frank opened a can of beer and talked loudly to cover her words: '. . . for these and all Thy other gifts we thank Thee.' If Sven heard her, he made no comment.

The simple three-generation family meal was frozen in Alice's Polaroid snapshot. Sven picked it up and said

353

through a mouthful of steak, 'We could reshoot it with professional models, right here. What do you think? It would make a marvellous Hansen's Food = Happy Family publicity campaign.'

'Uh-huh.' Alice took the snapshot from him. 'No business on Sunday. That's about the only rule you've ever stuck to, Granpa. And I'm not having you break it now.'

Even Frank, who went over the events of the nightmare a thousand times afterwards, found it impossible to unravel the strands of the tragedy that day.

If Sven had had a physically less demanding morning with his current girlfriend he might not have been asleep on the deck of the cruiser at the crucial time. If Frank himself had not had a bout of summer flu Alice would not have made him go back to the cabin for a siesta after the meal. If his mother had taken one glass of wine less at lunch she might have been more alert, and actually looking at the lake instead of sitting on a lounger, gazing into space. If the Mutt had not learned to chew its way through a leash when tied up, the day would have ended differently. If there had not been a squall of wind at the wrong moment . . .

It was impossible to reconstruct exactly what happened or in what order because everything happened fast and each person present saw only part of it.

Before the meal Frank had inflated a rubber dinghy for the twins to play in. It was moored to a stake firmly driven into what Sven called the beach. This was an area of lake shore a couple of hundred yards from the landing stage where he had had several tons of sand dumped on the shore and bulldozed flat for his grandchildren to play on. The little boat lay on the flat, calm surface of the lake, not even moving throughout the meal.

After eating, Alice took the children and the puppy to play in the dinghy, so that Sven and Frank could have a quiet rest. The Mutt was a nuisance, constantly trying to clamber into the tethered boat and threatening to overturn it, so she tied him to the mooring stake and watched the twins splashing happily in the warm water.

Before lying down on the bed, Frank looked out of the cabin window and saw Alice sitting on the sand watching the twins in their striped T-shirts facing each other in the rubber boat, as they did in the bath at home. The Mutt growled playfully as it tugged on its leash.

Sensing his eyes on her, Alice looked up and waved.

'We're very blessed, Frank,' she had said at the end of the meal.

Seeing her watching the children on the peaceful lake shore, his heart filled with warmth. For a moment he felt like taking a blanket and going to sleep beside her on the sand. But it was true, he did not feel on top form and the coming week was going to be tough, so he contented himself with waving back and lay down to sleep.

He was awakened by his mother's piercing shrieks. The surface of the water was broken by wavelets and the sky was dark. A sudden squall had struck the lake.

'The dog!' his mother called. 'It chewed through the cord holding the dinghy.'

The wind chose that moment to catch the shallow rubber dinghy and push it with its two passengers further away from the shore. Alice was already in water up to her neck but still unable to reach the little boat.

'I'm coming!' shouted Frank. He vaulted over the windowsill as he heard Sven, startled awake by his wife's cries, gunning the twin outboards of the cruiser into life with a roar that shattered the peace of the lake. In the fraction of a second before the noise erupted, Frank clearly heard one of the twins shout 'Mommy! Mommy!'

As he fought his way through the brambles and bushes, taking a short cut to the shore, Frank lost sight of the lake for a minute. Breasting a rise, he saw that Alice was no longer visible.

'She can't swim!' he called to Sven, who could not hear. He tore through the last brambles and ran past the buckets and spades and the book Alice had been reading, which was lying face down on the sand where she had thrown it. The Mutt barked excitedly in the shallows. There was no sign of Alice.

Frank threw himself into a crawl, heading for the spot where he thought she had disappeared. Just as he filled his lungs with air to dive for her, one of the twins – in their identical blue striped T-shirts he was unsure which of them it was – stood up and overbalanced the frail boat, tipping them both into the water.

With the agonising choice between Alice and the twins, Frank launched himself almost clear of the water, heading for the upturned boat. Sven was on the spot almost instantaneously, skilfully manoeuvring the cruiser to a dead halt with the engines and dropping the anchor. He dived off the deck before the echoes had died away and reached the capsized rubber boat at the same time as Frank. Neither twin was to be seen.

Frank dived repeatedly into the dark depths of the lake. Twice he caught at what he thought was clothing, only to find at the surface that he was holding a handful of weeds. Running out of air, his lungs filling with water, he surfaced underneath the cruiser and tore his scalp open on a propeller. He floated to the surface stunned, blood all over his face. The blood was flowing freely, diluted by the water, and diffusing in all directions in a dark stain on the green surface. Sven, who had climbed back on board by the stern ladder, tried to grab his son with a boat hook and pull him out of the water.

There was the noise of outboards growing louder as craft from other lakeside residences converged on the scene to find Frank gasping for breath, fighting the grip that Sven had managed to get on one arm. He was bellowing in pain like an injured bull, 'My kids! My kids!' His head vanished underwater as he broke free.

It was Jacksonville's chief of police, a lifelong friend of Sven's, who jumped into the water from the police launch and knocked Frank unconscious when he next surfaced.

Frank came to, head down and vomiting green water, on the deck of Sven's cruiser. He grabbed the police chief's arm with a grip that was amazingly strong for a man who had just almost drowned and was suffering from concussion. 'Tell me! Tell me!' he implored.

'You did everything you could, Frank.'

Frank's groan was the noise of an animal *in extremis*. He staggered to his feet, holding the shiny chrome guard-rail and scanning the placid green expanse that stretched back to the shore. The wind had dropped and the sky was blue again. There were two swimmers in the water with snorkels and face masks, supporting between them a small, lifeless body in a striped T-shirt. Inshore several men without equipment were searching on the edge of the shallows for Alice's body.

A mist of white pollen from the willows on the lakeshore drifted across the water, settling gently on the surface as though Nature was trying to wrap the dead children in cotton wool. A faint smell of blossom on the breeze dragged at Frank's memory. He wondered what plant could grow in the arid Wadi Ourène and beside an Idaho lake. The Arabs spoke of a tree of life. Perhaps there was a tree of death also which blossomed when he was near?

He could see everything clearly but heard nothing. An intangible glass wall separated him from the lesser actors in the drama. He felt remote from the scene in front of him, drained of emotion.

When anyone came near, he shook his head from side to side and kept repeating, 'I tried,' as though disbelieving his own words.

'I tried. I tried.'

14

The bar outside Castelnaudary's railway station was called Le Camerone. The décor was largely souvenirs of the Foreign Legion but the three dazzling white kepis on the counter were real. They belonged to Roger, Hans-Peter and Sean who had put them on for the first time at the ceremonial passing-out parade the previous day.

'For once, Irish,' said Roger Milton, 'you can join us in a drink to wash the dust of this place from our mouths.'

'If I tell you my old man was a drunk, that's the kindest thing I can say about him. I'll have an orange juice.'

'One drink,' urged Roger, 'won't make you a drunkard.'

'No.'

'Come on,' Hans-Peter joined in. 'We've got to celebrate getting out of basic training. After six months in hell with Grohmann stoking the fires, a drink will do you good.'

'I don't touch alcohol. And that's that.'

Roger sighed. To the barman he said resignedly, '. . . and an orange juice.'

Hans-Peter and Sean raised their glasses with Roger's to toast the caps on the bar. They had earned the right to wear them.

They stood and moved with a physical confidence that they had not had before joining the Legion. Their uniforms had been retailored several times as muscles built up. With regular meals and exercise, even Sean had grown three centimetres. Although shorter than his two friends, he no longer looked a small man.

The new intake which had arrived to replace them in the hands of Grohmann and the other training corporals looked a bunch of weedy, frightened schoolboys. It was not possible for the fully fledged legionnaires to remember that they had looked like that only half a year before.

Wearing their kepis, they had even been given a comradely nod by the military police sitting in a jeep outside the station. It made a pleasant change from the perpetual harassment that had been their lot while they wore the berets of recruits in training.

Roger rubbed the deep groove in the skin of his temples where the hard rim of the new kepi had left its mark. He was the only one of the three facing the door when a familiar figure darkened the entrance.

'Look out,' he warned in a low voice. 'Here comes trouble.'

The others turned to see Grohmann enter. Immaculate as always, he strode up to the bar. The barman stopped chatting with a group of civilians and hurried to serve the new arrival.

'The usual *marc*, corporal?' he asked.

'Make it four,' said Grohmann. He ignored the three men beside him until the glasses were on the counter and filled. Then he lifted one glass and pushed the others in front of Roger.

'Pass these along to your mates,' he said.

'Yes, corporal.'

Grohmann grinned at them. 'You think I'm a bastard, but I make good legionnaires. You three will be all right. I'll drink to that.'

Roger and Hans-Peter exchanged a glance. They raised the tiny glasses and waited to see what Sean would do.

To distract Grohmann's attention, Roger asked, 'Do you buy a drink for all your old boys, corporal?'

Grohmann's pale eyes held a hint of amusement. 'No,' he said. 'Most of them I never want to see again. But I owe you three a drink. My squad won the intake competition thanks to your shooting.' He nodded to Sean and Roger.

Hans-Peter waited with his glass raised for the corporal to drink first.

The fourth glass was still untouched on the bar.

'Drink,' Grohmann ordered Sean.

Under the corporal's unblinking gaze, Sean lifted the glass and swallowed the fiery spirit with the others.

Posted back to Aubagne for assignment, Roger, Sean and Hans-Peter discovered what had been Frank Hansen's favourite bar near the Old Port in Marseilles. It was still run by Larsen, the huge Swedish ex-para sergeant with a limp. He sorted out the *bagarres* with tolerant, good-humoured violence and never a call for help. He talked to the legionnaires who were lonely and left the others alone. A thick haze of Gauloise smoke hung in the air and a score of different accents desecrated the French language, or rather the legionnaires' peculiar mixture of argot, German, Arabic and Vietnamese.

Hans-Peter carried two beers and a bottle of Coke to the table where Roger and Sean were waiting.

'How did you get on?' Sean asked.

'OK,' said Hans-Peter. 'I tracked my father down.'

They were all three in uniform. They had many privileges now that basic training was behind them, but wearing civilian clothes was forbidden during the first five years of service.

By the flush on Hans-Peter's face, Sean thought his friend had had a few drinks already. 'What about your father?' he prompted.

'He was a sergeant. Killed at Dien Bien Phu when the outpost called Isabelle was overrun by the Viets.'

Roger whistled. 'One of those Teutonic hero types who fought to the last bullet.'

Hans-Peter pulled a creased and yellowed photograph out of his breast pocket. He tossed it on to the table. It showed six men sitting on a tank. Five wore bush hats. The sixth was bare-headed, stripped to the waist. There was a strong resemblance between his face and Hans-Peter's gentler features.

'That's him. The one without a hat. I stole the picture from the archives at Puyloubier. It came from Dien Bien Phu, taken a few days before he died. According to the librarian, the film was smuggled out from a Viet Minh prison camp underneath a plaster cast on someone's broken leg.'

Hans-Peter screwed the photograph up, tossed it into the ashtray and struck a match.

'Tough-looking bastard.' He set fire to the photograph and swallowed his beer in one gulp. 'Looked like he could lick the entire Viet Minh army with one hand tied behind his back.'

'Why d'you burn the photograph?' Roger asked.

'I don't owe him a thing.'

'How d'you mean?'

'I always felt I was a failure. I knew my father was that typically German warrior type. Strong. Brave. Tough. All my childhood I pictured him in Valhalla, swilling back the booze in the Bierkeller in the sky, singing those old *ein-zwei-drei* marching songs with his roughneck comrades and sneering at me for being what I am.'

Sean signalled to the barman, pointing to the empty glasses. 'And now?' he asked.

'I don't owe the bastard anything,' said Hans-Peter. 'He never did anything for me, so why should I do anything for him?'

'You've lost me, kraut.'

Hans-Peter grabbed Roger's lapels. 'So there he was sitting on a tank, looking like Rommel,' he said fiercely. 'That doesn't make him any tougher than we are.'

Larsen was limping in their direction with a tray of drinks. Despite increasing age, he was still a powerfully built man.

Sean disengaged himself. 'Let's go somewhere else,' he suggested. 'I think we've outstayed our welcome.'

Hans-Peter turned unsteadily. 'Who says so? As long as I have money, they gotta serve me. That's the law.'

'That's the law for civilians.' Sean grabbed his friend's collar. 'But start a fight in here and Larsen will crush you flat.'

Two hours later, they were all three pleasantly drunk after eating a giant bouillabaisse in a local restaurant, washed down with three bottles of white wine.

'Champagne!' Roger ordered. 'We have something to celebrate.'

Hans-Peter had been too full of his own emotions to pick up the hint of conspiracy between the other two. He realised now that he had been missing something. 'Celebrate?' he queried thickly.

'Go on, Irish,' urged Roger. 'Tell the kraut our news.'

'News?' Hans-Peter asked.

'The postings are up,' said Sean.

'And?'

'They're splitting us up.'

'Why celebrate that?' Hans-Peter grimaced.

'Because Roger's thought of a way round it.'

'That clever bastard would. How do we do it?'

'Simple. We volunteer for the paras.' Roger smiled.

Hans-Peter winced. 'You're kidding?'

'It's true,' Roger confirmed, pouring champagne into three glasses. 'The Second Parachute Regiment on Corsica gets the pick of the Legion to choose from. If we all volunteer and if we're accepted, we can stay together.' He beamed with pleasure and raised a glass: 'To the paras.'

Hans-Peter did not join the toast.

'What's the matter?' Roger asked.

Hans-Peter looked pale. 'I couldn't do that.'

'You're scared of jumping out of a plane? Or because the training's even tougher than what we've been through?'

Hans-Peter looked at his two friends. 'Yes,' he agreed soberly. 'I'm scared.'

Now that he had looked his father's ghost in the face he could admit that he was frightened. 'I'm scared,' he repeated. 'Anyone sane would be scared to jump out of a plane. The trouble is, you two are crazy.'

'Then they split us up.' Sean looked downcast.

'We swore an oath to stick together,' said Roger.

'We did not,' Hans-Peter disagreed. 'We said we'd stick together during training, that's all.'

Roger looked at Sean. 'That's it, then. We can't make him.'

Hans-Peter made a flash decision. What he decided was no longer anything to do with the man sitting on the tank in the faded photograph. He was free to do what he wanted. And what he wanted was to be with the other two.

So, wondering if he was mad, he blurted, 'I'll volunteer. If it keeps us together, I'll volunteer for the paras.'

Before he had finished speaking he found himself being hugged by both Sean and Roger. There was the sound of splintering wood as his chair collapsed under their combined weight. Customers at nearby tables looked uneasily at the three legionnaires lying helplessly on the floor.

'This calls for a celebration,' announced Roger when he had stopped laughing.

'And I'm gonna get drunk tonight,' said Sean.

15

The drive back to Wonderland in the wake of the ambulances was a dream. Frank's mind was unable to take in the fact that he had left the house that morning as a husband and father of twins, yet returned a widower with no children. As weeks went by and autumn became winter, the pain grew no less. He became convinced that the smell of blossom clung faintly to the skin of his palms, and washed his hands frequently but the smell was still there. Aftershave did not help either.

In a gesture to take his son's mind off the grief, Sven Hansen insisted on swapping jobs for a while, keeping Frank constantly on the move as roving ambassador and troubleshooter for the whole Hansen's Foods chain. On his brief visits to the head office at Jacksonville Frank saw that the death of his grandchildren had extinguished some of the essential fire in Sven. Gone was the compulsion to out-talk and outlive everyone else.

For weeks after the tragedy Frank could not re-enter his own house. He changed the name to a simple street number and had all the rooms re-painted but it took three months, until after Christmas, before he could spend a night there. Then he started to use the place like a hotel room on the nights he was in Jacksonville, bringing work back from the office to keep his mind occupied until he fell asleep downstairs over a pile of paper.

By mid-February 1968 the war in Vietnam was being shot on film, flown out of the battle zone, rapid-processed, edited on the spot and bounced by satellite round the globe. The Tet offensive provided regular evening entertainment for millions of American homes.

Frank sat slumped in a comfortable chair with a can of beer in his hand to watch the *Late Late News* on television. He was feeling tired after a sixteen-hour day which included business meetings in four different cities. The columns of figures in front of him blurred.

He knuckled his eyes and looked up at the screen. A network reporter was standing in front of the citadel in Hué, commenting on the mass executions of civilians which had been carried out by the communist troops during their occupation of the former capital. Thousands of bodies had been found stacked in common graves. Trimming his commentary, he skipped over the tragedies of the natives to the heavy losses of the American and ARVN infantry as they battled their way back into the city, house by house. One US Marine unit had lost a casualty for each yard gained in that day's fighting. The accompanying pictures told their own grim story.

Another reporter, in combat uniform with flak jacket and steel helmet, huddled behind a shattered house wall clutching his microphone as a mortar round exploded close by. His words reflected America's incredulity that the backward little yellow people who were trying to kill him could outfight the most highly developed war technology in the world.

The phone rang. It was a teenager apologising for a wrong number. Frank frowned with the effort of trying to get his mind back on track.

On the screen a couple of American marines were desperately calling for a Medevac helicopter.

In a flash of insight Frank grasped the truth behind the news: the United States was not going to win the war in Vietnam.

The two desperate men on the banks of the Perfume

River were surrounded by the bodies of the rest of their platoon. The picture went shaky as a Viet Cong rocket exploded nearby. Now only the marine sergeant was still on his feet. The camera whip-panned to show a Medevac helicopter dancing out of range of the green tracers arching up towards it. Again and again the pilot attempted to land but each time was beaten off by hostile fire.

On the ground, the sergeant had tears running down his face. He was talking to the helicopter pilot via a PRC-90 back-pack radio still strapped to the dead man beside him.

'You bastards!' he screamed, shaking his fist impotently at the sky. He could have meant either the Viet Cong machine-gunners or the pilot.

'Dust Off,' he pleaded, 'my men are dying down here.'

The phone rang again. It was the same teenager apologising.

By the time Frank had replaced the phone, the newscast had been interrupted for a commercial break. It was the advertisement for Hansen's Swedish Range that made everything come clear in Frank's mind. He stood up cold sober and tore the cable out of the wall socket, then lifted the television set and hurled it against the wall.

What am I doing in this empty house? he asked himself. I am twenty-eight, rich and successful but nobody needs me here. I should be where those men are.

I let De Burgh down. I let down Alice and my kids, but I don't have to let them down. They're Americans and they're dying. I'm a soldier. I could help them.

He sat down to write a letter to his father on the back of some computer printout. It was hard to find words that would mean the same to Sven as they did to him. When he had finished, he wrote a separate letter for his mother, ending, 'I love you both very much.' He signed both letters, 'Your son, Frank.'

The letters were unclear and rambling because the real reasons why Frank made his decision to join up again were veiled deep in his subconscious.

They had something to do with the guilt for De Burgh and a lot to do with the sense of identity he had felt during the years he had spent in uniform, but never found in civilian life.

It would have been hard enough for a man like Frank to write that. So how could he begin to explain to his parents the call of a lost cause, to which he was responding?

He was quite clear in his own mind that he was not going to Vietnam to help win the war but to fight and die if necessary in a cause that was already lost. Yet he felt an irresistible atavistic urge to take his place alongside those unknown men on the television screen, at whatever cost.

When he talked to me about it, I understood. Had not I and hundreds of others volunteered to be dropped into Dien Bien Phu knowing that the struggle was hopeless, the battle already lost, that we were unlikely to survive?

The call of a lost cause is the ultimate romantic reason for which a man will risk his life against all odds; the greater the odds, the louder the call. The impulse to answer it defies verbalisation, for it goes against logic. Probably no woman ever understands. To mothers, girlfriends, wives it looks as though the man who answers this call is throwing his life away pointlessly.

But Frank had no choice. He could be a man and go, or stay and be less than a man.

Frank sat in the darkened garage at the wheel of his car, looking out at the garden Alice had planted. It was partly lit by the street lamps. Across the tidy lawns of the houses opposite, in the homes where the neighbours had not yet gone to bed, the bluish light from television screens showed in uncurtained windows.

'You don't care,' shouted Frank.

'Care, care, care.' The echo from the house walls taunted him. It was all the same to his neighbours whether they were watching the commercials, a quiz show, an old cowboy movie or men dying for real on the other side of the world.

Frank had already started the engine when he remembered the Greyhound bus.

He pulled the key from the ignition, walked out of the

garage and back into the house. He placed his bunch of keys on top of the two letters and left, slamming the front door behind him. He had returned to Jacksonville, four-and-a-half years before, on a bus in the early morning rain. On a bus was the way he would leave it next morning, early.

Forty-eight hours after leaving Jacksonville, he was standing in a US Marine Corps recruiting office in downtown Washington.

'Age?' the recruiting sergeant asked.

'Twenty-eight.'

'Religion?'

'None.'

'Previous military experience?'

Frank wondered what the man would say if he answered 'Five years in the French Foreign Legion.' It was tempting, but service in the armed forces of a foreign power was illegal for citizens of the United States and he did not want any complications.

'None,' he replied.

'Why the Marine Corps?'

The posters on the wall behind the sergeant's back were of no help in answering this question. They showed marines in dress uniforms on parade, on sea and land, proudly holding hi-tech weapons, saluting the flag.

None of those images had been in Frank's mind when he made his decision to enlist. Sitting alone on the long-distance bus, he had been haunted by the ghost of De Burgh whose body lay in the hostile soil of Algeria. Like a reflection in the glass it had ridden alongside the bus, mile after mile. And no less real had been the recollection of the unknown marine sergeant on the television screen with tears running down his face as he shouted: 'Dust Off, my men are dying.'

For a moment, in the tidy office with the sound of early-morning commuter traffic filtering through the windows, Frank was tempted to say 'I'm joining up because we're losing the war.' But that did not make sense, even to himself . . .

'Why the Marine Corps?' the question was repeated.

None of the reasons could be put into words.

'Come on, fella, give me a break,' the recruiting sergeant urged. 'I have to fill in this form. Say something.'

'I heard it's tough in the Marines. How's that?'

The sergeant laughed and wrote the answer in the box provided. 'Recruits sometimes die in training at Parris Island. Is that tough enough for you?'

'I can hack it,' said Frank. The US Marine Corps, he thought, could be no worse than basic training at Sidi-bel-Abbès. He signed the form with a feeling of immense relief.

'Sit over there with the other two,' ordered the sergeant. 'I'll fix you some transport.'

He tossed a coin to Frank. 'Buy yourself a coffee from the machine, courtesy of the USMC. There are doughnuts on the counter. Help yourself. They're free.'

Frank caught the coin. He had deliberately left the house with no baggage, wearing only the clothes he stood up in: a pair of old jeans and a denim jacket worn over a rough work shirt. And he had taken no money above the cost of the bus ticket.

He sipped the hot coffee and bit into a doughnut. The decision was made; he could stop thinking for a while.

The sergeant was feeling expansive as he carried Frank's form into the lieutenant's office. For the first time in its history the US Marine Corps was using draftees to make good the high casualty figures of the Vietnam war. Three volunteers in one morning was a pretty good haul during the Tet offensive of 1968.

PART 4

MAY 1971–AUGUST 1973

1

I followed the worsening situation in Vietnam with a growing hopelessness as the clandestine skirmishing in Cambodia and Laos became open warfare. The possibility of anyone going back to Dien Bien Phu in my lifetime looked increasingly remote.

It seemed that my dream of recovering the gold which had cost me so much was just a dream, the obsession of a sick man who cannot come to terms with reality. So I decided to realise my other dream and started work on the conversion of the Templars' tower. My plan was to make it into the home that I had planned and lived in mentally, all those years before when I lay in the darkness and pain of Minh's cage.

As the builders tore away the decay of centuries they revealed more and more clearly the structure I had seen in my mind. They were surprised that I could tell them things about the upper storeys of the tower, since plainly a cripple could never have climbed up there to see for himself. I pretended to them that I had asked people to go up and make notes for me, but each time they found some small detail – like a bricked-up arrow slit not visible from the ground – I felt a minute upsurge of optimism. If one dream was coming true, perhaps the other would one day.

I heard little from my man on the spot. Koenig never wasted words; if there was no news, he didn't make contact. But I bought every publication that could tell me what was going on out there *and polished up my English so that I could listen to the BBC World Service, which was the best source of broadcast information. I knew more about what was going on in the former French colonies of South-East Asia than I knew about happenings in Paris. Daily I updated my maps as conscientiously as when I was Lépine's ADC.*

By the month of May 1971, Saigon had become a vast sprawl of rat-infested migrant shanties reached by duckboards laid over open drains. Even the centre of town retained little of the leisurely charm of French colonial times: the once-elegant rue Catinat had been renamed Tu Do Street and was a jungle of concrete and neon massage parlours, pick-up bars and brothels. Hustlers hustled everything under the sun, pushers offered a wider range of drugs than most Vietnamese hospitals could afford to stock, and beautiful girls sold themselves for two dollars upwards so that they could send money home to peasant families who had disowned them.

In pursuit of the myth that the war effort was devolving on to the Republic of South Vietnam, the US presence was wound down month by month. While most combat soldiers were happy to return to the world, some Americans chose to stay on because they no longer belonged anywhere else; the war had become their way of life. Frank Hansen was one of these.

Convinced that what De Burgh had called the smell of death still clung to him, Frank had avoided making any close friendships since enlisting in the Marines. His physical toughness, previous military experience, familiarity with weapons, a gift for languages and, above all, his selfless courage in combat had eventually earned for him what he reckoned the most appropriate job in the still vast military establishment which was designated Military Assistance Command, Vietnam.

He was a Special Forces sergeant attached to a montagnard tribe in the Central Highlands, near the Laotian border. Even among the hardened loners in Special Forces, Frank stood out as a tough and uncompromising man driven by demons. With the zeal of a Jesuit missionary and the reckless bravery of a Bronze Age warrior king he lived for months on end with his tribe, fighting the Viet Cong on their own terms in the jungle where stealth and cunning were a better armoury than gunships and Arc Light bombardment. Even on leave Frank preferred to be among Vietnamese rather than in some in-country American R and R facility or in Hong Kong or Thailand.

2

Hot and humid. Noisy and dirty. The bars and strip joints on Tu Do Street were just another kind of jungle, Frank reflected.

He was dressed in civilian clothes but the beggars and pushers had the sense to leave him alone. Nor did the bar girls bother the man who had Special Forces written all over him and who spoke their own language so well.

After two months in the mountains and jungle, Frank found the pollution and bustle of Saigon hard to take. He bought a couple of drinks in an American-owned bar where he might have stumbled across other Special Forces men on leave but drew a blank and ended the afternoon alone, waiting patiently across the boulevard from the new white concrete fortress that was the US Embassy.

Waiting was something he did well. Whether on a jungle trail or in a Saigon street leaning against a tree in the shade, watching everything that went on, he had an ability to merge with the background which was surprising in such a large man. The secret was stillness; only his eyes moved behind the dark glasses.

He was waiting for a woman, a librarian in the ethnological section of the Embassy library whom he had met eighteen months before while doing research on the montagnard tribes. Since then he had spent most of his leaves with her.

Phuong emerged from the side entrance of the building, wearing a patterned silk *ao-dai*, slit up the thigh, over white silk trousers. The sight of her classic Vietnamese beauty after the semi-naked montagnard women he was used to was enough to take Frank's breath away, even at a distance.

Phuong smiled at the Marine sentry, said goodbye to a Vietnamese woman colleague and crossed the street to a bus stop. Frank stayed well back in the crowds. He had no reason for the jealousy that made him spy on her, except her beauty and the fact that he was away from her so often.

He followed her bus in a taxi as far as what had been a suburb near open country on the north side of the city before the shanty towns engulfed the surrounding countryside. Alighting from the bus, Phuong entered a large European-style villa that had belonged to a French merchant. The architecture was suburban Paris 1930. Doors and shutters needed painting but otherwise the building was in good repair. It was a large house for just one old man and his daughter. On his first visit Frank had asked how the family afforded such luxury accommodation.

'My father was a mandarin at Hué,' she had explained. 'He wrote poems for which certain people still respect him. When we were driven from our ancestral home, they let us live in this house as –' she looked serious, as always when she sought a word in English – 'as caretakers, can I say?'

Phuong had told him little about her past, except that her mother and two sisters had been killed – by which side she did not say – during the Tet offensive in 1968. Her father had had some kind of stroke when he saw the bodies and still walked with one foot dragging as he opened the front door to his daughter's knock.

Frank waited until dusk before crossing the street from his observation point. He tapped on the door.

'Oh, Frank!' Phuong's porcelain features melted into a huge smile. 'It is so good to see you. Come in.'

'Give me a kiss.'

He had spoken in Vietnamese. Phuong turned her head away in embarrassment, in case passers-by should hear.

In English, she said, 'Please, Frank. You know it is not right the neighbours should see us kissing in public.'

'If you were an American girl . . .' He took her arm and squeezed it.

'I not American girl,' she said. 'That's why you like me. It make change from all the round-eye women you have had, I think.'

Frank let her pull him inside the house.

'Who is it, daughter?' The old man's frail voice interrupted Frank's embrace.

Phuong pulled away from him, blushing. Her father wore traditional Vietnamese robes and bowed to welcome the visitor who was honouring his house. Although he knew Frank spoke excellent Vietnamese, Phuong's father changed to French to show respect and invited him with old-fashioned dignity to take China tea. In the living room which was still furnished with the long-departed French family's three-piece suite and sideboard, they discussed current issues politely for ten minutes over the weak greenish brew. Then the old man excused himself and withdrew to his room. After waiting a while for decency, the young couple moved to Phuong's room.

'Your father doesn't like me much,' said Frank, pulling her to him and kicking the door closed.

'He likes you very much,' Phuong protested. 'Only he is old-fashioned. In his heart he wishes I did not have a lover from another country.'

'Then he's what we would call a racist,' grinned Frank.

'He is afraid . . .' She paused. '. . . that you will take me away from him when you return to America.'

Phuong's eyes avoided looking at Frank. 'I have told him that such a thing is unlikely.'

'I don't even think about it.'

Frank realised his blunder and added hastily, 'Going back, I mean.'

He watched her face in the mirror as his hands cupped her breasts and moved down to feel her flat stomach and slim hips. The rough skin of his fingers snagged on the silk of her *ao-dai*. In the glass, Phuong's smile was like the Mona Lisa's; it could have meant anything.

As Frank peeled her clothes off one by one, Phuong stretched an arm behind her and put out the room light.

'I want to look at you,' he said.

'No, please,' she protested.

'I say yes please,' he insisted.

She switched on a small lamp beside the bed and knelt on the covers for him to inspect her body. One hand lay modestly in her lap. Frank feasted his eyes on her slim curves. The natural grace of Phuong's posture, her golden skin lit from one side by the small bedside lamp, reminded him of a mass-produced print of a painting by Tretchikoff in the Special Forces sergeants' mess at Doc Lap. He wished he had a camera to freeze the moment.

'I love your body,' he said. He bent down and planted a soft kiss on one nipple. Among the rules he had made for himself, it was safe to say: I love your body. But never to say or even think: I love you.

She had asked him once why he would not say the words she wanted to hear.

'Because the people I love . . .' He had begun to explain and stopped. She had never asked again.

Phuong let him suck her flesh. As he sank down on to the bed, she cradled his head in the crook of her arm and stared past it at some private vision. 'I love you, Frank,' she said.

He wondered what the words meant to her. Her tapering fingers and perfect nails lay passive in his own much larger hand. His skin was cracked and scarred; hers soft and cream coloured, like a disembodied ivory carving.

Frank kissed the fingers one by one and looked up into her face. She showed no sign of pleasure or irritation. There was an explosion not far away – a single one, not gunfire – and the light went out.

'Power cut,' she said.

He felt her silken skin brush the hair on his chest as she

knelt astride him; she was shy about doing that when the light was on.

A flare ship circling high in the night caused silent lightning that bounced off the low clouds and lit the room faintly. For a long moment he saw Phuong towering over him like a dim statue of womanhood giving birth to him. Then there was blackness again. The mattress moved as she leaned forward. He felt her long jet-black hair brush against his face. Her lips kissed his brow. Frank pulled her down, crushing his face into her breasts, seeking her tight, hard nipples with his lips and wanting her with the sudden urgency of an adolescent.

'You were away a long time,' she breathed.

As she straightened up another flare reflecting off the clouds miles away etched her briefly in monochrome. Frank dropped his eyes from her face to her breasts cupped in the delicate hands whose touch he loved, to her flat belly and the pubic hair that was brushing the hairs on his own belly.

'You're beautiful,' he breathed as the light faded. 'I'm going to eat you alive, Phuong.'

'You like that,' she said, parting her lips for him in the darkness.

Frank slid down the bed, wanting her body to overwhelm him and stop him thinking. He inhaled deeply, sucking her smell into his brain.

'Oh God,' he shivered with pleasure. 'I miss your cunt when I'm away.'

She made little moans of pleasure as he tasted her, then twisted lithely round, reaching for him, sucking and licking as he swallowed mouthfuls of her. She knew just when to stop each time just before his climax, in order to prolong his pleasure.

Afterwards they dozed in each other's arms. Frank awoke, listening to the sounds of the distant artillery. He lifted Phuong on top of him, where she lay brushing his face with her hair. By the light of another distant flare he made her sit on him, clasped his large hands round her waist, feeling the swell of her pelvic girdle beneath her soft skin, and gently but firmly pulled her down on to him, impaling her as the distant light went out and left them joined in the darkness.

When the bedside light came back on, Phuong was asleep and her face, framed by the long black hair spread over the pillow like silk, was perfect in repose.

It worried Frank sometimes that she was such a good lover. The modest girl who would not let him hold her hand in public, who bowed to the household gods when she entered the house, was also the woman whose body obsessed him.

He woke her to ask the question that tormented him. 'What do you do when I am not here?'

She yawned. 'When you are with those savages in the mountains?'

'The montagnard tribes are not savages,' he said. 'They have their own culture. It's different from yours, that's all.'

'They kill Vietnamese people,' said Phuong.

'This was their country first. Your people drove them off all the fertile land and up into the mountains. No wonder they hate you.'

'They are savages,' she repeated. 'How can you live with them?'

'They are good soldiers,' he said.

'Like you?'

'Your people –' he was picking a fight – 'don't even have a name for this country. That shows you stole it from the montagnards. Viet Nam is just two Chinese words meaning far south.'

'Why are you angry with me, Frank?'

He looked at her face on the pillow. The flawless beauty seemed too painfully desirable to be his alone. He wanted to bruise her, to scar her and by marring her perfection, make it his.

The nagging question returned. 'What do you do when I am not in Saigon, Phuong?'

'You have asked me this before.'

'So tell me.'

She sighed, humouring him. 'I work. And in the evenings, I read poetry to my father. You know that. His eyes are not good.'

He wanted to make amends. 'I can get him some spectacles.'

'Thank you. But I think he prefers the sound of my voice to being able to read the words on the page.'

The worm of jealousy was eating at Frank's soul.

'I meant for fun,' he insisted. 'What do you do for fun? There must be a hundred American men in the Embassy who ask you for a date, who want to take you dancing and out for dinner.'

'I wait for you, Frank,' she said.

The thought of Phuong lying with another man made him feel ill, like a cramp in the belly. During sleepless nights waiting in ambush in the insect-ridden dark of the jungle, he was tormented by visions of her face radiant with love for another man, touching him with love in her eyes or being touched. He wanted Phuong to be his exclusive property, but would never make the commitment that involved . . .

'I wait for you, Frank,' she said with her quiet smile. 'Vietnamese woman very patient.'

At midday, every street in downtown Saigon was swarming with bicycles, trishaws and motor scooters that wove in and out of the mass of pedestrians with no apparent pattern or lane discipline. Adult beggars of both sexes and all ages squatted hopelessly with hands outstretched, while hordes of children tugged at the sleeves of passers-by and blocked their passage by sheer numbers. 'Give! Give! Give!'

The last person Frank expected to see getting out of a motorised trishaw on a busy intersection was Captain Koenig.

Through the dark wrap-around sunglasses he wore to protect his night vision Frank could not be certain that the tall figure in the creased linen suit walking away on the other side of the road was his one-time commander.

He snatched the glasses off just as the lights changed to

green and the white-uniformed traffic policeman blew his whistle. A tangle of Vespa scooters, Lambretta trishaws, bicycles, taxis, private cars, military vehicles and overloaded trucks broke from the white line like some mad, mechanised cavalry charge and bore down on the last pedestrians still crossing the road.

Through gaps in the traffic, Frank strained to keep his eyes on the man on the opposite pavement. The striding walk was almost certainly that of Koenig. Then came an abrupt, bird-like movement of the head and the black eye-patch confirmed the identity.

The lights changed to red. Frank sprinted across the road, catching up with Koenig on the steps of a large colonial-style building. The sign above the doorway read: *Cercle Sportif – Club Privé*. A thick-set Vietnamese doorman in uniform moved forward flat-footed to block Frank's entrance.

'Excuse me, sir!' Frank caught the sleeve of Koenig's jacket. Despite being in the peak of condition, he was sweating from the exertion in Saigon's clammy heat.

Koenig motioned the doorman to stand back. His pale blue eye took in the green beret and Special Forces insignia on Frank's uniform.

'*Alors?*' he queried without interest.

Changing to French, Frank asked, 'You don't remember me, *mon capitaine?*'

It took Koenig a couple of seconds to make the connection.

'Hansen,' he said. 'Corporal Hansen.' A smile of genuine pleasure softened his features. The right hand that was missing two fingers shot out and grabbed Frank's hand in a grip of iron.

Frank matched the pressure, his free hand indicating the stripes he wore. 'I'm a sergeant now, sir. In someone else's army.'

Koenig's one eye flicked over the badges on Frank's sleeve.

'Special Forces?' He seemed impressed and led Frank inside the club to buy him a beer at the bar, grilling him with machine-gun questions which gave Frank no time to drink.

'To sum up,' finished Koenig, 'you're on your third tour of Vietnam in the peak of physical condition. You speak Vietnamese, Laotian and several montagnard dialects. You can handle most modern hand weapons and know your way around the country pretty well.'

Frank swallowed the first mouthful of beer. 'That just about sums it up,' he agreed.

'I'll come to the point,' said Koenig. 'How'd you like a job?'

'That's what you said the last time we met,' Frank grinned. 'What's it this time? Bodyguard to some Mr Big in the opium trade, up there in the Golden Triangle?'

'I wouldn't insult you,' said Koenig coldly. 'This is a job for a man of honour. Are you interested?'

Frank shook his head. 'I just re-upped for another year this morning. That's why I'm in uniform.'

'Ah,' Koenig sighed. He sounded disappointed.

Frank took advantage of this first pause in the conversation to ask, 'It's kind of strange bumping into you in the middle of Vietnam, captain. What brings you here?'

Koenig laughed. 'We French were here a whole century before the White House could find Vietnam on a map, Hansen. I've lived here for eight years, planting rubber. This country's my home now.'

'Planting rubber?' Frank could not imagine Koenig doing anything other than soldiering. 'I thought the OAS trouble was all over. Surely you could go back to France now?'

'In 1961,' said Koenig bitterly, 'I was exiled from my own country with a price on my head. After nine years, they gave me an amnesty. I am now legally free to set foot on French soil, but I cannot forgive my nation for what it did to me.' There was a shadow of sadness on the lean suntanned face, swiftly concealed behind the glass as Koenig took a sip of beer.

'What about you, Hansen?' he asked. 'What are you planning for afterwards?'

'I ask myself that, sir. The answer is, I don't know.'

'You'll be going back to America?'

'No,' said Frank. He did not offer to expand

'Well you won't be welcome here much longer, the way things are going. Have you thought of settling in France?'

'I don't think much about the future.'

'The job I mentioned might still be available when you've finished working for Uncle Sam. It depends on circumstances.' Koenig took a piece of paper from the barman and scribbled an address on it.

'My plantation,' he said. 'It's near Pleiku. Not so far from your montagnard village. Promise me you'll come and talk to me before you re-enlist again.'

Frank got off the bar stool and slipped the address into his breast pocket. 'I'll do that, sir. And thank you for the drink.'

Koenig's hand gripped Frank's firmly. 'It's a date,' he said. 'You visit me eleven months from today, Hansen – if you're still alive.'

3

'I t's urgent,' said Marie. 'Please come.'

'Are you all right?'

'Gustave,' she said, 'has shot himself.'

'Oh God . . .'

There was a long silence before Raoul asked, 'Have you told the police?'

'I wanted to call you first.'

'I'll be with you in five minutes.' He slammed down the phone.

Most of the time he was reconciled to being wheelchair-bound, but at moments like this, it made him furious that he could not sprint down the garden, leap into his car and drive off. Instead, he had to lift himself into the chair, spilling a pile of accounts on to the floor. He left them there and propelled himself through the neat herb garden to the garage. It took several minutes to open the doors, manoeuvre himself into the driving seat, fold the wheelchair and stow it behind him.

Driving up to the château, he saw many changes since he had last been there. Work had started on the most urgent repairs to the house. Half the roof was off and new timbers were being hauled into place.

Raoul smiled wryly. Determined that her home should look beautiful once again, Marie had begun work on the huge, rambling house in the same week the builders had begun tackling the restoration of his tower. He had advised against it, arguing that it was premature to borrow money until the vineyards had begun to make a profit, but she had gone her own way on that and many other things.

She was standing in the courtyard, wearing an old anorak over her dress. There was mud on her shoes.

As Raoul opened the car door, he saw the pain in her eyes.

'Don't get out,' she said, not looking at him 'He's in the fields. You can drive me there.'

They spoke little except for Marie to give directions that ended by a small copse near the river where Gustave's body lay, the gun beside it. From the unnatural posture, Raoul had little doubt. All the same he asked, 'You're sure he's dead?'

'Oh yes,' she spoke dully. 'Half his face is missing. I looked.'

'It's a hunting accident,' he said.

She nodded. 'That's what he wanted it to look like.'

'Wanted?'

She met his eyes for the first time. 'He left a note.'

Raoul heard the rustle of paper in her pocket.

'Do you want to show me?' He would have liked to embrace her but was unsure of her reaction.

Marie shook her head.

'Then I'll burn it for you.' Gently he took the note from her fingers with the promise, 'I won't read it.'

'He knew about us,' she said.

'But that's not why he shot himself?'

'No. He said he was glad . . .' Her voice failed. 'He said he was glad that his old friend Raoul would be there to take care of me after he was gone.'

His old friend Raoul!

Perhaps Gustave was the only one of us incapable of betrayal, the only one who could not change his values and keep in step with a changed world? Was that why he drank? So that he did

387

not need to see what was happening all around him? Which included Marie and me betraying him, for we had taken our love pretending that it hurt no one else, but he must have known.

At times over the years I had despised Gustave for being weak, for not fighting back, for not grabbing the slings and arrows of outrageous fortune and hurling them back in fortune's grinning face . . . but perhaps he was right. For we who fought back – Koenig, Marie, myself – had all lost something called innocence, which he had kept.

Sitting in the car beside Gustave's body, Marie said that he had died for her years before. I said little, for I felt she must blame me in some way for what he had done. And I was cautious, having lately learned that women take their revenge slowly, sometimes after years have passed.

I lied to Marie that day. Of course I read the note before burning it. In it Gustave did not blame either her or me. He wished us happiness together but said – it was beautifully written, without any trace of what coroners call imbalance of the mind – that he could no longer face another pointless day and another and another. He said that since losing his fortune for the second time in Algeria he had failed to find another identity.

It was a packet of breakfast cereal on the kitchen table, he said, which had prompted him to take his life. Corn flakes of all things! I found it afterwards. There was a panel on the back of the box for children to fill in and enter a competition. One square read: I AM A . . .

I realised, wrote Gustave, that I could not fill in that blank. I have no identity. Without one, I cannot live.

I know how he felt. When I have to fill in some official form which asks my professional identity, I still find myself beginning to write: Sold. . . . It takes a conscious effort to write: Accountant.

Raoul took Marie's hand. It was cold. 'It's better this way, Marie. This was the old Gustave that we both knew. This was his way of resolving the problem I'll take you back to the house and I'll ring the police for you.'

'I don't have any tears left.' She pulled her hand away from his. 'I shed them all over you, Raoul. It seems so unfair for Gustave. He was a good man. He deserves someone to weep for him.'

'You never let me explain.'

'Huguette did the explaining,' she said. 'I don't want an apology from you.'

'I wasn't going to apologise.'

'Louise was wrong.' Marie had been too proud to show bitterness at the time. It came flooding out of her now. 'She said that you did not really love Huguette, but it seems after all this time that Huguette is the only person you do love, Raoul.'

He looked at Gustave's body, crumpled on the ground. It was inappropriate to try and explain everything at such a time and place, but there might be no other chance – and Gustave was past minding.

'I didn't know Huguette would come to visit you,' he said patiently.

'After spending the night with you . . .'

'She was being divorced. She was very unhappy. I couldn't refuse to help her.'

Marie snorted disbelievingly. 'That woman, unhappy?'

'Yes. That woman.' He clenched his fists, wanting her to understand. 'For the first time in her life Huguette had a husband who was hurting her, not the other way round. She was bewildered and unhappy. I tried to comfort her.'

'Like comforting a snake,' Marie said savagely.

Raoul drove her back to the château. He used the telephone in the farm office to call the police and the doctor while Marie sat in the visitor's chair, dry-eyed and saying nothing. He talked to the functionaries for her. When they had gone she let him drive away without touching him.

Time and again I tried to work out how Huguette did it.

I should have been on guard the moment she arrived at my house, driving herself in a small hired car, unannounced and late at night. Gone was the grand entrance with her chauffeur holding open the door. Gone too were the fine clothes; it was years since she had worked as a model and her last husband had made a point of not buying her the clothes she needed.

He was the first in her long line of men who managed to humiliate her. Humiliate! That's the word she used for his betrayals. She did not mind that he kept a mistress and had other women; she minded people knowing that she was now the one betrayed. She was dressed that night simply but elegantly in a blue tailored suit. She looked vulnerable.

'You're the only person I can trust,' she said. 'I need your advice.'

Did she believe what she was saying, about her husband deceiving her and humiliating her in public? Or was it all just a trick? With Huguette I never know. . . . And how did we progress from me wanting to advise her, to comforting her and finally being in bed together? Because after all the years of lusting for her, I couldn't stop myself undressing her, while she pretended to be a tearful little girl who needed reassurance.

I kept telling myself that we should just cuddle like the babes in the wood, but I knew I was lying. I wanted her with all the burning, heedless lust of youth. At the age of forty-five, I should have known better! As they say, you can't con an honest man. So Huguette deceived me because I was deceiving myself.

I wanted to believe when she hissed like a cat in my ear, 'Oh God, I want you, Raoul. I've always wanted you. You were so damned handsome. I always thought of you when I was with the others.'

Was I insane?

There was a moment just after I entered her when I saw the smile of triumph on her face and wondered what I was doing, but then the animal took over and we fought as we always had fought when making love, she with her teeth and nails – (Your beloved claws, I used to call them when we were young and obsessed with each other's bodies) – and I with the strength of my arms.

It was a contest of lion and lioness, with the strongest winning, at the risk of being mortally savaged by the loser, but in those moments of lust and passion I slaked the frustration of years.

Next morning she was like a cat that had been fed on cream and caresses. She must have planned everything from the beginning – I don't believe it was improvisation.

'No regrets?' she teased, leaning over the bed. Her huge violet eyes taunted me with memories, mine and hers.

'No regrets,' I said confidently. I was feeling strong and cured of my obsession with her. She took her time dressing and making herself up, deliberately drawing out the intimacy. Perhaps she hoped we'd be interrupted?

I remember thinking as she painted her lips, using the tiny mirror of her compact: How ordinary you are, Huguette. It was only youth and jewels and clothes that made you beautiful. Without money, getting older, you're nothing special.

But I was wrong. Ordinary she is not.

She turned from her toilet, lipstick poised, and licked her lips. Her eyes laughing, she smiled at me and I still did not know what was in her mind.

She drove straight from my house to the château and pretended to divulge a confidence to a friend.

According to Marie, Huguette told her breathlessly, 'Raoul and I are together again. Isn't it wonderful?'

Poor Marie! How could I have placed her in that position?

Huguette affected not to notice Marie's reaction . . . and went into all the details.

It was no wonder that Marie did not speak to me for three months afterwards, until that moment of need when Gustave killed himself.

Can she really have forgiven me for that?

4

Through the open car windows Raoul heard the bell of St Martin's little church tolling for Gustave.

He drove slowly back to his own house. The workmen had left. A green tarpaulin over the gaping roof of the tower flapped in the wind, but inside the barn it was silent, too silent.

Raoul put Mozart's Requiem Mass on the hi-fi, turned up the volume and sat with eyes closed, listening to the music and mentally burying his friend. The magnificent chords were like icebergs crashing together in the fogs of time, past and future grinding him and all his generation to pieces. Even the survivors were maimed one way or another.

At the end of the music he collected his mail from the box by the front door of the barn and tore open first the letter with the Vietnamese postmark. Like all Koenig's correspondence, it was short.

Dear Friend,

I have found Mr A: a man with the eagle and the snake on his arm who served under me in Algeria and is now in the American Special Forces. He is absolutely the right man for the job. But the war situation here goes from bad to worse. The Pathet Lao are fighting the Laotian government, the NVA are rampaging all over Laos and Cambodia. It would be like walking through a minefield. Did you ever get the feeling that time is running out on us?

Sincerely, K

The thought of time running out was an appropriate one at a funeral in the rain.

Raoul sat in the wheelchair at the rear of the party of mourners as they lowered Gustave's coffin into the earth of the small cemetery which sloped from St Martin's church down to the river, swollen with brown flood water. He watched Marie being comforted by her daughter.

Marie-France, he realised, had grown up a lot in her last year at university. She looked strong and beautiful and so like her mother when young that it cut him with a pang to think of all the years he had spent far from Marie and the stupidity of their current separation.

He wondered whether Huguette's main attraction for him all those years ago had been that her animal sexuality had overshadowed Marie's quieter beauty. Perhaps he had needed Huguette's brilliance to dazzle him and make him oblivious of the warm glow he felt whenever he saw Marie? Perhaps he had used Huguette to help him put aside the illicit love for his cousin? And now that he had found that love again, it seemed he had ruined everything for the sake of an old obsession . . .

The service over, he accepted a scoopful of earth from the sacristan to throw on the coffin of the man who had been trampled to death by history.

As the widow and her daughter passed him to return to their car, Marie-France pressed a note into Raoul's hand. It read: Please come to the château at aperitif time.

The handwriting was hers, not her mother's.

Raoul spent more care choosing what to wear than he had for any occasion in years. Suits he discarded as too businesslike, casual clothes as too casual. He settled in the end for a velvet suit and a button-collared shirt with a sober tie.

It was Marie-France who met him outside the château. She was in riding clothes, rubbing down a chestnut gelding that Gustave had bought for her years before. Straightening up she brushed a long strand of dark hair back from her face. The gesture and her complexion, flushed from the ride, reminded him again of Marie at her age.

Raoul complimented her on the horse.

She smiled at his awkwardness. 'Sorry for the drama of the note, but *maman* twice stopped me ringing you.'

'We' — Raoul felt inadequate — 'haven't been talking to each other for quite a while, apart from the day your father died.'

'You ought to be ashamed of yourselves,' she said mock-sternly. 'You're behaving like a couple of kids.'

He laughed. 'That's exactly what it feels like.'

'Well,' she grinned. 'I feel rather weird, acting as a marriage guidance counsellor for people of your age, but someone has to.'

He paused and spun the wheelchair to face her before going through the kitchen door. 'Has Marie told you what the break-up was all about?'

'No questions,' she said. 'You'll find her in the salon.' She led the horse across the yard to the stables, iron-shod hooves clacking on the cobbles.

'The salon?' he called.

She laughed. 'The old ballroom. They've nearly finished the interior restoration work.'

Raoul propelled himself along the corridors of the château. Workmen's tools were strewn everywhere and there was a smell of new wood, varnish and paint. From the progress that had been made since his last visit, he realised that Marie must have thrown herself into the restoration programme to take her mind off his infidelity. The salon had been restored, if not to all its former elegance at least to the status of a beautiful room lit by huge French windows through which was a view of the terrace, the lawns and the river beyond.

Marie was at a small writing desk, answering letters of

condolence. She remained sitting rigidly as Raoul approached.

'Marie-France told me I'd find you here,' he said awkwardly.

Her eyes searched his face, then her features relaxed and she smiled ruefully. 'I expect she told you off.'

'A bit,' he said guardedly.

'You should have heard the way she lectured me.'

He smiled.

'It was odd, being lectured by my own daughter on how to run my love life. She said I was behaving like a fourteen-year-old. We had a terrible scene. At first I screamed that it was none of her business. Then I realised she was right.'

'It was my fault.'

'No, listen.' Marie closed her eyes; the thought was too important to risk losing track of it when his eyes hypnotised her. 'I fell in love with you when I was fourteen, Raoul. And – perhaps because we did nothing about it – I haven't ever really changed my image of the person you are.'

She opened her eyes and looked into his. 'It's time to put that right.'

He tried to imagine the conversation she must have had with her daughter. 'She's grown up a lot, Marie-France,' he offered.

'In many ways,' she agreed. 'It shattered me when she said quite casually that she had four lovers before her twenty-second birthday. At twice her age, I've only ever known Gustave and you.'

Raoul relaxed. It was going to be all right. 'What did she say about you and me?'

'She assumed quite matter of factly that we'd been having an affair for years.'

'The young are different now,' he said. 'They accept things that would have shocked us at their age. Did you tell her about Huguette?'

She looked away then forced herself to look back. 'More or less. I couldn't use the words Huguette used – not to my own daughter. But she filled in the gaps for me. She had guessed it was something like that.'

There was a pause while Marie blew her nose. Raoul saw she was using a handkerchief he had bought her on a shopping trip in Bordeaux.

'I won't lie to you,' he said. 'If I was to say I'll never see Huguette again, I don't know whether that would be true – despite what she did.'

'I don't want promises.' Marie's voice was low, but controlled. 'As Marie-France said, it's not as if we were setting up house together or starting a family.'

'No.'

'But I need you, Raoul – as an adviser, a friend and a lover.'

I put out a hand. Marie hesitated, then took it in hers.

It was the first time we had touched in months. There was none of the electricity that had shot through my whole body when I put my hands and lips on Huguette's skin. Instead I felt at one with the woman beside me. I would have liked to put on some music and listen to it, holding her hand. How stupid, I thought, to risk my peace and happiness with this woman for the brief, extravagant excitement of that insane coupling with Huguette.

'It's been hell,' Marie whispered.

For a moment I thought we were both going to cry.

Instead she took both my hands in hers and said, dry-eyed: 'I'm not a woman who enjoys being alone and taking decisions on my own. I need you, Raoul. I need you to love me the way you do, not the way someone else might.'

My scalp tingled and goose-pimples crawled over my body. There were words I should have voiced then, but something stopped me saying them.

'It'll be easier now Gustave's dead,' said Marie. 'I pretended not to feel guilty, making love to you – but I did.'

'I know.'

'Kiss me.'

She made me come to her. 'Oh God, I've missed you,' she

breathed in my ear. 'Don't ever let me push you out of my life again, no matter what you do.'

The embrace was interrupted by Marie-France. She was still in her riding clothes and carried a tray bearing a bottle of champagne and three glasses. 'You can pay for this,' she told Raoul.

'To make amends?' He wiped his lips to remove Marie's lipstick.

'Rubbish!' She laughed at the thought. 'Do you remember the first day we came to St Martin? You promised me a bottle of real champagne and I never got it.'

He was easing the cork off when she took the bottle from him. The cork flew across the room.

'This salon,' she announced grandly, 'is a room which should ring with the popping of champagne corks.'

'I'm so lucky,' said Raoul. Borne on her youthful enthusiasm, he meant it.

'Now, to work,' said Marie-France. '*Maman* has told you we want you to draw up a deed of partnership?'

'Well, no.' He looked enquiringly at Marie.

'People of your generation are hopeless,' Marie-France scolded.

'I forgot all about it,' admitted her mother.

'Who's going to be whose partner?' asked Raoul, mystified.

'Mesdames Marie and Marie-France Laval.' Marie-France raised her glass in a toast and chinked it against her mother's.

'We had a long talk,' said Marie, 'about many things. I'm going to carry on running the estate, while Marie-France will concentrate on developing the wine business.'

'She will?' Raoul was taken by surprise.

'You've been saying for years that the price of wine must go up,' said Marie-France. 'Just because I was a kid, you thought I wasn't listening. Well, I was. I took it all in. The trouble is that we sell everything through the local *cave cooperative*. The price we get is the price of *pinard* – plonk.

As of this year, I'm putting a stop to that. I'm going to resuscitate the *appellation* of Château St Martin, blend the wine myself and make our label one of the great wines of the world.'

'Just like that?' Raoul wondered.

'One of the advantages of going to college in France,' she said calmly, 'is that one drinks a lot of wine. I discovered – and it will probably turn out to be the most valuable thing I learned at university – that I have an excellent palate. I always know if I'm drinking what it says on the label. You'd be amazed at the famous restaurants where I've sent the bottle back and called the wine waiter a liar. They treat me very well now.'

Raoul looked from one woman to the other. The midday sun pouring in through the tall windows and bouncing off the parquet floor was behind Marie and falling full on her daughter's face. In that light, the two dark-haired, olive-skinned women could have been sisters.

A mother and daughter partnership seemed bizarre. But why not? Raoul poured more champagne into their glasses. 'It's my turn to make a toast. I drink to Mademoiselle Marie-France Laval. You're a very extraordinary young woman.'

5

Midnight. Phuong was asleep. Wide awake, Frank turned on the radio beside the bed. It was a cheap medium-wave set she had bought in a street market. He tuned it to the AFN station in Saigon.

The bland voice of the newsreader crackled from the tiny speaker: 'Here is a round-up of the news worldwide. Air Force bombers, including B-52 Strato-Fortresses, pounded Hanoi, the North Vietnamese capital and its port of Haiphong today for the first time since March of 1968. Targets were fuel dumps and Eastern bloc merchant vessels unloading military supplies for the Northern war effort . . .'

Angry at the vague optimism of the official line, Frank turned the radio off and lit a cigarette. Smoke ruined his sense of smell, but that would be a blessing. . . .

Phuong had her eyes open, watching him.

'It doesn't matter,' she said pleadingly. 'You are tired, Frank. Sleep now. When we wake up in the morning, you will feel better. Then you can make love to me.'

He had been impotent for the first time in his life. It was as though someone had disconnected his brain from the nerves and muscles and organs of his body. Shamed by his limpness, he had rolled off her body and lain still. Unable to talk about it, he had turned on the radio, keeping his back to her.

She pulled him gently back to her and turned out the light.

'Phuong?' he queried after a while. 'You asleep?'

'I listen,' she said. Then, after a pause, 'You want to tell me about some new girl you have found? You want leave me? Is that it?'

'There's no other girl,' he said.

'Really not?'

He felt the mattress move as she leaned over him and kissed his brow.

'Oh, Frank, I was so worried.'

'Oh, God,' he whispered into her hair that smelled of roses. 'I'm sorry, Phuong.'

'It doesn't matter,' she repeated. 'I thought you were going to leave me, Frank. Oh, I know you will one day go back to what you call the world. But not yet, Frank. At least, I hope.'

'It's something that happened in the mountains,' he said.

'You can tell me.'

'Maybe.'

'I not VC spy, you know.' Her voice was quiet.

He grunted. 'I don't know that, but I don't any longer care.'

She traced his profile in the dark with one delicate fingertip. 'Strange. Your brain getting Vietnamese when you say things like that, but your nose stays American, so strong.'

Frank grunted. He was listening to the noises of the night. It was a habit that died hard after living for years in primitive villages high in the mountains near the border with Laos, where he was liable to sudden attack at any time, especially at night.

'What's that?' He half-sat up in bed.

She listened for a moment. 'Relax. That my father. He is old and must go to toilet in the night.'

Frank listened to the feet shuffling along the corridor. He had only recently discovered that, in addition to the two sisters killed at Hué, Phuong had also a younger brother who had escaped the massacre with his father and sister.

Neither Phuong nor her father spoke about the boy. It was Frank's guess he was with the Viet Cong.

A door closed somewhere in the house. Frank recalled the night when he had woken to find her gone from the bed. He had lain awake listening to the low murmur of men's voices in the kitchen and feigned sleep when she returned. All in all, her joke about not being a VC spy was probably . . . a joke.

But it didn't matter. Nothing mattered since he had smelled again the same sweet smell of blossom – this time mixed with the hot chemical stink of a bombardment in the middle of the dark jungle night.

'Tell me,' she whispered just at the moment he had decided to. Outside, the feet shuffled the other way. Another door closed.

Frank exhaled and talked to the smoke; it was easier than talking to a person. 'For two years, I've been working with a montagnard tribe in the mountains as part of the CIDG programme.'

'I heard about that.'

'The civilian irregular defence groups had a good record, carrying guerrilla war to the Cong, instead of waiting for them to hit us first. When that was phased out last year, I stayed on and used my tribesmen for intelligence collection.'

'I understand.'

He wondered to whom she would repeat what he was going to tell her. Not that it mattered. *Don't mean nothing*, was the grunts' motto.

'We'd been getting too clever over the last few months,' he continued. 'Convoy after convoy of heavy lorries was wiped out on the Laos side of the border, thanks to information from my scouts that I radioed back to base. Since Charlie badly needed those supplies for this year's spring offensive, he had to take us out.'

'Take you out?'

'Waste us,' he explained. 'So I moved the village to a new location where we could only be attacked from one side. The disadvantage was that we had cliffs on the other three sides, so there was no get-away. Then I did some trading with Cold Steel . . .'

'Who is he?'

'It's a call sign,' he explained, irritated by her ignorance. 'The AVRN divisional artillery. I did them some risky favours on the ground, in order to buy my village a priority entitlement to fire support.'

'You have to buy that?'

'It's the way it is.'

'And something went wrong?' she guessed.

The footsteps were in the corridor again.

'Something went wrong,' Frank confirmed. 'We were attacked by main-force NVA in the middle of the night. I used the radio to call div. arty and joined the men out on the perimeter. Since there was only one line of attack, we knew exactly where the NVA had to be. The co-ordinates were all plotted in advance. It should have been foolproof.'

'And then?' she prompted.

'We had a salvo of shorts.' Frank laughed; it seemed so inadequate to his own ears. 'The artillery major said after-wards there was a manufacturer's error in the batch of shells they were using, but I heard a whisper he owed a favour to the other side.'

'That's bad?' she said, not comprehending.

'Friendly fire,' said Frank harshly. 'That's what they call it. Those friendly American shells from the friendly ARVN guns fell not on the NVA attacking the village but on the huts, killing the women and children. And thanks to me, nobody could slip out the back door, because of the cliffs.'

'The women and children?'

'The men were on the perimeter with me, so some of them survived. I wasn't even touched. But my bright idea wiped out the village more effectively than the whole NVA could have managed in a year.'

'Many people died?' she asked.

'Almost all the women and kids.'

*

402

I was to become the confessor of all the men in my strange Legion of St Martin perhaps because, sitting there in the wheelchair, I was like a priest in the confessional – not quite a man. Or perhaps they sensed that I had had a lot of time to think about the things that preoccupied them. Whatever the reason, one by one they told me things they had not told anyone else.

Frank told me that when he walked through what had been the montagnard village there wasn't even much that could be buried.

He stood in the centre of the village, his nostrils full of the smell of blossom. The blast effect had stripped even the leaves off the trees, never mind any blossom. He turned his back on the tribesmen who were poking through the ruins, lifting a leg or an arm from the wreckage of their homes.

He turned his back in the hope that one of them would shoot him to assuage their anger or pain.

'Perhaps,' he said to me, 'they figured it was more of a punishment to leave me alive. They called me the one who never gets hit. I'm like a lightning conductor, Raoul. I bring down the wrath of the gods on those who are close to me or who depend on me. But I never get hit. The lightning leaves me unscathed each time, condemned to survive with my memories and my guilt.'

6

With the monsoon due any day, the weather in the Central Highlands was hot but saved by the altitude from the steamy oppressiveness of the coastal plain.

Frank drove his borrowed jeep off the highway and on to the bumpy track that led to Koenig's rubber estate.

Disregarding the pot-holes and wheel ruts in the concrete-hard earth, he kept the speed up; in this area the VC laid ambushes wherever bad roads compelled traffic to slow down. Red dust trailed behind the jeep and rose into the still air, announcing his arrival from afar. If you can't be secret, be fast, was a Green Berets' motto.

There was a checkpoint at the entrance to the estate, but it was unmanned and looked as though it had not been used for a decade. Termites had eaten half the boom once used to block the road; the remaining half with its useless counter-weight stuck up in the air. On either side of the track as Frank drove along, rubber collectors moved among the shady lines of mature trees. It was a peaceful scene; there was no sign of the war raging to the north, south, east and west apart from the sound of a distant artillery bombardment and condensation trails high in the blue sky.

The estate bungalow had been built on a hillock overlooking the rubber plantation. Beyond the house, a range of green forested hills stretched away into blue mountains on the horizon. Somewhere out there, he knew, was a village on the top of a cliff where no smoke from cooking fires rose into the cold air, where nobody lived any longer.

Driving up to the house, Frank was surprised to see no sandbags, no watch-tower, no defences of any kind. The large plate-glass windows of the bungalow were not shuttered or even barred. The estate office could have been in downtown Saigon, complete with telephones, production charts on the walls and two pretty, smiling secretaries.

As Koenig was out on the estate, one of the girls showed Frank into the cool and spacious main living room of the bungalow. A Vietnamese woman entered and offered him a choice of beer or tea. He chose tea.

One entire wall of the room was occupied by Koenig's books: 3,000 volumes packed in metal termite-proof travelling chests stacked one on top of another to make an instant library. Most of the books were non-fiction; almost all were on the subject of war. Frank browsed through them, picking out a few at random. From the feel of the books, the poetry section was the most used.

'Thanks,' he said casually when the woman returned with a tray of tea. 'Leave it on the table. I'll help myself.' Only after she had gone did he see there were two cups on the tray.

A book of poetry by men who had served in the Foreign Legion fell open to a page that startled him. In the margin was written Alice's name and her address at the trailer camp. The poem was by an American legionnaire called Alan Seeger who had died on the Somme in 1916.

Oh Alice . . . A hand gripped Frank's heart and squeezed. It was a long time since thinking of her had hurt this much.

He had a flash recollection of her sitting in her trailer, the pile of letters strewn across the table . . . and her voice saying: 'Captain Koenig sent me a beautiful poem. It helped a lot.'

405

Koenig appeared noiselessly on the veranda whilst Frank was reading the poem aloud to himself.

'I have a rendezvous with Death
At some disputed barricade ...'

Frank put down the book, recalling that his one-time commander had always had a trick of arriving where he was least expected.

They shook hands and walked out on to the veranda, where a table was set for lunch. The crisp starched table linen, shining cutlery and sparkling glassware – all the trappings of civilisation – contrasted with the exuberant green violence of tropical vegetation which began at the edge of the veranda.

The Vietnamese woman who had brought the tea reappeared in a new dress. When Koenig introduced her as his wife, Frank was embarrassed that he had treated her as a servant. She sat with them at the table where they were waited on by a white-jacketed Tonkinese who had been Koenig's batman years before.

The conversation was in French. Speaking his mother tongue had become an occasional luxury for Koenig. The meat course was wild pig, shot by the host himself the previous weekend, washed down with a good burgundy from his cellar. Conversation flowed easily. Frank found Koenig an interested listener who wanted to know about current weapons, the tactics of the NVA and Viet Cong, the problems of working with irregulars. The barrier between the veteran captain and the once awe-struck recruit was gone; now they were talking as equals. At the end of the meal, Koenig's wife excused herself, to leave the men alone.

'You see why I can't go back to France,' said the host. 'I can't leave her and my children, yet what sort of life would they have in Europe?'

Frank wondered how much he had hurt Phuong.

'But let's talk about you,' said Koenig. He poured brandy

into two glasses. 'It's time you got out of the Army, Hansen.'

Frank laughed. 'I've been wearing one uniform or the other for most of my adult life, sir.'

'You're thirty-two,' said Koenig. 'That's not too late to try something else.'

'Like what?'

'Like surviving, Hansen. D'you ever think how the odds begin to stack up against one, after a certain point? It only takes one bullet.'

Frank raised his glass, then put it down when he saw that his host was not ready to drink.

'What was the name of that friend of yours?' Koenig asked out of the blue. 'The one who got killed in the Aurès?'

'De Burgh.'

'I remember him. He turned out to be a good soldier. A tough little bastard. I thought you'd desert after that, Hansen. It hit you pretty hard, as I recall.'

'I still don't know if I've got over it,' Frank confessed. 'Despite –' He waved a hand in the air to indicate the pile of dead they had both looked in the face over the years.

Koenig took his meaning. 'So why did you join up again?' he asked softly.

Frank looked away. The edge of the veranda could have been the edge of the world; there was nothing but jungle and hill in front of them. Looking at the emptiness made it easier to talk. For the first time since leaving Jacksonville, he told someone of Alice and the twins.

Koenig covered his face for a moment. 'We give a hostage to fortune,' he said softly, 'each time we love somebody, Hansen.'

A hostage to fortune? Frank wondered. That sounded like a line from another poem. It had been a relief to talk openly about Alice and the twins. . . .

Koenig broke the pause. 'There's something else on your mind,' he said, 'that you haven't told me about. Something recent, I'd say.'

He listened as Frank explained what had gone wrong in the montagnard village and agreed it was likely the ARVN artillery commander had been taking bribes. 'But you can't blame yourself for all these things.'

'I can't blame anyone else.'

'I have a rendezvous with Death,' Koenig quoted softly in English, 'at some disputed barricade.'

'I don't follow, sir.'

The two fingers of Koenig's right hand scissored a Gauloise from the pack on the table and placed it in his mouth. The servant flicked an American Zippo lighter. Koenig inhaled. His eyes squinted through the smoke at Frank.

'You were reading that poem when I came in before lunch. Let me give you some advice, Hansen. I've known more than a few soldiers like you. You are a romantic: you have a dream of duty owed to your comrades who died. And to people you've loved. That's why you joined up again, isn't it? That's why you're staying on here when most Americans can't wait to get back on the right side of the Pacific.' He paused. 'Am I right?'

Frank was confused. He blamed the alcohol he had consumed with the meal. 'Something like that,' he muttered.

Koenig finished Seeger's poem from memory:

> 'But I've a rendezvous with Death
> At midnight in some flaming town,
> when Spring trips north again this year,
> And I to my pledged word am true,
> I shall not fail that rendezvous.'

There was a pause.

'That's what you feel, isn't it?' Koenig asked.

When Frank did not reply, his host leaned over the table and gripped his arm. 'Well, don't do it. We can't bring back our dead, Hansen, and I don't think they want us to join them too quickly because then they're doubly dead. Let them live for a while in our memories, even if it hurts. That's what we owe them.'

Frank stared at his glass and made no reply.

'It's time for a toast,' said Koenig, rising.

Frank stood and touched his glass to Koenig's. He had heard that some of the French settlers were drinking the health of the American 196th Infantry Brigade, whose units had mutinied on more than one occasion during the Communists' spring offensive, but he would not have drunk to that.

'You know what day it is?' The cold blue eye challenged Frank above the two touching glasses.

'Sunday?' guessed Frank.

'April thirtieth,' said Koenig. 'It is the anniversary of Camerone we are celebrating today, Hansen. *A la Légion!*'

Frank echoed the toast.

It was over the third glass of brandy that Koenig broached his offer of the previous year.

'What's the pay like?' Frank asked – not just because Koenig would expect him to need money but also because he did not want to draw on his bank account in Jacksonville: Sven would have ways of tracing him, once he did that.

Koenig laughed. 'Let's say that if you can pull off this one job, Hansen, you won't ever be short of cash for the rest of your life.'

'What do I have to do? Rob a bank?'

'Nothing criminal – or as easy as that.'

Frank was intrigued. 'Then I accept.'

Straight to business. 'Do you still have a French passport?'

'It's out of date.'

'The first thing . . .' Koenig's voice slowed down as something caught his attention, 'is to renew your passport at the Embassy in Saigon. If there's any problem, mention my name.'

Frank became aware that his host was staring fixedly at the road which led to the nearby village. A mile away there were six armed men walking towards the house. They stayed close to the tree-line. Even at that distance, Frank recognised their weapons as Chinese-manufactured Kalashnikovs. That and the black pyjamas they wore made them Viet Cong.

Koenig's good hand held Frank in his seat. 'Don't move,' he said. 'Above all, don't go out of the house.'

Frank reached for his M 16, which was lying against the windowsill. There was a magazine in it, with another taped on head-to-tail for a quick change. He understood now why Koenig had insisted he repark the jeep out of sight in a shed behind the bungalow.

'There's no danger,' Koenig reassured him. 'They're collecting taxes.'

'Taxes?'

'Each week the local VC cadres come to collect. They used to come by night. Now they don't even bother to wait for darkness.'

'And?'

'Like taxmen all over the world, they present an assessment of how much I owe them. They even give me a signed receipt for each payment on paper stamped with the seal of the National Liberation Front.'

Frank was incredulous. 'How long's this been going on?'

'For years,' said Koenig. He grinned wolfishly. 'In the OAS we robbed banks to get funds. The VC finance themselves by a system of parallel taxation. It comes to the same thing.'

The six Viet Cong were moving openly now, through a grove of spindly young rubber trees on the red earth of a field that had been cleared below the house.

Koenig unbuckled the heavy Colt .45 revolver he was wearing and left it on the lunch table. Unarmed, he walked out into the bright sunshine. He spoke to his wife and two children in the garden and headed downhill to meet the armed tax collectors.

7

'**T**ime spent in reconnaissance is seldom wasted, Hansen.'

The old maxim had been one of Koenig's first lessons for an eager recruit of eighteen. Frank smiled at the memory. The village of St Martin-sur-Dordogne was hardly new territory, but the habit of caution was hard to break. Before calling on Koenig's friend, he had decided to explore where the man lived and find out what the locals thought about this . . . Captain Duvalier.

Frank had chosen clothing as nearly military as possible. He felt ill at ease in soft thin garments after so many years in uniform and had opted for jeans and a denim jacket over an open-necked bush shirt. A new duty-free camera hung around his neck. He hoped his appearance and his American accent, exaggerated for the occasion, made him look like a tourist to anyone who was curious.

Time, he thought, stood still in the sleepy riverside village to which Koenig had dispatched him. It was far from any itinerary suggested by Michelin or anyone else. He noted that occasional cars drove straight through the place without stopping, using the bridge that spanned the Dordogne to speed away in the direction of somewhere more interesting.

The single street of houses and shops straggled along parallel to the river. There was a butcher's, a baker's and a small grocer's shop, but most of the stores in the village looked to Frank as though they had closed before the Second World War and never reopened. Pre-war posters hung sun-bleached in the windows, enamelled signs advertised products that had last been available a quarter of a century before and the tools of crafts long redundant lay in the windows of what had been a wheelwright's shop, a saddler's and a feed store.

In the abandoned garage in the main street, its rusty hand-cranked petrol pump built into the wall, lay a pile of worm-eaten cardboard boxes marked: *Red Cross – Official Parcel for Prisoners of War*. A small plaque on the corner of a house by the ugly stone bridge across the Dordogne marked the spot where two *maquisards* had been killed by the Germans in 1944.

The tiny village square's war memorial listed several dozen names of local men who had died in 1914–18. They overwhelmed the lesser sacrifice of the Second World War. Separate panels on the memorial recorded France's colonial wars in Indo-China and Algeria. Two faded wreaths lay crookedly against the base of the monument, while a small jam jar with fresh flowers in water showed that somebody in St Martin still cared.

The deserted terrace of the dilapidated cafe was large enough to accommodate thirty or forty tables. Frank sat at one of the two tables that were not broken and pulled a second chair close to rest his feet on. The newspaper he had picked up from the bar counter was full of the previous day's resignation of Gaullist premier Jacques Chaban-Delmas. The news meant nothing to Frank. He leafed through the pages, finding nothing of interest. The weather forecast on the back page was cloudy and rain. It was sunny and the sky was blue.

'Your beer, monsieur.' The old man who ran the café shuffled up in worn carpet slippers, a Gauloise clinging to his lower lip. His lethargy seemed typical of the few inhabitants of the village that Frank had met. But he was happy to talk to a stranger. Gradually Frank led the conversation round to the war memorial and ex-soldiers who lived in the neighbourhood.

'. . . and then there's our *ancien légionnaire*.' Ash spilled into Frank's beer as the old man gestured at the castle overlooking the village.

'He lives in that?'

The old man laughed and coughed on the smoke. 'Not him. The captain lives in the barn at the side of the tower. You can't see it from here because of the cliff.'

'What's he like, this Captain Duvalier?'

The old man spat the dog-end over the edge of the terrace. '*C'est un légionnaire. Ils sont durs comme cuir, ces gars-là.*' He laughed and shuffled away.

Tough as old boots, Frank thought. That sounded like a friend of Koenig's. He blew the ash off the top of the beer and drank it. There were workmen perched on scaffolding all round the tower; the sound of hammers and chisels on stone carried down to the village. Frank decided to kill time until they knocked off and then call on the man who owned the tower.

Below the terrace an immense quay of solid masonry sloped gently down to the green river that flowed slowly past. After the hair-trigger existence he had lived in Vietnam and the long-range penetration he had carried out with Koenig northwards along the Ho Chi Minh trail into Laos and back into Vietnam, Frank felt almost drugged by the somnolent beauty of the scene.

From the number of closed shops in the village, from the size of the café's terrace, from the width and length of the quay, it was obvious that St Martin had once been a prosperous little riverside town.

'Before the lorries came–' the *patron* was back to interrupt Frank's reverie with a clatter of small change on the metal table, '– the quay was covered in barrels, monsieur. Thousands of barrels of wine waiting to be ferried down the river on barges to Libourne and Bordeaux, for shipment all over the world.'

'Before the lorries came?'

'It's modern transport that killed St Martin,' the old man announced.

A replacement Gauloise bobbed up and down to the rhythm of his strongly accented patois. 'Once it became cheaper and faster to ship the wine by road, *le village s'est endormi. . . .*' Pleased with his turn of phrase, he repeated, 'The village fell asleep.'

A dozen working men appeared as the church clock struck noon, including the masons and joiners whom Frank had seen working on the tower.

They were clad in blue work clothes with large black berets. They greeted each other noisily and spent two hours on a five-course meal, during which they drank a litre of red wine apiece. Frank liked the simple food, the all-male atmosphere, the good-natured ribbing that went on.

Without anyone ordering, the *patron*'s wife placed in front of each man a bowl of *potage* followed by a huge plate of hors-d'oeuvres, then a dish of *lapin à la moutarde*, followed by a plate of cheeses and a dessert. Frank ate at the long oilcloth-covered table with the other men, and was included in their conversation without curiosity. It was like being back in the Legion and ten years younger, before the guilt began.

I could settle here, he thought in an unguarded moment.

The artisans talked freely about their employer. He seemed a man of mystery, but . . .

'An accountant?' Frank queried. That wasn't the image he had of a friend of Koenig's.

They winked at each other. 'Not just an accountant.' They stood up chuckling, full of good food and wine. 'You should see his women! Some man, our Captain Duvalier.'

Two o'clock struck. Quiet returned to St Martin, broken by the tapping of tools on stone from the top of the cliff. The July heat was mild by comparison with Vietnam. Frank took another stroll without meeting a single inhabitant out of doors. Only the occasional sound of voices reached his ears from some shady courtyard garden hidden behind high

414

lichen-covered walls of random limestone. The more he saw of St Martin, the more he liked the place.

The only two buildings of dressed stone were the ancient church which gave the village its name and the tower that brooded on the cliff above the houses.

Frank pushed open the heavy iron-bound door of the church and went down a flight of steps to what had been ground level more than a thousand years before. It was cool in the gloom, the light shafting through the narrow stained-glass windows. A flame burned in the sanctuary. From the head of a column, a strong woman's face carved in stone challenged him.

He sat on one of the flimsy wooden chairs. The joints creaked under his weight. It was the first time he had been in a church since the funeral service for Alice and the twins.

In one window, sunlight filtering between the branches of a tree dappled the image of a saint on horseback in the uniform of a Roman soldier, doing something with a sword. Through a hole in the glass, unfiltered light burned a white path through the dust motes.

'You are admiring the Charity?' a voice asked softly from the shadows.

Frank turned to find a priest in black cassock regarding him from the shadows of the confessional.

'The Charity of St Martin.' The priest pointed upwards at the window. 'He was stopped by a beggar who had no coat. So the saint took a sword and hacked his own cloak into two halves, and gave one half to the beggar.'

'Thanks for the information.'

'You're welcome. And the head on the column is of our other famous visitor: the duchess Eleanor of Aquitaine. She was an English queen too, of course.' A smile. 'Nothing much has happened in St Martin since her visit in 1152.'

Frank nodded.

The priest's next sentence caught him off guard. 'Do you have something to confess, my son?'

The simplicity of the question hurt. It shattered the mood

that had been building up inside Frank since his arrival in St Martin.

'No, I don't,' he said with sudden burning anger. 'Nothing at all.'

He got up and left the church.

8

Raoul turned down the voices of Tito Gobbi and
Callas. He wheeled himself out of the grandiose
dream world of *Il Ballo in Maschera* and back into
the present.

He opened the door and studied the man who had been
ringing his bell for several minutes. Local people rang once
and waited for him to come, knowing that he could not
hurry.

'I am looking for Captain Duvalier,' said Frank.

Raoul bristled at the title, which no one used to his face.
'Captain Duvalier is dead.'

'Oh.' Frank was taken aback.

'The captain's dead,' said Raoul. 'Ignominiously so. I
don't use my former rank, but I am probably the man you're
looking for.'

Through the gap between door and jamb Frank could see
the wheelchair and the wasted legs. A cripple? he wondered.
Koenig never told me his friend was crippled. And the men
at lunch said nothing about it. . . .

'I have a message from a certain Captain Koenig.' Frank
noted the flash of interest in the deep-set eyes of the man
in the wheelchair.

'Koenig!' The voice changed, came alive. 'How is my
friend?'

Frank grinned. 'Tired.'

'Why tired?'

'We went for a long walk together.'

'How long?'

'Right up the Ho Chi Minh trail to Dien Bien Phu. That's a long walk.' He waited for some reaction.

Raoul's pulse was racing, his heart thudding in the rib-cage. 'What's your name?'

'I'm Sergeant Frank Hansen, but Captain Koenig said to introduce myself as Mr A.'

Time stood still.

I looked at this man, unable to believe my ears.

Frank was obviously a soldier, who – if I had heard right – had lately been all the way back to Dien Bien Phu.

Koenig had picked him, done a recce with him and sent him halfway round the world to me.

Life was about to begin again. My plan to recover the gold wasn't just a dream after all.

There was a roaring sound in my head. I felt sweat break out on my temple. This was a moment for which I had been waiting and planning for nearly two decades. I thought I was going to faint and from the wary look on Frank's face, he thought so too.

'Are you all right, sir?' he asked.

I took several deep breaths. When I had regained control I mopped my temple and said, 'I am now, sergeant.'

I moved back from the doorway, to let him in. 'Welcome.'

'You must be tired,' said Raoul.

Frank yawned. The supper he had shared with his host had been only slightly more appetising than cold C rations eaten under a dripping poncho in the rain of a night ambush. The portions might have been sufficient for an emaciated man in a wheelchair, but Frank's well muscled frame could have consumed three times what he had been offered.

'I'm a bit jet-lagged,' he admitted.

'Have some more wine.'

'I'd rather have some beer, sir.'

'There isn't any.'

A cursory look at the food shelves above the tiny sink and single camping-gas burner made it clear to Frank that his host rarely entertained. 'Then I'll take some wine.'

He helped himself from the large jug on the table. The taste of the rough *vin ordinaire* reminded him of the *pinard* he had drunk night after night in the mess during his Legion days in Algeria.

The telephone rang and Raoul excused himself. As far as Frank could make out, the conversation was about a tax refund. The phone rang again: another client asking about an agricultural subsidy which had to be claimed that week or lost. At the end there seemed to be an argument about giving someone a job.

Whilst Raoul concentrated on the telephone, Frank studied the house. Everything was functional; there were few concessions to comfort. It was obviously a bachelor's pad; in fact, more of a command bunker than a home. One wall was covered in maps of Vietnam and Laos. Another was hidden by shelves which held hundreds of books on Vietnam and the war. There was an extensive card index and several filing cabinets. Half of the space on the large table was taken up by marked newspaper and magazine articles and half by accounts and correspondence with the tax office – a strange mixture, thought Frank.

Some framed black-and-white photographs on the wall caught Frank's eye. In one of them, a tall fair-haired man in the uniform of a Foreign Legion lieutenant was standing talking to a handsome man on horseback who had a polo mallet over one shoulder. The polo-player was laughing at some joke.

Something about the picture intrigued Frank. He kept coming back to it until the truth hit him: the tall man with two eyes holding his cigarette normally in his right hand was Koenig in his early twenties.

'How long,' Raoul asked, putting down the telephone, 'until the war in Vietnam is finally over?'

'Two years,' said Frank. 'I give it two years at the most.'

419

Raoul stared at his maps. 'That's what I had worked out,' he said. 'Giap will buy time by agreeing to talk. He'll agree to give some undertaking to respect the South's sovereignty. That will give him the breathing space to build up his forces and smash the Saigon regime once and for all. It's the way his mind works.'

'You know a lot about General Giap, sir?'

Raoul waved at the walls of books. 'I used to box,' he said. 'You watch your opponent's eyes, not his fists, Hansen. So in war it is more important to study the opposing general than to count how many men or tanks he has.'

'Sounds like an update of Sun Tsu.'

'You studied Sun Tsu?'

'Not my scene,' Frank laughed. 'But years ago, when Captain Koenig was my commanding officer in Algeria, he was always quoting Sun Tsu.'

'Koenig would,' Raoul nodded. 'We were contemporaries at St Cyr. In those days, he was the philosopher, poet and scholar . . . I was the man of action.'

It was dawn when Raoul swallowed the last mouthful of cold black coffee. They had consumed several potfuls during the night. His mouth tasted foul.

'Do you want to sleep?' he asked.

Frank stretched and yawned. 'It might have been a good idea a few hours ago, sir.' He had long since abandoned the one comfortable chair and was sitting on the edge of the bunk in the alcove.

After the night-long grilling, Raoul was impressed by Frank's on-the-ground knowledge of Vietnam and Laos; he had answered all his host's rapid-fire questions concisely and lucidly. Frank in turn had been impressed by Raoul's grasp of the political situation.

'Some time within the next eighteen months,' Raoul summed up, 'there will be a window of opportunity – a few weeks, maybe a month or two, when the NVA and Pathet Lao call off the fighting in north-east Laos in order to concentrate everything on a final drive in the South and topple the Saigon regime once and for all. That's the moment we have to be ready for.'

'Listen, sir,' Frank interrupted. 'I did this recce with Captain Koenig, but he never said what the operation was all about.'

'How much did Koenig tell you?'

'Just that you were planning a short, private war which involved a trip to Dien Bien Phu, the scene of the French defeat in 1954.'

'The point of the exercise?'

'He said you'd tell me that.'

'But you made some guesses?'

'He asked me about arranging porters – I speak Meo, the local montagnard dialect – so obviously you're expecting to bring something back from there.'

'Like?'

'Something valuable,' said Frank. 'Other than that, I can't guess. And something that would slow us down and make the party too big to slip in and out during the present hostilities.'

'What's valuable and heavy?'

Frank laughed. 'Lots of things. Gold . . .'

Raoul held up a hand. 'Stop right there. How would you like a one-sixth share in a million dollars' worth of gold?'

'A million dollars?'

Raoul smiled. 'At today's – July 1972 – values. But gold is going up all the time, so inflation's not a problem.'

As sole heir to Hansen's Food empire, I'm worth more than that already, thought Frank, but he could not disappoint the man waiting for his reply. 'I'd like it fine. Who do we have to steal the gold from?'

'Nobody,' said Raoul excitedly. He had passed the point of no return. 'It's mine. I earned it. I'll tell you how.'

At the end of the tale, Frank felt a bond with Raoul. Only a soldier could understand what Raoul had been through. The story of the court martial at Torrens did not surprise him. During his time in Special Forces, he had come across plenty of cases where politics overrode military considerations. At the military–political interface, people got screwed, hurt, wasted. . . .

It pleased Frank that what Raoul and Koenig were planning was a blow against the system on behalf of everyone who had been hurt by it. And the idea of a team consisting of Raoul, Koenig and himself felt good.

'The catch as far as you're concerned, Sergeant Hansen,' Raoul's voice interrupted his reflections, 'is that, afterwards, you can't rush out and spend your share of the gold. None of us can. It would attract attention.'

'So?'

Raoul felt his way. 'We'll have to keep it intact and sell it piecemeal over the years.'

'Which means sticking around here, afterwards?'

'It'll need a bodyguard, so to speak.'

'I could settle here.' The sound of his own voice surprised Frank's ears. Yet it was true, he thought. He had found here a peace that had eluded him elsewhere. . . .

'Then it's a deal, sergeant?' Raoul's intense eyes bored into Frank's.

Frank took the outstretched hand. 'It's a deal, sir.'

Raoul gave an enormous sigh. 'D'you mind if I call you Frank? And you call me Raoul from now on. I don't want local people to think I'm gathering an army around myself.'

Frank yawned. 'If it's OK with you, sir – Raoul – I'll get some shut-eye. Couple of hours should see me right.'

Raoul checked his watch. 'No time for that, Frank. Have a shower by all means and smarten yourself up. Then you have a job interview in half an hour's time.'

'Are you joking?'

Raoul looked serious. 'I am not. A man like you hanging around here, doing nothing for several months would be very suspicious as far as the locals are concerned. And remember, France has had a secret police since long before the Revolution, when old Fouché was able to tell Louis XV: "If four men meet and talk, one of them is my man, sire." So we must be careful. You must have a cover job, to account for you being here.'

A doubt crept into Frank's mind. The guy's paranoid, he thought. It's understandable after what he's been through, but . . . 'You've fixed me a job?'

Raoul felt heady with power. It was as though he had been gazing at a chessboard for twenty years, planning his game, and had just received permission to move the first piece.

'As a farm manager,' he said airily. 'It's all arranged. How do you feel about working for a woman?'

9

Marie Laval was angry. 'I don't need a farm manager,' she said. 'I have no idea what's in Raoul's mind, sending you here, Mr Hansen. Raoul is my accountant, not my partner. I decide who is going to be employed at Château St Martin, not him.'

Frank was amused at her reaction. It suited him quite well; he knew nothing about farming.

'It's a nice place you have here.' He looked out of the office window at the courtyard. The whole château was obviously in the throes of restoration. Some Arab labourers were relaying the cobbles outside the stables, taking it easy. 'But you're basically under-capitalised.'

'What does that mean?'

'You need an injection of maybe $100,000 to lift this place right off the ground.'

'We're doing very well,' she snapped, all her generation's prejudice against Americans rising to the surface. 'And we're doing it our way, Mr Hansen.'

'Well, I'm sure you're right.' He backed out of her office, not meaning to sound condescending. 'Thanks for seeing me.'

As he walked through the yard, one of the labourers remarked to his companion in Arabic, 'A Yankee stud come to fuck the Laval woman.'

424

Frank knelt quietly beside the man and said in the same language, 'You are the son of a whore. No, that is an insult to whores. You are a dog turd, drying in the sun. Furthermore, I have been watching you for fifteen minutes and you have laid two stones in all that time. So you are an idle dog turd.'

He left the two Arabs open-mouthed as he walked off.

It was a beautiful day, already hot at ten o'clock. He decided to take a stroll through the fields of the estate and see for himself how things were working at Château St Martin.

'Raoul?'

'Yes? Who is it?' He could never recognise voices on the phone.

Marie was staring out of the office window. The two labourers in the courtyard were working faster than she had ever seen them move. One touched his brow politely when he saw her looking and ostentatiously shouted at his companion to get a move on.

She turned her back, to concentrate on the telephone conversation. 'Look, Raoul, I told you when we spoke yesterday that I did not need a farm manager. So why did you send that American here, letting him think I would give him a job?'

Raoul was dumbfounded. His plan was so important to him that it did not seem possible Marie or anyone else should cause complications. He mumbled something indistinct.

'What's got into your head?' she asked. 'You don't normally hustle me or pressure me into anything? So why today?'

He muttered an inarticulate apology.

'And to cap it all,' she said, 'your Mr Hansen had the gall to tell me that Château St Martin is under-capitalised.'

'It is.' Raoul found his tongue at last.

'But how the devil does he know? He's only been here two minutes.'

'It's my fault,' Raoul apologised again. 'Your last accounts are on top of my desk. I didn't know Frank could read a balance sheet. I should have been more careful.'

'It sounds to me,' she was more amused than angry with him now, 'as if he's more qualified to work for you than for me.'

Frank sat in the shade, his back against the thick trunk of an old willow tree on the bank of the Dordogne. Its overhanging branches concealed him; it was a good place to have a doze.

Through the greenery, he thought Marie Laval's house had a certain style. The white-columned portico and the terrace that looked down over lawns to the river gave it the air of a Southern mansion. Very *Gone with the Wind*, he thought drowsily.

Through half-closed eyes he took in the scene: some labourers in one of the vineyards, lush green orchards. . . . A fish jumped, leaving circles in the slowly moving river. There was the sound of galloping hoofbeats growing louder as a chestnut gelding galloped towards him along the river-bank. As the horse got nearer, heading straight for his hide, he could see that the rider was a girl with long dark hair flying in the wind. Scarlett O'Hara herself, he mused.

'Who are you and what do you think you're doing on my land?' Marie-France reined the horse to a halt and tried to see him through the curtain of low branches.

Frank rose to his feet. 'Your land? I thought this place belonged to Marie Laval?'

The girl caught the accent and said in English, 'Oh, you must be the American that Raoul was talking about last night. I'm Marie-France Laval.'

He parted the curtain of willow and looked up at her, liking what he saw. For a long moment, they stared at each other. The resemblance to her mother was strong, he thought.

'You speak very good English,' he said.

The horse moved nervously, keeping a wary eye on the stranger.

'I spent four years at the Sorbonne reading English and Russian,' she said, slightly out of breath and calming the animal with a hand on its neck. *'Mais vous parlez bien français, Monsieur Hansen.'*

'J'ai passé cinq ans dans la Légion Etrangère.'

'Ah.' She understood. 'So that's why Raoul wanted to find you a job. Old legionnaires looking after each other . . .'

'Something like that,' he nodded. 'But I guess I wasn't exactly what your mother is looking for.'

She laughed. 'She's not looking for anyone. And anyway, Raoul put her back up by telling her to give you a job. He's not usually like that. If he had left the decision to her, she'd probably have found you some work.'

A film of sweat made the thin cotton shirt cling to her breasts. Frank was suddenly very aware of her body. Feeling his scrutiny, Marie-France ran her tongue round lips that were dry. She liked the look of this man: big, strong – and tough with it, she could feel that. 'What sort of job are you looking for?' she asked.

'It's not easy having a conversation with someone in the saddle.' As he spoke, he remembered the picture of Koenig talking to the polo player. It hit him like a cold douche that the glamorous sportsman on horseback in the photograph had been none other than Raoul before he became a cripple.

Marie-France thought for a moment, tossed a leg over the saddle and slid to the ground before he could help her. She tied the reins to a branch. 'That makes us equal,' she smiled.

'Except I'm on your land,' he said, fencing with her. 'That gives you an advantage.'

They shook hands, weighing each other up.

'Call me Frank,' he offered.

'You can call me Marie-France.'

She disengaged her hand from his strong grip. To tease him, she stepped on to the pebble beach below the high-water mark and called up to him on the bank, 'This is common land here, Mr Hansen. Now I've got no advantage at all.'

427

She untucked her shirt and fanned herself with the shirt-tail to dry the sweat of the ride. 'I'm hot,' she said. 'If you'll be a gentleman and look the other way, I can have a swim.'

'On one condition. Can I join you?'

'The river's common too,' she laughed. 'Please yourself.'

The water was cool and inviting. Frank slipped into the shallows and dived after Marie-France. She was a good swimmer. He had nearly caught up with her in the middle of the river when she vanished. There was a flash memory of Alice's head going under.

When she surfaced a couple of metres away, Marie-France was laughing. She shook her wet hair out of her eyes and saw his face, pale and with eyes staring. 'What's the matter? You look as though you've seen a ghost. Are you ill?'

He turned and swam to the bank without answering.

Marie-France finished her swim. As she walked naked out of the water, she saw Frank with his back to her, barefoot and clad in just his jeans as he stood talking to the horse.

'Carlo doesn't usually like strangers,' she called. 'Watch he doesn't bite you.'

'I'm used to horses,' he said without turning round. 'My father breeds them.'

'Professionally?'

'No, as a hobby.'

'What's his profession?'

'He makes money.'

'Oh. You can turn round now.'

Frank stayed talking to the horse. She climbed up on to the bank and put a hand tentatively on his arm.

'Are you all right? You looked pretty weird in the river, just now.'

'I'm OK. It's just that I haven't slept for several nights. I've been travelling.'

She came round in front of him and caught the look in his eyes full of pain. He blinked as though surprised she was not someone else.

It's none of my business, she thought. But he is a gorgeous hunk of a man. . . .

'Tell me about yourself, Frank Hansen. Maybe there's someone else round here could give you a job. I'd like to help.'

He took a deep breath. 'I'm a soldier primarily.'

She laughed and sat down on the grass in the shade. 'That's no good. Nobody in St Martin is recruiting an army.'

He shrugged. 'And apart from that I worked in the retail food business. I ran a production line and worked in marketing. My father has a chain of what you'd call hypermarkets.'

'So, if you've finished soldiering or whatever you call it, why don't you go back to America and settle down?'

He looked away from her. 'I can't do that.'

She wanted to touch him. Uh-oh, she thought. I'm falling for this strange, strong blond man with the pain in his eyes and his voice. But he's not just another soft-headed student you can play around with, Marie-France, so don't get involved. There's an aura of violence about Mr Frank Hansen and it's more than just the fact that he's a soldier. . . .

And then Marie-France had the idea that changed her life. 'Just supposing,' she mused, chewing on a grass stalk. 'Just supposing I wanted to market our wine in the States. With your background in marketing, would you know how to go about that?'

'Are you kidding?' He relaxed and laughed at the question.

'Tell me.'

'Well . . .'

Frank gave the horse a final pat and sat down on the grass beside Marie-France. It was a relief to think of something prosaic. 'This place you have here is pretty beautiful.'

He waved at the château, half a mile distant, at the vineyards, the river. 'I'd put a colour picture of the house – a watercolour – on every bottle. And the bottles should be a distinctive shape, so they stand out on the shelves. On the back label, I'd add the legend: *This beautiful wine is made from grapes picked on the banks of the Dordogne river.* And I'd put a photograph of you on your horse looking at the men working in the vineyards. And your signature, of course.'

'Oh no,' she burst out laughing. 'You haven't understood. We couldn't do that. Traditionally, we just have the conventional printed label like everybody else.'

'Are you asking me or telling me?'

Marie-France grimaced. 'You're right. I'm asking.'

He looked back at the house. Marie Laval was walking over the lawns towards them in a long white dress and a wide, soft-brimmed straw sunhat. The scene was like an Impressionist painting.

'You have to think big,' he said. 'I'd launch a whole range of French foods at the same time. Call it Hansen's French Farmhouse Food – pâtés, terrines, cheeses, sausages, confits . . . and we'd put a trained counsellor in French costume at each store to advise people what to buy and which wine to drink with it.'

Marie-France burst out laughing. 'You're so American, Frank. All I asked you was if you could help me sell our wine.'

He looked hurt again, but this time the wound was slight. She leaned forward and kissed him on the lips. Frank neither responded nor moved away; she was unlike any other young woman he had known.

Carlo's neigh warned them of Marie's approach.

Marie-France pulled Frank to his feet. *'Maman!'* she called, leading him through the curtain of willow branches. 'I want you to meet our new marketing manager.'

Marie did not look pleased to see Frank again as he emerged from the greenery, buttoning up his shirt. 'I told Mr Hansen we didn't have a job for him.'

Marie-France put her arms around her mother's neck. 'You told him that you don't have a job on the farm. The job I've given him is to help me sell wine to America. He's got the most wonderful plan already.'

Marie looked into her daughter's eyes and then at Frank standing well back, waiting for her reaction. 'I don't think that's a good idea,' she said coldly.

10

The tiny Kaman UH-2 Seasprite helicopter lifted away from the ledge on the side of a mountain high above the tourist beaches on the island of Corsica. Orange smoke from the marker streamed away in the gale-force wind.

'You bastard!' screamed Roger. 'You could have taken your pack – or at least the radio.'

Sean's two-finger gesture was the only answer as the little machine lurched sideways in a gust of wind and dropped fifty feet before clawing its way into undisturbed air.

Hans-Peter stood beside Roger watching the Seasprite disappear to the north.

'Lucky bastard,' he said. 'We train and train and he's the only one ever gets to do anything real.'

Roger kicked the abandoned pack. Inside it were several kilos of plastic explosive. 'I've a good mind to shove the whole lot right over the edge.' There was a sheer drop of 2,000 feet to a waterfall showing white between the rocks below.

'That'd teach him a lesson.' Hans-Peter laughed. 'He'd have to pay for every item lost. Cost him half a year's pay . . .'

'Shit,' said Roger, hefting Sean's back-pack over one shoulder. He grunted from the combined weight of his own pack and the extra one.

Hans-Peter grabbed the radio and started after him along the narrow sheep trail. 'Look on the bright side,' he said. 'Only fifteen kilometres back to base.'

Gusts of wind buffeted the tiny machine from side to side. Even the pilot was looking slightly sick.

The major seated beside him passed a set of civilian clothes back to Sean in the cramped rear seat. He had to shout to make himself heard and did not waste time or energy on explanations. 'Put these on.'

Sean did not expect an order to be explained. Especially not in the Fourth Parachute Company, which specialised in sabotage and infiltration.

As the chopper yo-yoed this way and that in the gale, he struggled in the cramped confines of the seat to pull off his wet and muddy uniform trousers and shirt. He donned the dark jeans, black sweater and black leather bomber jacket he had been given and stuffed the wet uniform into the small holdall out of which the clean clothes had come.

The major was taking instructions over the radio and making notes on the pad strapped to his knee. He said something to the pilot which Sean could not catch over the noise of the rotors, then removed his headphones and manoeuvred himself between the seats to squat beside Sean in the back of the tiny cabin.

'You've heard the news?' he asked, holding tight with both hands and looking ill as the helicopter dropped sickeningly.

Sean shook his head. 'I was on a mountain warfare exercise, *mon commandant*,' he shouted back. 'We'd been observing radio silence for two days until we were called up half an hour ago and told to pop some smoke for a helicopter rendezvous.'

He smiled at the thought of Roger and Hans-Peter taking it in turns to hump back to base his 60lb rucksack and the radio in addition to their own gear.

The major put his mouth close to Sean's ear. 'A job for you.'

Sean's pulse quickened. Three times during the last year he had been snatched from training and flown to wherever the President of the Republic was considered to be in danger at some public function. Together with marksmen from the Groupe d'Intervention de la Gendarmerie Nationale, he had been allotted a sniper's position overlooking the point of maximum exposure, with orders to kill by a single shot anyone who appeared to threaten the President's life.

So far he had never had to shoot, yet the adrenalin trip of the second-by-second tension and the sense that he was recognised as one of the best marksmen in the French armed forces made the jobs worth while.

He felt behind the seat.

'It's there!' shouted the major. 'With a fresh supply of ammo.'

'*Merde*,' said Sean. 'That means I'll have to doctor the noses.' It was a rule of the presidential protection operations that all bullets be dumdummed to give them maximum stopping power.

The major shook his head 'This is a different job. That's why I asked if you'd heard the news. A team of Palestinian terrorists took over the Israeli compound at the Olympic games in Munich early this morning. They've killed several members of the team and are asking for a plane to fly them and the remaining hostages to safety.'

Sean turned his head away to hide his blush of pleasure. This time, there was going to be a shoot-out. . . .

Below the helicopter the steel-grey surface of the Mediterranean was flecked with white wave crests. A few Vs marked the wakes of motorised vessels ploughing their way through a heavy swell. The aircraft lurched into a pocket and fell a hundred feet like an express lift.

The pilot's arm reached back and tapped the major's knee.

'We're going down,' shouted the major. He pointed out of the window on his side.

Sean levered himself up to look past the major as the

helicopter turned at a steep angle. A massive flat-topped grey ship appeared to be sliding itself underneath the chopper. The masthead flags stood out stiffly in the Force Eight gale. It was not going to be an easy landing.

There was one aircraft on the deck, with a cluster of figures around it. As Sean watched, twin belches of flame jetted from its engines.

'We're about to put down on the *Clemenceau*,' the major yelled as the helicopter danced in the turbulence from the ship's superstructure. 'She's France's biggest aircraft carrier.'

Sean raised an eyebrow.

'The President of the Republic gave orders that you should be got to Munich as soon as possible, so the Navy's flying you there in your own personal jet.' The major stabbed a finger at the plane on the carrier's deck. 'As soon as we touch down, you get into that Mirage and take off. You'll be in Munich in an hour.'

Several thousand armed police surrounded the Olympic village as the Mirage jet with French Navy markings circled above Furstenfeld military airport outside Munich, waiting for permission to hand. Nine surviving hostages' lives were at stake. Eight terrorists with a martyr complex held the attention of the world's media.

After landing, the Mirage taxied to a remote area where two black cars with diplomatic plates were parked. There were no immigration or customs formalities as Sean was led to one of the cars by the French military attaché from the embassy in Bonn. Accompanied by police outriders, they swept across the expanse of tarmac to the airport buildings. On the balcony above the control tower, the attaché pointed out to Sean where the terrorists' bus would park and where the getaway plane would be waiting, fuelled and ready to take off.

And then the waiting began.

West German Chancellor Willy Brandt flew to Munich to take personal charge of the negotiations. The terrorists bargained, threatened, insisted, changed their minds. Plans for their transfer to the airport were altered. Instead of arriving by coach, they would be flown to Furstenfeld with the hostages by helicopter.

In the crowded control tower, Sean checked the F 1 rifle. It was the one he always used. He had taken the precaution of scribing small marks on the telescopic sights, just in case anyone tampered with the settings since it had last been issued to him. Everything was in order. He would have liked to fire a few shots to get his eye in but there was no time for that. It was getting dark outside. He nodded at a new arrival, a marksman from the West German anti-terrorist squad GS9 against whom Sean had shot more than once in international competitions.

The French military attache from the embassy in Bonn was arguing in German with a group of officials about Sean's inclusion in the GS9 team. Sean felt adrenalin high as he always did before a job that was not, in legionnaire's slang, HBT – *habituel* or run of the mill.

Next to him, a group of Israelis were discussing in Hebrew a replay of a tape recording on a television monitor. Several of them were armed, Sean noted. Listening to the conversation and joining in was a British army captain from SAS in civilian clothes who had also competed against Sean in international shooting competitions. His cold eyes gave a flicker of recognition, which Sean did not return. He was speaking in English via a small walkie-talkie to the rest of the SAS team elsewhere in the airport.

Partly to shield his tired eyes, Sean slipped on a pair of dark glasses. There should be plenty of moonlight, if the previous nights in the Corsican mountains were any guide. He slumped in a plastic chair, dozing. For the past two nights he had had no sleep at all, thanks to Roger who had decided as corporal of the three-man squad to infiltrate the opposing team's positions under cover of darkness from the rear. A classic manoeuvre, except that there were two whole mountain ranges in the way. So they had spent the moonlit nights on forced marches over difficult terrain, trebling the distance of the shortest route.

Despite the hubbub all round him, Sean dozed.

'You took a long time at the château,' Raoul commented when Frank returned at dusk.

'There were some problems to solve.' Frank seemed pleased with himself. He had eaten well at lunchtime with Marie and her daughter and used his charm to try and melt Marie's hostility, without much success. Before returning to Raoul's home, he had gone into the village shops and bought meat, bread and vegetables for his own and Raoul's evening meal.

Raoul nodded distantly. His brain was feverish after a day of trying to analyse the latest, often conflicting, news from South-East Asia and come up with the answer to the question: when?

'So Marie didn't give you the job,' he grimaced. 'My fault.'

Frank grinned. 'Apparently you put Madame Laval's back up by ordering her to employ me. To get her revenge and show you who's boss across the river, she told me to piss off.'

Raoul closed his eyes, angry with himself for being so stupid.

'But it doesn't matter,' said Frank. 'I found another job.'

Raoul's eyes focused on the younger man with a glimmer of respect. 'In other words, you salvaged the mess I made?'

Frank shrugged. 'It turned out quite well. I got a job with her daughter.'

Raoul was incredulous. 'That's crazy. It's Marie who needs help managing those labourers of hers. Marie-France doesn't need any help.'

'You're wrong.'

Frank sorted out his purchases on the cooking surface and began to prepare the meal. 'Oh, I'll kick the *magrehbins* into shape for Marie, but what that place really needs is a deal which will finance the modernisation of the whole

437

wine-making side of Château St Martin. Marie-France showed me around the winery; it's positively medieval. And their ideas on how to sell are amateur – although Marie-France has got plenty of drive, I'll give her that.'

Raoul was now paying Frank complete attention. 'What kind of deal are you planning, to provide that sort of money?'

Frank was chopping vegetables. 'We've gone further than planning . . .'

'We?'

'I was on the telephone to the States for half the afternoon, with Marie-France beside me, okaying everything like prices, delivery dates and so on. It's all fixed. We leave tomorrow to sign the piece of paper. We get a plane from Bordeaux airport tomorrow morning to Paris, then from Paris to New York and . . .'

Raoul's fist slammed down on the chopping board. 'Hold on, sergeant. I said to get yourself a cover job, not devote yourself to some pie-in-the-sky idea that will cost a lot of money.'

Frank put down the knife.

'You listen to me, Raoul,' he said calmly. 'You said it was important for me to be accepted here in St Martin. So I've got to carve out a niche that suits me – one that's in character. Once I've fixed this deal for Château St Martin, everybody here will know I'm just the Yank with crazy ideas to sell wine on the wrong side of the Atlantic. Whilst they're busy laughing at me, your friends at the château will be getting quietly rich and I'll be free most of the time to work with you, planning your operation.'

Raoul was confused. It was as though one of the pieces on his chessboard had argued back – and been right.

'I apologise,' he said with difficulty. 'Your idea is better than mine. When d'you get back?'

'Well, Marie-France has never seen America, so we won't hurry. There are places she ought to see.' The real reason why Frank had arranged the trip had nothing to do with selling wine or showing Marie-France Niagara Falls and the Empire State Building. It had to do with confronting the past and all its pain, in order to start anew – but that was not something he was going to tell Raoul. Not yet.

'You're taking her with you?' Raoul shook his head with disbelief. 'Is that wise?'

Frank tutted. 'My! What an old chauvinist you are.'

There was a twinkle in his eye. 'I'm not taking her with me, Raoul. She's my boss, remember? She's taking *me* with *her.*'

Sean awoke and stretched. By the control room clock, two hours had passed. He felt refreshed. Once again his ability to sleep anywhere had stood him in good stead.

The polyglot wrangle was over. Most of the diplomats and policemen had left the control tower to report to their superiors. Despite all the extra lines which had been installed for the Olympics, non-priority international calls out of Munich were being delayed by up to three hours.

The French military attaché sat down beside Sean with a paper cup of machine-made coffee. Sean grunted thanks. 'What's the plan?' he asked.

The attaché made an expression of distaste. 'The authorities here do not want French, Israeli, British or any other help in sorting out the mess their lax security has brought about. Eventually they agreed that you will be working with the three-man SAS sharpshooting team in a back-up operation, in case the main plan to rescue the hostages does not succeed.'

Sean listened to his briefing without comment. He would have preferred not to be working with the British, but orders were orders.

It was already dark when he crawled stealthily on to the roof of a hangar and made himself comfortable beside the British sergeant. Two other SAS marksmen were several feet away. All four men were calm, silent, ready – professionals about to do a precision job.

The weather had been oppressive and sultry all day. As they waited for the terrorists' helicopter to arrive, the cloud thickened and obscured the moon.

'Just as well the whole place is floodlit.' The SAS sergeant spoke in French.

Sean grunted agreement. He did not want to talk to the man.

They waited in silence for an hour. Then came the *slap-slap-slap* of helicopter blades and a confusion of flashing lights in the darkness outside the brightly lit area of concrete between the hangar and the waiting Boeing 727. Sean nestled the stock of the F 1 against his cheek. He felt, as he always did on these occasions, a cold peace steal over him. The first two terrorists, counting from the front, were his. If he failed to get them or could not shoot because a hostage's body was in the way, they would anyway be taken out by German marksmen firing from the other side.

The helicopter landed, its escort putting down some distance away. The first Israeli hostage was pushed out into the floodlights' glare. He shielded his eyes from the light. Tightly behind him, a Makarov 9mm automatic pistol pressed against the Israeli's head, came Sean's first target. Sean licked his dry lips and followed the man's masked face in the telescopic sight. Without consciously thinking, his finger took up the first pressure on the trigger.

'Wait for it,' one of the other men on the roof murmured. The agreed cue to open fire was to be the third step taken by the last terrorist to leave the helicopter. The Germans' cue was to fire on the second step.

Seconds ticked by as the masked and hooded men below warily assembled their captives for the short walk to the waiting Boeing. The last terrorist emerged, took one step. . . .

All the lights in the airport went out. Sean's eyes and those of the other marksmen on the roof beside him, were blind. Blinking, they impotently willed their irises to adjust to the darkness. There was the whipcrack of rifle fire and the whine of ricochets as the German snipers opened up with infra-red sighted weapons. A sputter of sub-machine-guns and the explosion of several grenades. Then silence.

When the floodlights came back on, all the hostages lay

dead in pools of blood on the concrete. Four terrorists were also dead. At the foot of the steps to the Boeing was a milling confusion of police, soldiers and the surviving Palestinians into which no one could risk firing.

'Jesus!' The SAS sergeant swore. He smashed his fist on to the metal roof. 'What a cock-up!' He turned to Sean. 'How fucking stupid can you get, eh? They just threw those people's lives away. Did you ever see anything like it?'

Sean said nothing. He stood up and slipped the safety catch on. The whole fiasco seemed to sum up his time in the Legion. Roger grumbled often that they trained and trained, slogging their guts out to reach a pitch of perfection, but never actually went to war, which was what they had joined up for. Half of the paras had been rotated to the guerrilla war in Chad but Sean, Roger and Hans-Peter never got lucky. They had done courses on jungle warfare in French Guiana and desert warfare in the Sahara, they had taken part in winter exercises against French army troops high in the snows of the Alps, but they had never actually fought an enemy.

Despite the honour of being picked to protect the President of the Republic, even Sean had never fired a shot for real. There was nothing he could do about it, but he was fed up to the back teeth with peacetime soldiering.

11

Frank drove out of the executive parking lot of Hansen's Foods with a final wave to the group on the steps, assembled to wish him goodbye. Two press photographers were packing away their equipment and the local radio station's remote car had already left after a live interview with Sven, Frank and Marie-France.

'I really liked your parents, Frank,' she sighed. 'They made me feel so welcome.'

'People are friendly here,' he agreed.

'It's been a wonderful trip.'

'A business trip,' he reminded her. 'How does it feel to have the contract in your bag, all signed, and a banker's draft for the advance?'

She giggled and took a deep breath. 'I can't quite believe it. I feel like – what's that phrase of your father's? – like a million dollars.'

Frank laughed. 'You look like a million dollars.'

He drove out of town, heading for the Interstate Highway, the first step of the return journey to France and St Martin.

'It's so different from Europe.' Marie-France was looking at the houses they were driving past. 'People are very rich in America. I've never been in an air-conditioned car before. And all the homes in Jacksonville seem to have two cars in the driveway.'

'A lot of these people work for my father,' he said.

'He's sad you didn't want to come back here and settle.'

'I couldn't do that. Not yet. Maybe one day.'

'Your mother told me about the twins. I'm sorry.' She rested a hand on his knee for a moment, then took it away, wondering if that had been the wrong thing to say.

On a spur-of-the-moment decision, he wound the wheel and pulled the car round in a scream of tyres to face back towards Jacksonville.

'Where are we going?'

'A place I have to visit,' he said, keeping his eyes on the road. He sensed that in life as in combat, there were times when a man must accept a wound or stay holed up in shelter and surely die.

'Where's that?'

Frank did not reply. There was a strange set to his eyes, as though they were focused far ahead. He drove through a maze of identical residential streets and stopped the rented car opposite the house that had been called Wonderland.

The trees in the garden were bigger and thicker than he remembered. Some washing was airing on a merry-go-round and the two children who played with a dog on the back-yard lawn were about the same age the twins had been. A woman came out of the kitchen door and called to them. Through the tinted glass of the windscreen, with her back to the car, she could have been Alice.

'What is it?' Marie-France asked.

He let the clutch in and drove in silence out of town, in the opposite direction to where she knew they should be going.

They passed the sign for Jackson's Lake, where it had all happened, and bumped along the track between the trees which led to the Hansen cabin. Frank parked and switched the engine off. The birds sounded very loud.

'Stay in the car,' he said harshly, getting out. 'I won't be long.'

The clearing in the forest felt very deserted. Marie-France could not even see as far as the cabin.

'Where are you going, Frank?' she called after him.

'Just wait here.'

After a few minutes, she got out of the car and climbed the bank. When she saw the shine of water through the trees she knew that he had come to say goodbye.

The cabin, the landing stage, the forest and the lake made such a peaceful setting. It was hard for her to imagine tragedy here. She saw Frank in the distance. He was standing on the shore quite still, looking out over the water, his right hand raised in a salute or a gesture of goodbye.

Best to leave him alone, she thought and sat on a fallen tree to wait. The sound of another car approaching along the track alerted her. She looked up to find Sven Hansen parking his car beside Frank's.

'Hi, honey,' he said quietly, with no trace of his usual boisterousness. He climbed the bank, puffing, and hitched his belt over his belly. 'I'm getting unfit.'

'Frank's down by the water,' she said quietly. 'He told me to wait here.'

'I thought he'd come.' Sven patted her shoulder and walked through the brush towards his son. Marie-France watched the two men embrace. They stood a long time beside the water talking to each other while, out of earshot, she listened to the birds and the sounds of small animals scuffling in dead leaves.

When the men returned, Frank looked peaceful, as though the ghosts with whom he had communed had bathed him in the remembrance of shared happiness and washed away the sadness that had festered in him so long. All the grief was on Sven's face.

'Time to go,' said Frank, holding the car door open for her.

'Goodbye again.' Marie-France kissed Sven's cheek. 'And thank you for all your kindness to me.'

Frank's father looked her over. In the midst of his sadness, he still enjoyed the sight of a beautiful young woman.

'You're a lucky guy,' he said over his shoulder to Frank. 'I wish I was twenty years younger.'

He squeezed Marie-France's shoulders. His voice was husky. 'Thank you for bringing back my boy. Look after him, over there in Europe.'

'I'm not his wife, Sven.' She spoke seriously. 'I'm his boss.'

The bright blue eyes bored into hers. 'All the same . . .' he said vaguely, then stood aside for her to go. 'Have fun.'

A high-technology dot riding the jet stream seven miles above a dark ocean invisible under layer upon layer of cloud: they were somewhere over the Atlantic when Frank spoke for the first time since take-off.

'Tell me about yourself.'

Marie-France thought it would have been more interesting to hear about his life. Casual remarks he made from time to time betrayed the gulf of experience that separated them, but apart from what she had gleaned from his mother and the incident at Jackson's Lake, Frank had told her little about himself.

He was so unlike her student lovers or the balding poetry tutor who had seduced her in her first term at college that she was wary of being the one who lessened the gap between them, although the tension when they were alone was at times almost tangible. They were like two magnets with the like poles facing, held apart by invisible lines of force. One twist – a slight change in their respective positions – and the same forces would bring them crashing together, she was sure.

Frank had not made a pass at her. She had not invited one, but she would not have rejected it; it was just that she wanted him to make the first move. She could feel when he looked at her, especially last thing at night, that he wanted her physically. But the thousand changes of mood that his blue eyes telegraphed were sometimes bewildering.

She wondered if the curt instruction to talk about herself was his masculine way of beginning to build a bridge of intimacy between them. In which case, she asked herself,

445

why had he waited until the end of the trip? Most men would have tried to get her into bed much earlier. Was Frank's previous reluctance to make a move connected with what had been in his mind at the lake?

'I was born in Vietnam,' she began, 'on a rubber plantation 200 miles from anywhere . . .'

He was a good listener, silent and yet watchful of her face and perceptive to the nuances in her voice.

She recalled T. S. Eliot's phrase: *the still point of the turning world*. That's here, she thought, where we are suspended in our timeless metal tube hurtling through space, the globe turning far beneath. Are we still in America's evening or have we arrived in Europe's night?

The placelessness somehow made it easier to spill the trivia of her life in front of him. She poked into drawer after drawer of reminiscences, lifting out memories of places, incidents and people that might interest the silent man beside her.

'It's funny,' she interrupted herself, 'to think that you know most of the places I'm talking about, Frank – because you've been in Vietnam and Algeria too. In Oran, for example, you must have known the bar where we lived after the FLN burned down my parents' farm. It was called Chez Mimi, opposite the Legion depot in Oran. Lots of legionnaires drank there. I used to talk to them. Maybe I even talked to you.'

'I drank there.'

It was the first time he had spoken in twenty minutes, as though he had known all along where the conversation was going and been waiting for his cue. 'I wasn't often in Oran, but when I was, that bar was the nearest place to the depot for a quick drink.'

'Perhaps you even saw me there?' She was intrigued at the thought that their paths might have overlapped in the past.

'No,' he said. 'Like I told you, I wasn't often in Oran.'

Then he laughed. 'How stupid can you get? I'm trying to remember you as the woman you now are. When I first went to Algeria, I was only just eighteen myself so you must have been what . . . seven, eight years old? Oh Christ!'

He swivelled in the narrowed seat and stared at her in disbelief, seeing again in his mind's eye a little girl screaming in terror.

'What is it?' Wide-eyed, Marie studied Frank's face. It bore the same haunted look as when she had surfaced after diving underwater in the river, the first day they met in St Martin.

'The day. . . . No.' He shook his head, shuffling the pack of death cards he carried everywhere with him in order to take out the right one.

She put her hand on his white, clenched fist clutching the arm-rest. 'What's the matter, Frank?'

His blue eyes stared right through her, at a replay of the past. 'An Arab woman was assassinated. Outside Chez Mimi. The day I landed in Algeria. I ran across the road. There was a kid. The bullets had just missed her. She was surrounded by broken glass and blood. She was staring at the body, I remember, screaming. I picked her up and turned her face away but she wouldn't stop screaming. That was you, wasn't it?'

It was Marie-France's turn to pale. 'I don't remember,' she stammered.

Her nails were digging into the flesh of his hand. 'I don't remember anything about the shooting. I had nightmares and fits – tantrums, maybe you'd call them – for months afterwards. In the end *maman* took me to see a psychiatrist, but at that time in Algeria, most of the adults, let alone the children, had nightmares. So I don't think the doctor did much to help.'

He could see the scene so clearly, it seemed impossible she could have forgotten or repressed the memory. 'You don't remember me at all?'

She closed her eyes, trying to recall what had been so long suppressed. 'I think . . . there was a man who ran out of nowhere and picked me up. But maybe I was told that afterwards.'

She shook her head desperately. 'I don't know what I remember and what I was told.'

Frank gripped her arm so tightly that it hurt. 'Think! There was a man. There was! It was me. I was the guy who picked you up that day.'

Marie-France shuddered. She opened her eyes to find his face close to hers. 'I think I remember,' she whispered.

By an effort she made her voice normal. 'It must mean something, Frank. If, out of all the people in the world, you were there that day when I was in danger, it must mean something. Since then you've been literally round the world and lived through two wars to find me again. Think of the odds against that happening.'

The stewardess was trying to place a plastic meal tray between them.

'I want you,' he said.

Marie-France shook her head at the girl hovering in the background and received a plastic smile instead of the food. She wanted to touch Frank, but waited until the stewardess had moved on.

Then she said, 'I've been waiting for you to say that. Why now? Why did you wait until now?'

'I didn't want to drag you into my world,' he said hoarsely. 'But it seems you belong there already.' A girl who could survive what had happened to Marie-France the first time their paths crossed . . . perhaps at last he had found someone the jinx could not touch, someone he could love without smelling blossom again?

'What world are you talking about?' she asked.

A world of violence and pain: he didn't say it. 'I want you,' he repeated urgently.

'What are we going to do about it?' She lowered her voice, aware of the passengers in the adjacent seats.

'When we get off this plane,' he said, 'the first thing we do is check into an airport motel and catch up on the time we've been missing.'

Marie-France rubbed her arm. It hurt where he had

448

gripped it. She could see the marks of her nails on the back of his hand.

'Why, Mr Hansen,' she mocked him to cover up her own confusion. 'That's just about the least romantic proposition a girl ever had.'

'Would you like me to romance you a little first?' There was a hint of answering mockery in Frank's voice but his eyes were not joking.

'No,' she said. 'You did it just right. I always knew that one day I'd meet a man like you. Now I know why I knew that.'

He could not follow the feminine logic. 'What's that in American?'

'Work it out for yourself.'

Marie-France ran a finger down his profile, breaking the barrier of personal space yet gently preserving the distance between them. 'You're not responsible for me and I'm not responsible for you. Let's make a deal, as Sven would say. No promises, either side. Then nobody gets hurt. OK?'

The cool, slightly flip speech was not what her body was saying.

If only it was as simple as that, Frank thought. But people did get hurt, promises or no promises. He recalled Koenig saying: *We give a hostage to fortune.* But this time it was going to be all right, he knew.

Through the tiny windows the sky was night dark. Faintly in the plexiglass he saw the twin reflections: hers in profile and his full-face. He lifted Marie-France's hand and bent his head to kiss the backs of her fingers, one by one.

Eyes closed, she shuddered at the touch of his lips, as though he had reached inside her. She brought her legs tightly together and breathed, 'I want you, Frank.' It was the first time in her life she had really meant the words.

Frank felt her breath on his ear and then her lips. Her teeth closed on the ear lobe. The smells of her body rose

449

through the thin cotton dress she was wearing and filled his nostrils.

Frank closed his eyes and inhaled deep, deep, deep. No more blossom, ever. 'I want to eat you alive,' he murmured.

12

'Who's the brunette on the chestnut horse?' Koenig asked.

Raoul took the binoculars from his friend and adjusted them. As a belated legacy from his confinement without light, his eyesight was worsening rapidly and it frightened him. He swept the glasses over the valley and up to the limestone bluff overlooking the Dordogne, known locally as the Belvedere. Two figures on horseback sprang into focus through the powerful lenses.

'You remember meeting my friend Marie?' he asked. 'Well, that's Marie-France, her daughter.'

'Are she and Hansen having an affair?'

'I think so.'

'You don't know?' Koenig queried. 'It could be important if Frank talks in his sleep.'

Raoul dropped the glasses on to his knee.

He chuckled. 'Frank's fixed himself up as a sort of business partner of Marie-France, selling wine to the States. They've made several trips over there. In between they're modernising the winery at the château. Frank has a bed downstairs here but he also has a billet of some kind over at the château for the nights when he's working late. Yet Marie tells me they don't behave like lovers in the daytime – more like business partners, she says.'

Koenig grunted. He preferred simple answers to his questions.

'Well, you've done a good job here,' he said. He slapped the stone battlement. 'The Templars built this place to last. It's better than that dump you were living in, down below.' He spat at the last remains of the barn, which had been demolished to leave just a small garage. Once again the Templars' tower stood proud on the clifftop, as its builders had intended. From where Koenig and Raoul were talking, on the roof of the tower, the view spread over the village of St Martin, the river and the valley beyond.

In the months that had passed since Frank's arrival in St Martin, the restoration and conversion of the tower had occupied much of Raoul's time and energy. The old stones had lent themselves to his ideas for a dream house, blue-printed years before in his imagination. He had installed a lift to whisk him from the garage at ground level to his office on the first floor, from there to his bedroom on the second floor and from there to his dining and living-room above and finally to the roof where he could enjoy the view that had kept him sane in Minh's dark cage.

'The biggest bonus,' he told Koenig, 'was to find – when the builders started clearing out the rubble of the centuries – an underground dungeon below the tower. It makes a perfect place to hide the gold.'

'How many people know about it?'

'The builders will have forgotten by now. It was a nine-day wonder. Most of the houses in the village have habitable caves underneath and tunnels interconnecting them.'

'Why?' Koenig never took anything for granted.

'They were built during the wars of religion in the Middle Ages. This part of France was one long war from when the Romans left until just about the time of the Revolution. One year the Protestants would gang up on the Catholics and loot and burn their towns and villages. The next, it was the Catholics' turn to go on the rampage. So everybody had to have a refuge and an escape route.'

'If there's a tunnel leading out of your dungeon, then it's hardly a safe place to keep a fortune in gold.'

'There was a tunnel leading to a disused crypt underneath the church, but don't worry,' Raoul reassured him. 'Frank has taken care of that. He bricked it up. I just had the builders clean the rubble out of the dungeon, then it was covered over and they forgot all about it. Frank did the rest of the work down there for me at nights, even carrying the spoil out in sacks and disposing of it in the river, to leave no traces.'

'What do you think of Hansen?' asked Koenig. He had picked up the glasses again and was examining the two figures on the bluff.

'Frank? The best.'

'Mm.' Something seemed to be troubling Koenig. 'When I ran across him again in Vietnam, I was surprised he was still alive.'

'Why d'you say that?'

Through the glasses Frank and Marie-France, sitting on their horses a quarter of a mile away, seemed to be having an argument. Koenig grunted. 'You remember some men, even way back at St Cyr, had the smell of death on them? Hansen had it too.'

That phrase, from Koenig of all people!

As my insomnia grew worse I had taken to working in the daytime at my business and keeping the daily updates of the situation in Vietnam and South-East Asia for the small hours, when I sat poring over my maps and plotting the latest positions of all the forces involved. Frank too seemed to sleep less than most people. Frequently he arrived at two or three o'clock in the morning, having seen a light burning in the tower.

We sat and talked till dawn, mostly about the war, which seemed to have the same morbid fascination for him as it had for me. But sometimes, when I sensed he was depressed for whatever reason, I would lead the conversation round to his personal experiences and try to unravel the complex he had about causing people's deaths. Every time he used the phrase that his dead gypsy friend had implanted in his mind, it made me angry.

'Smell of death?' Raoul scoffed. 'That's a damned superstition. You might as well talk of a smell of life. We're still alive, you and I.'

Koenig grimaced. 'And how many others of our class? Two, three, maybe. All the rest are dead.'

'Then the phrase means nothing,' Raoul argued. 'Anyway, if you've got doubts about Frank, why did you pick him?'

'I have no doubts of his suitability for the job. You couldn't find a better man. He speaks the languages. Knows the country and the people. Tough as hell. It's just that . . .' Koenig paused, 'I always had a feeling about Hansen that he was a marked man, you know.'

Raoul hit his fist against the masonry and controlled his anger. 'Well, even if you're right, I'd say Marie-France has given him a new reason to stay alive.'

'Let's hope I'm wrong.'

Raoul changed the subject. 'You'll be going along on the mission with the men?' He tried to conceal his jealousy; he would have to hand control for the mission over to his friend, while he stayed at home watching maps, listening to the radio and worrying impotently.

Koenig picked up the intonation in his friend's voice. 'No,' he laughed. 'I'm too old to go all the way.'

'Too old?'

'Be honest, Raoul. We're nearer fifty than forty. I hope I concealed it from Frank, but when he took me on that recce we did last year, I thought I was going to die from heat exhaustion, or from exhaustion pure and simple. And remember, we were travelling light, not laden with a pile of gold.'

'And Frank?'

A grunt. 'Dammit, Hansen could have turned right round and done the whole trip over again. That's how tough he is.'

'The way they'll go in through Laos is much shorter.'

Raoul spoke swiftly to cover his relief. There was no need to be jealous. Not of Koenig, of all people. . . .

His friend grimaced. 'My place is at base, on the Laotian side of the border. My drug-running Corsican friends who are arranging transport of the loot back to France are not 100 per cent trustworthy. So I'll stick close to them and make sure that nothing goes wrong on the way out, and that transport's waiting when Frank and the others get back from Dien Bien Phu. I don't want the operation to end with some little Corsican short-arse pointing a gun at them and growling: 'Hand over the loot.'

'So Frank will be in command of the actual mission?' Raoul pictured the situation. All the midnight briefings had been necessary after all.

'We can trust him.'

'I agree,' said Raoul. 'One hundred per cent.'

'So let's hope,' finished Koenig, 'that he gets safely back here to enjoy what's sitting on that horse beside him.'

Catching a glint of the thin April sunlight on the lenses of Raoul's binoculars, Frank turned in the saddle and looked straight at the tower.

'I have to be getting back,' he said to Marie-France. 'Raoul's waiting for me.'

'We're agreed then?' she asked, putting a hand on his arm to restrain him. The horses moved, their breath steaming in the still air. 'We change the oenologist. I'm not satisfied with him.'

'He's the best man in Bordeaux.'

'The best chemist,' she agreed.

'The wine he blends tastes good to my father's customers.'

'What do Americans know about wine?' she snapped. 'It's my palate that blends Château St Martin, Frank – not that scruffy little chemist from Bordeaux.'

'Change him if you like,' he said, sulking. 'Why do you ask me, if your mind is already made up?'

His horse was already on the path that led down to the river.

Marie-France stared at his back. Lately she and Frank were squabbling more often than they made love. She knew there was something on his mind, but had given up asking what it was.

'Don't be cross,' she called, nudging Carlo after him. 'I want my wine not just in Sven's supermarkets but on the table of the White House and served at State receptions in the Elysée.'

'Why do you need a wine chemist anyway?' he asked, letting the reins go slack for the horse to find its own way down. 'It seems to me that you decide everything and spend the whole time arguing with the guy.'

'I suppose . . .' She thought an explanation might serve as apology. 'I suppose it's insurance. It's funny to have a gift like my palate. I mean, it's not as if I had learned how to taste wine. Maybe it's the same with all gifts: you don't know how you do it, so maybe one day you could be wrong and you'd never know until it was too late.'

He grunted. His mind was not on wine that day.

'Who is that man with one eye, Frank?' she asked.

'Koenig is an old friend of Raoul's. He was also my CO in the Legion.'

'What's he doing here?'

'On holiday.'

'*Maman* has met him. She says he doesn't look like the sort of man who ever takes holidays.'

'I'm taking a few days off,' said Frank, 'if you don't mind. Going on a trip with Koenig and Raoul to Corsica where the Legion's Second Parachute Regiment is based.'

'Can I come along?'

'Afraid not,' he said casually. 'It's a reunion. Strictly men only.'

The reception given to us in the officers' mess was warm and brotherly; the government might have court-martialled me and put a price on Koenig's head, but the Legion still welcomed us as two of its own.

On the parade ground I saw that Frank, standing not far away among a group of former NCOs, had been given a similar welcome home in the sergeants' mess.

It was the first time since my court-martial that I had been surrounded by men in the uniform of the Legion. White kepis and gloves, green and red epaulettes, the light stone-coloured uniforms, the weapons carried as though they had grown on the bearers like extensions of their own limbs . . .

The conflict of emotions within made it hard for me to breathe as I sat in my wheelchair in the Corsican sunshine and watched the men march past. There were other wounded veterans present, with empty sleeves and trouser legs neatly pinned up, on crutches and in wheelchairs. Mentally we were standing to attention again as the band played the music we knew so well and strong, whole-bodied young men sang the marching songs we had sung. Beside me, Koenig stood ramrod-straight. Neither of us wore medals. It was the only gesture we could make.

The anniversary of the battle of Camerone is traditionally an open day at Foreign Legion bases. That 30 April members of the public were sitting on the specially erected stands, mixed with relatives of the men in the Second Para Regiment who were on parade. In front of us, the toughest fighting men in the world marched across the blinding white concrete at the peculiar slow pace of the Legion. It was the best place in the world to seek the rest of the team that would go into Dien Bien Phu with Frank.

Citations were read out over the PA and medals pinned on chests by a general wearing white gloves. We listened to the familiar story of Captain Danjou's heroism which I had last heard nineteen years before over the Tannoy at Dien Bien Phu, against a background of gunfire. All the ritual sounds echoed around the hard barrack blocks, like mass in a cathedral.

The band finished playing as the last man marched off the parade ground. Over the PA, the commandant invited all the members of the public to join him for a vin d'honneur.

'Come,' said Koenig. 'We have work to do.' He grabbed the handles of the wheelchair. Frank shook hands with a couple of old comrades from Algeria and lengthened his stride to catch up with Koenig's brisk pace.

A classroom had officially been set aside for our use. In it was

a pile of personal files of men soon to be demobilised. It was a
favour done on the old basis: no names, no pack drill. . . .

Against a background of music from the band playing for the
vin d'honneur *and the sound of automatic rifle fire from a range*
where members of the public were trying their luck with a dozen
doctored FAMAS rifles, we interviewed a succession of young men.
All were fit, all highly trained and all wanted one thing – to see
some action before they were much older.

It was halfway through the afternoon when the last man was
shown out. The sounds of the traditional Camerone Day
fun-fair continued outside: the *pop-pop-pop* from the rifle
range, the excited voices of children, the regimental band
competing with the music from a giant roundabout and the
announcements over the public address system.

'It makes you wonder,' said Frank. 'When you're in combat, you pray for it to end. Yet all these peacetime soldiers
are praying for a war to fight. They all say the same.'

'Hopefully,' said Koenig, 'we're not fighting a war. As
Sun Tsu said, the best general is the one who avoids a
thousand battles. The last thing we want is to pick some
blood-freak who can't hold his fire at the critical moment.'

'The problem' – Raoul's fists were clenched in frustration – 'is that none of the men we've seen are the kind I'm
looking for. I want . . .'

Koenig was ticking names off a short-list. 'I know what
you want, Duvalier. Three battle-scarred German heroes
from the eastern front, am I right? Well, they're all dead
long since, *mon vieux.*'

He looked at Frank. 'And you won't find three more
Hansens.'

'I suppose you're right.'

'I am. We have to take what we can get. And we've got
to do it now. It's three months since Kissinger's cease-fire
was signed. And in Laos there's a shaky peace. Our window
of opportunity will be short duration. I know that part of the
world. I live there. We either accept the best men we can
find here, today – or kiss goodbye to the only chance of

walking quietly back to Dien Bien Phu we're likely to see during our lifetimes.'

'You're right,' Raoul admitted. 'I set my sights too high. All the men we've interviewed are possibles. Let's pick the best three.'

'There's a trio of possibles on my short-list,' said Koenig. 'And by coincidence, one of them is the son of one of your German heroes: Hans-Peter Muller.'

'I remember him,' said Raoul. 'We must be able to do better than that.'

Koenig scribbled three names on a piece of paper, which he handed to Frank. 'Call these men back. They're all due for demob. on the same day in August. I want to see again legionnaire Muller and his Irish friend, the marksman. Also that busted corporal with the broken nose: Roger Milton. Apparently they work well as an infiltration and sabotage team.'

Koenig leafed through the three personal files after Frank had gone. He grunted at something which caught his eye in the file marked: MULLER, *Hans-Peter*. He passed the file to Raoul, open at the handwritten life story.

Hans-Peter, Sean and Roger sat on the bench outside the classroom after their second interviews.

'What do you reckon this is all about?' Sean asked.

'They're recruiting mercenaries.' Roger had no doubts.

'Would they let them do that on Legion premises?' wondered Sean.

'More likely,' Hans-Peter suggested, 'they're from some secret service outfit that wants a handful of trained soldiers for a one-off job.'

Roger disagreed. 'That ex-officer with one eye, maybe. But the guy in the wheelchair and the Yank are nothing to do with the French secret service.'

'Whoever they are,' Sean said, 'we're the only ones they called back for a second interview. They must reckon we're pretty good. So let's agree that they have to take us all – or none. Right?'

They shook hands and sat back. After five years' soldiering, they knew how to wait. Sean fell asleep. From inside the classroom came the sound of voices raised in argument.

It was Frank who was being awkward. 'I talked with them. They're young,' he said.

'The German is twenty-seven,' Koenig observed. 'The other two are twenty-three. That's not so young.'

'I meant they haven't seen any action. Not one of them has ever been in combat.'

Koenig laughed scornfully. 'You and Raoul are in a dream world. These boys are the best we're going to find: highly trained, in the peak of condition, raring to go.'

'Well, the Irish guy's OK,' Frank conceded. 'Anyone who can shoot like him is a winner. On this mission, we'll only have the firepower we carry and no back-up. Each miss is a bullet we can't use again. So he's in. And the busted corporal is as strong as an ox, spoiling for a fight and good with automatic weapons. I'll take him too.'

'And the German?' said Koenig. 'What have you got against him?'

'He's gay. I can feel it.'

'So was Julius Caesar.' Koenig retrieved Hans-Peter's file from Raoul, who had not spoken since reading his life story. 'Muller is an unarmed combat instructor and some kind of mechanical genius. That could be useful. Remember Murphy's First Law of Mechanics: every machine that can let you down in combat, will.'

'I don't care,' argued Frank. 'I'm picking the men who go into the jungle with me and I don't want that guy. He'll cause trouble.'

Raoul spoke at last. 'Muller's also a medic,' he said quietly. 'That makes him a useful person to have along on this trip, I'd say.'

'I don't want him.'

'You're overruled, Frank,' said Raoul with finality. 'Those three men outside are a team. That's important not just during the mission but also afterwards. We can't risk hiring men who do the job and then split up and squabble over the money. So Muller comes too.'

Raoul's decision nearly cost Marie-France's life.

13

It was mid-August. The afternoon was hot and sultry. Nothing stirred among the fields and orchards of the Dordogne valley across the river from St Martin except the figure of a man on horseback.

Frank was riding Carlo, Marie-France's favourite gelding. He kept the horse at a walk on the verge of the dusty road; they were in plenty of time to meet the train he could hear approaching along the single-track line.

He just talked an excited Raoul out of coming to meet the three legionnaires himself.

'I'm the sergeant,' Frank had said. 'You let me meet them. They've got to be my men from the first moment they arrive.'

He had felt good saying that. Raoul was the officer and in command but he, Frank, was in charge of the men. *My men* was something he had not said in quite a while. He took a deep breath and stood up in the stirrups to get a first sight of the train through the dancing heat-haze. He was looking forward to welding into a tightly knit, fast-moving team the three young men who would shortly alight from it. It was a job he did well. He had not forgotten his reservations about legionnaire Muller, but they were all on the same side now and if Muller pulled his weight, they would get along fine.

A herd of almost white cows crowded together in the shade of a solitary plane tree, chewing the cud as their heads turned to watch him pass. The pasture was bleached a pale straw colour by the midsummer sun. To the south, the village was invisible through the haze. A distant hum of motor traffic came from the north where the main road ran parallel to the railway.

Frank heard the whistle of the train and sniffed sharply. His nostrils had caught a whiff of blossom on the air although no bushes or flowers were nearby. The hairs on the back of his neck stood up. He wheeled the horse in a circle and rode over the same ground three times seeking again the elusive hint of perfume that had alarmed him. There was nothing except the usual smells of hot earth and grass and animals, nothing to hear except the buzzing of insects, the distant traffic noise and the slow crescendo of metal on metal as the train drew nearer. But he was certain he had smelt blossom.

The automatic barrier swung down across the road. Frank felt a sudden chill of premonition and halted the horse under the next tree, staying in the shadow to watch as the two-carriage diesel train stopped at the station and three men climbed down. They seemed in good spirits. He watched them joking with each other. A whistle blew and the train belched exhaust fumes, gathered speed and rolled away westwards towards Bordeaux.

On the still air, the voices carried clearly to where Frank watched and listened, invisible in the shadow.

'What a dump!' Sean Carey expressed a town-dweller's reaction to the rustic simplicity of the railway halt which served St Martin and several neighbouring villages.

There was no platform, just a disused crossing-keeper's house and a small ticket office which was closed, the dusty windows almost opaque. A faded handwritten notice affixed to the door with rusty drawing pins advised travellers to pay on board the train.

The three ex-legionnaires stood on the cinders strewn beside the track, feeling strange in their new civilian clothes after spending five years in uniform. Three identical holdalls lay at their feet.

463

In contrast with Sean, Roger was taking deep breaths. 'Smell that air,' he said. 'You can almost eat it.'

'If you like eating cow shit.' Sean gestured to the fresh cow pats between the rails.

'I need a drink,' said Roger.

'You had enough at lunch-time,' said Hans-Peter.

'If there's no one here to meet us, we might as well stonk it to the village. There's bound to be a bar where we can get a beer and someone who can give us directions to where this Captain Duvalier lives.'

'We were told,' objected Sean, 'that we'd be met here at the station.'

'It wasn't an order, Irish. We're demobbed now. Civilians don't have to do exactly as they're told.'

'I say we wait,' said Hans-Peter.

'You krauts,' Roger mocked, 'always want orders. *Befehl ist Befehl und ohne Befehl bin ich nichts.*'

'Knock it off, Roger,' said Sean.

'I'm thirsty as hell.'

'You've got alcoholic dehydration,' was Sean's comment. 'That's what's wrong with you.'

Frank listened to the voices. This was not how he had planned to meet them: hiding and eavesdropping. Wrapped in a blanket inside the saddle-bag were four cans of cool beer for a welcome-to-St Martin drink. His mouth twisted. It wasn't going to be like that. He owed it to the three younger men he was going to take into the jungle not to get close, not to be too friendly, not to involve them with his jinx. Well, that wasn't difficult. He knew how to make men like him but he also knew a thousand ways to make them hate him.

'Stop squabbling,' said Hans-Peter. 'It's too hot.' He had shooed some cows away and claimed their shade under a tree.

'You two can wait if you want.' Roger draped his jacket over one shoulder, hefted his bag on to the other and started down the road. 'I'm off in search of an ice-cold beer.'

Sean looked at Hans-Peter, chewing a piece of grass as he lounged on his bag in the shade of the plane tree. Once out of uniform, he had reverted in a few hours to the languid manners of the hairdresser who had joined up five years before. It was as though he had packed away for the duration of the time in uniform all his natural gestures and was taking them out of a psychological closet to try them out again one by one and see if they still fitted.

Sean wondered whether he looked as odd in civilian clothes as he felt. Roger, striding down the road in open sandals with his bag slung over one shoulder, looked more like an artist in search of a scene to paint than a man who had been a professional soldier in one of the world's toughest armies only forty-eight hours previously.

'Roger! Come back and wait, you stupid bastard,' Sean shouted.

He watched his friend's figure getting smaller in the heat-haze, then carried his bag into the shade of the plane tree and dropped it alongside Hans-Peter's.

He squatted on it, making himself comfortable with his back against the tree and was asleep in minutes.

'Right, you two. On your feet!' barked Frank. He had ridden up quietly on the grass verge.

Hans-Peter and Sean opened their eyes to see Frank looming over them on horseback. He was dressed similarly to themselves in jeans and short-sleeved shirt, but the broad-brimmed cowboy hat struck a foreign note. Sean and Hans-Peter scrambled to their feet in a reflex induced by the tone of voice Frank had used.

'Names!'

'Hans-Peter Muller.'

'I'm Patrick O'Reilly.'

'And I'm Sergeant Hansen. Welcome to St Martin.'

As he shook hands with them perfunctorily, Frank's eyes behind the dark sunglasses were cold and unfriendly.

'Bags,' he grunted, straightening up in the saddle. 'Give me your bags. Unless you want to carry them in this heat.'

'There's no transport?' Sean asked, handing his bag up.

'For me, there is.' Frank lashed one bag behind the saddle and the other in front. He wheeled the horse round with a curt: 'Follow me, you guys. And keep up. If you get lost, I'm not coming back to look for you.'

He set off at a rapid trot along the dust-covered road.

'I think,' said Hans-Peter, 'that our friendly Sergeant Hansen means us to run after the horse.'

'Fucking cowboy!' Sean swore.

'A cross-country run in the afternoon heat,' he panted out of the corner of his mouth as they got into their stride. 'Just like old times with that bastard Grohmann. Remember him? We might as well have stayed in the mob.'

'Milton has gone on ahead, sergeant,' shouted Hans-Peter.

Frank raised a hand to show he had heard but did not slow up. He reined in the horse a mile down the road as he drew level with Roger sweating under the weight of a large holdall. Reflected in his sunglasses Frank could see Sean and Hans-Peter running at an easy pace along the road towards them.

'Am I glad to see you . . .' Roger wiped his brow, taking in the two bags tied on to the saddle.

He handed his to Frank who took it from him, swung it across the horse's back and dropped it deliberately into the roadside dust on the far side.

'You were told you'd be met at the station,' said Frank coldly.

'There wasn't anyone there.'

'You should have waited there, Milton.'

'Give me a break,' argued Roger. 'It's hot and I needed a drink.'

'You will.' Frank bared his teeth in a grin as Hans-Peter and Sean drew near. 'You can carry your own bag, Milton. I'd advise you to keep up with the other two. They're doing quite well so far. I told them I'm not coming back to look for stragglers.'

With a slight pressure of his heels he urged Carlo from a

466

walk to a canter. In the reflection on the sunglass lens he saw the two running men draw level with their comrade. One of them put out an arm and grabbed a handle of Roger's bag. The three running figures with the bag between them grew smaller as Frank pulled ahead.

Five hours later, Château St Martin's jeep was bumping up a track that led higher and higher into the Pyrenees. The weather had changed as they drove south and storm clouds were massed over the peaks with lightning forking in every direction.

'We're going up there?' queried Roger. He was sitting in the front passenger seat, map-reading. Sean and Hans-Peter were in the back, lying on a pile of kitbags and camping gear. Defying the noise of the storm and the motion of the vehicle, Sean was asleep.

'Just going for a little walk, to get to know each other,' Frank grunted. He stopped the jeep at the end of the track. As he switched off the headlights the scene was lit brilliantly by lightning. Almost instantaneously a crash of thunder echoed off the bare rocks all around and the downpour began.

The storm was still gusting to a hundred miles an hour on the peaks two days later as Frank led the three sodden, hard-pressed men down from a pass and back to where he had left the jeep. Three times they had sneaked their way along goat tracks past French and Spanish frontier guards, hiding in the storm. It was not exactly a rehearsal for a forced march through the jungle of Laos and Vietnam but it had been a useful test.

Lashed by wind and rain, it was hard to stand upright, harder still to keep open eyes that stung and ached with tiredness. At seven thousand feet above sea level, rain alternated with hail that lay thickly in a slippery, treacherous sheet on the bare rock underfoot.

By late afternoon, visibility was down to a few metres. It was dark and disorientating as only cloud on a mountain can be. Every instinct in Frank's mind urged him to find some boulder or overhang and bivouac early, to let the worst of the storm blow itself out. The pain from the ribs he had bruised in a fall as they came over the last pass, made breathing difficult.

They had just picked their way along the side of a precipice where wind-rent breaks in the cloud had shown a sheer drop to a foaming torrent hundreds of feet below. As they un-roped, Frank felt a tap on his shoulder and turned to see Roger shouting.

Frank pulled the parka hood away from one ear and caught the words: 'Stop ... fucking stupid, Hansen.' The rest of the sentence was torn away in the gale. The dark shapes of the other two men were just discernible behind Roger in the swirling mists.

Frank shook his head and gave the infantry signal for *follow me*. He peeled back a sodden cuff and stabbed a finger at his watch to make the point, then pulled the cuff down and turned to follow the boulder-strewn path which, according to his reckoning, would lead them off the mountain.

The moment's inattention nearly cost his life. A sodden piece of turf gave way beneath his feet without warning. He felt a push on one shoulder and crashed to the ground, where he slid helplessly on his back down the loose scree and towards the edge of the precipice.

Frank felt his feet go over the edge and hang in space. The whole slope was moving, lubricated by the rain. His legs scrabbled for purchase but found only thin air. Desperately he twisted round and clawed for a hand-hold. Broken nails slipped on smooth rock and loose shale but the downward progress continued. Then, with a wrench that nearly tore his shoulder from the socket, his scrabbling fingers caught hold of a projecting knob of solid rock and held tight. The writhing, sliding downward progress stopped.

Above him in the swirling mist he saw the other three men standing still, waiting. Frank groaned with the effort and pulled himself up inch by inch until his legs were no longer hanging in space. Cautiously he inched his way up the loose and shifting slope until he could stand.

He looked from Hans-Peter to Roger. The push he had felt must have come from one of them; Sean was last man and had still been coiling the rope.

Frank shoved his face close to Hans-Peter's and shouted above the noise of the wind: 'You fucking pushed me!'

Roger pulled Frank away. He seemed to have a grin on his face, but, shaded by the hood of the parka, it was hard for Frank to be certain.

'It was me,' he shouted. 'I tried to save you, Hansen.'

Frank looked at the other two men. Their faces were blank and gave him no clues.

Frank gestured with his torn and bleeding fingers to the edge of the precipice. 'You didn't try very hard when I was clinging on there by the skin of my teeth.'

'If I'd come down after you,' shouted Roger, 'I'd have started a landslide and we'd both have gone over the edge.'

14

I t was dawn when they arrived back in St Martin. Frank
dropped the three men at the primitive row of huts he
shared with Marie's North African labourers and gave
them orders to make themselves comfortable. From there
he drove straight to the tower.

It was snug in the first-floor office where Raoul was
already at work on his clients' accounts. He put aside the
sheets of paper and poured Frank a cup of the strong black
coffee he was drinking. A large fire was burning in the huge
medieval hearth.

Frank slumped into a chair beside the fire, hands clasped
around the hot mug. A stab of pain from his crushed ribs
made him sit up straight. His eyes were red from lack of
sleep, his face sore from exposure. His chin bore several
days' stubble and he had lost ten pounds in weight.

'Pour some brandy into your coffee,' Raoul suggested.
'You look as though you could do with it.'

Frank shook his head – the warmth was making him
drowsy enough without any alcohol – then changed his mind
and filled a glass with brandy, which he swallowed in one
gulp.

'I won't stay,' he said. 'I've dropped our three recruits off
at my billet.'

'Supposing people ask what they're doing there?'

'I've told them to say they are extra hands we're taking on for some building work up here at the tower.'

'How did they make out in the mountains?' Raoul asked. 'Was it really necessary to give them an endurance test, after they've just finished five years in the Legion's paras?'

'I wanted to shake them down, see how we got on together.' There was a wry expression on Frank's face. 'Those boys are tough and fighting fit.'

'We knew that much already.' Raoul studied Frank. He could tell there was something on his mind.

'It was a good way to get to know them,' said Frank doggedly. 'The Irishman shot us a couple of rabbits during lulls in the storm. He's one of those natural marksmen who doesn't have to aim. Like an old-time Western hero, he just grabs his gun and the target drops dead. It impressed me, I tell you.'

'And the others?'

'Milton is tough and strong. He has a nose for direction, didn't lose his way for a minute, even in zero visibility. He's also a good cook. Made us real meals with a couple of heat tablets under a dripping poncho in a Force Nine gale. A good man to have around.'

'Did you get on all right together?'

'Milton and I had a little tussle the first day, to see who was in charge. After that it was fine.'

'And Muller? You haven't mentioned him.'

'I still want to get rid of the kraut.'

'You just don't like him, do you?'

'He doesn't have what the other two have got,' Frank rationalised. 'They go easy on him, which means he reduces the speed of the team as a whole. That could be critical on the way out of Vietnam.'

Raoul thought about it. 'You're sure about this?'

Frank stood up. He winced from the pain in his ribs. 'I'll tell Muller we don't want him.'

'I'm the CO of this operation.' Raoul thought it time to remind him. 'You get some sleep, Frank. That's an order. And leave this to me.'

'No.' Frank sat down again. 'There's something else I've got to tell you, Raoul.'

I listened with incredulity to Frank's account of the near-fatal accident on the edge of the precipice.

'You're sure you were pushed?' I asked.

'I'm not making it up!' He was angry at me for suggesting it.

'I didn't say you were. But you think Muller deliberately pushed you?'

'Somebody did. I'm 99 per cent sure it was him.'

'So why would Milton say it was him you felt, trying to save you?'

'They've been a threesome for five years,' Frank growled. 'They stick together like glue. And Milton knows I'd take the kraut to pieces if I could prove my suspicions.'

When he had gone, I stared at the sheets of figures on my desk. I knew Frank was not paranoid, nor a man who exaggerated. If he said one of those men had tried to kill him, it was probably true. But what reason would they have? As yet they did not know anything about the true reason for their recruitment, so it was nothing to do with that. Pure mischief? Or to teach Frank not to hustle them? It was possible. . . .

I suspected – but it was only a suspicion – that Frank had been victimising Muller, who had tried to get his own back. But if that was the case, why had Milton intervened?

Looking back, that was the first moment when suspicion entered my mind. Until then I had assumed that we were all Boy Scouts, bound by a code of honour. From that moment, I kept a certain mental distance from Muller and Milton.

Now, seeking a traitor who could have led the masked raiders into my well protected tower, I would put Muller and Milton on the top of the list. Especially Muller, who installed the alarm system. Who better than him to brief the raiders on how to bypass it?

I should have listened to Frank that day. . . .

'That bastard Hansen,' said Hans-Peter sullenly. 'He's got it in for me.'

He sat on one of the camp beds that Frank had installed in the barrack, staring at the wall. Large patches of damp showed through the limewash and there was a puddle on the floor where Frank had been standing.

'I think you're right,' Roger agreed. 'But don't you do a thing, kraut. It's not up to Hansen to sack you. He's not in charge. I'll go up to the tower and talk to Captain Duvalier. Hansen thinks he's God, but it's the captain who's the boss.'

'He'll side with the Yank,' Hans-Peter prophesied gloomily. 'Officers always back up their NCOs.'

Roger hit him hard on the shoulder, knocking him full-length on the bed.

'Either Captain Duvalier hires all three of us,' he said angrily, 'or we piss off and he can shove whatever crazy operation he has dreamed up right up his arse.'

He turned to Sean. 'Is that right, Irish?'

'Agreed,' said Sean. He punched Hans-Peter in the belly hard enough to make him grunt. '*On se calme, le schleu.* Don't get wound up, kraut. Leave this to Roger and me.'

As the two of them left, Roger stuck his head back through the open doorway.

'Don't be in any hurry to pack your things,' he warned Hans-Peter. 'If you leave, we all leave.'

Hans-Peter brooded for half an hour before deciding to sort things out his own way. Since the incident with Cecchi, five years before, he had never backed down from aggression and did not intend to start now. The rain was easing off as he walked towards the château and found Frank in the yard underneath a tractor. There was nobody else about.

'Hansen!'

Frank grunted with the effort of forcing the spanner on the rusted sump nut of the ancient Renault tractor. He recognised the voice. All he could see of Hans-Peter was a pair of legs below the knees.

'Yeah?' he asked, tightening the spanner on the next nut.

'You're wasting your time.'

Hans-Peter squatted on his heels and twisted his neck to see the beads of oil oozing out of the sump. He ran a finger along the joint. 'The gasket's kaput. If you go on tightening those nuts, all you'll achieve is to strip the threads off the bolts.'

'When I want your opinion,' grunted Frank, wiping sweat from his brow with the back of a wrist, 'I'll ask for it.'

'You want a kick in the balls,' said Hans-Peter coolly. 'Are you asking for that too?'

Frank rolled out from under the tractor and levered himself up on one elbow. His face was inches from Hans-Peter's. 'Are you looking for trouble?' he asked.

Hans-Peter stood slowly and backed off to put a couple of feet between himself and Frank. 'You've been pushing me since I arrived here,' he said. 'Why, Hansen? What have you got against me?'

When Frank did not reply, he taunted, 'Frank the Yank. You're an old man. Why don't you pick someone your own age?'

'Go fuck yourself! I'm busy.'

Hans-Peter's foot lashed out without warning, aimed at Frank's testicles. A reflex body roll deflected the main force of the blow on to Frank's right thigh. A stab of pain shot up his leg from toe to hip.

'You stupid gay bastard,' he snarled.

Hans-Peter was standing, hands on hips, two paces away, waiting for Frank to get up and come at him. Instead, Frank pivoted ninety degrees and scissored his legs in the same movement, sweeping Hans-Peter off his feet. He broke his fall with one arm and had both hands clawing for Frank's eyes as the two men closed, each seeking an advantage.

They rolled, locked together, into the pool of oil underneath the tractor. Momentarily on top, with one of Hans-Peter's arms trapped behind his back, Frank scooped a handful of oil and earth, intending to rub it into Hans-Peter's eyes and blind him.

A jerk of the head beneath him and the filth smeared Hans-Peter's blond hair instead. His teeth closed on Frank's wrist and his free hand drove for Frank's eyes again and again.

As Frank jerked his head out of reach, he was aware of a semi circle of brown faces watching in silence. As usual, the *maghrebins* had appeared out of nowhere, the moment something was happening.

The German, he realised too late, was deceptive. Slow-moving and soft-spoken but well trained in unarmed combat, he knew all the dirty tricks there were.

As if to prove it, Hans-Peter slipped from underneath and ended behind him with a throat lock crushing Frank's larynx. His legs clamped around Frank's bruised ribs. A strangled groan escaped between Frank's clenched teeth.

Frank's only advantage as they rolled in the muck was his body weight; being a couple of stone heavier gave him more leverage. Deprived of his advantage by the throat lock, he blocked the pain in his chest and clawed at Hans-Peter's arm, then went suddenly limp. Hans-Peter's grip relaxed fractionally. Frank contorted his body in a spasm that slammed his head back into Hans-Peter's face, smashing the back of the other man's skull against the metal wheel of the tractor.

Being watched by the labourers made Frank coldly determined to finish the fight quickly, in order to keep his authority over them. He exerted all his strength to wrest an advantage as the throat lock weakened, and ended by having Hans-Peter pinned flat on the ground underneath him. The hold was too brief to have counted for points in a wrestling ring but enabled him momentarily to disengage one leg and knee Hans-Peter savagely several times in the groin.

Frank swung himself clear of the groaning man beneath him, heaved himself up on all fours and hung there, gasping to get his breath back. The pain in his ribs nearly made him pass out.

He pulled himself up by holding on to the tractor wheel. The circle of labourers started to clap.

'Bravo, Farrank,' one said.

The others started moving forward to threaten the still prone Hans-Peter, until Frank waved them back.

'Leave him,' he said thickly. 'If the *schleu* still needs teaching a lesson, I'll do it for myself.'

'The three of us are a team,' said Roger. He banged his fist on the oaken table, dislodging a pile of account books which fell to the floor beside Raoul's wheelchair.

'Don't raise your voice to me, corporal,' said Raoul coldly.

'I'm sorry, captain,' Roger apologised and bent to pick up the books. 'But we stuck together throughout our time in the Legion and we like it that way. Without Hans-Peter we don't want your job, whatever it is.'

'If you turn this down, you could be saying goodbye to a lot of money,' said Raoul calmly.

'It's better than saying goodbye to a friend.' Roger straightened up.

Very noble, thought Raoul. He looked at Sean, who had stayed silent so far. His face showed no emotion. 'What about you?'

'I go along with Roger.'

Raoul pursed his lips. 'Three musketeers? One for all and all for one.'

'That's the way it is,' agreed Roger.

'I respect loyalty,' said Raoul. 'But Sergeant Hansen says Muller's not as tough as you two. According to him, Muller holds you back – not a lot, but it could be critical, where you're going.'

'Come on,' Sean nudged Roger in the ribs. 'We're wasting our time.'

'With respect, Captain Duvalier,' said Roger. 'It wouldn't be the same without Hans-Peter. I'm sorry.'

His instinctive salute was transformed halfway into a gesture of take-it-or-leave-it.

'You've made us a problem, Frank,' Raoul sighed.

He blamed himself for letting it happen, for his chessboard mentality which assumed that all the pieces would want to move where it suited him.

'You've put yourself on the line by saying you won't take

Muller.' He was watching Frank's reactions carefully. 'Now the other two are calling your bluff by saying they won't go without him. How do we get out of this?'

'We could tell Milton and the Irishman what the job is,' suggested Frank. 'They'd be crazy to turn it down, once they know what's involved.'

'For security reasons, that's out of the question,' said Raoul shortly. 'And you know it.'

'On an operation like this is going to be,' argued Frank, 'I've got to pick my own team, Raoul. I don't want any passengers.' He gestured for emphasis.

Raoul noticed the skinned knuckles. 'You've been in a fight?'

'Spanner slipped when I was tightening a nut,' lied Frank.

'And what's so special about these three guys?' he asked. 'They're tough and well trained, but there are plenty of others where they came from.'

'Two things,' said Raoul. 'First, the timing. The Americans have virtually left Vietnam, in accordance with the Paris Peace Agreement, while Hanoi is systematically breaking every condition of that agreement.'

'So?'

'If Ho and Giap were playing for a lot of time, they'd observe some of the conditions of the treaty,' said Raoul.

He stretched a hand in the direction of the wall maps. 'It wouldn't hurt them, you can see that. The fact that they don't even bother to pretend the war's over tells me that they are preparing the final offensive on the South. We have to get quietly into Dien Bien Phu and out again while Hanoi is concentrating all its efforts on the war in the South, so now is the time. We haven't got long.'

Frank stayed sullenly silent.

Raoul enunciated each word separately. 'Secondly, I want these particular three men because of what happens afterwards.'

Frank looked blank.

'I've given a lot of thought to afterwards,' continued Raoul. 'Once we've got the gold, we run the same risk as a band of criminals after a successful robbery. A lot of people would like to get their hands on the gold of Dien Bien Phu.'

'And we won't have the law to protect us.'

'Right. So we can't afford to hire anyone who causes problems afterwards. Are you with me?'

'So far.'

'Now,' Raoul continued patiently, 'most ex-legionnaires are the sort of men who look for excitement, you know that as well as I do. They get drunk and talk to impress people they meet in bars. They get into fights. They crash cars. They spend too much or too fast, which always attracts the wrong kind of attention. They pick the wrong sort of women – the sort who'll give them away for revenge.'

'You've lost me.' Frank was tired. He had snatched two hours' sleep before answering Marie's call for help with the tractor, and was feeling all the sleep he had missed during the trip to the mountains. The fight with Hans-Peter had taken more out of him than it should have.

'These three are different,' Raoul continued. 'One: they want to stick together. Two – and this is rare in men of their age, especially rare among ex-legionnaires – a quiet life in St Martin would suit them down to the ground, collectively speaking.'

'How can you know that?'

'The Irishman,' said Raoul cryptically. 'He's the key. What do you make of him?'

'A mean little bastard,' grunted Frank.

'Exactly,' Raoul smiled. 'Yet he only stepped out of line once in his five years with the Legion. Now, I don't know if that means anything to you, but I recall my first CO telling me when I was a fledgling second lieutenant that mean little bastards who behave exceptionally well are usually in the Legion to lie low.'

'And?'

'In his *deuxième bureau* file I found a note that our Irish friend corresponds remarkably closely with the physical description in an Interpol notice for murder which originated in Belfast, Northern Ireland. The suspect's name – I made a note of it – was Sean Carey.'

'He says he's Patrick O'Reilly from Dublin.'

Raoul laughed.

'The Legion wouldn't protect a man from a count of murder,' observed Frank.

'*En principe*, you're right.' Raoul's thin smile was still in place. 'However, reading between the lines, the Irishman had already proven himself to be one of the best snipers the Legion has ever known *before* the Interpol notice caught up with him. Nobody wanted to lose the marksman who could outshoot the Army and the other services in inter-service competitions, so an umbrella was put up to make our Irish friend invisible.'

'I know the system,' Frank yawned. 'On my first tour in Vietnam, I was with a Spec Four who had a golf handicap of three. When the colonel found out, the Spec Four was made up to sergeant and spent the whole year playing golf in Japan. Never saw so much as an M 16 or heard an incoming round.'

Raoul nodded thoughtfully; all armies were the same in some respects. 'I think we need another talk with Mr Carey/ O'Reilly,' he said.

15

The three men sitting on camp beds in Frank's barrack stopped talking and glared sullenly at him. They were drinking coffee Hans-Peter had made on the small camping gas burner in one corner but no one offered him any.

Frank pointed a finger at Sean.

'You, Irish,' he said. 'The captain wants to see you.'

They made the journey across the river to the tower without speaking. Even standing close in the small lift which was just big enough for a wheelchair, the two men stayed silent.

Sean stepped into the office on the first floor of the tower and stood warily in front of Raoul, who studied him closely for several minutes. Sean returned the stare, aware of Frank standing behind him, lounging against the lift door.

'Name?' asked Raoul.

'Patrick O'Reilly.'

'Name?' Raoul repeated.

'I told you.'

'We'd like you to tell us your real name,' said Frank flatly.

Sean did not turn round. 'Paddy O'Reilly was good enough for the Legion.' He stared at Raoul without blinking.

'Your name is Sean Carey and you're from Belfast, not Dublin.' Raoul spoke softly.

'Who says I am?'

'A lot of people,' said Raoul. 'Like Interpol. I'll ask you again: what's your real name?'

Sean took his time, weighing up the odds, then: 'Sean Carey. I'm from Belfast.'

'You were on the run,' said Raoul. 'That's why you joined the Legion.'

It was a relief to say it. 'That's correct, captain.'

'There was – probably still is – an Interpol notice that you killed a man.'

'I killed several.' It was not a boast, just a statement.

'For what reasons?'

'I was ordered.'

Raoul exchanged a look with Frank. 'Right, Carey. You can go.'

Sean stood his ground. 'What are you going to do about it?'

'Nothing.' Raoul looked from Sean to Frank standing by the door, arms crossed over his chest. 'Apart from Sergeant Hansen and Captain Koenig, nobody will learn from me. I promise you that, Carey.'

'And if I don't believe you?'

'Then you keep running all your life. But if you accept my word, go and get Milton and Muller. Tell them they've got the job.'

Sean had half turned away before he took in what he had heard. A grin of pleasure creased his ugly face.

Frank's voice was that of the orderly room sergeant. 'Dismiss, Carey. On your way.'

The look Sean gave him as he went past said: Up yours, Yank.

Frank was watching from the window as Sean left the tower and walked down the road to the village.

'Now,' said Raoul. 'Do you see why the Irishman is the key?'

Frank was tired. 'No guessing games,' he said. 'You tell me.'

'For a man on the run –' Raoul was feeling expansive; the chessmen were moving to their appointed squares – 'a dozy little place like St Martin is the ideal place to hide. With his Legion discharge papers we'll get him French citizenship and he's free to start life again. His old record will never catch up with him here.'

'And why will the other two want to stick around?'

'They're comrades,' said Raoul. 'Like the three musketeers, one for all and all for one.'

'If you say so.'

'I'm Sean Carey from Belfast.'

He stood on the bridge over the Dordogne, talking to the river. Raoul had been the first person to use his true name since he had said goodbye years before to Father Callaghan in the waiting room for the Liverpool ferry. It seemed a lifetime ago.

'I'm Sean Carey from Belfast,' he repeated.

He tossed a symbolic pebble into the vortex of water where the river swirled around the old stone pier beneath him. 'And you I bequeath to the deep, Patrick O'Reilly, whoever you are.'

Over the years Sean had known nightmares in which various people – the SAS sergeant he had met at Munich was one – threatened to disclose his real identity. In the dreams he had been dragged by faceless men back to scenes of his childhood, back to the places and the horrors that had made him what he was. In the dreams his father and uncle had been there gloating. Their drunken, sweaty faces had closed in on him, as large as they had been when he was a child. He had awoken screaming.

Yet he felt no fear that the two men in the tower would betray him. The captain, he thought, was still a Legion officer, despite being crippled and in a wheelchair. And Hansen, although flint-hard, was ex-Legion too. . . .

Sean recalled the time when he was in prison for attacking Cecchi. An Italian legionnaire had been thrown into his cell on a charge of absence without leave.

'How did they catch you in Italy?' Sean had asked. He was still planning to desert.

'They didn't,' was the reply. 'I was home with my family. I chose to come back.'

'Knowing you'd be chucked in the *gnouf*? You must be crazy.'

The Italian had smiled ruefully at himself. 'Perhaps, Irish, I came back because the Legion is the only place nobody ever lied to me.'

Sean skimmed a stone into the sunset. It bounced four times before sinking. It was time, he thought, to tell Roger and Hans-Peter his true identity. He looked up and saw Marie-France on the towpath, riding her chestnut horse at a slow walk. She waved and Sean gave a grudging wave in reply.

From his vantage point in the tower Frank was uneasy. Marie-France's daily rides were usually exuberant outbursts of energy for both horse and rider. He wondered whether she had been following the Irishman, and realised that they would have to tell her something soon.

It was a parade. No one shouted orders, stamped their feet or stood at attention, but it was a parade, all the same.

The sun was going down and the houses in the village were lost in the shadow of the bluff, giving an effect of total isolation to the five men on the flat roof of the tower.

Roger, Hans-Peter and Sean made a loose line facing Raoul. They stood at ease by habit, not because anyone had told them to. Frank stood at right angles to them, his back against one of the battlements, hands hooked in his belt loops, waiting. He was chewing gum, an old habit he had taken up again.

As the sun sank below the horizon, Raoul turned the wheelchair to face the line of men.

'You've made your point,' he said. 'You're a team and you want to stay together. Sergeant Hansen and I respect that. We're taking you as a team.'

'I told you.' Sean cuffed Roger's ear. 'You did it, you bastard.'

Roger ducked the blow and looked pleased.

'See?' he said to Hans-Peter.

*

I noticed the bruising round the German's eye and a livid graze on his temple. A spanner slipped, indeed!

For a second I wondered what he and Frank had been fighting about. But it was none of my business. Frank had to show those three men that he was as tough as they were in order to impose his authority on them. With no stripes on his sleeve, how he did it was up to him.

Then the dream took over. The years dropped away and in my imagination, I was standing again on a hilltop known only by a number which represented its height in metres above sea level. Below were the smouldering remains of a convoy which had been ambushed by the Viets on Route Coloniale Quatre. The new lieutenant's bars were shining on my collar. I was surrounded by seasoned fighting men whom I was about to lead into combat. It was my first command.

I looked at Frank and the others standing there waiting for my orders and felt what I had thought never to know again: the feeling of being in command of a group of fighting men, my Legion of St Martin.

Even the knowledge that I was stuck in a wheelchair and would not be going on the mission with them could not spoil the pleasure of that moment.

'Tomorrow . . .' Raoul came back to earth. 'Tomorrow you'll get a full briefing. For now, you'll find there's 500 francs apiece in the envelopes Sergeant Hansen is about to give you. Go into Bergerac. That's the nearest town. Buy yourselves a good meal, get drunk, or celebrate however you like. But keep your mouths shut. If anyone asks, you're here to build a wine cellar underneath my tower.'

Roger and Sean took their envelopes and shook hands with Frank. Hans-Peter was last.

Frank handed him the envelope. 'If you're looking for trouble, Muller,' he said neutrally, 'I'll give it to you. But if you pull your weight, we'll get on fine.'

He stuck out a hand which Hans-Peter shook warily.

*

Frank walked into his barrack naked to the waist, his work jeans held up by a thick leather belt with a heavy cowboy buckle. His face and hair were dripping wet from showering himself in cold water with a garden hose to chase the tiredness away.

Sitting on his bed was Marie-France.

Frank groped for a towel. 'Hi, what are you doing here?'

'I own this place,' she said frigidly. 'I don't have to explain myself.'

He grunted. 'I walked right into that one.'

She watched him dry himself. 'You've got scratches on your face and your ribs are all bruised, Frank.'

He touched himself gingerly. 'I know. They hurt like hell.'

'And look at your hands. They're torn to pieces. Have you been in a fight?'

'Horse threw me,' he lied. 'It was my fault.'

'When?' she asked. 'You haven't been out riding for days.'

He dropped the towel, kicked the door to behind him and made to embrace her. 'I've missed you.'

She avoided him. 'Where have you been, Frank? I've hardly seen you for days.'

'I've been sorting something out for Raoul.'

'And who are the three men you've got staying here?' Marie-France pointed to the clothing strewn over the camp beds. 'They're telling people they've come to build a wine cellar for Raoul.'

'That's right.'

'Don't lie to me.' She sounded angry. 'There are plenty of builders to do that sort of job and those three don't look like labourers.'

'What do they look like?' He was trying to work out what to tell her. Raoul had said grandly, 'Fob her off with some story.'

Marie-France was not in the mood to be distracted. 'Soldiers,' she said curtly.

485

'Not surprising.' Frank decided to stay as close to the truth as possible. 'They've just been demobbed from the Legion and need a job.'

'They're something to do . . .' She was guessing. 'Something to do with your mystery trip to Corsica with Raoul and his one-eyed friend.'

'Raoul –' Frank talked through a T-shirt he was pulling on to cover the bruises – 'belongs to some old comrade association that finds work for men who've finished their time in the Legion. You know, to help them settle into something honest and not take a wrong path and end up as mercenaries, that sort of thing.'

Marie-France touched the bruises on his face. 'Am I going to see you tonight?'

Frank lifted her chin and smoothed the dark hair back from her face. 'No,' he said.

Too proud to ask why not, she pulled away.

'Because you're going to see me right now,' he said, as lust chased the fatigue away and his lips found hers.

She heard the squeak of metal as he undid the buckle of his belt, then the sound of his zip.

When she broke free from his powerful grip, she was panting. 'You can't stop my questions as easily as that, Frank.'

He grinned, loving her anger. 'No, but I can sure as hell delay them a bit.'

He felt the letter in the hip pocket of her jeans. 'What's this? A billet-doux from a boyfriend?'

'Oh, I forgot. It's for you. An airmail letter from Vietnam.'

A shutter came down behind his eyes.

'What's the matter?' she asked.

'Give it to me.'

'OK.' Disturbed by his change of mood, she pulled it out of her pocket. 'It's a man's handwriting, very old-fashioned.'

'I know who it's from,' he said harshly, taking it from her.

486

'Frank! Where are you going?'

'Leave me alone, will you?' He pushed past her like a stranger.

Puzzled and hurt, she stood in the doorway watching him go.

16

That evening I received two telephone calls from Marie-France, asking whether Frank was with me.

I was too busy with my planning for the next day's briefing to do more than wonder why he had gone missing. It was 3 a.m. when he turned up on my doorstep looking haggard and – I had to admit it to myself – mad.

'Blossom,' he said.

I asked him twice to repeat it before I understood. He wasn't able to talk coherently, but thrust at me a letter which had been crumpled up and smoothed out several times.

Monsieur (the letter began)
J'ai le triste devoir de vous informer . . .

The language was stilted and formal, like an official communication. Phuong's father was a mandarin to the end, concealing emotion behind politeness and formality.

. . . my daughter is dead. She was on a visit to relatives in Hué when the bus on which she was travelling was stopped by armed men. It is not known to which side they belonged, nor does it matter for we cannot avoid our destiny. All the passengers were killed. My son, with whom I have contact sometimes, tells me that it was not done by his people. I have

waited several weeks before writing to you, in the hope there
was a mistake of identification . . .

'You see?' Frank was staring at me red-eyed as I finished reading.
'I never told Phuong that I loved her, but the jinx knew all the
same.'

'Don't talk like this.' I grabbed his arm. 'In Vietnam people
are dying all the time, Frank. What about the other passengers
on the bus? Are you going to blame yourself for their deaths too?'

'Just hers,' he said thickly. 'That's enough.'

We talked for hours. I wanted to help him but selfishly I was
worried that Frank would want me to call off or at least postpone
the mission, feeling the way he did.

To my great relief he said just before dawn, 'Let's get on with
it, Raoul. Perhaps with all this –' he waved at the maps all
round us – 'I can fill my head with details and stop thinking.'

'Are you sure?' I asked.

'There's no point running away.' He seemed quite clear, as
though he had made a decision while we talked. 'I have a rendezvous with death. Koenig was right. But it'll happen when it
happens. There's nothing I can do.'

I should have postponed the operation but I was frightened that
time was running out on us. That very day Koenig had flown to
Vientiane, the Laotian capital and started the countdown. And I
suppose a part of me thought that the best thing for Frank was to
be occupied, not brooding. Or was that just the way I justified
things to myself?

Frank led the three men the long way round to the tower.
It avoided walking through the village.

The old towpath under the cliff was overgrown and little
used. It was half a century since horses had pulled the wine
barges upstream against the Dordogne currents.

Roger, nursing a monumental hangover behind dark
glasses, was walking alongside Frank. The others were a few
paces behind.

'You could give us a hint what the mission is about,

sergeant,' suggested Roger. 'We're going to find out in a few minutes anyway. So why not?'

'OK.' Frank's voice held no emotion. If anything he seemed bored. 'Listen up.'

He stopped by the rotting hulk of an old wine barge abandoned long since. Most of the planking had gone, only the oak structure surviving. He heaved himself on to what was left of the decking.

'I'll give you two hints,' he said. 'First, this is a clandestine mission, so we use no ranks. It's Roger, Sean and Hans-Peter from now on. And forget I was a sergeant. Call me Frank.'

'And the captain?' asked Sean.

'Call him Raoul.'

'And the officer with one eye?'

'Call him Koenig. He doesn't have a first name.'

The three men exchanged glances. The idea of a clandestine mission excited them.

'What's the other hint, sarge . . . Frank?' asked Roger.

'How do you three guys fancy being very rich?' His voice was so deadpan that it took them a moment to absorb his meaning.

'How rich?' asked Hans-Peter quietly.

'Difficult to say exactly,' Frank shrugged. 'Probably as much money as you'll ever need.'

'All from this one job?' Sean wondered. The idea of being rich had never occurred to him as a practical possibility until that moment.

'That's right. From one job.'

'We're going to raid a bank?' from Sean.

He spoke at the same time as Roger said, 'It must be dangerous, if the pay's so good.'

'Wrong,' Frank told Sean.

'Right,' he said to Roger. 'Operation Gold is the recovery of *une caisse noire*. Do you guys know what that is?'

'A treasure chest?' from Roger.

'The pay-chest of a whole fucking colonial army that had to be abandoned in a battle we lost two decades ago.' Frank watched their eager faces. 'It's a pay-chest packed with gold coins.'

'Where is it?' asked Roger.

'The captain . . . Raoul will tell you that.'

'How does he know?' Sean asked.

'He's the officer who was in charge of it during the battle.'

'I was right.' Roger punched Hans-Peter's arm in excitement. 'Vietnam. I guessed that Captain Duvalier had been a prisoner of war.'

He turned to Frank. 'Dien Bien Phu. Yes?'

'You're fast,' Frank admitted grudgingly.

Hans-Peter grabbed Roger and danced a polka on the grass.

Frank slipped to the ground. 'Come on,' he said to Sean. 'If you can stop those two girls dancing, we'll be on our way. Raoul doesn't like to be kept waiting.'

'Miserable bastard,' muttered Sean to the others. 'What's on his mind?'

Balance sheets, trading accounts and tax correspondence had been relegated to filing cabinets. Raoul's office was a command post, the walls papered with maps, the huge desk covered in photographs, diagrams and schedules.

He looked at Frank as the men filed into the office. Frank nodded good morning, apparently in control of himself. The faces of the three younger men betrayed their excitement.

'It looks as if Frank has given you some idea what Operation Gold is all about,' Raoul began.

'Gold,' said Roger.

'How can we be certain it's still there,' asked Hans-Peter, 'after twenty years?'

'Nineteen years,' Raoul corrected him. 'And it is still there because only Frank and I know exactly where it is.'

He spoke with an assurance that was feigned. There was always the chance of a peasant stumbling on the pay-chest by chance as he hoed his field, or an animal digging a burrow and turning up golden coins. Treasures hidden centuries before were often discovered by purest accident.

Three hours later, the office transformed into operations room was thick with cigarette smoke. Both Roger and Hans-Peter were heavy smokers. Between them, they had got through a packet of Gauloises during the briefing. Sean sat near an open window. Frank was chewing gum.

'To summarise,' Raoul wound up, 'Operation Gold is a lightning raid inside North Vietnam. Make no mistake, speed is our main weapon. We can't fight our way in and out. So hopefully we can do both trips without firing a single shot. Since Dien Bien Phu is only ten miles inside the border, the amount of time you'll spend on Vietnamese soil is a matter of hours only, if all goes well.'

'There's a war going on over there,' interrupted Sean, from the window. 'How can you be so sure we can just sneak in and out without half an army falling on our backs?'

'The fighting is a thousand miles away, in the South,' Raoul spoke with authority. 'There's no action on the border with Laos. The area you'll be going through has no strategic importance to either side in this current war, so Hanoi has milked all available strength away.'

'There are some border defences,' Frank said, 'but the jungle is the main obstacle.'

Raoul wheeled himself from the wall map of Vietnam, past a smaller-scale map of Indo-China to the large-scale military map covering the area around Dien Bien Phu. His pointer tapped the outline on the map where the French camp had been.

'Several hundred French and Legion troops got away after the surrender but almost all of those gave up trying to fight their way through the jungle and turned themselves in to the Viets, rather than starve to death.'

The news sobered them.

'It's not impenetrable, though. My friend Koenig was one of the ones who got away. And last year Frank and Koenig went back to Dien Bien Phu to check that the operation on the ground is feasible.'

The pointer moved along the road leading into Laos. 'Here, where the military road crosses the border, there's a

492

detachment of NVA. Maybe a dozen men. It's augmented from time to time for reasons that are not clear. Usually it's not much more than an armed customs post.'

'In our case,' Frank cut in, 'we won't be using the road. We're going in and out cross-country.'

'But here –' the pointer tapped the map again – 'at Dien Bien Phu itself, there are about 200 infantry in what appears to be a training camp.' He picked off the desk the enlargement of a photograph Frank had taken through a telephoto lens. The three intent faces pored over it.

'That camp,' said Raoul, 'is only a couple of miles from where you'll be recovering the gold. Although the recruits probably don't amount to much, their instructors will be battle-hardened veterans.'

Sean licked his lips. The idea of nicking the gold from under the Viets' noses added spice for him.

'How are they armed?' Roger wanted to know.

'Automatic rifles,' said Frank. 'Chinese AK 47s, captured M 16s. They also have heavy and light machine-guns, and some light mortars.'

As a further note of caution, he pointed to the radio mast on the photograph. 'They can also call up reinforcements and aircraft if need be.'

'What about the Ho Chi Minh trail?' asked Hans-Peter. 'I've heard that's pretty heavily defended by the North Vietnamese even though it's on Laotian territory. Won't we have to cross that?'

'It's a long way further south.' Raoul gestured to the map of the whole country and Frank indicated with a forefinger where the trail crossed from North Vietnam on to Laotian soil just above the demilitarised zone in central Vietnam.

Roger raised a hand. 'The way you've described it, the three of us are essentially to be Frank's bodyguard.'

'That's correct.'

'All the arrangements for the native guides and porters we'll need, he makes.'

'Frank speaks the languages.'

Roger looked from Raoul to Frank and back again. 'But

none of us three will actually know where we're going. If anything happens to Frank, what then?'

Raoul wondered which of them had tried to push Frank over the precipice. 'Just make sure nothing happens to Frank.'

Sean had a question. 'We also don't know a thing about the arrangements to get us out of Vietnam and back home after the recovery operation.'

'That's right,' said Raoul. 'Only Frank and Koenig know what those arrangements are.' He raised an eyebrow at Frank.

'If something should happen to him,' said Sean, 'how do we get home?'

'Each man gets a money belt,' answered Raoul. 'Sewn into it will be enough dollar notes to buy an airline ticket back to Europe. If you can make it to an airport, that is. I hope it doesn't come to that.'

There was silence.

'Well,' ended Raoul. 'If there are no more questions, gentlemen, I propose that we adjourn for lunch.'

The men stood and stretched. Raoul quietened their exuberant chatter with a clap of his hands. 'Frank tells me that my diet is not quite adequate for healthy young men like you. Upstairs on my roof you will find wine and an assortment of charcuterie and cheeses which I hope are to your liking. Eat and drink as much as you like . . .'

'. . . for tomorrow we die,' finished Hans-Peter.

Catching Frank's glare, he added, 'That's a joke.'

The meal was noisy, the three young men plying Raoul with questions. He caught their infectious enthusiasm. Only Frank was withdrawn and silent.

It was Sean who named the operation. 'We can hardly go around talking to each other about Operation Gold. It's a bit obvious, if anyone overhears, don't you think? Why don't we call it just Rainbow?'

'*Arc en ciel?*' Raoul queried.

'Why rainbow?' Frank echoed in English.

'Because back home,' drawled Sean, 'they say there's a crock of gold at the end of every rainbow.'

'It's a good name.' Raoul was thinking ahead: 'Rainbow Productions.' He handed Frank the tray from his knee. Overexcited by the tension of the long-awaited briefing, he had been able to swallow very little food.

'A party of men like you can't expect to arrive in Thailand and war-torn Laos without attracting the wrong kind of attention,' he explained. 'Remember the whole country is overrun with spooks and informers. So you have to have a *raison d'être*, a cover story which explains why you are there – one that accounts for you wanting to go up-country.'

'Which is?' Frank prompted. This was new to him.

'You go in as a freelance camera team shooting a travelogue film for French television. You'll have paperwork identifying you as employees of ... we'll call it Rainbow Productions.'

'We don't know anything about filming,' objected Roger.

'You will do in a week from now,' Raoul promised. 'I've arranged for you to spend five days with a real film crew, learning enough to impress outsiders. The company is owned by a client of mine. He won't ask any questions because he thinks he's doing a favour for the secret service.'

He pointed at Roger. 'You will be the cameraman. Sean is your assistant. Hans-Peter is the sound-man. And Frank will be the producer, which accounts for him giving orders.'

Frank was taken aback. 'You never said anything about this, Raoul. And I don't know a thing about production.'

'You don't need to,' smiled Raoul. 'As producer, you just stride around looking important. Your cowboy hat and dark glasses are just right for the part.'

He ignored the suppressed smile that passed between the younger men. 'But the other three have to learn at least to operate their machines properly. Hence the five-day training course.'

Slightly drunk, Roger was pleased with the role he had been allotted. He grabbed Raoul's clipboard off the lunch table and smacked it with the flat of his hand. 'Scene One. Take One. Action!'

An empty wine pitcher became a camera in his hand, Roger peering through the distorting glass at Sean.

'Pan right to close-up of Miss Bardot,' he shouted, twisting round and tracking in to Hans-Peter's right eye. 'Now cut! Print it!'

Raoul and Frank left the three fooling about on the roof and took the lift down to Raoul's office.

Getting out of the lift Frank stared at the large-scale map of Dien Bien Phu marked with chinagraph arrows. He picked up the enlargement of the photograph of the NVA camp. Twelve trucks and a couple of light armoured vehicles were visible, circled by chinagraph.

'They think all this is a fucking game,' he snarled, meaning the men upstairs. The back of his hand slapped the map. 'Those poor bastards don't realise there are people at the end of this particular rainbow who will be trying to kill them.'

17

'**D**on't treat me like a fool,' said Marie-France.

Frank was bending down, snipping off the *pampres*, the unwanted growth which would otherwise take sap needed by the fruit-bearing branches of the vines. Behind him the labourers were talking among themselves in Arabic.

He stood up, slipped the secateurs into his pocket and led her out of earshot. 'What's the problem?'

There was a determined set to her mouth. She shook his hand off her arm. 'Those three ex-legionnaires you said were here to build a wine cellar have gone. And they've stolen my jeep.'

'I said they could have it. They're taking a few days' holiday, that's all. They'll be back.'

'Oh,' she said sarcastically, 'I didn't know criminals took holidays.'

He turned and gestured at the Arabs whose disembodied heads were watching them over the rows of vines. The heads bobbed back below the level of the leaves, like divers plunging simultaneously into a green sea.

Marie-France stood two paces from him, feet apart and angry. 'This morning, when I was walking past your billet, I overheard the German and the Irishman talking about guns. Everything fits. They're crooks, aren't they? And now they've gone off to commit some crime. The papers are full of armed hold-ups of banks and . . .'

'You're wrong,' he said, trying to calm her.

She hit his arm to keep him away.

'And you're even worse,' she cried. 'You're in it with them. You came here and wriggled your way into our confidence like some . . . like some worm getting into an apple. Just to make a hideaway for yourself and your crooked friends, you used me! How could you do that, Frank? How could you?'

She turned and stumbled away in the direction of the house.

Frank ran after her. 'Keep your voice down,' he hissed.

He caught at her arm. 'It's not what you think, Marie-France.'

'No?' she challenged him with tears in her eyes. 'You've been lying to me all along.'

He led her further away from the labourers' listening ears. 'You don't think Raoul's a crook, do you? Well, I suggest we go up to the tower right now and he can tell you what's really going on. Will that put your mind at rest?'

She leaned her head against his chest. 'Oh, Frank, I don't know what to think. You've changed. What's happened between us?'

She lifted her head and searched his eyes. It was like staring at glass.

'Take this as a warning,' said Frank. 'The wrong conclusions Marie-France has jumped to may occur to other people as well. I think we have to tell her what's actually going on and be more careful in future.'

'Don't make it sound such a big favour,' she cut in. 'They've gone off in the farm jeep. That makes me an accessory before the crime if they're caught. And Frank is the ringleader of this gang of crooks.'

Raoul raised a hand for silence. 'I have news for you, young lady. Frank is not the ringleader. I am.'

'You?' Marie-France stared at the man she still sometimes

called her uncle. A bank raid planned by him was beyond feasibility. She sat down on one of the chairs still there from that morning's briefing and noticed the ashtrays full of cigarette ends. 'I don't understand.'

The outline of Operation Rainbow which Raoul gave to Marie-France was a simplified version of the full briefing he had given to Sean, Roger and Hans-Peter.

Her eyes travelled from Raoul to Frank, to the maps on the wall and back to Raoul. 'So that's why you've always had these maps and things, Raoul? *Maman* said it was an obsession of yours, but the whole time you've been planning this Operation Rainbow – all these years.'

'All these years,' he agreed.

Her next question caught him off balance. 'What can I do to help?'

'Keep your mouth shut,' suggested Frank. 'That's what you can do. We want to come out of this thing alive. If anyone talks . . .'

'Don't be stupid,' said Marie-France. She turned to Raoul. 'I meant what part can I play in Operation Rainbow? I want to help.'

Frank grunted derisively. 'Are you kidding? There's no part for a woman . . . a kid of your age.'

'I was old enough for you to fuck,' she retorted without turning round. 'Look, Raoul. I'm twenty-four. By my age, both you and Frank were professional soldiers, risking your lives every day.'

'That was different,' snapped Frank before Raoul could speak.

'Because I'm a woman?'

'Yes,' he shouted at her. 'Because you're a woman. That's what I'm trying to tell you.'

'So –' She spun round on him furiously. 'You think my place is to stay quietly at home knitting like Penelope while the man I love risks being killed on the other side of the world? Is that it?'

Frank refused to meet her eyes.

'Let's calm down.' Raoul manoeuvred the wheelchair

between them. 'And let's not exaggerate the risk element. Frank and the other men are highly trained soldiers. In a short-duration clandestine operation like this, there's far less danger than a civilian would think. It's reduced to a minimum by training, by everyone in the team knowing his job and doing it so fast and so quietly that the Viets don't even know we've been there.'

'Can you promise me there's no real risk?' she asked.

'None until the Vietnamese border and very little after that.'

A smile stole over Marie-France's face. 'In that case, there's no reason why I can't go along at least as far as Laos. In the jungle, I'd be a nuisance but in the early stages of the operation, I'd be an asset.'

Raoul laughed. 'I'm sorry, but . . .'

We cannot avoid our destiny. . . . The words from the old man's letter had been haunting Frank. He had tried to protect Phuong by never telling her that he loved her, and that had not worked. He wondered how many lives the jinx would take before it was satisfied. There was nothing he could do, either way. Now that he had touched her, it made no difference whether Marie-France came with them or stayed in peaceful St Martin. After all, Alice and the twins had died in just-as-peaceful Jacksonville.

He had tried to distance himself from Marie-France emotionally, but realised now that would not save her. Nor would physical distance; Phuong had died when he was half a world away. Better, he thought, to keep this woman close and not leave her unprotected while he was thousands of miles away. This time, he determined, when the jinx came he would move so fast it would have to take him and not someone else. . . .

Marie-France was still trying to persuade Raoul. 'This film crew idea is a good cover, but there's a flaw in your plan. To make it work you need a production secretary.'

'No.'

'Oh yes. A four-man crew –' she stressed the word *man* – 'will look like what it is – a cover for something else. Think about it. Frank looks pretty tough and anyone can see that the others are soldiers – in or out of uniform. Their haircuts . . .'

'You're right,' Raoul agreed. 'Their haircuts worry me a lot. No civilian has hair that short. Even allowing a few weeks' growth . . .'

'You see,' Marie-France turned triumphantly to Frank, 'without me as the continuity secretary, you four haven't a chance of passing as a real film crew.'

'But you don't know anything about filming, my dear,' objected Raoul gently.

'Nor do the others.' Frank's voice startled them both. 'Let's send Marie-France to this film company of yours, Raoul. She's right. A crew with a continuity girl is far more likely to pass any suspicious examination. She can stay safe with Koenig when the rest of us go over the border.'

Frank was repairing a fence damaged by a neighbour's sheep when the jeep returned at the end of the week.

'Well, what do you think of us?' Marie-France was perched on the bonnet of the jeep, a stop-watch in one hand and clipboard in the other.

With a sweep of her hand, she indicated Roger at the wheel, with Hans-Peter and Sean in the rear seat. All available space was taken up with cans of film, a tripod, an Arriflex 16mm camera and a pile of spare lenses and magazines.

But it was not the borrowed equipment that caught Frank's eye.

Roger was dressed in a bright red shirt and vivid green trousers. His fair crew-cut hair was augmented by a growth of beard. He sat at the wheel, grinning at the effect on Frank.

In the back of the jeep, Sean's head was completely shaven but a straggling gingery bandido moustache was starting to cover his upper lip. There was a gold ring in his right ear. He was dressed in a baggy army-surplus camouflage shirt and trousers to match. Hans-Peter, beside him, wore a white shirt and white trousers, with white sneakers on his feet. He was clean-shaven with his blond hair smartly brushed and parted.

'Don't we look good?' Marie-France asked happily. 'Nobody would know now that the boys are only a couple of weeks out of uniform.'

'Whose idea was this?' Frank asked.

Roger stabbed a finger at Marie-France.

'Action!' she cried.

On the cue, Roger twisted in his seat, grabbed the heavy Arriflex camera and jammed the shoulder mount on to his right shoulder, squinting through the reflex view-finder. Simultaneously, Hans-Peter slipped a pair of headphones on and stepped out of the jeep. An expensive-looking Nagra tape recorder hung from a shoulder strap, with a cable leading to the camera and another to a thick gun microphone he was holding.

Sean stepped in front of Frank and held a clapper-board just in front of his face. Hans-Peter aimed the mike at Sean's mouth.

'Rolling,' said Roger, adjusting focus on the board.

'Frank's Astonishment,' called Sean into the microphone. 'Shot One. Take One.' He clapped the board and stood aside.

'What the hell. . . ?' began Frank.

'Cut!' cried Marie-France. 'Wait for it! Always wait for your cue, darling! Cut!'

The board, rechalked, was in front of Frank's face again, as though Sean had spent years at the job.

'Rolling,' calmly from Roger.

'Frank's Astonishment. Shot One. Take Two.'

'Cue Frank,' called Marie-France.

Frank wiped sweat from his brow. 'You're all amazing,' he said. 'But dressed like that you'll attract more attention than a flock of penguins arriving in the middle of the Sahara.'

'Wrong.' Marie-France slid off the bonnet of the jeep and embraced Frank as Roger zoomed out to a two-shot. 'You should have seen the real film crew, Frank. They looked a lot weirder than us.'

She kissed him on the mouth.

'Beautiful,' murmured Roger. He crabbed sideways and zoomed in to a close-up of their faces. Frank tried to pull away, but found her arm wrapped tightly around his neck.

It was Marie-France who ended the kiss with a smile for the camera. 'Cut,' she said.

'Have you got film inside that machine?' asked Frank.

'Colour negative stock. One hundred ASA,' replied Roger.

Hans-Peter was balanced on one leg, fiddling with the tape recorder. He concentrated on the sound in his head-phones. 'A good take,' he said, straightening up. 'The sound's fine.' He punched a button and Marie-France's voice came out of the small integral speaker: '. . . looked a lot weirder than us.'

Frank stood, hands on hips. 'Very impressive,' he said, meaning it. 'You look very professional.'

'I'm taking this seriously,' said Marie-France. 'I want us all to come back alive. That may not be what men think about when they go off to play with guns, but I think it's important.'

'OK. OK.' Frank calmed her down. Used to working exclusively with men, he had expected Roger to compete for dominance of the team. The idea that Marie-France might want to be boss had never occurred to him.

PART 5

SEPTEMBER 1973

1

I *could never have been a general like my father, content to sit*
calmly at headquarters watching symbols and arrows on maps
and thinking of logistics while other men did the fighting and
took the risks.

As Marie pointed out more than once, I was like a cat on hot
bricks from the moment that my brave little Legion of St Martin
drove off to the airport. My proper place was with them in the
thick of the excitement, which was now just a faded memory for
me. I was, to be honest, jealous that Koenig and Frank were
leading my men on my operation. Angry with the useless body
that kept me at home, I fumed and fretted and vented on Marie
my sudden outbursts of pointless anger.

To occupy my mind I checked and rechecked every detail of
Operation Rainbow. If anything went wrong, it would be my
fault. It is always the general's fault.

The situation in Laos was crazy enough even without anything
going wrong. The communist Pathet Lao guerrillas had signed a
cease-fire with the government, so in theory the country was at
peace. Yet Koenig on his recce in Vientiane, the Laotian capital,
had seen on the runway at Wattay airport a Chinese transport
plane taking war material to Hanoi politely giving way to a
taxiing Russian Ilyushin loaded with arms and ammunition for
the Pathet Lao and itself being waved ahead by the pilot of an

American civilian plane carrying bombs to drop on the same people!

The day that Frank's party flew into Vientiane, I was listening on short-wave to the Voice of America Far Eastern Service:

'Here are the headlines for this Friday 3 September 1973. President Nixon has made a statement to the nation about his involvement in the Watergate cover-up. This is the first communication from the White House on the subject since May. Also in Washington, the Supreme Court today ruled that US bombing of targets along the Ho Chi Minh trail in Cambodia is illegal under US law and must stop. And in Cambodia, a relief convoy carrying urgently needed medical supplies has broken through to the besieged capital, Phnom Penh.'

Koenig and I both reckoned that the confusion of this mad war would count in our favour, with everyone being too busy to pay attention to Frank's small party going up-country. We even had some allies on our side, for the opium trade in the Golden Triangle had traditionally been in the hands of the Union Corse – the organisation that had smuggled Koenig and others in and out of France during the time of the OAS. So long as the French ran Indo-China, Corsicans had smuggled the dope to Marseilles where it was processed into heroin for sale in the United States.

As a side effect of the colossal American involvement in South-East Asia, they had been bulldozed out of the sordid trade by a hush-hush operation that involved the US Mafia, the CIA and its clandestine airline called Air America. Not surprisingly, the Corsicans were happy to win a trick from the Americans by helping us.

Meanwhile I had to sit impotently at home in sleepy St Martin and wait for coded cables which could tell me little except that everything was going more or less as planned.

Marie-France spent the flight from Bangkok to Vientiane trying not to be airsick as the vibrating Air America twin-prop plane battled through turbulence and clouds of smoke from slash-and-burn forest fires raging down below. In the smoother moments she compared the distance that had grown up between her and Frank with the closeness they had felt the last time she sat beside him in an aircraft. His unexplained behaviour puzzled her more and more.

In a precaution against anti-aircraft fire, the pilot chose a steep angle of approach to Wattay airport. There were no seat-belts; indeed the seats themselves looked only temporarily bolted into the sparsely appointed C-123. Instinctively Marie-France gripped Frank's arm as the plane went into what seemed a suicidal dive. A beefy red-faced Texan – one of a party of oilmen who had been drinking steadily during the flight – slid from his seat and careered all the way down the gangway to crash against the door leading to the flight deck. As the undercarriage creaked and groaned from the bumpy landing on the much-repaired runway, he drained the bottle he was holding, urged on by hoots of laughter from his drunken friends.

'We made it,' he leered at Marie-France, as though there had been some doubt.

Frank was staring out of the window.

She nudged him. 'You haven't said a word to me, all the way from Bangkok.'

A grunt: 'Got things on my mind.'

'Obviously.'

He stared, seeing her for the first time since takeoff.

'What was in that letter from Vietnam, Frank?' she asked for the hundredth time. 'You've been strange ever since you got it.'

His mouth twitched, as though he wanted to talk but could not find the words.

'Was it from an old girlfriend, Frank?' she persisted. 'You can tell me.'

He shook his head. 'I'll tell you when all this is over.'

The plane taxied to a halt. Steps were wheeled into position and a pretty smiling Laotian hostess welcomed the passengers to Vientiane. The temperature was in the mid-nineties and humid. Walking across the tarmac to the arrivals building, Marie France felt the cloying tropical dampness settle over her skin like spray from an atomiser.

They sat waiting inside the Customs hall while the baggage cooked in the sun outside. Sean fell asleep. A Chinese family of three generations sat down calmly on the floor and ate a meal from a selection of bamboo baskets. Some Buddhist monks in saffron robes chanted a prayer over and over again. Two very beautiful Thai girls who had been on the plane were accosted by the Texans with offers of money. There were armed soldiers lining the walls of the shed, watching the passengers.

'So ho' in Vientiane.' The two Thai girls came to sit next to Marie-France in the hope she would keep the Americans at bay.

Marie-France nodded. One of the girls handed her a small bamboo fan and what looked like a piece of soft leather.

'Suck this,' she said. 'It take away thirs'.'

Marie-France looked doubtfully at the gift.

'Iss dry mango,' the girl reassured her. 'You like it.'

The desiccated fruit tasted better than it looked.

'You don' like to be kep' waitin'?' the girl asked.

'Does anyone?'

'We are Buddhists,' the girl explained. 'For us, all life is waitin'. We may jus' as well wait here as somewhere else.' Her friend laughed gently.

There was no air conditioning in the bare concrete hall. The sticky heat made even talking an effort. The drunken oilmen departed with their hand baggage, leaving one morose drunk behind to wait for the other bags. A resigned quiet fell over the hall. After twenty minutes, two men hauled the baggage trolley lethargically into the Customs shed.

As Frank's team started checking and assembling their baggage, they looked every inch like a pro film crew going about their jobs. Trouble came when the Customs officer shook his head and handed back the paperwork Roger was holding out. He announced that a special permit was necessary before filming equipment could be brought into the country. There was no way round; they would have to return to Bangkok.

Frank argued for ten minutes before settling the size of the bribe at fifty American dollars and two packs of Camels. The Customs officer opened a drawer in his desk, slipped the notes and cigarettes inside, stamped the *carnet* and waved them past.

They walked through a staggered anti-grenade screen into the main concourse of the airport, past youthful soldiers fingering their loaded sub-machine-guns. Koenig, sans eye-patch but wearing wrap-around sunglasses, sat reading a newspaper on one of the concrete seats. He gazed right past them and looked disappointed as though the person he expected to meet were missing.

A horde of small boys lying in wait for tourists grabbed their bags and scuttled away to the taxi rank, leaving no choice but to follow. The taxis looked as if they had been borrowed from a breaker's yard in one piece because nobody wanted to risk using the individual parts. Frank comman-deered three vehicles that he thought might just make it into town.

The hotel he had booked was a dream of cool spacious verandas overlooking the Mekong river. Casually dressed Europeans lounged in rattan chairs and were brought jugs of iced lime juice by soft-footed servants. The architecture was an exotic fantasy of white-painted wooden tracery imitat-ing the outlines of Khmer pagodas. It looked fragile enough to blow away in a strong wind.

'We have no rooms,' the reception manager assured Frank smilingly. 'There are so many journalists, diplomats and military people staying in Vientiane since the cease-fire.'

A handful of money changed hands after a prolonged harangue in Laotian by Frank and they were conducted to three adjacent rooms which had obviously been waiting for them all the time.

Marie-France luxuriated in a shower and clean clothes. She emerged on to the balcony of their bedroom as the sun was setting across the river under a curtain of heavy monsoon clouds. The dramatic lighting made a perfect backdrop for a honeymoon, she thought.

Frank, unbothered by the heat, was still in the tropical shirt and slacks he had worn to travel. He was talking on the extension telephone and checked his wrist-watch as she came in. '. . . see you in the Café Central in one hour from now.'

The phone buzzed as the party at the other end hung up.

'Who are we meeting?' she asked.

'Not we,' he corrected her. 'I go. You stay here and eat dinner with the boys.'

'Frank . . .' She was about to argue with him, then changed her mind. The view of the setting sun across the river was too romantic to waste. I'll show you, Frank Hansen, she promised herself as the door slammed behind him.

The Café Central in downtown Vientiane could have been on the boulevard St Michel. It had the same cheap chic and thick fug of Gauloise smoke as any French pavement café. But the talk at the zinc-topped tables was not of politics and philosophy. It was of arms, drugs and money, the three currencies of the area.

To get there, Frank took a taxi that drove at breakneck speed through streets jammed with pedestrians, piles of merchandise and wandering pigs and chickens. Stepping out of the taxi, he inhaled the moist air thick with smells, sweet and pungent, that told him he was back in Asia. He felt a surge of excitement.

On the side of the street opposite the café, a row of Chinese shops were wide open to the night. A swirling blizzard of kamikaze moths were trying to copulate with the naked bulbs strung above the entrances to illuminate the merchandise piled on the floor below. A naked toddler wandered between sacks of rice, watched by an immobile grandmother of indeterminate age who squatted like a Buddha statue atop an empty packing case. Men and women of all ages haggled and dealed in high-pitched Cantonese. The clacking of mah-jong tiles from an upper room carried clearly through the open window and across the street.

Frank chose a table as far away from the pavement as possible and ordered an iced coffee. Koenig entered the cafe from the rear. From behind a bead flyscreen, he surveyed the crowd seated at the tables before slipping unobtrusively into the spare chair at Frank's table.

The claw hand gripped Frank's meaty fist. 'Good to see you, Hansen. Smooth journey?'

'Fine. No problems, sir.'

'How is Raoul?'

Frank grinned. 'He's shed ten years since we started gearing up for Operation Rainbow.'

'I can imagine,' said Koenig. He ordered a chilled Perrier water from a passing waiter and, as usual, went straight to the point. 'The girl, Hansen – whose crazy idea was it to bring her with you?'

Frank was glad the lighting in the café was dim, in case he was blushing. 'Well . . . Raoul thought it was better cover – less suspicious than a party of four men.'

'He did?' Koenig grunted. In his book, women always complicated things. 'You can't leave her here in Vientiane And you're surely not planning to take her with you?'

'The idea is for Marie-France to stay at the forward base with you while we're across the border. She can act as communications officer and keep Raoul advised.'

Another grunt.

'How are your wife and family?' asked Frank.

Before Koenig could reply, a young Chinese in white shirt and dark trousers slipped between the tables and made his way to them. He bent and whispered something in Koenig's ear, then scuttled away. Koenig stood and pulled Frank with him through the fly screen, hurrying out of the café by the rear exit. They had gone a hundred yards along the rubbish-strewn alley when the sound of an explosion reached their ears, followed by screams and a few scattered shots.

'What was that?' Frank asked unemotionally. 'I thought the war was over here.'

'Suspended, adjourned, postponed,' said Koenig. 'Not over.'

His pace was relaxed as though they were strolling down the Champs-Elysées. 'But the bang we just heard was an internecine Chinese matter being settled. It was something to do with the protection money for the mah-jong game.'

'Nothing changes,' said Frank. 'Where are we going?'

'Remember Stanton?'

'If that crook is still alive, there is no God.'

'Stanton is our transport officer,' Koenig laughed mirthlessly.

'Oh no.'

'He lives in a converted Khmer palace run as a luxury whorehouse outside town. I think he owns it. At any rate, that's where we're going to negotiate the price of two-way helicopter facilities up-country.'

'Christ!'

'We don't have any choice, Frank. He can give us access to any Air America plane in Laos. And since there aren't any others, we either fly courtesy of him or not at all.'

Frank knew that road travel was out of the question. Even if roads had been built within 200 miles of where they were going, it would have taken a convoy of tanks to get through.

'There's another delicate matter.' Koenig opened the door of a taxi that was waiting in the alley for him. 'Our jumping-off point at Muong Ngoi is also owned by Stanton.'

'No way! It's supposed to be a CIA facility.'

In the faint glow of the taxi's illuminated sign, Frank saw the cynical grin on Koenig's face. 'The CIA has suffered budget cutbacks. So Stanton put a proposition to Langley. He offered to build a chain of listening posts in Laos and Thailand which the CIA staff and operate.'

'Magnanimous! In return . . . ?'

'They let him use all the Air America planes he wants to, with no questions asked.'

'So that's how he did it.' The taxi's light went out. To Frank it seemed symbolic. 'Very neat. Very Stanton.'

'Affirmative.'

'I don't like this one bit,' said Frank.

Koenig got into the taxi and slammed the door. 'If you have a better idea, tell me fast.'

Frank stood by the taxi, drumming his fingers on the roof, thinking. Stanton was the last person he would choose to trust. But Koenig was right: there was no other way.

'Get in, Frank. We're invited to dine with the big man himself and I don't want to be late.'

Frank gave a gigantic yawn. 'We'll need a long spoon.'

2

Beneath the slowly turning ceiling fans in the restaurant of the hotel, Marie-France was enjoying the company of Roger, Hans-Peter and Sean. They were far more relaxed when Frank was not around. During the days they had spent with the film company, learning their parts, the trio had adopted her as part-boss and part-mascot. It was a relationship she liked.

As though sensing that Frank had upset her, Roger had taken her aside when she went down to dinner. His back to Sean and Hans-Peter, he pressed into her hand a package gift-wrapped in the paper of the hotel shop and murmured, 'You look very beautiful tonight.'

She opened the parcel to find a figure-hugging Thai silk dress.

'Oh, it's so pretty, Frank.'

'My name's Roger.'

'I'm sorry.' Marie-France kissed him on both cheeks to make amends. 'Do you like my hair? Hans-Peter did it for me.'

'I know.' He kept his voice low so that the others did not hear. 'Will you wear my present for dinner?'

When she came downstairs for the second time even Sean had a gleam of approval in his eye and Hans-Peter applauded, causing heads to turn in the crowded foyer. Feeling like a queen, Marie-France took Roger's arm and was escorted into the restaurant. All the attention made up for Frank's curt rejection.

At table, Roger acted the host with evident pleasure that Frank was not around, ordering for everyone and selecting a different wine for each course. It was obvious to Marie-France that he knew little about wines, but she kept quiet and let him act the connoisseur.

By the dessert course she was feeling light-headed as alcohol combined with jet lag. It was hard to concentrate on the fantasy of coloured ice cream and unfamiliar fruit in front of her. There seemed to be two spoons in her hand.

Sean swore at a waiter trying for the tenth time to pour wine into his glass.

'Why don't you drink alcohol?' Marie-France asked him.

'Because he's an uncivilised Irish bog-dweller,' answered Roger.

'Because he doesn't like drunks,' Hans-Peter corrected him.

Marie-France had never met a man like Sean. He intrigued her. She watched him across the table. The hard, unsmiling face and shaven skull were how she had imagined a legionnaire would look. The hostile grey eyes, his terse sentences and long silences all made her nervous of him. It suddenly came home to her that Sean, his two friends and Frank were all soldiers and that the trade for which they had been trained was not parading and saluting, but killing people.

Emboldened by the mood of the moment and the beautiful setting, she leaned forward and put a hand on Sean's arm. Among his several tattoos she saw the same green and red design of an eagle and a snake as on Frank's arm, only the colours were less faded.

'One glass,' she pleaded. 'Drink a toast to Rainbow, please.'

He moved his arm away. 'No,' he said flatly.

'I've never been to Belfast,' she said, trying to make contact. 'What's it like?'

'You wouldn't want to know.'

She gave up.

If Sean was her image of a legionnaire, the other two men, she reflected, were nobody's idea of brutalised killers. Hans-Peter with his rather wistful smile and soft, girl's eyes, was hard to picture in uniform.

He was always polite to Marie-France, holding doors open and helping her into cars like royalty. When he had offered to do her hair, she had accepted as a joke but he had done a good job, chatting easily about clothes and hair-styles as he used the drier on her long hair. She liked him and felt it was a pity he was gay. He seemed very fond of Sean and watched the Irishman's face a lot of the time, which made her think they must have a physical relationship.

Roger was a mystery: a mixture of Frank's rock-hard physique and a whimsical intelligence that, she thought, could not have been much appreciated in the Legion. Perhaps that was how he had got his nose broken? It gave his face an air of distinction unusual in someone so young.

So young! she thought. They're the same age as me, give or take a few months. I've got too used to Frank and his attitudes. . . .

Sean smiled crookedly as Roger gave a signal behind Marie-France's back. He stood up.

'Come on, kraut,' he said to Hans-Peter. 'Let's find some action. Take a taxi into town, see what the bars are like. There's a stripper at the White Rose called Susie who can smoke cigarettes with her . . .'

'Hey, you two! Don't get into trouble,' Roger ordered.

They grinned. Hans-Peter put an arm around Sean's shoulders and said, 'Don't worry, I'll look after him.'

'I like your friend,' Marie-France said to Roger as the two men walked out of the room. 'Hans-Peter, I mean.'

He laughed. 'Nobody likes Sean. Even in the frigging Legion he didn't make friends. He's an ugly little bastard that nice girls instinctively steer clear of.'

'Why's he so . . . ?' She stopped, not wanting to intrude on their friendship. 'Sometimes when he stares at me, my flesh creeps.'

'That's Sean. Grew up in a Belfast slum. Shit of a life he's had. Doesn't talk much about it, but despite his looks he's a really great guy.'

She felt his hand reach for hers under the tablecloth.

'I don't understand how someone like you can be friends with that sort of man.'

He tried to explain. 'We've been through a lot together in the Legion.'

'But you're civilians, so why stay friends?'

'You don't understand. If, twenty years from now, one of us was –' he released her hand and gesticulated, trying to find the right words through the fog of jet lag and alcohol in his brain – 'in prison on the other side of the world, let's say . . . the other two would go there and get him out, whatever the odds.'

He wasn't joking, she could see. 'I don't think women have that sort of relationship,' she said wonderingly.

'It's the *sine qua non* of the all-male tribal hunting group and the war party,' said Roger. 'Each man will take enormous risks because he knows the others will back him all the way.'

Macho mystique, thought Marie-France. She shook out her hair. 'I like Hans-Peter. I can see him in a chic hairdressing salon, but why ever would a man like him join the Foreign Legion?'

Roger placed a finger on her lips and spoke in English. 'In the Legion, it's considered frightfully bad form to ask why a chap decided to join up. Didn't you know?'

She giggled. 'You're two people, Roger. When you speak French, you're a rough-tough legionnaire, but when you speak English you sound like a poetry professor I had at the Sorbonne.' Who seduced me in my first term, she did not add.

'It wasn't –' his eyes travelled round the room to see who was watching – 'just a casual thing on my side, the other night.'

'Why did you join the Legion?'

'It's a silly story.' He withdrew his hand and lit a cigarette. 'Well, if you really want to know, it was because of a woman.'

'A woman? That sounds romantic. Tell me.'

He blew a stream of smoke at the fan over their table. 'Her name was Vanessa. She jilted me. I ran away to get over it.'

He said it so seriously that Marie-France had to laugh. 'Wow! So men really do run away and join the Legion because they've been jilted – to get away from it all?'

He smiled uncertainly. 'No kidding. Lots of men, even today.'

'You were engaged to this Vanessa?'

'Nothing like that,' he laughed, relaxing. 'She was my headmaster's daughter.'

'You were at school?' How incredible, she thought, to run away from school and join the Foreign Legion.

'Yes.' He looked rather wistfully at Marie-France. 'Vanessa and I were virgins. We held hands in the moonlight after the sixth form end of term dance. She quoted Wordsworth to me and I recited John Donne. Maybe you know the poem?

> Go and catch a falling star.
> Get with child a mandrake root.
> Tell me where all past years are
> Or who cleft the devil's foot . . .'

He stopped, unsure of her reaction.

'Nowhere lives a woman true and fair,' she quoted, teasing him.

Roger relaxed. 'Vanessa let me kiss her but – as they used to say in Victorian romances – rejected my further advances. I had a crush on her and thought it would be terribly dramatic to write her a letter, saying I had joined the Legion suffering from unrequited love.'

He laughed at himself. 'Actually I was suffering from an overdose of P. C. Wren at the time.'

'Do you really mean,' she persisted, 'that you actually joined up and served five years, just because a girl said no?'

'Raoul asked me that. Somehow he had found out that I could have got out at the very beginning. My father pulled some strings. He has friends in all the right circles.'

'What kind of man is he?'

Roger's mouth was twisted. 'Clever is the first word that comes to mind. Possessive is the second; he loves owning people.'

'That's why you didn't let him get you out?'

He nodded. 'I suppose I wanted to show the old man that he didn't own me, that I wasn't a well trained gun-dog he could just call to heel.'

Roger shook his head as though to shake the memories loose. 'I think I also wanted to show him I could do something he couldn't do. Come on.' He stubbed his cigarette out and stood up. 'You're worse than Raoul. He grilled us all for hours on the roof of his castle back in St Martin.'

They went upstairs and stood on the balcony looking at the lights of Vientiane and some lightning on the horizon.

'Are they a couple, Hans-Peter and Sean?' she asked.

'Does it matter?' He sounded defensive.

She smiled at him. 'So long as you're not the same.'

Roger pulled her gently to him but did not kiss her. 'How can you ask that after the last night we spent with the film crew?'

He held her gently but firmly so that he could look into her eyes. 'Once,' he said, 'might have been just your itch and mine that needed scratching. Twice is something else. And four times in one night means I love you.'

He kissed her lips very gently. She closed her eyes and thought of Frank. He was so *heavy* by comparison – like Sisyphus forever carrying some burden from the past, while Roger was young and free and uncomplicated. Frank would never have held her this close without crushing her in his arms and kissing her on the mouth. His sometimes brutal love-making aroused her physical core but left her brain fighting him. How different, she thought, it is with Roger.

The tantalising anticipation she felt standing close to him in the perfumed tropical night, wearing the dress he had bought for her, was the most erotically stimulating moment of her life.

Roger's lips brushed hers very lightly. She felt his hands lift the hair away from her neck. The feel of the night breeze on her moist skin was like a caress. Roger's lips touched her neck once more on each side.

'You have beautiful skin,' he breathed.

Touch me, she screamed internally. *For God's sake, take me now!*

Instead he stepped back, holding both of her hands in his. In the flickering light he looked gentle and innocent.

'Marie-France,' he whispered.

'Yes?'

He searched her eyes. 'Such a beautiful name.'

She felt in a trance as he led her by the hand into his bedroom. They spent an hour without saying one word. When she tried to leave, he caught her hand and pulled her back on to the bed. 'Do you love Frank?'

'I don't know.' It seemed the safest thing to tell him.

They looked at each other for a long time, not touching. 'I must go.'

He nodded. 'I know.'

'What about Sean and Hans-Peter?' she asked at the door. 'Do you think they know?'

'They won't say anything to him.'

3

'N o more alcohol,' said Frank. 'It's the worst possible thing for jet-lag.'

Marie-France could not wake up. 'I didn't have much to drink.'

She felt drugged. As far as her body clock was concerned, it was midnight: time to go to bed, not get out of it, whatever Frank's watch said.

She lay between the sheets drowsily recalling the details of the previous evening's love-making with Roger – and then with Frank. He had returned at 2 a.m. from his visit to the brothel where Koenig and he had refused the free run of the house. But the offer had made Frank feel randy and he had half-woken Marie-France to make love to her on his return.

She would have liked to stay in bed remembering, but Frank had other ideas.

'Five minutes,' he said, pulling the sheet off her with one hand and shaving with the other. 'We leave in five minutes. Get dressed or you have to come naked.'

She staggered out of bed, half asleep and with an aching head, to pull on a pair of cotton pants, jeans and a light T-shirt. In the hotel car park she saw Roger, Hans-Peter and Sean loading filming equipment into a white Volkswagen bus.

Frank bundled her into a waiting taxi. The ride to the airport was a blur of trying not to be sick as the car lurched and bumped its way out of town and through a series of road-blocks manned by armed soldiers. They were stopped at each one. The soldiers, who seemed little more than boys, looked nervously in the boot and under the seats. There was a lot of shouting.

Marie-France came to look forward to the searches. They gave her time to breathe some crisp morning air and stop feeling nauseous for a moment.

Dawn was still fighting the heavy thunderclouds in the eastern sky when they arrived at the airport. The taxi drove past the civil buildings to the military base, where Frank had an argument with a guard which was settled by a couple of notes changing hands.

Once through the checkpoint, they were in another country, of which Major Foxwell Stanton was king. To Marie-France's eyes, he was the archetypal Anglo-Saxon from the top of his crew-cut head to the sweat-stained shirt and the olive fatigue trousers tucked into the tops of his combat boots. He kept his feet on the desk, ignoring Frank's greeting.

There was no unit or rank insignia on his uniform, just the name STANTON above the breast pocket from which a row of thin cigars protruded. He lounged at a desk in the airport control tower, chewing gum and looking as though he was perpetually angry: a coiled spring liable to lash out at any moment.

The control tower was full of noise: a radio playing music, telephones, the air conditioner, communications receivers crackling with terse VHF transmissions in Russian and English breaking through the squelch. The words were in code or jargon of which Marie-France could understand not a word in either language, however hard she strained her ears.

'This why you didn't take up my offer to stay the night, Hansen?' Major Stanton leered at Marie-France's nipples showing through the thin T-shirt. He licked his lips. 'Can't say I blame you.'

The frankly carnal examination made Marie-France feel as though she had forgotten to put on any clothes. She turned sideways and felt Stanton's eyes lock hungrily on to the profile of her breasts.

'Muong Ngoi,' said Frank without preamble; the man had already been paid his advance. 'Which machine?'

Stanton jerked a thumb angrily out of the window. 'There's a chopper in the third bay along,' he drawled. 'Air America ass-and-trash run. Pilot's name is Faulkner. He'll take you along, if you get there in time.'

A telephone rang on the desk. Stanton started shouting into the receiver about some delivery that was overdue. Frank took advantage of the interruption to usher Marie-France out of the control tower.

'Who was that horrible man, Frank?' she shuddered.

He ignored the question and led her at a run past a row of sandbagged helicopter emplacements, unable to talk because of the noise of engines and rotors all around. In some servicing bays mechanics were working under floodlights. Marie-France felt Stanton's eyes burning through her clothes like laser beams stripping her naked and turned to see him lounging in the doorway of his office, staring at her.

'Hi there, Hansen. Heard you were back.' The speaker was a black mechanic crouched on a footplate on top of a Huey, screwing back an access plate in the engine nacelle.

Frank hung a loose salute in reply.

'You gonna ride in this bird, man?'

'That's the general idea,' Frank shouted back.

The black man laughed – a high-pitched falsetto laugh – and made a throat-cutting gesture. 'You're crazy to go up in this heap of shit, Hansen. You know that? Crazy.'

'Don't take any notice of Doc,' Frank advised as the mechanic climbed down to the ground.

'You're a doctor?' Marie-France asked, confused.

The black man turned to her and held out a hand.

'Machine doctor, lady,' he said politely. ''Cept nobody listens to my diagnoses – not Faulkner and not dear ex-sergeant Hansen here. Nobody want to know what the doctor say.'

He picked up a toolbox and departed laughing at his own jokes, or maybe God's.

As she climbed into the Huey, an uneasy premonition seized Marie-France. 'Why is Stanton staring at us like that, Frank? It's as though he knows something we don't know.'

'It's his prerogative,' Frank shrugged. 'If he wants to stare, I can't stop him.' The noise of a neighbouring Huey taking off precluded further conversation.

There were several crates lashed down to rings in the floor and a large American asleep in one of the sling seats, snoring.

'Cargo kicker,' explained Frank.

The pilot of the UH-1 Iroquois helicopter – the ubiquitous Huey of the Vietnam war – was dressed in a combination of military and civilian clothing, eyes hidden behind mirror-lenses. The co-pilot was wearing a flak vest, shorts and plimsolls. When Frank tapped the pilot on the shoulder and shouted something into his ear over the noise of the machines in the neighbouring bays, he was almost at the end of his cockpit check and seemed no more interested than a bus driver would be in a passenger who has just boarded his vehicle.

Only when he caught sight of Marie-France out of the corner of his eye, did the pilot turn to have a better look. She read the name FAULKNER written in felt-tip on the front of his helmet.

An American voice that could have been Stanton's crackled in the earphones lying beside the sleeping kicker: '. . . clear for take-off.'

The pilot yawned and stretched. He turned for another look at Marie-France, on the pretence of: 'You guys strapped in, back there?'

Marie-France nodded. The lightweight nylon mesh seat was uncomfortable already. It was the first time she had been in a helicopter. She watched wide-eyed as the pilot rolled the throttle open and squeezed the trigger switch on his collective stick. The powerful electric starter motor whined shrilly with the effort of turning the engine against the inertia of the huge forty-five-foot span of weighted rotor blades. There was a loud hissing noise audible over the moaning of the starter motor which meant that the jet gases had ignited in the turbine.

Faulkner was staring at a gauge marked EGT. As the temperature of the exhaust gases mounted, the needle moved into the red and the rotors spun into a blur overhead. The needle moved back into the green. There was a smell of warm kerosene in the air. The pilot leaned forward to tap the gauges in front of him. A gloved hand gave a thumbs-up to his passengers.

Frank leaned across from his seat to shout in Marie-France's ear. He pointed to the side of the helicopter. 'Hold on. No doors.'

The noise of the motor rose to a scream that hurt the ears as Faulkner used collective and cyclic together to lift the Huey's nose off the concrete, correct drift and move. The machine lurched forward. As it gathered air speed, they lifted to skim low over barbed-wire entanglements and sand-bagged bunkers that lined the edge of the field. Then with a lurch that had Marie-France screaming with momentary panic, the pilot stood the Huey on its side and turned on to his flight heading.

'Takes some getting used to . . .' Frank's strong arm was around her shoulders.

She nodded, pointed to the ground receding through the open door just two feet away from where she sat. 'Why no doors?' she shouted in his ear.

He grinned. 'This chopper is what's called a slick. It's stripped of virtually everything unnecessary to give it maximum load capacity, speed and manoeuvrability.'

The noise was less painful now that the ground was too far below to reflect the sound of the rotors.

'You stay strapped in,' ordered Frank. 'I want to talk with the driver.'

He hauled himself from hand-grip to hand-grip.

In the main cabin, Marie-France braved the sight from the open doorway and looked down. A hot wind blew in one door and out of the other. Racing past below was a chequerboard pattern of rice paddies worked by buffalo and people up to their thighs in the brown water. Then the Huey gained altitude and the paddies were replaced by jungle-covered hills, green and featureless. An occasional river or hamlet of palm-thatched huts broke the carpet of treetops.

As they climbed, the air grew colder. The sleeping man pulled a blanket over himself without opening an eye. Hoping for another blanket, Marie-France opened a metal crate that was attached by web straps to hooks bolted into the floor. She found herself staring at a machine-gun. The bracket in the doorway, which she had thought was a boarding handle, was the mount for a gun, she realised. She closed the lid and looked around the cabin to see what the pilot was carrying to wherever Frank had said they were going. A stack of metal boxes, also lashed down, bore a stencilled legend in Cyrillic script. She deciphered the letters one by one and pronounced the word aloud: '*Patrony – 7.62mm.*'

Patrony? Nothing to do with the French word *patron*. No, *patrony* was the Russian for bullets. Marie-France wondered why an American helicopter was taking Russian ammunition to men in the middle of the Laotian jungle.

She felt suddenly alone and wished Frank would come back and sit with her. This was his world, not hers: a world of killing machines and men who did not smile, but looked at her as though she were a piece of meat, and where it was normal to hitch a ride beside a machine-gun, surrounded by enough ammunition to arm a regiment. As the Huey lurched in an air current, she felt sick again and wished she was safe in bed.

Hans-Peter was driving the van very carefully. There were only a few inches either side of the wheels as they travelled along a narrow dike between two irrigation canals. In the paddies peasants with water buffalo were already at work.

Hans-Peter was singing to himself the song which drove Roger mad: 'The Happy Wanderer.'

'Shut up, kraut,' ordered Roger. 'I've got three different maps. Each one shows the rendezvous co-ordinates at a different place. So be quiet and let me concentrate.'

'How are we doing?' asked Sean from the back seat.

'I'm guessing that the map with Japanese markings is more accurate than the ancient French one or the American one.' In fact none of the maps agreed exactly with the terrain they were on. Roger's navigation was more by instinct and the sun than by cartography.

'Don't be early,' Koenig had told him. 'I don't want any-one hanging around at the RV point and attracting attention.'

'And don't be late,' Frank had said. 'If your white vehicle isn't there, we may not find the RV at all from the air – depends how good the pilot is.'

Fuck you both, thought Roger.

Sean was staring into space, alone with his thoughts. Out of the blue, he asked 'What's she like, Marie-France?'

Checking the maps and the terrain against his watch, Roger muttered: 'You've known her as long as I have.'

'I meant in bed.'

'Mind your own business.'

'Is she a nympho?'

'They don't exist. They're just a figment of your fevered barrack-room imagination.'

'She got plenty last night.'

'What's that mean? No, left here,' Roger screamed. 'Left!'

'Try telling me before the junction . . .' from Hans-Peter.

'Is this vehicle amphibious?' asked Sean. 'We had about two millimetres' clearance between our rear wheels and the canal on that turn.'

'If you want to drive –' said Hans-Peter, taking both hands off the wheel.

'Stop fooling about,' said Roger.

'I mean . . .' Sean returned to his obsession. 'You gave it to her last night after dinner. Right?'

'Mind your own business.'

'It could be my own business if Hansen finds out.' Sean grinned at Hans-Peter in the rear-view mirror. 'Frank the Yank doesn't strike me as a guy who'd want to share his woman. So . . . little Marie-France had it from you and then Hansen banged her when he came in, at whatever time that was.'

'You're dreaming,' said Roger. 'Right here. Right!'

'We had the room next to theirs,' said Hans-Peter. He was grinning openly. 'We could hear everything.'

'Every little moan of pleasure,' said Sean.

Roger turned in his seat. 'Shut your fucking mouth or I'll shut it for you.'

Hans-Peter was giggling. 'Now, girls,' he said. 'Don't squabble.'

4

Frank waited until a range of low hills put them out of radar sight of the control tower at Wattay before handing Faulkner the piece of paper with the rendez-vous co-ordinates.

Faulkner passed it to the co-pilot who juggled with some maps. 'It's in the middle of nowhere,' he shouted.

Five minutes later Marie-France looked down to see the white Volkswagen minibus driving cautiously along a dike between a rice paddy and a canal. On the canal an outboard motorboat of the kind Thais call a long-tail was cutting a deep wake through the still water, which was covered in a vivid green weed. There were two men in the boat which appeared otherwise empty.

The Huey touched down with its skids overhanging the dike on both sides. Frank jumped out and ran to greet Koenig, who was just stepping on to dry land. The other man in the boat was also European but his skin had a yellow tinge from living too long in the tropics. He jerked a woven rattan mat off two stoutly made crates lying in the bottom of the boat.

'*Macht's schnell,*' he said.

Frank waved an arm as the minibus braked to a halt. Out of the side door came Sean and Hans-Peter, leaving their filming equipment behind. They clambered down into the unstable boat and grabbed the rope handles of the first chest, grunting with the effort of lifting it and keeping their balance in the round-bottomed boat. The long-tail rocked alarmingly with each movement. The second chest was lighter.

'*Les fringues et la bouffe*,' explained the boatman tersely in a thick Corsican accent: clothes and grub.

No sooner were both crates on dry land than the boatman backed the long-tail off, turned it by manoeuvring the long shaft of the outboard motor and headed back the way he had come. Vivid green weed lapped together, healing the scar of his passage.

On land, Koenig wasted no time either. Hans-Peter had left the van's engine running. With a wave of his hand to Frank, Koenig drove off along the dike.

'Jesus, this is heavy.' Sean crouched in the doorway of the Huey with Frank also pulling and the other two men lifting. Gradually, the heavy crate slipped over the sill and on to the floor, to be slid past Marie-France's knees to the centre of the craft where the kicker lashed it down. The second crate followed. There was no floor space left, so Sean and Hans-Peter scrambled on top of the crates.

'What the hell is all this, Hansen?' Faulkner complained. 'Nobody told me about cargo. Just three bodies, Stanton said.'

'The customer's always right,' said Frank. 'Let's go.'

Less than five minutes after touching down, the Huey was straining to get airborne again. The blades of the overloaded craft bit into the soggy air, straining for lift.

Heat and humidity reduce the lifting capacity of a helicopter; it was both hot and wet. Faulkner twisted the Huey sideways and bumped the skids along the narrow dike, trying to gain forward momentum but lifting no higher with each hop.

'Are we going to make it?' Frank asked.

Faulkner indicated with his eyes the rotor revs needle which was well into the red quadrant as the engine screamed in protest. A warning siren added its note to the din in the cabin.

'Doc was right,' Faulkner shouted. 'You get some good choppers and you get some bad ones, Hansen. This is one of the bad ones. If you'd told me we were carrying lead, I'd have checked out another machine this morning.'

'Come on,' said Frank. His fists were clenched, willing the Huey to move. Instead, the entire craft started to shake with the excess revs stressing the worn-out engine.

'Gonna have to take a chance.' Faulkner licked sweat off his upper lip.

He nudged the cyclic control stick sideways, at the same time applying a light pressure to the right pedal. The rotor disc tilted and the pitch of the tail rotor reduced fractionally its resistance to the main torque, which in turn released a margin of power to the main rotors. On its next hop, the Huey turned forty-five degrees and slipped over the side of the dike. It dipped towards the surface of green slime, a hole of dark brown water appearing as the down-draught blew the weeds away.

Convinced they were going in, Marie-France screamed and wet herself in fear.

'Geronimo!' yelled Faulkner. Using all the advantage he had left, he let the Huey slide forward and down until touching the surface. As they turned into the sun, a spider's web of stress lines turned the plexiglas canopy blindingly opaque. It was like heading into a searchlight and left both pilots completely blind.

The movement was just enough to put the blades into undisturbed air and gain translational lift. The Huey lifted suddenly, nose up, until it was once again level with the dike, green slime dripping off the skids. Then the dike was behind and below and they were skimming away across the paddies, narrowly missing a peasant and his water buffalo.

Marie-France's last image of the take-off was the man's face under his conical hat staring upwards into the cabin with neither anger nor fear, just animal-like resignation.

The shaking ceased and the buzzer stopped as normal flight was achieved.

'You can let go now,' Roger shouted in Marie-France's ear.

She looked down and saw that she was gripping his arm. 'I was scared.' She felt ashamed.

'We all were,' he grinned. 'The first time I went up in one of these things, I wet my pants too.' He would have liked to say something kinder but it was impossible to speak to her without Sean or Hans-Peter hearing.

The noise lessened as they gained height. Marie-France shivered as the gale drove in through one door and out of the other. Her back and chest were wet with sweat from the tension of the takeoff and her crotch was wet. She could not ever remember feeling as physically afraid. Sean, she saw, had wedged himself between the two new crates and the Russian ammunition. Like the cargo kicker, he was apparently asleep, despite the cold and the noise. Hans-Peter gave her a smile.

Muong Ngoi was more of a trading post on the river Hou than a proper village. A small and rickety jetty of bamboo poles projected into the sluggishly flowing river of red-brown water. Smoke drifted upwards from cooking fires in outdoor hearths where women and children were making food.

The jeep Faulkner had summoned to the landing area by radio roared through the cluster of low thatched huts, scattering squawking chickens and squealing black pigs, and braked to a halt outside a large Thai house on stilts. The construction looked as though some apostle of Frank Lloyd Wright had been ordered to test bamboo to its limits. A series of cantilevered platforms were suspended by steel wires from a tall palm tree that jutted through the centre of the roof like the king pole of a circus tent. Aerial walkways led from one to another, like a children's fantasy treehouse.

Frank had left Roger, Hans-Peter and Sean to unpack the crates in the clearing where Faulkner had landed while he went with Marie-France to sort out the next step of the journey.

The house on stilts was full of Americans. An oddly assorted bunch to find in the middle of the jungle, thought Marie-France. All appeared to be civilians, refugees from the time of flower power. The men had moustaches and beards. The women wore loose printed cotton Indian dresses or sarongs and walked barefoot on the woven bamboo floors, making the whole house creak like a ship under sail as they moved around. There were two girls for each man. Without any apparent jobs, they drifted around the main living area in a mildly happy daze.

While Frank talked with some of the men over a beer, Marie-France wandered off on a tour of the premises. Every room in the house reeked of pot. In the kitchen dirty dishes were stacked high in a stainless steel sink. There were three well-stocked refrigerators in a room whose main purpose was to house some powerful-looking radio receivers. A couple of college boys in their early twenties were listening on headphones and scribbling on log pads. They took no notice of her.

Outside, an array of aerials on a tall pylon near the house completed the hi-tech side of the outpost, for which a Honda petrol-driven generator supplied the power.

A tall blond academic type who seemed to be in charge introduced himself to Marie-France as Carl Jorgensen and said he was a professor of ethnology from the University of Indiana. Despite the hippie costume and long hair, he appeared to be in his late thirties. His second-in-command was a thin, bespectacled young man in his early twenties called Stanley who, according to Frank, spoke five of the local languages. Another scholarly looking man with completely shaven head was introduced by one of the girls, with a chorus of giggles, as 'the guy who knows more about frogs, would you believe, than anyone else who isn't one.'

Apart from the radio monitors, the only non-academic male was the young black with a New Orleans accent who had driven the jeep up to the clearing to collect them. He lay now in a hammock slung between two posts on the veranda, smoking and listening to soul music on a ghetto-blaster nestled against his left ear.

'What do you do?' one of the girls asked, squatting beside Marie-France on the mat floor, trying to be friendly.

'I'm a student.'

A gentle confusion of giggles. 'No, honey, I meant what's your stuff? We've got everything here. Even good old-fashioned alcohol, if you want it.'

To escape, Marie-France went in search of Frank. She found him sitting on the jetty with the young man in the thick glasses. They were talking in what she supposed was Lao to a small thick-set Asian dressed in the simple black pyjamas of a peasant. After a while, Stanley seemed to lose interest in the conversation. He excused himself and walked off.

Marie-France had the feeling that some kind of a deal was being negotiated. Repeatedly the Asian smiled and went silent, puffing away at his cigarette with eyes closed until Frank came up with what was apparently a better offer.

Finally they seemed to reach agreement. The man got into a dug-out canoe and poled away lethargically upstream.

'So far, so good.' Frank sounded satisfied.

'Who was that man?' she asked.

'Name of Trung. He's a second-hand buffalo dealer.'

Seeing the look on her face, he explained, 'It's like the used-car business back home. Each peasant with a rice paddy needs to buy a new buffalo every few years – or trade in the one he's got for a stronger or younger animal – so Trung is the Asian equivalent of a used-car dealer. In his business, he travels from village to village the whole time, so he can come and go as he likes without arousing suspicion. It makes him very useful.'

'You were talking Lao?'

'That was Vietnamese,' said Frank. 'Trung's a Viet. He's going to do a little recce of the area around Muong Thanh for me, strictly for cash.'

'Muong Thanh? I thought this place was called Muong Thanh?'

He smiled at her. 'Where we're at is Muong Ngoi.'

'It's all so confusing.'

'To your ears. The people here are Lao. Muong Thanh, which is the Thai name for Dien Bien Phu, was settled by Thai-speaking people.'

'But it's in Vietnam?'

'Doesn't mean a thing. The international frontiers of South-East Asia were only laid down by Europeans in the nineteenth century. A million Thai-speakers living over there didn't emigrate just because it suited the French to draw a line on a map.'

Marie-France decided there was no point in trying to understand. The man called Trung had stopped his dug-out in mid-river and was having a conversation across the water with two men in another boat travelling downstream.

'Can you trust a man like that, Frank?' she asked.

'I don't trust Trung,' he laughed.

'Oh. And who are those other men?'

'Montagnards,' he said. 'Meo hillmen. They come here to buy salt.'

'Oh?'

'They produce just about everything else they need. The salt is brought upriver from the coast and traded village to village, like in Stone Age Europe.'

It was the longest conversation she had had with him in weeks. 'Thanks for the lecture, professor,' she smiled.

Frank gave her a gentle push. 'You go on back to the house.'

Marie-France grimaced. 'I don't like those people, Frank. They all seem to be on drugs and there's a room packed with weapons.'

'It's a CIA listening post,' he said.

'Listening to what?'

'They interrogate traders going up and down the river and refugees who come across the border. It all gets co-ordinated by some computer back in Thailand which feeds a digest to Saigon, which feeds it to some computer in Langley, I suppose. And back comes permission to carry on carrying on.'

She gestured at the aerials festooning the radio pylon. 'That's what the radio is for?'

'No,' he explained. 'That's another side of what goes on here: SIGINT, analysing radio traffic on the other side of the border.'

One of the antennae swivelled backwards and forwards then settled, like a dog hungrily scenting the air. 'DF-ing,' said Frank.

Marie-France was lost again. 'I didn't understand a single word you just said, Frank.'

'Never mind.' He put an arm around her for the first time in weeks. For a moment his smile was like the old Frank.

'You're liking all this, aren't you, Frank?'

'Sure,' he grinned. 'I belong here. Everything's going to be OK. Just trust me, honey.'

5

'I'm worried about Marie-France.'

It was nearly dawn in St Martin. Raoul looked up from the map over which he was poring. There was a red cross on the position of Muong Ngoi with K & M-F written beside it. An arrow led north-east across the border marked F+3.

'Don't be worried,' he said to Marie. 'Frank's looking after her. I know you don't like him, but she couldn't be in safer hands – you have to admit that. He knows the country and the people out there like you know your own fields and vines.'

'All the same, I can't help worrying about her. She's so young, Raoul, to be mixed up in all this.'

'It wasn't my original idea,' he said irritably.

Marie slipped a peignoir over her nightdress and came to stand behind him. 'You didn't sleep at all,' she accused him.

In the light of the desk lamp he looked old and wrinkled.

Raoul took her hand with the grip that always surprised her by its strength. A grin made him look young again. 'Think of Operation Rainbow – or at least Marie-France's part of it – as an exotic holiday she's having. There's no more risk to what she's doing than that or I shouldn't have let her go.'

He picked up a cable reading: PRORAINBOW EXRAINBOW

539

'You see?'

'So they've arrived in Laos?'

'Everything's in code. FIRST RUSHES TOMORROW – this
was sent yesterday – means that they are already up-country
here.' His finger settled on the red cross.

She stared at the map, remembering the sounds, the
sights, the smells of Asia which it signified.

'There are two weeks to go till the *vendange*,' she said,
trying to rationalise her premonitions. 'Without Frank and
Marie-France, it'll be a disaster.'

'Don't worry.'

Raoul squeezed her hand. 'The plan is for Marie-France
to sit tight in the relative civilisation of Muong Ngoi with
Koenig and wait for Frank and the others to return. Each
day I get a cable from her, which tells me she and Koenig
are OK and everything's going according to plan. Five days
from now, the cable will say: RETURNING ON FLIGHT SO-
AND-SO. You'll see.'

'This,' said Frank, 'is the pig.'

He lifted from its packing case an ugly matt-black M 60
machine-gun – the weapon which had provided US troops
with the bulk of their platoon-level fire support throughout
the Vietnam war. 'It's so called because it's heavy to lug
through the boonies and because the bipod and gas cylinder
are permanently attached to the barrel . . .'

'. . . making it a swine to change barrels,' commented
Hans-Peter.

All five, including Marie-France, were dressed identically
in anonymous faded olive fatigues, unpacked from the Corsican's crates. Trousers were bloused into the tops of jungle
boots, rubber soled with canvas uppers to allow moisture to
escape. The only civilian touch in the whole team were the
few strands of Marie-France's dark hair escaping below the
back of her peaked forage cap.

Roger, Sean and Hans-Peter had spent the afternoon

examining the unfamiliar American weapons. Frank had taken nothing for granted, insisting that each man shoot off a dozen magazines with the M 16 assault rifles which had characteristics different from those of the Legion's FAMAS to which they were accustomed. Then they had got the feel of American grenades by lobbing a few into a nearby pool, which had provided fresh fish for supper. They had even used some of the American C-4 plastic explosive to fell a few trees.

It was a short but comprehensive familiarisation course. The pig was the last item to be unpacked. Frank hefted the heavy machine-gun in one hand and balanced it, feeling the weight as though it brought back memories. It weighed twenty-three pounds.

'Straight line layout, working parts concealed in the butt. You can see for yourselves, it's a direct descendant of the krauts' MG 42 in the Second World War.'

He tossed the weapon to Roger in mid-sentence. Roger caught it in both hands with a grunt and tossed it back to Frank without warning. Frank twisted and caught the gun awkwardly. Without a word, he tossed it back to Roger, who made a point of catching it in his left hand this time.

'Not heavy at all,' Roger grinned.

Marie-France watched the tussle between the two big men, wondering if it was to do with her or not. Hans-Peter and Sean stayed on the sidelines.

'Spare barrels are heavy.' Frank pulled one out of the case and tossed it to Roger, who caught it with his free hand. 'Now let's see you shoot the thing,' he ordered.

Roger spread the bipod legs and lay behind the M 60, wriggling himself comfortable and squinting down the sights. Hans-Peter knelt beside him, feeding the belt of 7.62mm Nato shells.

'Fire?' from Roger.

'Short bursts,' ordered Frank. 'The pig can loose off 550 rounds a minute, but you'll find with practice you can fire short bursts and even single shots without a selector lever.'

There was an ear-shattering burst of noise. A palm tree

541

fifty metres away hovered for a moment in mid-air, then fell sideways and crashed to the ground, a section of trunk disintegrated before their eyes as the heavy full metal jacket bullets impacted. His ears ringing, Roger adjusted the snap-up rear sight, resighted and felled the next tree in line, severing the trunk neatly a few centimetres above ground level. Then he fired a succession of single shots.

He looked up at Frank enquiringly. 'Happy, Hansen?'

'Are you?' asked Frank noncommittally. 'You're the one that's got to carry the pig and its ammo.'

Roger stroked the housing below the carrying handle. 'I love it already,' he grinned at Frank. 'Consider us married.'

In retrospect, Frank wished he had been less thorough about the weapons familiarisation. If they had been making less noise, he might have heard the helicopters inbound and worked out what was happening while there was still time to do something about it.

The first thing he knew about Stanton's double-cross was when the two heavily laden Hueys staggered over the clearing on a southerly heading which would take them back to Vientiane.

Frank stared upwards. The angle of ascent of the two Hueys indicated that they were loaded to the limits. Each could carry up to fifteen passengers, which meant . . .

'That bastard Stanton!' He ran across the clearing to the jeep where Marie-France was sitting, and leaped behind the steering wheel. The midnight deal in the pagoda-turned-brothel had been too quickly settled, the arrogant major not greedy enough.

'What's up, Hansen?' Roger shouted.

Frank's reply was the sound of the jeep's starter motor.

Marie-France clung tightly to the seat and windscreen as they bumped down the rutted track that led to the river. Frank kept his foot flat on the floor right through the village until they skidded to a halt outside the house on stilts.

It was deserted. All the CIA people and their hangers-on had gone: most of the radio equipment had been stripped out of the communications room. The still-burning lights, the well-stocked refrigerators, clothes strewn about untidily and a collection of *Playboy* magazines were the only evidence of recent occupation to be seen.

Frank went from room to empty room in a rage. He overturned the fridges, hurling food in all directions, smashed equipment and tore down flimsy partition walls. The entire structure rocked with his fury.

Marie-France found herself thrown out of the way by a man whose eyes stared right through her.

'Get out of here!' he growled at her through gritted teeth. She slipped out of the house and sat in the jeep, hoping that she never got on the wrong side of Frank's rage.

There was a muted *whoomp!* when Frank threw a twist of burning paper into the petrol he had splashed all over the building. He ran from the house as it ignited in one gigantic bamboo-popping fireball.

'Shit,' he snarled through clenched teeth, gripping the wheel as though he wanted to pull it off the jeep. 'Have I been taken for a ride!'

He jammed the gear-stick viciously into reverse and reparked the jeep at a safe distance, to sit watching the conflagration as though it gave him deep satisfaction. Then suddenly his nostrils flared and he stood up, sniffing the air. All Marie-France could smell was burning bamboo.

'What's happened, Frank?' she asked.

He sat down, looking calmer.

'There must be another clearing where choppers can land and take off.' He was thinking aloud. 'I should have noticed: where we landed the tree stumps have been freshly cut. Someone cleared the ground up there just for us – so we'd be well out of the way.'

'Where have all Jorgensen's weird people gone?' Marie-France asked.

He watched the house on stilts collapse in great belches of flame.

'They've abandoned the base.'

'How can they do that?'

He laughed wryly. 'They had no choice if Stanton wanted

to close it down.' He filled her in briefly. It was a relief to talk.

A novice to the Vietnam war, she found it incredible. 'But . . . surely one man couldn't tell the CIA to close down its operation here?'

'He probably fed them a rumour that the place was going to be attacked – in which case their standing orders since the Pueblo affair are to get out fast and save the classified documents and equipment.'

There was no point in panicking. Calmly she asked, 'Where does that leave us, Frank?'

He lifted a hand slowly above his head. 'Up to there in brown stuff.'

There was a figure carrying an M 16 running through the village, where the natives were standing in groups nervously watching the fire. It was Hans-Peter.

'Did I tell you to follow me down here?' Frank snarled as he ran up.

'Fuck off, Hansen.' Hans-Peter was alert, not out of breath. 'The others are guarding the equipment. When we heard the noise, Roger thought you might need help.'

Frank swallowed his anger. 'Well there's nothing you can do here, kraut. Jump in behind us. Let's get back to the others.'

Frank was feeling more rational after the outburst of pyromaniac rage that had destroyed Stanton's property.

'We have a problem,' he announced. 'Our plans are working out rather differently than intended.'

They had made a rough bivouac for the night in sparse jungle, fifty metres away from the clearing. While the others ate the fish Roger had fried in oil, Sean was on guard, invisible somewhere in the undergrowth.

'Listen Frank,' Roger interrupted. 'You're playing this thing so close to your chest, nobody else knows what's supposed to be going on. I know that's the way you and Raoul planned it back in St Martin. I didn't argue about it then because it made sense from a security point of view. But now you've got to loosen up and bring us into the picture. You never know, one of us jerks just might have a useful idea.'

Hans-Peter said nothing. Marie-France had noticed that he and Sean left the talking to Roger. Her voice startled Frank. 'I think you'd better tell him what you told me.'

In the gloom of dusk Frank's eyes flicked from her to Roger and back. 'I've been working too long with native irregulars,' he grunted. 'Made it a rule never to tell them anything further ahead than their noses.'

It was as near an apology as he could come.

He filled Roger in with the situation, ending, 'The plan was for Koenig to sit here at forward base, making sure our return was safe. Marie-France was to stay with him. Now there is no base, Koenig isn't coming and she can't stay here.'

'That gives us two choices,' said Roger.

'You make it sound so easy,' Frank sneered.

Roger ignored the sarcasm. 'Either we abort the mission or we take her with us.'

'Very smart,' said Frank. 'If we abort, Operation Rainbow is off for good. Stanton doesn't know exactly what we're up to, but when it comes to money, he's a good guesser. He won't give us another chance. Anyway, we can't abort . . .'

'Because?'

'There's no way home without Stanton's choppers. We're stuck.'

'You and Koenig must have fixed some alternative transport,' Roger reasoned, 'in case something went wrong. You wouldn't have trusted this man Stanton to provide our only escape route.'

'Timing,' said Frank cryptically. 'Koenig won't have had time to set up the fail-safe transport yet. And we can't stay here till he does because Stanton and Co. will be arriving at first light tomorrow to take over Operation Rainbow. If they get here before we're gone, we'll be lucky to get away with our skins and Raoul will certainly never see any of his gold.'

Before Roger could speak, Marie-France announced with a shudder, 'We have to be gone before that man arrives, Frank. He's a killer.' The words sounded melodramatic in her own ears.

'So there's no choice,' Roger summed up. 'We have to take her with us, Hansen.'

They were silent. The light faded – fast, as it does in the tropics. It was completely dark when Frank spoke again.

'Have you any idea what this'll mean, Milton? Taking a girl through jungle on a forced march lasting several days? I did a recce last year with Koenig. We were travelling light and fast – just the two of us – but it almost broke him.'

'Tell me the other options.' It was Roger's voice, dis-embodied in the blackness.

'There aren't any,' Frank admitted reluctantly.

'I want a gun, Frank,' said Marie-France.

'No way,' he laughed sourly. 'If you manage to carry your-self, you'll be doing pretty well.'

'Don't talk about me like that!' she retorted. 'I may not be as tough as you men, but I'm fit. I'm used to working all day in the fields and on a horse I can ride you into the ground any day.'

'We'll be on two legs, not four.'

'Give me one of the M 16s,' she argued. 'They're light. I could carry that and a couple of magazines. My father taught me how to shoot. He used to take me hunting.'

'Jesus Christ!' Frank swore. 'Once across the border, we're not going to be up against rabbits. I tell you one thing, kid. If we get into a fire-fight, anyone shooting back immediately becomes a target. The cleverest thing for you to do is lie flat and not move. Except for shitting yourself from fear, which you will.'

Marie-France lay in the dark, trying to identify the jungle noises all around and wondering whether it were possible to be more afraid than she had been that morning in Faulkner's helicopter.

She felt Roger's hand steal over her thigh, grope for her hand and squeeze it. With Frank lying only inches away on the other side of her, she panicked. How had she got into this situation? What would Frank do to Roger if he found out? It was all his fault for rejecting her after that mysterious letter. What had been in it and why hadn't he talked to her about it? Perhaps then she wouldn't have let Roger make advances. No, that was a fabrication. The truth was that she had set out to seduce him on her first day with the film company.

Marie-France squeezed Roger's hand and felt his answering pressure, then realised she had been holding her breath from suspense. She let it out audibly.

'You all right?' Frank asked softly. 'I didn't mean to shout at you, honey.'

He rolled over and reached for her. She grabbed his hand quickly before it could touch Roger's and lay holding a lover's hand in each of hers.

'That's OK,' she murmured drowsily. 'I understand.'

No, you don't, Frank thought. He clenched his free fist involuntarily. If Stanton had been there, he could have strangled the man with his bare hands.

Frank sniffed the night air. There it was again . . . He lay beside Marie-France in the velvet blackness wide awake, smelling blossom and raging silently against his destiny.

6

Thirty-six hours later Marie-France was stumbling through the early morning fog. The jungle nights were far colder than she would have thought possible and the days – once the fog had cooked off – were appallingly hot. The nightly downpour soaked everyone to the skin. Until dawn they lay trying to sleep, plagued by swarms of mosquitoes which navigated between the huge raindrops and homed in on any exposed skin despite the foul-smelling insect-repellant.

Frank and the other men seemed unaffected by being wet, hungry and bitten to death. She wondered whether they felt the fatigue and discomfort less than women or whether they were just acting tough in front of each other.

Her eyelids puffed up by insect bites, Marie-France stumbled into one of the Meo tribesmen whom Frank had recruited as porters. The man put out a hand to steady her and she saw that the file had closed up. On point, Frank was talking in whispers with Roger and the tribesman who was acting as guide. As the light grew, they ate a breakfast of cold American combat rations washed down with some coffee that Roger made over two smokeless heat tablets. Marie-France nibbled a biscuit and tried not to feel sick.

'We just crossed the border,' Hans-Peter whispered.

She nodded, not really absorbing the meaning of what he had said.

And off they set again. If walking was the generic term to describe their progress, the specifics were scrambling up slippery banks by holding on to projecting tree roots, sliding down muddy inclines, bending under low branches, climbing over fallen trunks and being pricked, torn and slashed by thorns that rent clothes and skin alike.

The fog was swirling between the trees, making every trunk seem identical. In the disorientating greyness, it was like negotiating the same five paces again and again. Marie-France wondered how Frank and Roger, who shared the navigating with one of the tribesmen, could know which direction to take.

The first sign of the heat to come was the occasional vision of brightly sunlit treetops above their heads as they struggled over the summit of a hillock where the fog was thinner. An hour later they were sweating in a steam bath caused by the sun's heat drawing back into the atmosphere much of the rain which had fallen in the night.

When Frank called the midday halt Marie-France lay against a fallen tree with her head resting on a cushion of moss.

Part of the tree moved.

I'm hallucinating, she thought. Then she saw the snake's eyes watching her, less than a foot away. Forcing herself not to move, she whispered, 'Frank!'

She heard movement behind her. 'Don't move,' said Frank's voice. 'Don't even blink. It isn't poisonous, but if frightened, it may bite.' His voice was calm and reassuring. 'And if you get a bite in the jungle, it may go septic, honey. So just stay very still and it will go away.'

She heard a snick of metal as Sean flicked the fire selector lever of his M 16 to vertical for a single shot. He sighted carefully down the barrel, all his movements slow and controlled. None of the tribesmen moved. There was a noise of leaves being crushed as Sean inched sideways for a clearer shot. The snake lifted its head, looking past her at the men standing behind. It slid towards Marie-France's face: an infinity of gleaming yellow and black scales. She felt its body weight on her shoulder as it slithered past. And then it was gone.

Frank lifted her to her feet, shaking.

'It's OK,' he said, hugging her. 'You're all right.'

'What was it, Frank?' she asked when she could control her voice.

'A krait,' he said.

'A krait?' She pulled back to look at his face. 'You said it wasn't dangerous.'

He was trying to calm her. 'I didn't want you to be alarmed and make a sudden movement. If a krait bites you, you're dead in three minutes.'

'No sweat,' laughed Sean. 'If it had been going to strike, I'd have blown its fuckin' head off and sod the noise.' He grinned at Marie-France, put the M 16 back on safe and sat down calmly to finish his drink.

Five minutes later they were on their feet again, moving along a trail where, according to the hillmen, there was a danger of mines. Marie-France wondered how anyone could tell one trail from another. In the middle of the file of men, she was concentrating on putting her feet exactly in the footprints of the men in front.

'Who laid mines in the middle of the jungle, Frank?' she had asked.

'The Pathet Lao maybe. Or perhaps the NVA. Does it matter?'

She recalled the childhood game of walking along railway sleepers. When Sean was on point, the footprints were not too far apart but the longer legs of Frank or Roger made a stride too long for her to match comfortably. Then each step became agony.

They had walked for ten hours the previous day. Every muscle in her body ached, but Marie-France was determined not to admit her degree of tiredness in front of the men. She wished she had not been so proud about insisting on carrying a back-pack; the straps were cutting into her collarbone. Frank had several times suggested lightening it, but she had refused the concession. The men's back-packs weighed four times what hers did. Counting their weapons and ammunition, they were carrying sixty pounds apiece. Roger with the pig was carrying more, but nobody complained, so neither would she . . . .

At the next halt, Hans-Peter asked, 'How are you feeling?'

'A bit dizzy.' She tried to smile.

He took her hand gently. She realised he was taking her pulse. 'What's the diagnosis, doctor?'

He felt in one of the pouches on his belt, took out a large white tablet, stripped off the foil and passed it to her with his canteen of water.

'Salt tablet,' he said, thrusting the foil back into the pouch. 'It'll cut down your sweating.'

She took it with a grimace. 'I'll lose weight.'

'You'll lose consciousness if you go on perspiring like that. And heat exhaustion can damage brain cells permanently.'

'*La ferme*,' hissed Sean.

At the head of the halted column Frank was holding up one arm. The unarmed montagnards were listening to the sounds filtering through the jungle. From the north came the faint sound of a heavy truck grinding up a gradient in low gear.

Roger and Frank looked pleased as they checked the map. Roger turned to grin encouragingly at Marie-France.

'Not far now,' he said in a low voice.

The closer they drew to Dien Bien Phu, the more agonisingly slow progress became: a recce by the point man was followed by an advance of fifty metres or less, then another recce and another short advance. They crossed two small tributaries of the Nam Youm in flood and dozens of streams in what had been trenches dug by the Viet Minh round the French positions.

Each time they heard voices on a trail, there was a wait of ten minutes until Frank decided it was safe to cross. They hid behind a screen of vegetation as groups of peasants walked past only metres away, oblivious of their presence. Villages called for wide detours.

They knew they had arrived at the old battlefield when Sean, on point, stubbed his toe on a rock which turned out to be a piece of reinforced concrete. The Meo guide pointed through the undergrowth at a concrete blockhouse which had been part of the French strongpoint named Anne-Marie. The masonry was undamaged by man, for the outpost had resisted the encircling Viet Minh forces for only two days before the Thai colonial troops had deserted en masse and thus spared Anne-Marie the months of siege that had levelled the rest of the French positions.

What man had failed to do in seconds of violence, nature was accomplishing at her own pace. The entire blockhouse had been lifted on one side by the roots of a forest giant so that its own weight had cracked it in two halves. Lesser trees had taken root in the cracks. One trunk grew out of the main gun embrasure, completely filling the opening as though the roots were set in solid concrete.

Frank scrambled on to the top of the mound to use his binoculars. There was nothing to see except green trees and some smoke he judged to be a mile or so distant. He was halfway back down to ground level when he heard the sound of an aircraft.

A small reconnaissance plane was flying slowly and low over the jungle to the north of their position, along what Frank guessed was the motor road that led to the border and through the pass into Laos. Through his glasses it looked like a captured American L 19, the modified military version of the Piper Cub.

He beckoned Roger to join him atop the mound, where together they watched the plane's movements for several minutes. Their patience was rewarded when it turned southeast and flew directly overhead to land on the airstrip in the valley. By following the line of the plane's glide-path, it was possible to determine exactly where the runway was and therefore their own position.

'Shit!' said Frank softly. 'We're three miles off-track.' He moved his finger from where they were to the point Raoul had marked with a red X. Somehow, due to the cumulative effect of a hundred small detours, their line of march had drifted steadily to the north.

'It was still pretty good navigation,' Roger said.

'Not good enough,' replied Frank. 'The last thing I want to do is go trudging around the valley in daylight. We'll have to keep to the hills. It'll take us hours.'

It did take hours. Hours of diversions around hamlets, walking a few paces then waiting and listening.

The longest hold-up was when a military patrol stopped for a smoke break less than twenty metres from their hiding place. The soldiers, mostly armed as Frank had predicted with captured American M 16s, were young. They looked about sixteen and unhappy. There were two older men with them, presumably NCOs, though neither wore badges of rank. One was armed with a mean-looking Chinese type-50 sub-machine-gun and the other unarmed. As Frank and the others lay aching to stretch themselves, the unarmed commissar took a small book from his green canvas satchel, selected a text and gave the boy soldiers a long political harangue.

A column of red fire ants attacked Frank and Marie-France. As their bites burned her skin, she marvelled at the control Frank had. He paid no attention to the ants on himself, but helped her silently to brush away the voracious insects. He lifted up her right sleeve and pointed. Two huge leeches clung to her skin, swollen with her blood. When she went to brush them off, he shook his head, and silently drew Hans-Peter's attention to the leeches.

The lecture ended, the soldiers began what seemed to be a sort of catechism, punctuated at intervals by slogans which were shouted in chorus. At last they were permitted to march away towards the valley. Frank's hidden party breathed freely again, rubbed cramped muscles, stood up and shook out of their clothing the insects that were tormenting them. With a lighted cigarette, hastily stubbed

553

out afterwards, Hans-Peter burned the leeches off Marie-France's arm.

The doorbell in Raoul's office continued ringing. Thinking it might be the overdue cable, he turned off the hi-fi and rolled to the door control.

'Hallo, darling,' drawled Huguette's voice from below. 'I did push the door, but it seems locked.'

'It is.' He recognised her voice and felt a trace of the old panic.

'Very unfriendly,' she tutted. 'Does it mean I'm not welcome?'

He cast a look at the office filled with maps that he did not want her to see. But if he told her to go away, that would be suspicious. . . .

'I did look to make sure there wasn't another car in the garage – so that I wasn't interrupting anything, darling.'

Damn her! Raoul decided to let Huguette in and get rid of her fast on some pretext or other. He would tell her Marie was coming later. That should frighten her off. Whenever the two women met, they circled each other like fighting cats.

He pressed the button to open the door.

When Huguette swept out of the lift, she exclaimed at the sight of his office. 'My God, darling! Whatever's all this? Are you playing soldiers again, at your age?'

'I follow the war,' he said. 'Like you read fashion maga-zines. Guns for me, frocks for you. They're still our toys, aren't they?'

'I suppose so.' She placed a cigarette in her mouth and waited for him to offer her a light.

'I'm just going out,' he said.

'Aah,' she blew smoke and perched on the corner of his desk. Marie-France's cable fluttered to the floor. 'What's this?'

'Give it to me.' He held out a hand.

She picked it up and read it slowly. 'Marie-France send-ing you a cable from Vientiane. That's in Vietnam, isn't it?'

'No.' He remembered her appalling sense of geography. 'It's a resort in Thailand. She's on holiday there. A honeymoon.' He folded the map of South-East Asia that was lying next to her.

She laughed. 'Well, well. I never thought that American hulk would make an honest woman out of the Laval girl.'

Raoul smiled. 'It just goes to show.'

'Why the funny language in the telegram?' she drawled. 'And who's Rainbow?'

'Cablese,' he said.

Huguette said nothing.

Ten feet away from her the wall map was marked with a series of arrows leading from Vientiane to Muong Ngoi and thence to Dien Bien Phu. Raoul relied on his ex-wife's shortsightedness not to see what was in front of her very eyes

What is it about women like Huguette?

She is devoid of intellect and not even particularly intelligent, yet she has an instinctive shrewdness that always outwits me. I can never tell what is in her mind – certainly I couldn't that day as I tried to keep her from seeing anything too compromising and managed finally to get rid of her on the pretext of a meeting with some clients.

Yet why had she chosen that day of all days to visit me after an absence of two, maybe three, months? What did she see in the office? I found out later that she who had always been too vain to wear glasses except for driving, had bought her first pair of contact lenses. Was she wearing them on that visit? I could hardly ask her afterwards. But if she was, she must have seen the map on the wall. Could she have connected map and cable and guessed about Rainbow?

I didn't have time to wonder then, for as I showed her out and prepared to get into my own car, Koenig's cable arrived. I waited until Huguette had gone before tearing it open to read:

PRORAINBOW EXKING RUSHES GONE ASTRAY STOP HOPE TO SHOOT STANDBY FOOTAGE ENDS

I sat at the wheel of my car wondering how to tell Marie that the

perfect plan over which I had laboured for so long had gone wrong – so badly wrong that her daughter, Frank and the others were stranded in hostile jungle on the other side of the world with no way of getting back alive unless Koenig could pull off a miracle.

7

The late afternoon shadows were lengthening in the valley below when Frank called a halt in thick secondary jungle fifty metres in from the treeline.

Marie-France had been sleepwalking for the last couple of hours, alternately pushed and pulled through the clinging, slashing vegetation by Hans-Peter. She slumped against a tree and was asleep before she had sagged all the way to the ground, despite the insect bites and a thousand stinging small cuts from thorns on her hands, legs and arms.

Frank's instructions to the montagnards were simple: 'No fires, no smoking, no talking. Eat now and sleep. Tonight we work.'

With Sean posted as sentry, the other three men immediately stripped down their weapons. Rust had not yet had time to be a nuisance; they did it because of their training, without thinking why. They also honed the long, matt-black stilettos they carried in ankle sheaths.

Roger took over sentry. Sean cleaned his M 16 and curled up to exercise his odd gift of instant sleep.

Almost immediately he was shaken awake. 'Got a job for you,' Frank whispered.

On the march a mutual respect had grown up between the big American and the runtish little Irishman who reminded Frank in many ways of De Burgh. Sean had a natural talent as a scout: he saw and heard small things that even the montagnards missed and seemed able to float between the trees like a shadow despite a weapon in his hand and a heavy pack on his back. In return Sean had learned a hundred tricks by watching Frank. Of the three young ex-legionnaires only he appreciated just how good a jungle soldier Frank was.

Sean opened his eyes, instantly awake. He picked up his M 16 and followed Frank silently towards the jungle edge. It was a relief to travel light, leaving their packs with the montagnards. Avoiding trails and using all the cover available, the two men made their way along the tree-line to that night's jumping-off point, where they lay concealed to observe the valley.

The road the French had designated Highway 41 crossed the Nam Youm about a mile away. Through glasses, the slowly flowing river itself looked to be about fifty feet across and swollen with the night's rain. Problem? No, thought Frank, it had been high on the last night of the battle also. Raoul had been specific. So that should be OK.

With Sean beside him keeping a 360-degree watch, he adjusted the glasses and scanned the area northwards to his left. The valley bottom was flat and seemed to be a mixture of scrubland and fields. There were two villages, one approximately where the main French positions had been and the other further away to the north. He was looking for the army camp which he and Koenig had spotted the previous year.

He located it at the southern end of the airstrip and passed the glasses to Sean. Sean watched as a file of armed men made its way back to camp along a trail between waist-high grass. He passed the glasses back to Frank.

In the camp itself two jeeps and several trucks were parked under a bamboo awning next to the parade ground. Too close for comfort, thought Frank. If the alarm was given, it would take the Viets only a few minutes to reach the bridge over the Nam Youm.

His tired brain slipped out of gear for a moment and

drifted back to a boyhood holiday when his father had taken him to visit some Civil War battlefields. He had had the same feeling of subdued disappointment at Gettysburg that day. After looking from Lee's positions on Seminary Ridge across Plum Run to the Confederate trenches on Cemetery Ridge opposite, young Frank had feigned excitement for Sven's benefit. In Dien Bien Phu as at Gettysburg, there was nothing to show for the heroism and the suffering. The earth, fertilised by all those thousands of bodies, was no better or worse than elsewhere.

Frank turned the glasses to the right. A convoy of canvas-covered trucks was driving northwards over a metal girder bridge across the river. Raoul had said the bridge was made of stone. Frank held his breath and steadied the glasses. The piers, he could see, were older and made of masonry. He sighed with relief. If the Viets had demolished the old bridge in order to build their new one on a different site, that could have been the end of the story.

Sean knelt, stared at something and tapped Frank on the shoulder.

Frank followed the pointing finger. To the south, about half a mile from the bridge was a watchtower approximately where an unnamed hamlet was shown on Raoul's map. He could see the figures of two guards but no sign of weapons.

He wished he had brought Roger with him to discuss the night's plan. Since the confrontation at Muong Ngoi, he had come to value his second-in-command's logical approach and speed of thought. He seemed to do the talking for both Hans-Peter and Sean.

'Where?' asked Sean softly, mind-reading.

'By the bridge.'

Sean assessed the problem. 'Then the watchtower is a problem. Me and Roger'll take care of the boyos in the tower.'

Frank rolled on one elbow. 'With no noise?'

Sean patted the sheath on his ankle. 'They won't hear a sound.'

Less than two feet separated them. Frank stared into

Sean's face. 'Can you do it, Irish? Can you creep up behind a man and slit his throat?'

Sean's cold grey eyes looked at Frank. 'If I could do it to you, Hansen,' he said slyly, 'I could do it to them.'

Frank recalled Raoul's suspicions. Oh yes, he thought, this little runt beside me was something to do with the IRA. Sean Carey may never have killed anyone during his time in the Legion, but he knows what it feels like.

'Good,' he pointed. 'That leaves your German pal to cut the road a klick or so to the north, between the bridge and the camp.'

'There's a better place,' Sean nudged his arm sideways. 'See that culvert where the road crosses a stream running into the main river. Blow that and at least one lorryload will fall right in the hole.'

'You've got good eyes, Irish.'

'I tell you something, Hansen.'

'What?'

Sean grinned. 'If you'd given me a real rifle instead of this toy –' he tapped the M 16 beside him – 'I could take out those two boyos on the tower from here.'

'That'd be some shot, Irish.'

'I'm some shooter, Yank.'

As the sun went down, Frank kept the briefing simple, his map a sketch of the valley drawn in the soft leaf mould with a stick. The getaway was the simplest part: if anyone got left behind, one of the montagnards would remain near the jumping-off point until daybreak the next day, to act as guide for the stragglers.

'But I don't want a fight,' Frank emphasised. 'Speed and silence are our best weapons. If we get into a fire-fight, we'll have the problem that we can't move fast enough to disengage without leaving the gold behind. Do I make myself clear?' His chin jutted to make the point.

Roger repeated the instructions to him: 'Sean and I make our way to the watchtower he spotted this afternoon.' He indicated its position on the makeshift sand-table.

'If it's manned, we kill the men inside silently. If not, we lay a charge in the road, halfway between the hamlet and the bridge. We then come up the road to join you and the digging party. When we get there, Sean acts as lookout and I take over the M 60 that you will have set up ready for me. That releases you to supervise the digging. On the way out, Sean recovers the charge we laid – so we don't leave any evidence behind.'

'Right. And you, kraut?'

'I come with the main party as far as the bridge, looking after Marie-France. I leave her there with you and continue northwards solo.'

Hans-Peter traced his path in the earth. 'I follow the road until I reach the stream where I place a charge in the culvert to be detonated by the first vehicle passing. I return to the bridge across the Nam Youm. When the digging's over, I recover the charge from the culvert. I return to the bridge. On withdrawal, I take Marie-France with the main party, leaving you, Roger and Sean as rearguard.'

He sounded almost bored. This was a game he had played with Roger and Sean for five years. Little did Hans-Peter imagine as he repeated Frank's orders what horrors lay ahead of him that night.

'OK,' said Frank, scuffing the earth flat. 'Now don't try and carry the detonators away. They could blow your hand off. Just disengage them carefully from the C-4 and leave them behind. But the C-4 is a giveaway so we bring that back with us. Understood?'

At the prospect of action, the tiredness had gone from his muscles; he was running on hundred-octane adrenalin and the other three had the same zipped-up look. The montagnards watched them with anxious eyes. Only Marie-France slept.

The tropical dusk happened fast.

'Time to black up,' Frank decided. 'Then eat something and rest. We move off at 2200 hours.'

'That's early,' commented Roger. 'We may bump into a peasant on his way home.'

561

Frank disagreed. 'The people who live here rise early and go early to bed. The sooner we get moving, the further away we'll be at dawn.'

He knelt down beside Marie-France. She did not move even when he blacked her face. Hans-Peter was to give her a couple of benzedrine pills when she woke up. Frank debated whether to leave her at the jumping-off point with one of the montagnards and decided against it. If they had to withdraw by another route, trying to link up in the darkness would be a nightmare.

He lay down beside her and closed her eyes. Roger rolled over and nudged him. 'You worried about the girl, Frank?'

'What do you think?'

'She'll be OK with Hans-Peter,' Roger reassured him. 'He's stronger than you think. If necessary, he'll carry her.'

'If we're not disturbed during the digging,' whispered Frank, 'there's no danger. It just seems crazy, having her here at all.'

'You didn't have any choice.' Roger patted Frank's shoulder. 'Don't worry, we'll all look after her.'

Frank grasped the hand on his shoulder and shook it. 'You're a good guy, Roger.'

'So are the others.'

Frank looked at the wall of vegetation behind which Sean and Hans-Peter were on sentry. 'I think so,' he agreed.

Roger grinned. In the half-light, his teeth showed white in a black face. 'I thought at first we weren't going to get along, Frank. Now I think we make a pretty good team.'

Frank grunted. He would decide about that when the night was over.

8

The march to the river was uneventful. Puffy little clouds were scudding across the sky. The strong moonlight was double-edged: it enabled Frank's team to move faster but also increased the possibility of being seen.

Reaching the bridge ahead of the main party, he posted Sean as lookout and climbed down the slippery bank to follow Raoul's instructions, learned by heart in the tower that overlooked a different river in far-off France.

Frank slipped on wet mud and fell into a deep waterhole, swearing under his breath. Above him, the figure of Sean leaned over the rail and hissed, 'You OK, Hansen?'

Frank cursed himself silently.

The hole he was floundering in must be the crater made by the buried shell that blew Minh's first team of diggers to pieces. He hoisted himself back on to dry land, where Raoul had lain while the second group of *bo-doi* continued the job.

And that, thought Frank, is one possibility we didn't take into account. There must still be unexploded shells lying all over this valley. After two decades of decomposition, they will be pretty unstable by now. If we hit one . . .

The memorised directions could not have been simpler. He found the ledge at head height which Raoul had described and the place where a Viet shell had taken a neat

V-shaped nick out of the stone. Moving right, he counted stones to the corner. Twelve. Correct. A twelve-times table. Very neat, Raoul.

With his fingertips Frank counted forty-eight stones on the second side of the masonry. And lastly, on the side opposite the cache Raoul had betrayed to Minh, thirty-six stones led to where the other half of the *caisse noire* had been buried, two paces out from the footings – diametrically opposite the other cache. Raoul's plan was simplicity itself: simple enough to memorise in the din and confusion of a battlefield, simple enough to communicate twenty years later.

Frank's heart was beating fast. Where were the montagnards? They should be here, ready to dig. What was holding them up?

Hurry. Hurry. Hurry, he prayed.

And then the tribesmen were there beside him, silent and tense. They feared the valley, for their ancestors had lived in it before the Tonkinese came and drove the Meo into the mountains. The montagnards believed that their ancestors were angry that their graves had been abandoned; it was not a good place to be in darkness.

Frank set the men digging, explaining what he wanted in whispers, then climbed back on to the bridge and set up Roger's M 60 to face either way, north or south. There was no sign of the other three men who had departed as briefed.

The pile of wet earth excavated from the growing hole glistened in the moonlight. The diggers were already up to their knees in water seeping in from the river.

Roger and Sean had returned with the news that the watch-tower was not manned. Now they were on guard on the bridge.

'It's going fine,' Frank murmured in response to Marie-France's question.

'Hansen?' A low whisper reached them from Sean on the bridge above.

'What is it?'

'Roger said to tell you that Hans-Peter is still not back!'

'What the fuck's he doing?'

Frank scrambled up on to the bridge. A dark huddle by the parapet of the bridge was Roger and the M 60. Sean stood shading his eyes from the moon and staring northwards. Moonlight glinted dully on the matt-finish plastic of the M 16 in his hand.

'Do you want me to go look for him?' he asked.

'Yes,' said Frank. 'But if he's in any trouble, get back here fast. No shooting. And don't try any one-man-band rescue tactics.'

Sean moved off at a silent run northwards in the direction Hans-Peter had gone. Frank stood beside Roger and the pig. There was nothing to say to each other as they waited. In the moonlight, the landscape appeared deserted in all directions.

This is it, thought Frank. This is what a man can't find in civilian life: this feeling of being alive that you only get when your life's at risk, the feeling of speed and keenness that overrides hunger, tiredness, even the pain of wounds. . . .

From the dark shadows on the other side of the bridge came the sound of men digging quietly, the occasional slosh of a shovelful carelessly lifted falling back into the water.

Five minutes passed. Frank debated whether to go after the two missing men or to send Roger. He decided to wait another two minutes, then go himself.

Thirty seconds before the expiry of the deadline, Roger pointed up the road. 'Here they come. Looks like Hans-Peter is wounded. Sean's helping him to walk.'

Frank strained his eyes.

'Stay by the pig and keep your eyes peeled in both directions,' he hissed and walked up the road to meet the two men returning.

As they drove closer he could see in the moonlight that Sean was half-carrying, half-pulling his comrade.

'What's up?' Frank demanded. 'What happened to the kraut?'

'Leave him alone,' said Sean protectively. He tried to brush past, explaining, 'There was a gook sleeping in the culvert where he had to set his charge.'

'And?'

'He slit the bastard's throat, of course,' said Sean.

'Good for you, kraut,' Roger called softly from the machine-gun.

Frank shoved Sean aside. He placed both hands on Hans-Peter's shoulders and turned him until they were face to face.

'You did what had to be done, kraut,' he said slowly. 'Good man.'

Hans-Peter shuddered. His skin was shiny with perspiration and his eyes were glazed.

Frank shook him roughly. 'Did you place the charge as instructed?'

A shuddering nod.

'I want an answer, Muller,' Frank insisted. 'Did you place the fucking charge?'

'Yes.'

'OK.' Frank released him.

As he scrambled down the embankment to the group of montagnards, he heard vomiting.

'Keep that man quiet, for Christ's sake,' he hissed to Sean on the bridge above.

The short outburst of triumphant laughter from the tribesmen sounded to Frank's ears as loud as machine-gun fire in the silent night.

He leaped into the hole where they were up to their waists in water, shushing them. A rusted ammunition box was thrust into his hand. It was as heavy as if filled with lead. With an order for silence and another to continue digging, Frank heaved the box up to Marie-France on dry land. It weighed ten kilos or so. He wondered how much gold that was and what it was worth.

The rusted lid defied her efforts to open it and the wire handle came away in Marie-France's hand. Frank took an entrenching tool and levered the metal apart to reveal a layer of mud in which the untarnished coins gleamed in the moonlight.

'That's gold?' Marie-France asked. 'It doesn't look exciting.'

'Not in the moonlight,' he grinned at her. 'But it'll look a whole lot prettier made into a necklace and fastened around your neck.'

Another ammunition box was passed up from the hole. And a third. Raoul had said there were twenty-four – the missing link in the twelve-times table.

Slightly high on the benzedrine, Marie-France threw her arms around his neck.

'We've done it, Frank.' She was almost crying with excitement. 'We've found Raoul's gold.'

For a moment, her euphoria connected with him. He kissed the lips of her blackened face and hugged her tight.

The water seeping into the hole was slowing the digging and the Meos – brave fighters and willing porters though they might be – showed their resentment at being used for the women's work of digging by easing off despite Frank's exhortations.

His watch showed 0220 hours when the first grumble of thunder from the east confirmed the approach of the nightly storm. Dripping boxes were still being passed up from the hole and stacked on the edge. Slowly the pile grew.

Frank put Marie-France in charge of the diggers.

'Keep them moving,' he ordered. 'I've told the guide that he doesn't carry anything. Understood? But each of the others gets three boxes of gold in his back-pack. That leaves six boxes for us to carry: two each for Sean, Hans-Peter and me. Roger has to carry the M 60. That's heavy enough, so he doesn't carry any gold. Got it?'

'Yes, sir,' she grinned at him mischievously.

'And above all,' he said, 'keep the montagnards quiet.'

'Go,' said Frank, tapping Sean on the shoulder.

Sean departed southward at a silent lope.

Roger rose from the M 60. 'I'll do Hans-Peter's charge,' he said. 'He can stay here and look after the pig.'

'No,' said Frank. 'The main party will be moving off any minute. You're the core of the rearguard, Roger. I want you here. Muller must do his own job.'

'I can't go back there, Frank.' The low murmur came from Hans-Peter, hunched over on the parapet. 'Please don't make me go back.'

Frank pulled him roughly upright and shook him.

'You selfish bastard,' he hissed. 'You'd sacrifice everyone else to save yourself looking at a dead gook, wouldn't you?'

Hans-Peter stared glassily at him. Deliberately, Frank stepped back and punched him hard on the side of the face.

'You shut up,' he snarled over his shoulder at Roger's protest.

Hans-Peter pulled himself together, rubbing his cheek. After a moment he said, 'You're right, Hansen. I'll go.'

He turned to leave, but Frank stopped him.

'Now take it easy, kraut,' he said gently. 'Remove the detonator real smooth, put it down somewhere out of the way and bring the plastic back with you. I want to see it when you return.'

He patted Hans-Peter's shoulder. 'Off you go.'

On an afterthought, he called, 'Your knife, Muller. Where is it?'

Hans-Peter stopped, his back to Frank. 'I left it there.'

'Recover it,' said Frank, 'and show it to me when you get back.'

'Why'd you hit him, Hansen?' Roger asked quietly when Hans-Peter's figure had been swallowed up in the moonlit terrain.

'He's in shock,' snapped Frank. 'It was a way to snap him out of it.'

There was a pause. 'You were right,' said Roger.

'I know,' said Frank shortly. 'I've been here before, many times.'

He looked east. There were black clouds massing under the moon and lightning flickering in the distance as the storm built up. He scrambled down to the hole again.

Marie-France turned a worried face to him. 'There was one box missing, Frank. We've spent five minutes looking for it and I've rechecked every man's load, but it's still missing.'

'Shit!' Frank checked every load. Had Raoul miscounted? In the middle of a battle, it would have been an easy mistake to make. . . .

There was no time for discussion. 'Leave it,' Frank decided.

In Meo dialect he gave the order: 'Two men, refill the hole. The rest of you, saddle up and be ready to move out, the moment I give the order.'

He translated the instructions to Marie-France and moved through the group collecting up the tools; he wanted nothing left behind.

The tribesmen were happy to be leaving the valley of angry ghosts. The two men refilling the hole were working like demons at the thought they might be left behind. As the others shucked their back-packs to get the loads comfortable, there was a general murmur of relief and a touching of amulets.

A man came slithering down the bank. It was Hans-Peter.

Frank dropped the entrenching tools and caught him by the shirt-front, pulling him close. 'You OK?'

There was a look of pure anguish in Hans-Peter's eyes.

'Did you defuse the charge?' Frank insisted.

'The plastic is in my hand,' Hans-Peter snarled. 'What do you want me to do, Hansen? Shove it up your arse?'

'Cool it,' said Frank, releasing him. 'Stow the C-4 in your rucksack and take off with Marie-France and the montagnards.'

He had collected up the entrenching tools for the second time when he remembered the knife and called, 'The knife, Muller. Where is it?'

He felt the point dig into his back just above the left kidney. Hans-Peter's free arm was locked around Frank's neck, forcing his head back and constricting the windpipe.

The voice of a man near breaking point hissed in Frank's

left ear: 'Can you feel my knife, Hansen? It's still wet with another man's life-blood. I killed a man tonight, do you understand? I didn't waste a dink or a slope or a gook. I killed a man like you and me. That makes me a killer. One shove of this blade . . . two, maybe three inches deeper into your body and you're a dead man.'

Frank stood very still. His own warm blood trickled down the small of his back from where the razor-sharp knife was digging in.

Very calmly, despite the stranglehold, he said, 'You've done a good job, Muller. Get your pack from Marie-France. You're in charge of the first party: her and the tribesmen. Roger and I will follow as soon as Sean is back. Now go!'

He felt Hans-Peter's arm trembling and counted the seconds until the pressure of the knife point was withdrawn.

9

The truck was a three-ton Russian ZIL 151 that had been supplied as part of a Sam-2 missile site. It ground its way through the night at a steady thirty miles an hour.

As it came round the bend, Frank looked away, not wanting to spoil his night vision by staring into the lights. To his horror, he saw the beam of the headlights swing out across the valley as the truck turned, clearly lighting for a moment the column of marching figures less than a quarter of a mile away. After a moment's panic, Frank reasoned that the driver could not have seen anything. Hauling a heavy truck round a tight bend at night, he must have been watching the edge of the road, not the far end of the beams.

The ZIL slowed and went into second gear to negotiate the roughly made ramp on to the bridge. As it drew level with Roger and Frank, a figure dropped off the back of the truck and lay flat.

Sean picked himself up and laughed. 'Hitched a lift back. How about that?'

'Let's go,' said Frank.

'That's a lucky feller,' said Sean as the lights disappeared round the bend. 'If his truck had happened along one minute earlier, he'd have run right over my charge and bang!' He sounded disappointed.

Roger unloaded the M 60 and grunted at the combined weight of his rucksack, loaded mainly with ammunition for the pig, plus the weight of the gun on his right shoulder.

'Ready?' asked Frank. He slipped his own pack on and hefted Sean's on to his shoulders.

'Jesus,' said Sean. 'How many people are hiding in my Bergen?'

'Only two,' joked Roger. 'Mr and Mrs Gold. They're nice people. We said you'd give them a lift.'

The thunder started as they slid down the embankment and set off after the others.

'Move it,' said Frank. 'I want to catch the others up before that storm loses us the moonlight.'

'Don't talk to me like that.' Sean shucked the back-pack higher. He giggled. 'I've just become a millionaire, Yank, so be polite.'

Frank sniffed the air. A stench of rotting vegetation rose from the reed-beds that lined the river. He could smell nothing else. Maybe it was all going to work out. . . . Infected by the suppressed hilarity of the two younger men, he would have liked to leap in the air and give a yell of triumph.

Feeling as though they had enough reserves of energy to climb a mountain, the three heavily loaded men ran along the path to catch up with the main party. Behind them, dense black storm clouds built up, obscuring the moon and promising all the rain they could wish to obliterate their trail before morning.

Marie-France shivered in the pre-dawn gloom. The argument between Frank and the tribesman acting as guide had been going on since she woke up, cold wet and stiff in every joint, feeling worse after two hours' mosquito-tormented sleep than if she had stayed awake all night.

She moved close to Roger as the tribesmen took off their back-packs and dumped them on the ground. Roger's face was streaked with camouflage, mud and blood from thorn scratches. The eyelids were puffy from mosquito bites. Marie-France realised that she must look the same.

'What's the argument about?' she asked.

'The guide wants to go back the same way we came.'

'Why not? If it's the quickest way.'

'Never use the same trail twice. Frank's right. If a Viet border patrol stumbled across our tracks on the way in, they'll have set up an ambush to catch us on the way out.'

Roger crossed the small clearing to where Hans-Peter was sitting on a moss-covered stump staring into space. He knelt down, put an arm round his friend's shoulder and shook him gently. 'It's OK, kraut. It's OK.'

Marie-France looked at them curiously. Roger's voice had the tenderness of a mother comforting her child while his friend's face looked as if he were ready to burst into tears.

She turned to Sean who also looked worried. 'What's wrong with him?' she asked quietly.

The cold grey eyes looked into hers. 'He never killed a man before.'

She put a hand to her mouth to stifle a cry.

Sean patted the sheath strapped to his ankle. 'Knife,' he explained.

'That explains the vomiting I heard . . .' Marie-France felt sick in sympathy and turned her head aside to retch into the bushes.

It was Frank's strong wrist that caught her arm and pulled her to him. 'Shut up,' he hissed. 'That noise travels.'

She clung to him. 'I just heard about Hans-Peter.'

'I didn't want to bring the cock-sucking fairy here in the first place,' snarled Frank irrationally.

'Shut your mouth, Hansen,' said Sean coldly. 'He did his job. You leave him alone. Roger and I will take care of him.'

Frank swore. Hans-Peter's conscience was not the cause of his anger. He called Roger to him.

'I'm having problems with the little people,' he announced. 'The guide says that the only alternative route back over the mountains involves a climb of 2,000 metres.'

'And?'

Frank sighed. 'We can't carry all the gold and they won't do the climb. So they win.'

Roger kicked the pig, which was lying on the ground. 'Maybe we will need this thing after all.'

'I don't like it.' Frank felt he had failed as a commander. 'But there it is.'

'Shit,' said Sean.

Frank buttonholed him. 'I want you on point the whole time, Irish. Keep your eyes skinned for any signs that people have moved along the track since we came along it on the way in. If you see anything, however small, tell me.'

He crossed to where Hans-Peter was sitting and squatted to bring their faces level.

'Your job is to look after Marie-France,' he said. 'Will you do that?'

The German's eyes were sunk far back in their sockets.

'Right,' he said, getting to his feet with an effort. 'I'll take care of her, Hansen.'

They stood face to face for a minute. I hate you, thought Hans-Peter. You gave me the orders to do what I did tonight. By doing it, I made myself what you are. And that I can't live with.

'You going to be OK?' Frank asked.

'Sure,' Hans-Peter smiled crookedly. 'Why not? What's one gook more or less in the world, Hansen?'

The fog dissipated and left them sweating. Hans-Peter passed Marie-France a salt tablet and his canteen. She spat the water out; it tasted foul and was brown.

'It's OK,' he whispered. 'We refilled the canteens at the river, but there's a purifying tablet in each canteen. It's safe to drink.'

She took another sip and forced herself to swallow.

One of the tribesmen tapped Hans-Peter on the forearm and made a gesture for silence. Marie-France looked at the half-naked porters. Their eyes were scanning the greenery on all sides. There was nothing to see but the unending chaos of trees, creepers, moss, rot and rebirth. Further along the trail, she saw Frank standing beside Sean and the guide who was pointing to a punji-pit.

As they passed the pit, Marie-France looked down. A wild pig had fallen at some time in the night through the mat of woven leaves and twigs. Transpierced by the needle-sharp bamboo stakes sticking upwards from the bottom of the pit, it had died in agony. She shuddered and passed on.

The bloodied pig impaled on the pointed stakes brought back vividly to Hans-Peter all the horror of the night. He concentrated on watching Marie-France's boots ahead of him, tapping her gently on the shoulder when fatigue made her stumble or place a foot outside the safe footprints of the men in front. It saved him thinking of himself and the nightmare moment when he had crawled into the drain to lay the charge and found himself looking into the face of the peasant sheltering there from the nightly storm to come.

Half-asleep, the man had taken him for another peasant seeking shelter for the night. He said something quietly, not alarmed. Hans-Peter had just time to draw the knife, knowing he would have to kill. Then came the peasant's panic as he saw that the man who had just entered his shelter had blond hair, which no Vietnamese could have.

Hans-Peter had done it in textbook fashion; Corporal Cecchi would have been proud of this pupil who had chanted with the others by the mud pit at Castelnaudary:

'One: left hand over the man's mouth to stop him crying out. Two: slam his head back hard against the wall to stun him. Three: draw the knife once, twice to make sure, hard across the windpipe, severing the trachea and the arteries. Four: keep the hand over the mouth until all movement ceases.'

'And what's it called?'

'Killing from the front soundlessly with a knife, corporal!' It was easy to do as a drill when the recruits practised in twos. Reality was that the dying man's arms clutched his attacker, the nails tearing flesh. Reality was the dying man's legs thrashing wildly so the killer had to embrace his victim's body as though for sex in order to keep the hand in place over that desperate mouth. Reality was the final contractions of the victim's heart spurting blood into his killer's face. Reality was the concrete tomb resonating with the murderer's heavy breathing and blood everywhere, glistening, warm and wet.

Beneath the mud that covered them all, Hans-Peter knew his fatigue shirt and trousers were stiff with blood and that he would never again be clean.

The ambush was only half a mile beyond the punji-pit.

Before he hit the ground, Frank had flicked the fire selector of his M 16 to the rear position for automatic fire. From the volume of fire being directed at them, he judged that they were up against half a dozen automatic rifles and one machine-gun firing wildly at waist height, well above men lying flat on the ground. There was no fire from the rear, which probably meant that Sean had sprung the trap too soon by seeing a telltale sign.

Frank shouted an order for the porters to retrace their path fifty metres. Half-naked men wriggled past him on their bellies. One was groaning, with blood running down his thigh.

Frank's voice was lost as Roger got the M 60 into action on its tripod. Carefully aimed short bursts told Frank that Roger was in control. The 7.62mm slugs from the pig shredded the vegetation. The problem was that Frank's fire could not reach the Viet machine-gun, which was hidden from him by a hummock of earth.

Nor could Frank see the actual position of the gun from where he lay. Glancing left, he saw Sean on one knee behind a tree, coolly taking note of where the fire was coming from. From his pack, Frank pulled an M 79 grenade-launcher, familiarly known as a bloop-gun. It was loaded with one round of HE. He tossed the stubby weapon to Sean. Roger slid behind a tree trunk, stood up then swung round and loosed off a whole belt from the pig in the approximate direction of the enemy position. At the same time Frank lobbed two grenades. The enemy machine-gun continued to fire. Then Sean fired. There was an enormous explosion as the single round from the bloop-gun took out the Viet machine-gun and all the men near it. Shrapnel zinged overhead.

Then a ringing in their ears as they strained to hear movement. Frank changed magazines, stood up cautiously, rifle at the ready. The whole engagement had lasted less than two minutes. There were moans from near the Viet machine-gun position and a scuffling in the undergrowth on his left, near Sean.

A single shot from Sean's M 16 and the movement ceased. He moved from tree to tree like a ghost, flanking the main position of their attackers from the left. On the right flank Roger rose, carrying the heavy M 60 ready to fire from the hip, with a new belt of ammunition coiled over one shoulder. He stepped softly off the trail and vanished into the green on the right flank.

Frank gave them a couple of minutes before moving directly towards the groans, M 16 held across his body, ready to fire.

There were two wounded soldiers in NVA uniform who had been firing M 16s and five bodies lying near the machine-gun. Thanks to Sean's marksmanship the grenade from the M 79 had exploded right on the Viet machine-gun, laying the crew out in a neat star shape on the ground around it. Both the wounded men had multiple wounds, one with half his intestines hanging out in purple obscenity on the ground. Frank put one shot into each head. He looked up to meet Roger's eyes.

'Anything?' he asked.

Roger looked at the bodies with distaste. 'No.'

'I got a blood trail,' said Sean, appearing through the wall of green on the other side. 'I'd say two or three got away. Do you want me to follow them?'

'No.' Frank indicated the bodies. 'Take their ammunition. Let's get out of here.'

He saw the spreading patch of blood on Sean's left shoulder. 'You're hit.'

'A scratch. It's clean.'

'Get the kraut to dress it, right now.'

'It wasn't much of an ambush,' commented Roger.

Frank pointed the muzzle of his M 16 at the bodies. 'Look at them. They're only kids. My guess is they got nervous and opened up too soon when Sean signalled us to drop.'

There was a shout in Vietnamese from the trail.

With the adrenalin speed of reaction that combat engenders, Frank hurled himself through the vegetation back to the trail. He took in the frozen tableau. Hans-Peter was standing paralysed, Marie-France lying at his feet. Facing them was a wounded NVA soldier who was just as startled, having blundered out of the jungle to find himself confronted by an armed enemy. The Viet was recovering fast from his surprise while Hans-Peter stared with open mouth, his M 16 pointing uselessly at the ground.

As in slow motion, Frank saw the Kalashnikov swing round in the direction of Marie-France. There was a sudden resolve in the Viet's face that – as he was going to die anyway – he would take with him these two Europeans. His finger tightened on the trigger. Frank twisted and fired one-handed from the hip as a single shot rang out over his shoulder. Sean's bullet hit the man between the eyes a fraction of a second before the entire contents of Frank's magazine mashed the Kalashnikov into the man's shredded belly and slammed the whole mass bodily against a tree. He was dead before he stopped moving.

Marie-France watched the whole drama played out from her position on the ground. At one moment, she faced death, aware that Hans-Peter would do nothing to save her. Then Frank appeared out of nowhere like an avenging green angel and the Viet's body vanished in a red mist.

Frank was standing over her. 'It's okay,' he said, changing magazines by habit. '*Ça va. Ça va.*'

They were the same words he had used on the morning the Arab cook was assassinated on the terrace of Chez Mimi.

For the first time in years, Marie-France recalled the details of what had happened and saw Frank clearly as the man who had rescued her that morning in Oran. She wanted to tell him so, but could not speak.

He pulled her to her feet with his left arm, at the same time slamming his M 16 into Hans-Peter's chest to bring him to his senses.

'Come on, Muller!' he snarled. 'Wake up, you useless bastard. Dress the Irishman's wound and let's get the hell out of here.'

10

E ven Frank found himself waking up on the move and wondering how long he had been sleepwalking. It was impossible to keep awake all the time. Like zombies they plodded across the border into neutral Laos. There they buried the pig, most of the ammunition and all the spare food. Although lighter, they moved no faster. At 2 a.m. they stopped and slept where they lay on the trail.

Marie-France awoke the next morning with stomach cramps that obliterated the now customary discomforts of being cold, hungry, tired and wet. She blamed the river water she had drunk, wondering how effective the purifying tablets were.

Her feet were painful. From walking for days in wet boots, the skin was the consistency of wet blotting paper and looked grotesque, painted daily by Hans-Peter with gentian violet. Her leg muscles ached. Her face was bloated from all the insect bites. She took a drink of water and retched again. It was already dawn but nobody was astir. Only Sean, on sentry, sat looking at her from under his poncho hooked over a bush.

She started to rise on one elbow and felt vertigo, vomiting weakly on the ground where she was lying.

Sean prodded Hans-Peter with one booted foot. When there was no reaction, he kicked harder.

'Get up, medic,' he said quietly. 'You've got a customer.'

Half asleep, Hans-Peter knelt over Marie-France. He took her pulse and looked at her eyeballs, pulling the lids back with his grimy thumb.

'Take these,' he mumbled.

'What are they?' She hated taking pills, especially when she did not know what they were.

'Salt tablet and anti-malaria pill.'

'They'll make me feel worse.'

'Take them all the same.'

Hans-Peter stooped under the dripping branches to check the condition of Sean and the injured tribesman. Neither was bleeding, so he left the dressing in place, confining his aid to jabbing a syrette of antibiotic into each man.

It was mid-morning when Frank dreamed he heard a familiar sound. Suddenly aware it was no dream, he shouted, 'Take cover!' seconds before the first NVA helicopter skimmed low above the treetops.

'So much for the border,' said Roger.

They reached the Meo village half an hour later and stood in brilliant sunlight looking over the valleys stretching eastwards into Vietnam. The landscape below was like a Chinese silk scroll painting, with sheer-sided islands of tree-clad limestone outcrop floating on a sea of green trees and mist. In other circumstances the panorama would have evoked feelings of wonder and beauty.

Frank was settling the deal for the porters in the headman's hut when Sean called him outside.

'Those two dots in the sky –' he pointed east – 'look like choppers to me.'

'Good guy,' Frank could see nothing. He raised the binoculars. 'They look like choppers to me too.'

Through the lenses he watched the two small blips hovering over a ridge of jungle approximately where Roger and Sean, as rearguard, had ambushed a small NVA border patrol the previous day.

'I'd say they are rappelling men down into the jungle to pick up our trail.'

'That puts them a day behind us,' said Roger.

'And Stanton a day in front.' Frank lowered the glasses. He pointed to the line of waiting porters. 'Get those guys moving, Roger. If either of the helicopters back there comes snooping around, I don't want them picking up any trace of us near this village.'

'What'll they do to these people if they connect us with them?'

'Drop germs.'

'Bombs?' Roger thought he had heard wrong.

'Biological weapons are cheaper. And people don't run away from a few small canisters that burst open without exploding. To primitive people they seem harmless until it's too late.'

'Jesus!'

'Have you got a minute, Frank?' Hans-Peter interrupted.

'I'm talking to Roger.'

'I can see that.' Hans-Peter stood his ground. 'I just thought that you'd like a word in private about Marie-France's condition.'

'Don't go.' Frank caught Roger's sleeve. He turned to Hans-Peter. 'What's the matter with her?'

Hans-Peter stood, arms crossed over his mud-spattered and bloodstained uniform. 'She's been sick a lot the last few days.'

'A bug she's picked up,' said Frank dismissively. 'Keep feeding her the Lomotil. If all goes well, we'll get her to a doctor soon.'

Roger was monitoring the exchange.

'Listen to the kraut,' he said quietly. 'He's trying to tell you something.'

'This bug that she picked up –' Hans-Peter smiled. He was enjoying this – 'is called morning sickness, Hansen. You know what that means?'

Frank was silent.

'That girl is pregnant,' Hans-Peter announced.

'She can't be,' Frank muttered.

Roger looked startled.

'Hasn't had a period for six weeks, Frank.' Hans-Peter's eyes flicked to Roger and back. 'It's the sort of thing you'd want to know, if you're the father. Isn't it?'

'I'm bleeding, Frank.'

Marie-France lay on a rude sleeping platform which, like nearly everything else in the Meo village, was made of woven bamboo. There was hardly any light in the windowless hut. Some of the smoke went out by a hole near the ridge but most stayed inside.

'You should have told me,' he said, trying to keep anger out of his voice. Roger had already set off ahead with Sean and the porters.

He slammed a fist into the king-pole of the hut. 'I'd never have brought you even as far as Muong Ngoi if I'd known.'

'I kept hoping I'd made a mistake. Then, when I knew, I didn't dare say anything.'

He suppressed his anger, stroking her hand. 'You'll be all right,' he said gently. 'I'll look after you.'

She pulled him to her. 'I'm frightened, Frank. I'm so frightened.'

As his eyes grew accustomed to the smoke-filled gloom, he saw her clearly for the first time in days. The Meo women had washed her face. She lay looking up at him, pleading with her eyes for him to take care of her. Frank blamed himself for the insanity of the situation. From his experience of combat wounds he could guess which casualties might live and which would certainly die, but he knew nothing about women's problems like pregnancy and spontaneous abortion.

'There's no danger for the moment,' he said soothingly, hoping he had misunderstood Hans-Peter. 'Have a sleep, honey. We'll be on our way in an hour or so to catch the others up. You'll be OK when you're rested.'

He felt her body shudder. 'You don't understand, Frank. I get cramps as soon as I stand up. I can't walk half a dozen steps, never mind fight my way through the jungle for another day or two. I'm so sorry to let you down.'

'She's right.' Hans-Peter's voice was quiet but decisive in the gloom behind Frank's back. 'She can't be moved.'

Frank squeezed her hand again and put it down. 'Give me a minute to work this out.'

He pulled Hans-Peter out of the hut. 'How bad is she?' he asked in a low voice.

'If she lies still, she may be OK.' Hans-Peter spoke calmly but with authority. 'But there's no question of her walking.'

'Then she'll have to be carried,' Frank decided. He turned away and made for the headman's hut to ask for two more porters and a litter.

Hans-Peter caught up with him after a few paces and swung him round, face to face.

'Listen to me, Frank. I'm only a medic, not a doctor. But I'm telling you that if you move that girl and have her carried through the jungle on a bumpy stretcher, she may lose the baby. Maybe you don't care too much about that, but in this festering filth –' he swept an arm round to encompass the refuse and excrement between the huts and the perpetual cycle of rot and regrowth that was the jungle beyond the perimeter of the village – 'she'll almost certainly get an infection and die.'

'What do you expect me to do?' Frank glared at Hans-Peter.

'Are you really asking my advice?' Hans-Peter drawled.

'Damn it!' Frank grabbed Hans-Peter by both shoulders and shook him viciously. 'I just did.'

Hans-Peter knocked Frank's hands away and took a pace back. 'Can you do some kind of deal with Stanton and call up a chopper to lift her out of here?'

At the word chopper, Frank looked to the east. One dot was gone. The other was casting back and forth over the jungle half a day's march away. He shook his head as an answer. There was no point in sending someone ahead to Muong Ngoi to summon help. Stanton had no humanitarian instincts. To tell him they had a woman bleeding to death in the jungle would be handing him a trump card.

Hans-Peter watched him without pity. 'It's your call,

Hansen. You give the orders around here, so make your mind up.'

Frank returned to Marie-France's hut. A little light from the smoke hole in the roof fell on her face. Her eyelids flickered.

'Frank?' she asked, drowsily aware of him through the medication.

'I'm here, honey.'

Her hand found his and pulled it under the rough woollen blankets to place it on her warm belly.

'I love you, Frank. No matter what happens, it's you I love.'

'What's that mean?'

'I wanted to tell you.'

'I know that,' he whispered. 'We're going to be OK. All of us.' He included the unknown life in her belly.

'Mm.' She sighed and the rhythm of her breathing grew more regular.

He had cramp in one leg but did not move until he was certain she was asleep again. Then he gently disengaged himself and flexed his leg. He squatted a while in the darkness beside her, thinking.

They made good time. It was downhill most of the way. With empty back-packs Frank and Hans-Peter took turns with the porters carrying the litter. They caught up with the advance party in mid-afternoon.

During the first break Roger found a pretext to be alone with Marie-France on the litter.

'I love you,' he said. This time he was not smiling, but serious like Frank. 'I want you to know that.'

She closed her eyes without replying, not wishing to think about the complications.

To reduce the size of the party as they approached Muong Ngoi, Frank paid off all except four porters who were promised a bonus. Thirteen of the boxes were distributed among them. The remaining ten were split between Frank, Sean and Hans-Peter. The lightest load was Sean's, which he carried despite the pain in his injured shoulder. In addition each man carried one M 16 and two full magazines. Roger's load was his Bergen rucksack converted into an emergency seat in which Marie-France was to travel the last few miles.

'Saint Christopher Milton,' he joked.

By the time Frank halted the straggling column at what he reckoned was about a quarter-mile short of Muong Ngoi, Roger was almost unconscious from heat exhaustion. He lay flat beside Marie-France, breathing shallowly as Hans-Peter fanned his face with a wide leaf. The porters left, relieved to be paid off.

Sean was white-faced and pale as a ghost, but refused to rest. He posted himself twenty metres ahead of the others and stayed awake on guard.

Frank woke with a start. He remembered lying down under a bush to study the tented camp which stood where the house on stilts had been, then nothing.

He wished Sean was with him to do a silent recce, but the wound in the Irishman's shoulder was looking ugly and Frank wanted him to regain some strength if possible for the night's activity which lay ahead.

Stanton was making no attempt to conceal the camp. A generator was running and lights were on. Plainly the drug-dealing major thought that Frank's party had no choice but to show up openly sooner or later – or starve in the jungle. Music was coming from a radio. Frank counted six armed men in addition to Stanton himself. One of them was Faulkner, the pilot. Frank toyed with the idea of bringing Sean up to take out Stanton with one shot, but where would that get them?

The dug-out canoe lay heavy in the water, loaded with half the gold plus Hans-Peter, Marie-France and Roger as passengers. The second canoe rode a little higher under its load but had a hole or split in the wood at the stern which was barely above the waterline.

Frank cast off from the jetty and grabbed the rope Roger was holding out as he drifted past the other canoe. If they were separated on the river at night, they would never find each other again. He tied the rope firmly to the seat on which Sean was slumped and began paddling as silently as he could manage, trying to draw the two boats harnessed together out into the current. They had only been able to find one paddle at the jetty and Frank had vetoed Sean's offer to search for another among the huts.

There was no sign from the bank that their departure had been noticed.

The silent trips back and forth through the night laden with the gold had been the last punishment. Apart from Frank sitting upright and steering with the solitary paddle, all the others lay in the boats, inert with exhaustion.

'Where are we heading, Frank?' Sean's voice came out of the darkness as the current tugged the overloaded boats into midstream.

'To the emergency rendezvous,' said Frank. He was praying that Koenig and his Corsicans had not been outmanoeuvred by Stanton. If they had, there was no emergency rendezvous, but he was not going to tell anyone that.

The first drops of rain began to fall. Within a minute the nightly deluge was a solid curtain of water threatening to sink the overloaded boats. They had only two empty C ration cans to bale with.

11

Where are we, Frank?' Marie-France asked weakly. She reached across the gap between the canoes to hold his hand.

'Somewhere on the Hou river in north-east Laos.'

'I've lost track of time.'

He looked at his wrist. The gold watch, a welcome-home present from his father which he had worn for ten years, was gone – lost somewhere in the river or on the bank when they were loading the gold into the dug-outs. He hoped it was in the river.

The Huey came looking for them as the morning fog cleared. Faulkner was too old a hand at search-and-destroy missions to give them advance warning. He stayed low, using the trees on the banks to muffle the rotor noise until the moment he swung round the bend upstream of their hiding place.

One minute the river was a peaceful expanse of primeval brown water flowing sluggishly between the jungle-clad banks; the next it was a gale of noise and wind from the downblast of the rotors.

From their hiding place behind a screen of overhanging branches which threatened to blow apart in the turbulence caused by the rotors, Frank and the others watched the Air America helicopter skimming past low above the river. In the cockpit, Faulkner was clearly visible at the controls. Sitting in the left-hand seat with a rifle between his legs and a pair of field-glasses in his hand, was Stanton. In the rear cabin, two other men manned M 60 machine-guns mounted in the doorways.

As the Huey flew away downriver, Roger commented, 'A real bird of prey.'

'And we're the chicken,' said Frank.

'Or the goose that has the golden eggs,' offered Sean. He laughed excessively, making Frank wonder if he had a fever.

After several minutes' wait, Roger suggested moving off but staying close to the bank in case they heard the Huey returning.

'No way,' said Frank. 'Once those guys found the dugouts missing, they know to concentrate the search on the river. They'll be back. Again and again. There's no point in trying to travel in daylight. We wait until darkness grounds the Huey.'

As if to prove him right, the peace of the river was shattered as the Huey turned the bend downstream and flew slowly past for the second time.

The morning passed slowly. They dozed in the steamy heat despite the swarms of voracious insects. At irregular intervals they were awoken by the noise of the Huey's passes. In between, they lay hungry in the low boats. Frank was worried about Sean, whose shoulder was discoloured, swollen and painful.

'Let me have a shot at his petrol tank,' he begged Frank thickly.

'And if you miss? It's not an easy shot.'

'I won't miss.'

'No,' decided Frank. 'Be patient.'

From time to time a low mutter of appreciation greeted Frank's catch of a fish. He had extracted a dozen fish hooks from a small survival pack in a side-pocket of his rucksack and set lines from the spars that ran to the outriggers, using swatted mosquitoes as bait. His catch were ugly looking creatures and there would be no fire to cook them on. The last water in the canteen was being kept for Marie-France. The men had to slake their thirst by sucking the juices from the flesh of the raw fish. It was not much, but it would keep them alive.

They had been drifting on the river for two days and three nights.

Sean was delirious. They had taken his M 16 away and thrown it in the river. It had required all Hans-Peter's and Roger's remaining strength to stop him diving in after it. He lay in the bottom of the boat rambling, 'You're gonna die, son.' and 'I shot Jesus in the eye, father. What do you think of that?'

Roger thought that he too was hallucinating as the canoes slid slowly past the lantern. His half-starved brain grappled with the problem of how a green hurricane lantern could be hanging in the middle of uninhabited jungle. There was no sign that Frank, on lookout in the other canoe, had seen anything. Then a red light appeared beside the green one.

Green and red, thought Roger. The colours of the Legion. The rain had stopped some time before and the mist had not yet started. It was around 5 a.m. He blinked his eyes and twisted round. The two lamps were still there, hanging from a branch on the left bank. Below them was an olive-drab awning of some kind.

He leaned across to shake Frank. 'Wake up,' he croaked.

Frank was instantly awake, his heart racing as adrenalin pumped into his overstretched system. 'What is it?'

'Those lights.' Roger pointed.

They had already drifted a good distance. Frank tried to shout. The only noise that would come out of his throat was a croak. If the lights were Koenig's, it was their last chance. If it were anyone else, they were already so out of luck that it hardly mattered. He grabbed his M 16 from the bottom of the boat and fired the whole magazine straight up in the air.

Gripped in one of the river's sporadic currents, the canoes

accelerated. The lanterns grew smaller and vanished. Frank and Roger stared at each other, wondering if they had imagined them. They had almost lost hope when a searchlight slashed the dark and swept the river until it picked up the two dug-outs, blinding the five pairs of eyes in them. There was the roar of a powerful aero engine as a hovercraft pulled out from the bank in pursuit and rapidly overhauled them.

Three minutes later they were in tow and heading back upstream to the hovercraft's mooring. No conversation was possible with their rescuers until the powerful aero engines shut down.

Frank allowed himself to be helped out of the canoe by two of the mixed Laotian and Corsican crew of the hovercraft. His legs refused to work properly. After the pounding of the forced march and forty-eight hours unable to move in the unstable boats, they collapsed under him. He staggered like a drunk on the narrow walkway above the deflated skirt of the hovercraft and tottered unsteadily into the cabin.

'You look terrible,' said Koenig. 'And you smell worse.'

The US Navy Patrol Air Cushion Vehicle, to give the armed hovercraft its proper title, was a gift from the taxpayers of the United States to certain non-taxpayers in the kingdom of Laos. It had travelled fifty miles since the fog lifted. A machine that took mud flats, water and even low scrub in its stride, it was gliding over some shallow rapids when Faulkner's Huey caught up just before midday.

The rotor noise added to the scream of the hovercraft's engines combined to wake Frank, who watched through the tinted cabin windows as Faulkner brought the helicopter almost down to water level to buzz them. In the left-hand seat, Stanton was shouting through a powered loudhailer, calling on the hovercraft to stop. The noise was deafening, but Marie-France, Sean and Hans-Peter slept without moving.

Roger joined Frank to see what was going on. Apart from looking thinner, he was his normal self. With one hand he grabbed an open can of C ration ham and beans. With the other he emptied a can of beer down his throat.

The Lao soldiers on deck shook their heads at the helicopter in a pantomime of incomprehension. The Corsicans were all out of sight below decks. When Faulkner swooped ahead and dropped into the hovercraft's path, the steersman shouted an order. Two of the soldiers ran to man a pair of loaded .50 calibre machine-guns which they trained point-blank on the Huey. Out of Frank's line of vision on the front of the hovercraft, a 20mm cannon also threatened Faulkner's craft.

'Shoot the bastard down,' said Frank.

'We can't,' Koenig contradicted him tersely. 'This vessel is flying the Laotian army flag.'

'So?'

'So the crew won't do anything directly against an American chopper unless it fires first. General Dan Van Tong – he who lent me this miracle vessel for a share of the gold – lives on American handouts.'

'Stanton's not stupid,' Frank argued. 'He won't fire first. But if he gets back to Vientiane before us, we're fucked. There's no way he'll let us get out of Laos with these.' He kicked the pile of muddy boxes on the deck.

'Keep your fingers crossed,' said Koenig. 'Stanton doesn't know you're aboard.'

The Huey hovered right in the path of the hovercraft, forcing it to change course.

'Oh yes, he does,' said Frank. 'He knows me.'

They had been so intent on watching the helicopter that neither had seen Sean. He had awoken clear-eyed and momentarily free of fever. He heaved himself off the floor to see what the noise was all about. A nod of his head to Roger, who grabbed one of the M 16s. Steadying it against the side of the window, Sean aimed and fired one-handed.

Frank and Koenig turned at the sound, to see Sean collapse on the deck unconscious with the pain of his injured arm.

Roger was watching the scene outside, fascinated. The

Huey hung in mid-air for a moment, lifted, slipped sideways and exploded neatly in a self-consuming fireball, the aluminium and magnesium airframe producing a funeral pyre for the occupants which reached several thousand degrees centigrade. A few twisted pieces of burnt metal hit the water sizzling and vanished in the turbulence of the hovercraft's passage.

The yellow-skinned Corsican who had brought the supplies to the rendezvous on the first day in Laos made a gesture with one finger at Stanton's watery grave: Up yours!

Frank took in the faded tattoo of a snake and an eagle on the man's forearm. He rubbed at the coating of grime that covered his own arm.

'Snap,' he said.

He could hardly keep his eyes open.

'That was a hell of a shot,' he yawned.

Roger opened another can of beer. He nodded at the recumbent form of Sean. 'And that's a hell of a shooter, Yank.'

Frank lay down beside Marie-France. She moved and put her arm out to touch his face. 'Are we safe at last?' she wondered.

'Safe as houses,' Frank echoed Koenig's promise.

She kissed him on the mouth. 'I love you so much,' she said and fell asleep half on him and half off.

Over her shoulder he saw Koenig watching.

Frank grinned wearily. 'We did it,' he said.

Koenig raised his mutilated hand in a slow salute. '*Repos*,' he said: at ease.

INTERLUDE

The robed figure of a Buddhist novice stood at the water's edge, begging bowl in one hand. The other hand was open and empty, symbolising the pointlessness of possessions.

A vivid sunset splashed red, orange and gold off the moving surface of the river, daubing his robe and the bare skin of his shoulder with a shifting patina of colours that made his stillness the more unnatural, like that of a statue rather than a living being. The gaunt face could have been carved from ivory. The day had been warm for March, but the evening breeze was now chill on his shaven skull and the river water lapping at his bare feet was snow-melt from the Massif Central.

His feet blue with cold, Hans-Peter ignored the pain, trying to empty his mind of thought by concentrating on the sunset. It was harder than usual that day, with so many old thoughts crowding his consciousness.

On the opposite bank of the Dordogne, Sean squatted by the cooking fire outside his tent. Satisfied that it was burning well, he settled down to wait until the embers were ready for cooking. To while away the time he took a flute from its case, raised it to his lips and played Debussy's haunting fantasy, *Syrinx*. The shimmering cascade of sound was the perfect accompaniment for the sunset and the river flowing timelessly to the sea. On hearing the first notes, Hans-Peter turned and smiled then went back to his meditation.

Sean had been helping Roger with some building work in St Martin's ancient bar and restaurant that morning when Hans-Peter walked back into their lives.

They stopped hacking old plaster off the walls and gazed at the robed figure standing in the doorway.

'It's a fucking ghost,' said Sean.

'An apparition,' agreed Roger. 'A thin, underfed, washed-out copy of the original.'

'Bears a faint resemblance to the kraut, you could say.'

'Not really,' Roger disagreed. 'Take no notice and it'll go away.'

He returned to his hacking. A large piece of plaster fell to the floor, deluging all three men in choking lime dust. They staggered outside into clean air on the terrace of what was to be Roger's bar, hugging and pummelling Hans-Peter.

'You bastard. Where've you been?' from Sean.

'I like your dress,' from Roger.

'You had us worried,' from both of them.

It was several minutes before the conversation became coherent enough to learn that Hans-Peter had been living in a monastery in Thailand since the day he had walked out of their lives at Bangkok airport.

'I was dyin',' said Sean. 'Fine medic you are to clear off and leave me like that.'

'Dying? Not you,' smiled Hans-Peter. 'Take more than a shoulder wound to put you out of action permanently.'

'You could have written to us.'

'I had things to work out. . . . Tell me what's been happening in your lives.'

Roger gestured at the chaos in which they were standing. 'Thanks to Raoul, I'm now the proud owner of this heap of rubble. Supposedly it's going to be a riverside bar by the time the summer holidays start.'

'What happened to the old guy who used to serve us drinks here?'

'He died and Raoul talked me into buying the place.'

'And Sean?'

Sean pointed across the river. 'See that?'

'What?'

'That campsite.'

'No.'

'Well, it's not there yet. But it will be. I own all that bank.'

'Do I detect the hand of Raoul in that too?' Hans-Peter looked at them both covered in plaster dust. 'It wasn't anyone's plan, was it, to settle in St Martin? We talked about heading for South America with our share of the loot.'

'Ah well,' Roger grinned sheepishly. 'Raoul was marching to a different drum. Only after we got the gold back here did he tell us we couldn't have our shares.'

'Why not?'

'He was right. You can't walk around with a suitcase of gold coins without getting into trouble. His idea is that we sell the stuff slowly over the years and invest it, giving us all a nice income to play with for the rest of our lives.'

'And you two agreed?'

'What do you think?' said Sean. 'There was a bloody mutiny, wasn't there, Rog?'

'Damn right,' said Roger. 'After all that hacking through the stinking jungle, to be told we couldn't have our share seemed a very dirty trick.'

'But Raoul won?'

'I suppose so,' agreed Sean. 'He tricked me into gettin' made gamekeeper for the commune.'

'Gamekeeper?' Hans-Peter thought about it. 'That's a good job for you.'

'Irish was made for it,' said Roger. 'When the local hunters saw the way he can shoot and track game, they couldn't believe their eyes.'

'And you?' Hans-Peter asked. 'Are you happy living in St Martin? Or shouldn't I ask?'

Roger grinned ruefully. 'I always fancied having a bar of my own.'

'How is Marie-France?'

*

She waited in the trees until Sean had finished playing, and shivered not just from the evening chill. Marie-France pulled her cardigan around her shoulders and walked up to Sean after the last note had died away to greet him with a kiss on the cheek.

'I love that tune,' she said quietly. 'I wish you played more often.'

'Nah. All that was in another lifetime.' Sean returned the kiss and moved away.

'Mind if I sit down out of the wind?' she asked, shivering.

He tossed her a blanket. It was not easy for her to get comfortable, lying on the ground in the lee of his small tent.

'When's it due?' he asked.

'Soon, I hope.'

She felt her swollen belly. 'I've been cleaning the house all day. I felt I had to get out for a walk in the open air or I'd go mad. Well, to be honest I'd have preferred a ride on my horse, but that would be stupid.'

He was pouring hot water into two mugs. 'Tea?'

'Thanks.'

She took the mug from him and changed the subject, knowing it embarrassed him. 'Nobody thought you'd live in this tent all winter, Irish. Don't you feel the cold?'

Sean grinned sideways at her. 'I only did it for a bet with Roger. By the end of this year –' he jerked his head at the partly built wooden hut not far away – 'I hope to have something more comfortable to spend the winter in, like.'

'Are you really going to make a campsite here?'

'Why not?' he said. 'In winter I'm a gamekeeper. In the summer, I'll run the campsite. The two jobs fit nicely.'

Marie-France sipped the tea.

'It shows how little you really know what's in people's minds,' she mused. 'Now you, Irish . . . I had you down for a real townie who'd never settle in a dozy little place like St Martin.'

The embers were ready. Sean melted some butter in the frying-pan, broke two eggs into it and stirred them with a fork. The relief at seeing his friend alive and well made him feel expansive for once. They had spent the whole afternoon talking before Hans-Peter excused himself and walked away to be alone.

'I tell yer something,' he said quietly. 'There was this priest in Belfast organised an outing once for a whole lot of kids like me. We spent a couple of rainy days and nights camping in leaky tents on a farm right out in the country. It was the first time I'd seen animals apart from alley cats and mangy dogs and one old nag that pulled the milkcart through the streets of Clonard.'

He raised his face to the darkening sky, remembering. 'There was cows and horses and chickens and ducks on the farm. And one boy who was thick as pig-shit came running round the tents to tell everyone he'd seen apples growing on trees. Somebody bashed him for having us on. Then later we saw them for ourselves in the orchard.'

'It was important to you, that holiday?'

'The only one I ever had.'

The robed figure on the opposite bank had not moved.

'It's good to see Hans-Peter again,' said Marie-France.

'The kraut just came to say goodbye.' Sean sounded sad. 'He won't stay long.'

'It's taken a load off Frank's mind, him turning up like this. He was sick with worry about Hans-Peter.'

'Frank never liked the kraut,' said Sean gruffly.

'Maybe he didn't,' she admitted. 'But he felt responsible. I used to argue that there wasn't anything we could do, but Frank said that one of his men was MIA. He wanted to go back and search the whole of Asia till we found him. I think he would have, if Raoul hadn't talked him out of it.'

'There's us here worrying about him,' Sean laughed, 'and all the time the kraut was eating his rice in a Buddhist monastery, meditating and chanting his prayers all day.'

'A robe suits him,' she observed.

'Better than a uniform. He never looked right in uniform. If you knew the times he was put on jankers . . .'

'I asked him this afternoon if it wasn't a bit drastic for a man of twenty-five to renounce the world. Do you know what he said, Irish?'

'Tell me.'

'He said: "All my life I was pretending. Now I don't have to any more."'

Sean crouched Neanderthal-like over his fire. The food was ready. He tipped it out of the pan on to a plate. 'We were all trying to prove things,' he said.

She gave a little grunt as the child kicked within her. 'In the Legion?'

'Yeah. And . . . d'you know the best thing about Raoul's Operation Rainbow?'

'Tell me.'

'We don't have to prove a fucking thing to anyone for the rest of our lives.'

She shifted to get more comfortable. 'So if Hans-Peter wants to be a monk . . .'

'. . . and I want to look after the wildlife round here and run a campsite where kids can have holidays, that's OK.'

'You'll have kids of your own one day,' she said.

'Nah,' he sneered at the idea. It was getting dark and the flames sidelit his face, softening the hard features. 'I won't get married.'

'You never know,' she teased him. 'Even an ugly bog-dweller may find a nice girl who dreams of living on a campsite or a titled lady who wants to have an affair with the gamekeeper.'

Marie-France sat quietly enjoying the dusk while he ate his simple meal. The moment of silent intimacy drew its power from the timeless tableau of the monk on the water's edge. Sean picked up the flute and played again the beginning of Debussy's music. He lowered the flute but continued fingering the notes absently. The noise of the keys made a quiet plopping sound in the silence.

'I never told anyone this before.' He avoided looking at her, then spoke fast to get it all out before he changed his mind.

'When I was a kid . . . my father and my uncle used me.'

Marie-France had not understood. 'Used you, Sean? What for?'

'Like a girl,' he said. 'You know.'

She let the pause run for several minutes before saying softly, 'It wasn't your fault, Sean.'

He turned on her, a defensive wariness coming back into the cold grey eyes. 'I didn't like it, if that's what you're thinkin'.'

She would have touched him, to bridge the gap that words could not, but he always moved away when she did. It seemed pointless to say I'm sorry, so she said nothing at all.

'You won't tell anyone?'

She shook her head.

The shadows crept in like curtains drawn around the small area lit by the fire. The monk and the river vanished. Lights came on in the village houses and a flash of light appeared in a window of Raoul's tower on its cliff above the village, then vanished again.

Marie-France turned her head and listened. On the breeze came the sound of a pneumatic drill which Frank had hired. He was personally drilling the foundations of the new winery at Château St Martin. The sound of hammering came from the bar across the water where Roger was still at work.

'I'm sorry,' said Marie. 'I didn't know you were sitting here in the dark.'

Raoul blinked at the light. He had a pair of field-glasses in his hand. The recent damp weather had made his injured legs painful. He had not been out much, but the glasses and the telephone kept him in touch with the members of what he called the Legion of St Martin. It was a name they were beginning to use amongst themselves.

He had watched Marie-France walking along the river and Sean cooking by his tent. He had seen Roger working on his new restaurant, Hans-Peter meditating by the water's edge and Frank labouring under floodlights at the distant château. It felt good to know that he had peopled the land-scape of his dream with a band of legionnaires.

For one mystical moment as the light failed he had seen an illusion of laser beams crisscrossing the valley like lines of force joining these people who related to each other so strongly because of him.

Marie switched the light off again and stood blinded in the gloom.

'Huguette was here,' she said. It was more of an accusa-tion than a question.

'Yes.'

'Did you give her money?'

'A bit,' he admitted. 'I can afford to. We're sitting above a fortune in gold, you know that.'

'You haven't told her about the treasure?'

He laughed. 'I don't trust Huguette with the time of day. I just give her some reassurance and a bit of cash for her needs now and again.'

'No more rich husbands?' she could not resist asking.

'No more loving from me, either.'

She came and stood behind the wheelchair with her hands on his shoulders. By following his eye line she could see, framed by the narrow window, the view of the Dordogne valley which Raoul thought the most beautiful place in the world. It was in shadow with just a few splashes of light on the high ground. Through the middle, like St Martin's sword dividing the cloth of his cloak, the great metallic slash of the river divided and united the two sides of the valley.

'Can you stay the night?' he asked.

'Not really. I ought to be with Marie-France. It won't be long now.'

He reached for her hand.

'What were you thinking about, all alone in the dark?' she asked.

'I was thinking . . .' He paused. 'I was thinking that it's all worked out like a dream.'

PART 6

SUMMER 1974
AND AFTER

1

'**C**aptain Duvalier!' The voice was like a whisper on the wind from far away.

Raoul groaned and twitched his head as though to shake the unwelcome sound from his ears, then slipped back into the cloying blackness.

An order had to be obeyed. Someone had said: 'When you wake up, you must obey this voice.' So he tried to heed the summons, but lacked the strength to lift himself out of the blackness.

'Captain Duvalier!' The voice with its hint of Oriental singsong was persistent but calm, almost gentle. 'You have been very ill and delirious. But you are feeling better now. Can you hear me?'

Raoul forced open one eyelid. It was dark. He felt cold, chilled to the bone. The voice he knew so well was calling from a long way away. He had to listen to it but it was hard to concentrate.

'Captain Duvalier! Listen to me.'

There were whispers in the background, like a consultation at the foot of the bed which the patient is not supposed to hear. The language was Vietnamese.

And now the familiar voice, insisting in French, 'Listen to me, Captain Duvalier. You have been delirious but now you are getting better. I shall turn on the light so we can talk. It will hurt your eyes after all these months in the dark, but you will get used to it.'

Raoul screamed as light pierced his closed eyelids like hot steel.

He tried to lift his hands and cup them over bruised and throbbing eyeballs but his arm muscles would not obey the brain's commands. Sobbing with pain from the stabbing, burning light, he lowered his head like an animal awaiting the slaughterer's blow. It was no good; there was no refuge anywhere. Light seemed even to reflect from where his chest must be. And there was light inside his skull, ricocheting backwards and forwards through the cells of his brain.

'Please,' he gasped through cracked lips. 'Turn off the light. Please turn off the light.'

Miraculously there was darkness. Raoul heard himself whimpering with relief from the excruciating pain.

'Is that better?' the voice asked solicitously.

'Better,' he heard himself croak. The sound came long after the thought. There was a delay between the brain and the vocal chords, as though he had not used them for months.

'Good. Then we can begin, Captain Duvalier. I am going to turn on another light. It is a smaller bulb. It will not hurt your eyes this time, or maybe just a little to begin with. But it will enable us to see each other.'

The second light did not blind and burn its way through the skin and brain but even so, Raoul hid his eyes from it by dropping his head until the chin rested on his breastbone.

'Now you can open your eyes, Captain Duvalier.' The voice was both soothing and authoritative at the same time. 'Just a little. Don't look up yet. Let your eyes get accustomed to the light before you open them fully.'

Raoul squinted through almost closed lids. In the foreground of his vision, his hands lay limp on his knees. The fingers were like animal claws: clenched, dirty, covered in tropical sores. The nails were broken, some of them missing where fingers terminated in bleeding, oozing stumps. He tried to move a finger. The result was uncoordinated jerking, as though the nerves had all been disconnected at the exchange and wrongly rewired.

He was clad in grime-stiffened black cotton pyjamas. A coarse rope of woven fibre cramped his chest, binding him to the chair so that he would not fall. There was a pool of light on the floor where his dirty, twisted feet lay.

Raoul concentrated hugely, with an effort that hurt behind the eyes. Lungs and heart straining to pump oxygen to reluctant muscles, he managed with a colossal effort to close the index and thumb of his right hand and open them again.

'You have been ill,' the voice reminded him. 'Very ill indeed.'

Raoul let the hand fall on to his knee, where it rested leadenly. His eyes hurt. As the lids drooped, the command came like a whiplash: 'Keep your eyes open!'

He blinked and slowly raised his head. The dirty earth floor came into focus and bamboo walls on either side. In front of him were the legs of a table and between them a pair of feet in Ho Chi Minh sandals made from an old tyre.

'Look up,' the voice commanded.

He tried to comply but his head would go no further.

Someone standing behind him took hold of Raoul's head under the chin and raised it millimetre by millimetre so that his field of vision travelled slowly upwards to include a pair of hands resting on the bare bamboo table. Beside them lay a notepad, a simple cotton cap with a red star above the peak and a bottle of the locally brewed beer which the camp guards all drank.

As his head continued its involuntary pivoting motion, the next thing that came into Raoul's field of vision was the torso of a man dressed in black pyjamas, identical to his own but clean. The man was seated behind the table.

Raoul realised that the light in the bamboo hut was dim; it had only seemed bright to eyes adjusted for complete darkness. The single low-wattage bulb was somewhere behind the man opposite, leaving his face mostly in shadow. Yet Raoul recognised the jet black hair, the outline of the head, the slight angle at which it was held, the way the ears projected and the way the hands lay patiently on the table — even without the voice.

'Would you like a drink?' Minh asked.

A drink? thought Raoul. Drinking a whole swimming pool would not slake this thirst. . . .

'You must answer my questions, Captain Duvalier.'

I must not answer his questions. I must not. . . .

'A drink?'

'Yes.'

The monosyllable rang in Raoul's ears like a great betrayal, telling him that he would answer all Minh's questions because he had no choice.

An earthenware cup was placed against his lips. The supporting hands helped him to drink. He swallowed greedily but much of the water slopped down his chin and dribbled cold on to his dirty, naked chest where the pyjamas gaped open.

'Is that better?'

'Yes. Better.'

'Good. Now listen to me, Duvalier. You have been very ill with malaria. The fever was in your brain. You nearly died.'

'Yes. I nearly died.'

'In your delirium you were raving about a fantasy world in which you thought you were living, complete with imaginary friends called Roger and Frank and others whose names I don't recall.'

A low, conspiratorial chuckle from Minh evoked a grunt from the guard holding Raoul's head. 'You lived in a dream house: a tower of stone overlooking a river. In the dream you created a whole landscape and peopled it with a group of men called the Legion of St Martin. You even had women whom you loved. Am I right?'

'You are right.'

'You see. I know everything, Duvalier. All your private thoughts.'

Minh laughed again. 'Your dream was, I think, the perfect

fantasy to comfort a sick man in solitary confinement, abandoned by his comrades and his country.'

He paused and lit a cigarette, his hands cupped around the flame. 'You know what I am talking about, Duvalier?'

'I know.'

'You are not the only one.' There was a little sadness in Minh's voice, as though he did not like to destroy a prisoner's last pathetic possession: his private fantasies.

He exhaled and plucked a piece of tobacco off his lips. 'Most men kept in solitary confinement for a long period invent a fantasy world into which they can escape. For some, it's a way of keeping sane; for others, it is the madness into which their brains retreat for ever. You are a highly inventive man, so you created a very complicated fantasy.'

Minh took a drink from the bottle of beer on the table.

'Sensory deprivation had already lessened your hold on reality even before the malaria fever intensified the hallucinations to the point where they may now seem more real than me. . . .'

He extinguished the half-smoked cigarette by dropping it inside the nearly empty bottle, tantalising the prisoner.

'Do they seem more real than me, Duvalier?'

You are the dream, Minh, he wanted to say. You are the bad dream and the others are real. Please God, the others are real, not you. . . .

'Answer my question, Captain Duvalier!'

Raoul battled for control of his mind, telling himself that the Legion of St Martin was real, that Louise and Marie existed, that Frank and Roger were not just figments of his imagination. . . .

He watched in slow motion as Minh's right hand lifted off the table. It swept through the air between them and out of his field of vision then crashed against his right eye in a powerful back-hander. Again. And again. The restraining hands held Raoul's head steady as the blows came faster and from both directions.

With a scream of rage, Minh kicked over the flimsy table and stood in front of him, blocking out the light, hitting and kicking at Raoul's head and body until he abruptly sat down, apparently tired by the effort.

'Now which is real?' he snarled. 'Your fantasies, or me?'

Raoul could no longer see out of his right eye. He felt liquid running down his cheek and hoped it was just blood, not the matter of the eye itself.

I don't want to be blind as well as crippled, he prayed. Please God, I don't want to be blind. . . .

The pain in his eye was bad. Even worse was the pain of betrayal inside his brain.

'You are real,' he admitted. Speech was growing easier. 'At any rate, the pain is real and you caused it.'

'Now we are making progress.' Minh sounded relieved. He was still breathing heavily.

Someone replaced the table between him and Raoul. An arm from the shadows placed another bottle of beer on the table in front of Minh. He took a long drink from it. There was a stab of fire in Raoul's right arm as a needle went into the vein.

'Now,' said Minh. 'You are going to tell me where the gold is.'

'By the bridge. I showed you. By the bridge over the Nam Youm.' His own voice grew distant in his ears.

Minh stood up and walked round the table. He sat on it and bent down until his face was only inches away from Raoul's. A little light reflected off Raoul's own face lit up the eyes watching him. They seemed very large, like a deep pool into which Raoul was being pitched forward. Panicking with vertigo, he wanted to pull back from the edge of the pool, but could not.

'I know all about the two caches of gold, Duvalier.' Minh's voice was crystal clear in Raoul's brain, as pure and pleasant as birdsong in the hush of a deep forest.

'It was clever of you,' he continued, 'to split the *caisse noire* into two halves and bury them separately. You were cleverer than I thought. But you see, in the end I am cleverer than you. I find everything out sooner or later, do I not?'

Raoul tried to say no, but what came out was 'Yes.'

He tried to take his eyes off Minh's, but could not.

Minh was smiling.

The smile told Raoul that he could never escape from the *can-bô* who had saved his life on the battlefield of Dien Bien Phu. He knew that release was just a dream and that the Legion of St Martin was only the fantasy of a madman whose brain had snapped while caged in a black box.

Despairingly, he croaked, 'I will tell you what you want to know.'

'Aah!'

This was the moment for which Minh had waited so long. 'The second cache, Duvalier. You are going to tell me where that gold is now.'

2

'Frank?'

'Who is it?'

'Roger. I'm calling from the bar. You sound weird. Are you pissed or something?'

'Course not.' Frank switched on the bedside light which had been flashing intermittently. It was 2 a.m. 'I just got to bed. I've been at the hospital all evening with Marie-France.'

'She had it yet?'

'Nope. She sent me away. Said I was more nuisance than help.'

'Listen, Frank, I know you've got other things on your mind but something has happened up at the tower. Raoul's emergency signal is flashing and bleeping its guts out.'

Frank yawned. 'My light is flashing too. If I hadn't been so deeply asleep . . .'

'Now, it could be a technical fault.'

'Have you asked the kraut? He's the one who installed the system.'

'He's standing beside me now.'

There was a mumble of voices at Roger's end of the line. Then he said, 'Hans-Peter has checked out the circuit with some kind of meter. There's no malfunction. He says that Raoul must have activated the alarm.'

Frank sat up in bed. 'He could be ill, Roger.'

'In that case he'd have telephoned. The alarm is only for –'

'You're right.'

Frank stood up, holding the phone with one hand and reaching for his shirt with the other. 'Someone had better slip up to the tower and see what's going on.'

'I've sent Sean. He's the best man to move around at night without being seen or heard.'

'Check. I'll be with you in ten minutes.'

'Ten?'

'I'll come on a bike so as not to show any lights.'

The kitchen of Roger's bar was a jumble of plasterboard, hanging wires and half-installed equipment. On the burglar alarm console an indicator lamp flashed on and off. The buzzer had been disconnected by the time Frank arrived.

Hans-Peter was sitting in his robe, barefoot at the kitchen table. Roger was wearing a suit of old fatigues dyed black. Frank was dressed in a dark shirt and trousers, with black trainers on his feet.

'How long has Sean been gone?' was his first question.

Roger checked the wall clock. 'Nearly a quarter of an hour.'

Frank took the cup of coffee that Hans-Peter held out to him.

'If that was a false alarm,' he said, 'our little Irish friend would have been back by now.'

The night was pitch dark. Sean kept well back in the trees, clear of the field swept by the infra-red detection devices mounted on the walls of the tower. If there were intruders inside the tower, the alarm system was now on their side.

With a non-smoker's keen sense of smell his nostrils picked up the unmistakable odour of fresh blood. Sean knelt on the ground and felt around in the darkness. There was a patch of damp earth where one of the dogs had had its throat slit as a *coup de grâce*. He rubbed his fingers in the wetness and raised them to his nostrils to make sure then squatted on his haunches in the shadows, analysing the other smells and sounds of the night while he reconstructed what must have happened.

There was a slight sound from the top of the tower: a scuffing of cloth on stone. A sentry, thought Sean. Maybe more than one. He crawled silently under a bush and tossed a stone well away from where he was hiding. It fell into dead gorse and long grass, making a noise like a startled deer.

The sentry leaned over between the battlements, straining to see what had made the noise. The starlight scope had been detached from the crossbow and was used now to scan the ground below, revealing only bushes and grass. An electronically intensified image of Sean's left leg was studied for two or three minutes before being dismissed as a fallen branch because of its immobility.

Sean waited ten more minutes before moving. He snake-crawled silently through the undergrowth until he was sheltered by the overhang of the rock, then scrambled down the cliff and ran crouching through the village to Roger's bar, taking advantage of garden walls and houses to screen him from any observer on the tower.

'You took your time,' was Roger's greeting.

'Well?' asked Frank.

'Something's up.'

Sean winced at the light in the kitchen and slipped on a pair of dark glasses to protect his night vision. 'Whoever's in the tower has killed the two guard dogs. The bodies aren't there so they must have taken them inside.'

'Very tidy,' commented Frank.

'How did they get inside?' asked Roger. 'It's one thing to kill the dogs, but –'

'I've worked that out,' Sean interrupted. 'Crossbow. They shot a line over the tower, hauled a rope up and let themselves in by the door on the roof.'

'There's no moon.'

'They have some kind of starlight scope.'

'Professional,' said Frank.

'Very,' Sean agreed. 'And there's a vehicle.'

'Where?' asked Frank.

'Neatly parked in the garage with Raoul's car so there's no outward sign anything's wrong.'

'Except the dogs and that.' Roger nodded at the flashing light.

'Any idea who they might be?' Hans-Peter showed interest for the first time.

'After I chucked a stone into some bushes,' said Sean, 'the guy on the roof reported into a walkie-talkie. He spoke in some tonal Asian language. I guess it was Vietnamese.'

He sounded puzzled. 'I thought the sentry's voice could have been a woman's, but maybe I imagined that.'

3

'**C**aptain Duvalier! Can you hear me?'

Minh's distant voice was drowned by a rhythmic sound like waves on a pebble beach. The roar of each incoming wave was followed by the grating of the undertow. The noise grew gradually fainter, until Raoul identified it as the sound of his own breathing. As it faded, Minh's voice became louder and more normal.

Raoul opened his eyes to find himself lying on his bed in the Templars' tower. A surgical dressing was taped above his right eyebrow. The cut throbbed but his vision was unaffected. His mouth felt parched. Otherwise the rest of his body was normal. He lifted one hand clear of the bed sheets. It was clean, the fingernails unbroken but with traces of rubber solution clinging to the cuticles.

'Make-up,' explained Minh. 'It had to be realistic, however good these modern drugs may be.'

Raoul was mystified.

'I wished to take no chances with an old adversary as cunning as you. We gave you scopolamine and a Molotov cocktail – a mixture of drugs invented at the Serbsky Institute in Moscow to obtain very rapid confessions.'

Raoul's brain was clearing, but he felt physically weak. Another pillow was thrust beneath his head by a black-clad woman seated beside the bed. Minh barked an order at her.

She filled a syringe with liquid from a coloured plastic phial, placed it on a table outside Raoul's reach and left the room.

Raoul was busy looking about him, checking that everything was as it should be. A great elation hit him as he realised that the room, the tower and everything else about his life in St Martin was real and not just the hallucination of a madman.

The final confirmation lay in Minh's features. Seen clearly in full light, it was the face of a fifty-year-old. Minh had aged. His hair had been dyed black to conceal a few grey hairs and back-combed to make it look thicker.

'They did a make-up job on you too,' Raoul observed.

'The ravages of time . . .'

'So . . . Thanks to your drugs, I told you what you wanted to know?'

'You did,' Minh confirmed. 'My people have broken into your hiding place in the dungeon. They are bringing the gold up to ground level now. Then we shall load it on our vehicle and depart swiftly.'

'Just like that?'

'There will be one last injection for you.' Minh's eyes strayed to the syringe beside him. 'But I can promise you at least no more pain.'

He lit a cigarette from the stub of the previous one. 'Strange, to be smoking a Gauloise again after all these years. I acquired a taste for them when I was a student in Paris.'

Desperate to keep the conversation going, Raoul asked, 'What did you study? Politics? History?'

'Theology,' Minh sniggered. 'I was intended for the priesthood.'

The explanation made sense. 'I used to think of you as a Jesuit,' said Raoul slowly.

He wanted to slow the whole pace of the conversation; Operation Rainbow's End depended on timing. 'I saw you as a man serving a red star as others serve the cross. You had that implacable faith which consigns living bodies to the flames in order to save their souls.'

A nod. 'I was educated by the Jesuits at Hué – such a promising student that the brothers sent me to France to complete my studies. It was in Paris that I became a communist.'

'The Order of Jesus made a mistake.'

'Not at all,' Minh disagreed. 'I have been a devout, unquestioning Marxist. Jesus or Karl I should have served with equal devotion. Changing sides was simply a matter of transferring total allegiance from one master to another.'

The tunnel which began underneath the church, in the sealed-off crypt where they had stored the equipment for Rainbow's End, swiftly became a steep flight of subterranean stairs leading upward to the top of the cliff, underneath the tower.

Frank removed his caving helmet and wiped beads of perspiration from his blacked-up face. He was breathing heavily. Roger followed him into the chamber hollowed out centuries before. He too was sweating from the rapid climb as he unwound the cable of a field telephone. He placed the hand-set on the damp floor and wound the handle for a test ring. At the other end of the cable, Hans-Peter's voice was calm.

Frank checked his watch. 'We've got about five minutes to Go. That should be enough.'

In front of him was a wall of dressed stone. On the dungeon side it appeared solid; on Frank's side the blocks were held in place by wooden wedges, easily knocked out with the hammer that hung ready from a rusted hook. Frank handed Roger the .22 civilian version FAMAS assault rifles he had been carrying. Each had two loaded magazines taped back-to-back. They also had a couple of stun grenades per man.

Cautiously Frank knocked out the wooden wedges. The stones were now held in place by only a few millimetres of soft lime mortar, ready for swift removal. He unstopped a small eyehole and peered through into the dungeon beneath the Templars' tower. All was dark.

He put his ear to the hole and listened for a moment before announcing, 'Nobody there.'

Roger braced himself firmly against the rock wall behind them and raised a booted foot to kick in the marked stone in the dungeon wall which was designed to give way. He kicked twice, swore and kicked a third time, harder.

The heavy stone slid, tottered on the edge of the one below and fell. There was a dull thud as it hit the dirt floor of the dungeon. Roger peered inside.

'What can you see?' Frank asked in a whisper.

'Doesn't make sense.'

Roger kept his voice low, turning his head to pan the narrow beam of the light on his helmet round the interior of the dungeon. 'The raiders have brought a whole lot of gear down here. There's a chair and lights rigged up. A bamboo table. And the walls are lined with bamboo matting.'

'Let me see,' said Frank. Ignoring the bamboo hut décor that had been so convincing to Raoul in his drugged state, he played his lamp on the wall opposite. The secret cavity, known only to him and Raoul, was open and empty.

Minh moved to the window and glanced at the eastern sky, wanting to be gone before dawn.

It seemed through Sean's telescopic sight that the Oriental face was staring straight at him. Then the hooded eyes were replaced by the back of Minh's head as he turned to face his old adversary in the bed.

'When I became a Marxist,' he said, 'I discovered that it is surprisingly easy for a religious to discard one philosophy for another which gives a more relevant answer to life's problems.'

'I suppose so.'

'In a few minutes we shall leave your tower,' Minh promised, 'and you, Duvalier, will know the answer to the greatest of all questions.'

He stubbed out the cigarette and touched the syringe the nurse had left on the tray.

Delay, thought Raoul, each minute counts. . . . To play

on Minh's vanity, he begged, 'Tell me how you tracked me down. Tell me that at least.'

Minh smiled, unable to resist playing with his captive to the end. 'How do you think I tracked you down, Duvalier?'

'The last box of gold turned up, I suppose. When I heard it was missing, I had a premonition of this. But Frank was right to abandon it.'

'Frank the American? You see, I know them all.'

Minh laughed, coughing on the Gauloise smoke in his lungs. To Raoul's surprise, he continued laughing and coughing until tears were running down his face.

'It was not the missing box of gold,' he gasped at last. 'Oh no, Duvalier, that has nothing to do with why I am here.'

Raoul was genuinely puzzled. 'You mean it wasn't found, after all?'

'*Mais oui*,' conceded Minh, when he had got his breath back. 'It was found by peasants the following morning when they explored the hole your people had dug during the night.'

'And?'

'They did what peasants have always done. They buried the gold again!'

Raoul blinked. He had not thought of that possibility.

'Only when odd coins started turning up on the black market in Hanoi were enquiries made which ended up on the desk of the new political commissar for the region of Dien Bien Phu.'

'And what did he do?'

'You are looking at him,' said Minh slyly.

'Then, what did you do?'

'No one likes to confess failure. You know that as well as anyone, Duvalier. When I put two and two together, I realised that you had fooled me all those years ago by dividing the gold into two caches and revealing only one to me.

'I was ashamed, for I should have been more astute. I realised from what the peasants revealed under examination that someone – obviously not you – had come back and dug up the second cache, missing one box. I went through all the reports of cross-border incursions until I found one that fitted: your Legion of St Martin, on the operation you called Rainbow.'

He stopped, head cocked to listen to the sounds of loading coming from below. A voice cried something in Vietnamese.

'They are ready,' said Minh. He picked up the syringe. '*Nunc dimittis.*'

'And then?' Raoul prompted. 'What did you do then?'

'I dispatched the peasants to work camps and destroyed all the evidence of what had taken place. I did a good cover-up job for you.'

'Why?'

'I told you,' said Minh irritably. 'No one likes to confess failure.'

'So why are you here?' insisted Raoul.

He had a terrible feeling that he already knew the answer. 'If you covered up for us, why are you here now?'

'It's very simple.' Minh put down the syringe. He watched Raoul's face closely, enjoying the effect his words were having. 'You were betrayed.'

Raoul groaned.

'You were betrayed to Hanoi. This time, there was nothing a humble district commissar could do to cover his own shortcomings.'

'So one of my Legion of St Martin is a traitor?' Raoul shook his head, not wanting to believe what he knew was true.

'Yes.'

There was another cry in Vietnamese from downstairs. Minh shouted something in return. He picked up a cigarette from the pack beside the syringe and moved to the window to peer out into the pre-dawn light. He could see nothing through the small leaded panes.

'One of the members of your futile little community, all bound by your unbreakable code of honour, has betrayed you.' Minh interrupted himself to strike a match and light the cigarette, savouring the pleasure of what he had to say.

621

4

It was almost an exact repeat of the first time Sean had killed a man.

He lay on a bare rock looking down on the tower, the rifle stock nestled against his cheek. His world had narrowed to a single lit window – and from that to the field of the telescopic sight in which the enemy's face was lit briefly by a match. The pinpoint reflection in Minh's eye would last only a second, then the moment would be gone.

Sean squeezed the trigger by reflex. Centred in the telescopic sight was Minh's eyeball. The bullet sped through the air, impacted on the glass and neatly removed one pane from the leaded frame, leaving the rest intact. The fragmented glass, travelling at slightly less than the speed of sound, shredded the facial skin and muscles as efficiently as shrapnel. Damage from the glass was superficial because Minh's body was already travelling backwards, driven by the impact of Sean's dumdummed bullet, which had mushroomed inside the target's skull, removing the back of his head from ear to ear. The lifeless body with its unrecognisably gory head was thrown halfway across the room, to lie inertly across the foot of Raoul's bed.

The right hand that had been holding the fatal cigarette lay awkwardly across the body as though Minh were trying to confer one final benison. There was a groan as the air left his lungs and bubbled through the lacerated throat. The hand subsided, its blessing done.

His robe held high, Hans-Peter sprinted down the steps of the crypt. One sandal fell off and then another. He grabbed the field telephone and wound furiously at the handle.

The shot he had just heard was early. Realising that Sean must have had an irresistible target to make him jump the gun, Hans-Peter screamed into the hand-set, 'Come on, Roger! Answer the damned thing.'

At that instant the door of Raoul's bedroom burst open. The woman in black leaped through the door, a 9mm Makarov automatic pistol at the ready. She took in the scene: the broken window, the body of Minh and the invalid lying half-trapped beneath it with his hands raised in the air.

Shouting something in Vietnamese she advanced into the room, taking careful aim at Raoul's head with the Makarov held in both hands. She was halfway across the room when Sean's second bullet neatly removed another pane of glass and impacted on her shoulder.

The third shot followed instantaneously, the dum-dummed bullet removing her face in a spray of atomised pink globules and hurling her remains back through the doorway where she disappeared from Raoul's view to roll and fall soggily down the spiral stairs. Another raider, running upstairs three at a time, collided with the faceless body coming down. They fell in a tangle to the next landing.

'Go! Go! Go!' shouted Hans-Peter, the second he heard Roger's voice.

At the other end of the tunnel, Roger slammed down the hand-set.

'That's Hans-Peter's cue!' he shouted. 'Never mind the time. Let's go.'

He lifted one leg to slip through the small gap in the stone wall. As he bent to pick up his FAMAS, the beam of his helmet lamp wavered.

Frank's peripheral vision picked up something furry just

inside the hole. 'There's an animal in there,' he said.

Roger moved his head to let the torch play on the lifeless form of one of the Alsatian guard dogs. 'Never mind that. It's dead.'

His leg was halfway through the opening when Frank grabbed him off balance and pulled him back into the chamber.

'What the fuck are you doing?' Roger snarled, adrenalin pumping. 'We've got to move fast.'

Frank's memory had moved faster than reason to connect a dead Alsatian, a hole in the rock and a comrade in danger. . . .

He shouldered Roger aside, to be first through the hole. His shoulders jammed in the gap. With a grunt, he wriggled them through and pushed down with his hands to lift himself over the stone sill, never feeling the thin black nylon trip-wire press briefly against his forehead or hearing the *thwack!* of the bowstring.

The raiders' trap had been well set. The crossbow, securely jammed into a crack between the stones in the far corner of the dungeon, did not budge as the release mechanism dispatched the barbed metal bolt on its short flight. The shaft entered Frank's body, horizontal in the hole, between his left collar-bone and the trapezius muscle. It tore through the skin and muscle, fat and lung tissue, transfixing the subclavian artery. The impact drove his body back through the hole to collapse on the dirty floor at Roger's feet.

'Jesus!' Roger knelt and ripped the shirt away from Frank's shoulder.

The wound was not bleeding but it was obvious that it was mortal. Eyes wide with shock, Roger stared down at the small piece of metal protruding from Frank's body.

He saw the lips moving and bent his ear to Frank's mouth, barely catching the words 'apple blossom', then 'Cold. So cold.'

Roger cradled the dying man in his arms. 'It's OK, Frank. You'll be OK. I'll get Hans-Peter here right away and he'll take care of you.'

A strange gurgling came from Frank's throat. Even if the words had been clear, Roger would not have recognised the song or known that the old Buddy Holly number had been De Burgh's jukebox favourite.

'That'll be the day . . .'

Just before the life left him, Frank opened his eyes wide. In the faint yellow light of Roger's helmet lamp, he saw a man bending over him. Mistaking the blacked-up, sweat-streaked features, Frank reached out his right hand, smiling. The years dropped away from his face and for a second he was a young man of twenty again.

'Hi!' he said clearly. 'How you been, man?'

Roger laid the lifeless body on the ground and took a deep breath. He could do nothing for Frank but hopefully Raoul was still alive. . . .

Defying the possibility of another trap, he scrambled through the hole into the dungeon, ran up the flight of stone steps, switched off his helmet lamp and kicked open the door at the top.

Silence and blackness. He took one step, then a second. The muzzle of a gun was rammed firmly into the back of his neck.

'Freeze!' a low voice ordered.

'It's me, you fool,' whispered Roger. He switched on the lamp of his helmet.

'I got two of them,' said Sean. His eyes showed white in the blackened face staring at Roger. 'What kept you and Frank down there so long?'

'Keep your voice down. Frank's dead. I'll tell you later. What's happening up here?'

'You don't need to whisper. They've gone. Piss-panic. Just drove straight out of the garage and down the track like they was on two wheels.'

'You let them go?'

'Once I saw they'd left the loot behind, neatly stacked on the garage floor, it seemed more important to get in here fast and see what they've done to Raoul.'

They inched their way up the twisting staircase, stepping

over the inert and faceless corpse of the woman sentry. It was the first time Sean had seen at close quarters what the combination of his outstanding marksmanship and a dumdum bullet could do to a human body. He hurried upward in Roger's footsteps.

Raoul picked up the syringe with which Minh had been toying. He pressed the plunger and spilled colourless liquid onto the stone floor. Operation Rainbow could so easily have finished with him lying dead, not Frank. It was unjust, he thought, that an old man should survive and a young man with so much to look forward to, be killed. . . .

Roger and the other two men had cleared away most of the evidence of the night's violence. The bodies of the two dogs and the Viet casualties were lying, weighted, at the bottom of the river. Lack of reaction from the village made it seem that the three shots fired by Sean from the top of the bluff had caused no alarm in St Martin. If anyone had woken up, they must have thought they were hearing poachers.

Raoul jumped at the sound of the telephone. 6 a.m.? Who would be calling at that time? Possibly the call was for the raiders – some kind of warning they had arranged. He picked up the receiver and listened without saying anything.

'Raoul, is that you?' It was Marie's voice, calling from a phone box.

'Yes.' The anticlimax was so great, he sounded disappointed.

'Are you all right?'

'I'm OK.'

'Did I wake you up?'

'No.' He tried to keep his voice normal. 'I was awake.'

'I'm calling from the hospital. I've been trying to ring Frank at the château, but I get no answer. Can you try and get through to him?'

'Listen, Marie . . .' he began to explain.

'I can't hold on, the money's running out. Just tell my handsome son-in-law that he has a gorgeous, healthy son.'

Marie laughed: 'It's funny, some babies look like nobody except themselves, but this one looks unmistakably like a miniature Frank. He's so like his dad, it'll make you smile. And tell the proud father that Marie-France is fine. She sends her love. Tell him to hurry down here and see them both.'

A series of pips cut off Marie's voice. Raoul replaced the receiver.

He made a list of what had to be done and began ringing the gendarmerie, the doctor, the ambulance service It was mid-morning when he steeled himself to dial a series of twelve digits that connected with the other side of the world. The dialling tone continued for a long time before a woman's voice answered.

'Hallo,' he said. 'Is that Madame Koenig?'

There was a long pause with a ringing echo on the line, as though the circuit had been broken.

'Hallo?' he repeated. 'This is Captain Raoul Duvalier '

'Yes,' she said. 'I recognise voice. My husband not here He is on estate, cannot come to phone.'

Raoul remembered her stilted French from previous conversations. He spoke clearly and slowly for her benefit. 'Will you please give him a message? Tell him that I rang with some bad news. His friend Frank Hansen has died. Koenig was Frank's commanding officer. We shall delay the funeral for a couple of days, to give him a chance to get here.'

'Oh,' she said, her voice empty of emotion. 'Such sad news. My husband very fond of Frank Hansen.'

'You will give him the message?'

'Of course,' she said. 'Goodbye.'

5

They buried Frank in St Martin's small cemetery beside the Dordogne, beneath a simple white head-stone carved with the same device which had been tattooed on his arm: the eagle and the snake of the Legion.

Koenig appeared in civilian clothes shortly before the ceremony was due to begin. He brought with him a firing party of four recruits and a bugler from the Legion's nearest base at Castelnaudary. As the four young men in uniform bore the coffin from the church of St Martin to the burial ground, Koenig merged with the throng of mourners.

After the priest had ended the prayers at the graveside the tall man with the black eye-patch stepped forward to the edge of the hole and recited unbidden the poem which he had quoted to Frank in faraway Vietnam. His firm voice rang out as clearly as it once had on the parade ground at Fort Lesieur when Frank and De Burgh had been raw recruits sixteen years before.

> 'I have a rendezvous with Death
> At some disputed barricade,
> When Spring comes back with rustling shade
> and apple-blossoms fill the air . . .'

The words in English meant nothing to the assembled villagers but no one moved or spoke.

'It may be he shall take my hand
And lead me into his dark land
and close my eyes and quench my breath . . .'

Raoul's face was drawn and sallow. He blamed himself for
leading Frank into the dark land. When things went wrong,
it was always the general's fault.

Beside the wheelchair Marie stood dry-eyed, wanting to
comfort Sven Hansen who was weeping openly. Roger and
Sean stood a little way off with Hans-Peter in his robes.

'And I to my pledged word am true,' Koenig finished, 'I
shall not fail that rendezvous.'

He saluted and stood a moment with head bowed, looking
down at the coffin. He took one pace to the rear. The bugler
played the Last Post. Commands rang out. The volley was
fired. Earth was thrown on to the coffin and people started
to move out of the graveyard.

Then Raoul raised his voice in the slow cadence of 'Le
Boudin', the most famous of the Legion's songs. First to
join were the four young soldiers of the firing party and the
bugler. The sound swelled as Roger, Hans-Peter and Sean
added their voices.

Only Koenig kept silent, his mouth a thin, hard line.

Roger surveyed the remains of the buffet supper he and
Hans-Peter had arranged. The trestle table on the roof of
Raoul's tower was covered in half-eaten snacks. Nobody had
eaten or drunk very much.

It was a beautiful golden summer evening with an idyllic
view over the village and the fields, orchards and vineyards
of the Dordogne valley. Most of the guests had departed,
leaving only Sven Hansen to finish his goodbyes.

He nodded at the view. 'This is a beautiful place, Captain
Duvalier. I can understand why Frank wanted to live here.'

He stepped into the lift with Marie, bound for the hospital
to visit Marie-France and the baby.

'I'm proud to have met so many of Frank's friends,' he
called as the lift sank below floor level. 'God bless you all.'

Raoul kept his sad smile in place until the lift was gone. Now only the Legion of St Martin was left.

It had been hard to act a part at the funeral, but he owed that much to the mourners. He took a deep breath.

Suspicion! Unless Minh was lying for some inscrutable reason, one or more of the men standing on the roof of the tower within a few feet of me, is a traitor who caused Frank's death. Now that man of dishonour must be unmasked and the appropriate action taken.

Of course the traitor could have been a woman. . . .

Which one would be capable of such an act? Huguette of course. F⌐ ₃ share of two million dollars, she would do anything. Against ₁₋ , he knows little that could have been useful to Minh. And whoever helped Minh to plan his attack, knew a lot about the defences of the tower. The raid was too slick, too rapid to be improvised. Every last detail had been planned in advance. No, not Huguette.

Marie? No, she hates Communism, which twice destroyed her life, and I doubt if she would be capable of treachery anyway. Her daughter? Again no. Since the end of Operation Rainbow, Marie-France has been too radiantly happy for a person planning deceit and betrayal. Although . . . it does seem that she betrayed Frank, in the carnal sense of the word, with Milton. At least, so her mother told me.

Raoul shook his head in answer to Roger's gesture, holding out a glass of wine. He wanted to keep a clear head.

And what of these men, my legionnaires of St Martin? Koenig? Roger Milton? Sean and Hans-Peter?

Motive? Opportunity? Reward?

What would make one of them betray the others?

But is a traitor motivated by reward? Or is treachery almost always the act of a misfit wanting to hurt the class or society which has hurt him or failed to recognise his talents? Once uncovered, a traitor may pretend that he committed treachery for this or that grand cause, but the fact is that betrayal is always a negative act.

Raoul's glance strayed to the cemetery down by the river. He missed Frank's no-nonsense approach to any problem.

'Rubbish!' Frank would have said. 'Forget the philosophy, Raoul. Look for opportunity . . .'

Like most Westerners of my generation, I suspect any European who embraces an Oriental religion.

If Frank were here, he'd point the finger of suspicion at that German clad in Buddhist robes. He never liked the man. From the start, he warned me that Muller was unreliable. And Muller hated Frank, so what kind of a monk does that make him? Muller was inexplicably missing for months after Operation Rainbow. Why did he come back here? Was it out of friendship for Milton and Carey; or was he the advance party?

And what an ally he would have made for Minh! For Muller planned and installed the whole alarm system. He could have told Minh everything he needed to know.

When I asked Muller where he had been all these months, he smiled vaguely and said 'In a monastery in Thailand, working out my own salvation.' Maybe. But perhaps he took a side trip to Hanoi. . . .

The sun glinted on Sven's hired car as it crossed the bridge on its way to the hospital. A bitter sense of loss hit Raoul like a pain. Unmasking and punishing the traitor was not just a duty owed to Frank, it would satisfy the primitive need for revenge: a hurt to cancel out a hurt.

Take the Irishman.

You never know what's going on in his mind, behind those grey eyes that give nothing away. He is a cold, repressed man who rarely smiles. He doesn't seem to want women. At first I thought he and the German were a couple. But he doesn't want men either, as far as I can tell. He doesn't drink or smoke. He has shown no interest in his share of the gold, except to buy that campsite of his, which cost peanuts.

But he's another misfit, like the German. If he'd not been born in a slum, he would never have become a soldier. I've heard him playing the flute and talked to him about music. He had it in him to be a great musician. I can understand a man like that being consumed by bitterness about the way life has cheated him of his birthright. I can understand that man wanting to hit back at society, at me, at everyone. . . .

And Milton? What do I know about him? Intelligent. A dreamer. A good soldier, so Frank said. Strong and brave. Of the three, Milton was closest to Frank. But in my book an honest man doesn't steal a friend's wife. Of course, Frank wasn't actually married, but it amounts to the same thing.

This is insane. How can I, of all people, judge a man for seducing his friend's wife? The truth is that I have no grounds to suspect Roger Milton of anything. On the contrary, I owe my life to the way that man and his comrades carried out Rainbow with split-second timing. If Carey had delayed his shot another minute, Minh would have given me that last injection and I'd be lying down there in the plot of ground by the river next to Frank.

I am only suspicious of those young men because they are not of Koenig's generation and mine. How do I know what they understand by honour or duty? Definitions change. Koenig taught me that.

'Am I interrupting your reverie, old friend?' Koenig's voice cut through Raoul's unhappy thoughts.

'Perhaps it's just as well. Sit down and keep me company.'

Koenig sat heavily in the crenellation next to Raoul's wheelchair. Despite his efforts at self-control during the funeral service and after, his face was scarred by pain.

'It's over now,' said Raoul. 'All done.'

Koenig sat forward on the edge of the stone, hands clenched in his lap. With an effort, as though a great burden were pushing him down, he forced himself to raise his head and meet Raoul's eyes.

'You're looking for a traitor, *mon vieux*,' he said.

Raoul stared at the three young men on the other side of the roof.

Koenig's claw hand grabbed his friend's arm.

'Look this way,' he said hoarsely.

At first Raoul did not understand. And then he saw that the haunted look in Koenig's eyes was deeper than comes from the grief of losing a friend, even one who has been like a son. It was the anguish of a man destroyed. If his thoughts

632

since the funeral had not been preoccupied with the pathos of a man's untimely death at the hour his son was born, Raoul would have seen it earlier.

'Old friend,' he gasped. 'What's wrong?'

6

The conversation between Roger, Sean and Hans-Peter stopped in mid-sentence.

Instinctively they stayed where they were, leaving space for Koenig to unburden himself. He rose and stood back-lit by the sunset, hands hanging at his sides as though inviting them to strike him.

In a hoarse voice, he said, 'I am the traitor you are looking for. I was standing beside my wife when Raoul telephoned about Frank's death. I was too ashamed to talk to him.'

'What are you saying?' Raoul thought his friend had gone mad. 'How could you of all people, Koenig. . . . How could you betray us to the Viets?'

'Suspicion,' said Koenig, 'is a terrible thing between friends. I did not come here today to pay my respects to Frank. I had no right to do that. But I owed something to people, so I went through the motions of a proper grief down there in the graveyard, convincingly I hope.

'The true reason I came is that I knew you would be sniffing out the man who had betrayed you all.'

Raoul turned his wheelchair to look at the three men listening to Koenig's confession. He had suspected them, yet they were loyal and the traitor was his oldest friend. . . .

Koenig rested one arm on the battlement. Below him, the

wall fell sheer to the cliff and the terracotta tiles of the village roofs a hundred metres below.

'I told the Viets everything about your defences, your alarm system. I gave them all the details I knew so that their raid could be swift, allowing you three men and Frank a minimum reaction time. I planned for them to get away before anyone could be hurt.'

He gave a half-bow in their direction. 'But I underestimated what good soldiers I was up against. You didn't lose any time, did you? If you had arrived even a few minutes later, there would have been no casualties.'

Seeing in memory the way Minh had toyed with the lethal syringe, Raoul asked, 'You trusted the word of the Viet Minh – the Viet Cong or whatever they call themselves now? It's not possible, Koenig. You have known them for what they are, over more than a quarter of a century.'

'They said . . .' Koenig lost his voice.

It was Roger who silently handed him a glass of water. No one else moved.

'They said they would use drugs to make you tell them exactly where the gold was and promised there would be no after-effect.'

'Minh's plan,' said Raoul, 'was to kill me with one last injection. You must have known they would do that.'

Koenig lurched sideways, grabbing the battlement for support.

For a moment, Raoul thought his friend was going to jump. He leaned half out of the wheelchair and pulled at Koenig's arm.

'Sit down,' he pleaded. 'And tell me why you have done this thing.'

Koenig pounded his fists on the old stones. 'You want excuses for something inexcusable.'

Chest heaving, he allowed himself to be pulled down to a sitting position. His face, painted red by the sunset, was a portrait of misery.

'Tell me how this all came about,' ordered Raoul. 'Yc owe me that much.'

Koenig met his eyes briefly and looked away. 'You know how it is in Asia. There are no secrets. Whether the Corsicans talked, I don't know. At any rate, Stanton's people fingered me for Hanoi, as a sort of belated revenge.'

'But what made you co-operate,' asked Raoul, 'instead of telling us?' He had an intuition that they had not heard the worst yet.

'They took my children as hostages.' Koenig's face was twitching. 'They gave me a choice of getting the gold back for them or receiving my children's dead bodies.'

He raised both hands in front of his face, to screen it from their eyes until he had regained control of himself.

'And do they still have your son and daughter, old friend?' Raoul asked softly.

Koenig's eye swept over the three silent men listening on the other side of the roof. He avoided looking at Raoul and focused wretchedly on the distance.

'When I refused to do this thing, they gave me back my daughter.'

'Why?'

'To teach me a lesson, they hooked her on heroin and returned to me a little girl of eight whose brain was damaged beyond repair.'

Koenig lifted his hands and examined them, palms up. 'With these hands I helped her to die.'

As though asking Raoul to explain, he clutched him. 'They were local people who had done that to her. I knew them. They knew me. They had watched her grow up. And . . . they threatened me that my ten-year-old son would be returned in the same condition if Hanoi did not get the gold back.'

'You should have told us about this.' Roger's harsh, angry voice made both Raoul and Koenig turn in his direction.

'And what could you have done?' asked Koenig bitterly 'Mounted another Operation Rainbow to rescue my children?'

'Yes,' said Sean. 'With great pleasure.'

Koenig clasped his head in his hands.

'I didn't even know where they were being held,' he groaned. 'It was probably only a mile or two from my estate. Beneath each village the Viet Cong have dug miles of tunnels. They have underground hospitals, living quarters, classrooms, armouries. You would never have found them in that underground maze, even if you had stumbled on the right entrance.'

'Then it's all over?' asked Raoul.

Koenig did not look up. 'When I said goodbye at the graveside, I was talking to my son as well as Frank.'

'Supposing,' said Roger. 'Just supposing Hanoi got the gold back – or what we've got left, which is most of it ... would they hand back your son?'

'Probably,' said Koenig dully. 'I don't know.'

'Well,' Roger shouted. 'Get off your arse and find out, captain.'

Raoul stared at him. 'What are you suggesting?'

'Now Frank is dead, the gold belongs to the five of us standing here at this moment. We can do what the hell we want with it. Right?'

'Correct.'

'Well, if those bastards want a couple of million dollars' worth of loot to help finish off their war in the South, let 'em have it, I say. It won't make any difference to the outcome of the war if we give the gold back to them in exchange for that kid's life.'

Koenig listened to the exchange, his eyes flicking from one speaker to the other.

Raoul held up the five fingers of his left hand. 'They can have Koenig's share and mine, for a start.' He folded the thumb and index, leaving three fingers outstretched.

'After what that gold cost you?' Koenig wondered.

'Getting it back was a fixation,' said Raoul. 'It was the obsession that gave me the strength to go on. But do I need it now? I live in a beautiful place. I have enough money to live. I have friends. I have a woman who loves me. What more should I want?'

Roger walked across the roof and knelt in front of Koenig.

'The gold was morally Raoul's and yours. Yours is the generation that paid the price for it. So you can have my share.'

He folded Raoul's middle finger.

Hans-Peter smiled at Fate. 'Buddhists believe that by disposing of their possessions, they make themselves free.'

Raoul held up just the little finger. Four pairs of eyes dwelled on Sean's back. He was facing away, staring at the belvedere from where he had fired the shots that killed Minh and the woman.

'What the fuck would I do with a third of a million dollars?' he grunted.

'Why?' asked Koenig of everyone. 'Why would you do this?'

'Fuck it,' said Sean, turning round to face him. 'We'd have done Rainbow just for kicks, *mon capitaine*. There didn't have to be any gold there in the first place.'

'We trained for five years,' explained Roger. He was still on his knees, talking to Koenig urgently, trying to bring him back to reality fast.

'You know how tough it is in the Legion's paras, captain. For five years, night and day, we took all the punishment they handed out. It was different for your generation and Raoul's. You had a real war to fight, but we never knew whether we had what it takes until that trip to Dien Bien Phu.'

'How can we contact Hanoi?' asked Raoul, being practical.

'That's easy,' Koenig said. He seemed stunned. 'Call my house. All the servants work for the VC. We can talk through them.'

'And is your son still alive?' asked Hans-Peter.

Koenig climbed unsteadily to his feet. He was aware that his brain was working slowly, unable to grasp the new possibility. He was almost unwilling to hope.

'I have a word-code I use with my wife when I am away because the VC always monitor the telephone lines. When I rang this morning she called me husband. That means she has reason to think my son is still alive.'

'Come,' Raoul wheeled himself into the lift. 'Let's make a phone call – and pray to God she was right.'

The handover took place three days later outside the concrete fortress of the USSR Embassy on the edge of the Bois de Boulogne. Under the curious eyes of a busload of CRS embassy guards commanded by a former legionnaire, Roger drove a decrepit, *deux-chevaux* van on to the pavement.

It was an hour before dawn and the only cars swishing past along the boulevard Lannes in the light drizzle were driven by pimps ferrying their sodden charges home after a hard night's grind in the Bois. The few drivers who slowed down to watch the last act of the drama of Operation Rainbow were waved energetically on by armed riot policemen with lit batons. They took the hint and accelerated away.

Roger stopped at the head of the ramp which led to the underground car park. The rear bumper was just inside the line of studs in the pavement that demarcated the limit of Soviet territory. A small group of well-muscled Russian guards stood by the van, waving back the cordon of French police. Roger removed the keys from the ignition and stepped backwards on to French soil. Two Vietnamese hurried out of the Embassy under umbrellas and began checking the contents of the van.

Two minutes after they had vanished inside the Embassy, the main door opened and Koenig appeared with his wife. A boy of ten, looking pale and frightened but otherwise healthy, stood between them. As they drew level with Roger, one of the Soviets put out his hand for the ignition key.

Roger handed it over and walked behind the family group as it crossed the road through the line of CRS in their blue battledress, with FAMAS rifles at the ready. Sean and Hans-Peter were sitting on the bonnet of Raoul's car, ignoring the rain. As Roger opened the rear passenger door, the ex-legionnaire in CRS uniform blew a whistle and waved his men back into their bus.

Raoul twisted round and stretched a hand towards Koenig's wife as she got into the back seat. She smiled uncertainly, recognised the faded tattoo on his wrist and shook his hand.

'I'm Raoul Duvalier,' he said. 'Your husband and I have been friends for a very long time. Welcome home.'

7

For days the sky had been black with smoke from burning oil wells. Even the mid-afternoon sun of the Persian Gulf could not pierce the mile-thick pall that hung over Kuwait to provide the retreating Iraqi army with the largest man-made smokescreen in history.

In the ravaged city itself life had almost stopped. Electricity and water had been cut off for weeks. The only food available was hoarded, looted or black-market canned goods. The senseless violence of the occupying forces kept most people off the streets. Through the debris-strewn gloom of what had been one of the city's most prestigious shopping streets a few figures moved in search of food or water, scuttling from one doorway to another like nervous animals.

Alerted by the clatter of approaching tank-tracks, they darted for cover as a convoy of Saddam Hussein's Republican Guards roared past in yellow-painted Soviet T-72 tanks, heading for the six-lane motorway leading to Basra and home. The *crump-crump* of exploding demolition charges was audible in the middle distance interspersed with small arms' fire as Iraqi firing squads settled some last scores with the Kuwaiti resistance. Invisible in the clouds of smoke a flight of French Jaguar fighter bombers screamed overhead, their course marked by exploding shells from radar-guided anti-aircraft batteries. The bomb-loads exploded in a tight pattern on an Iraqi bunker less than a mile away. High overhead a manta-like American Stealth bomber headed north for Baghdad, inaudible and invisible from the ground.

A loud squealing of metal on metal startled two teenage looters as the bullet-pocked metal shutter of an underground garage beneath a large apartment block was cranked up laboriously by hand. As it rose, the looters caught a glimpse of four men wearing Arab head-dresses over nondescript civilian clothes, two straining at the reluctant handle and two heaving at the shutter itself. Outnumbered, the boys took to their heels. The shutter finally jammed just high enough for a white Volvo family estate with an overloaded roof-rack, which was parked on the ramp inside, to pass underneath. The men leaped into the car. Unfamiliar with the Volvo, the driver swore when he saw the sidelights automatically come on with the ignition. The last thing he wanted was to attract attention.

He leaped out of the vehicle again and smashed the bulbs in the side and rear lights with the butt of his machine pistol, then jumped back behind the wheel and accelerated up the ramp and on to the street with a screech of tyres, heading northward through the drifting smoke in the hope of catching up with the Iraqi tanks before they reached the city limits.

Beneath the nondescript disguises, he and two of the other men wore the uniform of US Marines. They had volunteered to rescue an American businessman who had been hiding out with his family in the apartment of a Kuwaiti employee since the Iraqi invasion months before. The mission was not for humanitarian purposes: the 'businessman' was also a CIA undercover operative with information urgently needed for the last stage of Operation Desert Storm. But the extraction plan had gone wrong. The Marines and their nervous charges had arrived at the rendezvous point on the beach the previous night, only to find the oil-covered sea had been set on fire for miles in both directions and seaborne extraction was out of the question.

The Marine sergeant at the wheel of the Volvo was staking

everything on his gamble that the safest alternative way out of the city was to tag on to the ragged convoy of loot-laden vehicles which was following the column of tanks.

The dirty windows of the Volvo were kept tightly shut. It was stiflingly hot inside with the air conditioning switched off to save fuel. From the front passenger seat, the CIA man gave terse directions to the driver, suggesting side streets to use in the effort to catch up with the tanks. Behind, his wife cuddled their two children with another Marine riding shotgun beside her. The third Marine sat side-saddle in the rear seat, his weapon out of sight under a blanket. The woman was wearing a baggy Arab dress that covered her from head to foot with a veil concealing her pale face that had not seen the sun for months. The blond hair of her children was covered by dirty bandages which the Marines had wound around their heads. Nobody had the right papers to survive a close examination. They were relying on confusion and the nerve of the man at the wheel to get them to safety.

They bumped over small debris and between random barbed-wire barriers and stalled, looted and burnt-out vehicles. Every so often the driver stopped and switched off the engine, to strain his ears for the sound of tank-tracks. At one halt, three desperate and half-starved Iraqi soldiers staggered through the smoke and tried to hijack the car at gunpoint, so they could join the panic flight northwards.

'Don't fire!' the driver ordered. His right hand knocked the CIA man's revolver out of sight below the dashboard as he slammed his foot flat on the accelerator and headed straight at the Iraqis, scattering them and receiving in return half a Kalashnikov magazine of 7.62mm bullets that missed the Volvo's petrol tank and shattered the rear window, lightly wounding the Marine in the back seat.

Rounding a corner, the driver slammed on the brakes just in time to avoid colliding with an Iraqi army truck that loomed out of the gloom, crammed with armed men and suitcases. Two men were standing on the bumper. They jumped down and shouted at the Volvo, ordering it to stop and give them a lift to Baghdad. The CIA man wound down his window just far enough to shout in Arabic with what he hoped was an imperious Iraqi officer's accent, 'No room. We are full. Stay on the truck.'

The convoy ground through the suburbs in second gear for half an hour, passing two road-blocks where the guards took no notice of the dust- and smut-covered Volvo which had sporadically queue-jumped its way to the centre of the motley line of vehicles.

As they crossed what had been the Iraq–Kuwait border, the driver spoke in a voice that had more than a hint of a Canadian accent, 'So far, so good.'

'We're heading the wrong way,' the CIA man disagreed.

A grin. 'Don't worry. As soon as the traffic thins out, we turn left, head across the desert, make a radio call and get ourselves lifted out. You'll be eating steak and ice cream for dinner yet.'

'If we don't run out of fuel first after all this crawling along in second gear . . .' The passenger was nervous of the trigger-happy, footsore and hungry soldiers trying to hitch lifts by the roadside. 'If we stop, those guys'll be on us like a flock of vultures.'

It was dusk as the straggling convoy cleared the overhead smoke and reached the main highway to the north, bordered by burnt-out trucks, tanks and civilian cars. The Republican Guards had timed their departure to take advantage of night. Just in case, they made a brief halt to intersperse the civilian vehicles between the tanks and trucks as an impromptu deterrent against air strike. The Volvo had inches to spare between two huge T-72s as the column got under way again.

'That makes us the jam in the tank sandwich, if anything goes wrong,' commented the CIA man. 'Those things weigh forty tons apiece.'

The driver grunted. He was watching the fuel gauge.

The air strike came minutes before nightfall. A flight of French 'Hot' Gazelle helicopters bore in from the west and raked the front and rear of the column with anti-tank rockets and 20mm cannon fire. With the convoy halted and unable to retreat, the Gazelles concentrated on taking out the desperately manoeuvring tanks while the civilian cars scattered across the desert in all directions.

'Hold tight! Here we go!' The driver hauled the Volvo off the roadway seconds before the tank in front went into reverse. The heavy-duty Swedish suspension crunched sickeningly as the car bounced off the asphalt and headed west across the featureless expanse of desert.

Both the children were crying at the noise of the explosions. Their mother and the Marine in the centre seat tried to comfort them as the car lurched and crashed over the uneven surface.

It was sheer bad luck that one of the Gazelles was having a fuel problem. The pilot chose to break off the action early and turned for home, leaving the smoking column of tanks behind, his head busy with sums about fuel reserve and flying time. To his left and beneath him he saw a white car trying to escape. There was a man hanging out of the rear window trying desperately to pull suitcases off the roof-rack. The pilot's thumb squeezed the red button and emptied the last rounds from his magazines, puncturing both the Volvo's front tyres and smashing the radiator. As he overflew the stricken vehicle, he caught a brief glimpse of an American flag sticking out from beneath the suitcases.

The car stopped as though it had hit a brick wall. The front-seat passenger was unconscious, his head lying at an awkward angle against the shattered windscreen. The driver too was groggy. He heard the Marine in the back seat smash the remaining glass in the rear window with the butt of his pistol.

'Don't get out of the vehicle,' he shouted.

'Why not?' The man in the back was halfway out already.

'I think ... we're sitting in a minefield. That's why.' The driver had to shout to make himself heard over the children's screams. The effort seemed to drain him. He felt so heavy that he would never be able to climb out of the seat. A great weight was pushing him down and down into the upholstery.

'Aw shit, Raoul.' The man at the back wriggled back inside. 'You really fucked up this time!'

'No sweat.' The Marine in the middle seat disengaged himself from the child clinging to him. 'I'll call up Search and Rescue on the radio. They'll have us out of here in no time.'

'They won't want to land in a minefield,' said the driver slowly.

'So we spend the night here. At daybreak, they'll drop in a Nedex team and clear a landing zone. We're safe enough till then. Nobody's going to come looking for us in the dark.'

'That would be the safest thing.' The driver's voice was getting fainter. 'Except I'm bleeding a lot. I've been hit in both legs.'

He sounded drunk and half-turned to the men behind. 'Sorry, you guys. I fucked up.'

'Raoul?' The Marine sitting behind him on the cramped centre seat grabbed the driver's shoulders and shook him. 'Talk to me, Raoul!'

The Mayday call from the US Marines stuck in the minefield was picked up by hundreds of military units on the allied side. Among the nearest ground troops was a reconnaissance squadron of the Legion's Second Parachute Regiment, returning from a clandestine mission behind the Iraqi lines.

I heard all about it from Koenig's son, who caught a snatch of the interchange on the common emergency frequency.

He heard a laconic Southern voice saying 'Ranger Five, this is Bluejay. Repeat the name, rank, number of your casualty. Over.'

And faintly, from the radio in the Volvo, an American voice answered, 'Fuck you, Bluejay! Get us a Dust Off immediately. There's a man bleeding to death here.'

'Negative on that, Ranger Five. We have zero availability of Medevacs in this sector at this time. We're working on it. Stay on this frequency. Meantime repeat name, rank and number of casualty.'

'What the hell are you playing at, Bluejay? Oh Christ, the

guy's name is Raoul Duvalier. Sergeant Raoul Duvalier, US Marine Corps. You want me to spell that for Chrissake?'

Louise could have given our son her surname. In which case young Koenig would not have risked driving his all-terrain P 4 jeep through a minefield to save a stranger's life and I would be looking at a telegram now.

Instead, I am watching the stairs wheeled up to a plane at Bordeaux airport. The first passenger to appear in the doorway is a tall, handsome young man with one leg in plaster. He smiles at the stewardess and hobbles down the steps, leaning on a stick.

I recall the awful, soul-numbing fear when I heard Raoul was injured in both legs. I couldn't believe Fate could be that cruel. But the surgeons did a good job on him and, with a physiotherapist like Louise to help, he'll be walking normally in a few more weeks.

He moves slowly towards the arrivals building, being overtaken by all the other passengers except a middle-aged woman who has slowed down to walk at his pace. I hardly recognise Louise.

Now Koenig's son has left us. He is striding across the concrete in the sunshine, his sand-colour Legion uniform starched and immaculate, to greet the young man incoming. He pretends to kick the plastered leg. The invalid defends himself with his stick and knocks the white kepi off young Koenig's head. They embrace, laughing.

I look at my old friend Koenig standing beside my wheelchair. His hand grips my shoulder tightly. Neither of us can say anything.

Warner now offers an exciting range of quality titles by both established and new authors. All of the books in this series are available from:
Little, Brown and Company (UK) Limited,
P.O. Box 11,
Falmouth,
Cornwall TR10 9EN.

Alternatively you may fax your order to the above address. Fax No. 0326 376423.

Payments can be made as follows: Cheque, postal order (payable to Little, Brown and Company) or by credit cards, Visa/Access. Do not send cash or currency. UK customers: and B.F.P.O.: please send a cheque or postal order (no currency) and allow £1.00 for postage and packing for the first book, plus 50p for the second book, plus 30p for each additional book up to a maximum charge of £3.00 (7 books plus).

Overseas customers including Ireland, please allow £2.00 for postage and packing for the first book, plus £1.00 for the second book, plus 50p for each additional book.

NAME (Block Letters) ....

ADDRESS...

....

☐ I enclose my remittance for _____

☐ I wish to pay by Access/Visa Card

Number ☐☐☐☐☐☐☐☐☐☐☐☐☐☐☐☐

Card Expiry Date ☐☐☐☐